A Garden
to Keep

Jamie
Langston
Turner

BETHANYHOUSE
MINNEAPOLIS, MINNESOTA

Published by Bethany House Publishers
A Ministry of Bethany Fellowship International
11400 Hampshire Avenue South
Bloomington, Minnesota 55438
www.bethanyhouse.com

Printed in the United States of America by
Bethany Press International, Bloomington, Minnesota 55498

Library of Congress Cataloging-in-Publication Data

Turner, Jamie L.
    A garden to keep / by Jamie Langston Turner.
      p. cm.
    ISBN 0-7642-2154-X
    1. Church attendance—Fiction. 2. Women teachers—Fiction. 3. South Carolina—Fiction. 4. Married women—Fiction. 5. Adultery—Fiction.
I. Title.
    PS3570.U717 G3 2001
    813'.54—dc21
                                                2001002501

FOR
BETA GAIL LANGSTON STERYOUS
my sister Betsy
whose life is an ornament of grace

"Strength and honour are her clothing;
and she shall rejoice in time to come.
She openeth her mouth with wisdom;
and in her tongue is
the law of kindness."

PROVERBS 31:25–26

JAMIE LANGSTON TURNER has been a teacher for thirty years at both the elementary and college levels and has written extensively for a variety of periodicals, including *Faith for the Family*, *Moody*, and *The Christian Reader*. Her first novel, *Suncatchers*, was published in 1995. Born in Mississippi, Jamie has lived in the South all her life and currently resides with her husband and son in South Carolina, where she teaches creative writing and poetry at a university in the Southeast.

Part One

Part Two

PART ONE:

Sure there was wine

Before my sighs did dry it;

There was corn

Before my tears did drown it.

GEORGE HERBERT

Against Thy Mandolin

1

Though the roots go back many years, the story begins to bloom around a kitchen table after Sunday dinner. Not my own kitchen table—I'm here as a guest. Let me warn you from the start that this story might make you angry. I know for a fact it defies everything I've always believed in—logic, justice, self-preservation, equality, recompense, accountability, moderation, common sense. But hear me out. Close your eyes and picture it all with me. We're in the kitchen of a duplex on Cadbury Street in Filbert, South Carolina. I can see it exactly as it was that day.

The man of the house said grace before we ate dinner. That's what he called it—saying grace. I remember thinking at the time what a pretty word that was—*grace*. It's a word I hadn't heard that often. I wondered why I couldn't have thought of it when we were trying out names for our daughter twenty-five years ago. Grace Landis. That has a shimmer to it, like expensive crystal. But the name Grace hadn't entered my head when we named our baby, so we finally picked Jennifer, the same name a gazillion other parents picked back during the seventies.

But back to grace. The man said it, and aside from thinking briefly about the sound and feel of the word, the thought going through my mind as I sat at the kitchen table of these two people I barely knew was this: *A wasted afternoon*. At this same moment an odd scrap of a Bible verse echoed in my mind: *"I was a stranger, and ye took me in."*

I had heard the words at church that morning, a place I rarely visited. How I got there this particular morning is a story I'll get to later. But the verse struck a chord now. Indeed I was a stranger to these two people—or practically so—and they had taken me in, though not entirely willingly on my part. I wished I had had the presence of mind, or whatever it takes, to decline the invitation. But I hadn't, and here I was, stuck for the duration.

But don't whine, I told myself. It's your own fault. No one forced you to accept this invitation. This was a familiar lecture that I delivered to myself regularly.

I gave the kitchen the once-over before the man said grace. Get a picture in your mind as I look around—the blue-and-white plaid tablecloth, the matching dishes imprinted with a border of morning glories, the folded white napkins edged with white tatting, the vase of daffodils, the shiny hardwood floor, the yellow tab curtains at the window, the clock in the shape of a teapot, the gleaming white of the stove and refrigerator, the wall calendar showing a close-up of a pale purple crocus pushing through the snow. If there are such things as clichés in the world of photography, this crocus-in-the-snow image surely must be one. No microwave or dishwasher that I can see.

Over on the counter beside the porcelain sink, which is also white, I note a ceramic canister set shaped like little cottages, with the residents' names over each ivy-draped front door: Sugar, Flour, Tea, Coffee. Beside these sits a shiny silver percolator with a little glass bubble knob on top, the kind my parents used before the days of coffee makers. Well, well, here we go, I'm thinking—Sunday dinner at the Retro Cafe.

When the prayer was over, the woman, who was wearing a bibbed apron over a light blue dress, proceeded to take the lids off the hot casserole dishes and lift the foil wrap from the meat platter. Her husband looked at me and said, "Hope you're hungry, ma'am," and I smiled back and said, "It smells delicious." That's me, polite all the way. All kinds of scathing, critical things can be running through my mind, but you'd never know it from the outside. My mother taught me good manners to a fault. You mention my name to anybody, and probably the first word they'll think of is *polite*. Polite Elizabeth Landis.

Or *dumb*. Here's what a roommate of mine used to say in college every time I took on something extra: "For being so smart, Elizabeth, you sure are dumb." Laurie thought she was funny, and sometimes she was. "The word is *no*," she would say in an exaggerated drawl. "Here, let's practice it, honey. Watch me do it." And she'd say it again. "No-o-o-o. See there, easy as pie. Now you try it all by yourself, darlin'." All of this was dripping with sarcasm, of course.

So every time I end up doing something I really don't want to do, Laurie rises in front of me like some cantankerous genie, shaking her finger and her head at the same time. "The word is no," she says to me. "For being so smart . . ." And I'll always interrupt her and think, Yeah, yeah, I know. I sure am dumb. And the funny thing is, although I see Laurie regularly, floating around and wagging her finger, I don't even know where she is now. I do know one thing, though. Laurie would consider *dumb* much too mild a word to describe the story I'm getting ready to tell.

I had already seen her that Sunday, of course—twice actually. The first time was when I stepped into the church that morning, and the second was when I agreed to come to dinner. "For being so smart, you sure are dumb," she said both times. Laurie's eyelashes and bangs touch each other, both of them long and dark, the way I knew her in college.

So back to the kitchen on Cadbury Street. It's a mild February Sunday afternoon, and from where I sit, I can see the dark filigree of bare tree branches through the kitchen window. The sky is pewter gray in the open spaces among the trees but brighter, the white of beach sand, higher up where the sun hides behind a curtain of cloud.

Contrary to what Laurie always said, I am not dumb. I want to get that settled early on to eliminate dumbness as the reason for what I'm leading up to. Back in high school, in the "Senior Prophecies" issue of our school newspaper, somebody wrote this about me: "Elizabeth will continue her career as curve wrecker in college courses such as Advanced Electrodynamics and Metaphysical Philosophy," two subjects I never even saw listed in my college course catalog. For sure I never took them. Once Laurie said to me, "How come you always make A's? That's dumb." It wouldn't have done any good to point out the irony in what she said. She would've said, "Irony? What's that? That's dumb."

So okay, I'm smart. Maybe not off-the-chart smart like a bona fide genius, but somewhere at the upper end of the scale. Maybe not summa-smart but for sure magna-smart. To say schoolwork came easily is an understatement. So there's Elizabeth Landis in a nutshell. Smart and polite, a combination that implies another characteristic—boring. I would never write a book with a main character like me. Nobody would read past the first page.

My polite exterior hides some pretty snobbish attitudes, though. For instance, I categorize people into two groups—Aware and Unaware. Every now and then I'll come across someone I'm not sure about, and if I can work up my courage I might test them with a joke: A guidance counselor tells a father his kid is in the lower fifty percent of the class, and the shocked father says, "I knew he wasn't in the upper fifty percent, but I never dreamed he was in the lower fifty." If somebody responds right to that joke, I know he's Aware. And it's not just *if* the person laughs; it's more in how he laughs.

And so, instead of finding myself outdoors playing tennis on this nice February Sunday, which would probably be my first choice after a very long dark winter, or browsing in a bookstore, which would be my second, I'm sitting at a kitchen table with two people I hardly know. I've already realized I can't even remember the woman's first name, and it's a name I should know since she's been sitting at the end of my row in an evening poetry class I've been attending for four or five weeks now.

On the few occasions when she has spoken in class, eyebrows have been raised. While most of the rest of the class scratches and pokes timidly at lines of poetry, this woman digs. She lifts words to see what's underneath, and I'm always impressed by what she pulls out and holds up to the light. I can't help wondering why she's taking the course. I'm taking it partly to shake off a long winter that started way too early, but mostly I'm taking it because I love poetry, pure and simple.

Who can tell why a person chooses what he chooses to love? My sister grew up in the same house I did, and her opinion about poetry, which she expresses every time we're together, is that "the measly little ounce of pleasure you get out of it isn't worth the ton of trouble it takes to try to understand what in the world it's talking about." Her passion is growing orchids. Talk about a ton of trouble. My brother, Greg, who also grew up in the same house with Juliet and me, devotes most of his free time to watching ESPN and ESPN2. Talk about an ounce of pleasure. His idea of a poem is a clever advertising jingle.

I love the way words in poetry play off one another like shadows across the floor. I had a professor once in graduate school who handed back a paper I had written and asked to see me after class. "Your writing reminds me of Jane Austen's," he said when we were alone. I was speechless. "You have that same way of setting plain words beside exquisite ones and letting them reflect off one another," he added.

I guess part of the reason I couldn't think of what to say was that I thought that kind of compliment, about the light of words bouncing off one another, belonged to poetry. I had, in fact, always found it fascinating to see how a single short poem could contain very disparate pairs of words. *Speckles* and *preconceptions*, for example. *Escutcheon* and *die*. *Cherish* and *woodchuck*. *Clutter* and *rainbow*. Give me a minute, and I could cite examples by the hundreds. But I'm digressing again.

I could never write a book that held together. My mind doesn't stay still in one place long enough to follow through with a line of thought. It charges over the countryside, catapults through the air and lands in a neighboring county, crosses state lines, leaps oceans, and travels abroad.

Part of the problem is that words set off fireworks in my head. Growing up, I found endless hours of entertainment between the covers of my red Thorndike-Barnhart dictionary and later my rusty brown *American College Dictionary* by Random House. This isn't to say I was a frail indoor child. I remember climbing up to the top of a sycamore tree in our backyard with my dictionary and another book or two and spending hours reveling in words.

This is the absolute truth—I climbed trees to read my dictionary. I once came across something the Chilean poet Pablo Neruda wrote: "It's the words that sing, they soar and descend. . . . I love them, I cling to them, I run them down, I bite into them, I melt them down." I have no trouble at all understanding someone who gets so enraptured over words that he imagines hugging or eating them.

I can't look at the letters on a license plate without imagining all the words they could form if other letters were filled in. *LVA* could become so many things: lava, larva, lavatory, leviathan, lovable, livable, leverage, levitate. It's a game I like to play.

Up until a few weeks ago, it had been over twenty-five years since I'd taken a poetry class, though not a day goes by that I don't read poetry or read about it or quote it to myself. Occasionally I even try to write some. So when I saw "Modern Poetry" listed in a flyer advertising after-hours classes at Clarke-Forsythe Community College between Greenville and Spartanburg, I decided to sign up.

I needed something to do with myself in the evenings, and though I tried not to expect too much from the class, I couldn't keep from hoping. After all, sometimes you'll find these incredibly aware people teaching at some out-of-the-way school on the back side of nowhere. Take my husband, for example, who comes later. I'm working up to him.

Happily, the poetry class proved a nice surprise. The professor seemed to know his stuff, and I immediately pegged the woman sitting at the end of my row—my present dinner hostess—as somebody who would make up for any deficiency in the course material. The chairs were arranged in three semicircles in front of the podium, to give the class a friendlier atmosphere, I suppose, and the professor sat on a high stool, swiveling his head from one end of each long row to the other.

While some of the others in the class took notes halfheartedly and slack-jawed, this woman sat as if she had a rod for a backbone. She fixed her eyes on the teacher as if to snatch up every word that dropped from his mouth. I think everybody else in the class was awed by her, and I think the teacher was, too. Professor Huckabee, who was probably in his early sixties, always wore long-sleeved white shirts and neatly cinched neckties, and sometimes in the moment between her asking a question and his responding, he would hook a finger inside the front of his shirt collar, tug at it, then swallow hard.

Hers was a discordant name, with first and last names that didn't quite go together—I remembered that much. I'm usually very good with names, so it irritated me that I couldn't come up with it. I knew I'd think of it sooner or later, though. A clue was bound to drop sometime during the meal. If I could catch either her first or last name, I was sure I could remember the other half.

The woman played the organ at a church, which I hadn't known before a couple of hours earlier, when I had seen her in the very act. I had been surprised to find her there. It didn't seem to fit together. She was obviously intelligent, so why would she be attending church, especially this one? The preacher had taken his text from the book of Ecclesiastes, and if he said, "All is vanity" once, he must have said it fifty times. So why did a smart woman study poetry during the week and go to a church like this on Sunday? It was a riddle to me, mainly because of my experience with the Moffett family and Rex Harkness. They come later, too.

I had sat near the front of the church that morning because, you see, if I'm going to do something, I'm not going to cower in the back. I want to be able to see. Maybe also it's one way I punish myself for saying yes when I should have said no.

Actually, part of the reason I say yes so often is due to something else entirely besides my habitual politeness. I can't help thinking about the slight possibility of missing out on something big if I say no. What if I say no to being on the library's used book sale committee, for example, and I'm not there when an early edition of Elizabeth Barrett Browning's poems, printed on tissue-thin paper with gold edges and bound in a black leather cover like a small Bible, comes along? That's what happened one time, except I had said yes, of course, and I was the one who opened that box and pulled that book out.

The Poetical Works of Mrs. Browning was its title, and it contained over five hundred pages with eight original engravings. I bought it and have it at home. Somebody back in time had penned her name in the front—Eva Worthwaite—along with a page number, which, when I turned to it, bore the fourth of Mrs. Browning's forty-four *Sonnets from the Portuguese.*

Each word of that fourth sonnet had been underlined in blue fountain-pen ink that bled through to the other side. And beside the poet's line "My cricket chirps against thy mandolin," someone had written in a lovely script, presumably Eva Worthwaite herself, "Yet tell me, love, that I do not spoil the music." I knew at that moment that the book was mine. My husband is a musician, you see, and I am not. I felt an instant bond with Eva Worthwaite.

So when I had first been invited to attend church that morning, I suppose the thought came to me almost subconsciously: What if I say no and miss out on something really spectacular? I had read in the Derby paper a few years ago about a student at a theological seminary somewhere in the South who found a lottery ticket blown up against his windshield one day after class, and it ended up being a winning ticket. The man, who said he didn't believe in gambling, did some heavy-duty negotiating with his conscience before claiming his prize. He gave ten thousand dollars to a missionary, I think the article said.

But back to the church. After the service that morning the woman had slid off the organ bench, headed straight for me, and welcomed me to church, saying she recognized me from poetry class. She even called me by name. Then before I could blink twice, I heard myself saying yes to her invitation to take Sunday dinner with her husband and her at their house.

All it usually takes for me to say yes is one simple question, especially if I make the mistake of looking into the person's eyes. In fact, that's the very reason I was at church this morning. Somebody else—a kid I barely knew—had asked me to come hear him sing. That's another thing I'll get to later. Anyway, that's the way it goes. One yes leads to another one and another and so on until you're blowing around in the wind like milkweed.

So we're now at the kitchen table, which I somehow keep wandering away from. Here we sit, a cozy threesome: the organist, her husband, Thomas—I've got *his* name all right—and me. And I'm still halfway grumbling to myself for wasting my afternoon. Not that this one is really all that bad, since Thomas is a pretty comfortable old guy to be around—talks a lot like my daddy used to, and by that I mean not only the amount of his talk but also his rambling, good-humored, folksy manner. At first I assume he's retired, but not so. He fixes vacuum cleaners down at Norm Lang's hardware store, he starts telling me.

His wife begins picking up dishes of food on the table and passing them to me, and they just keep coming. I can't believe she really cooks like this every Sunday, and I make a note to ask her about it later. How would you put all this together after being in church all morning? It looks good—pot roast, those little red potatoes, carrots. It's that kind of meal, the kind your mother cooked when you were growing up. It's been a long time since I cooked a meal like this. I know how, don't get me wrong, but I rarely do it anymore.

"My husband is going to wish he had come to church with me this morning when I tell him about all this," I said just to have something to say. I was smiling, and I heard the cheerful tone of my voice. I could be suffering a thousand deaths, but I would never let on in these situations. But really, I asked myself now, what was so awful about spending a Sunday afternoon like this? I'd get a good meal, have some polite conversation, then leave as soon as I could. Besides, this woman had a certain mystery about her, and I liked mysteries. She was smart and religious—not a combination you ran across every day.

"Oh, you got a husband, do you?" Thomas said. "Here I was thinking you was a single gal."

"Single?" I said, scrunching up my face as if I were thinking hard. "I must have skipped that stage. I went from childhood to college to marriage, with marriage being the longest."

The woman, who had gotten up to pull hot rolls out of the oven, returned to the table. "We would be happy to have your husband join us," she said. "Could you telephone him now?"

I shook my head. "Oh, heavens no. He's probably on the tenth or eleventh hole about now. He likes food a lot, but nothing could make him give up his Sunday golf game, except maybe a concert."

"Your husband likes music?" the woman asked. She handed me the basket of hot rolls.

"He *lives* it," I replied. "He's a conductor. A composer, too."

"You got children?" Thomas said.

"Two, but we kicked them out of the nest," I said, and when I did, I felt like a wad of cotton was suddenly stuffed down my windpipe. A picture of Travis flashed into my mind, and I wondered what he was doing right at that moment. I'd like to have thought he was sitting in his dorm room studying, but I knew better. Without me there to organize his schedule, he was probably lying on his back listening to music or taking a long, solitary nature walk or watching something inane on television or just staring into space.

I asked myself again what kind of world it is we live in that expects eighteen-year-old boys to know what they're going to do for the rest of their lives, to go away from home, where no responsible adult is going to be checking up on them regularly, and to apply themselves to mastering some field of study over the next four years. And I still couldn't get over the fact that I had gone along with it—his mother! Well, "gone along with it" isn't at all true, but I had finally given up. I, the one who knew him better than anyone else in the world, didn't have the courage to keep saying, "This is a ridiculous educational tradition, and I won't have it."

I thought back to Travis's Christmas break a couple of months ago. The week before he had left to go back to college in January, he had lost his new leather jacket, backed over the Yarnells' garbage cans next door, and knocked over a two-liter bottle of Mountain Dew on the den carpet. After each incident I had asked myself one question: *And this kid is going to be a physical therapist in a few short years?* I can see him now, accidentally breaking people's arms and legs as he takes them through rehab exercises. I guess it's a good thing his sister is a lawyer. She can advise him about malpractice insurance and then handle all his lawsuits.

As I took another bite of roast beef, I glanced at the teapot-shaped clock. Jennifer was probably just crawling out of bed about now. I wanted to call her today but wouldn't. I had called her three nights ago and could tell she was busy, not necessarily with anything urgent but just busy with her own life. When you're twenty-five and just getting started in a law firm, you don't have time to sit around and talk to your mother on the telephone. The first thing she had said on the phone three nights ago was "Is something wrong?" and the second was "Then why are you calling?"

"You all right there, ma'am?" Thomas said to me.

"Oh, sure, sure," I said.

"Thinking about those two birds you kicked outa the nest?" he said, and I nodded.

"You never get over wondering if they can really fly, you know," I said. "Do you have kids?"

He shook his head. "Nope." He made a funny face and glanced at his wife. "Well, she might disagree. She thinks I act like a kid." His wife smiled and dabbed at her mouth with her napkin. She was a pretty woman, younger than her husband by a good fifteen or twenty years, I'd guess. I figured she was close to my age, maybe even a little older.

"You've gone and fixed up another mighty fine spread, Rosie," Thomas said, and I looked at Rosie, who was refilling my tea glass from a green ceramic pitcher.

I must have looked puzzled because she stopped pouring and asked, "Do you prefer water? Forgive me for not asking sooner."

"No, no. The tea's very good," I said. "It's your name, that's all. I didn't think your name was Rosie."

She shook her head and smiled. "My name is Margaret," she said. "My husband calls me Rosie."

Margaret, that was it—I had it now. Margaret Tuttle. She was last on the class roll when Professor Huckabee read it off the first couple of nights of class. I remember thinking it was strange in a class of thirty-five or so that there were no names after hers—no Vaughns, Weavers, or Youngs.

"There's a reason I call her Rosie," Thomas said.

"There is most often a reason for doing anything," Margaret said solemnly, though her eyes twinkled as she said this.

"Pass me another roll from that basket there, please, ma'am," he said to me, "and I'll tell you about it."

"I doubt that Elizabeth is interested in such trivia," Margaret said.

I laughed. "You've made me curious now," I said. "Besides, I love trivia."

I take a quick look at the food on the table, then help myself to another serving of the green-bean casserole. The steam isn't rising from the dishes anymore, but it's all still plenty warm. I take more potatoes, too, more carrots, and a small helping of roast. Oh, what a *congress* of flavors at this table, to borrow from Theodore Roethke, though he used the word to describe unpleasant smells. Professor Huckabee had us read that poem in class one night—"Root Cellar," it was called.

Sometimes when I hear a word like *congress* used in such a different but altogether suitable way, I wonder how long it would have taken me to come up with that same word if I had been given the same subject to write about. I doubt that I would have ever come up with that one. The last line of the poem came to my mind now: "Even the dirt kept breathing a small breath."

A "congress of flavors"—I liked the sound of it. When was the last time, I wondered, that I had sat in front of this much food? Ken had taken me out to dinner for our twenty-eighth anniversary in January, a week after Travis had left to go back to college, but it was a fancy place over in Greenville, and the portions were small. The waiter was round and bald, with a sweet face. I could see him in a monk's robe tending a garden. He brought the dishes out one at a time and set them before us with soft flourishes of his hands.

I felt like telling him to quit teasing us and bring us out a real plateful of food, but I was afraid it would hurt his feelings. He had the look of someone who would take teasing too seriously. Besides, it would have embarrassed Ken, and then I would have been annoyed at him for being embarrassed. You learn these things over the years.

By now Thomas was telling me the story about how Margaret had gotten her nickname of Rosie, and I was listening. They had met in a hardware store, of all places, and he had thought she looked like the World War II pictures of Rosie the Riveter. She was buying a hammer, and he had waited on her, then followed her out to her car. I'm always interested in stories like that about how couples met. Flood me with details, all of them.

"That's interesting," I said when he had finished. Then I turned to Margaret. "You know, that word *rivet* reminds me of you in another way."

She lifted her eyebrows and tilted her head. "Yes?" she said.

"That's how you look in our poetry class," I said. "Riveted. You always have your eyes riveted on Professor Huckabee." I looked at Thomas. "That was the word that came to my mind the first night in class when I saw how tall she sat and how focused she was on everything he said." I looked back at Margaret. "So I guess Rosie the Riveter fits in more ways than one."

She smiled. "I suppose so," she said. Then changing the subject abruptly, she asked, "Do you mind telling us why you visited our church this morning, Elizabeth? Are you looking for a place to worship regularly?"

I told them no, I wasn't looking for a church but had been invited by someone. Which brings me to the earlier yes I mentioned before, the one that brought me to the church in the first place. The kid who invited me was singing in a quartet. His name was Hardy Biddle, and my acquaintance with Hardy consisted of four or five memorable contacts in different classrooms over the course of several years.

Substitute teaching has its drawbacks and its advantages. One of the drawbacks everybody knows about is that students love to give substitute teachers a hard time. They try things. And it's funny how similar the pranks are all the way from first grade to twelfth. I've subbed in every grade at some time or other, and one of the favorite things students like to do—I'm talking mostly about boys here—is make vulgar noises when your back is turned. It doesn't matter if they're six or sixteen—that has to be the most common test for substitutes.

But subbing has its advantages, too. There's the little bit of pay you get, the flexibility of being able to work on the days you want to, plus a few golden moments here and there when you really connect with a class.

I had met Hardy Biddle in several different classrooms before the day he invited me to church, and let me tell you that as a student he was notorious enough to be listed, all by himself, as a major drawback to substitute teaching. To lump him in with a whole category like "unruly students" just didn't do him justice. He had a reputation among the regular teachers that no doubt accounted for many absences and sick days among their ranks, and I had heard of three different cases of teachers who quit teaching after having Hardy Biddle in one of their classes.

I always try a low-key approach with uncooperative boys. I've found that if I adopt a quiet, somber attitude, acknowledging that I'm well aware of the misbehavior but consider it so highly immature that it doesn't warrant a public address, I can usually survive the attacks. I assess the trouble spots quickly and set about to get the other students on my side with some kind of engaging story or activity. Showing them you have a sense of humor helps, also, but it can't be too spirited. Wry and offhand works best.

To be truthful, I can't help sympathizing at times with the disruptive students. So much of the teaching that goes on in our schools seems to be so incredibly boring! Travis had a World Geography teacher in ninth grade, for example, who *read the textbook aloud* to the students *for the entire class period every day of the school year* except on test days. I'm not making this up. That's exactly how that man taught.

But back to Hardy Biddle. The week before my Sunday dinner with Margaret and Thomas, I was called on Friday morning by Morton Hollings, the principal of Berea High, to substitute for a sophomore English teacher. The teacher was having her wisdom teeth pulled. Fridays are the worst days for substitutes, of course, and I sometimes turned down those requests, though not directly. I could hardly ever say no once I answered the telephone, but sometimes I let the answering machine take the message and then didn't return the call.

I answered this time, though, and accepted, but as I was pulling into the teachers' parking lot at Berea High, the thought hit me: Hardy Biddle is a sophomore at this school! Suddenly the prospect of having my wisdom teeth pulled seemed like a pleasant alternative to what I was about to do. Even if they were impacted with roots two inches long. I was pretty sure that all the sophomores had the same English teacher unless things had changed. I didn't know whether I preferred to have Hardy first hour and get it over with or last hour and have time to brace myself. As it turned out, I had him second period.

I spot him immediately since he's hard to miss. Hardy likes to dress in costumes—that's the best way to describe it. He shops the secondhand stores, according to the teacher gossip I've heard, and the more outlandish the article of clothing, the more likely he is to wear it. On this particular day he's actually rather subdued compared to other times I've seen him around the school. He's wearing a referee's shirt—black and white vertical stripes— with a bright blue plastic toy whistle around his neck, the kind you'd get out of a gum machine. As I see him enter the classroom, I'm thinking of all the potential for mischief in that little whistle. Over his referee's shirt he's wearing the zip-out lining of a coat, as if it's a long vest.

Well, not to belabor this any more than I need to, Hardy Biddle shocked me that day. He was totally different from what I was prepared for. It was as if another boy had taken his name and was inhabiting his body and wearing his clothes. It certainly wasn't the same Hardy Biddle I had met in other classrooms. He sat up reasonably straight, listened intently, even raised his hand and said some really perceptive things about the story we were discussing that day, which was Stephen Crane's "A Gray Sleeve." I kept waiting for the real Hardy Biddle to take over, but he never did.

Afterward when he was leaving class, I called his name, and he came up to my desk. I went right to the point. "Hey, Hardy, what's happened to you?"

Now listen to his response. First he grins—he really is a good-looking boy in spite of his bizarre clothes—and says, "It's a long story, Mrs. Landis." Then he pauses a second and says, "Well, no, really, it's pretty short. I met somebody who changed me, see, and now . . ." Someone calls to him from the hallway just then, and he looks away, then back at me and says, "Say, Mrs. Landis, tell you what. You do me a favor and come to my church on Sunday morning 'cause our quartet's gonna be singing, see. I think you can figure out what's going on with me if you come. It starts at eleven. Church of the Open Door in Derby."

He points to me as he backs out of the classroom. "Be there, okay? I'll be looking for you. I mean it."

So this is how the invitation came about. He paused at the doorway. "Okay?" He cocked his head to one side and raised his eyebrows imploringly.

And like the spineless creature I am, I nodded and said, "Okay."

In case anybody is wondering, I know my verb tenses are wildly erratic. I know all about verbs. I can conjugate them in my sleep. But verb tense is one of the most irrelevant parts of reviewing your life. I know I shift tenses disgracefully. Present, past, present perfect, past perfect, future, future perfect—what's the difference?

As you relive events, the past bleeds into the present, the present turns into the future, and the future reverts to the past. It's all part of the same long line called life. There are no shut-off valves, no neat walls between then and now and someday. Ken used to say at times that I lived in the past, but he didn't understand. I live firmly in the present, but the past always escorts me like an enormous, devoted entourage.

And yes, I know all the rules against *you* in scholarly writing. But this isn't scholarly. It's definitely not scholarly. It's like I'm sitting on a sofa in somebody's living room telling my story as it comes to me, hoping my voice will eventually find its true pitch and settle into the song.

Maybe somebody will read this someday and say, "Oh, so that's the way life works. That's what love means."

Home of Long Tides

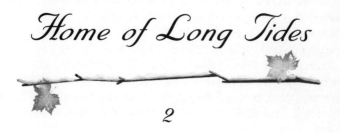

2

Hardy had spotted me at church that morning. After having been way-laid by Margaret and Thomas, I was heading for the exit when I heard his voice behind me. "Hey, Mrs. Landis! You came! Whoa, wait up!" People smiled and stepped aside so he could work his way through the crowd and catch up to me.

I was out of the sanctuary by now, inching through a small crowded foyer. A man clapped Hardy on the shoulder and said, "That's a mighty fine quartet you boys got!" and I heard a woman behind me call out, "You make the coleslaw, Shirley, and I'll do a Jell-O salad!" Another woman touched my hand and practically yelled, "We're so happy to have you visiting with us this morning! You come back again real soon, you hear?" I nodded and smiled.

"Come on, I'll walk you to your car," Hardy said, and as soon as we were outside, he asked, "Well? So how'd you like it?"

"I have to agree with the man back there," I said. "You've got a mighty fine quartet." I meant it, too—I wasn't just flattering him. I might not be a trained musician, but I like to think I could have done something in music if my father had signed me up for piano instead of tennis lessons when I was a kid. I have a pretty good ear for pitches and harmonies. Once when Ken and I were newly married, I was passing through the room where he was listening to a tape of an orchestra concert he had recently played in. "The oboe sounds flat," I said, and if Ken had worn dentures, they would have fallen out. He was always surprised, and still is, whenever I identify something correctly in music.

"You're right. It *was* flat," he said. "That girl had the distinct honor of ruining an entire concert single-handedly." He often takes that tape with him now when he goes somewhere as a guest conductor. He plays excerpts of it to stress the old proverb that one bad apple can spoil the whole barrel.

Hardy was telling me now about how he and his three friends practiced twice a week in a garage. "Strictly *a cappella*," he said. "That way we get the harmony down pat. We don't want to have to depend on a piano, see." Somebody called to him from across the parking lot, and Hardy threw back his head and made a sound like a howling coyote. "He just moved here from Texas," he said, jerking his thumb toward the boy.

"So you howl at him?" I said.

He grinned. "Yeah, he likes it. His name's Kyle Wolfe. So anyhow, we got five songs learned now, and we're gonna start singing the third Sunday of every month." He went on to tell me that he and one of the other boys switched off singing bass.

"Will There Be Any Stars in My Crown?"—that was the title of the song Hardy and his three friends had sung that morning. I recognized two of the other boys as twins who went to Berea High. I thought the other boy might have gone to Derby High, but I wasn't sure. When you sub at different schools, the faces start blending together. I wondered if anybody else in that church thought it strange that four teenaged boys would get up and sing a song about doing good on earth so you could be rewarded in heaven. If teen-aged boys sang at all, it usually didn't have anything to do with heaven. More often it sounded like the other place.

I tried to imagine my son singing "Will There Be Any Stars in My Crown?" He sang along with his Nat King Cole CDs, but that was about it— "Mona Lisa," "Route 66," "Paper Moon," things like that, always in his room by himself. Travis had never gotten into hard rock. He liked an odd mixture of things—blues, big band, swing, classical, show music, calypso, and of course Wynton Marsalis, his hero. He liked Yo-Yo Ma, too, especially the CD he made with Bobby McFerrin, called "Hush." I'm not complaining. Give me Wynton Marsalis or Yo-Yo Ma any day over Marilyn Manson.

I wondered if Hardy Biddle was going home today to listen to Pearl Jam and Nirvana after having sung "Will There Be Any Stars in My Crown?" at church. I was seeing a shiny surface, but I was wondering what would be underneath if you scratched it. I can't describe what this kid used to be like. Surely there was still some residue of the old Hardy.

We were standing by my car now. I had parked in one of the spots marked *Visitor*, right beside two spaces reserved for the handicapped. The way I had seen it all my life, anybody who attended a church like this regularly would qualify to park in a handicapped parking place.

"Thanks again for coming," Hardy said.

I looked him up and down. Picture this: He was wearing a red-and-white striped vest with a white shirt, white pants, and a red bow tie. Corny to the hilt, but somehow he managed to pull it off. In fact, the other boys in the quartet had seemed rather lackluster standing beside Hardy. He's one of those people who can wear outlandish clothes with confidence. "I wouldn't have missed it," I said. "Thanks for inviting me." I stuck out my hand.

"I've invited all my teachers," he said, "but you're only the second one to come." He shook my hand vigorously, then opened my car door and flashed me a smile.

"And I probably shouldn't even count, since I'm just a sub," I said.

Quick as a wink he said, "Yeah, I been meaning to talk to you about that, Mrs. Landis. You oughta settle down and get you a regular class. You keep popping up in all these different classes. What's the matter? You afraid of making a commitment, or what? How come you don't go after something permanent?"

"Oh, I'm the restless type," I said. "This way I get to teach a little bit of everything." I got into my car and dug my keys out of my purse.

"Yeah, but—hey, not so fast. Hold on," he said. "I gotta ask you something before you peel outa here."

"Shoot," I said, looking up at him.

He appeared to ponder something for a moment. "Well, okay, then," he said. "I was gonna use a car wreck, see, but I'll change it to a drive-by shooting."

I laughed. "I see that the sermon this morning put you in a cheerful frame of mind."

Hardy stuck a finger in the air as if making a point and said, "Ah yes, a good dose of Ecclesiastes will purge out all that silly optimism. 'Vanity of vanities; all is vanity. . . . Behold, all is vanity and vexation of spirit.' " He stopped and frowned. "But, hey, I'm not making fun. What the preacher said—it's all true, you know."

"Well, he seemed convinced of it," I said, "and I don't think I'd want to argue any of it with him." Actually, the minister, to my surprise, had been quite polished as a public speaker. I wasn't expecting anything remotely close to the controlled, articulate sermon the man delivered. "Brother Hawthorne" sounded to me like somebody on the same level with the Moffetts and Rex Harkness, whom I'm coming to in a minute.

"Now stay with me here," Hardy said, making a fist of one hand and pushing it into the palm of the other. "Okay, let's say we're standing here like this when somebody drives by out there on the street and shoots you— or they could wait till you got out on the road and smash into you head on, doesn't matter."

"Do I get to pick?" I said.

"Hold on. I'm not done," he said. "And let's say you die."

"It's getting better all the time," I said. "Is there more, or is that all?"

"Well, actually, that's sort of what I wanted to ask you," he said. "After you die, what happens? Is there more, or is that all?" He stuffed his hands inside his pockets and smiled down at me. He didn't look in the least bit uncomfortable. He could as easily have been asking about my favorite kind of pizza instead of what happens after death.

I pretended to be stumped. "Uh, well, usually there's a funeral, isn't there?"

"To *you*—what happens to the real you, Mrs. Landis? To your soul? Where does it go?"

It was hard to look at this kid and get mad at him. These same words coming from somebody else might have pushed me past the limits of my politeness, but Hardy's manner was so friendly and sincere, I couldn't work up even a trace of irritation. You'd have to see the kid and listen to him to know what I mean.

"Well, now, I don't know the answer to that," I said. "Nobody I know of has ever died and come back to give us all a report." I said it kindly, though, and then reached out to pat his sleeve. "You're a good man, Hardy Biddle. Thanks again for inviting me to your church." I started the car and closed the door gently, then waved good-bye.

"Think about it, okay?" Hardy called through the glass as I slowly backed out. I nodded and waved again. But I want you to know I was nervous as a cat driving over to Margaret and Thomas Tuttle's house for dinner. Don't be ridiculous, I kept telling myself. You've been driving since you were seventeen and not once has anybody shot at you or smashed into you.

Why did these people have to be so morbid? When the preacher had talked about the "long home" in the last chapter of Ecclesiastes, I couldn't help thinking what a mournful sound the words had, with those long *o* vowels, all the more so after the minister identified them as a reference to the grave.

But the same words can sound entirely different depending on the context, I reminded myself. I thought of Elizabeth Bishop's poem "The Moose." One of the lines was something about the "home of the long tides." It had the same two words in it but sounded far more hopeful. She wasn't writing about death but about the rhythms of life, about changes within a larger pattern. But death is the ultimate change within a larger pattern, so I suppose she was writing about death after all. Somebody once said that all the best poetry deals in some way with death.

I meant to leave the Tuttles' house as soon after eating as I possibly could and still remain on the sunny side of courteous, but before I knew it, the teapot clock on the wall said it was almost three o'clock. By then we had eaten slices of apple-spice cake with vanilla ice cream for dessert, and after that Thomas had left to go visit somebody in the hospital. I stayed to help Margaret with the dishes, and in so doing we had begun discussing poetry. I told her of my lifelong passion for it.

I discovered she was taking the poetry class out of nothing more, or rather, nothing less, than a deep love of the genre. She was even teaching, or "guiding," as she called it, a local poetry club that met once a month and was using some of the same poems we discussed in class. Well, this was pretty amazing—a poetry club in these parts. South Carolina is a state that's full of incongruities.

I've always considered myself a voracious reader, but I soon realized that Margaret gave the term *widely read* a whole new meaning. And she didn't limit her reading to poetry—oh, goodness, no. As a matter of fact, she read more fiction than anything else.

When we went into the living room after finishing the dishes, she invited me to sit down and visit a while longer. From my end of the sofa, I spotted five new books in glossy book jackets neatly stacked on a table on the other side of the room. These she had just ordered from the Penguin Putnam Literature Catalog, she told me. The titles were intriguing, though I was embarrassed to admit I had never heard of any of them: *The Tent of Orange Mist*, *Winter in the Blood*, *The House Behind the Cedars*, *An Octave Above Thunder*, and *Banished Children of Eve*. From where I was sitting, I could read all the titles, which were in large print, but not the names of the authors.

I felt a little better when Margaret told me that she had seen three of the titles for the first time herself when she had recently looked through the catalog. "I cannot recommend any of them yet," she said to me, "for I received them only yesterday. I am afraid I have done a very foolhardy thing in ordering them, but they were a gift."

She proceeded to tell me about a friend in Tuscaloosa, Alabama, a man named Mickey Freeman, who had mailed her the catalog, along with a check for one hundred dollars made out to Penguin Putnam, and instructed her to choose whatever she wanted to order. "He is a generous man in every way," Margaret said. "His wife was a dear friend of mine." She said that Mickey Freeman had also sent Thomas a new electric ice cream maker.

"Perhaps I should have selected works with which I was familiar," she went on to say. "I could have ordered the complete poems of Tennyson, for example, or *The Life of Samuel Johnson* or the *Portable Faulkner*. Or Jane Addams' account of Hull-House or a book about the Dead Sea Scrolls or a thousand other things—oh, it was a painful process. There were too many choices, and I wanted them all. Since placing my order, I have spent part of each day rereading the catalog and rebuking myself for choosing hastily." She smiled over at the stack of books and then turned to me. "By 'hastily' I mean an entire week of concentrated effort, revising my selections many times a day."

I understood exactly what she meant and told her about receiving a gift certificate to a bookstore one time for my birthday. I made four trips to the store, trying to decide which books to choose, before finally giving up in frustration and using the gift certificate for a new dictionary.

But back to Margaret's books. Here's a little quiz for you, one that I took and failed. Knowing that she was trying to broaden her knowledge of poetry, I asked her if all five books were modern poetry collections, and she said that only one was. The other four were novels.

"Wait, don't tell me," I said. "Let me guess which one. I like games like this." Smiling, I lifted my chin and added smugly, "Usually I'm quite good at them."

She moved as if to pick up the five books but stopped and looked at me. "Most likely you already recognize the names of the writers," she said, "especially since one of them is a poet."

I shook my head. "Maybe so, but I can't read them from here."

She nodded. "All right. I suppose I can trust you." She smiled as she sat back down on the other end of the sofa and turned to face me. "Now, which title do you think is the poetry collection?"

"Okay, let's take them one at a time," I started out. "Let's eliminate *The Tent of Orange Mist* first. That sounds like some pseudohistorical novel set in China or Korea. Or something sociological maybe. Some American goes to the Far East and has all his romantic illusions about the Orient shattered. Or maybe it's the opposite. Cynical American flees Western civilization and camps out on the banks of the Yangtze, where he discovers the meaning of life. Or I guess it could be a Vietnam War story. Wasn't Agent Orange the name of that stuff they sprayed all over?"

The expression on her face didn't tell me a thing, so I kept going. "Let's see—*The House Behind the Cedars* probably isn't it either. That sounds too much like a memoir—even sounds a little ominous, don't you think? Like somebody dumping all his childhood baggage. Of course, some people might think it sounds warm and fuzzy like something by Laura Ingalls Wilder, but they're not picking up the clues. It's a *house*, not a home—and then it's *behind* the trees, not *in* them. The whole title sounds scary. Maybe it's a mystery. That's a possibility. But whatever it is, I don't think it's a book of poetry."

Margaret smiled again but made no comment. I looked at the other three titles. "It gets harder now," I said. "*An Octave Above Thunder* has possibilities, but I think it's too obvious. I mean, poetry is all about sound, so what self-respecting poet is going to pick such giveaway words as *octave* and *thunder* to stick in a title? I guess some poets might want a neon sign like that on their covers, but not the really good ones. I actually think it's a pretty good title for something, but not for a collection of poetry. And, really, I think *An Octave* Below *Thunder* would be better, don't you? I mean, thunder is already low, so almost any sound could be above it. But what's *below* thunder, now that could be interesting."

Margaret simply shrugged and blinked her eyes twice. I was left with only *Banished Children of Eve* and *Winter in the Blood*. "Either one of these has potential," I said, "but I don't think it's *Banished Children of Eve*, and I'll tell you why."

I had to go slowly here because I wasn't sure how this part would come out. Somewhere in my reading I had run across the phrase "banished children of Eve" and was fairly sure it was part of a Roman Catholic rosary prayer. "There's got to be a *story* to go with that title," I said to Margaret. "Something with a plot, characters, setting, all that. And even if it were a book of poetry, something tells me it would have a feminist slant." I paused. "And I hope you won't be insulted at this, but frankly I can't see you ordering a book of feminist poetry."

She looked away as if miffed, but I sensed that she was only teasing. "Of course, I don't know you all that well," I continued, "but I'd venture to be pretty dogmatic about the fact that most feminists have dishwashers, for example, which you don't. And all the cooking and the apron and . . . oh, I don't know, you just don't seem that . . . well, I don't know, that *narrow* or rabid in your outlook, I guess."

"I doubt that feminists would appreciate your assumptions as to the outfitting of their kitchens or their culinary skills or your choice of the words *narrow* and *rabid* to describe their outlook," she said gravely.

"Probably not," I said, "but didn't you just refer to them in the third person instead of first? Doesn't that prove my point? But anyway, let me continue. That just leaves *Winter in the Blood*, doesn't it?" I said. "Actually, I have a few problems with that one, too, but it's the only one left, and my objections to it aren't very big ones. I can see a poet picking a title like that. Poets are always talking about winter, both literally and figuratively. It's everybody's favorite symbol of death."

"So that is your final guess?" Margaret asked.

"Yes, that's it," I said. "How did I do?" I tried not to look proud of myself, but I was fairly certain I had guessed right. It just takes a little systematic reasoning, that's all.

"*Winter in the Blood* is an American Indian novel," she said. "It is set on a reservation in Montana."

"Oh, so it is *Banished Children of Eve* after all," I said. "Sorry, I didn't mean anything by all those things I said. I just didn't think you'd—"

"*Banished Children of Eve* is a novel set in the Civil War era," she said. "The poetry collection is *An Octave Above Thunder*."

I made a face. "Dumb title for a book of poetry," I said, and we both laughed.

Do you know how it feels when you forge a bond with somebody as a friend? All your instincts tell you, "This is something rare and fine." You feel as though that person is a spring of cool, clear water, and you know that however many times you put your dipper in, it will always come up full. This hadn't happened to me often. I wasn't ever the type to make friends easily, and I didn't have anyone I'd really call a "best friend"—and all of a sudden I'm sitting here thinking, *And three hours ago I didn't even want to be here!* This is what I mean about saying no and missing out on something big.

Margaret reached down to the magazine rack beside the sofa. She pulled out a catalog and handed it to me. "I ordered the books from this," she said. It was the Penguin Putnam catalog.

I flipped it open. It seemed to offer everything. I saw American colonial literature and contemporary Japanese drama. There were Icelandic sagas, Confucian texts, anthologies of prison writing, translations of Euripides, Irish fantasies—you name it.

"I love titles, don't you?" I said. "Good ones, that is. *Watching Our Crops Come In*—that's good. *Learning How the Heart Beats, Daughter of the Queen of Sheba*—good, good. *I've Known Rivers*—I don't usually like complete sentences as titles, but that one works."

I was at the end of the catalog now and started flipping back toward the front. "*Ring of Bright Water*—good. *The Music of Chance*—okay. *White Noise*—so-so. Here's a good one—*The Land of Little Rain*. And *Shadow Play*—I like that. *Where the Rivers Flow North*—good. *Kill Kill Faster Faster*—stupid. *The Frequency of Souls*—no. *Rocking the Babies*—okay. *Him with His Foot in His Mouth*—a little on the silly side, but I like it. *Miss Gomez and the Brethren*—yes. *The Interesting Narrative*—oh, please." I sighed and closed the catalog. "If only they'd check with me first, I could give them so many good pointers."

We both laughed again. "And I thought before right now that you were such a kind, gentle, soft-spoken woman," Margaret said.

"Yes, that's what everybody thinks," I said. "You know, the sad thing about book titles is that the good ones don't always go with the good writing. The best book out of all those titles I just read is probably that last one—*The Interesting Narrative*."

Margaret put the catalog back in the magazine rack. "Titles used to be far less metaphorical," she said.

I nodded. "They used to just stick the main character's name on the cover and call it the title. Like *David Copperfield* or *Robinson Crusoe*."

"*Jane Eyre, Silas Marner*," Margaret added.

"Or else the theme," I said. "*Pride and Prejudice, Crime and Punishment, War and Peace*. I guess they must have used up all their creativity before they got around to choosing their titles."

Enough of book titles. I said earlier that my story began to bloom at Margaret's kitchen table but that the roots went back a lot further. I also said the end of the story might make some people angry, and I also said I thought the word *grace* had a beautiful sound. Remember all of this.

Remember, too, that it's a Sunday in February when all of this takes place—the church service, the conversation with Hardy, the dinner with Margaret and Thomas. It's on that same Sunday that something else happens, two big things—two enormous things, in fact—and if anything proves that God has a special way of timing things, this does it.

But first, the Moffett family and Rex Harkness. I've got to come back to them before I get to the other part. They were the ones who had given religion such a bad name in my opinion, and I had to get past them that day in February before I left Margaret's house. As nice a person as I pretend to be on the outside, I'm going to demonstrate now on a big screen in living color how snobbish I can be. But every word of this is true. Don't forget that. I'll tell it in order—the Moffetts first, then Rex—and I'll try to be brief.

The Moffett family lived next door to my family when I was growing up in Burma, Georgia, where my daddy owned and operated the first Putt-Putt and Bat-Bat in the state. I got to play all the miniature golf I wanted to, and most of our birthday parties during those years were held at our Putt-Putt. Daddy set up three or four picnic tables and a Coke machine by the entrance, and Mother would bring the cupcakes and Kool-Aid and balloons out there. There would be free games of Putt-Putt and rounds of Bat-Bat for the birthday guests, of course, so they were popular parties, even though I was anything but popular myself.

I loved the Putt-Putt, but the Bat-Bat I despised. Part of my spending money came from retrieving all the balls in the field, and let me tell you we had some powerful batters in Burma, Georgia, during those days, which meant I had to roll that cart for what seemed like miles and miles picking up all those baseballs. Juliet and Greg had to help, too, of course, but they were younger, so I was always convinced that I did most of the work.

But back to the Moffetts. They lived next door to our family, and Mr. Moffett made a living by doing other people's yard work. He had a little rattletrap riding mower held together with baling wire and duct tape, and Daddy hired him the first year or so to help him keep the Bat-Bat field mowed.

That was something else I got to do, but instead of riding on a mower like Mr. Moffett's, I got to walk along with the push kind. We'd do the part up closer to the cages, and Mr. Moffett would do the big area out toward the back fence that separated our property from the drive-in theater, which wasn't the friendliest of neighbors for an enterprise like the Bat-Bat.

The owner of the drive-in theater was certain that our baseballs were going to cause all kinds of personal injuries to his customers and their cars, and even when Daddy sat down with him calmly and showed him all the regulations for field size and distance from other businesses and so forth, the man still painted grim scenarios of innocent teens in convertibles dying from baseballs dropping on their heads.

Mr. Moffett, on the other hand, thought that that would be the best thing that could happen. He saw every single tragedy on the face of the earth as a visible sign of God's judgment on wicked men, and he believed it was a Christian's job to point out the link between cause and effect for all the people who didn't see earthquakes and sickness and car wrecks and the like as the hand of God. And if a man could help God along by meting out a little judgment himself whenever he saw sin, well, he was only doing his Christian duty.

In Mr. Moffett's opinion every one of those teens in convertibles *ought* to be thwonked on the head with a baseball for partaking in the devil's business, which included paying money to support Hollywood, feasting their eyes on lustful images, and doing who-knew-what-else in those cars in the dark of night.

And believe it or not, Mr. Moffett was mild compared to his wife. Mrs. Moffett was short and round and always seemed to be out of breath. She'd have to stop after every few words to rest a little, but that didn't keep her from talking at great length. She had a disconcerting way of smiling while she said the gloomiest things.

She'd come out to the driveway while my mother and I were bringing in groceries and say things like "The world can't last much longer. . . . Did you read in the paper about that man that killed his wife and baby girl over in Spartanburg? . . . Bludgeoned them with a steel pipe. . . . I hope they electrocute him. And it's too bad they can't do it twice. . . . Kill him once, and then resurrect him back to life . . . and kill him all over again. Maybe hang him with a rope the second time around . . . pay for them two lives he took."

And she'd be smiling the whole time. Granted, it was a sad sort of smile, but still! Mrs. Moffett thought criminals should pay for their crimes by having certain body parts cut off, such as a hand for stealing, a foot for a drunk-driving felony, and I don't need to keep going.

"Pare 'em down to stubs . . . and they'll quit their evil ways," she'd say. Repeat offenses by criminals on parole was one of her favorite subjects, and she could tell story after story. She'd usually end her speeches by prescribing a remedy, which was always the same. "Men's hearts are blacker 'n the pit of hell . . . and nothing's going to change . . . unless we have a revival in our nation. . . . Folks need to be born again . . . before it's too late."

And I haven't even gotten to the Moffett children yet, although I guess they deserve pity more than anything, having such parents. I heard my mother tell my father one time that all the various deficiencies of the Moffett parents were multiplied in the children. The oldest boy, Freddie, used to gather all his younger siblings in the backyard and preach long sermons to them. They'd sing hymns, take an offering, pray out loud—the whole works.

Lila Moffett, who was my brother Greg's age, told me several times over the back fence that I was going to be sent to the lake of fire for wearing shorts, and Dwight Moffett, who was younger yet, used to point his little finger straight at us and lisp, "For the wageth of thin ith death." I never even knew that verse had a happy ending until Margaret read it to me that Sunday afternoon in February. But I'm getting ahead of myself.

The Moffetts went to a church over in Cornwall, Georgia, about twenty miles from Burma. It had a flamboyant name, something like the Holy Temple of Mount Zion Fellowship of Believers. It didn't have the name of any standard denomination in it—I remember that much.

Keep in mind that the Moffett family, as daily observed by me in my impressionable youth, was my first and only up-close contact with avidly religious people before Rex Harkness. Rex was in my class in seventh and eighth grades, and even though we went to different rooms for each subject, the same students were kept together. For some reason Rex latched onto me as a friend. It was probably because I was the only one in the whole class who would lend him a pencil or piece of notebook paper, which he always seemed to be in need of. I was the only one who didn't treat him like dirt.

Rex was a swarthy kid with a wiry build. I imagine he grew into a handsome man, but he moved away after junior high, and I never saw him again. He was good in sports, but none of the other boys ever wanted him to play on their team. He joined in anyway but always on the fringes of games, and on Field and Picnic Day at the end of the year he took prizes in all the sprints. He wasn't dumb in school, either. He could do math problems in his head and was runner-up in the seventh-grade spelling bee, which I won on the word *glowworm*. Rex had spelled it with only one *w*.

So with all this going for him, it seems like he should have had friends. But he had two things against him, and in the mid-sixties at Burma Junior High School they were two big things. He was poor, and he was religious. Being poor affected the way he looked, of course, and like kids down through the ages, our school was no different in its treatment of those who didn't dress right. His clothes usually had some kind of obvious defect like holes or patches, and they never looked very clean. Kids don't stop to think things through. These exterior faults canceled out all the good things about Rex.

As for his religion, it manifested itself in the facts that he carried a New Testament in his shirt pocket, didn't participate in gym class on the days we danced, and bowed his head in the lunchroom before he ate. Chuck Pratt liked to tell Rex dirty jokes just to see him turn red. Once when Chuck asked him why he didn't laugh at his jokes, Rex said, "Because I'm a born-again Christian." I heard this with my own ears. He spoke up boldly, and he used that same term I'd heard from the Moffetts—born again.

This religion part is funny because most of my classmates in Burma, Georgia, attended church with their families. But church never was anything that interfered with your normal life. You never talked about it at school, for example. Besides, most of us went to one of the three socially acceptable churches in downtown Burma—the big brick ones with white columns and lots of steps, either the First Baptist, the First Methodist, or the First Presbyterian.

It was rumored that Rex Harkness went to a little country church where they rolled around on the floor and shouted out loud, but somebody probably just made that up out of meanness. I do know that none of us ever saw the Harkness family at our safe, sanitized churches.

If anybody's reading this who goes to one of those kinds of churches—either the country kind or the big-city kind—don't get offended. I'm not passing judgment. I'm just telling my story as I remember it from my childhood. You can find plenty of good and bad people in both kinds of churches.

You might think smart and athletic would be enough to outweigh poor and religious, but in Rex's case it wasn't. He was an outcast. Maybe if he'd had a more assertive personality or a goofy sense of humor or if he didn't seem to care so much, it would have made a difference. But he was shy and meek and conscientious, so the other boys found him a soft target. And if he'd been *cleaner*—that would have helped, too.

Part of me felt sorry for him, and when he looked at me with his sad brown eyes and asked if he could please borrow a pencil, I usually gave him my best one, which he always returned sharpened. Another part of me hated him for finding the weak spot in me, for being too nice, for not wearing clean clothes, for carrying his Bible to school, for being so different. I was relieved when he moved away after eighth grade, but I've never quit wondering what happened to him, where he is now, what he's doing, if he's married and has kids, if his wife keeps his clothes clean. Something in me hopes he's a millionaire.

So that's the way it was. I had viewed the Moffetts almost every day of my life for the six years we lived next door to each other, and I had been in classes with Rex Harkness every day for two years. So although I now realize my sampling was far too small for a reliable survey, I concluded what any other kid would have: People who called themselves born-again Christians were weird in some elemental way and should be avoided. And like most other assumptions formed during childhood, I carried this one with me into adulthood. I didn't make a big deal out of it, but whenever I thought someone might be too religious, I quietly turned and went the other direction.

End of Act One. Curtain drops, intermission lasts a few decades, then the curtain goes up again, and Hardy Biddle and Margaret Tuttle enter, about as different from each other as people can be, yet very much alike in one important way. I had heard the pastor use the phrase "born again" in his sermon that Sunday morning, so I knew the Moffetts and Rex Harkness would have felt right at home in this church.

But instead of the Moffetts and Rex, I see a bright, likable, witty teenager named Hardy and a beautiful, intelligent, generous woman named Margaret, neither of which fits my stereotype of born-again Christians, sitting there soaking up everything the preacher says. I liked them both very much, and what's more, I felt something very akin to respect for them. I had already labeled them both Aware.

So what do you do in a situation like this? You reevaluate. You've got the Moffetts and Rex on one hand and Hardy and Margaret on the other, and you realize you didn't do enough research before you drew your conclusion.

So when Margaret turned to me in her living room that afternoon after our conversation about book titles and said, "Elizabeth, may I ask you a rather direct question?" I think I must have known what was coming. I had put Hardy off in the church parking lot with some lighthearted banter, but I gave Margaret my full attention. Not because she had me trapped in her home and made me feel obligated after the good dinner she'd fed me, but because she was winsome in every way. I wanted to hear what she had to say.

We talked for almost an hour, during which time Thomas came back home, looked pleasantly surprised to see me still there, and went into one of the bedrooms and closed the door. At the end of the hour, my understanding was enlightened, to put it mildly.

I saw things differently—not only the whole idea of Christianity in general but also my new friend in particular. Her experience of being born-again hadn't come easily. The labor had been intense, and by that I don't mean she had to work hard to win her salvation, but she had suffered greatly before she was ready to accept it. My life in comparison to hers had been a rose-strewn garden path.

When I said the biggest *yes* of my life before I left her house that day, I had no way of knowing that I was about to be slammed up against the wall. As I said earlier, God's timing of all this couldn't have been an accident. It could seem cruel to have the two events happen this way, so close together. Or merciful. You could look at it both ways I guess.

Whose Hands Shipwreck Vases

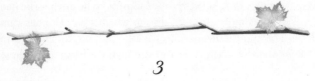

3

The way Ken and I met doesn't make an interesting story like Margaret and Thomas's encounter in the hardware store. It was at college, and I happened to be with Laurie, who was my roommate at the time—the same one who always said, "For being so smart . . ." I was dragging her to the library to help her get started on her sophomore literature paper, which was due in a week and which was the only thing that could salvage her grade. It was pretty clear, though, that I cared about her grade a whole lot more than she did. Laurie had not come to college for academic reasons.

We had settled on Othello's tragic flaws as the topic of her paper, but first I had to straighten out the characters for her. She had Othello confused with Iago and thought Desdemona murdered somebody and tried to wash the blood off her hands. It was a Saturday afternoon late in the spring term, and the trip to the library was interfering with Laurie's plans to sunbathe, which meant she was in a bad mood.

I tried to tell her that the paper would be easy to write once she got going, that we could think of tons of stuff to put in. The hard part, I told her, was going to be keeping it under six pages. "Good grief, I mean Othello is probably only the best example of the tragic hero in all of Shakespeare!" I said, but she wasn't impressed. On our way to the library, I tried to prime the pump with some questions and comments about Othello's character weaknesses. I didn't want to just *feed* her all the information. The teacher instinct in me wanted to draw it out of her. I should have known better.

"His most obvious tragic flaws are that he does a couple of things too much—things that are normally good, but he overdoes it," I hinted. "Do you remember what they are?" I was sure her instructor must have covered this in class. I was still operating under the delusion that she had actually read the entire play, which I learned later was not the case at all. Nor had she heard much of what the professor had said, since she hadn't been in class very often lately. I didn't realize all this at the time, however.

When she didn't answer immediately, I prodded a little more. "They're both verbs," I said. "Come on, you know this. Othello *blanks* too much— what is it?" I was thinking, of course, of *loves* or *trusts*.

Laurie shrugged. "Did he eat too much? Was this Othello guy a porker? No wonder he turned Desdemona off."

"He didn't turn her off," I said patiently. "She loved him."

"Yeah, some girls like fat guys," Laurie said. "I knew this girl in high school who fantasized about marrying one of those humongous sumo wrestlers. Can you imagine?"

"Othello didn't eat too much," I said.

"Then how come he was fat?" she said. "Did he have a glandular disorder?"

Laurie was good at avoiding anything she didn't want to discuss. We were walking up the steps of the library now, and that's when it happened. A guy pushed the door open from the other side and started down the steps toward us.

"Hey, Ken," Laurie said. "Want to trade places?" He looked confused and gave a little half smile. "I'll go wherever you're headed," Laurie continued, "and you can go with Elizabeth, the warden, here to write a paper about Othello the Rotund."

I sighed and grabbed her elbow. "Excuse my friend," I said to the guy. "She's disoriented." And I shoved Laurie toward the door. "Who was that, anyway?" I asked her once we were inside.

"Ken somebody," Laurie said. "He sits next to me in Civ Survey." It was popular in college to shorten all our course titles. Civ Survey was actually A Historical Survey of Western Civilization, but who's going to say all that? The paper we were getting ready to write was for a course called Introduction to British Literature, or Brit Lit, as we called it.

"They've got us all in alphabetical order," she went on, "so I guess his last name's got to start with an *l*." She emitted a short cackle of laughter, which drew several disapproving looks from people studying. "Ken L," she said. "Get it? I'm going to start calling him Kennel. 'Hey, Kennel, I hear you're going to the dogs.' Wonder if he'll think it's funny. He doesn't laugh very much." She paused, then laughed again, drawing more frowns. "I guess he wouldn't be going to the dogs if he were a kennel, though, huh? The dogs would be going to him." Laurie could be incredibly silly.

I saw him a few days later, at the library again. The thought came to me that he had probably been hanging out there all year, as I had, but I'd just never noticed him before. He saw me first as he passed by the table where I was studying. He stopped and leaned over. "You're Elizabeth, aren't you?" he whispered, then glanced quickly toward the check-out counter, where a

large sign read *QUIET, PLEASE*. I always liked that sign. The fact that someone had thought to add the word *please*, which would have cost more, said a
lot about the college in my opinion.

I nodded and whispered back, "Hi, Ken." And even though my contact
with him had been minimal, I jumped to three conclusions: He studied a lot,
he had a good memory, and he followed rules. Unlike my faulty assumptions
about Christians, these three turned out to be mostly correct, except the one
about following the rules, of course. I'm coming to that.

The next thing I found out was that he was a music major. I saw him
carrying what looked like a little black suitcase a few days later. I was on my
way to the typing lab to type Laurie's paper, which was due the next day, and
he was turning onto the sidewalk leading into the music building. "What's
that?" I asked, pointing to the case.

"My trumpet," he said.

"You play it?" I felt my heart racing. Initiating conversations with guys
wasn't something I did a lot of.

"I try to," he said. He stopped and swallowed, then looked up into the
trees. He shifted his trumpet case to the other hand. It hit me then that he
was just as nervous as I was.

"I bet you do more than just try," I said.

He smiled a little and cleared his throat. "Well, I've got my eye on first
chair, but I have to squint to see it from where I'm sitting. I'm eighth chair
right now." He looked briefly apologetic, then quickly added, "But the first
four chairs are graduating, so next year I'll move up."

"I'm sure you will," I said, even though I didn't really understand about
chairs graduating. Then, because I couldn't think of anything else to say, I
politely said good-bye and went on my way. That's me all right, polite. And
boring. As I continued to the typing lab, I thought of several other things I
could have said to demonstrate my keen wit and charisma, but these things
always came to me too late. I think there's a phrase for it in French—something like *l'esprit de l'escalier*, which means "staircase wit." It's that perfect
remark you should have made, but you don't think of it until you've left the
room or wherever. My "staircase wit" file folder is jam-packed, let me tell
you.

I knew enough about music to know that orchestras rarely had as many
as eight trumpets, so I figured Ken must be in the band. By telephoning the
music building later that day, I found out there was a band concert the next
weekend, and I went to it by myself. Laurie had two dates that night, one
for a hamburger at Father Barlow's, a college hangout run by a former priest
turned hippie, and another for a movie at nine.

When I think about the movies we used to go to, I have to throw my
head back and laugh—or else cry. They were so tame compared to today.
There was a movie house near campus, the Gold Sabre, that showed old

black-and-white movies almost exclusively, and in the upside-down way that fads are often born, it became the fashionable place to go. The movie that night was *Bringing Up Baby* with Cary Grant and Katharine Hepburn.

Laurie had no idea how she was going to make the transition from Date Number One to Date Number Two that night, but she wasn't worried. "It'll work out," she said. "It always does." By now the spring semester was almost over, her Brit Lit paper had been turned in, and she was devoting the rest of her sophomore year to her favorite course, called Having a Good Time. Exams were looming, but they didn't start until Wednesday. No need to let them spoil a perfectly good weekend—that was her attitude.

So I went to the band concert alone, which was held in a big auditorium with a vaulted ceiling dating from the midtwenties, when the college was founded by a South Carolinian aristocrat who deplored the fading emphasis on moral values, social graces, and cultural accomplishments at state universities. He gave the college his own name—Randolph Shelby Piper College of the Humanities. Randolph Piper had enough connections in the state, not to mention his own private resources, to fund the college liberally. In later years the sciences, education, and business were added, so Humanities was dropped from the name. Today it's commonly known as Piper College.

I sat in the back of the auditorium. Above me was the domed ceiling, painted silver, and around me were dark paneled walls. The crowd was surprisingly small, I thought, but what could you expect when you scheduled a concert for six-thirty on a Friday night? The size of the crowd didn't seem to affect the musicians' spirits at all, though.

I had never heard the Piper College Symphonic Wind Band before, so I had no basis for comparison with earlier concerts, but I didn't see how anything could have possibly surpassed this one. And though I've already admitted my limited knowledge of music, I still knew enough to realize that this group wasn't just average. So why didn't more people come to hear them? Why hadn't I ever heard anybody talk about them in glowing terms? Why weren't there ads stuck up all over campus announcing their concerts? Was all this supposed to be a *secret*? Maybe it had been promoted and I had been too wrapped up in other things to pay attention.

They started with a lively piece called "Israeli Wedding Dance." I don't know exactly what gave it its Middle Eastern flavor, but I felt like I was swirling around in the middle of a roomful of very happy Jews. When the players ended the piece with a unison shout of "Hey!" what I wanted more than anything at that moment was to hear the whole thing all over again.

I don't remember every piece they played that night, but I do remember the first and the last. The last one cast a spell over me that I still feel whenever I hear the piece today. You know how the arts can do that—take you back to a time and place and re-create the whole mood of the original experience for you. Before that band concert, I had felt that kind of transporting power only in poetry. I never knew before that day that music could come so close to poetry.

Anyway, the last piece was listed in the program as "Elsa's Procession to the Cathedral," a band transcription from Richard Wagner's opera *Lohengrin*. What this piece did was ambush me. Listen to it sometime. Here's what happens. You're sitting there in the beginning totally unsuspecting. It starts out soft and slow, majestic really, but very restrained and sedate, and you're expecting it to be like that all the way through, though I've learned by now not ever to expect that out of music.

What you're not prepared for in "Elsa's Procession" is the gradual steady swell of volume and intensity that happens so subtly you're not even aware of it. It's the aural equivalent of the frog being boiled to death in the pan of water, which I know isn't a very aesthetic comparison.

At any rate, you suddenly realize that whereas you were just ambling along the shore enjoying the wet sand and gentle tide a few moments earlier, you've somehow been picked up and plunged right into the middle of the ocean, and the waves are so big and powerful you can hardly move. You're not sure if you're scared or delighted, but one thing is certain—you're completely overcome. You know for a fact that Elsa has made it all the way to the cathedral, has maybe even climbed right up inside the huge pipe organ.

I couldn't see Ken from where I was sitting, but I listened especially hard for the trumpets. The whole section sounded good to me—no weak links that I could detect—so I concluded that there couldn't be more than a grain of difference between the first-chair player and the eighth. The juniors and seniors probably got the higher chairs just because they'd been in the group longer.

When the band concert ended, I noticed some of the people in the audience going up onstage to speak to the conductor and the players. Ken walked offstage, but I knew I never would have had the courage to go speak to him anyway. In a daze I headed for the exit, intending to go back to my dorm and start studying for exams, granted that I could get the stunning effect of "Elsa's Procession" out of my mind. I planned to walk slowly to give myself more time to recover.

So I've already given it away that I wasn't exactly a social butterfly in college. The dorms were always quiet on Friday and Saturday nights, which meant I didn't have to go to the library to study on weekends. And, really, in case anybody is feeling sorry for me, don't. I loved studying and being by myself in my dorm room. I'd get a bag of popcorn and a Coke at the campus snack shop, which was called the Cove, and sit at my desk for hours, happy as a flea on a fur farm, as my mother likes to say.

So I went by the Cove first for my popcorn and a Coke in a glass bottle, because a Coke always tastes better from a glass bottle than any other way, and this time I was the one coming out as Ken was going in. We met each other right at the door of the Cove a little after eight o'clock on a Friday night in May. We were both by ourselves. He had taken his jacket and black bow tie off but still had on his white shirt, open at the collar.

The very first time I saw him I had the vague thought that he looked sad, but the second time I realized it was mainly the shape of his eyes. Everything else about him looked pleasant enough, but his eyes, even when he smiled, pulled down a little at the corners. And they were so dark they looked black behind his glasses, which had square brown frames. His jawline was square, too, and his thick hair, which was much lighter than you'd expect with such dark eyes, was parted and combed to one side, with just the slightest hint of a wave in it.

So was he handsome? Well, by the third time I saw him, going into the music building with his trumpet, I was convinced that he was. But in my way of seeing things, *handsome* has so much to do with other things besides actual looks that it might be a little misleading. Laurie, in fact, laughed when I first used the word in connection with Ken. "He's a nice guy, honey," she said, "but handsome he ain't" were her exact words.

But trust me, he was. He was about five ten when I first met him but grew another inch before we graduated. So he wouldn't be called either short or tall, just medium. I had always imagined marrying somebody really tall, since I was tall myself, but then there was something to be said for not having to crane your neck too much. He looked serious and studious, and he was, but underneath was a sense of humor that could be both dry and downright goofy. Most people rarely saw this side of him, though.

And a music major? I had never expected to be attracted to one of *those*. I guess I had thought all along that I'd marry somebody in business who would earn enough money so that I could stay home and dabble in whatever suited my fancy. Of course, I would want him to like all the things I liked, too, so we could have something to talk about. He'd have to be interested in more than just numbers. Let me back up and explain that my problem was never finding something I liked and could do well in, but it was narrowing down the multitude of possibilities.

My first love was poetry—it had been since my mother first read Mother Goose rhymes to me before I could talk. It had surprised me the first time I realized that the average person didn't have a repertoire of Mother Goose rhymes like mine. I mean, most people knew the ordinary ones like "Hickory, Dickory, Dock," "Humpty Dumpty," and "Jack and Jill." But one time when I was only ten or eleven, I remember someone asking me at school what a new boy's name was. When I said, "Charley—you know, like 'Charley, Charley, stole the barley, out of the baker's shop,'" I got a very funny look.

Later, when I made a close friend in seventh grade, a girl named Katie, I asked her once if she had ever heard of Tommy O'Linn. "Who? Is he in eighth grade?" she had asked, and I started quoting, "Tommy O'Linn was a Scotsman born, His head is bald, and his beard is shorn." She frowned and interrupted me to ask what in the world I was talking about.

I went on to quiz her about others, and it turned out that Katie had never heard of the Three Wise Men of Gotham or Old Father Graybeard or Little Betty Pringle, Parson Darby, Sulky Sue, or Hannah Bantry. Why, she'd never even heard of Bobby Shaftoe or Margery Daw! But she did finally manage to quote "Little Miss Muffet" all the way through. We weren't friends for very long before she got even more boy-crazy than she already was and told me we didn't have much in common anymore.

And art—that's another thing I've always loved, but mostly as a spectator. And sports—I was always the best in girls' P.E. The trouble was, I never specialized in anything. Most people who love poetry, for instance, will zero in on a particular period or a certain poet and devote themselves to exploring that acre of the field. Not me. I like to wander over the whole farm.

Most art lovers have a favorite style and era. But not me. I flit around from flower to flower. I love Thomas Moran's landscapes as well as Mark Rothko's abstractions, and John Singleton Copley's family portraits as well as Martin Puryear's red cedar baskets. I could soak for hours in Georgia O'Keeffe's watercolor of *Light Coming on the Plains* and then turn to one of Joseph Cornell's eccentric box creations like *Hotel Eden* and baptize myself all over again.

I adore George Bellows' sensational treatment of light and dark in that famous painting of the two boxers and the way Edward Hopper depicts solitude in *Nighthawks*. And I love Winslow Homer's simple paintings, such as the one of the man scything wheat, that end up being full of symbolic overtones. I'm fascinated by it all, by all the millions of ways of making something out of nothing. Of course, these are all American artists, so I guess I have narrowed my interest a little.

Considering my love of poetry and art, it's funny, I suppose, that I never ventured into music. Maybe I sensed that music was so big that if I ever stepped in, I'd be swallowed up. And not having a musical background—that is, no one at home playing or studying music, except for the stuff Greg and Juliet listened to on the radio when they hit adolescence—there were just too many other things to take up my attention. I guess I haven't mentioned yet that I was on the tennis team in high school and college.

And ironically, Ken, though consumed with music, had never dug very deeply into poetry or art. There must have been some sense in both of us, then, of having met our complements.

I had no idea what to major in when I graduated from high school. I liked literature, I liked math, I liked history, I liked art, I liked cooking, I liked sports—and I not only liked them all, I was good in them and had the potential to be very good. The only thing I was sure I didn't want to be was a seamstress or a scientist, although I had earned the highest grade percentage of all the chemistry students my junior year of high school.

So taking my cue from the original name of the college I attended, I majored in good old humanities. It pleased my parents well enough. All they really wanted for me was a solid, well-rounded education and a good husband at the end of four years. And really, that's all I wanted, too. I didn't have dreams of becoming the first woman to excel in this or that. I didn't want to be famous.

I wanted to do well and enjoy the things I was interested in, then graduate, get married, and have a family. I tried to keep my lack of ambition quiet, but I'll bet you one thing. I'll bet most of the girls in my college class felt exactly the same way. Sure, feminism was very alive and very well back in the late sixties and early seventies, but deep in the hearts of most girls, this wife and mother thing was beating strong.

Ken had started piano lessons at the age of seven but abandoned them two years later when he first picked up a trumpet. He never once doubted what he would major in: Music Education with a trumpet proficiency. He wanted to be a conductor first but was also interested in composition, and luckily for him, the college his father had chosen for him to attend—Randolph Shelby Piper College—offered courses in both conducting and composition from a knowledgeable professor.

Yes, professor, singular. The man's name was Dr. Graham Lockheart, and he was practically the whole music department by himself. He taught two courses in instrumental conducting as well as beginning, intermediate, and advanced composition as needed. Fortunately for the students, he was very, very good. In addition, he was the band director, so Ken got to observe him from several angles. I think I can safely say that Ken's dream as a college student was to be exactly like Dr. Lockheart someday. He worshiped the man.

But I didn't know Dr. Lockheart when I first met Ken. I didn't even know our college had a band, much less a good band. I knew it for sure after the night of the concert, though. And I knew that the eighth chair trumpet player's name was Ken. And when I think of Ken right now, today as I write this, thirty years after that day I first saw him coming out of the college library, part of me wants to weep quietly and part of me wants to break something made of glass.

That night after the band concert, he turned around at the door of the Cove and walked me back to my dorm. I can't remember anything we said in those first moments, but I do know that he took the Coke bottle to carry for me, and somehow before we had walked half a block, he managed to lose his grip on the bottle, which had been in a cooler and was cold and slippery. It fell onto the sidewalk and broke into several thick pieces. "Whose hands shipwreck vases," I said aloud as we watched the Coke gurgle out onto the concrete.

He looked at me curiously, and I told him it was from a poem by John Frederick Nims. I didn't tell him that the title of the poem was "Love Poem" because I didn't want him to get the wrong idea. I just told him it was a poem about somebody who was clumsy in a lot of ways but graceful in others. I could tell he was embarrassed, and I was wishing now I hadn't said anything.

He lifted his hand and held it up in front of me. "Actually, I'm really very good with my hands," he said in all sincerity. "I'm studying to be a conductor."

"I didn't think conductors used their hands much," I said. "I mean, all they have to do is hop on and off trains and say, 'All aboard!' " I knew it was dumb, but it came out before I could stop it. I guess I had been around Laurie too much.

He laughed a little, then rose to the occasion. "Sure, they do," he said. "They have to give hand signals to the engineer."

I smiled. "Well, don't worry about it. I can get another Coke."

He looked down at the sidewalk and shook his head. "I might as well tell you. I've got a bad habit of dropping things when I'm nervous."

"Remind me not to pick you for my softball team," I said. All this was new to me. I wasn't usually like this with guys, joking and quipping. Laurie would be proud of me. Or maybe something about Ken brought it out in me. I felt sorry for him and wanted to impress him at the same time.

"Let me get you another one," he said. He stooped down and picked up the pieces of glass. "Here, let's throw these away, then go back to the Cove." We started eating the popcorn as we walked.

By the time we got back to the Cove, we had somehow decided to go to the Gold Sabre to see *Bringing Up Baby*. I had told him by now, of course, that I had been to his band concert, and when he asked if I knew somebody in the band, I said, "Yeah, you." I don't know if he ever really understood that he was the only reason I went to the concert that night. I'm pretty sure I never told him, although I don't know why.

Ken passed his habit of dropping things on to his son, but he never seemed to see the connection. I've seen him lose his patience with Travis a hundred times for breaking or spilling something, and I've wanted to say, "Hey, remember the bottle of Coke on our first date?" But this is getting things way out of order. First, we went to see *Bringing Up Baby*, which Ken had never seen before. And who should we run into in the lobby of the Gold Sabre but Laurie. She was getting popcorn with Date Number Two, who looked a little bit like Ringo Starr.

"Well, well. What have we here?" she said. "Does Barbie know you're two-timing her, Ken?" We all laughed, even Ringo, who probably didn't even catch the joke. Laurie squeezed her eyes shut, then opened them again wide and gave her head a little shake. "Wow, I can't get used to the sight of Elizabeth with a *man!*" she said, and I shot her a reproving look, which she ignored.

It turned out all right, though, when she added, "How did you do it, Ken? I mean, Liz here is only the world's hardest-to-get woman." She winked at me, and when Ken walked over to buy two Cokes, she said, "Hey, what *is* this? Shouldn't you be back in the room studying? I mean, what if you make an A *minus* on one of your exams?"

Just as the movie was getting ready to start, Laurie found out Ken had never seen *Bringing Up Baby*. She grabbed his arm and said, "Well, you know Baby really isn't a *baby*-baby, don't you? It's this big black catlike animal—a panther or something." I had planned to let him find out for himself, but that was Laurie—she couldn't stand to keep an interesting tidbit of information to herself. She was the kind who would tell you that Rosebud was the name of the sled right before you watched *Citizen Kane* or that Darth Vader was Luke Skywalker's father. If you were getting ready to read *The Scarlet Letter*, she'd say, "Dimmesdale's the one who got Hester pregnant." Of course, that one's a bit of a stretch since Laurie never read books.

Ken liked *Bringing Up Baby*. Laurie had said he didn't laugh much, but that night he did. He laughed a lot, and I liked his laugh. It wasn't a very loud laugh, but it was real. I spent a good part of the time watching him instead of watching the movie. I'd already seen it four or five times anyway.

So you see what I mean about how I met Ken. Pretty uneventful story. We were both sophomores at the time, and we got married two and a half years later. I look back now on that first date and wonder if there were signs I should have picked up on that were telling me we weren't right for each other. I knew we were alike in a lot of ways, but I didn't know how dangerous it was to marry someone too much like yourself in critical ways.

But there was one good sign, a big one in my opinion. In fact, this was what probably blinded me to some other things. Coming out of the movie, we heard Ringo ask Laurie, "You want a ride, sweetheart, or you gonna use your broom to fly back to campus?"

I looked at Ken and without thinking said, "There was an old woman who rode on a broom."

Without missing a beat, he said, "And she took her old cat behind for a groom."

I'm sure my mouth fell open. "Do you know that nursery rhyme?" I asked, which was a stupid question.

It was hard to tell, but it looked like he blushed. "My mother was big on nursery rhymes," he said. "I got them all first, and then I heard them all again with my two brothers, and then I got another dose when my sisters came along. I'm sure I was the only boy in sixth grade who was still listening to nursery rhymes before bedtime."

"Did all the kids at your house share a room or something?" I asked.

He looked embarrassed again. "Well, for a long time we did, but it was a great big room," he said. "It was practically the whole upstairs of the house. The boys' bunks were at one end, and the girls' were at the other. We had a wall put up in the middle when we got a little older."

"Neat," I said. "I think that's really neat." And I wasn't talking so much about his sharing a room with all his brothers and sisters as I was about his thorough knowledge of nursery rhymes. For some reason I took this to mean that we were destined for each other.

I do remember one of the last things Ken said that night. I'm sure he said other things after this, because he walked me all the way back to my dorm after our discussion about nursery rhymes outside the Gold Sabre, but this is the last thing I remember. "Did you ever notice," he said, "how many of those nursery rhymes have unhappy endings?"

And he went on to prove his point. "Think of it—Polly Flinders got whipped for messing up her clothes, Barney Bodkin broke his nose, Lucy Locket lost her pocket, and what else? Let's see, Little Tommy Tucker didn't have enough to eat and Tom the piper's son stole a pig and got a beating and Wee Willie Winkie ran around town in a nightgown." I thought he was done when he added, "And the three blind mice had their tails cut off, and . . ."

"But Old King Cole was a merry old soul!" I said. "And Little Jack Horner ate pie and was a good boy."

"Ah, but he was sitting in a corner, remember. Why was he sitting in the corner if he was such a good boy?"

I laughed. "Did anybody ever tell you you've got a good sense of humor?"

"Well, yes," he said, "but I always figured my mother was a little prejudiced."

The Edge of the Receding Glacier

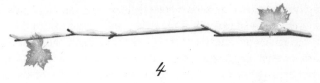

4

Life insists on being lived. The last line of Theodore Roethke's poem "Dirt Cellar" keeps coming back to me: "Even the dirt kept breathing a small breath." The idea comes to me to take that last line and write a poem from it, working backwards. This is something I like to do—write poems from the last line to the first.

I'd come out with an entirely different poem from Roethke's, of course. Not a better one, but different. I might start with a line like "And though the wind died as we sank to the black deep," which would fit snugly into the closing line. The pleasure of writing a poem this way is that while you know the end, you don't yet know the beginning. It's the opposite of life.

So I have this much: "And though the wind died as we sank to the black deep, / *Even the dirt kept breathing a small breath.*" I'm putting Roethke's line in italics to set it apart from mine. Maybe the next line, or rather the previous one, could be something like "Snatching our words, flinging sand into our eyes." I'm working backwards from the wind here, and I'm casting the wind as a culprit. It may even create itself into a symbol, but all it is right now is just a nuisance, getting in the way of hearing and seeing clearly.

It's funny to observe a symbol backwards. It's like looking at a full-blown flower and contemplating what the seed looked like. Before it can start representing bigger ideas, a symbol has to exist literally, so at least I've gotten that far with the wind.

I now have three lines: "Snatching our words, flinging sand into our eyes. / And though the wind died as we sank to the black deep, / *Even the dirt kept breathing a small breath.*"

Of course, the rule is you *have* to work backwards. It's cheating to think the whole thing through frontwards and then just set the lines down in reverse order. And anyone can see that to do this right, you have to force some run-over lines. You can't have each line contain a complete thought—that would be dull and "pedestrian," a word Professor Huckabee likes to use when he points out a poetic phrase that stands flat-footed on the page. "Or how on the open beaches it held us apart"—that could be the next line.

> Or how on the open beaches it held us apart,
> Snatching our words, flinging sand into our eyes.
> And though the wind died as we sank to the black deep,
> *Even the dirt kept breathing a small breath.*

Real poets do this, you know—borrow lines from each other and weave them into their own poems. Read the poetry of Donald Justice if you don't believe me. Start with a really easy one like "Counting the Mad" and ask yourself, "Is it just my imagination, or does this poem really sound a lot like 'This little pig went to market'?" Then move on to something like "After a Phrase Abandoned by Wallace Stevens." You have to laugh at a title like that. Nobody can accuse Justice of trying to hide the fact that he borrowed a phrase from another poet. "The Tourist from Syracuse," "The Grandfathers," "Young Girls Growing Up"—on and on it goes. Donald Justice took a little from here and a little from there but always ended up with something his very own.

It's a little like nest building. In between all the twigs and grass woven together in a bird's nest you'll see that bright little scrap of paper or string or fabric from the human world—something that happened to catch the bird's eye and make him think, "Hey, I can use that." The point is, as T. S. Eliot once said, that a good poet like Justice will fashion something totally different from the original, often even better. "The good poet," Eliot said, "welds his theft into a whole of feeling which is unique." Who else but Eliot could have said it that way?

One more line in my backwards poem, and then I'll go on with the story. "Or how in the woods it clamored through the trees." To this point in the poem the wind has diverted our attention in the woods by making a racket in the trees, has kept us from talking on the beach, and then has finally died. I have to remember, though, that "even the dirt kept breathing a small breath." I can't ever forget that last line.

> Or how in the woods it clamored through the trees.
> Or how on the open beaches it held us apart,
> Snatching our words, flinging sand into our eyes.
> And though the wind died as we sank to the black deep,
> *Even the dirt kept breathing a small breath.*

And don't forget what I said about life: It insists on being lived. I'm talking about the lives of sane people here who might be driven to the edge of madness but will always take that final step backward, away from the chasm.

I guess it's appropriate, then, that I should be writing a poem backwards. In searching for the beginning of the poem, perhaps I'm searching for the beginning of something else. I'm trying to move away from the chasm.

I left Margaret Tuttle's house in Filbert, South Carolina, shortly after four o'clock on the eighteenth of February and drove slowly to my own house in Berea. There's so much I haven't yet explained, but it will come. One step at a time, as my mother used to say. "Take your little red wagon by the handle and pull it behind you one step at a time," she'd tell me when I got in a hurry. Go too fast, and you'll catch your heel and trip. One thing follows another. Everything in its time. My mother was big on orderliness.

Mothers, in fact, were on my mind that day as I drove home. Margaret had told me a little about her mother that afternoon, how she had nurtured and protected Margaret, how she had talked with her, sung to her, read to her, cultivated her mind in every way. Yes, she had read nursery rhymes to her—I asked about that. Margaret had spoken tenderly of her mother's beauty, her intelligence, her love, her faith in God. But her mother had died when Margaret was thirteen, and the years that followed at her grandparents' house were full of a pain she didn't describe but at which I could guess.

Margaret's mother, I knew, had given her more in thirteen years than many mothers give in a lifetime. She had stamped her mark upon Margaret, making her the woman she is today. Though Margaret had rejected the faith of her mother for many years, she had come back to it. Her mother had given her a home base.

These thoughts led me to ask myself on the way home that day what I had given my own children. I had always awarded myself high marks as a mother. Motherhood was what I considered my crowning achievement, and I had spared nothing in my efforts to be a good one. Motherhood is that part of a woman's life, I think, that comes closest to being completely selfless.

But I was coming home a different person than when I had left. Looking at what I had gained in the last hour, I couldn't shake the idea that I had wasted a great many years. I felt as if I had spent my whole life nibbling a piece of stale white bread in a closet and had missed the banquet table on the other side of the door. And, what's worse, I had kept Jennifer and Travis in the closet with me. I saw plainly how the gospel, as Margaret had presented it to me so clearly today, could be the most powerful, enriching force in a person's life, and I couldn't help regretting the fact that I had not equipped my children with it.

The only gospel I had taught was the gospel of good manners. I had pounded the Golden Rule into my children's heads. True, there are worse gospels to preach, but it fell so short of the real one.

Over the years people had commented on how polite my kids were, and I had always taken this as a badge of success. I had stressed good morals, but morality was part of my general creed of courtesy, nothing more. As I glanced down now at the Bible on the seat beside me, which Margaret had given me before I left her house, my heart ached to realize what I had withheld from my children. This was a major omission. And I had wanted to be such a good mother.

After Ken and I were married, we both did graduate work at the University of South Carolina in Columbia. I took some education courses, thinking I might like to teach someday, and worked part-time in a gift shop. Ken had a graduate assistantship with the conductor of the USC marching band and eventually ended up with a doctoral degree in conducting, which some people in his family didn't understand. "How can you get a doctoral degree in something like that?" his aunt Shasta asked. "I mean, what do they do to fill up all those class periods? Really now, how much can they say about waving your arms around? How long does it take to learn the difference between four-four and six-eight?"

After Jennifer was born, I didn't have an outside job again for a long time, but I did put some of my education courses into practice. Oh, how I loved the children's homework! School was in my blood, and I always wanted my children to love it as much as I did. It started with Jennifer. When she would come home from school, we'd get her homework all laid out on the kitchen table and tackle it systematically. She rebelled in seventh grade, though, and started refusing to let me see her assignment sheets. After school she would take her books directly to her bedroom and close the door.

By then Travis was starting school, however, and being far less willful and independent than Jennifer, he made an ideal pupil. Bright and docile, he was content to let me supervise his homework. We always made a game out of it, and he rarely objected when I added practice drills, oral reading, and such to his assigned homework, which I often thought was pitifully small in quantity. As he got older, things started encroaching on our time, but to some degree we maintained our ritual at the kitchen table right on through high school, even though it shifted from the afternoon to the evening.

So there it is. It looks pitiful to see it reduced like this on paper, but those were my goals as a good mother—good manners and good grades. Two things that could have been part of a much bigger, more colorful picture became the picture itself, a very small black and white. By those two standards I was a good mother, a great mother, a splendid mother, but by my newer, higher standard, I was a failure.

So I'm on my way home after having my whole view of God revised, and I'm thinking about how miserably I've failed as a mother in spite of all the things I did to get my kids shaped up into my idea of model kids. I pull into our driveway on Windsor Drive and just sit in the car for a while. It's almost four-thirty now, and Ken isn't home yet from golf. I look at my house and think about Margaret's duplex, or her half of it, which would probably fit into our house three times.

But unlike me, Margaret seemed so content and so busy in her duplex. She had a job, but not at all the kind I expected a woman like her to have. She was not a teacher or an editor or a librarian or a journalist. No, she worked in the lunchroom of an elementary school! I felt as if my whole diagram of life had been scrambled up by Margaret. Here was this supremely Aware woman who, first of all, was a born-again Christian and, second, had a pretty menial job according to my way of looking at things and, third, came home to a two-bedroom duplex every day to cook meals for her husband and, fourth, seemed perfectly happy to live this kind of life.

I was sitting in the driveway feeling exhausted, even though it was a good six or seven hours before bedtime. I couldn't even muster the energy to get out of the car. Margaret had invited me back to church that night, but I told her I needed to go home and spend the evening thinking. I promised to come back the next Sunday, though.

I picked up the Bible she had given me and opened it. It fell open to the ribbon marker, and the first verse my eyes lighted on was in Psalm 116. "I will take the cup of salvation, and call upon the name of the Lord." This was what I was going to do tonight for a long time. I had already taken the cup of salvation, and now I was going to call upon the name of the Lord. I had a great deal to learn.

A movement in the corner of my eye made me look up. Our retired next-door neighbor, Wallace Yarnell, was flapping a rug over the iron railing of his front porch. As I tried to imagine Ken doing something so domestic, Wallace's wife, Eunice, came charging out the front door clapping her hands and crying, "Ferdinand! You stop that, you bad, bad dog!" Ferdinand was the Yarnells' Chihuahua, and as far as I could tell, the only thing he was doing was sniffing around a pair of gray stone rabbits situated among the low shrubbery beside their front door.

Eunice is very particular about the rabbits from what I've observed. She hoses them off and changes the ribbons around their necks regularly. This month the ribbons were bright red to match the ribbon on Eunice's February heart-shaped door wreath and the ribbon on the lamppost at the end of the sidewalk. She also had one of those little cast-iron coach boys holding up a lantern beside the driveway. You can guess what color the ribbon around the lantern was.

Out on the road a jogger ran past, and Ferdinand's attention was suddenly diverted from the rabbits to something alive and mobile. He went dashing out to the curb, yipping hysterically at the jogger, who was already past by now. I turned around and watched him dancing sideways at the edge of the yard, bouncing up and down the curb on his little twiglike legs. Meanwhile, Eunice raised a commotion all her own. "Ferdinand! You stop that!

You stop that right now! I never ever thought I'd have such a bad, bad dog!"
Her voice is rather shrill, with an edge to it.

Wallace had finished his rug flapping and disappeared well before Eunice
finished scolding Ferdinand and shooed him back inside. I turned and
looked at the house on the other side of ours. The Ellises, Pete and Sandy,
were a young couple who had the nicest lawn on the whole street. They were
"DINKs"—double income, no kids—and kept pretty much to themselves.
They had a large, gentle golden retriever named Lucky that wore a red bandanna tied around his neck and roamed the neighborhood quite harmlessly.

I had expected a great outpouring of neighborliness when we moved here
last summer, but it never happened. Things were different these days. Growing up, I remember my mother fixing entire meals for new neighbors. In our
old neighborhood over in Derby, I had always at least baked something, a
cake or a loaf of pumpkin bread, and sent it over when somebody new
moved in. But people didn't do that much anymore. Wallace Yarnell had
given Ken some grass seed back in the fall, and that's about as neighborly as
it got on our street.

I hadn't wanted to move here. Our old house over in Derby was fine.
Good grief, I told Ken, why would we want to move into a bigger house *after*
the kids leave home? He gave me two reasons. Number one, because we
could, referring to the fact that Ken's aunt Shasta had died a year earlier and
left Ken two hundred thousand dollars, and number two, so we'd have a
place big enough for our kids and their families to visit someday.

I laughed at this one. The prospects for grandkids were pretty bleak, I
reminded him, seeing that Jennifer had vowed never to trust another man as
long as she lived. She had suffered through a completely disastrous relationship with somebody she had met in law school named Marsdale—that really
was his first name—and had since declared that "Men are a pain." She was
"perfectly content" to be "unattached," she said, and she had "all kinds of
plans" that didn't include "a man with an ego the size of a barn." What
about a man whose ego wasn't the size of a barn, I asked her, to which she
replied, "There isn't any such creature."

And Travis—well, he got stuck in the preadolescent stage where boys are
scared to death of girls. I should be ashamed to tell this, but I'm going to
anyway. Here's what Travis did on prom night his senior year of high school
less than a year ago. *All by himself*, of course. He ordered a large pepperoni
pizza and watched eight straight hours of old *Columbo* reruns he had video-
taped. Something struck his fancy about the bumbling detective in the rumpled raincoat and rattletrap car who always triumphed over the suave so-
phisticates. Travis must have identified with Columbo because of all their
mutual blunders—running over curbs, bumping into people, knocking
things over, and what have you.

In between *Columbo* episodes that night, Travis made himself a milk shake, during which process he got a spoon caught in the garbage disposal and splattered chocolate ice cream all over my kitchen curtains. Besides the pizza and milk shake, he ate almost an entire box of Cheese Nips, half a bag of Chips Ahoy cookies, and three granola bars, washing it all down with a six-pack of Mountain Dew. And do you know what? He loved every minute of prom night. He talked about it for weeks afterward.

I've worn myself out worrying about my son and his preference for his own company, and I think I can honestly say I've finally given up after eighteen years. If there's one thing I've learned from it all, it's this. You can't force a personality on a kid. You can try, and you can try valiantly and persistently. You can run yourself ragged trying. You can drag other children over to your house by the droves, throw elaborate birthday parties, sign your kid up for every club or team that comes along, and shuttle him to parks and pools and camps and anywhere else that kids congregate, but you can't make him mingle. You can buy him his very own telephone, but you can't force him to pick it up and use it to plan social events with other kids.

I don't know if there are other college freshmen who have never had a date, but I know there's one at Piper College right now. If I were to look up someday and see Travis walking toward me with a girl by his side, people standing nearby would say, "I don't know what happened, but all of a sudden she just collapsed." My son is a good-looking kid, smart, funny, polite, athletic, musical—all the things that should make a person popular. But popular people generally talk, and in public Travis hardly opens his mouth except to smile and say, "Yes, ma'am."

So I've said all this to say our future doesn't look too promising in the area of grandchildren. And I got off on grandchildren to explain why we didn't need to move to a new house. As for Ken's first reason, because we could afford it, that's pretty lame, too. We could afford to go on a dogsled ride across the Yukon, but it doesn't mean we ought to.

We left a wonderful neighborhood over in Derby, and I had been sulking about it ever since. On this February afternoon as I sat in the driveway, however, I think I was ready to admit that I had made it worse than it needed to be. It wasn't a really bad house at all. In fact, it was a very, very nice house in a lot of ways.

There were other things I needed to face squarely, but I didn't know if I was ready to. I was sitting there in the car taking note of a couple of unimportant things like how the wrought-iron railing beside the front steps needed to be repainted and how a brass door knocker would look nice on the front door while I let my mind inch toward some important things like how my new relationship with God was going to affect my old relationships with people.

I thought of Ken. I knew our marriage had been blown off course—no, that implies a single ship. It would be closer to say that we were separate ships going in opposite directions. We were in dark arctic waters with ice floes all around. In Margaret Atwood's poem "Habitation," she calls marriage "the edge of the receding glacier." But at the end of the poem the couple learns "to make fire," so you have to take heart from that.

I was sitting in the car thinking of other lines of the poem when I heard the trill of my cell phone. It had been my Christmas present from Jennifer, and I had developed the habit of turning it on whenever I was in the car, even though I rarely used it. I had never even gotten an incoming call on it during the two months I had had it.

This is where the plot sickens, as my father used to say about bad movies. But first a memory has come to me suddenly, and it makes a good pair of lines for my backward poem. I think it must be important somehow. It's about the wind again, and it happened at our old house in Derby. "Or how it toppled our new sapling, the ball of roots / Wrenched from earth in spite of tethers and stakes." It was an extremely gusty wind that day, and that poor little spindly plum tree didn't have a chance. Okay, so I guess it's not really playing by the rules of the poetry game to think of two lines together like that, but it's my game, so I guess I can amend the rules.

And I've thought of another line, too, to go before these two: "How our red kite plunged to earth when it stilled." I remember how the wind suddenly stopped one spring day as Ken and I were flying a kite—something I had never done growing up. This was early in our marriage, before Jennifer was born, and Ken couldn't believe it when I told him I had never flown a kite. He went out and bought a red one with a yellow dragon printed on it, and we went out to a field near the USC campus in Columbia. It was going great until the wind for no reason just quit blowing. "How it thwarted us when we ventured out of doors" will be the line before that one, leading into the kite, the sapling, and all that.

> How it thwarted us when we ventured out of doors,
> How our red kite plunged to earth when it stilled,
> Or how it toppled our new sapling, the ball of roots
> Wrenched from earth in spite of tethers and stakes.
> Or how in the woods it clamored through the trees.
> Or how on the open beaches it held us apart,
> Snatching our words, flinging sand into our eyes.
> And though the wind died as we sank to the black deep,
> *Even the dirt kept breathing a small breath.*

Things are coming to me in a rush now. I'm thinking of looking out through a window and not being able to hear the wind but seeing its effects. So the next line should be indoors to lead into the outdoor section, something like "Through the glass. And let us not forget." That could fit the two parts together. You want to be careful about putting a period in the middle of a line of poetry, but sometimes it's exactly what's needed.

When I was a child, we had a creek behind our house, and my mother must have planted a hundred jonquil bulbs along the bank. This picture comes to my mind now, along with a line to add: "Only sight—a trembling bank of jonquils." In the springtime those jonquils were never standing still. From my upstairs bedroom window I could see them. Sometimes they appeared to be dancing, but other times trembling. Maybe the condition of the sky had a lot to do with it. I imagined on sunny days that they were happy but on cloudy ones they were scared.

As a kid I thought of the wind as a person with many different voices, somebody you never quite got to know very well because he would arrive without warning and then leave as suddenly, a lot like my uncle Clayborn, in fact, who was a bachelor and an amateur ventriloquist. He might pop in suddenly on a Monday evening, on his way to Atlanta maybe, and then leave before dawn on Tuesday so he wouldn't hit the early morning traffic.

I hated to be outdoors in a strong wind. I'd always run inside and look out through a window. I liked it when the wind was strong enough to be swooshing things around but not strong enough that I could hear it through the window.

So I have another line: "A voice that through the pane had no sound." I can feel the beginning of the poem bubbling up like a fountain. Counting my lines, I realize I have twelve so far.

> A voice that through the pane had no sound,
> Only sight—a trembling bank of jonquils
> Through the glass. And let us not forget
> How it thwarted us when we ventured out of doors,
> How our red kite plunged to earth when it stilled,
> Or how it toppled our new sapling, the ball of roots
> Wrenched from earth in spite of tethers and stakes.
> Or how in the woods it clamored through the trees.
> Or how on the open beaches it held us apart,
> Snatching our words, flinging sand into our eyes.
> And though the wind died as we sank to the black deep,
> *Even the dirt kept breathing a small breath.*

The beginning is easy now. "Let us not forget the voice of the wind" comes next, followed by "And as we sift our past for blame to share" as the opening line. Generally you don't want to start a poem with *And*, as if you're picking up right in the middle of something. But that's exactly what I'm doing. I'm in the middle of something big, trying to look back and ahead at the same time. So much has happened before the beginning of this poem that the only honest way to launch it is with *And*. *In medias res* can apply to poetry as well as drama.

If it's unclear what the wind stands for in the poem, it will come. I'm still working through it myself. It's far, far from a perfect poem. For example, I'd like to add a few more images after the second line, things I saw the wind doing through the window. And it doesn't rhyme, of course, nor does it bounce along in a steady meter, so some will condemn it for this, though these aren't things I will change.

Those who insist on rhyme would have to condemn Milton's *Paradise Lost* for the same reason, not that I'm suggesting for a second that my poem comes anywhere close to Milton's. And those who insist on meter, well, they shouldn't. A poem doesn't have to have a regular beat.

Now, to return to the telephone call. The cell phone rings as I'm sitting in the driveway, and two thoughts quickly cross my mind. First, I hardly ever receive calls on it, so it's probably a wrong number. Second, I've given my cell phone number to only four or five people. This last thought is what makes me scramble a little faster to get to it. Maybe Travis or Jennifer needs me. It surprises me to realize how much I'm hoping one of my children needs me.

As well as I can remember, here's how the telephone call went. But first, remember what I said earlier about the timing of the events of this day. The thought came to me later that I must be following in the steps of my father, who got a phone call from his doctor on the morning of my wedding day telling him that the lab tests didn't look good and he needed to come in for a biopsy right away. In his case, though, the bad phone call came before the happy event. In mine, it came after. Keep in mind that I've just undergone a wonderful, life-changing spiritual awakening, and now I'm sitting in my driveway saying "Hello?" into my cell phone.

I recognized Ken's voice at once. "I'm on my way," he said. He didn't quite sound like himself, but I knew it was Ken. There was a tone of something very close to eagerness.

I couldn't figure out why he'd be telling me this, but I said, "Okay."

"Where are you?" he said.

"Home," I said. "In the car."

He laughed a little, and then there was a pause. "What are you doing? Sitting in the driveway waiting for me to call?" he said.

"Sitting in the driveway, yes. Waiting for you to call, no."

He sounded puzzled now. "Hey, you asked me to call you as soon as—" He broke off, and when he spoke next, his voice had changed. I can't think of the right word for it—panicky is too strong. There was a definite change, though. Some awful revelation had clicked in his brain. "Elizabeth?" he said quietly.

"That's my name," I said.

"Well, I thought you were"—he broke off to laugh as he tried to recover—"you were going to . . . be out at the tennis courts all day." He sounded relieved to find his way to the end of that sentence. It was actually a pretty good way out, since earlier in the week I had mentioned signing up for the YMCA spring league, which would be starting up again in March. I had even gotten my racket out of the closet after a six-month layoff from tennis and had checked the strings and grip.

If he had spoken less haltingly, if his voice hadn't crept into its upper register, I might have fallen for it, but suddenly my mind was flooded with unthinkable thoughts.

"No," I said, "I went to church instead." I tried to speak lightly, but my heart was pounding in my ears. I wondered if I was talking too loud.

"Church?" he said. "You went to church? Well, I'm sure that was interesting." I knew by this point that my suspicions weren't just in my head. Something about the cautious way he was proceeding told me.

"It was," I said. "Very much so." Then, though I knew this whole conversation was a charade, I added, "Then someone invited me over for dinner."

"Oh," he said in a brighter tone, "well, speaking of dinner, that's why I was calling." He was grasping at straws now. "I was wondering if you wanted me to pick up something to eat on my way home." Neither one of us spoke for a few seconds. As far back as I could remember, he had never once called me after a Sunday golf game to ask if I wanted him to pick up something for dinner. We always fended for ourselves on Sunday nights. "You might not be hungry, though, if you ate dinner," he said. He was trying so hard to sound cheerfully offhanded.

"No, I'm not."

"Well, then, I'll just grab something for myself and . . . well, I'll be on home in a few minutes."

I switched my cell phone off without replying and saw that my hands were shaking. I sat in shock for several long moments, during which for some reason I started counting, and when I reached forty-three, I thought of something to do. I didn't know Ken's cell phone number from memory, since I rarely called him on it, but I had it written down on a slip of paper I kept in my billfold. I found it now, then switched my phone back on and slowly dialed the number. It was busy, as I had known it would be.

It wasn't hard to figure out what had happened. In spite of his organized mind and generally tidy habits, Ken often wrote down phone numbers with no names beside them. Somewhere he had my cell phone number written down, and somewhere else he had another cell phone number written down. Evidently, he had checked his records and dialed the wrong one.

So if someone were to ask me what happened on February 18, I'd say, "Well, first God claimed me for all eternity, and then an hour later I drove home and found out my husband had a girlfriend. That's what happened to me on February 18."

And as we sift our past for blame to share,
Let us not forget the voice of the wind.
A voice that through the pane had no sound,
Only sight—a trembling bank of jonquils
Through the glass. And let us not forget
How it thwarted us when we ventured out of doors,
How our red kite plunged to earth when it stilled,
Or how it toppled our new sapling, the ball of roots
Wrenched from earth in spite of tethers and stakes.
Or how in the woods it clamored through the trees.
Or how on the open beaches it held us apart,
Snatching our words, flinging sand into our eyes.
And though the wind died as we sank to the black deep,
Even the dirt kept breathing a small breath.

I haven't come far in all of this, but I've written a poem. It doesn't have a title yet, and it needs considerable revision, but it's a first draft. Sometimes you say more than you mean to when you write a poem. I used to think a poet had his message all thought out first and then he just sat down and put it all on paper, but I know better now. The words you put down on paper lead you to the message. Ask any good poet, and he'll tell you the same thing. The words come first, and the truth grows out of them. Sometimes you feel your way through a poem like a blind man, and sometimes at the end you're healed and can see.

I have a continent of sorrow to explore. But as I do so, I know what else I must do. I must call upon the name of the Lord. And I must go on living somehow. And I must remember that *Even the dirt kept breathing a small breath.*

Where a Garden Once Was Kept

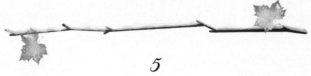

5

I sat in the car several minutes longer, thinking of nothing and everything. The Bible was still open in my lap, and when I looked down at the verse in Psalms, I felt a momentary flood of anger. So this is what happens when a person takes the cup of salvation? Is this how God works it so that you'll be forced to call upon him? Wasn't it only fair to warn people that there was something missing in the middle of the verse? Number one, you take the cup of salvation; number two—here's the missing part—you get flattened by some horrible turn of events; and number three, you call upon the name of the Lord and beg for rescue.

Even as these thoughts were coming to me, however, I knew they were just filling up space. I knew that deep down I didn't really mean them. Underneath, other thoughts were seething, crowding in on each other. This is probably not the exact order they came at me, but it went something like this.

First, the most obvious and devastating thought was that Ken had been unfaithful to me. I could find no other explanation for his strange phone call. When I timidly suggested to myself that maybe there was some really innocent explanation that didn't have anything to do with another woman, I said right out loud there in the car, "Get real." Ken's manner on the phone had told me the truth. In conjunction with the enormous sense of betrayal I felt, I couldn't believe I had missed all the clues that must have been dropped. So much for being Aware. "For being so smart, you sure are dumb," I told myself.

And yes, of course, another thought was shouting itself at me. "Who is she?" Then back again to "Maybe she's just a good friend." Then, "No, it's true. Ken is having an affair." But somehow I just couldn't bring this picture of Ken into clear focus. Never mind that I had just been confronted with some pretty convincing circumstantial evidence.

Always before, when somebody on television or in the newspaper would say that so-and-so couldn't have committed such a crime because "I *know* him, and I know he'd never do such a thing," I would always say to myself, "Well, honey, you've just announced to the whole world that you're a total idiot." And now here I was, part of me wanting to gouge Ken's eyes out but the other part of me saying, "He couldn't do this. I know him, and I know he'd never do such a thing." It would have been enough to make me laugh if the situation hadn't been so serious.

I knew Ken like the back of my hand. Every habit, every expression, every gesture, every preference, every hang-up, every mood. They all added up to picky, predictable, intense, focused, steady, and reserved. It was a joke in my family that Ken always managed to get out of hugging anybody. My sister, Juliet, who was a liberal hugger, used to try to corner him at family functions, but he was skillful at dodging. He'd sometimes stand behind me and stick out a hand for shaking.

I remembered all of a sudden something Juliet had once said to him on one of these occasions. "I can only hope you're more affectionate in private than you are in public." Then she had turned to me and said, "It's a wonder you two have any kids." It was all very good-natured, with everybody laughing, but it was pretty clear that Juliet considered the avoidance of physical contact a major character flaw. Ken teased right back, though, telling her kids they ought to call her "Smother" instead of "Mother."

To be honest, it had never bothered me when we were first married that Ken shied away from public displays of affection. In fact, I remember thinking it was sort of romantic the way he was so different at home than he was in public. At some point I quit thinking it was romantic, though, and a couple of times I had even said things to him like "I wish you'd stop treating me like your great-aunt in front of people." For years I had watched Juliet and her husband kiss and give each other full-body hugs right out in the open, and I had wished at times that Ken could be more like Tony, but without the bushy beard and spare tire.

Once a waitress leaned over behind Ken at a restaurant and gave him a little half hug. He jumped as if she'd touched his bare flesh with a red-hot poker. She jumped back herself, then giggled uncomfortably and said, "Y'all come back again real soon, hear?" She looked at me in a way that I interpreted as sympathetic before she laid the check on the table and left. I remember chiding Ken for embarrassing her. I think I even told him he needed to loosen up. "I mean, good grief, she couldn't have meant anything by it if she hugged you in front of your wife!" I said.

So now, of course, I'm sitting in the car with dreadful images flashing across my mind of Ken loosening up in a way I never intended. I'm seeing someone else besides me on the receiving end of his hugs, and I'm so mad I can hardly think straight. The only other woman I remember seeing him hug was his mother.

Though I've been a very polite person publicly, this isn't the first time I've been angry, of course. I've experienced those moments every woman goes through of saying things you wish you'd never said—maybe on a few occasions even *shouting* them. I've been so irritated at things my children have done that it's been easy to forget all those tender moments when I thought they were angels dropped down out of heaven. I've had urges over the years to put my hands around Ken's neck and strangle him for something he did, like the Valentine's Day when he brought home a single red rose in a cheap blue vase with a bright pink Winn-Dixie sticker still on it. That gift had "tacky" written all over it. Also "last-minute" and "obligatory."

I became so infuriated once during a tennis match, when I knew beyond a doubt that my opponent was calling shots out that were clearly in, that I even made what could be called a modest little scene right there on the court in front of a lot of people I didn't know. It was during a tournament, and a referee had to come over to mediate the situation. Going further back, I was once so mad at my brother, Greg, that I took his favorite pop bottle from his collection, then leaned out a window in the second story of our house in Burma, Georgia, and dropped it very deliberately onto the driveway. It was a Barq's cherry soda bottle, and he was never able to replace it. He still brings up the incident.

But I could take all those other angers over all my years of living and put them on one side of the scale, then take this new anger and put it on the other side by itself, and the side with the new one in it would bang down fast and hard, as if the other side had only a few feathers in it. This was a completely new level of anger.

Another question battled its way through all the anger: "How long has this been going on?" And, believe it or not, this is what led me back to the verse in Psalms. I had a pretty good idea that whatever was going on between Ken and this other person—and I didn't think they were getting together to play Chinese checkers—hadn't gotten started just today.

And, amazingly, I was even thinking clearly enough to realize that if I had found out about it a week ago or even just yesterday, I would have had to face the whole thing unfortified. And, really, wasn't *now* a better time to find out than three weeks from now, or four months, or a year? There was so much I didn't yet know about God, but I think I did know from the first hour of my conversion that even in something as terrible as this, God's mercy was evident.

The anger I was feeling was real, of course, but I wonder now if I wasn't using it to cover up some other emotion that was even bigger, one that was even harder to deal with. Anger is really an easy emotion in a lot of ways. You can just let go and flail around and wallow in it. It verges on enjoyment the way you can throw yourself into it so completely, especially when you've been undeniably wronged. I guess it's a lot like sorrow, too.

Maybe there are really only two big emotions—sorrow and joy—and everything falls under one of those. Maybe sorrow includes everything from guilt and hatred to disappointment and fear and, of course, anger and hurt. I imagined my present sorrow as a bitter drink already mixed and stirred and placed to my lips. I couldn't separate the parts—I had to drink it all.

The car suddenly seemed very stuffy. I closed the Bible and got out, standing for a minute on the driveway, feeling slightly dizzy and wondering what I should do. If I went inside, I might see something of Ken's—his moccasins by the door, say, or a stack of mail on the counter that he hadn't sorted through or his dirty cereal bowl in the sink—and I might suddenly start smashing things. I want you to know I felt perfectly capable of this at the moment. I considered getting back in the car and driving somewhere, but I had no idea where I'd go, and I didn't trust myself behind the wheel right now. So I walked through the carport, which was presently too crowded with other things to accommodate the full length of a car, and into the backyard.

Before we had moved in last summer, the house had been vacant for over a year, and it had been on the market a full year before that. The former owner had finally just moved out, out to California I think, and left it in the hands of a realtor. This owner, a retired man, had a firm price in mind, so it's not hard to guess why the house didn't sell. Combine an overpriced house with a stubborn seller, and you've got a For Sale sign planted in the front yard for a long, long time.

When Ken made an offer on the house, the realtor had laughed. "The last guy offered more than that," he told Ken, "and Mr. Sherman told me not to insult him again by calling with such a ridiculous offer." When Ken insisted on trying anyway, the realtor finally gave in. "You don't know what you're asking me to do," he said, "but, hey, it's part of my job description to be abused by my clients. So okay, I'll call the old coot. I'll tell him your offer, then hold the phone a foot away from my ear while he gives me what for. And then I'll call you and say, 'I told you so.'"

When the realtor called Ken back the next day, he started laughing again. "Go ahead and tell me," Ken said. "I'm a big boy. I can take it."

And the realtor laughed some more, then told Ken that Mr. Sherman made a counteroffer of only three thousand more than the offer. "It's unbelievable!" he told Ken. "This man is absolutely the worst skinflint I've ever known. He hasn't countered *anybody's* offer. Something must have happened. Maybe he's got a girlfriend, and he needs cash to take her around the world or something. Whatever it is, we must have caught him at the right time. Let's get the paper work out to him before he has time to change his mind."

When he stopped talking, Ken told him he wanted to counter the counter-offer. Suddenly the realtor wasn't cheerful anymore. He told Ken he was crazy. "I'm telling you, this guy is the type to blow up and call the whole thing off," he said. "You better take a good thing while you got it. It's a bargain, and we both know it."

But Ken insisted, and anybody can guess the outcome, since we're living in the house now. And what would you expect out of a house that had sat empty for over a year and before that had been occupied by a tightwad who, according to the realtor, went to bed at sundown so he wouldn't have to burn any electricity?

That's what all this has been leading up to. The house was a bargain, yes, but there's a downside to most bargains. The downside of this one was that Ken's vision of what the house *could be* required a lot more money than just the cost of the house itself, not to mention all the sweat. The neighbors must have been eager for someone to move in. In a neighborhood of well-maintained, upper-middle-class homes, the place had been an eyesore for a long time. All the more reason you'd think they would have done a little more to welcome us.

So I'm outside our house right now, walking into the backyard, which is the only part of the house that remotely interested me when Ken first coaxed me over here to look at it early last summer. He actually tricked me into coming, taking me out for barbecue first and then "swinging by" the house, which was way over in Berea, a good seven or eight miles from where we ate over in Filbert and the opposite direction from our home in Derby.

In its run-down condition, I wasn't impressed with the house itself, but I felt something like a spark of inspiration when I stepped into the backyard. It's hard to explain, but it was a definite feeling I got deep inside. I could imagine spending whole days out here watering flower beds, walking along pathways, reading poetry, watching fireflies, standing in the middle of it all and looking up at the sky through the treetops.

So forget about the roof repairs right now and the new furnace and the insulation and all the inside stuff we had to do, like new paint and carpet and kitchen cupboards, and look with me at the yard. Picture me walking through the backyard, still holding the Bible that Margaret gave me and still reeling from what I've just discovered about my husband of twenty-eight years.

There's a swing back here, made of cedar and treated for rain. Ken bought it for me for Mother's Day when Travis was just a little boy, and I had read *Stuart Little*, *Charlotte's Web*, and *Trumpet of the Swan* to Travis in that swing on late summer afternoons that year—it must have been at least ten or twelve years ago. Mostly I had avoided the swing since he had outgrown my reading to him. The sight of it made something hurt inside me.

I sat down in it now. The swing was situated close to the kitchen window facing the whole backyard. It's a deep yard, full of tall pine, poplar, and oak trees, and I remembered even in the middle of hot summer days last year how dim and cool it felt back here. It was plain that somebody who lived here in the past had fancied yard work and had tried to make the backyard into a garden retreat with stone-lined pathways laid out.

In the center was a large circular area bordered with liriope and red bricks set in at an angle so that they formed a pointed edge all the way around. An old birdbath and two small stone benches sat in the middle, along with a brown bird feeder on a tilted pole and a couple of small dogwood trees, stunted because of the lack of sunlight.

Azalea bushes had been planted in clusters, interspersed with forsythia, hydrangea, gardenia, lilac, and others I couldn't identify. I'm not really that much of a horticulturist myself, and in February they all looked pretty much alike anyway. I knew there were irises and lilies in a bed close to the house, though they had already finished blooming by the time we moved in last summer, and there were peonies under the den windows.

A thick mat of dead leaves and pine needles covered most of the ground, and the back of the lot had been taken over by ivy. Oddly, though, the effect wasn't one of decay so much as just rest. The backyard seemed to be waiting for something. They could have filmed *The Secret Garden* here if only we'd had a tall stone wall and a gate with a key. I could imagine Dickon and Ben Weatherstaff bringing things to life here.

And then there were the daffodils. This was the most conspicuous feature in February, although I had no idea last summer that I would be assaulted by their sudden and profuse blooming eight months hence. Daffodils were the furthest thing from my mind back then. Whoever the garden person was who used to live here, he must have run across a closeout sale on daffodil bulbs. There were even more blooming in the front yard than back here, with all the trees to block their light, but I could tell the backyard was going to be lit up before it was all done.

Daffodils come in so many varieties. Just the week before, Professor Huckabee had read to us a poem called "Dooryard Flower." I couldn't help picturing my own backyard when he read the line that spoke of a place "where a garden once was kept." The poem was about someone gathering armfuls of daffodils to take to a sick friend, and the poet, Ellen Bryant Voigt, described them all with such delicate precision that I could barely breathe while he read the poem aloud.

Talk about snarled thoughts and conflicting emotions. I'm sitting in the swing practically incapacitated with the knowledge of Ken's unfaithfulness, yet looking around at my beautiful backyard, once cultivated but now grown wild, taking note of all the details and feeling something almost like a physical hand comforting me. The backyard had been the right place to come, I guess, if any place can be right at such a time. Or maybe it wasn't the yard at all, I thought. Maybe it was God reminding me that I wasn't sitting out here in the swing all by myself.

Sitting there, I could see through the trees to the house directly behind ours over on the next street. I had often seen their lights at night and wondered who the people were, but I had never taken the time to make my way through the undergrowth at the back of our lot to meet them. Anyway, as I had told myself in the first few months, they should be the ones to come visit us first. I wondered if they even had any idea that they had new neighbors living behind them. Did they ever look at our lights through the trees and wonder about us?

I think Aware people do this—they wonder about the lives of other people. Part of being Aware is realizing what a tiny particle of humanity you are and contemplating all the vastness of the rest of it. But even while I'm understanding that my husband's indiscretions and my current pain aren't even making a blip on the large screen of Life in General, that doesn't keep me from feeling like it's the end of my life in particular. There's no sense of perspective at a time like this. Your own life is what matters most. It's selfish, but it's true. It's no comfort to say, "This is of no consequence in the scheme of the universe." A person's universe is himself.

The light was fading now, but still I sat in the swing. Looking at my watch, I saw that only twenty minutes had passed since I had talked with Ken on the phone. Twenty minutes, and my life was turned upside down. But even as the dramatic, alarmist part of me was asking, "What in the world am I going to *do*?" one very insistent answer kept repeating itself: "Call upon the name of the Lord."

Suddenly the words of the preacher at the Church of the Open Door that morning came to my mind. *"Vanity of vanities; all is vanity."* Other thoughts from the passage came to me, too, something about youth and old age and something about the sun and moon and stars. I turned to the list of books in the front of the Bible and found Ecclesiastes. It was hard to read in the dim light, but soon I had found the words I was looking for and could make them out.

The whole chapter was full of poetic metaphors. "While the sun, or the light, or the moon, or the stars, be not darkened, nor the clouds return after the rain." It was talking about the days of one's youth. And the verses that followed, with their almost whimsical descriptions of old people's failing eyesight, missing teeth, and chirpy voices, led into those solemn words "Then shall the dust return to the earth as it was," and after that the inevitable "Vanity of vanities . . . all is vanity."

A pretty grim picture of life. You have a few days of youth and sunshine before the windows darken and you get old and die. I read to the end of the book, and here's what I came to. The last two verses claimed to give the "conclusion of the whole matter," and here it was: "Fear God, and keep his commandments." That was it. And then I noticed this heading above those last two verses: *"The best thing possible to man under the law."* And just what, I thought, does "under the law" mean? It sounded heavy. I couldn't help thinking there must be something better than "under the law." I had questions to ask Margaret.

My eyes wandered across the page to the first chapter of another book called the Song of Solomon, and just as my eyes settled on the words "but mine own vineyard have I not kept," I heard the sound of Ken's car in the driveway and saw his headlights sweep across the side of the Yarnells' house and settle into the trees behind the carport, then go dark. No sound of the car door slamming, though.

I could imagine him sitting in his car, trying to figure out his next step. He had to feel like anything he did next was going to be the wrong thing. Like filling your mouth with scalding coffee—do you spray it out or swallow it? Neither one is good. How would you go about approaching your wife after making such a monumental blunder as he had just made? Ken used to like jigsaw puzzles. He'd work a big one-thousand-piece one every year during our summer vacation. So now here was a new puzzle for him, one of those great big challenging 3D ones with trillions of pieces.

And how was I feeling as I sat waiting for him? I'll be honest. Part of me was feeling satisfied over what he must be going through right now. I was pretty sure this wasn't really a *Christian* feeling, but something perverse in me wanted him to be suffering a million agonies. I wanted his stomach to churn, I wanted his knees to turn to jelly, I wanted his heart to race and his palms to sweat. I wanted him to stammer, and I wanted his voice to crack.

I wanted him to feel like a lump of dirt, unworthy to breathe the same air with decent, ordinary people. My earlier thoughts of God's mercy had evaporated. At the moment I wasn't thinking about calling upon the name of the Lord. I was thinking of all the names I could call Ken.

Finally I heard the door slam. A few seconds later I heard the trunk slam shut, and the next thing I heard, of course, was the door of the storage shed open and close as he locked his golf clubs away. How like Ken to take care of all the mundane details first. He wouldn't have thought of leaving his clubs in the trunk of the car overnight, not even on a night like tonight. Here's how his thoughts would run: First you put away your clubs, then you brush off your golf shoes and store them in the cupboard by the back door, then you go inside and own up to your marital infidelity. I'm sure it made perfect sense to him.

Moments later I saw the kitchen light go on. I guess he must have thought I was sitting inside in the dark, and as I saw the lights in other rooms flick on, it pleased me to think of him hunting for me, wondering perhaps if I was going to spring out from behind a door with a carving knife in my hand. I imagined him going from room to room, calling softly, "Elizabeth? Elizabeth?" He would retrace his steps after that, calling a little louder, maybe even opening closet doors and looking under beds this time. I guessed wrong about that, though, because before I knew it, he was coming around the side of the house into the backyard.

"There you are," he said, stopping in front of me.

"Here I am," I said. My hands were resting on the open Bible, and I didn't look up at him.

I suddenly realized I had no idea what was coming. Though I thought I knew Ken inside and out, I couldn't begin to predict how he was going to handle this. And what's more, I didn't know how I was going to respond to whatever he said. It could all be very civil or very, very ugly. It could be very businesslike or very emotional. It could be short or long.

"Can I sit down?" he asked.

"I'm sure you can," I said and moved over.

He ran a hand across the seat of the swing before sitting down, then brushed both hands together. "Did you wipe this thing off?" he said. It was a lucky thing for him that I wasn't holding a shotgun in my lap right then. "Oh, well, it doesn't really matter," he added quickly, and he sat down beside me. The swing rocked a little, then grew still.

Ken sighed. It wasn't one of his exasperated sighs, but one filled with dread of what's ahead, the kind that says, "Okay, here we are, now what?" Only he didn't say anything. We sat there together with the night closing in, neither of us speaking. This won't surprise anybody who's married. How do you go about initiating a conversation like this one was going to be?

It was an owl that prompted the first words. He lives somewhere in the vicinity of our house, and he chose that moment to hoot. Ken lifted his head and scanned the treetops. The owl hooted again, sounding closer than usual. "Don't owls hibernate?" Ken asked, then said, "No, migrate—that's the word I meant." I couldn't believe my ears.

I must have made a disgusted sound, because he quickly cleared his throat and said, "I'm sorry."

"Oh, don't apologize," I said. "This is a perfect time to discuss how owls spend their winters."

The owl hooted again, and Ken let out another sigh. "Oh, Elizabeth," he said, and after a long pause, he added, "What do you want me to do?"

Looking straight ahead, I answered steadily, "Maybe you should have thought of that question earlier. Maybe if you'd given just the least bit of thought to what I wanted you to do, all this wouldn't be happening."

It's funny how your mind can be operating on two levels at the same time. I wanted to be mature and reasonable, but I knew I wasn't going to be. There is no reasonableness at a time like this. I was thinking of all the years that had passed and wondering how we could have come to this point. Oddly, I suddenly remembered very vividly a time twenty years ago when

Ken and I used to go to an open field near our house in Derby and throw a Frisbee back and forth.

This is why the art of conversation is such a difficult one, I think. It's not merely a two-way exchange of words with another person, but you've got this other whole conversation going on in your head at the same time. When somebody says something that seems irrelevant in a conversation, you have to assume he's slipped off to his interior track.

But anyway, I knew that "mature and reasonable" was impossible in a conversation like the one that was unfolding between us. What kind of woman would accept her husband's unfaithfulness maturely and reasonably?

And here's another funny thing. At the same time that I wanted Ken to be eaten up with guilt, I remember feeling grateful to him for one thing at this point, two really. At least he hadn't tried to invent an excuse for the phone call to make me think it was all a simple mistake. He could have tried that. A lot of husbands would have. He also could have just chosen not to come home. A lot of husbands would have done that, too. But he had come home, and he wasn't trying to make up a story. I never would have said any of this out loud, though. Can you imagine? "You've done a horrible, unforgivable thing, Ken, but thank you so much for coming home to face the truth."

"So what do you want me to do?" he said again.

And until the moment I spoke, I had no idea I was going to say this. "I think you'd better leave," I said.

"You mean, go inside?" he said.

"No, I mean . . . leave," I said.

How like me to say something drastic like that, and how like Ken not to argue. He used to just ignore the extreme things I'd say from time to time, knowing the moment would pass and I'd never act on them. But all the rules were different now. We had never come to a bend in the road like this one.

He stood up, and I could feel him looking down at me. "All right," he said at last. "If that's what you really want, I'll leave." He waited a few moments as if to give me a chance for revision, and when I didn't speak, he turned and slowly walked away. I heard him sigh again.

Now here's a question for you. Is that really what I wanted? After Ken went inside and as he got his things together, I sat in the swing and asked myself that same question over and over. *Is this really what I want?* It was getting cold now, more like February should feel. I pulled my sweater up around my neck and held it tight. The sky through the trees wasn't completely black yet, but I could see a few lonely stars glimmering halfheartedly through wispy clouds. The moon was fuzzy and lopsided. I had never seen a night sky so bleak.

After he took his suitcase out to his car, Ken came again to the backyard.

"Well, I'm going now," he said, and although I thought of a thousand things to say, I didn't say any of them. Again he paused as if waiting for something, but I didn't speak. So he walked away, got in his car, and backed out of the driveway. I don't know how much longer I sat in the dark listening for him to come back.

Three Foggy Mornings and One Rainy Day

6

The world is a very small place, mainly because there are so many people living in it. It sounds like a contradiction, but it's not. What I mean is this. Because so many people are bunched together in towns and cities, their lives are bound to intersect on many planes.

They say you could take five people at random from five different places in the United States and within a few minutes find a personal connection between two of them. I believe it. I believe I could probably go up to somebody on a park bench in New York City or in an airport in Los Angeles, strike up a conversation, and soon discover that we both know the same person who's a postal clerk in Kankakee, Illinois, or both had an ancestor who fought in the Battle of Cowpens during the Revolutionary War, or both attended the same junior high school in Georgia.

And television, radio, newspapers—they all make the world smaller. "Where were you when you heard the news about Kennedy's assassination?" this person on the park bench might ask me, and after I answer, "In eighth-grade science class watching a filmstrip on comets," we might sit quietly, absorbing the knowledge that we shared a particular moment of national shock. The truth is that people are linked to other people, whether they want to be or not.

I was convinced of the world's smallness again four days after the Sunday evening Ken got in his car and drove away. I won't go into the details of those four intervening days except to say I functioned in a daze. I didn't eat a single bite of food those first two days, and I remember drinking only one glass of water in the middle of the second night. But after each fresh gush of anger and pain would sweep over me, something would call faintly to me, as if over a great distance, and I would open my Bible to Psalm 116 and read my verse again. "I will take the cup of salvation, and call upon the name of the Lord." It was always there, right in the same place every time.

I didn't know where Ken had gone. I imagined him backing out of our driveway, dialing a number on his cell phone—making very sure he had the right one this time—then heading down Highway 11 to . . . where? I tried to keep my mind from forming the pictures, but they kept coming. Where did this other person live? Over in Derby? Filbert, maybe? Surely not here in Berea. Maybe Greenville or Spartanburg.

It couldn't be too far away, I knew, because Ken had planned to go see her on his way back from playing golf, then make it home before it got late enough to worry me. I kept imagining him pulling up to an apartment building and parking. I don't know why I insisted on an apartment instead of a house, but that was the picture I had.

He would get out of his car, carry his suitcase up a flight of stairs, and knock at her door. And she would open the door almost instantly, then pull him inside and . . . I tried to stop the film there, but it usually kept going until finally I remembered I needed to start breathing again. Then I would think of the verse once more and start reciting it. "I will take the cup of salvation, and call upon the name of the Lord."

I guess at first I thought this was the only verse of comfort in the whole Bible, but it was on Tuesday afternoon that I unglued my eyes from that thirteenth verse and saw another verse earlier in the chapter. "I was brought low, and he helped me," it said. I liked that. I skipped up to the first verse and read, "I love the Lord, because he hath heard my voice and my supplications." I started looking through the rest of the Psalms and suddenly felt as though I had stumbled upon a treasure chest. And other books of the Bible, I found, contained promises and words of comfort, also.

I wasn't very experienced in praying, but I spoke to God earnestly, repeating over and over, "Help me know what to do. Help me to be strong." I won't lie and say that the verses I discovered and my simple prayers healed my pain and erased my sorrow, but I will say that they helped to sustain me over those first darkest days. They gave me something to hold onto and something to say aloud over and over.

They also gave me instruction, for when I read in Ecclesiastes—yes, I made my way back to that happy book for some reason—"Whatsoever thy hand findeth to do, do it with thy might," I knew I must get busy doing something. Sitting inside with all the blinds shut and the doors locked, crying my eyes out, surely hadn't accomplished anything useful.

So I closed my Bible Tuesday night, determined to answer the phone if it rang early Wednesday morning as it had on Monday and Tuesday mornings. For two mornings I had let the answering machine take the calls from two different school principals, and of course, I hadn't called back.

February is always a prime month for substitute teachers. Christmas vacation is long gone, winter is growing tedious by now, and even though the daffodils are blooming, spring break still looks very far away.

Besides the principals' calls, the phone had rung eight other times on Monday and Tuesday, most of which I didn't answer. Three times it was Ken, and he asked me to call him at his office at the college, which I didn't do. Once it was my mother, and I picked up the phone as she was leaving a message. Her first question was "Well, how are things going, honey? I hope they're going better for you than they are for me. The older I get, the more convinced I am that man is born to affliction."

Juliet was there visiting her for a couple of days, and the two of them had just gotten back from a home decorating show, which was pretty much of a disappointment overall. "A lot of really silly things," my mother said. "Just trinkets and useless froufrou mostly." She wanted to know when I was coming to see her, reminding me that Juliet had been twice already since Christmas. "Juliet says Tony gets along fine when she's gone," she said to me, "and I'm sure Ken would, too. You never come to see me. And don't try to tell me you don't have the time, with Travis away at school now."

I told her I'd have to see what I could work out. I didn't tell her I had something far bigger on my mind than a visit to Georgia.

After telling me about the annoying side effects of her new medication, she ended the call by saying, "Wait a minute, Juliet is saying something. Oh, she says to give Ken a big hug for her," and I could hear Juliet laughing in the background. "And a kiss, too, she says," my mother added. "A big slurpy one."

Another call, one I didn't pick up, came close to ten o'clock on Monday night. It was from Margaret Tuttle, wondering why I was absent from poetry class that night and asking me to call her if I needed anything. She also told me she was praying for me and was thinking of our nice visit together last Sunday with many pleasant memories. That's exactly how she said it—"with many pleasant memories." She said she hoped it would be the first of many such visits.

I couldn't help wondering what the people at the Church of the Open Door would say if they knew I had asked my husband to leave home and that he had done it. Would they reach out and shake my hand in the same friendly way they had last Sunday? How did these people respond to messy situations? I guess Margaret knew a thing or two about messy situations from her own past, but what about the rest of them?

For all I knew, that church might be full of people just like the Moffett family and Rex Harkness. Maybe the Church of the Open Door was just a bunch of losers and eccentrics who stuck together because the rest of the world shunned them. Maybe they lived for Sunday, the one day of the week when they could feel accepted among people who were as strange as themselves.

Maybe this salvation thing was risky in a social sense. What if all these people were communally Unaware? Of course, I already knew Margaret, Thomas, and Hardy, but what if they were the only Aware people in the whole church? Did I really want to join up with a band of misfits?

The YMCA director also called and left a message asking if she could put me down again to help plan the end-of-season luncheon in late May for the tennis league. She was working ahead and getting things lined up, she said, and she reminded me that the matches would be starting in a few short weeks, so she hoped I was getting all warmed up for a good season. She had made some new contacts and was looking forward to a larger pool of participants this year. She's one of those people who wear you out with their cheerfulness.

The other two phone calls were for Ken, one from a man and the other from a woman named Heather Moody. And yes, I did call the woman's number back out of curiosity and suspicion. The voice that answered said, "Hello, thank you for calling Sears Pest Control, where our goal is to meet your needs. Total satisfaction or your money back. This is Heather. How may I help you today?" Imagine having to say all that every time you answered the telephone.

Heather sounded very brisk and efficient. She sounded very happy also, as if working for Sears Pest Control was a gold medal and she was the lucky one who got to wear it. It turned out that they were doing a free termite inspection for new homeowners in our area and had "tentatively scheduled Mr. and Mrs. Ken Landis for an appointment next Friday morning, the second of March, at ten o'clock." She spoke with great confidence. "May I confirm the appointment time?"

I struggled to think of words to put together in a sentence. "Well, it's . . . well, next Friday? I don't . . . let's see, well . . ." I trailed off lamely. I *could* have said, "No, my marriage is falling apart, and I can't think ahead to the next minute, much less next Friday," but she sounded so young and hopeful that I couldn't bring myself to turn her down flat. Politeness can be such a weight around your neck. It can choke the words right out of you, and for certain it can waste a lot of your time. I didn't have the least bit of interest in a termite inspection, but I couldn't bring myself to say it.

"They can just *destroy* your home, you know," Heather said, "and sometimes the damage is done before you even know it." I saw the parallel right away.

"Oh yes," I wanted to say back, "lots and lots of damage can be done to your home before you know a thing about it." What I said, instead, was that I'd have to think about it and get back with her, that my schedule was a little topsy-turvy right now. It didn't come out that smoothly, but she finally let me hang up without setting an appointment.

Her last words were "Well, Mrs. Landis, I can appreciate a busy schedule,

I sure can, so if I don't hear from you within a week or so, I'll call you back. Okeydokey?"

And even though I didn't want her to call back, ever, I said, "Okeydokey."

But anyway, back to the world being a small place. Four days after Ken left, I was walking out to the mailbox to get the paper and check the mail. It was on Thursday afternoon after I got home from substituting in an eighth-grade math class all day. The fact was impressed upon me every hour of the day now how routinely things continued to happen in spite of my own present distress. Of course, anybody knows it has to be that way, but it's still just one more thing to lower your morale when junk mail continues to show up in the mailbox and the newspaper continues to be dropped at the end of the driveway, the front page carrying the same news about murders and border skirmishes and strikes and budget deficits and pollution and car accidents and all the rest of it.

Wallace Yarnell continued to put a leash on Ferdinand and take him for a walk every afternoon, Pete and Sandy Ellis continued to leave for work in separate cars and arrive home after dark, and Theresa Dillman across the street continued being visited by the man who drove a mustard-colored Volkswagen van. She had told us once that he was an artist, but since I had never seen any of his work, I didn't know if he really was or if he just thought he was, which is more often the case with people who call themselves artists.

I heard the same distant train whistle every night around midnight and the same drone of airplanes regularly passing overhead from the municipal airport nearby. Nature also seemed to take no note of the upheaval in my life. The daffodils continued to bloom, the clouds continued to move across the sky, and the sun continued to rise and set.

Joggers and walkers continued to pass our house. Even though it was February, we seemed to have moved into a neighborhood bent on fitness. So anyway, now I've come to the point of all this. I'm ready to open the mailbox when I see two women ambling up the street toward me. I had noticed them walking down our street before, ever since the beginning of January, in fact, which seemed like a strange time of year to be going on a walk, especially the way these two did it. They walked slowly, pointing to things and talking, sometimes stopping dead still and studying something like a tree branch or something in the sky. The only thing getting any exercise appeared to be their tongues.

Catching sight of me at the mailbox now, one of the women called out, "Maybe there's a check for a million dollars in there!" And for some reason I can't begin to guess, I answered the first thing that popped into my mind, which was "Vanity of vanities; all is vanity."

Normally I would have just smiled and said hello, but I had been reading in Ecclesiastes again just that morning, and the words fell right out before I could stop them. Then, so they wouldn't think I was a total dimwit, I added, "All we seem to get is bills, never checks." By the time I had pulled the mail out of the box, the women were almost right beside me.

The one who had spoken first tilted her head and looked at me closely. I was sure I had seen this woman before, but I couldn't place her. "I can't believe what you just said about vanity," she said. "I wonder . . ." She narrowed her eyes and appeared to be thinking. "I mean, it's such a coincidence, isn't it, Della Boyd?" She looked at the other woman now. "You know what that's from, don't you? 'Vanity of vanities'? Remember where we heard that recently?"

The other woman, Della Boyd I assumed, was looking up into the bare branches of the Japanese maple tree beside our mailbox with a dreamy sort of look on her face. "We met a man down at the end of the street," she said in a soft lilting voice, "who said he's won over five thousand dollars in different sweepstakes. Remember him, Barb? He won two thousand alone when he matched up some cards in a Burger King contest." She turned her gaze to our house, smiling past me as she gave it the once-over. "Five thousand dollars *he* won, but not me. No, not me. I've never won a red cent on those sweepstakes." She suddenly pointed behind me. "I've always admired your pretty bay window. We walk along here every day or two, and I always tell Barb, 'Look there, isn't that the prettiest bay window?' Don't I, Barb?"

Barb laughed. "Yes, you do, Della Boyd." Then she turned to me and said, "Evidently she didn't hear my question, so I'll ask you. You must know where that's from—'Vanity of vanities'?"

I nodded and said, "I do."

"Our preacher's sermon was all about that last Sunday morning," she said. "That's why I was so surprised to hear you say it."

That's when I remembered where I had seen her. It was at the Church of the Open Door. Midway through the preacher's sermon, someone had slipped down the center aisle of the church and whispered something to someone sitting at the end of a pew. A message was passed down, and then a woman farther down the row had gotten up, made her way to the aisle, and walked out. This was the same woman. I remembered watching her, thinking what a pretty, wholesome-looking person she was. I wondered at the time if she had an emergency phone call about some trouble at home, or maybe she had a baby in the nursery who needed her attention.

"Yes," I said. "I was there."

"You were? You were at the Church of the Open Door?"

I nodded. "I went to hear Hardy Biddle sing, and the Tuttles invited me over for dinner afterward."

Both women started talking at once, and I finally sorted it all out. Hardy Biddle, it turns out, was Della Boyd's nephew, and she was there at church that day also. And two of the boys singing with Hardy were Barb's sons. And both Barb and Della Boyd knew Margaret Tuttle and acted like they thought she hung the planets. "Oh, that Margaret is such a smart, smart woman," Della Boyd said.

And even though I knew it was trite, I said it anyway: "Well, it's a small world, isn't it?"

"Oh yes, it is!" said Della Boyd, leaning forward. "It certainly is a small, small world. And did Margaret tell you about our poetry club?" she asked. "We meet once a month, and, oh, it's just the most wonderful thing you can imagine!" She cast her eyes upward and closed her eyes briefly as if the thought were too blissful to bear. This woman was funny—I wasn't sure if she was actually a little short on gray matter or if she was just one of those who seem like it. The world is full of both kinds, you know. I was leaning toward the first choice with Della Boyd, but something in her eyes made me hesitate. I could see a light on, so somebody must be home.

"Maybe you'd like to come with us to our next club meeting," Barb said. "We love to have visitors." Then she stuck out her hand. "Forgive me for not introducing myself earlier. I'm bad about that." She took my hand and shook it gently. "I'm Barb Chewning, and this is Della Boyd Biddle. We both live over on Brookside."

I smiled. "I'm Elizabeth Landis, and I live here," I said, motioning behind me. "It's nice to meet you both." I closed the mailbox and stepped back. I sensed that I could extend this conversation indefinitely, that both of these women would be more than willing to come into my house for a visit.

I knew if I told them how my afternoon with Margaret Tuttle had ended last Sunday and then what had awaited me when I got home, I could find out right this minute how the people at this church would respond to messy situations. I figured from just these few minutes of conversation that I would have a sympathetic audience in these two, but while that would have appealed to a lot of people, I suppose, the last thing in the world I wanted to do right now was pour out my heart. Here's a trick you learn as you go through life: Keep the corners of your mouth turned up so everything stays in.

Della Boyd suddenly fixed me with a wide-eyed look and said, "Do you get hummingbirds?"

"Do I what?" I said.

"Get hummingbirds," she said. "I have a hummingbird feeder, but I haven't had any little visitors yet." She pointed. "I see a feeder hanging from the eaves on the side of your house, and I thought maybe you knew about birds."

"Oh, that was there when we moved in last summer," I said. "I don't know much about hummingbirds myself. My mother likes them, but she lives in Georgia." I was suddenly overcome with a desire to get back inside.

Della Boyd looked so disappointed about the hummingbirds, though, that I added, "It's probably too early for them, you know. It seems like my mother's are always around in the summertime."

She nodded sadly. "That's what I'm afraid of. But I'm not sure I'll still be here this summer, you see."

"I'm sure they have hummingbirds in Mississippi, too, Della Boyd," Barb said. Then to me she explained, "Della Boyd is talking about moving back home to Mississippi in the next month or two."

"That's nice," I said, then wondered if that might sound a little insincere. "I mean, if you want to, that is," I added.

Della Boyd's eyes brightened. "Oh, I do, I do!" she said. "It's just that I wanted to see the hummingbirds before I left."

"Well, you've still got some time," Barb said. "We won't give up yet."

I raised a hand and waved my mail at them. "Well, I'll let you get back to your walk now," I said. "Thanks for stopping to chat. Tell Hardy I said hi."

"Do you play tennis?" Barb asked. "I see the tennis magazine." I looked down at the mail in my hand. "Sorry, I'm not trying to be nosy," she added. "I just wondered is all. I signed up for the YMCA league this spring, and I thought maybe . . . but I guess that would be too many coincidences in one day if you played tennis, too, wouldn't it? It's probably your husband's magazine, right?"

Well, here was even more proof of the world's smallness. "No, it's mine," I said. "I do play tennis." My words were all used up now. "Maybe we'll play each other sometime," I said. I waved again and walked backward a couple of steps, then turned around and headed quickly up the driveway toward the house.

I heard their good-byes behind me, and Della Boyd said, "Now wasn't she an attractive lady? I used to have nice thick hair like that, but then Old Father Time went and thinned it all out." She laughed. "Yes, sir, he thinned it all out, and now I can feel the wind clear down to my scalp." She laughed again. "I do like that bay window, don't you? When I have my own house again someday, I'd love a bay window." Their voices grew fainter as they continued on their way, and finally I reached the kitchen door and went inside.

The light on the answering machine was flashing, and when I pushed the Playback button, I think I already knew it would be Ken. "Elizabeth, please . . . I need to see you. Call me, won't you? I know you don't . . . well, I know I'm the last person you want to talk to, but please, Elizabeth, I've got to tell you some things. And . . . well, the guy was supposed to come either this week or next and look at the carport, you know, and give us an estimate for . . . well, I don't know what we're going to do about that now, but . . . call me, okay? I'm at my office. Call me *now*, okay? I'll be here till seven, then again after eight or so. Call me, Elizabeth, please. I need to talk to you."

I played it back two times. I'm not sure why, but I think I was trying to hear something more than what was there. Or maybe I couldn't believe what was actually there. Would someone please tell me how a man can talk about an estimate on enclosing a carport at a time like this?

I don't think any poet has ever captured the differences between men and women as effectively as Robert Frost in "Home Burial." For the life of him, the husband in that poem can't figure out why his words are always the wrong ones, and the wife can't get past the fact that only moments after digging a grave for their dead baby, he could actually talk about how his birch fence was rotting. Read that poem sometime. The tension is thick enough to slice. No, it's more than that. The tension in this poem is brick solid. You couldn't begin to slice it. Nobody's giving, nobody's really hearing, nobody's moving forward, because you can't do any of these things through a brick wall.

"Three foggy mornings and one rainy day," the husband says, is all it takes to rot a birch fence. His spade still has mud on it from digging the grave, and he comes inside the kitchen and says that. And then he has no idea why his wife acts like she despises him!

And Ken Landis in Berea, South Carolina, calls his wife four days after she finds out he's been fooling around and talks about the *carport*. After I listen to the message a third time, I want to turn my eyes to heaven and say, "God, I'm not criticizing or anything, but would you please explain to me why you made men this way? Is this another result of the Fall?" On Sunday Margaret had talked to me about the results of man's sin in the Garden of Eden. Maybe she just forgot to mention the complete removal of emotional sensitivity in the male species.

I've done everything I can think of to make Travis different from this. I don't know how it will test out when he has a wife, but considering his total avoidance of the female population, I may never have a chance to observe my training put into practice. Of course, there's so much that goes on in private between a husband and wife that I probably wouldn't have a chance anyway. Things can look all peachy on the outside, but at home it's a different matter. You've heard the same stories I have, and when the truth breaks, everybody goes around saying, "I just can't believe it! They seemed so happy!" *Seemed*—that's the key word.

I looked at the clock after playing the message the third time and saw that it was a little past four. According to the answering machine, Ken had phoned around two. And he said he'd be in his office until seven and then again after eight. So what was he doing—living there? He did have a full-size couch and a coffee maker in his office, along with a bathroom and the faculty lounge down the hall, but surely he wasn't spending nights there.

What were other people thinking, seeing him wandering around the college all hours of the day and night?

I had a professor in college who everybody said slept in his clothes in his office. He taught psychology, of all things, and loved to tell us about case studies, never seeming to catch on that he could be the subject of a very wild and wacky case study himself. What if students were starting to talk about Ken as we had talked about Professor Gillespie?

I couldn't imagine Ken going to class with rumpled clothes, though, seeing that he's as fastidious as the day is long. Up to a point, that is. Let me illustrate.

On Friday, the next day, when I came home from substituting for this same eighth-grade math teacher, who it turns out has mononucleosis, I could tell right away that Ken had been home sometime during the day. This is what I mean by "up to a point." He probably thought when he sneaked in and back out that he hadn't left a trace, but I knew he'd been there the minute I walked in. I saw three clues.

First, a chair at the kitchen table was pulled out about eight to ten inches, and I knew exactly why. The first thing Ken does when he enters the kitchen is take off his shoes so he doesn't track anything in. He sets his shoes by the door very precisely, then pads around the house in his socks or a pair of moccasins he keeps by the door. When he gets ready to leave again, he pulls out a kitchen chair, sits down, and puts his shoes back on. It's the chair closest to the door, the same one I usually sit in when I'm gulping down a bowl of cereal in the morning. I knew I had pushed the chair in that morning until it touched the table, but here it sat away from the table, and I knew it hadn't slid out by itself.

Second, a few moments later I saw the tiniest tip of white sock sticking out of one of the drawers of Ken's bureau. At one time it had been the source of joking between us that he so often failed to get his underwear drawer closed snugly without something peeking out, but we hadn't joked about it in a long time now. Whenever I put his folded clothes away, I always stack them neatly, then press the stack down before I push in the drawer. He always skips the pressing-down step and just shoves in the drawer, never noticing that something got caught.

Let one of the flutes in his wind band miss the cutoff, though, and hang on just a nanosecond too long, and he would notice *that* in a heartbeat. Or let one of the tubas, who sit at the very back of the band, try wearing a plain white shirt instead of the formal tux shirt that goes with the band uniform, and he'd notice that, too. Let the score for a piece of music have the tiniest mistake in it—say a missing flag on a thirty-second note in the third trumpet part or a wrong note printed in the second clarinet part, which makes a fleeting chord sound just ever so vaguely off-kilter—and he'd be on that like a cat on a canary. But a sock or T-shirt sticking out of his drawer he won't see.

So I see the chair and the sock, and you can guess what the third thing is. It's the classic sign that a man is around—the toilet seat. It's not in the master bathroom but in the hall bathroom, which I hardly ever enter except to clean it. I didn't see it when I went by the first time, walking from the kitchen to the bedroom, but coming back down the hallway, I glanced into the bathroom and there it was, signal number three, raised like a white flag of surrender, only nothing was being surrendered, of course.

He had evidently washed his hands carefully and dried them just as carefully because I saw no evidence of drips or crooked towels, but in all his tidiness he forgot the toilet seat, which I knew had been down when I left because I had cleaned both bathrooms after midnight the night before, when I couldn't sleep. I knew I had left both the toilet seat and lid down.

If you want to feel sorry for yourself, clean a bathroom at two in the morning when you finally get out of bed after not being able to sleep all night. It surely hadn't been the wisest choice for a sleepless night's activity, especially when I got to the hall bathroom, which was the one Ken most often used. And it's not that the condition of the bathroom itself was so dirty. Not at all. Ken, as I've said, is a neat freak in a lot of ways. He always wipes down the tile after a shower, rinses out the tub, cleans off the mirror, all those things. He always hangs his towel back just so.

The only thing he forgets to do, and this is on a regular basis, is to put the toilet seat down. When Travis was at home, the two of them shared the hall bathroom, and since they considered it the men's bathroom, they saw no need to put the seat down. I finally gave up fussing about it.

But I'm spending far too long talking about the toilet seat. The point is that my postmidnight cleaning session ended with me lying face down on our bed crying, and here's why. Everybody knows that you always want things you think you can't have, often things you once had but have since lost. So instead of making me mad at Ken and glad he wasn't around to create extra work for me anymore, cleaning his bathroom only made me sad. And you know what it was I heard the whole time I was in that bathroom? I heard whistling. It was something I guess I hadn't paid any attention to for years, but it suddenly hit me that I hadn't heard Ken whistle for five nights.

I'm not talking about the common old ordinary tuneless whistling that people do to pass the time of day. Ken is a virtuoso whistler. Whenever I go to one of his concerts, I recognize all the pieces, not because I'm so familiar with the standard band repertoire but because I've heard Ken whistling them all in the shower over the past months. He has a very pure, piccololike tone when he whistles, always right on pitch.

So it's after two o'clock in the morning, and as I'm cleaning his bathroom, I'm looking around at the walls wondering how many different whistled melodies have bounced off them in the eight months or so we've lived here and wondering if I'll ever hear another one. Isn't it a mystery how a woman's mind works? I had never in my life been so angry at Ken for what he had done to me, and I had never in my life missed him so much.

How Lucky, Little Tree

7

Three telephone messages awaited me that Friday when I arrived home after another day with eighth graders and math. I ignored the blinking of the answering machine at first, dreading all the obligations that come with recorded messages, but by and by my curiosity won out, and I sat down by the telephone in the kitchen to listen to them.

The first message, recorded at ten o'clock that morning, was from Margaret Tuttle, and she asked me simply to call her. I hadn't attended last night's poetry class again, so I was sure she wanted to find out if I was sick. She must have called from work because I heard voices and muffled thunks in the background. She gave me both a work and home phone number.

When I thought about Margaret now, it seemed like five months instead of only five days ago that I had spent an afternoon with her. I was certain that what I had taken away from her house was genuine, but I'll admit I was struggling to put it together with my present crisis. I was still calling upon God and clinging to the verses I had found, but I had no idea how a Christian was supposed to make it all work. It wasn't an easy thing.

The idea came to me, though, that maybe it wasn't up to me to "make it all work." Maybe my job was just to trust God for however long it took for *him* to work it out. It didn't seem like this was going to be a speedy proposition, though. God didn't appear to be offering me any quick fixes.

I knew it would probably help to talk with Margaret, but the thought of telling anybody about my trouble was something I couldn't face yet. I couldn't imagine the humiliation of actually speaking the words aloud and then seeing the changed look in the other person's eye, the look of new knowledge, and then having to hear the other person's response. I knew that more than a little pride was mixed in with my grief.

And fear. I knew some of that was mixed in, too. I was angry, I was hurt, and I was scared. When I asked God, "What am I going to do?" I was talk-ing about more than just the next day. The whole huge picture overwhelmed me. I already expected that Ken would be leaving for good, that we would eventually divorce, that he would marry this other woman, that I would have to call my family and tell them, that I would be alone for the rest of my life. My prayers were for God to give me strength somehow to endure it all. I wasn't praying at this time for a reversal of the situation.

And a host of worrisome details flooded my mind. At the same time that I was crying, "How could he do this to me?" I was also crying, "Where will I live? How can I keep up a home by myself? How will I take care of my car? Who's going to figure my taxes in April?" A woman left alone starts thinking about all those kinds of things.

Other thoughts like "What will everybody think?" kept popping up, too, along with the inescapable fact that my new identity would be that of "re-jected wife." So *"What am I going to do?"* was an enormous question.

Today when I hear those Sunday School songs that say something like "Give your heart to Jesus, and he'll take away your burdens," I want to add a word or two. "It's not quite that simple," I want to say. "You don't check your problems at the door when you step across the threshold into the king-dom of God. You take them all in with you. And sometimes you even get new ones after you get in. Salvation doesn't erase all your problems."

I'll be honest. I had spent the week reading verses and praying for help, but by Friday afternoon I felt that I was hanging on by a slender thread, and I could picture its microscopic strands snapping and unraveling like those ropes in cartoons that always give out when the hero is hanging over a can-yon or a snake pit or a crocodile-infested swamp.

I couldn't help wondering, though, how I ever would have made it this far if I hadn't gone to Margaret's house last Sunday and come home a differ-ent person. I was still angry, not at God but at Ken. I've heard of people blaming God for their problems, but it never occurred to me to do that. Ken was the one who had created this mess, not God. Something told me God wanted to help me out of it.

The second phone call was from Heather at Sears Pest Control saying that I might be interested in knowing that "Sears had just this week dem-onstrated its concern for the tremendous financial strain on today's families by actually *reducing* the cost of a year's contract for full pest control service from \$410 to \$385." She went on to say that she hoped we would schedule an appointment "without delay." She then gave me her phone number, re-peated it slowly, and closed with a cheery "Bye-bye now!"

The third message was from Ken, recorded a little past one o'clock. He started out by saying, "All right, Elizabeth . . . you've got to call me. We've got things to discuss. So here's . . ." I heard a knock in the background, and he broke off to say, "Just a minute, Matt, I'll be right with you." But maybe that was just a cover-up. Maybe it wasn't Matt at all.

He dropped his voice a little and continued. "So here's what I'm going to do. I'm coming over tonight at nine o'clock, and we're going to talk. I want you to be there, so don't make up some reason to be gone. Please. It's Friday, Elizabeth. It's been five days. We've got to talk." He paused a moment, then said, "I ran home this morning to get some clothes." As if this was news to me. Then, "I'll see you tonight at nine."

Part of what I was listening for as I replayed this message, followed by all the others I had saved during the week, was something I wasn't finding. It was a tone of apology. I'm not sure whether I really wanted to hear it or was hoping I wouldn't. Maybe if he had sounded penitent, it would have angered me more. Isn't this what errant husbands do—play on a woman's emotions? Act sorry, grovel a little bit, and she'll give in and take you back and forget it ever happened. Then act meek and reformed for a little while until enough time has passed that you can act like a jerk again, at which point the whole process starts over. I wasn't born yesterday.

It's not that Ken sounded proud of what he'd done. He just sounded patiently neutral and firm, like a businessman trying to get in touch with an evasive client or a parent trying to reason with a stubborn child. Part of me admired him for his emotional reserve and sense of purpose, for having a mind always in perfect control, but the other part of me was wanting to scream, "I'm not a client, and I'm not a child! I'm your wife, and you're the rat in this scenario, so don't be telling me what you're going to do or what I've got to do!"

In playing those messages back, I was begging to see some of his heart. That's what a wife wants sometimes—some sign that her husband does more than just think and plan and analyze and critique. Some sign that he *feels*. Even back in the good days of our marriage, Ken was always low on sympathy and high on advice. If I'd share a problem with him, he would respond with what he considered a sensible solution, followed by steps to prevent it from happening again. He never once just folded me in his arms and said, "Hey, I'm sorry, babe."

Once I showed him a blister on my foot after I had played two matches one Saturday in a tennis tournament over in Greenville. He studied it for a moment, then said, "If you'd wear two pairs of thick socks, that wouldn't happen." I finally quit telling him about my problems.

But there was another thing I couldn't help marveling over as I replayed the messages. Ken, the consummate avoider-of-conflict, was actually pressing for a face-to-face talk. In all our years of marriage, his least favorite activity had always been opening up and discussing touchy or potentially embarrassing subjects. I couldn't remember that he had ever urged me to talk to him. I was always the initiator whenever there was one, though it had been a long, long time since I had started a heart-to-heart talk. Some things you just give up on after a while.

Which brings me in a roundabout way to a title for my backwards poem: "Wild and Whirling Words." *Hamlet*, act 1: "These are but wild and whirling words, my lord." I don't normally like titles that explain the central metaphor so blatantly, but this one seems right.

Anybody reading my poem would probably wonder how the wind could be a symbol for words, especially when the wind snatches words in line twelve. How can words snatch words, you're saying. Well, they can, let me tell you. Your words can do all kinds of things to other people's words, including suffocate them. I'm not sure I even knew where this poem was leading as I was writing it. Sometimes the truth creeps out without your meaning for it to. Maybe I still don't know where it's leading.

The truth about Ken and me is this. We never learned to talk, not really. Oh, I mean, we went through the literal, physical motions of talking all right—of forming words and speaking them aloud, telling each other what time we'd be home, who called and left a message, how much something cost, things like that—but we rarely did that real kind of talking where you sit down, look each other in the eye, and lay your soul bare.

Here's a brief summary of my talking habits over the years. Growing up, I talked freely at home, though everybody outside our family thought I was the quiet one. Whenever I had a best friend at school, which happened only in second, fourth, and seventh grades, I would talk her head off, but I hardly ever started a conversation with anyone else. Teachers thought of me as "that smart, shy girl."

Then I got a job during summers in high school working as the receptionist at a photography studio, and to my surprise, I found out I was good with customers. I would politely ask the older ones about grandchildren and the middle-aged ones about children and little kids about pets. And I always remembered their names when they came back to see the proofs. I'd ask engaged couples how they met and what their plans were for the future. I never ran out of things to talk about with customers, and Mr. Cannon, the photographer, sometimes had me come to the back while he was doing difficult sittings—babies with keyed-up parents or children with their dogs. He thought I was a calming influence.

When Ken came along, I started talking to him, of course, and he seemed to soak it up. I was a great curiosity to him. He would lean on one elbow and watch me talk, smiling a quiet smile as if he were hearing a new musical composition. In spite of coming from a family of five kids, it had been a fairly quiet house, he told me. I found out why later, when I learned more about his parents.

I saw a little bonsai tree on Margaret Tuttle's piano the Sunday I was at her house, and I thought immediately of a poem by Marge Piercy called "A

Work of Artifice," which in turn made me think of Ken's mother and father. The poem appears to be describing a bonsai tree, but it's really talking about a woman whose potential has been stunted. And when the gardener snips off branches and turns the tiny trunk to fit his whim and says, "How lucky, little tree" to make the bonsai think it's happy being a dwarf tree in a little pot, you know that the poet doesn't think it's a lucky tree at all. Ken's mother was a lot like that bonsai, and his father was the gardener.

I continued to talk a lot after Jennifer and Travis were born. I read to them, played games with them, explained things to them, laughed over things they said, taught them songs, made up stories with them, instructed them in good manners, and all those other things Super Moms do.

And then at some point—who can ever say exactly when these things happen?—I started noticing that when Ken came home at the end of the day, I didn't have as much to say to him anymore, that my verbal reservoir, which for most women is fairly sizable, was almost drained after being a mother all day.

I know it's the opposite with a lot of women. They're so hungry for adult conversation by the end of the day that they start talking as soon as their husbands walk through the door and don't stop until after they're asleep in bed. It didn't work that way with me, though. I was suddenly too weary to keep trying, and Ken didn't seem to mind really. It was like we were traveling in two different, nonintersecting orbits. So even if I did speak, the distance would be too great for the sound waves to travel across.

I doubt that Ken ever thought, *Wow, Elizabeth's sure not talking much these days. I wonder if anything's bothering her.* Even if he had ever thought something like that, he never would have said it to me—that's not his way. The very idea of talking about why we weren't talking seemed pointless. It would just take too much effort.

So where did the "wild and whirling words" come in? Oh, marriage is so complex. It tires me out to think about trying to untwist all the threads of our twenty-eight years.

As I sat by the telephone after listening to Ken's most recent message and the sound of his voice died away, I was struck again by the silence all around me. Our new neighborhood was situated well away from the busiest streets, and with all the tall trees and large lots, there was a feeling of isolation in spite of the houses on every side.

Our other house over in Derby had been just off a main thoroughfare, and though I didn't think of it as being a noisy neighborhood at the time, I felt that sound had suddenly ceased to exist when we moved over here to Windsor Drive in Berea. Ordinary things that used to be part of everyday life were suddenly gone—screeching tires, honking horns, sirens, children's voices, yapping dogs. Some days I welcomed the sound of Eunice Yarnell fussing at Ferdinand next door.

Too few children lived on our new street. Right after we had moved here, I would close my eyes at night and dream about summer evenings at our old house when the kids were young. I could hear their feet running across the yard, the slamming of doors, the shouts and squeals and laughter of all the neighborhood children. It was a place rich with sound, and in those summers everything seemed to be part of the sound. I could almost hear the blinking of fireflies, the moon hanging above the treetops, the glimmer of porch lights.

Those were Travis's favorite times to play, when the darkness made him anonymous and relieved the pressure to socialize. The next day in the glare of the sunlight he might ride his bike right past someone he had played tag with the night before and pretend he didn't see him. Or maybe he wasn't pretending. It was hard to know with Travis. Maybe he was thinking deep thoughts about chipmunks or blue jays or reliving a *Lassie* rerun he'd seen on Nickelodeon.

Anyway, the silence had been a hard adjustment for me. Most people crave silence, pursue it, consider a quiet neighborhood prime real estate, and pay good money to move into one. But it made me ache to sit inside and hear nothing but the air conditioner clicking on and off. I had started listening hard for the faraway train whistle, for airplanes overhead, for the owl, and for Eunice Yarnell. I discovered that silence has a sound of its own. It's a high, steady buzz, like a multitude of cicadas humming a single shrill note, but without the throbbing pulse. Sometimes it was so loud I had to cover my ears.

When Travis left for college back in the fall, I felt as if I had tumbled into an abyss. I imagined myself spiraling downward at a high rate of speed, all alone and in total silence. There was no sound, not even a whimper from my own lips, not even a rush of air as I plummeted to a bottom I knew would never come. I remember walking around the house, wishing I had the courage to break out all the windows to let the sound in.

It was the hottest part of August when he left, but during the day I would swing the front door wide open, hoping to hear the birds or a passing car or a neighbor's lawn mower. I wanted to stand on the front porch and scream, "Let there be sound!" Then Ken would come home, comment on how hot the house was, close the door, and adjust the thermostat on the air conditioner.

But that was last summer. Right now I'm sitting by the telephone in the kitchen, and it's not summer. It's February. I realize that the house is cold, but walking to the hallway to turn up the heat seems like too great a labor. Nine o'clock will be here in less than five hours. I look at the door leading from the carport, the door Ken will enter.

I can't imagine what he'll say to me or what I'll say back to him. What is there to say? There are questions I want to ask, but will I? "Why did you do this to me? Who is she? When did it start?" and the hardest one, "Do you love her?" which is really just an indirect way of asking the one I really mean: "Do you love me?"

So back to the subject of talking. After the good years, I gradually stopped finding things to talk to Ken about. He never had talked much to me, so there was no change there. But I found the silence hard to take.

After so long, I would erupt with a flurry of words, often accusatory, something about how wrapped up in his work Ken was. And then he'd look at me with a mixture of surprise and helplessness, and I would launch several more volleys of words, all of which missed him entirely since he would have retreated by now. He saw from behind a glass pane far away that I was upset, but he couldn't hear anything that gave him a clue as to why.

I don't know if he really didn't care or if he just gave up trying to figure it out. One thing he must have figured out, though, was that there was a pattern. I would blow up; he would hide. I would stew; he would bury himself even deeper in his work. Then gradually the waves of my mood would die down, and the sea would grow still again.

I don't remember when it all started. When we were first married and still going to school, we talked a lot about our classes. We were both working and studying, and I thought we were happy. No, we *were* happy. I'm sure we were happy. And even when a little voice says to me, "Maybe you only *thought* you were happy," I have to reply, "Well, okay, but if we thought we were, then we were."

Then Jennifer came along a couple of years later, and I started my career as a mother. By that time Ken had finished his master's degree, and he took a job as the band director at a high school in the thriving metropolis of Derby, South Carolina, where he stayed for several years. I'm trying hard to put all this in order. I want to get it right. He started doing a few weekend band clinics, started spending more and more time composing and arranging, and somewhere in there I started keeping everything locked up inside me. There were big things I should have told Ken, but I didn't. There were sorrows I kept as secrets.

I wonder now how many of my words during the early years Ken ever really heard. I thought they were so essential for a while, that they buoyed up our relationship. If I didn't talk enough and fill up the emptiness, then our little kite of a marriage would stop flying and take a nose dive. That's what I thought. I guess I thought any words at all were better than silence.

But then, on the other hand, we planted a tree once at our old house— the plum sapling in my poem—and Ken followed all the directions for supporting it against the elements. The very next day a bad storm blew up, though, and that little tree didn't have a chance. Isn't this the way it is with most things? They can be both good and bad. The wind can hold things up, and it can also knock things down.

And take that bonsai I was talking about earlier. In "A Work of Artifice" Marge Piercy used it as a symbol for something bad—the suppressing of natural growth—whereas Margaret Tuttle had shown me a poem of her own titled "Tree of a Thousand Stars," in which the tiny flowers of the bonsai represented not only the blooming of faith but also the fruit of good works. So there you have it—the same thing serving opposite purposes.

My mind went back to the plum tree Ken had planted all those years ago, and I was just forming a thought that started out, *But one good thing to remember is . . .* when the telephone rang. It startled me so much that I instinctively reached for the receiver and answered it instead of letting the machine record the call.

It was Margaret Tuttle. Life is full of coincidences like this. One minute I'm thinking about her bonsai, and the next minute I'm talking to her. My father used to love to tell the joke about the little boy who asked another one, "What does the word *coincidence* mean?" And the other kid says, "That's funny—I was just getting ready to ask you the same thing."

As soon as I heard Margaret's voice, I imagined her sitting at the little telephone table in the living room of her duplex. I remembered the earnest appeal in her voice and eyes last Sunday as we sat together on her sofa. A picture of her kitchen table laden with food sprang to my mind, and I saw her husband's kind eyes turned toward me as he spoke. I thought of the game we had played with book titles and of the Bible she had placed in my hands before I left.

Without any warm-up chitchat, Margaret came right to the point. "Are you ill, Elizabeth?" she asked. "You were absent from class this week, and I have been concerned about you."

Margaret's voice reminded me of how much I liked her. Even though I was in no mood to talk, I felt drawn to her. Maybe God had urged her to call me at this exact moment for a specific purpose. Was this possible? Maybe he had distracted me to the point that I reached to answer the telephone without even meaning to. Maybe he meant for me to talk to her right now. Was my God the kind who synchronized details like this? Maybe he cared not only about what happened but also when it happened.

"I haven't been feeling very well this week," I said to her. This was certainly the truth.

"Could you use my help in any way?" she asked. "May I bring over food? Do you need medicine? Have you seen a doctor?"

"No, no, no, no," I said. "There—did I answer them all?" I tried to laugh, but I knew it sounded fake. "It's not really that serious," I said, then immediately realized how false that was and added, "Well, I mean, it's not a physical thing, and . . . oh, I just haven't felt much like getting out this week. You know how things can come up, and . . . and all." It was odd—I both desperately wanted to share my trouble with Margaret and to keep it from her.

She paused as if searching for direction. "Do you want to talk about something, Elizabeth?" she asked. "I do not pry into other people's business, but I want to help you if I can." She paused, then continued slowly. "I find this difficult, and perhaps my imagination is too active, but I sense that you need to talk, and though I feel poorly equipped to give counsel, I am willing to listen and even now am praying for God's wisdom in responding." She paused again, then added, "And if I am presuming, please forgive me. I only want to help."

Just as it had done when she explained to me the wonderful plan of salvation the previous Sunday, Margaret's effortless formality, rather than sounding stiff and putting me off, moved me. "Oh, Margaret," I said, "it's too much to tackle right now. Maybe later I can . . . I don't know, it's something I never . . . well, I never expected to have to face."

"I want to help," she said again.

"I know you do," I said. "I believe you. But I can't even put it into words right now. It's just too much to . . . well, okay, wait, I do have a question. Only one right now. Can you tell me how a husband and wife can"—I realized that I didn't have a clue about how to end it. It was far too big to put into a single question—"how a husband and wife can . . . be happy?" I almost whispered the last two words. And just as I sensed she was about to speak, I added, "Only one sentence, please. I want the condensed version. Happiness in a nutshell."

She waited several seconds, and I knew she was thinking, maybe praying. Her answer, when it came, seemed too simple. "I think that each one must learn to see through the eyes of the other," she said.

I couldn't think of a reply. I guess it was pretty much what I expected her to say, yet it surprised me, too. It seemed both empty and full. Both glib and sincere. I didn't like it at all, yet I knew I should examine it carefully.

I told her I had to go, thanked her for calling, and said I'd probably see her next week in Dr. Huckabee's class.

"He asked us to read chapter six for the next class and also Keats' 'Eve of St. Agnes,' " Margaret said.

"Keats?" I said. "That's not modern poetry."

"He said it ties in with something we will be discussing about the matter of poetic inspiration," Margaret said. "He also said that he always finds Keats to be a great cleanser of the palate after too many sips from some of the impotable works of modern poetry. That was precisely how he phrased it."

Neither of us spoke for a few moments, but the silence was companionable. "Are you sure I cannot . . ." she started, but I interrupted with a gentle "No, thank you, Margaret. I have to go now. Good-bye."

And almost immediately upon hanging up, the thought I had suspended when the telephone rang completed itself. *But one good thing to remember is*

this: Ken did replant the sapling, and before we moved from that house, we ate plums.
Let me tell you, this surprised me—not that we ate plums, but that I re-
trieved and finished a thought. So often in the past year it has seemed that
my thoughts have fled from me. One minute they're there, almost close
enough to grasp, and then as I reach out they're gone. And it also surprised
me that I was trying so hard to find hopeful things to latch onto. I am not a
natural optimist. I have a lot of my mother in me.

"I think that each one must learn to see through the eyes of the other,"
Margaret had said. I wondered if Ken had ever sat down and considered
anything from my point of view. No, I knew the answer to that. Ken was
consumed with his own world—his teaching, his composing, his conducting.
It had always been that way. It would never occur to him to look at a situation through my eyes. That would require taking his eyes off his staff paper,
off his computer screen, off his band score, off the careless saxophone, off
the piccolo waiting for a cue, off the televised concerts he never missed on
the arts channel, off his golf ball on Sundays.

After he got his doctoral degree, working on it for three summers and a
year, he wanted a change from high-school band, so he left Derby High and
took a job at the brand-new Derby Middle School back in 1980. By this
time the sixth graders had been taken out of elementary school and put in
with the seventh and eighth graders in middle school. Junior high schools
were now passé. So here's a man with a *doctoral* degree in conducting and
composition trying to teach a bunch of preadolescents how to blow into
band instruments and make something loosely resembling music.

This is what he wanted to do, though. He said he enjoyed younger kids,
and it would give him more time to compose. He had hated working with
the marching band in the high school, so that was another advantage of
changing to middle school. Of course, he took a lot of heat from everybody
for this move. His father came right out and told him he was a moron to
waste his degree in a public middle school, and his doctoral advisor sent him
a list of private colleges in the Southeast with strong band programs and
urged him to send out resumes. Even his mother, in whose eyes Ken could
do no wrong, asked him if he wasn't a little overqualified for his job.

I didn't say much. I knew he'd be making more money because of his
new degree, in spite of moving down to middle school. I was keeping busy
with Jennifer, and as long as he was satisfied and I didn't have to work, his
job didn't much matter to me.

But on Friday evening, between playing back all of Ken's messages on
the answering machine and waiting for him to come at nine o'clock, I'm
thinking about Margaret's answer to my question, and all of a sudden I realize that his job probably should have mattered a lot more to me. And then
I get mad. What am I doing anyway? He's done an awful thing to me, and
here I am thinking about how I could have done better as a wife.

I get back on track and remind myself that Ken could have done a lot better as a husband. Husbands need to see past the end of their noses, to look at things from a wife's perspective once in a while. But something else keeps intruding even though I try to push it away. I'm still sitting at the kitchen table near the telephone. I have a pencil in my hand, and I'm tapping the eraser end against the tabletop.

Here's the thought I can't shake: I remember the first time I went to one of Ken's middle-school concerts that first year he switched from high school. And here's the part I don't like to think about. *I remember experiencing an overwhelming desire to laugh that night.* That's the honest truth.

It struck me so funny all of a sudden that these fifty or sixty twelve-, thirteen-, and fourteen-year-olds were sitting up on a stage blowing into all these different-looking instruments that made such a variety of piping, honking, tooting sounds. And such different shapes and sizes of kids, too, all of them trying so *hard*. They looked so earnest all slicked up in their good clothes clutching their instruments and frowning intently at their music.

Kids are so gawky at that age, and a couple of clarinet squeaks and French horn wipeouts made the whole thing even funnier. Midway through the concert a trombonist knocked over his stand with his slide, and during one dramatic silence, a lone tuba blatted briefly. When I laughed later and told Ken that the concert was cute, he had looked puzzled and disappointed, as if I had said awful instead of cute. And that was what came back to me now—that look on his face when I said *cute*.

Six years after Ken took it over, that middle-school band received a "Superior" rating at Concert Festival and was invited to play for the annual meeting of the South Carolina Band Directors Association over in Greenville. He had turned "cute" into something people sat up and took notice of.

He threw himself into composition also and turned out some original pieces and arrangements that he tried out with his band and later submitted to different places for publication. They were snatched up by publishers, and before very long he was getting phone calls with requests to compose pieces for certain occasions and other phone calls to serve as a contest judge here or a guest conductor there.

So by the time Travis was born, Ken was doing a lot of traveling—conducting for band clinics, civic functions, regional and all-state band festivals, things like that. This little middle-school band director had made a name for himself. And though I was proud of him, his success was his alone. I had no part in it. I had taken no interest in his work. I hadn't really respected it. I mean, after all, I had laughed at his first middle-school concert.

Sorrowful Noise Overhead

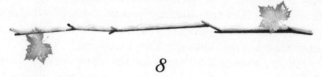

8

I have a lot of time to think while I wait for Ken to come at nine o'clock, and while I sit at the kitchen table it comes to me that maybe instead of "Wild and Whirling Words" the title of my poem should be something about silence. I think now that the voice of the wind in that poem probably has nothing to do with my occasional outbursts. Maybe it's the voice of silence in our marriage, the words we needed to say but never did. Silence can rage like a storm. Too much noise and you can't hear. Too much silence and you can't hear, either. Different causes but same results.

"Thunders of white silence"—that's a line from Browning that comes to me now. I think it might make a better title for my poem than the line from *Hamlet.* My rush of words could have been only a result of the storm, not a cause—the debris in the wake, not the meteorological forces that churned up the storm. I believe that silence was the destructive force in our marriage. My own poem is opening up to me, you see, and revealing the truth layer by layer.

One reason I didn't want to move from our old house in Derby, besides the trouble of it all, was Polly Seacrest, who had been my next-door neighbor for six years and probably the closest thing to a best friend I've ever had during my entire married life. I knew two things for sure about Polly. First, when she was with you, she was really, really *with* you. She was always ready to drop anything she was doing for a chat in the backyard, at the kitchen table, in the driveway, just wherever.

Polly was a funny person in a lot of ways, full of contrasts. She was a great conversationalist, but part of her was very guarded. She let you get only so close. She loved to read romance novels, but in everyday life she was a realist. She had never been to college, but you could tell she was very smart. She liked to listen to Dr. Laura Schlessinger on the radio and discuss the situations with me afterward. Mostly she agreed with Dr. Laura even though her own kids, contrary to Dr. Laura's philosophy of child rearing, basically ran wild. Polly had a strict code of right and wrong, but she had trouble laying down the law with her kids.

But the first important thing about Polly was that she was totally focused on you when you were together. She would fix her eyes on you and look as though what you were saying was the most important thing in the world. She would cock her head sympathetically, ask pertinent questions, and offer her opinions tactfully.

But the second thing I knew was this: The saying "Out of sight, out of mind" was never more true with anybody than Polly Seacrest. One day I could divulge some problem to her, receive her apparently undivided attention and feedback, and then the next day have to remind her all over again what it was I was so worried about, even to the point of reviewing the main facts. I knew that if I moved away, our friendship would be over. We might say we'd get together and call each other, but it wouldn't happen. I knew it wouldn't. I knew Polly. And I knew myself. I knew I probably wouldn't work at it, either.

I knew if I moved, Polly would take up with someone else, adjust herself to this new person's temperament, and it would be like she had walked out of the room where I was, turned out the light, and closed the door. Once she was in a new room, she never went back to old ones. Her life was one of walking straight ahead down a long corridor and never turning back. I knew that.

Part of it was that she had grown up on military bases, where the word *neighbor* meant somebody different every year and the word *friend* was whoever happened to be handy at the time. It gave her a lot of variety but not much permanence. She liked people, but she didn't get attached to them because she knew they wouldn't be there for very long. She told me once that her best friend growing up had been her tabby cat—he was the only one that stuck with her every time she moved.

I thought of calling Polly that Friday night before Ken arrived, but I didn't. For one thing, I didn't want to run the risk of hearing her say, "Elizabeth? Elizabeth who? Are you that woman I met at the car wash last week?" For another, talking on the phone is never the same as talking over the hedge or on the back porch. A disembodied voice isn't my idea of a real confidante. And for another, I wasn't ready yet for anybody's sympathy. You have to relinquish so much of your privacy to get people's sympathy.

One thing I had both loved and hated about Polly was the fact that she had a nearly perfect marriage but didn't really appreciate it. Here's a brief bio. After the military-base upbringing and high school graduation, she went to work at an A&W root beer stand someplace in Virginia and stayed there for ten years, eventually becoming a partner and then running the place. She met her husband, Morris, one summer at the A&W, which was next to a big empty lot, while he was on a construction crew that was filling up that green meadow with a shopping center. She was bearing down on thirty by this time.

After they married, they moved down here to South Carolina, where Morris started his own home repair business—did everything from siding to insulation to roofing to pouring concrete, you name it. He bought an old white van and had *Seacrest Home Improvements* painted on the side. Polly and Morris didn't waste much time having children, and they did that thing where all your children's names start with the same letter, *E* in their case—Estella, Edwin, and Eaton.

Estella, the girl, was rowdier than both boys put together, but somehow in a five-year-old it came across as comical, probably because she lived next door instead of at my house. Edwin and Eaton were three and four when we moved away last summer. I remember when they brought each of the children home from the hospital. I took supper over all three times.

Though Polly was younger than I was by a dozen years, a difference in age like that never means much once you get married and have kids, although when I was eighteen and she was six I probably wouldn't have been much interested in having extended conversations with her.

So Morris works all day fixing up other people's houses, and then he comes home at night and guess what he does? No, he doesn't vegetate on the sofa with the remote control. The first thing he does when he pulls his van up in the driveway is turn on the gas grill out in the carport. Then he goes inside, finds Polly, and gives her this really extravagant back-bending embrace and says something like "How's the most beautiful woman this side of the Mississippi?"

And she'll break free and act offended and say something sassy like "So who's the most beautiful woman on the *other* side of the Mississippi? Have you been looking 'em all over, huh?" And he'll grab her again and laugh and say something like "Uh, let's see, I need to think fast here—oh yeah, it's my sister."

Morris really does have a sister who lives in Colorado. And Polly will keep up her offended act and say something like, "Thanks a lot. I'm so flattered to know that I rank up there with your two-hundred-pound sister." Morris's sister really does weigh two hundred pounds. But I haven't mentioned yet that Polly herself is a far cry from beautiful. I mean a really far cry. She's got a long narrow face and small close-set eyes and—I hope she never sees this—a nose that could fit under the category of "Beaks." You forget all this when you get to know her, of course.

Anyway, how many other couples who have been married seven years carry on like this at the end of the day? The two of them will go on this way for a while, with the kids joining in and hanging all over Morris, until he says to Polly, "Okay, beautiful, what you want me to grill tonight? Is it thawed out yet, or have you been too busy with these three little leeches to get anything out?" Before it's all over, of course, Morris is down on the floor with Estella, Edwin, and Eaton, and all you can see are little arms and legs spinning like windmills. Even Jester, their poodle, gets in on it. Jester has several physical abnormalities, the most conspicuous being that he has only three legs and one good eye. I promise.

I've witnessed enough of these scenes to know they're not staged. I can't count the number of times I've been right there in the kitchen talking with Polly when Morris's van pulls in, and she says, "Oh, good grief, what time is it? I haven't even thought about supper!" She has just enough time then to jump up and grab a package of chicken or hamburger meat out of the freezer and throw it in the microwave to defrost before Morris bursts in calling, "Where's that gorgeous wife I live with?" and Polly shoots back something like "You got another one somewhere you don't live with?"

These little homecoming scenes are everyday affairs with Morris and Polly. They hug each other all the time, though mostly it's Morris doing the hugging and Polly squirming and saying things like "Wait, I've got to go put the clothes in the dryer!" And while Morris cooks whatever meat they're eating for supper—he grills outside even in the dead of winter—Polly tears around the kitchen getting together something to go with it, usually some kind of potato and a vegetable out of a can, maybe some brown-and-serve rolls. I would sometimes stay a few minutes and help Polly—peel carrots, slice cheese, whatever—before going home to get our own supper on the table.

The days when our family ate supper together now seem like something from another lifetime. Once he got to high school, Travis sometimes didn't get home from school until after five—soccer, piano, trumpet, science lab, things like that. He was the only kid at Derby High who rode a bicycle to school, which is completely off the subject except for the fact that it explains why I didn't have to interrupt my visits with Polly in the late afternoon to go pick him up.

Even after he learned to drive midway through his senior year, Travis preferred to ride his bike, and it wasn't because we insisted, believe me. I could have taken him to school, even *wanted* to do so and offered repeatedly, but he wasn't interested. I told him he could drive my car on the days I didn't sub, but he'd shake his head and say the parking lot was too crowded and he'd just ride his bike. Travis was the kind of kid who fell into a routine and couldn't be budged.

I tried over and over to talk him out of riding his bike to school, frequently mentioning the boy who was struck and killed on a bike out on Fredericks Road. That boy was ten, Travis would remind me, and he wasn't wearing a helmet. The main reason I tried to discourage him, though, was that I knew riding a bike to school was considered a nerdy thing to do. I could just imagine the looks he got from the other kids, who no doubt already thought he was uncool enough as it was.

Like with other things, though, I finally gave up. Travis was just Travis. He refused to be anybody else. He lived in his own galaxy. This past Christmas when we got him a used Dodge Colt to drive back to college, I said, "There, don't you wish you'd had this last year?" And he said—these were his exact words—"Nah, what for? I had my bike."

But back to the Seacrests. Here's the odd thing. In spite of the fact that he was hardworking, loyal, humorous, attentive, helpful at home, and all of that, Polly didn't seem to think Morris was much of anything special at all. In fact, she would often gripe about things like the way his clothes were always so dirty when he came home from work ("What did you do today, roll around in the mud?") or his loud voice ("Shhh, I'm not deaf!") or, believe it or not, the way he helped with the children ("Those are the wrong pajamas you put on Eaton" or "You don't need to take her temperature *again!*"). Once she even told me it really bugged her the way he was always in such a good mood.

One day I remember Polly complaining about what Morris had done the night before. "And then after he spent all that time down on the floor acting out Peter Rabbit and Mr. McGregor and got all three of them so wound up they were ready to bust," she told me, "he let Estella talk him into *curling her hair* with my curling iron. You should have seen him trying to figure out how to work it with those big fat hands of his." She heaved a sigh as if having endured a terrible ordeal, then ended with, "They were in bed way later than they should've been!"

These stories showed me how wrong I was to make assumptions about men, but they also made me think a lot about my own husband's shortcomings. Sometimes when Polly got too cranky about Morris, I would speak up and remind her that a lot of women would give their eyeteeth to have a husband who actually *talked* to them and always told them they were beautiful and even helped with the cooking and the kids and all the rest.

And she would always agree but very reluctantly. "Yeah, I know," she'd say with a sigh. "He drives me crazy, but I guess he's got his good points."

Over the years we were neighbors, I got too caught up in Polly's life. I know that now. I always felt that the colors next door were a little brighter, the sounds were louder and clearer, the whole business of living a lot happier and more *real* and spontaneous. I loved watching it all and developed something like an addiction. When one of the kids spilled grape Kool-Aid all over the kitchen floor or dressed Jester the poodle up in baby clothes or when Polly chased a roach down the hall with a rolled-up newspaper, it was like a scene in a funny movie, except it was much, much better because these were real people, not actors. I'd go home after an hour or two in Polly's kitchen and feel I had experienced something zany but absolutely authentic.

I'd watch her and Morris together and get that pit-of-the-stomach tightness I get when I read a good poem. Sometimes I'd look across the driveway at the Seacrests' house at night and wonder what they were doing. When the light went out at their bedroom window, I'd imagine them lying there in the dark talking. I liked the living proof that postchildren marriages could still have life.

After the lights went out in our bedroom, we never talked. Ken rarely stayed awake long enough, or when he did, I could tell he was working through a piece of music in his head. He would blow out little rhythmic passages as he breathed, he'd tap a finger against the covers, he'd rub his feet together. If I said something, he would say, "Uh-huh" in that mindless way that says, "Don't bother me."

So in a way, Polly was a big part of the reason I didn't want to move, yet also a big part of the reason I probably needed to. The more fascinated I became with the Seacrests' lives, the more inadequate my own life seemed to be. Not that I wasn't doing other things—a lot of other things really. During those years we were neighbors, I played a lot of tennis and started substituting in the schools a few days a week. I kept track of Travis and cleaned my house and did laundry and cooked and read and helped out on different committees.

I even wrote some poems of my own now and then. I tried writing one inspired by Polly, as a matter of fact, called "Housewife," but it was awful. One line included the phrase "spreading jam and joy," a pathetic attempt at zeugma. Poets walk a tightrope "constantly risking absurdity," as Lawrence Ferlinghetti put it. Nothing is more embarrassing than to read something you've written in an attempt to capture the sublime, only to realize how ridiculous it is.

In spite of all my busyness, though, I'd still find time to run next door for two or three late-afternoon visits every week. You always find time for what you want to do. Polly's house was always vibrant, which is a word I would never use to describe our own house, even when our children were young. Looking back, I would have to say our home was pretty boring in a lot of ways. Orderly and predictable. Ken wasn't exactly a party animal, though he did remind me of an animal in other ways. A mole, to be specific—that's what I told him more than once.

"A mole in a hole" was what I always thought of when I saw him hunkered at his desk in his study at work on a new composition. He burrowed in deep and rarely saw the light of day. Up until the last few years, he always wrote his pieces by hand first, and the scratching of his pencil on staff paper reminded me of the busy little paws of a mole. But why am I speaking in past tense? He still writes music, just not in our house anymore. I think the thing Ken's mother was most proud of was that he wrote music. "My son, the composer" was how she thought of him.

Which brings us back to Ken's mother. But first, "The River-Merchant's Wife." All these different parts will come together eventually. I have to believe that. Oh, to have the eyes of God, to see it all plainly. But I have only recently taken my first taste from the cup of salvation, and my eyes are the newly opened eyes of a baby. There must be a correlation between tasting and seeing, though. The more I taste, the more I'll see. I read a verse about that in the Bible. "O taste and see," it said.

Which reminds me of how all the senses are connected. At the Church of the Open Door one Sunday, for instance, they sang a hymn that started out "O worship the King." Immediately I saw the color yellow—a very bright pulsating yellow—and felt a prickly sensation like something very hot being held too close to my skin, and I tasted something almost metallic, as if I had bitten down on a penny. All of this from a few measures of a hymn I'd never heard before! I used to worry that these sensory transfers were evidence of a miswiring in my brain until I read one day that Sir Isaac Newton, a perfectly sane and intelligent man from all accounts, also associated colors and musical notes to the extent that he consistently saw the color red when he heard C, orange when he heard D, and so forth.

I had an aunt, my mother's oldest sister, who slowly lost her mind as she grew older. One of the last times I was at her house in Georgia, I remember sitting on her sun porch and listening to her talk. Aunt Philippa was her name. My mother's parents had hoped for many sons, but all they had were daughters, five of them. So they kept giving them feminized boys' names like Philippa, Wilhelmina, Ronalda, and Georgette. My mother, the youngest, they named Danielle, which I thought was the best of them all.

But anyway, returning to Aunt Philippa on her sun porch, I was stunned at the way she kept up a steady current of talk, none of which seemed to fit together and make much sense. She talked about the wonderful taste of macadamia nuts, I remember, and then went right into listing the last twenty Kentucky Derby winners in order. She followed that up with a story about two former neighbors named Ted and Annabelle, who collected fountain pens and belonged to the Georgia Pen Collectors Club and had in their collection a little Japanese pen with lacquered inlays that looked like a . . . She never finished that sentence but switched to an account of a fishing trip she'd taken the week before, though I knew my mother had told me Aunt Philippa hadn't stepped foot outside her house for almost ten years. I remember my mother and Aunt Willie, who was there at the same time we were, giving each other meaningful looks that afternoon as Aunt Philippa talked on and on.

My thoughts are like Aunt Philippa's speech that day. If I spoke them aloud, people would exchange meaningful looks behind my back, too. I've wondered at times if Aunt Philippa's madness started out like this, if her thoughts first started skipping wildly here and there and then one day she just opened her mouth and spoke exactly what she was thinking and from that day on was judged to have lost her mind.

Well, anyway, my point is that I believe all of this is going somewhere. It just takes time. I believe it all must be part of the design somehow. So back to "The River-Merchant's Wife," which keeps nudging at my mind. It's a poem translated by Ezra Pound but written hundreds of years ago by someone named Rihaku, which was the Japanese name for the Chinese poet Li Po.

The poem is a letter from a wife to her husband. She's young, still a teenager, and her husband has been gone for five months. She grew to love him after they married, and now she languishes at home waiting for word from him while "the monkeys make sorrowful noise overhead." We don't know if the husband is still alive. Maybe he won't even get the letter. All of that is part of why the letter breaks your heart.

I have a big map of the world that came with a *National Geographic* subscription one time. On my map Japan is green, Korea is pink, China is yellow, and Vietnam is lavender. I close my eyes and imagine it spread out in front of me, and I'm looking at the pastel countries in the Far East, trying to imagine this young wife whose heart is aching for her husband's return.

I remember years ago during the Vietnam War I saw a newscast that showed a Vietnamese mother weeping over the body of her son. She wasn't weeping softly. She wailed, a high, piercing sustained note, and her face was a wreck of pain. To my shame, this thought came to me. *Why, those people must love their families as much as we do.* I was surprised at the intensity of the mother's sorrow. I guess these thoughts aren't anything to be ashamed of, but I am. I had gotten to the age of whatever I was at the time—maybe sixteen or seventeen—without realizing that the deepest emotions of the heart are universal.

So the young wife in Ezra Pound's poem keeps a vigil every day, hoping for news of her husband, walking to the moss-covered gate through which he left, watching the falling leaves of autumn in the garden and the yellow butterflies that go in pairs, and she yearns for him. And do you know what? Nowhere does she come out and say in that letter, "I love you," but every line makes it clear that she loves him past all telling.

So why does this poem haunt me so? Even in my anger and indignation at being so badly treated by Ken, why does it get to someplace soft inside me? I think it's because it shows me a glimpse of what the love between a husband and wife could be. It's the same reason I both loved and hated being around Polly and Morris Seacrest.

As I've said, Ken travels off and on. It started years ago after he made a name for himself as a middle-school band director, and it continued as he kept composing and having his pieces published, and then by the time he took the position with Harwood College, he was receiving so many invitations to speak, conduct, and judge that he had to turn a lot of them down. After all, a teacher has to be on site unless he's teaching correspondence courses, which wouldn't really work with music. I know there's a world of difference between my situation and that of the river-merchant's young wife, but the one thing I keep thinking of is this. Until now, I never, ever felt sad when Ken left. And even worse, I hardly ever felt particularly happy when he came back.

So there. I've put it down on paper. It sounds awful, but I mean to write an honest record. Not that it excuses what Ken has done. The law is very clear, and he has very clearly broken it. I'm not saying that if I had been sadder to see him go and happier to see him return, all of this could have been prevented. It's a bit late for prevention right now anyway. I'm just going over the facts.

When Travis broke my hand-painted ceramic urn from Romania, all the lectures in the world about not messing around with a baseball bat inside the house wouldn't put that urn back together. Maybe they'd keep another vase or china teapot from getting broken, but that urn was destroyed. It was history. I knew *why* it was broken, but that didn't alter the fact that it was shattered into thousands of pieces. And even if I hadn't known how it had happened—say, we had walked in one day and there it was in tiny shards all over the floor and nobody knew why—it still wouldn't change its present condition. It was ruined for good.

So I picture my marriage like that for a moment—something irreplaceable smashed to smithereens. And I ask myself, "Does it do any good to go over all the possible actions leading up to the demolition?" In the case of the Romanian urn, I could have blamed myself for Travis's brief interest in baseball, for I had signed him up for Little League and chauffeured him to practices and games and rigged up a pitching target for him in the backyard and bought him a brand-new aluminum bat—the same one that dealt the blow to the urn.

Or I could have blamed Ken, since he was the one who decided the urn should go on a teakwood pedestal right beside the front door on the hardwood floor. I wanted to put it in the living room on the carpet. I could have replayed every step Travis took that day that led him to the fateful accident, and I could have stopped the tape at any number of points and said, "If only he had done this instead of that, maybe he wouldn't have ended up inside the house with that bat in his hands." I'm sure I could have dragged Jennifer into it somehow so she could partake in the blame with the rest of us, but what I'm getting at is this. None of the "what if's" and "if only's" would do a thing to fix the damage.

So why was I sitting here feeling something like guilt that I enjoyed Ken's absences from home? I don't know. Maybe because in the midst of all my confusion, this was something I could latch onto as fact. But even if it had anything to do with all this, the big fact remained that Ken was the one who had broken the cardinal rule of marriage, not me. I didn't know how it had come about or why or how long it had been going on, but none of that changed the act itself.

"Thou shalt not commit adultery" was one of the Ten Commandments. I had known that long before Margaret explained to me God's plan of salvation. I knew the Bible probably had a lot to say about those who broke that commandment, and I decided right there that evening as I waited for nine o'clock to come that I'd do some research on it. I would be well armed with Scripture by the time Ken arrived. I knew there was a concordance in my Bible. I had already used it to look up the words *trust* and *fear*.

To my surprise, however, the word *adultery* wasn't even in the concordance. That was odd because I was sure the word was in the Bible. I kept going over the column where it should have been, but the list skipped from *adorn* straight to *advance*. Then I discovered something called the subject index right before the concordance, and there it was. *ADULTERY* in all capital letters with a number of subheadings and Scripture references underneath. I saw two categories that interested me especially: "Forbidden" listed five verses, and "Penalty of" listed four.

I grew up hearing my mother blame herself regularly for other people's troubles. Maybe it's typical of pessimists not only to expect bad things out of life but also to hold themselves accountable in some way. "I should have been more alert when she first started acting funny" was her most common remark about Aunt Philippa, for example, as if she could have somehow warded off the dementia if she had only seen it earlier, and "It was probably all those starches and sweets I used to fix" was her explanation for my father's cancer. The biopsy he got the phone call about on my wedding day turned out to be bad, which was no surprise to my mother, of course. "I knew it would be malignant," she said when the report came back. She had known he would die, too, which he had.

That could have been why she was so drawn to nursery rhymes. As Ken had often pointed out, a lot of them were pretty negative when you started thinking about it. My mother would read them to me over and over, morning, noon, and night, nodding the whole time as if they confirmed her own dim view of life and what could be expected of it. Old Mother Hubbard's dog got nothing to eat, the poor children who lived with the old woman in a shoe got spanked and sent to bed without supper, and the innocent, hardworking maid in "Sing a Song of Sixpence" got her nose snipped off for no good reason.

Here's something that illustrates my mother's mindset as well as anything I can think of. I remember going to Atlanta with my mother and Juliet one time when I was a teenager. We passed a new office building just off the freeway that was so shiny you could hardly look at it. The whole outside was covered with what looked like big overlapping mirrors. You could see everything reflected in it—cars, trees, sky. Juliet, who would have been eleven or twelve at the time, said in her usual gushy way something like "Wow! Isn't that the most *beautiful* thing you've ever *seen*?" To which my mother replied—Juliet and I still joke about this—"I bet it wouldn't be so beautiful after a good hailstorm let loose on it."

She was a good mother, though. I want to make that clear. She was the reason I wanted to be a mother. She worked hard after my father died so she could send Juliet and Greg to college, and she was always very interested in everything we did. I guess her melancholy streak served a good purpose in that she was never disappointed when we suffered setbacks. She expected them at every turn. So when we had our little successes in school, as Greg did in football and Juliet did in gymnastics and I did in academics and tennis, she was always happily shocked and made grand celebrations out of each occasion because she was sure they wouldn't be repeated.

So anyway, I start looking up the verses listed in the subject index under the word *adultery*, and when I finish I feel satisfied. God doesn't leave any doubt about the seriousness of this particular sin. In the references under the "Forbidden" subheading, I read four passages citing all or part of the Ten Commandments and another one listing adultery as one of the "works of the flesh," declaring that those who do it "shall not inherit the kingdom of God."

The "Penalty" verses are even more severe. One says adulterers should be put to death, and other verses put them in the same category with drunkards, thieves, and extortioners. The Hebrews 13:4 verse makes me take a deep breath and hold it for a long time. "Marriage is honourable," it says, "and the bed undefiled," and then it goes on to say that God will judge adulterers.

This is the last verse I read, and though I've decided not to blame myself for anything, I can't help seeing a picture of our marriage bed in my mind, and I can't help remembering how much I liked it when the whole bed was mine. But somehow the picture I see now is a shameful one. A queen-sized bed is way too big to be a permanent bed for only one person.

I wonder briefly about divorced couples and their beds. Do they usually sell them afterward, or does one partner keep the bed? Or maybe they divide it up—one partner takes the frame and headboard, the other the mattress and box spring. Would somebody dare to use his first marriage bed in a second marriage? Has anyone ever chopped up the bed after a divorce and burned it in the front yard? Has anyone ever hauled it out to the curb and put a sign on it that said "FREE—PLEASE GET IT OUT OF MY SIGHT"? Maybe you could advertise it in the want ads with something like "Bed—used ten years, defiled by adulterous husband, cheap now."

The verse about the marriage bed reminds me that I have another night to get through. I've slept alone many nights in our married life but never more alone than the past five nights. Earlier I said Ken's absences weren't times I dreaded, and that's the truth. I've always liked being at home by myself, setting my own schedule, sleeping smack in the middle of the bed, eating whatever I want, watching TV, reading past midnight if I want to, playing CDs of music Ken considers substandard—such as "Bolero" and the Mantovani Orchestra and Floyd Cramer on the piano—not having anybody around to pick up after, and all that.

And I don't think I'm all that different from most women, with certain exceptions like the river-merchant's young wife in ancient China. She was only a teenager, though. Give her enough years with the same man, and I bet she'd be glad for an occasional separation. Maybe she wouldn't, I don't know. Shortly before we moved from our house in Derby, Morris Seacrest flew to Michigan for his grandfather's funeral, and Polly said those were the worst three days of her life. The day he came home she got a spiral-sliced Heavenly Ham to serve for supper, then took a bath right in the middle of the afternoon and put on a *dress* with a ruffled collar just to go meet him at the airport. But there again, they had been married only seven years or so, and you have to take that into consideration.

But anyway, when Ken was away from home before, I always knew it was only temporary. Now I feel aloneness like something cold and wet and smelly oozing in under the doors. I've never been afraid when Ken was gone overnight. Never. That wasn't the way I was.

When Travis was still home, I always felt safe, knowing he would do anything he could in a threatening situation. Travis might have some personal quirks that would disqualify him for Mr. Popularity, but he's not a coward. Years ago when he was only five, I remember when a stray dog went after Jennifer in a park over in Derby, and before I could jump up and rush to her, Travis had grabbed that dog's tail and was pulling and screaming and kicking for all he was worth. The dog turned on him, of course, but by then several adults had converged and it was all over for the dog. Discounting the tetanus shots, no one got really hurt.

Even after Travis left for college last fall and nobody else was home when Ken went out of town, I still wasn't afraid at night. Of course, I was in a fog for months after Travis left, so that was part of it. I wasn't thinking clearly enough to be afraid of the dark or anything else, except of losing my son. But generally, the women in my family have never been prone to nighttime fears. A dozen years ago or so, my aunt Ronalda's house in Clydesville, Georgia, was burglarized in the wee hours of the morning—or I should say a burglary was attempted.

Aunt Ronalda collected art, mostly local stuff she ran across at bookstore galleries, sidewalk displays, student art shows, that kind of thing. I think I must have gotten some of my love of art from her. She had a good eye for quality and knew talent when she saw it. One of her pieces was an abstract metal sculpture with a marble base. It looked like a cross between a set of measuring scales and the inside of a grandfather clock, but it had a certain grace you couldn't explain. The piece was displayed on a low table at the end of the hallway underneath a huge pen-and-ink drawing of feathers—nothing but feathers, all in black and white—executed by a disabled veteran who held the pen in his mouth.

Anyway, the burglar must have thought nobody was home, since Aunt Ronalda's car was at the auto repair shop. When he came around the corner from the living room into the hallway in the middle of the night, however, Aunt Ronalda was ready for him. She was holding that metal sculpture by the top end, and she brought the marble base down on his head from behind. Then she picked up the telephone and calmly called the police, who got there before the burglar came to. While she waited, Aunt Ronalda emptied the burglar's bag and returned her sterling flatware, her gold-plated candlesticks, and her pewter mugs to their places in the china cabinet. She was seventy years old at the time. Of all the art Aunt Ronalda owns, this metal sculpture is the piece I hope to inherit and add to my own art collection someday. It has a story behind it.

But back to my past five nights alone. That very first night, Sunday, I lay in bed and ran my hands all along the bottom sheet on either side of me. I couldn't see it in the dark, but I knew it by heart. It was pale yellow, all cotton, soft from many washings. The top sheet was newer, a crisp white with a design of yellow flowers and ivy imprinted on it. Ken had been lying right here on these same sheets just the night before.

In recent years Ken had begun sleeping on his left side mostly, meaning his back was to me, but I never took it personally. I preferred it that way, actually. When he used to sleep facing me, I kept hoping he would want to talk at night. With his back to me, I didn't have to keep hoping. I wondered now if he had kissed me before we went to sleep the night before, but I couldn't remember. Usually he didn't, but every now and then the old habit resurfaced. I tried hard to think. It wouldn't have been more than a perfunctory peck lasting about a tenth of a millisecond, but it somehow seemed very important that first night to remember whether he had kissed me. I ended up pretending I couldn't remember, but deep down I knew he hadn't.

That night I thought about all the bedtimes of years gone by. During the early years, Ken used to kiss me right after he turned out the light, then take a handful of my nightgown and clutch it as he drifted off to sleep. He would start out over on my side of the bed, jammed against me, and he'd be asleep before the first sheep could jump over the stile. That would last about ten minutes—I could have timed it almost to the second—and then he'd shift his position to his back and rest his hand palm down on my nightgown for

another ten minutes or so. Finally, he'd stir again and move over a little farther and lay his hand on his chest.

That first night I slept alone after discovering Ken's adultery was one
long night, believe me. One thought led to another as it always does, and I
was still awake three hours later, my eyes aching in their sockets. I got up
and turned on the light, then rummaged in the medicine cabinet for something to help me sleep, then changed the sheets on our bed. Then I picked
up a book from the top of my little desk in the bedroom. For another hour I
read, or tried to, from *A Book of Days for the Literary Year*, a birthday gift from
Juliet some years earlier. She had bought it in Ireland when she and Tony
took a study tour of the British Isles.

All this was Sunday night as I said—the Sunday night of the revelation.
I know I'm backtracking, but I must be granted that freedom. Things unfold
at their own rate. A story like this isn't linear. It's full of compartments. This
book I was reading in the middle of the night—*A Book of Days*—has entries
for all the days of the year, telling what happened on that day in literary
history.

It was February 18 at the time, so I turned to that page first and saw that
on that day in 1678 John Bunyan's *Pilgrim's Progress* was published, in 1885
the author of *Zorba the Greek*, Kazantzakis, was born in Crete, in 1884 Tol-
stoy's *What I Believe In* was confiscated by the Russian police, and in 1931
Toni Morrison was born in Ohio. Well, imagine all that.

The thought came to me that I should write my own *Book of Days*. Beside
February 18 of this year, I would write "Elizabeth Landis, lover of great poetry and writer of mediocre, learns of husband's infidelity and discovers the
meaning of the word *alone*."

The next night I tried sleeping in Travis's room, but I got up and moved
after an hour. The glow from the streetlight seeped through the cracks in his
blinds and made a pattern on the ceiling. I imagined I could hear his music
playing, the silly dialogues he used to stage with different voices, the soft
thump of his Nerf ball against the door, all the sound effects he was so good
at—birds, police sirens, catfights, crying babies, and so forth.

I studied the outlines of all his childhood treasures arranged on a high
shelf above his desk: the carved giraffe, the clay unicorn, the figurine of
Bilbo Baggins, the onyx egg. And I was supremely conscious of his bedraggled old stuffed bear sitting on his desk, even though it was just a vague
shape in the shadows. Travis called the bear UFO, which stood for Unnamed
Furry One. I imagined UFO staring sternly at me with his scratched glass
eyes. All through his teens, Travis had steadfastly refused to retire UFO to
the attic or a closet shelf. No doubt he's the only college freshman who still
has his stuffed bear from childhood prominently displayed in his bedroom.

I finally threw off the covers and fled from the room. What had ever made me think I could endure a night alone in Travis's room? Part of me had ceased to live when he left for college, a very big part. But "ceased to live" is way too mild for what happened inside me when he left home. "Died a horrible death" would be closer.

Like a Map of All the World

9

An hour before Ken was to arrive home on Friday night, after I had looked up all the references to adultery, I opened my Bible again. It was now dark outside, the only light coming from the one over the kitchen sink. The pages fell open to the book of Psalms, and I saw a verse, actually only the first four words of a verse, that I immediately made my prayer. It was in Psalm 119:18, and the words were "Open thou mine eyes." Later I saw the rest of the verse and thought it was beautiful—"that I may behold wondrous things out of thy law." But I didn't even notice that part until weeks and weeks later. Being a new Christian, please judge me mercifully.

So I plucked out these four words—"Open thou mine eyes"—and I said right out loud to God, "Yes, please do this. Open my eyes and help me make some sense out of this whole thing. Help me to get all these parts laid out. Show me what I need to know." Without prayer and the knowledge of God's presence with me, I'm certain I would have panicked. I had been through deep waters before, and I knew my usual response was not to swim or float, but to sink to the bottom like a stone.

I have to say something here. I know there must be fine books and excellent counselors available to help with problems like mine, but I didn't consider seeking them out. I'm not saying these things shouldn't be used, however, or that you're some kind of inferior Christian if you do look for such help. To be truthful, going to a good counselor probably shows a healthier attitude than the way I did it. I told myself that the Bible had all the help I needed, and though I believed that, I also know that my pride was a factor in keeping everything to myself.

To be honest, a lot of what happened during these early weeks is a blur in my mind now. I'm trying to put it all in order the way I remember it, but when your life collides with forces out of your control, the frame gets bent, and it takes everything you have just to keep up some semblance of moving along. You keep your eyes on the ground and creep along one slow inch at a time. The scenery you pass and the things that occur along the way get muddled. At times I wish I had kept a record during those earliest days, and at other times I'm glad I didn't. It would help me in what I'm writing now, but I'm not sure I'd want a daily log of my sorrow sitting on a shelf somewhere. That would be one heavy book.

But anyway, almost immediately after I prayed for God to open my eyes, two faces came to my mind. You might think that Ken's face would be one of them, but it wasn't. One was Travis, and the other was Ken's mother. I took a deep breath and said, "Okay, God, I'll take a good look at them both."

But which to look at first? I suppose I could flip a coin. Or I could go with the hardest one first. That would be Travis. Or the one who has drained me dry. That would also be Travis. Or the one who has always filled me up again. Travis. Or the one who has consumed most of my thoughts during my waking hours. Travis again. Or the one I had grown to feel was the reason for my existence. How would a kid like Travis ever have made it this far without a mother to coax him along? I had asked myself this question many times.

Travis. When I say his name over and over, it starts to sound funny after a little while. It reminds me of a piece of equipment or something hard and utilitarian, some small part in the carburetor of an engine maybe or a tool for prying things apart. Can't you hear somebody saying, "Here, hand me the travis"?

I never liked his name really. It wasn't my choice. I mean, loving poetry as I do, I'm fond of slant rhyme and all, but Travis Landis sounded a little corny to me. Ken pushed for it, though, saying the middle name, which would be Brandon after my father, would smooth it out, and in the euphoric generosity of having a new baby after seven long years—a *son*—I gave in. The middle name only made the whole name sound funnier, of course, like the first line of a limerick: "Travis Brandon Landis / Consumed a praying mantis." But at least, I thought, I could someday teach Travis the poetic device of assonance by using his own name as an illustration.

Thinking back over it now, I believe naming Travis might have been the last decision Ken ever made for a long, long time concerning his son. He could claim the name, but not the child. Travis was mine from day one, just as sure as Jennifer was Ken's. But even more so, of course, because I did all the purely functional mother things for him all day long, and then I had his heart besides.

Where to start—now there's the question. It seems that Travis has always been. Actually, I guess the best place to start is seven years before Travis was born. That would be Jennifer. Jennifer was Ken's child, as I just said, which wasn't at all fair considering the amount of time, energy, and love I lavished on her. She made me a mother, and I adored the feeling of having my very own child. I remember lying beside her the day after we brought her home from the hospital, examining each toe and finger over and over, touching her tiny ear lobes, tracing the curve of her nose, and whispering, "You're my own baby girl."

I had dreams about our mother-daughter relationship. She would admire and respect me, copy what I did, want to be exactly like me. She would pour out her heart to me and listen intently to my advice. She would be the life-long best friend I had never had. We would laugh together, go shopping, play tennis, share clothes, talk late into the night, all those sisterly things that Juliet and I never did together because we were so different from each other.

I was certain things wouldn't be the way between Jennifer and me that they usually are between mothers and daughters during those difficult teen years, the way it had been between my own mother and me when I had withdrawn and she had tried to press in closer. The relationship between Jennifer and me would be so special that she would want me to be matron of honor at her wedding, and I would have to talk her out of it, telling her it just wasn't done that way. "But I want you standing beside me when I get married," she would say, "not sitting behind me."

Long before her first birthday, I think I began to realize these dreams would never come to pass, although I hung on to them for many years, sure that ours was one of those relationships that start off slow and go through some rocky times but then evolve into something beautiful later on. Patience—that's all it took, and I actually thought at one time that I was a very patient person.

One of my earliest clues concerning the adversarial nature of our relationship was one afternoon when I was trying to nurse Jennifer. She was probably only six or seven months old at the time. It was an exhausting day, I remember that. She had slept fitfully, only short little naps, and now she was hungry and fractious yet wouldn't settle down to the meal right in front of her. It was hers for the taking, but she writhed and fussed and turned her little face away. A couple of days later I discovered that the underlying cause was really an ear infection, but I didn't have any idea on this particular day.

I was holding her in the rocking chair in the nursery when I heard the back door open. Ken came to the door of the nursery and looked in. We must have been a sight. I was worn out, and Jennifer was full of infant rage. This wasn't at all the picture I had conjured up when I used to dream of motherhood, let me tell you.

The reason I remember this specific day was that it was the first visible evidence that Jennifer wasn't really my daughter, but Ken's. He spoke to her from the doorway, something like "Whatsa matter wif my wittle Jen-Jen?" He usually kept his distance when I was nursing her, so he didn't come into the room. I no doubt replied for her, something like "Your wittle Jen-Jen is acting like a spoiled brat, that's what, and her wittle mother is wiped out."

But here's what happened next. Now imagine this. One minute Jennifer's face is beet red from her wailing and all scrunched up like a little troll's. And then Ken walks over and kneels down beside us. He cups a hand over Jennifer's head, leans in close to her, kisses her ear, and whispers, "It's okay, Jen-Jen. Daddy's here. Don't fret, pumpkin. Eat your din-din like a good girl." And the next minute, it's like magic. He gently turns her little head toward my breast, and she quits crying and latches on as if she's starved. The only sounds she's making now are the little slurping, sucking noises of a hungry baby.

He stays there the whole time with his hand on her head, and she keeps cutting her eyes over to look at him. She really did, I promise. Ken fixed his own eyes on the floor except for occasional glances to check on Jennifer. Private moments have always embarrassed him. He wouldn't have stared for the world.

And this is the way it has been ever since. I was always the one who fed her and dressed her and bathed her and read to her and the million other things a mother attends to, and I loved doing them, I really did. And she needed me to do all these things. Ken was always the one she really *wanted*, though. She was always wiggling out of my lap and running to him when she was a toddler. I had been so hopeful that her first word would be *Mama* and would be spoken as she lifted her little arms to me beseechingly. It didn't happen, though. Her first word was *no*, and the only reason she was lifting her little arms to me was to try to push me away as she threw a fit. Her second word was *Dada*.

From the moment she started kindergarten, it was always Ken she looked for at school programs, several times even waving and calling out, "Hi, Daddy!" And she wanted nothing to do with dressing up in her mother's clothes and high heels. No, she'd clomp around the house in Ken's shoes and old sport coat for hours. He had an old fishing hat she wore everywhere when she was eight or nine. In middle school, even before baggy was the fashion, she liked to wear Ken's shirts with the sleeves rolled up, sometimes as a jacket over a T-shirt. In high school everything I said she viewed with skepticism or outright derision, whereas she'd turn around and listen to Ken's opinions as if his middle name were Oracle-at-Delphi.

As she got older, I had suggested off and on that she consider becoming a teacher because she was so good at breaking down complex ideas, relating easily to others, and putting thoughts into words. She had always said she was going to travel every summer when she grew up and got a job, so I thought it was only logical that she go into education so she'd have her summers free.

One night at supper, however, when she was in eleventh grade, we were talking about something that had been in the newspaper that day, something about a man in Columbia who had been accused of murdering a police officer but got off scot-free because of a trial technicality. Her government teacher had discussed it in class that day, and Jennifer was mad about it. After she had spoken at length, I remember Ken saying sort of offhandedly, "Well, Jen, maybe you ought to be a lawyer and keep things like that from happening in your cases. A lot of those situations are the fault of careless lawyers."

He was eating a piece of corn on the cob, I recall distinctly, and as he picked up his napkin to wipe a trickle of butter from his chin, I remember feeling something like an electrical tingle in the air. You see, I realized that what Ken had just said wasn't just a casual remark, but a prophecy. I don't know how I knew, but I did. *You wait and see,* I said to myself. *She'll study law as sure as you're sitting here stabbing broccoli florets with your fork.* And that's exactly how it turned out.

Oh, I'm proud of her, no question about that, even though she's not exactly the daughter I had put in an application for. I had not expected a fussy baby or an aggressive tantrum-throwing toddler. But at least she learned to smile prettily and behave like a little lady in public. By the time she was four and five, people assumed she was the perfect child because she was so precocious and well mannered. She was beautiful also, with cameolike features. Her angelic looks threw people off. They assumed she was delicate and gentle. They didn't live with her, though.

What was strong willed at home, however, came across as focused and confident at school. Teachers always wrote things like "classroom leader" and "respected by others" and "assertive yet courteous" on her report card. Considering her willfulness, I guess we got through her teenage years with relatively few scars. Needless to say, she and I didn't share clothes and secrets, we rarely played tennis or went shopping together, and the only times we stayed up at night talking were when we were arguing about her coming home too late.

Now that she's grown and on her own, Jennifer is what you'd call a dutiful daughter. She sends me birthday presents and cards right on time. She knows exactly what sizes and styles I wear in clothing and often says things like "I remember you saying you didn't have a white cardigan you liked, so that's why I got it." She gave me a pretty lamp last Christmas for the top of my dresser because she had heard me say I could never find what I was looking for in my jewelry box. She buys me original artwork when she sees something at a good price that she thinks I'll like, which I always do. She telephones the first Sunday of every month, and she sends a hundred dollars a month to pay for a car we financed for her in law school. She's a good daughter, and I would lay down my life for hers without a thought. But she's always been more Ken's than mine.

And now, Travis. It's still hard to think about the morning he left for college. Ken drove him down to Piper College the last week of August less than a year ago. The memory of Travis walking out of the house is a great wound in my heart. It's still painful to the touch; it hasn't healed over. I stood in the doorway of our bedroom and watched him make his way down the hall, through the kitchen, and out the side door into the carport, and then I followed along behind him, still hoping there was some mistake and this really wasn't the day I thought it was. Or hoping he'd suddenly stop and say, "I've changed my mind. I don't want to do this. I want to stay home."

I couldn't begin to count the number of times I've watched Travis go down the hallway and out the kitchen door, but this wasn't like any of those other times when he went to school or to a piano lesson or soccer practice. He wasn't going to be coming back after just a few hours, and even when he did, it would never be the same after this.

Don't tell me I'm making too much out of this. Don't tell a mother whose only son is leaving home to go to college that it's no big deal. I honestly didn't see how I could keep living in this house after that day.

So Travis is going down the hall away from me, and I know he'll never again make a trip down the hall exactly like this one. Of course, it's not seeming to hit *him* as anything unusual. He could just as easily be going off to another day of his summer job at the barbecue place for all the ceremony he's putting into this final walk.

Travis didn't look like a college freshman that day, and he surely didn't act like one. He was walking down the hallway the way little kids do, trying to touch anything above their heads that's attached to the ceiling or walls. The only difference was, of course, that he didn't have to jump since he could touch most of it standing flat-footed except for the ceiling itself—he did have to stand on his tiptoes a little to touch that with his fingertips. Here again, this is something you think of young boys doing, not college freshmen. I could get up from this kitchen table and go out into that hallway right this minute and find dozens of Travis's fingerprints on the ceiling. We've lived here only a little over eight months, remember, and Travis has been away at college for most of that time, so these aren't fingerprints left over from when he was nine and ten.

And if you were to ask Travis, my son who's a college freshman, why he feels the urge to put his fingers against the white ceiling, he would say—and I can quote him verbatim on this—"I don't know." Isn't this a boy's favorite answer to almost any question?

On the day he left for college, besides touching the hall ceiling with his fingers, he swatted at the little pull chain hanging down from the attic door, put his entire hand around the globe over the hall light as if he were laying hold of a large doorknob, flicked the little doorbell chime box with his thumb and index finger, knocked twice on the smoke alarm and said,

"Who's there?" then ran a finger across the top of the bathroom doorjamb. "Rats! The dust monitor is foiled again," he said.

Back in those days I used to pride myself on my thorough dusting—baseboards, tops of doors, picture frames, and so forth—and Travis liked to tease me about it. "Watch out, Mom's flitting again," he'd say when he saw me with my feather duster. As I'm writing this right now, I can't honestly remember the last time I used my feather duster for all those extra places. The dust monitor would find plenty if he visited today.

I know now that Travis was just trying to cheer me up that day, but it wasn't working. Right at the end of the hallway is a large framed display of his senior pictures—five different poses of Travis taken at a photo studio several months before his high school graduation. He stopped briefly in front of them, pointed, and said, "Wow—quintuplets." I saw nothing humorous in any of this.

It was only six months ago that he left home, but it seems like six years—no, more like six decades. But why am I starting with something so recent? As I said earlier, it seems that Travis has always been. Jennifer was almost eight by the time Travis was born. I had wanted another baby for a long time, had gone through some hard times because of it, had shut down in a lot of ways, so when I heard Travis let loose and wail in the delivery room, I felt like I had been reborn.

All the dreams I had for motherhood were transferred to Travis, most of them having fallen through with Jennifer. I knew they'd have to be modified, of course. We couldn't really share clothes, for instance, but as I saw Travis's personality and temperament taking shape, I began to see that maybe a mother-son relationship could transcend even the best mother-daughter one.

Thoughts are flying at me all out of order. Here's one from way back, for instance. One time when he was around seven, I was worrying aloud over Travis's apparent disinterest in developing friendships with other children his age. I was describing to Ken what I had observed when I went to Travis's classroom at school that day to help out with the Christmas party.

We were in our bedroom that night. Ken was already in bed, and I was getting ready to take a bath. Ken is probably one of the few men who actually wears pajamas with a matching top and bottom, and he had on his maroon pair that night. He was sitting up in bed, propped against the pillows, leafing through some sheets of a brass arrangement he was currently working on. He would look at it a few seconds, then lift his eyes to the ceiling as if searching for something. I was getting undressed, but he never once looked my way. Does this tell you anything?

Anyway, I finally got his attention away from his music long enough to describe what I had seen that day. "He just sits there *watching* everything," I said. "Kids will be talking right over his head to somebody else—like he's not even there. I mean, I didn't see him say *one word* to anybody else. Well, I take that back." And I told Ken about some boy coming by Travis's desk and noticing that he hadn't touched his big Santa Claus cookie. "So he asked Travis if he could have it," I said, "and you know what Travis did? He wrapped the whole cookie up in a napkin and handed it to the kid and said, 'Yeah, here, you can have it.'"

"That was nice," Ken said. But he was frowning. Maybe he had gone back to thinking about his music by now, or maybe he was looking at me in my underwear, thinking something like "Elizabeth's put on a little weight lately," or maybe he was trying to remember when he last checked the air in the tires. Or maybe he really was thinking about his son's poor social skills. Who knows what goes on in the mind of a man?

"Maybe it was nice," I said, "but it was also *weak*. That's not the way to make friends. That's the way to teach people they can walk all over you."

And then Ken said to me, and I'll never forget this, "Well, Elizabeth, you know what I think?" He laid his sheets of handwritten music down on the bedspread and clasped his hands behind his head. He leaned back against the wall and looked up at the light as he spoke. "You're not going to like this, but I'm going to say it anyway. I honestly don't think he's going to be making many friends until you let go of him a little." I remember all this as if it happened an hour ago.

I was stunned. "Where did *that* come from?" I said.

Ken pointed to his mouth. "From right here," he said, and then he got out of bed, took his music with him, and left the room. When I came out of the bathroom later, he was back in bed and was turned over on his side away from me. I slipped under the covers and lay very still, right on the edge as far away from him as I could get. Neither one of us said a word, though I knew he wasn't asleep. I could tell from the way he breathed.

This was the extent of our talking. One of us might venture on rare occasions to say something from deep inside, or it might slip out by accident, but there was never any real follow-up discussion of it. It would just hang there in the air for a while like a vapor. Our home was full of these vapors that had wafted up into the corners and coated the walls and ceilings over the years.

So I'm still sitting at the kitchen table, and it's completely dark outside and rather chilly inside. I'm right in the middle of remembering what Ken said all those years ago. It must be around eight-thirty by now on a Friday night a good eleven or twelve years later, but I can still feel the indignation that welled up inside me at Ken's suggestion that I was somehow to blame for Travis's lack of friends. I was surprised not only by *what* he'd said but also by the matter-of-fact tone he had used.

Now I'm sitting absolutely still in the dark kitchen, thinking, when all of a sudden I hear a light knock on the kitchen door and the sound of a key in the lock. I hadn't even heard Ken's car pull into the driveway or the car door slam, but here he is standing at the door. He flips on the kitchen light and sees me. Oddly, he's carrying a pizza box. At least he has the good sense to look sheepish about this.

"I know I'm a little early," he said, closing the door. "I hope you don't mind the pizza. I was on my way over, and . . . well, I realized how hungry I was, and I thought maybe . . . have you eaten anything?" He saw the open Bible on the table and frowned a little, then added, "Aren't you cold in here? What's the thermostat set on? How come you were sitting in the dark?"

Something inside me wanted to erupt. I wanted to scream at him and ask how in the world he could dare to bring a pizza into our house tonight of all nights. How could he be *hungry* when he was coming over to talk about the dissolving of our marriage? How could he talk about the *thermostat* and the *lights* at such a time?

But a curious thing happened instead. At the very instant I opened my mouth to say something harsh, I caught a whiff of the pizza and realized that, like Ken, I was very, very hungry. On the one hand, I wanted to lift up my voice, point to the pizza box, and say, "Get that abomination out of my sight!" But on the other hand, I wanted to grab it out of his hands, open the box lid, and start eating. Another thing that hit me, too, was that I knew he was right about the temperature in the house. I felt again how cold it was.

I felt a rolling kind of ache in the pit of my stomach that I knew to be hunger. Had I eaten that day? I tried to think back to lunchtime. I'd had a free hour between the morning and afternoon pre-algebra classes. What had I done with it? I remembered sitting at the teacher's desk in the classroom and staring for a long time at the equations on the chalkboard. I remembered seeing the overhead projector on a cart against the wall and wondering if the regular teacher used that instead of the chalkboard.

I had gotten up from the desk at some point and gone to the rest room in the teachers' lounge, and what else? Oh yes, I had dug some change out of my purse and gotten an Orange Crush out of the vending machine since it was out of Coke. I remembered speaking to another teacher, who asked me how it was going, giving her the standard vacuous answer of "Fine," and I remembered sitting on a sofa by the window after that and listening to a conversation between two other teachers about the ease of keeping track of grades on a computer instead of the old way in a grade book. A box of Krispy Kreme doughnuts sat on one of the tables, and I had eaten one, not even thinking at the time that maybe I should ask someone about paying for it.

Ken was still standing by the door, waiting for an answer or some kind of cue. I waved him over to the table. "Oh, set it down," I said wearily. "It's okay. You know where the plates are. I think there's some Sprite in the fridge. You know where the thermostat is, too."

"I don't need a plate," he said. He set the pizza down and walked to the refrigerator. I wondered if he was thinking about how he used to open it without an invitation from me. He got out a two-liter bottle of Sprite and set it on the counter, then took a glass out of the cupboard and filled it with ice cubes. I couldn't even remember when the Sprite had been opened. It was half full, probably flat by now. But when he poured it, I could see tiny bubbles and fizz forming on top, and he stooped to suck in the foamy part, then resumed pouring.

"Would you like some?" he asked, and I nodded. He poured another one. Then he opened another cupboard, took out two plates, and brought them to the table. "I guess plates would be good," he said. He set them down, then walked to the hallway to turn up the heat. I heard the hum of the furnace as it clicked on. He came back to the table with the glasses of Sprite and sat down across from me.

"Well, isn't this cozy?" I felt like saying. "Why don't we light a candle and make a special evening of it?" But I didn't say it. Instead, I reached behind me to the pass-through window and took two napkins out of the napkin holder and laid one beside each plate. He stretched out his legs under the table and bumped into my feet in the process. "Sorry," he said, quickly repositioning himself.

I wasn't going to talk first. I had made up my mind about that. It was Ken's turn. I had been the one to start our conversations all these years, but now it was up to him. I could tell it was an awkward moment for him, and I admit I found some small bit of pleasure in that. At the same time, and I can't explain this really, I felt a little sorry for him being thrust into such an unfamiliar and uncomfortable role.

He pulled back the pizza lid but didn't take a piece at first, as if thinking he probably shouldn't seem too eager to eat at a time like this. He cleared his throat, then gestured to the pizza. "Do you want a piece?" If I took a piece first, that would release some of the tension. With both of us chewing, it would be a little easier to get through these first few dreadful moments. I knew that. So I shook my head no and took a sip of my Sprite instead. I didn't look at him but directed my gaze to the napkin beside my plate.

He worked a moment at pulling out the first slice, then set it on his plate. He cleared his throat again and repeated, as if by way of apology, "I'm really hungry. I didn't eat anything for supper yet."

"I didn't either," I said, and I'm not sure why. Maybe simply because it was the truth, but more likely because it would suggest a superior level of seriousness, illustrating that I was taking this the way it should be taken, forsaking food.

"I'm sorry, Elizabeth," he said as he lifted the slice of pizza to his mouth and took his first bite. I felt like asking him what he was sorry for—the pizza or committing adultery—but I didn't say anything. He took two more bites, chewing at great length.

I thought of the verse in the Bible that said, "Marriage is honourable," and I felt the sudden fullness around the eyes and the tightness of throat that comes when you know you're on the brink of crying. I hate this part of being a woman, this assault of feelings that comes without warning. I want to sit here stoically, waiting him out as he struggles to find words in his vocabulary to put together for the speech he must deliver as the unfaithful husband. I don't want to fill the void and rescue him by crying. I don't want to divert his attention from the subject he must address in plain words.

I blink rapidly and look up at the light above the table, forbidding the tears to spill over. A horrible vision has come to me, you see. I have suddenly seen two faces again, two different faces than before. I don't know if these two images are from God. Surely they're not. Maybe they're from Satan. But here they are anyway.

The first is my own as I saw it in the mirror that morning while I was getting dressed for another day of substitute teaching. It's not the young face it used to be. It's not a face that young men turn to look at a second time. It's a face that might as well have *MIDDLE AGED* stamped across it. It's a face that has labored valiantly to keep the years from showing, but it's slowly losing the battle, and I know it.

I think of Diane Wakoski's poem "Sour Milk," which is really not a poem about sour milk but about getting older. I love this poem. Everyone should be required to read this poem once a week between the time he's thirteen and thirty to remind himself that time lays claim on everybody eventually and that all these old people who are getting in his way right now might have something to teach him.

Diane Wakoski talks in this poem about all the virtues of sour milk, its distinctive texture, its unique properties for cooking, and so forth, all of which are recognizable only by those who are willing to examine it closely "like a map of all the world." In a way, old people *are* a map of all the world. They've traveled all the roads and rivers, climbed all the mountains, descended all the valleys. Their journeys become a map for everybody coming after them. But back to milk. Milk of advanced age can do wonderful things regular milk can't, but it takes a skilled cook to know that, and as the poet points out, there aren't many of those in the fast-food world we live in.

So anyway, I see my face, presentable enough for my age but already settling into what it's going to be when I'm old. And then in the same instant, right next to it, I suddenly have a vision of the woman Ken thought he was calling last Sunday on his cell phone. I have no way of knowing what she really looks like, but in my imagination, as I sit across the table from my husband, I see her as a finalist in the Miss America contest.

If I'm sour milk, she's milk fresh out of the cow, pinging warm and white and sweet into a spanking clean bucket. She has a complexion like the cream that rises to the top and eyes the color of meadow grass and lips like wild red poppies. Her hair is long and luxuriant like a field of golden wheat, as far from my dust mop of a hairstyle as you can get. Okay, so I'm going overboard here, but the point is that in my mind she's gorgeous and young.

And even though I told myself I wasn't going to open the conversation, I can't stop the words that spring from my lips. "Do you love her?" I say, lifting my eyes to Ken's. He stops chewing and looks at me for what seems like an hour. I can't remember the last time he looked me right in the eye for this long. His eyes are jet black in the dim light of the kitchen, even dimmer than usual because one of the bulbs in the small copper fixture above the table has burned out. He has a trapped look.

"It's not that simple, Elizabeth," he finally says. "It's a lot more complicated than that."

"Okay," I say. "I can accept that. But I still want to know. Do you love her?" By asking this, of course, what I'm really asking, as I've said before, is "Do you still love me?" and maybe even more importantly, "Are you going to leave me?" I'm not for a minute suggesting that love is secondary to living together, but for some reason I can't begin to explain, I felt at that moment that I could bear the news that he didn't still love me if only he would assure me that he wouldn't abandon me.

Don't ask me to make sense of this. How can I be so angry at him that I'm sitting here thinking hard about the deadly slicing power of the deluxe set of razor-sharp Cutco knives I purchased less than two years ago when Polly Seacrest briefly tried her hand in the area of home sales, and yet still feel that my world will collapse if he leaves me? If somebody can explain this, he's a lot smarter than I am.

My question hangs in the air. He takes another bite of pizza and stares at the knotty pine paneling on the wall as he chews. My heart is pounding, and I see my hand reaching out to get a piece of pizza for myself. I see it peeling away the side that's attached to another piece, and I see it transfer the slice to my plate. I feel myself barely breathing as I pick the pizza up and bring it to my mouth. I'm looking at Ken now, and he shifts his gaze from the wall back to me.

Months later I can still feel the deafening stillness of that moment. The heat was on now, blowing through the wall vent behind me, and we both sat there chewing our pizza, looking at each other. I tasted nothing except fear and hope, which makes a strange combination, let me tell you. I had read the phrase "from everlasting to everlasting" in the Bible sometime during the past several days, and I began to get a glimmer of what it meant in that long stretch of time between my question and Ken's answer.

At last he opened his mouth and spoke. "I don't know," he said, which I should have predicted.

PART TWO

Footfalls echo in the memory

Down the passage which we did not take

Towards the door we never opened

······················

T. S. ELIOT

Great Expanse of Green

10

February ends, then March creeps by, and now it's April. It's a Saturday morning, and I'm finishing a tennis match, my fourth one of the YMCA spring season. At least it was morning when the match started, but I can tell by the sun that it's probably close to noon now. It's a great day for tennis, around sixty-five degrees and no wind. Still, I can feel my shirt wet against my back. We've been going at it for probably a good two hours.

Remember the chatty woman who hailed me at my mailbox back in February—Barb Chewning? She's on the other side of the net, and it's match point, again. I won the first set 6–4, she won the second 7–5, and at 6–6 we're in a tie break in the third. I have six points to her four in the tie break, so if I can win this next one, I'll have the match. She's fought off three previous match points, though, so I'm not counting on anything with this one. I'm serving, which should give me the edge, though it hasn't made much difference so far. We've broken each other's serves a lot in this match, a sign that we're not ready for the pro circuit yet.

This has been the hardest match I've played so far this season. The previous three were easy two-setters, all of which I won. I haven't been concentrating as I should today, for one thing, but for another Barb Chewning is a better player than my previous opponents. With most people you can assume a weaker backhand than forehand, so you naturally take advantage of that. Unfortunately for me, Barb's backhand is every bit as strong as her forehand, and she's quick on her feet, which means my drop shots aren't always winners.

And she won't give up on a point. She latches on like a bulldog, runs everything down, has a lot more stamina than a fortyish mother of four should have. So the points go on and on, and so do the games. One game we had ten deuces before she finally won it. That many points could make a whole set. We do a lot of base-line hitting, but every now and then one of us will get brave and rush the net. She's got a great passing shot and a pretty consistent lob, though, so mostly I stay back.

I bounce the ball a couple of times in preparation for serving, and then suddenly, without meaning to, I think of what I saw last night. I bounce the ball two more times, trying to erase the scene so I can focus on serving an ace. I try to envision myself delivering such a deadly serve that the impact breaks the strings on Barb Chewning's racket and the ball goes right through, leaving a hole, the way Pete Sampras did against Patrick Rafter that time.

This is what Coach Kendall in college always told us to do in those moments right before lifting the racket to serve—think it through and get a quick mental picture of yourself serving with textbook form. Don't let yourself think about the score or your opponent's return or the time or the weather or the last bad shot you made or what you're going to eat for supper—just zero in on the serve you're about to deliver. He liked to talk a lot about what he called "imaging your game." Coach Kendall was into New Age before its time.

The only picture I can see right now, though, has nothing to do with my serve. Instead, the image I can't get rid of is what I saw for real the evening before—Ken standing beside the driver's window of a blue Mazda in the parking lot of an Italian restaurant over in Greenville, talking to someone sitting inside the car. His hands are spread apart, palms up, and as he talks he's shaking his head. I have just come out of a bookstore where I've purchased a book titled *Making Your Own Days* by a poet named Kenneth Koch.

I guess it's obvious by now that I freely exercise the right at any point in my story to skip over entire weeks and months or, more often, to stop and fill in background. Sometimes when I'm reading a book and the author stops to muse over some extraneous detail, I say, "Come on, get on with the story and stop all this stalling." But now I'm the writer, see, and anybody who's writing something gets to make the calls. And anyway, think of Henry James. He got away with writing slow digressive stories. To which you're probably replying, "Right, but he was Henry James, and if I wanted to read Henry James, I'd read Henry James and not some poor imitation."

So this is one of those places where I stop to muse before the story goes on. I'm freezing the frame right before I raise my racket with my right hand and toss the ball with my left, and I'm going to say a word here about a poet named Kenneth Koch, who wrote the book that I went over to Greenville to buy last night when I saw Ken in the parking lot of Luigi's Little Italy.

Professor Huckabee brought Koch's new book to class two weeks earlier and read aloud from it. I knew I had read a poem by Koch sometime in the past, a poem I liked a lot, so I went home after class that night and, after some searching, found "Fresh Air" in a book on one of my shelves.

The poem convinced me to go to Greenville the next day and buy the new book by Koch, *Making Your Own Days*, so I guess I can say if it hadn't been for "Fresh Air," I probably wouldn't have been walking out of the bookstore that day, which means I wouldn't have seen Ken beside the blue Mazda in the parking lot, which would have been one less thing to divert my attention while trying to serve a tennis ball. But I read the poem, I went to the bookstore, and I saw Ken, in that order. What happens happens, and you can't revise the past, which are two of my mother's favorite things to say when she's discussing life and its ups and downs.

I had forgotten what a funny poem "Fresh Air" was, both curious funny and amusing funny. It's clear that it's a satirical attack on stuffy, pedantic attitudes about poetry. At the end of the poem, Koch talks about the elements of "clarity and excitement" in poetry and calls them a "great expanse of green." He greets them with an affectionate hello as if they're beloved grandchildren he's seeing after a long separation. Green is a perfect color for poetry, with its connotation of life and freshness and vitality. This poem made me smile the first time I read it. It made me feel as if I had just had cataract surgery and could see words on the page so much more clearly now.

So it's around five o'clock when I walk out of the bookstore, where I've bought my new book by Kenneth Koch, and I walk around to the back, where I like to park, and I look at the springtime green of the empty field behind the parking lot and immediately think of that phrase from "Fresh Air." Who knows, I may have even said it aloud—"you great expanse of green"—but nobody is nearby to hear me, so it's okay. I feel the weight of *Making Your Own Days* in the bookstore bag I'm carrying, and I imagine I hear it rustling around trying to get out. I'm eager to get home and let it loose.

I fill my lungs with the mild April air and lift my head to the sky and give thanks that I haven't drowned in my sorrow, not yet. I have been upheld by my new friend Margaret, by my poetry, by my teaching, but most of all by the right hand of God. I have felt a strength that is not my own. Not that I have come out on the other side yet. Not at all. The vale of sorrow is long and dark, I'm learning. But every time I've stumbled, I've felt a hand lifting and steadying me, and I get up and go a little further along the trail.

As I open the car door on this green spring day, I glance toward the parking lot of Luigi's Little Italy Restaurant next to the bookstore, and this is when I see Ken. He doesn't see me because his attention is directed elsewhere. I can't see the person in the car clearly, but I can see enough to tell it's a woman. She has long hair, which confirms in my mind that she's young. In the days when Ken used to express preferences about the way I dressed and wore my hair, he once said that no woman over thirty-five should have long hair. I don't know what was so significant about thirty-five, but this was some rule he had come up with. It could have been something he heard his mother say. Anyway, I always remembered it, although by the time I turned thirty-five, he had pretty much quit noticing if I had hair, much less how I wore it.

The sight of him talking like that to another woman cuts deeply. I see immediately how good he looks. Things like this are sometimes easier to see from a distance. He holds himself with an easy grace, and his hands move expressively. If I didn't already know him, I might look at him standing like that and think, "That man must be an artist."

He's talking earnestly, it appears, and I can't help remembering how seldom he has talked earnestly to me in recent years. We often sat on opposite sides of the kitchen table eating cereal in the morning and never said a word to each other. Not that we were mad at each other, but we just didn't have anything much to say anymore. When we went out for our last anniversary back in January, I looked at Ken across the candle and bud vase in the center of the table and almost felt embarrassed that I couldn't think of anything to generate a conversation, at least not a civil one. Travis had gone back to college for his second semester a couple of days earlier, and my heart felt like an empty sack.

But here's my husband now in a parking lot talking animatedly and at length to another woman. Apparently he has plenty to say. I can't tell you what this does to me.

In the newspapers I receive, which continue to report tragedies other than my own, I recently read about a horrible collision on I-85, another of the many that happen all too frequently on the freeway that passes Greenville. In this one, an eighteen-wheeler came over a slight rise and barreled toward a line of cars that had come to a complete standstill because of road construction.

Who knows what the truck driver was doing. Maybe he was gazing toward the horizon, thinking about making it home in time for his daughter's tap dance recital or his son's baseball game, or maybe he was adjusting his mirrors or trying to find a better radio station. He didn't even notice the cars in time to brake. He hit them going seventy miles per hour, and four of them burst instantly into flames and were burned beyond recognition, along with the people in them.

One eyewitness told about how nobody had time to react. This man was sitting at the end of the right-hand lane of traffic and through his rearview mirror saw the truck bearing down on the cars in the left lane. He looked over at the car next to his in the other lane and started yelling and honking to get the driver's attention, but the woman had her windows up and the visor flipped down and was checking her makeup. She must have had the radio turned up pretty loud, because he said she appeared to be bobbing up and down in time with music. Then the truck hit, and she was dead before she knew what happened.

This man who witnessed it all, whose voice was still shaking three hours later when he talked about it for a TV camera, was able to escape the explosion and fire by driving his car off the shoulder of the freeway just seconds before the collision and then tearing off down the grassy stretch next to the line of other cars. I can imagine some of those other drivers saying, "What does that idiot think he's *doing?*" right before they heard the crash behind them.

I don't mean for a moment to trivialize what happened to those people who were killed, and I've never been slammed into by an eighteen-wheeler going seventy, but when I saw Ken standing by that car talking with a woman that day, I felt something like a sudden, fiery impact inside. Among the five people who died in that I–85 accident were a fifteen-year-old boy and his mother on their way to an exhibition soccer game in Charlotte. When I read that, I was glad they were in the car together. What mother would want to live if her son died and she didn't?

End of digression. So guess what happens to the ball I'm serving as this picture of Ken talking to a woman fills up the screen and obliterates the one of me delivering a perfect ace? Well, interestingly—and this is contrary to what Coach Kendall said would happen if you allow yourself to be distracted—that ball zips over the net, kisses the sideline, and bounces up with so much spin that Barb only tips it with the top of her racket, and it flies off wildly into the adjacent court. To think it's taken all these years to discover the fallacy of my coach's instruction about serving. The key to a good serve is as simple as this: Think of something that makes you really mad, then pack all your anger and frustration into the tennis ball and blast it as hard as you can.

Barb approaches the net, smiling, and says, "Boy, you pulled a new trick out of your bag with that one." She extends her hand and says, "Good match, Elizabeth. I'm exhausted."

I've talked to Barb several times since our first meeting by my mailbox. Her friend and neighbor Della Boyd Biddle has just recently left to move back to Mississippi, so she now takes her walks alone or sometimes pushes a stroller with her toddler in it. Once she was with an attractive red-haired woman I recognized as Hardy Biddle's mother, Catherine. I've seen Catherine Biddle at church a couple of times since that first Sunday I attended back in February, and I was introduced to her once.

So the tennis match was over. After Barb and I said good-bye and left the court, I drove home. As I got out of my car, Theresa Dillman beckoned to me from her front yard across the street. The mustard-colored van was there, and her artist boyfriend was on his knees up by the front steps, planting something.

Have I mentioned yet that an amplifier was mounted on top of the mustard-colored van? Instead of a regular horn-honking sound, other sounds emanated from the van every time it pulled up into Theresa's driveway. Once I distinctly heard the sound of a mooing cow and another time a Woody Woodpecker laugh. Another time it was a saxophone rendition of "Stardust," and once it was Peter, Paul, and Mary singing "Blowing in the Wind," with the sound of hurricane-force winds in the background. I have no idea how her boyfriend rigged it up, but it was always something different. If the guy had been a teenager, you could understand it, but you have to wonder when a grown man does things like that.

Well, anyway, here was Theresa waving her hands at me from her front yard, calling out, "Elizabeth! Can you spare just a minute? I want to show you something!" I didn't want to talk to anybody right then. I wanted to go inside and take a long cool shower, then fix myself a sandwich and read some in the book I had bought the night before.

In addition, I wanted to go back and read something I had run across in the Bible a couple of nights earlier. It had come to me just a few minutes earlier on the way home from the tennis courts, when I saw a geyser of water gushing from a fire hydrant on Pembroke Street. A truck from the Upper Carolina Water System was just pulling up nearby, and a man in an orange vest was getting out.

"He brought me through the waters"—that was what came to me as I drove slowly through the flood, and I remembered that the words were in the book of Ezekiel. I had found them before bed one night and had meant to reread the whole chapter later but had forgotten until now. Everywhere I turn in the Bible I keep finding something I want to go back to and read again. In this Ezekiel passage, there was something about a "river that could not be passed over" and waters that "shall be healed," and I wanted to see how it all tied together.

I was discovering that the Bible was full of wonderful poetry. Very lyrical, elegant lines, not rhyming, of course, but poetry nevertheless. In the introductory pages of my Bible, I had found a grouping of the books of the Bible under the heading "A Panoramic View of the Bible," and one of them, in all capital letters, was POETRY. Job, Psalms, Proverbs, Ecclesiastes, Song of Solomon, Lamentations. I had read them all by this time, many passages aloud, although I had to take Song of Solomon in small increments. A spurned wife finds that book hard to read, let me tell you.

But back to Theresa Dillman calling me from across the street. She looked so friendly and full of hope that I couldn't turn her down. My long years of showing good manners kicked into action. A few minutes wouldn't matter, I told myself. My shower and lunch could wait. My new book wasn't going anywhere. So I set my tennis bag down beside my car and walked across the street. Maybe if I did this right, it wouldn't take long.

"Another tennis match, huh?" Theresa asked as I approached.

"Yes, a long one," I said. I pushed my hair back off my forehead and fanned my face with one hand. "I'm ready to drop." I was laying the groundwork for a quick escape.

"I wanted to tell you I'm getting married next month," Theresa said. She was wearing gardening gloves, though she didn't appear to have any intention of getting them dirty. "Well, I mean, *we're* getting married." She looked down at her boyfriend proudly.

Something flipped over inside me. I remembered looking at Ken that way many years ago. Isn't it odd how when you're about to lose something, you suddenly deem it precious and start remembering all the good things about it? And all around you, I was learning, are reminders of what you used to have but don't have anymore.

Theresa was shaking her head. "All these months you've lived right across the street from me, and I don't think you've ever met Macon, have you?" she said. "I've kept meaning to bring him over to introduce him, but . . . oh well, anyway, this is Macon Mahoney. Macon, this is Elizabeth from across the street. Be nice. She's going to be your neighbor."

Macon stood up, then turned up his right palm and examined it. "Unclean," he said sadly. Then clinching it into a fist, he closed his eyes and said, "But let us imagine our spirits shaking hands." Before I could think of anything to reply, he opened his eyes again and smiled brightly at me. "There now," he said, "my spirit is pleased to make the acquaintance of your spirit, Elizabeth."

"Macon, you are so weird," Theresa said, but anyone could tell by the way she said it that she didn't mind his weirdness one bit.

Standing this close to Macon Mahoney, I saw that he had a soft, smooth-shaven face like a young boy's and blue eyes behind rimless glasses. If it hadn't been for a weathered look around the eyes, he could have passed for eighteen. He was wearing jeans, dirty at the knees from kneeling on the ground, and a plain white T-shirt with paint smears all across the front.

He dropped to his knees again. "What Theresa says is true," he said, glancing back up at me. "The conjugal knot shall be tied betimes." He began digging into the earth with great fervor. "I have grown weary of bohemian bachelordom, so rather than hire a housekeeper and cook, I thought I'd marry one. It will not only be financially advantageous, but the companionship may prove over time to be suitable." From his tone of voice, you'd never have known whether he was teasing.

Theresa seemed to know, however. "Don't be so sure about that companionship part," she said as she pretended to kick him, in fact did kick him just enough to leave a little splotch of mud on the seat of his jeans. She yanked off one of her gardening gloves and whapped him on the head with it several times. "And the prenuptial contract I've just decided to see a lawyer about says *you'll* be doing most of the cooking," she added. "My specialty is sandwiches," she said to me.

"Ah yes, the sandwich," Macon said, still digging. "'A most delicious, nourishing, and wholesome food, whether stewed, roasted, baked, or boiled.'"

To say that my senses were stunned by Macon Mahoney would be putting it mildly. Just another example proving once again that you might miss something extraordinary if you don't say yes.

"We're going to live here in my house," Theresa told me.

"Yes, she demands that I forfeit my palace for hers," Macon said.

"His palace is an apartment above a mattress store," she said. "It's all one big room—bedroom, kitchen, living room, studio, bathroom. The toilet and bathtub sit over in a corner without a door or anything."

"Concise living, I call it," Macon said.

"Crude, I call it," Theresa said.

She held out her left hand to show me her engagement ring—a beautiful, enormous emerald-cut diamond flanked by rubies. If this guy bought this ring with cash, I thought, he must be a legitimate artist. Maybe he had more money than he knew what to do with. Or maybe he bought the ring with some inheritance money, or maybe it was his grandmother's. And right on the heels of this thought, I wondered what in the world the grandmother of a man like Macon Mahoney would be like.

This is what happens when you meet new people, especially interesting new people. You start wondering about their family backgrounds, their personal problems, and so forth. Sometimes I might be standing behind a woman in a check-out line, and she piques my curiosity for some reason. Maybe it's a hat she's wearing or the wisps of hair at the base of her neck or a long leopard-print scarf draped around her neck. But whatever it is, it's all I can do to keep from grabbing her, swinging her around, and saying, "Tell me about yourself! What's your name? Where do you live? Do you have children? What are your hobbies? Do you read poetry?" I've never done it yet, thank goodness, but I constantly fight the urge.

But back to Macon. I still hadn't seen any of his work, but Theresa had told me one day from the driveway that he had landed a commission from three banks in Spartanburg and a children's hospital in Greenville for some paintings and wall murals. One day I had seen him carrying what looked like a huge framed picture from his van up to Theresa's front door. The picture was the size of a dining room table with all the leaves in. He was having trouble carrying it and had to set it down a couple of times to adjust his hold. Finally Theresa came out and helped him. I saw it only from the back, however, so I had no idea what kind of art he did. He didn't carry it back out, so I assumed it was still in her house somewhere.

"I hear you're an artist," I said to him now. I tried to imagine what kind of pictures a man like this would paint. Nothing predictable and traditional I was sure, maybe nothing even sane.

" 'Art is a jealous mistress,' " he said to the dirt. He was digging a second hole now and piling up the dirt neatly beside it. Uprooted weeds were in a bucket beside him, and four potted hydrangeas sat on the sidewalk, ready for planting. He raised his trowel, waved it briefly, and proclaimed oratorically, " 'It's clever, but is it art?' "

Theresa sighed and shrugged at me. "I'm sorry, Elizabeth. He's being bad. He always talks in circles, but some days it's worse than others."

" 'Weave a circle round him thrice!' " he declared.

"Landscapers are so expensive, though," Theresa continued. "If he wasn't so good with dirt, I wouldn't even consider marrying him."

Macon stabbed the ground with his trowel. " 'Half the soul is dirt!' " he said.

"And I've got some bills to pay off," Theresa went on. "You can put up with a lot from somebody who's got a little bit of extra money put away."

" 'Hath a dog money?' " Macon said. He set one of the hydrangeas into the hole he had just dug and began to tamp loose dirt around the base with his hands. The backs of his hands were sinewy, I noticed, and his fingers were incredibly long and slender.

"Catch him on the right day," Theresa said to me, "and you can have an almost normal conversation with him. We'll try again some other time, okay?"

I smiled at her, then looked down at Macon. "Life is so full of surprises, isn't it?" I said. I was referring to Macon, of course. From the other side of the street he looked so average coming and going. Discounting his van, which I'll admit should have prepared me, he could have been any normal thirtyish man, but here he was—like *this*, digging in the dirt and spouting non sequiturs. I was sure by now that whatever Macon painted, he must use colors no one else had ever dreamed of.

He sat back on his heels and looked up at me. "Surprise mingled with profound respect, I trust?" he said.

I smiled at him. "More like surprise mingled with bewilderment," I said to him.

"Don't worry," Theresa said. "Nobody ever knows what he's talking about."

"I think I might have caught a snatch of Emerson," I said, "and of course a line of Shakespeare, but I'm afraid the rest of it went right over my head."

Macon picked up his trowel again and pointed it at me. He nodded his head slowly and made a purring noise deep in his throat. "You shall be rewarded," he said at length. "You shall be rewarded, and great shall be your reward." He glanced at Theresa. "Why didn't you tell me your neighbor was Keen? Keen and Regal."

I laughed. "Oh, yes, I'm very regal as I stand here dripping with sweat."

"As a Regal person, I know you already know this," Macon said, "but I'll say it anyway. Regal is an attitude. Many, many degrees higher than Seren-dipitous, where happiness begins, but even higher than the more rarefied attitudes of Aligned and Attuned." He pointed his trowel at me again, then repeated, "Yes, you shall be rewarded. You shall indeed."

"Well, that's nice," I said. "I could use a reward or two about now. Do I get to pick?"

He gave a little dismissive snort. "And what kind of a world would it be if it worked that way?" he said. "Rewards can't be ordered from a catalog." He closed one eye and studied me for a moment. "But if you could, what would a Keen and Regal person like yourself pick for her reward?"

The answer came to me quickly. "I'd like to see some of your art," I said.

"Art is edible, you know," he said.

I nodded. "Yes, I know. I often have ink running out my mouth." I was thinking, of course, of that poem by Mark Strand called "Eating Poetry," where the poetry-loving narrator becomes a mad dog romping in the library.

"Get the muzzle," he said to Theresa as he stood up. "She's a dangerous one." He brushed off his hands and knees, then led the way up Theresa's front steps.

So here it is again. Being polite has opened up another door. Not only do I get to meet this artist—whom my mother would call a dingbat—but now I get to see his art. If I had said what I *felt* like saying when Theresa called to me from across the street, I never would have been invited inside her house that day to see three of Macon Mahoney's paintings.

And how do I describe his art? I feel like I need a whole new medium of communication instead of plain old words. The three pieces were wildly different from each other, yet the sharply defined detail in each suggested a single artist. Not to mention the sense of humor in each one.

Try to see it all with me. I follow Macon up the steps. I apologize for being sweaty and promise not to touch anything, but they pass it off, of course, and we step into Theresa's house to see Macon's art. I untie my ten-nis shoes and take them off by the door.

The first painting is directly in front of me as I step across the threshold. There's a little arched doorway leading from the entryway into the hallway, and the picture is hanging in the hallway, framed by that arch. It looks like something alive, and I imagine sounds coming from it. It might even be moving. I stand there for a few moments, then start walking toward it.

It's an oil painting about three feet square. In the foreground are clothes-lines crisscrossing, and everything here is at very close range. The wooden clothespins are a good three or four inches long, and you can see every crease in every piece of fabric hanging on the lines. They're not definable clothes as such, but broad stretches of cloth like sheets or towels. And the colors take your breath away—a blue lavender the color of a pulsing vein, a yellow with the sweet timbre of a songbird, and a soft green you could eat like chilled sherbet.

Beyond the clothesline is the whole wide world. Children are playing in the streets, a house is under construction, a dog is chasing a truck, normal things like that. Then you start noticing the amusing little twists like the mailman sitting on a tree stump eating a banana, the cement mixer with cement dribbling out the back onto the hood of the car behind it at the stoplight, a boy on a bicycle with a parrot on his head, the street sign that says Street Sign on it instead of the name of a street, and other things like that. I think of the Richard Scarry books Travis loved as a kid.

I could go back and spend an entire week looking at that painting. Above it all is the sky, a rich, true unbroken blue. He didn't do anything goofy with the sky, just made you want to drench yourself in it.

The next piece must be the really big one I saw them carrying inside that day. The frame, believe it or not, is made out of long bamboo poles lashed together at the corners with something like jute or sisal. It's a watercolor painting of three Chinese pagodas in the middle of a lake with mountains in the background. The colors below the sky are mostly muted blues and greens and tans, though the railings around each tier of the pagodas are bright red. But the sky—well, the sky paralyzes you for just a minute. It's a sunset sky with streaks of coral and purple and gold swimming across it like exotic fish.

And here's the humorous part, the Macon Mahoney touch. At the bottom and along one side of the picture, Macon has printed captions. He means the painting to represent a giant postcard, you see. In fact, he tells me that the painting was inspired by an actual postcard he received from a friend who visited Taiwan. The caption along the side is made up of Chinese characters, which look quite authentic to me, lined up in a long column top to bottom. The caption at the bottom is in English, but Macon tells me it's a translation from Chinese into English. It was the exact one printed on the back of his friend's postcard, apparently composed by someone who studied English in school but hadn't learned the nuances of the language. Here is what it says: "It is the nationwide known olden structures in the setting sun scenery of Tsuo-Ying."

"Don't you love the cadence of that?" Macon says after I read it aloud. "I've got a dozen postcards this guy sent me, and the captions are the best part. The pictures are all alike—way too much turquoise and so perfect they're boring—but the captions, now they take off and fly." And who could disagree with that? Today, months later, that caption dances in my head: *"It is the nationwide known olden structures in the setting sun scenery of Tsuo-Ying."* I adore it.

The third picture was a pen-and-ink drawing on what appeared to be a brown grocery sack. It was a woman sitting next to a boy who was playing a violin. Several kittens were rolling around at their feet. On a small table beside the woman sat a mug and a clock, along with a single sunflower in a vase and a pair of glasses. It was all very spare, no superfluous lines but just enough to let you know what each object was.

Macon had named it *A Study in Earl Grey*, and he explained that it was a sketch of his mother teaching a violin lesson. His mother was fond of Earl Grey tea and always had a cup of it nearby as she taught. So Macon got the idea of brewing up a pot of strong Earl Grey tea and soaking some paper in it. After several hours he took the paper out, wadded it in a ball, and spread it out flat to dry. Later he drew the picture on it with pen and ink.

"I offered it to my mother," he said, "but she didn't like the paper—said it needed ironing. She was also afraid it would attract ants because of the tea."

Theresa laughed. "The real reason she didn't want it was she thought he made her look too fat," she said. "She went on a diet the day after he showed it to her."

"I call her Mother Superior Worrier," Macon said. I laughed. I could imagine my mother and Macon's forming a close friendship.

By the time we came outside again, I felt as if I had traveled to a fantastical country and back. "Thanks," I said, extending my hand to Macon. "My reward was indeed great."

"See? I'm a prophet," he said.

"I like your name, too, by the way," I told him. "Macon Mahoney has rhythm and style."

"I was named after my mother's hometown," he said. "She was born in Macon, Georgia. I'm just glad she wasn't born in Oglethorpe or Valdosta."

I looked at Theresa. "Keep him," I said.

She nodded. "I plan to."

"Congratulations on your engagement," I said to them as I started down the front steps.

" 'O sweeter than the marriage feast!' " cried Macon from the front door.

I knew where that one came from. "Coleridge," I said, turning around. " 'The Rime of the Ancient Mariner.' "

Macon nodded solemnly. "I memorized the whole thing when I was seventeen," he said. "Just to have something to do one summer when I had a stupid job. Lifeguarding."

"And what would be sweeter than the marriage feast?" I said to him.

He was standing behind Theresa, and he put his arms around her neck, then with utter seriousness said, "The marriage feast is only the beginning. Much sweeter are all the days that follow."

I took a couple of slow breaths. "I don't go to many weddings," I said to both of them, which was true even before Ken had left home. Going to a wedding right now would be painful, I was sure, in ways I couldn't even imagine. "But I'll come to yours," I said, "if I'm invited, that is."

"You will be," Theresa said.

I saw Ken's car the same moment Theresa did. "Oh, there's your husband," she said.

I watched Ken pull into the driveway. For several weeks now, he had been showing up at odd times, uninvited and never for very long. Usually it was to pick up something he needed. He had mowed the lawn a couple of times on Saturdays. Sometimes he came while I was gone, and later I saw signs that he had been there. Whenever he came while I was home, we rarely said much to each other. Once he had climbed up on the roof and cleaned dead leaves out of the gutters, then left without a word.

I wondered what he wanted this time. Maybe he had come for the rest of his handkerchiefs and socks. That was about the only thing still left in his chest of drawers.

Under the Gypsy Moon

11

Of course, my mother knows now. If you have a mother like mine, you can't keep things from her very easily. It didn't take her long to pry it out of me. She could tell something was wrong, she said, that first time she talked to me on the phone back in February after it happened. She called me three more times during the following week, and the third time, after she had asked how things were going and I had again deflected the question with something vague, she thought of a plan. "Well, then, let me speak to Ken for a minute before I hang up," she said. "I have to tell him something."

I hesitated. "He's not here right now."

"I didn't think so," she said. "He hasn't been there for a while, has he?" We were both silent for several seconds before she said, "Do you want to tell me about it, Elizabeth?"

I cried some, of course, but told her the truth. She wasn't surprised. That's another advantage of being a pessimist. Nothing bad that happens surprises you because you're always expecting awful things anyway. Though she and Ken had always gotten along well enough, the fact was that she had tried to discourage me from marrying him the first time she met him. "I'm worried that he's not a long-haul kind of husband" was what she had said. She went on to say that men who were too passionate about something—it could be anything from gardening to billiards to politics—never truly "bonded" with their wives. I remember that was the exact word she used. It wasn't as popular a word back then as it is now.

This other part of a man's life, she warned, was too powerful, too seductive. It was like a demanding mistress. It drove a wedge between him and his family, she said. She had seen it happen time and time again. All these grim prognostications were uttered on a Saturday night during my junior year, when my parents drove to Piper College expressly to meet Ken. We spent two hours at a restaurant together after a concert he played in. My mother told me afterward, before she and Daddy let me off at my dorm, that she was afraid Ken's love of music bordered on lust. I had laughed at her.

My father had no such fears. Although he had hoped his daughters might marry into money since his own means were so modest, he thought Ken was "bright and likable." Those were his words. My father was cheerfully adaptable. Maybe he had always been that way, or maybe living with my mother had forced him to make constant adjustments. Anyway, he knew that most music majors ended up teaching in public schools and that the music programs were the first to get cut in a budget crunch, but he also liked certain types of music and knew that some musicians made it big. I think he was already beginning to imagine how it would sound to tell his friends that his son-in-law conducted the New York Philharmonic or led the band on *The Tonight Show*. One thing Daddy wasn't afraid to do was dream.

I've often wondered how different my adult life would have been if my father had lived longer. He could have taken Travis fishing and hunting, maybe could have drawn him out of himself more. Travis could have said to his classmates at school, "My granddaddy took me hunting over the weekend, and we got a six-point buck and saw a skunk den." The other boys would have wanted to know all about it, and Travis would have told a colorful story. They would have crowded around him at the lunch table, jockeying to get the seat closest to him. "And then what happened?" they'd want to know.

But my father died, as my mother knew he would, and now years later Ken had left home, which also didn't surprise her one bit. So now she calls me every few days in case I want to confide anything else. There's not much else to tell her, though. I've already told her that Ken has an apartment at a place called Home Away from Home, advertised as an "extended-stay" motel. She wants to know all about the place, but I don't have any details to give her except that it's over between Greenville and Spartanburg, just off the interstate and far enough away from Berea and from Harwood College, where Ken teaches, that nobody would even have to know he was staying there.

Our neighbors probably haven't noticed anything since he was always gone so much of the time anyway. But who knows, maybe they have. At least no one has let on, and I'm not about to volunteer any information. I've been a little surprised, frankly, that it's been so easy to keep it a secret, but everybody is busy, and Ken still drops by enough to be seen regularly. Like I said, he often comes while I'm away. He loves this house—no doubt this is the hardest part of the separation for him. He still pays the bills for the mortgage, power, water, things like that. I leave them on the kitchen table when they come, and he goes through them when he stops by.

His continued interest in the house sometimes makes me hopeful for just the briefest moment, thinking it might be an indication that things will someday return to the way they used to be, but then I remember what he's done to me, and I know nothing will ever be the way it used to be. The way it used to be wasn't so great anyway except for the fact that it was familiar and secure.

Why would he keep coming home, though, if he didn't want to live here again? Then it hits me. Maybe he's hoping to live here again someday *without me*. He's just keeping an eye on his future home until things work out and he can get me shuffled off somewhere else. I'll just bet that's what he's thinking.

We haven't talked much since the night back in February when he brought a pizza with him. And now I realize that I never got around to mentioning that I found out three things that night. Number one, he loves this other person. What he said was "I don't know" when I asked him if he loved her, but I knew what he really meant was "I don't want to tell you." I suppose she's the same one who was sitting in the blue Mazda in the parking lot at Luigi's Little Italy, although I don't know exactly who she is. It's not that I don't care. I wonder about her day in and day out. I wonder if she's his first girlfriend on the side. I try to look back at the past several years for clues, but my mind locks down.

My mother keeps asking me about all this also. Who is she? Where did he meet her? How long has it been going on? And my answer is always the same one Ken and Travis have always given for everything: I don't know, I don't know, I don't know. In my case it's true, however. The truth is, I'm scared to find out too much. It hurts enough as it is. In a way I want to know every detail of how it all developed, but in another way I don't want to know a thing. It's safer sometimes to be ignorant.

I wonder if everybody at the college where Ken teaches knows all about it. I can't help wondering how many people here in Berea knew about it as I was blindly going my way all that time, confident of my membership in the Aware sector, when all along I couldn't see what should have been as plain as the nose on my face. Maybe I just *think* my neighbors don't know what's going on. Maybe people are looking at me everywhere I go, pitying me for being the rejected wife. "There goes poor Elizabeth Landis. You heard about her husband and . . ." But I can't even fill in a name for her.

I haven't asked Ken what her name is even though I think about it almost constantly. At times I wonder if it's something exotic like Veronica or Desiree or Sophia, although I can't for the life of me imagine Ken making an advance on someone like that. But then, I'm not sure what kind of name I can imagine him making an advance on. Becky, Sally, Linda, Joanne, Sheryl—none of those seem right either. To be honest, it's hard to picture him touching another woman when he's never even liked to shake people's hands.

Maybe Esmerelda or Betty Sue or whatever her name is goes after the hard-to-get type. Maybe she chased him until he gave in. Maybe he tried and tried to resist, but she kept laying traps for him. I keep reading in the Bible where God tells me to love my neighbor as myself, do good to them that despitefully use me, be kindly affectioned to all men, and all the rest, but I can't dredge up even the slightest bit of goodwill toward this woman. I try not to hate her, but I really don't try very hard. And my feelings toward Ken are too complex to label. I'm learning that the theory and practice of Christianity are sometimes hard to reconcile, which I hadn't intended to include in the list of three things I learned that night in February. But believe me, it is something I'm learning.

The second thing I learned the night Ken came over back in February was that he wasn't ready yet to talk about divorce, or at least that's what he said. For sure he must have known I wasn't ready to. He must have been able to tell by the high brittle edge to my voice and the way I couldn't keep my hands from shaking even after he adjusted the thermostat. "I'm not ready to talk about divorce" was exactly what he said, but I know he was watching me out of the corner of his eye. He was being thoughtful as he diced my heart into little pieces.

I imagine him even now waiting for some sign, even the smallest little hint, that I'm capable of hearing the word *divorce* without going over the brink. He'll be leaving the house after one of his stopovers, and he'll look at me for just the briefest second as if saying to himself, "Is she ready yet?" Sometimes he'll even open his mouth to say something, then close it again and walk out the door.

The third thing I learned that night was that besides me and this other person, there was a third woman involved in all of this. It was his mother. In the back of my mind I'm sure I already knew this. Hadn't Ken's mother been involved in everything in our lives from the word go? Such a quiet deferential soul, you never would have guessed she could be such a disruptive factor, that she could have managed to position herself right in between us time and time again. We had never argued about her outright, but she had always been there. I thought of her as a huge Casperlike presence haunting our house, but not nearly as friendly as the one in the cartoon.

We didn't talk about her the night Ken came over—not directly. Oh, we skated around things that night! We were like hockey players doing agility drills. Those orange cones were the important topics we needed to discuss, and we didn't touch a single one as we wove in and out. Ken came over to talk that night, but what we did was pass riddles back and forth. They zipped between us like pucks on ice, but never once did we sink one into the net.

One thing he said before he left, though, made it clear to me that his mother was still in the middle of things even though she had been dead for over five years now. And he didn't even finish what he said but let it trail off into nowhere. "For the last five years I've felt so . . ." he said. "If only Mom hadn't . . ." That was all he said before he fished his keys out of his pocket and walked out the door. Wives can usually complete their husbands' sentences, though, and I knew exactly what words went in the blanks. "For the last five years I've felt so *guilty*," and "If only Mom hadn't *died*."

But she had. She died once a little over five years ago, and she had continued to die every day since then. For five years the two of us had worn our guilt over her death strapped to our foreheads like a phylactery, inside which the words of the fifth commandment were inscribed, the commandment we had violated together. "Honor thy father and thy mother." Ken's mother weighed barely a hundred pounds when she died, but let me tell you, she was heavy. The term *dead weight* had special meaning for Ken and me.

Remember that poem every schoolchild used to read, the one about the blind men and the elephant over in India? They're trying hard to figure out what the elephant is, but each one of them latches on to some isolated part, like a tusk or the trunk, and ends up with a distorted idea about elephants. They don't ever put all the parts together into a whole. Well, right now I'm one of the blind men, and my marriage to Ken is the elephant I can't comprehend.

I can't see the whole thing, only random parts of it, and even though Ken is much more of a big-picture person than I am, I'd be willing to bet he can't either. I've taken some upper-level math and science courses in my academic past. In high school I was on the math team that made it to the state tournament. I've taken statistics and worked with formulas a foot long, but let me tell you, nothing is more complicated than marriage. Nothing. Normal rules like one plus one equals two are suspended in marriage.

I try to open it up and analyze it, and I realize I'm only an amateur poking around inside a cadaver. I don't know enough about anatomy to know what anything is. Or I'm sifting through the rubble after an explosion, looking for clues, but all I pull out are effects, not causes. She does get carried away with analogies, you're probably saying, and I freely admit it. But don't scorn analogies. I've heard that a great deal of Thomas Edison's remarkable inventiveness was due to his ability to reason through analogy, that the incandescent light bulb, the phonograph, and all the rest were conceived through this way of thinking.

They say that analogy is how poets get to the heart of life. Besides, thinking up analogies can be a good distraction. When you can't figure out a puzzle, such as your marriage, you at least feel like you're doing something halfway constructive if you come up with an analogy or two. So on it goes. I'm an apprentice in a machinist's workshop with a million metal parts laid out in front of me, but I can't tell what connects with what. When put together, it might turn out to be anything from a printing press to a cotton baler, but

I don't have a clue at this point. Oh, I could go on all day. I'm a translator, and I'm hearing words, but I don't recognize the language.

This one reminds me of something. The art of translation has always fascinated me. I mean to find out someday how Ezra Pound went about translating "The River-Merchant's Wife." Did he know the language, or did he hire a Chinese translator to help him? Maybe he got a Chinese dictionary, figured out the gist of the original, then made up his own poem.

Give the same piece of writing to ten different translators, and you'll get ten different versions. I have in a book of mine several translations of Federico Garcia Lorca's "Romance Sonambulo," and the variety of the translators' word choices, syntax, and line layout is fascinating. Someone named Rolfe Humphries wrote the one I like best, that seems the most poetic. In it he speaks of things "under the gypsy moon," which is the only phrase I can recall exactly. As I remember, a woman in the poem is outdoors at night being watched by something, but she can't see what it is. I know exactly how that woman feels, believe me. I know what it's like to be confused in the dark.

Well, I've digressed again. I hope my grandchildren, in the unlikely event that I ever have any and that they ever read this, won't lose their patience and use these pages for kindling. Maybe one of my grandchildren or a niece or nephew will love poetry as I do. Maybe they'll find these tedious poetry parts more interesting than the dissection of my marriage. Maybe they'll go back and reread these things about poetry, then skim over all the other stuff about Ken and me.

What got me started on all this was that last analogy. I'm a translator, but the words I'm hearing are from a language I haven't begun to master. Let's say I've got a whole book I'm supposed to translate, but I'm struggling with the first couple of sentences. I'm trying to decipher the past twenty-eight years of my marriage, and so far I haven't made it through the first few weeks.

So anyway, let me get the buggy back on the road, as my mother used to say. Or at least move it in that direction. But first, a picture has come to my mind, and this is relevant in a roundabout way, trust me. It has to do with a visit from one of my neighbors a few weeks back. One visit from Miriam Ramsey and I'll never look at my house exactly the same way again.

On the way home from Derby to Berea, you pass by a little shopping center called Utica Corner right where Highway 11 intersects Lake Utica Road. When I say *little* shopping center, I mean it—like about five businesses total when they're all in operation, which is not very often. It seems that one or the other is always going under, but then something else comes in to try to make a go of it. It's a funny little cluster of stores, a mishmash of backwater enterprises.

I can imagine tourists from big cities passing by here and almost having a wreck from laughing so hard. Currently, one little storefront has a sign that reads *Tatum's Taxes and Tuneups*. You go in through the front door for help with your taxes and drive around to the back for your tuneups. Another one is *Ballenger's Upholstery and Alterations*, and another is *Frank and Pattie*, a hot dog and burger place.

I can't remember what's on the far end now, maybe a barber shop or a bakery, but on the end closest to the flashing red light at the intersection is the newest business with the biggest sign, on which is printed in block letters the straightforward name *CASKETS*. It's not the kind of business you'd expect to see along the side of the road, although the owner must have thought the location would be good because of all the fatal accidents that seem to happen along Highway 11. Maybe it has made people a lot more careful. One of our local papers, the Filbert *Nutshell*, reported that the owner had been waiting almost a year to open his business until a bill passed concerning the licensed sale of funeral merchandise at places other than funeral homes.

Driving by, I always try to keep my eyes straight ahead, but I never can. At the last minute I always weaken and look over. The front of the store is a plate-glass window with several models of caskets displayed on a large multi-tiered velvet-draped platform. The casket in front, closest to the window, has a shiny pink satin interior. Very shiny and very pink.

These days I see the sheen of that casket with the pink satin not only every time I drive by Utica Corner but also every night when I take a bath. Here's how it works.

You see, my bathroom is pink, exactly the same shade as the satin lining of that casket. Whoever built our house must have either really liked pink or else found a closeout sale on pink floor tile, wall tile, soap and toothbrush holders, and—this is where it gets really extreme—all the standard bathroom furnishings such as sink, toilet, and bathtub. Except for the ceiling and the little bit of wall that's not tiled, it's a completely pink bathroom. "Terminal pinkness" was what Travis said when he first saw it before we moved in. Since Ken always shared the hall bathroom with Travis, the pink one was all mine.

Well, okay, so one night a few weeks back I stepped into my bathtub and eased myself down into the water. That was when the thought hit me over the head like a hammer. *This is exactly the same color as the inside of that casket.* The fact that the pink was also a *shiny* pink and that the bathtub was shaped like a casket didn't escape me either. Usually I slide down a little so I can lean back in the bathtub and relax for a few minutes, but that night I sat bolt upright and made quick work of bathing. But there's a reason my mind came up with the bathtub-casket link, you see, and it all had to do with a surprise visit earlier that night from a neighbor I'd never met.

This particular neighbor lives in the house behind ours. Remember the lights I saw through the trees in the backyard when I sat in the swing? Well, those were her lights. More than once I had wondered about that house through the trees, though not so much lately as before Ken left home.

So on this night back in March, several hours before I take my bath, I'm in the den with the television on when somebody knocks on the back door, the one just six feet behind where I'm sitting on the couch. Whoever it is knocks three times, and I hear the scrape of feet on the little stoop. I can't remember anybody ever knocking on that door before, and it throws me for a loop. It's one of those heart-stopping moments of sudden terror. It's when the bad guy lunges out and grabs Audrey Hepburn's ankle in *Wait Until Dark*. It's that kind of fear.

Thoughts race through my head. Somebody is in the backyard. It's dark out there. I'm all by myself. If I open the door, he'll grab me and stuff a gag in my mouth. If I don't go to the door, he'll know I'm afraid. If I get up and try to sneak to the telephone, he'll break the door down and come in after me. He knows I'm here. He can probably even see me through the little slits between the blinds. I look around for something heavy, something the equivalent of Aunt Ronalda's sculpture, but I see nothing I can use as a weapon. I never used to get afraid like this, and I'm ashamed that it hits me before I even think to pray.

Then I heard a voice, a woman's voice. "Hello! Is anybody home? It's your neighbor!" From what I could tell, it was a robust voice, a little on the raspy side, but not a young one. It didn't sound like Theresa Dillman or Eunice Yarnell or Sandy Ellis, all of whose voices I would recognize, and the only other neighbors I had talked to before were Juliana Sam, a native Jamaican who spoke halting English, and Tula Oglesby, who was ninety-two years old and never walked any farther than her mailbox. There were several other neighbors I sometimes waved to, who lived up and down the street on both sides, but why would any of them be coming to the back door?

I thought I saw the beam of a flashlight against the blinds. "Hello!" the voice came again. "Can anybody hear me? I need some help! I'm your neighbor!" She sounded a little panicky, but I had heard about tricks like this. Still, something told me this woman, whoever she was, wasn't trying to pull anything over on me. She sounded exactly like what she claimed to be—a neighbor who needed help.

I went to the door and pulled back the blinds a little. A woman stood on the other side leaning forward with her head cocked. She aimed the flashlight at her face and called out, "See, I'm just a harmless old lady come a-begging! I live back there." She waved the flashlight toward the trees to the house behind ours.

I unlocked the door and invited her in. She was a small woman with tightly curled gray hair and an abundance of nervous energy. She started talking as soon as she stepped in and barely stopped to inhale for the next few minutes. Her eyelids fluttered, and her hands gestured the whole time she talked. "I was so glad to see your light through the trees. I can't find anybody home along our own street tonight, and Spencer needs some cough syrup something terrible, and I was wondering if you maybe had some on hand. He was fine when he got here, but now I've put him to bed and he can't get to sleep for coughing and wheezing. He's got some allergies, like dust mites and strawberries and mold, so I'm wondering if it could be the cat."

Her voice was shaking a little, but she didn't stop. "It was a stray cat I took in a couple of weeks back, you see, but it's real clean and stays in the laundry room most of the time. Spencer did go in there and was playing with it a little before bed, though, and then he started up coughing and sneezing, and I just don't know what to do. His mother and daddy are away for the whole weekend, and I know they'd worry themselves sick if I called them up, so I'm trying to keep my head glued on straight and figure out what to do. Do you know anything about little boys and allergies? Do you have anything he could take?" She stopped suddenly and put a hand over her mouth briefly, then continued. "I'm sorry, I haven't even introduced myself, and here I am begging for help. I'm Miriam Ramsey."

She stuck out her hand, and I shook it quickly. Her hand was dry and cold, not at all what you'd expect from someone with such lively eyes in the throes of a crisis. "My boy used to have allergies, too," I said. "Wait right here and I'll go see what I have."

A couple of minutes later I was walking with her through our backyard to her house. Spencer was her only grandson, I learned, and this was the first time his parents had left him anywhere overnight. They were at a class re-union in Conyers, Georgia, where Miriam had raised all three of her sons. When she found out I was from Burma, she put her hand over her heart and said, "Well, did you ever? I thought I recognized a kinship as soon as you opened the door." She knew right where Burma, Georgia, was, she said—had driven through it numbers of times going to and from Conyers and even remembered the Bat-Bat and Putt-Putt my father owned, which were just off the old highway.

Spencer was six, with a tangle of black curly hair and eyes as dark as onyx. He didn't have a fever, only a bad case of watery eyes, tickly throat, sniffles, and sneezing—the classic symptoms of an allergic reaction. We got him out of bed and gave him Benadryl, then another bath since he had played with the cat after his first bath. Miriam changed his pajamas, and I helped her put clean sheets on the bed.

"My boy used to like something warm and sweet to drink after he took his medicine," I told Spencer when he got back into bed. "Would you like that? Something like hot cocoa maybe?" I glanced at Miriam, and she nod-ded.

"How old is your boy?" Spencer asked.

"Eighteen," I said. He looked disappointed.

"But I already brushed my teeth," he said soberly.

Can you believe it? A six-year-old hung up on dental hygiene. I rolled my eyes and smiled at his grandmother. I used to have to stand right beside Travis to get him to brush his teeth.

Miriam laughed. "No rule that says you can't brush them again, Spence," she said. "How about some cocoa for all three of us?" Spencer crawled out of bed cautiously and followed Miriam to the kitchen. "Who knows?" she said. "We might even have us a cookie or two with our cocoa."

She's sure dragging this out, you must be thinking. Okay, I'll wind it up. What I'm leading up to is what I found out from Miriam after we'd had our little snack and put Spencer back in bed. It turns out Miriam Ramsey was a very close friend of the woman who used to live in my house, the woman who loved gardening and planted all the flowers and laid out the pathways in the backyard. The one who, I learned from Miriam, had used some of her own money she had saved up to pay for the completely pink bathroom she had always dreamed of having.

Dorothy was her name. Dorothy Sherman, the wife of the temperamental man we'd bought the house from, the man who had let the house run down, then had moved out to California and finally shocked us all by accepting Ken's outrageously low offer. Here's what I learned about Dorothy Sherman, and here's why I step into my pink bathtub now and think somber thoughts about caskets.

Dorothy Sherman died in our house, right in the same bedroom where I sleep now. She was "eat up with cancer," as Miriam described it, and she was in agony for many days at the end. "I was with her for four straight days and nights," she told me. "She wanted to go to the hospital to die, but Ernie wouldn't let her. She had her suitcase packed, but he wouldn't take her. I tried to get her to let me take her, but she was afraid of him. Said he'd get back at me somehow if I did. I said I didn't care, but she wouldn't do it. It was money. That was the reason. His hospital coverage had a four thousand deductible, and he wanted to save that four thousand."

Miriam shook her head sadly. "Dory was my dearest friend, but I hated Ernie. That man didn't have an ounce of human compassion, not even for his own wife." She looked down into her empty cup and said, "I can still hear her screaming that last day. He stayed outdoors chopping wood all day so he wouldn't hear it. When I went out and told him she'd passed, I remember exactly what he did. He looked up at the sky, took his ax and sank it into a log, rubbed his hands together and said, 'Well, thank goodness, it's over.' I wanted to grab that ax and hew him in half."

So why does any of this matter? Well, it does. I look at my house through different eyes now. I always knew someone else used to live here, but it was always general, not specific, although I did know her name from all her third-class mail that still comes to our house: seed catalogs, brochures from charities, and the like. But now when I lie in bed at night, I'm intensely aware of the fact that Dorothy Sherman died within these four walls, that she screamed with pain, and that her husband stayed outside chopping wood while she passed from this life to the next.

When I step into the pink bathtub, I can't help thinking of her. She sat right here where I'm sitting, and she knew while she was sitting here that she had cancer and was going to die. This pretty pink bathroom had seen all the ravages of cancer and chemo. Dorothy Sherman dragged herself in here during those final days and begged for death to come and release her.

By the time I leave Miriam Ramsey's kitchen, Spencer has been asleep for over an hour, and I feel as if I've traveled down a long, long road. If the story of a death like this one in your own house doesn't give you a new way of thinking, I don't know what would.

If I had heard all this before I knew of God's gift of salvation, it would have spooked me. I would have wanted to get as far away as I could. But that night as I walked inside my house, I went to the kitchen and stood right in the middle, then looked all around. Dorothy Sherman stood over there by the sink and washed dishes, I thought. She walked across this very floor and set dishes on the table. She looked through the window at her flowers and her bird feeders and watched her children playing in the backyard. At some point she walked in through that door over there after a doctor's appointment at which she had heard the diagnosis of cancer for the first time. She lived in this house with a husband whose money meant more to him than her pain.

I had thought I was Aware before this, but what did I know? A huge part of being Aware, I knew that night back in March standing in my kitchen, is understanding in a very personal, direct, almost supercharged way all the different kinds of suffering there are. It doesn't erase your hurt, of course, but it makes you yield to it a little more. You feel a confederacy with other people, especially other women who have been through valleys.

And so, naturally, I've come back to Ken's mother. As much as I've tried to shove her away, I know I have to face her. Dorothy Sherman opened my mind to what I have to do. Could it be that God sent Miriam Ramsey for this purpose? That he synchronized that whole evening for my benefit? That he brought along a stray cat, planned the reunion for Spencer's parents for that weekend, timed the allergic reaction, arranged for all the other neighbors to be away from home, made the light from my den shine through the trees to Miriam?

Listen, I'll stand on the housetops and proclaim what I'm realizing more and more. There's no such thing as Randomness in the life of a Christian, but there is a great big something called Design. Miriam Ramsey comes along, then Dorothy Sherman, and finally I'm ready to take a good hard look at Ken's mother, another woman who suffered.

I see very clearly what I have to do. I must step into my mother-in-law's shoes, which were little ones—she wore a size five. I used to look at her feet and think of the days when Japanese women bound their feet—or had them bound. I doubt that they bound their own. My mother-in-law knew all about being wrapped, bound, and stunted, believe me.

And Buried It Deep, Deep

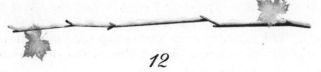

12

The urge to find analogies is what comes of reading so much poetry I guess. I'm thinking now about peeling an onion. Some of the most mundane actions are full of interesting sidelights if you take the time to notice them. I don't like raw onions, but there's nothing to substitute for the flavor of onion in cooking, so I've done my share of peeling onions.

When you peel an onion down to a new layer, there's this thin, slick little membrane that separates the layers. You don't even notice it if you're just slicing a whole onion, whacking it into disks to separate into rings and lay on top of a casserole or a piece of meat, but if you're going down methodically through the layers, you keep running into it. At first you can't even see it, but you can feel it as you run a finger across the surface. So you scratch at it a little and slide it off like a piece of moist tissue paper.

That little membrane is nothing really, but without it the onion wouldn't have all those layers. It would be just a solid texture all the way through, like an apple or carrot. So that little bit of nothing between the layers is actually what gives an onion its uniqueness. It separates all those layers and lets them nest inside each other like those little Russian dolls that keep opening up to reveal another smaller one inside.

So there you have it, another analogy. The things you can't see, usually don't even notice, are often the things that make something what it is. It's not a very good analogy, really, but it's the one that comes to me when I think of Ken's mother. I wasn't with her much during the twenty-some years I knew her, but she was always there like that little invisible membrane between onion layers, always a subtle divisive factor in our marriage. And every time I think about her now and the life she was dealt and my attitude toward her, my eyes start to burn the way they do when I chop an onion. One of my mother's favorite questions as we were growing up was "Aren't you ashamed of yourself?" I hear it now, and my answer is yes.

But I never finished the part about Ken arriving home as I was leaving Theresa Dillman's house that day. It's hard when you're moving through an upheaval in your life to remember everything in order. And when your mind jumps from one thing to another at the least provocation, the story line tends to have a lot of loose ends. But stick with me. This is a big house, and it takes a while to furnish all the rooms.

So quickly—to finish up the day I played tennis, then visited Theresa and met Macon Mahoney and then saw Ken pull into the driveway. It's April now, remember. It's not all that much to finish up, really. By the time I went into the house, Ken was back in his study noisily opening the drawers of his desk and shuffling through papers in folders.

I took off my socks and shoes in the kitchen, put my tennis bag away, then pulled off my headband and shook out my hair. I needed a haircut, but it seemed like so much trouble to make an appointment, then keep it. I knew a woman who attended the Church of the Open Door named Dottie Puckett, who had a beauty shop in her home out on Highway 11. I had passed her house hundreds of times over the years, then actually met her at church one Sunday when the song leader had everybody shake hands and greet one another. Maybe I would call Dottie Puckett sometime in the next week or two about an appointment. I heard she did good work in spite of the fact that she looked a little on the frumpy side herself and lived in a house the color of a swimming pool.

Anyway, as I walked down the hallway to the back bathroom, I passed Ken's study and glanced in. His back was to me, but I heard him click his tongue the way he does sometimes when he's frustrated. This is the only habit Ken has that has ever struck me as the slightest bit unmanly. When he conducts a band or orchestra, his hands are graceful and expressive like a ballet dancer's, but not at all effeminate. He'll hold his favorite rosewood baton lightly, with the pinkie of his right hand poised like a Victorian tea sipper but without the least hint of sissiness. If you want an aesthetic experience, watch a good male conductor. The combination of power and delicate precision is a kind of music all by itself.

Well, okay, so the top of Ken's desk is strewn with papers he's taken from various folders and spread around. Two drawers are pulled open. I stand there knowing I'm going to be peeved if he doesn't tidy everything up before he leaves and also knowing this is exactly what's going to come to pass. I can tell he's not in a tidying mood. At times he can be as meticulous and picky as an old maid, and at other times he can look right past a mess as if he doesn't see it. He sees me at the door now. "You haven't seen a piece of handwritten music for a trumpet solo, have you?" He sighs and runs both hands through his hair.

I laugh a little to show how ridiculous his question is. "I don't ever come in here," I say. How like a man to expect you to know where everything is that he hasn't had the foresight to keep up with.

"Well, I need it," he says. "It ought to be in this folder right here, but it's not." He picks up a folder and throws it back down. He's wearing a short-sleeved navy plaid shirt I gave him for a birthday years ago. Or it used to be navy. He's worn it so much that it's now the color of washed-out denim. Ken's standard practice is to wear a shirt once, then put it in the laundry hamper, so there's no telling how many times this one has been washed and dried. He prefers them ironed, of course, but for the past few years he was lucky to get them washed.

I wonder how he's managing his laundry now. Does he take it all to the cleaners? Or maybe *she* does it for him. The first week after he left home back in February, I found the laundry hamper full of his clothes. I slung them into the washing machine, dumped in some detergent without even measuring it, and slammed the lid. Then I let them sit for a whole day before I yanked them out and threw them into the dryer. Later I folded them roughly and haphazardly, then shoved them into the right drawers. After that he had come home and removed all his clothes a few at a time to take to his new living quarters.

Standing there watching him open another desk drawer, I'm hit with a sudden, blinding memory of the birthday when I gave him that shirt. That's the trouble with having an active memory. Your days are filled with these relived scenes from the past. You'll be going along fine when history once again turns into a current event, reenacted in living color and sound right in front of you. Memories are like live-in relatives. They impose themselves on you day in and day out, whether you want them there or not. They interrupt your routine, take up a lot of space, and don't know when to leave.

I'm coming back to my mother-in-law, but first there's this memory to deal with. Sometimes you can ignore a memory, just pass right by it. It's like when you're leafing through one of those women's magazines in a waiting room somewhere and looking for something substantial. You might catch a blur of something that has potential and think about going back to it. You know you could find it and lay the page open flat and read it carefully if you wanted to, or you could just keep going and hope you run across something else better.

As far as women's magazines go, I usually do keep going. I might stop and read something a little sensational such as how a woman discovers that her husband likes to wear women's clothes, but generally those magazines are nothing but fluff. Once, though, I did find a poem hidden in the back pages of one, and it made my scalp tingle when I read it. Some poet I'd never heard of before named Isabella Cubbage. The poem was about walking through a neighborhood at night and observing houses from the street, and how you never knew what went on inside them. There was an image I've never forgotten of a woman's silhouette behind a rose-pink shade, then the turning out of the light. That poem shimmered. I ran my fingers over it and was surprised that the words weren't raised on the page.

Without asking permission from the owner of the Hair Today Shop, where I was waiting at the time for Travis to get his hair cut, I cut the poem out with a pair of nail scissors I keep in my purse—the kind with tiny curved blades, which made cutting a straight line a little difficult. The edges turned out scalloped in a ragged way, as if I'd tried for a decorative effect and failed. I still carry that poem folded up in my billfold.

So there—you see, life is never predictable. A decent poem in a women's magazine—who would have ever thought it? Of course, the editors didn't have the sense to feature it in the front of the magazine on a page all by itself, but used it instead as a filler, the way they do recipes or jokes or ads for blinds and futons. But anyway, I found it as I flipped through, and Isabella Cubbage, whoever and wherever she is, has no idea that her poem is being carried around in somebody's purse in South Carolina.

But back to this memory of Ken's birthday, the one when I gave him the shirt he's wearing. I can't flip past it. I stop, open it up, and step into it. It must have been six or seven years ago now, in July. Ken's birthday comes five days after Travis's, so Travis must have been twelve or thirteen. Wait, I remember exactly—it was when he was thirteen. I remember because he had been wanting a new bicycle for almost a year, and we kept putting him off, telling him we'd get him a teenager's bicycle for his thirteenth birthday that summer.

I wanted Travis's thirteenth birthday to be a huge event. I wanted it to be a turning point in his social life. Remembering how I had begun to come out of my own timidity a little by the time I reached my teens, I had big plans for Travis in this area. He would gain confidence in himself over the summer, start opening up to other kids, and by the time school started in September he would be a different boy, ready to land in eighth grade right in the center of the action instead of at his usual outpost on the fringes.

Kids did this—developed new personalities when they hit adolescence. I remember a girl in Burma, Georgia, who suddenly turned into Miss America material during the summer between eighth and ninth grades. Oh, yes, puberty can reverse things in a hurry. One day the boys were treating her like she had cooties, and the next day they were falling all over themselves trying to impress her.

And you see the same kind of thing happen to boys, too. Major transformations. The class midget hits a growth spurt and turns into a hunk. And this kind of physical drama is often accompanied by a huge leap in the kid's self-confidence. Oh, I was full of hope that summer Travis turned thirteen. He hadn't turned into a hunk, but he had grown a full two inches since school was out.

We made up a guest list for a birthday party to top all birthday parties. Actually, I did the guest list pretty much by myself. Travis kept shrugging his shoulders when I'd suggest a name and saying things like "I don't even hardly *know* him, Mom," but I'd put the kid's name down anyway. I had been a room mother every single year during his elementary school years and had carted him around to Little League Baseball and county league soccer games since he was six, so I knew the names of the boys who always led the pack, who tossed off catchy comebacks that made everybody laugh, who had outgoing older brothers and sisters who taught them the ropes of being cool and well liked.

As far as social tutoring went, Jennifer had been a total failure as a big sister. She went her own way and largely ignored her little brother. Of course, when Travis was starting first grade, she was already a teenager, so you can't much blame her. But still, she could have helped if she had tried at all.

So we had the guest list all made up—fifteen names. I called the school office even though it was summertime and got the addresses for every one of those boys, and we made invitations and put them in the mail two weeks before the day of the party so they'd all have time to clear their schedules and make plans to come. I imagined all those boys calling each other or talking around the pool or over at the park, saying, "Hey, are you going to Travis's party? Me too!"

I planned a whole lineup of games I knew thirteen-year-old boys would love, nothing too structured but plenty of competition and nifty prizes. The last event, before we came back for birthday cake, home-churned ice cream, and a whole cooler full of cold pop, was going to be a soccer game over at the park two blocks from our other house in Derby. I talked Ken into agreeing to be the referee, complete with a striped shirt and silver whistle. He had played soccer for two of his four years at Piper College, so he knew the game. We rigged up two portable goals and transported them over before the party.

The party came and went, and that night I cried in bed. Not because nobody came. Oh, plenty of boys came—twelve out of the fifteen we invited. We have a picture somewhere of all of them in our backyard eating cake and ice cream. That picture tells a lot. We had borrowed a neighbor's picnic table to put beside ours to make one long table, and the boys are all sitting there, with Travis in the middle. Ken must have taken the picture because I'm leaning over the table at one end, cutting the cake into slices.

The boys don't seem to notice a picture is being taken. Nobody is posed, and nobody is looking at the camera. Several of them are standing up and reaching across the table with various aggressive gestures, as if providing a perfect illustration for the caption "Boys Can't Sit Still and Can't Keep Their Hands Off Each Other." Others have their heads thrown back in laughter, and others are blowing hard on the little noisemakers I had set beside everybody's fork and napkin. One boy has his shirt off and is waving it around his head like a banner. He's on the end, standing with one leg propped up on the seat, eyes crossed and tongue lolling, no doubt making one of the many vulgar sounds that thirteen-year-old boys can make so well.

Everybody in that picture is interacting in some way, or at least vying for somebody else's attention—except, of course, Travis. It's as if there's this little bubble of space around him where nothing is going on. He's sitting down smack in the middle of mayhem with his head tilted upward, his eyes focused on something above him, and his mouth slightly open as if he's just breathed, "Oh!" Completely dissociated from the social occasion of which he's supposed to be the center, he's otherwise occupied, as usual. It's not hard to guess what he's doing—probably observing two squirrels chasing each other through a tree, or maybe a bird's nest, or a butterfly, or maybe a bank of clouds scrolling by.

After the party I tried to tell myself it had been a great success. I looked at the stack of nice gifts the boys' mothers had wrapped and sent with them, and I thought of the dozen happy, sweaty boys marching back from the park to our house after the soccer game, running and laughing and swatting at each other the whole way, and I thought of the rambunctious rendition of "Happy Birthday" around the picnic table and the way the cake and ice cream had disappeared. Several of the boys had even remembered to say thank you before leaving.

I knew when I went to bed that night, however, that the party had accomplished nothing, that Travis was still an onlooker among his peers, that when school started again in the fall, his classmates wouldn't even notice he was there, that given the choice between a corner and the center of a room, he'd pick the corner every time. I cried awhile over the wasted effort of the party, but even as I cried, I knew that I wasn't about to quit trying with Travis. I knew that as soon as this disappointment wore off, I'd try something new. Hope springs eternal in the heart of a mother.

If Ken felt the party was a failure, he never said anything. In fact, I don't remember that either of us said anything at all about the party afterward. He had to get cleaned up in a hurry to make it to a summer park concert he was playing in over in Filbert that evening, and I was busy clearing away all the party litter.

Travis disappeared into his room, I remember, and when I stood outside his door an hour or so later to ask if he wanted to go with me to hear his dad's concert at the park gazebo, here's what I heard. Behind his closed door he was staging his own basketball game. If I didn't know better, I might have thought it was a radio or TV, but I had heard all this before.

He produced all the sound effects himself—the announcer's hyper-emotional, fast-paced narrative of the court action, the referee's whistle, the crowd's frenzied hurrahs and groans of disappointment, the buzzer signaling the end of a period, the cheerleaders' perky chants, the whole works. Even the little squeaks of the players' shoes on the gym floor. During the entire drama, of course, I knew he was scooting around the miniature basketball goal secured to the back of his door, making show-off shots with his Nerf basketball, snagging rebounds, pivoting to lose a guard, then rushing in for a lay-up, taking three-pointers that might give his team the lead with two seconds left on the clock.

I waited for several long moments, then knocked on his door. The noise behind it ceased immediately, and he called out, "Who's there?" As if it could be anybody but me. When I asked if he wanted to drive with me to Filbert to hear the park concert, he opened the door and said, "Okay, I guess so." His face was flushed and happy, and I knew if I were to ask him which he thought was more fun, the party I had spent lots of time and money on or his imaginary basketball game, he would say the party to spare my feelings. Both of us would know it was the basketball game, though. And when I looked over his shoulder into his room that day on his thirteenth birthday, I knew there were actually two rooms there. There was the regular bedroom you could see, and then somewhere inside those four walls was another place, an invisible private place where no one else was allowed.

If I had stopped to think about it, though, I would have realized that we were a family of private places. While Travis wove fantasies, Ken retreated to his music, and I to my poetry.

Anyway, I was so distracted by that party and all my motherly worries about how to integrate Travis into mainstream adolescence that when Ken's birthday arrived five days later, I had made absolutely no plans. For the first time in our married life, I had forgotten about his birthday, and when his mother called at seven-thirty that morning to wish him a happy birthday— she always called before eight o'clock to get the cheapest rate—I lay in bed listening to his end of the conversation and trying to figure out how to throw together a celebration that wouldn't look as quick and easy as it was going to have to be.

His mother must have asked him what our plans were for celebrating his birthday because he said, "Oh, I don't know. She hasn't told me yet." She said something else, and he replied, "Yes, I'm sure she will. She always does." I wondered what it was that I always did. It probably had something to do with a gift and a cake. Those were things I always did on his birthday. It's funny how programmed you can be. Ken and I might not have spoken more than a few sentences a day to each other for weeks, but let his birthday roll around, and I headed to the kitchen to bake a cake and to the mall to buy a gift.

Maybe a big part of it was that I knew his mother would ask about those things later, and I wouldn't want her to find out I hadn't produced anything by way of celebration. I wouldn't want my chief rival to know I had failed. She had outscored me in a lot of ways, but a birthday cake was something I could do and do well. Oh, the cakes I had baked for Ken's birthdays! Not for his sake really, but more for his mother's. They were beautiful work-of-art cakes—Lord Baltimore Cake, Williamsburg Orange Cake, Mocha Layer Cake, Blackberry Wonder Cake, Miss Betty's Fresh Peach Cake, Tennessee Ambrosia Cake, Honey Praline Cake, Sour Cream Cherry Cake, and on and on.

I ran out that day and bought the navy blue plaid short-sleeved shirt, which is no longer navy blue, for his gift, and I made a Peppermint Checkerboard Cake with cream-cheese frosting. I even stopped at some point and made three quick phone calls to put together a little party of sorts, feeling proud of myself that Ken could give a good report to his mother about his birthday. We had no idea that day, of course, that Ken's mother wouldn't be alive on his next birthday.

Four people came to the party—the choral director at the college where Ken teaches, along with his wife, the bachelor band director who had taken Ken's place at the middle school back in 1980, and the only member of Ken's trumpet quartet I could get hold of that day, a divorced man in his fifties. It was a weekday, a Thursday I believe, and they all showed up bearing humorous cards they had hastily purchased on their way to our house.

Everyone was polite and tried to make the most of the party, but they had to know it was a thrown-together affair. After an attempt at playing Rook, during which the trumpet player took the bid and went set three times in a row and the choral director's wife never caught on to the idea of following suit, the middle-school band director started talking at length about a trip he'd taken to Mexico and everybody else started stifling yawns. I'm sure they all considered it an act of mercy when I served the cake and gave subtle hints that the party could be over anytime they needed to leave.

The only thing Ken said later about his birthday party was "That was sure an odd combination of people," which made me bristle a little since I had at least made an effort, which was more than he ever did for my birthday. This is something I've observed over the years—a wife usually does more for her husband's birthday than the husband does for hers. That's just usually the way it goes. Maybe because wives are trying harder to impress their mothers-in-law than husbands are. That was the last time, though, that I ever tried to put anything together for Ken's birthday.

After that, by the time I had shopped and planned and baked and schemed for Travis's birthday, it was easy to convince myself that Ken didn't really want a big deal made out of his. I might buy him a little something and wrap it up, and I might mix up a sponge cake from a box mix and top it with strawberries or buy a cheesecake or a Baskin-Robbins ice-cream cake or do something easy like that, but I was pretty well drained of celebratory energy after going all out for Travis. Besides that, Ken's mother wasn't alive after that birthday to check up on me.

So this is the memory that sets me back as I stand in the doorway looking at Ken searching through his desk. He opened his gift that night almost six years ago after the birthday guests had left and I had put the rest of the cake away. I was busy rinsing off the dessert plates at the sink, so I wasn't even watching him when he opened it, but I heard him say, "I can really use this. All my shirts are about shot."

And do you know what? When I hung it up in his closet the next day after I had washed it—he won't wear a new shirt until, as he puts it, "all the chemicals are washed out of it"—I was surprised to notice that he was right. The condition of his shirts was pretty pathetic. Somehow I guess I hadn't been paying attention, which was funny in a sad way because this was a frequent complaint I had about him. I felt that he didn't pay any attention to me anymore, that he hadn't done so in a long time. So my mother's fears had come to pass, you see. His heart belonged to his music, not to me. And I wasn't really paying attention to him anymore, either.

I remember a brief flicker of hope about midway through Travis's ninth-grade year, when it appeared that he was developing a friendship with a boy who had moved from Nebraska. I didn't know much about him except his name was Ricky and he had a pet ferret and his father was a veterinarian. He had been assigned to sit next to Travis in the back row in geography class, and for some reason he really latched onto Travis. This was the class where the teacher read aloud from the textbook, during which time Ricky told Travis all about himself that first day.

He called Travis that night about a homework assignment in algebra and told him he'd look for him at lunch the next day, which he did. At the end of the week Ricky asked Travis to spend Friday night at his house. He wanted Travis to see his aquarium, his ferret, and an old car his dad was going to let him have after it was fixed up. He collected all kinds of comic books, too, and asked Travis to bring his *Far Side* collection. Travis took his cleats so they could play soccer on Saturday morning after breakfast. Oh, they were full of plans for a great weekend, at least Ricky was. And I was full of hope that this friendship would be the beginning of a new life for Travis.

But they didn't play soccer on Saturday because Travis ended up not even making it through Friday night. Around midnight on Friday Ricky's mother called and said Travis wasn't feeling well. I thought she sounded a little irritated, but maybe I was wrong. Anyway, Ken and I drove over to Ricky's house and collected Travis and all his stuff. He said his stomach hurt, and he wouldn't talk on the way home. He headed straight for his room as soon as we got home and flopped down on the bed and turned his face to the wall. In bed that night, when Ken suggested with no hint of sympathy that Travis had been merely homesick, I wanted to slap him.

Anyway, the friendship with Ricky fizzled out after that. Ricky's mom dropped by one afternoon the next week to deliver Travis's pillow, which he had left at their house, and when I asked Travis a few days later if he and Ricky were still eating lunch together, he shrugged and said, "Yeah, I guess, sort of." What that meant, I finally pried out of him, was that they usually ended up at the same table but didn't really sit together. Ricky had become friends with an older boy in tenth grade who had just gotten his driver's license and drove a remodeled Chevy Impala to school.

For some reason I decide to say something else to Ken on this day that he has come home and is looking for the piece of music. I've already told my mother about going to Margaret's house and accepting God's gift of grace, but I haven't told Ken yet. I would have told him about it the same Sunday it happened, but things went haywire before I had a chance.

So after I step out of the birthday memory, I find that I'm still standing in the doorway of Ken's office, and he's dragged several more folders out of desk drawers and is riffling through them. "I've been going to church," I say to his back. He doesn't reply but turns his head slightly as if to hear better. "It's that church over in Derby close to where Jennifer's piano teacher used to live—the Church of the Open Door."

He may have found the music he's looking for because he stops all of a sudden and pulls a single sheet from a folder. "And I've been reading the Bible," I continue. He holds the music in front of him, studies it, and nods his head. "And praying, too," I add.

Ken turns around now and looks straight at me. "Well, good," he says. "If that helps you, then that's good."

"Oh, it helps all right," I say. "It helps a lot." He nods again absentmindedly, then looks down at his music once more. "In fact," I continue, "my prospects for the future are great. I'm going to live forever now."

He looks up at me quickly, and his expression is suddenly distrustful. "Elizabeth, what are you talking about? This isn't some kind of extreme church, is it?"

"Oh yes, I think it is," I say calmly. "It's extreme about spreading the truth. I've found out some very extreme things about God's power and love."

He walks toward the doorway, and I move aside so he can pass. He stops, though, and looks into my eyes. "Be careful, Elizabeth. Religious groups like to find people who are going through a hard time. They know vulnerable people will fall for anything."

"I found out about God first," I say. "The hard time started after that."

He looks puzzled. He glances down at his music again, then looks at his watch. "I'm glad I found this," he says. "I've got to play it for a wedding tonight." He looks suddenly embarrassed, and I wonder if he's thinking the same thing I am. He played his trumpet at our own wedding twenty-eight years ago.

Someday I'll try to write a poem about the way a sharp memory can slice right into the deepest, tenderest part of your heart. Poetry is the only way you can deal with a subject like that. I close my eyes as Ken turns and walks down the hall away from me, and I put out a hand to touch the wall so I won't lose my balance. I'm hearing the piece he played at our wedding, a piece he had written himself called "Stella's Song." He said "Elizabeth's Song" would be too obvious. "Stella's Song" was the name of a quilt pattern my mother was working on the summer we were married.

Ken was fascinated by the design of the pattern, a furiously colorful circle of interlocking flowers and leaves on a black background, and he studied it at great length the first time he saw it. He said it was so gorgeous it gave him the sensation of actual physical pain. My mother looked at him suspiciously when he said this, but anybody could see she was pleased at the compliment.

He set about writing a trumpet solo called "Stella's Song" that night while he was visiting at our house for the weekend, and it turned out to be the most beautiful melody I've ever heard. Oh, I could write up a whole list of beautiful melodies. If you've ever listened to Malcolm Arnold's *Four Scottish Dances*, a piece Ken's wind band played the year he took the college job, you'll remember an oboe solo in the third movement. Nobody could ever forget that melody. It makes you sit absolutely still and ache with joy. And "Londonderry Air"—that's another melody I love. As well known as it is, it has never become trite. And "Ivan's Song" and "Novelette," both of which Travis used to play on the piano as I sat in another room with my eyes closed and my hands clasped together very tightly. And Gabriel Fauré's "Elegie" for cello is another one. And "Morning Mood" from Grieg's *Peer Gynt Suite* and "Air on G" and some of the Gershwin tunes—oh, I have a long list of Melodies I Love. But as pretty as all of these are, "Stella's Song" has them beat. "Stella's Song" is liquid silver, pure and sweet.

My mother ended up giving us the quilt as a wedding gift when she finished it, so I had two "Stella's Song"s made by two different people in two different media, one to look at and one to listen to. But standing in the hallway that day, I was thinking of the musical version, not the quilted one, and I wondered if a person would know when he started losing his mind. I wondered if this was how it felt. Like you had just stepped off shore and plunged straight into the deepest part of the ocean.

Someone in our poetry class recently asked Professor Huckabee why so many poets slipped over the brink into insanity. He thought a moment, then said, "Perhaps it has to do with the exploitative nature of a writer's life." He tugged at his shirt collar, then added, "Your question is interesting because I've actually thought of this many times over the years and keep coming back to this possibility. I have no proof, of course, but perhaps as one makes repeated use of other people in order to furnish his writing, he becomes dissociated in some fundamental way from himself and the edges of reality begin to erode."

He quoted from a poem called "Your Dog Dies" by Raymond Carver, in which the poet comments on the way writers snitch little pieces of sorrow from everyday life and then stitch them together for profit. "Of course, in this day writing poetry can hardly be called profitable in the monetary sense," Professor Huckabee said.

I wonder if his theory has merit. Maybe as some poets retreat into their private worlds, they lose contact with the common man and also therefore lose a sense of purpose. We all know, of course, that it's the common man who is best equipped to deal with everyday life, not the most gifted nor the grossly disadvantaged. Common men hold the world together. But for some poets, I'm convinced, it's their poetry that keeps them on the sunny side of sanity, that reminds them of the universals that make every man a common man.

Professor Huckabee did go on to say, also, that emotional depression could serve art well. "Think of the great masterpieces that have been written and painted by artists in despair," he said. This whole business of the emotional rhythms of writers, painters, and musicians, especially their downswings, gives me much to think about. The low tides of life can be useful, I suppose.

Well, anyway, blah, blah, blah, as Jennifer likes to say when I get carried away with theorizing. "Get back to the facts," she'll say. But one more thought. You can overdramatize things in real life and mess yourself up royally, poet or not. In Raymond Carver's poem, you see, the writer's daughter has a dog that gets hit and dies, and the writer delves into that whole experience right down to the part where he carried the dog's body to a place in the woods "and buried it deep, deep."

And of course—oh, *of course*—he has to write a poem about it, which turns out pretty good, so he goes on borrowing other people's tragedies to write about and never realizes that he's a living, breathing tragedy himself. He's digging a grave for himself as he slowly loses his ability to sympathize and participate and experience firsthand. I wonder if T. S. Eliot was thinking along these lines when he said what he did about an artist's life being "a continual self-sacrifice, a continual extinction of personality."

Anyway, so much for the dead dog and the sad life of a poet. Actually, I think we ought to give poets the benefit of the doubt. I think it's possible to be a poet and be actively involved in real life. I think the best poets see life as it really is, right down to the foundation and studs. And they not only see *what is* but *what can be*. I think poetry is one way to blow away all the fog and see life in full light. A certain kind of poetry can prettify and falsify life, no doubt about it, but the right kind can boil it down to its essence.

And furthermore, my personal opinion about poets who commit suicide is this. I'm still working this out but think I might share it with Professor Huckabee sometime. First, because of a poet's heightened awareness, a good poet can't help realizing the shallowness of a life without an ultimate eternal purpose. "Nothing gold can stay"—Frost and all the others find their own way to say the same thing.

Now follow me here. Since the only religion a lot of poets seem to believe in is their own deified intellect and sensibilities, which they know will die along with their bodies, they inevitably lose hope. Since poets spend more time than the average person probing the mysteries of life, the smart ones come to the same reasonable conclusion quite early: *Why live if there's nothing better than this?* But of course, it's the *if* that they don't investigate thoroughly enough. So some of them take an early exit at their own hand. Oh, I know this is a broad, sweeping, simplistic way of looking at it, but I believe there may be a lot of truth in it.

So here I land, having leaped from Ken's plaid shirt to the high incidence of suicide among poets. I'm used to these wild flights and hairpin curves my mind takes. Nothing much surprises me anymore.

But to get back to Ken, I told him that day in a bumbling, backward sort of way about my faith in God, and he shook his head on his way down the hall as if he felt sorry that I had sunk so low.

He left his study a shambles, as I had known he would, and after I heard his car pull out of the driveway, I went to my pink bathroom to take a shower. It has to be a shower after a tennis match, never a bath. A bath comes at the end of a regular day of low-key or moderate activity. So it was a shower that day, and though I turned the water on high and let it beat hard against me for a long time, I don't need to tell you what I heard above it.

"Stella's Song" goes from a low G to a high C, a wide range for a trumpet. Ken played it flawlessly on our wedding day, and as he did, I stood in front of the preacher bawling like a baby, thinking it was impossible to be happier than I was at that very moment.

How Dark the Hemlock Wreath

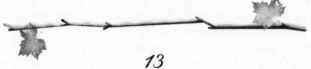

13

Seven years ago Ken's mother came to stay with us for a week. An entire week of seven very long days. She was sixty-four years old at the time but looked at least ten years older. Her hair had thinned drastically. It looked like a loose web you could see right through. She nevertheless faithfully had it styled once a week at a beauty shop in Charleston, where she lived in a small house a few blocks from the beach. The house used to be a vacation cottage but had been her permanent home since Ken's father had left her high and dry on the eve of her fiftieth birthday. I guess I haven't mentioned yet the fact that Ken's father had set a precedent for extramarital shenanigans.

My mother-in-law was a meek woman in many ways but a flinty, resolute one at the core. You didn't find out about the core at first, however. To see her with her husband, as I first did the day before Ken and I were married, you'd think she had invented the word *submission*. Ken had talked about her, of course, always very respectfully, almost worshipfully at times, but I had never met her face-to-face until the day of our wedding rehearsal.

I was expecting somebody much different, not the timid person who appeared to be afraid of her own shadow. Her eyes darted everywhere, I remember that. She didn't move her head much, but her eyes took in everything. On someone else her expression might have looked shifty, but on her it looked scared. It irritated me right from the beginning. I never stopped to wonder what she might be afraid of.

I wasn't really much concerned about her at the time, however, since my mind was taken up with the wedding. She supervised the rehearsal dinner in a low-key way, watching everything with her quick eyes and whispering a word to the head waiter from time to time. We had the dinner in a private room off the main dining room at an old hotel in Burma, Georgia, just a couple of blocks from the big Methodist church where we were married. My parents were still members at that church, though I'm quite sure they hadn't darkened the door of it for many years.

Ken's mother had made all the arrangements for the rehearsal dinner by telephone from Orangeburg, South Carolina, where they lived at the time. If she was disappointed in what our little town had to offer in the way of dining accommodations, she never showed it.

She wore a pale green two-piece suit to our wedding, I recall, and in our pictures she's standing a good six or eight inches from her husband, though everyone else is standing shoulder to shoulder. She's not looking right at the camera like everyone else, and from the expression on her face she appears to be thinking of something mildly disturbing.

She's also in the background of the picture where I'm throwing my bouquet. You can see her standing off to the side watching while Juliet and Ken's two younger sisters, Sue and Mary, position themselves to be the catchers, along with a few assorted cousins and friends who attended the wedding. She looks worried. Maybe she was afraid one of her daughters would catch the bouquet and she'd have to endure another wedding.

Ken and I went to the Smoky Mountains in the middle of winter for our honeymoon, which lasted only three days because we had to get to Columbia in time to move into our apartment and enroll for second-semester classes. We didn't see my in-laws for seven or eight months after that even though Orangeburg isn't far from Columbia. Ken and I were busy with our schoolwork and our jobs, and the Landises weren't the type to take weekend trips, even short ones.

They never called us on the telephone, but Ken sometimes called them on Sunday afternoons. I could always tell which parent he was talking to. With his father he used a cautious, formal tone, but with his mother he relaxed and even laughed sometimes. If his mother wasn't home, the phone calls were very short.

Well, anyway, I've said all this to make the point that I didn't really know my mother-in-law when Ken and I were first married, and I had formed only a dim impression of her by the time our first anniversary rolled around. It took me a couple of years into our marriage to figure out that she turned into somebody different whenever she wasn't in her husband's presence. "Hey, what's this—a *personality*?" I felt like saying the first time I noticed it. She was laughing with Ken, I recall, and she actually said something moderately witty, though I can't remember now what it was. My father-in-law wasn't anywhere around at the time, though. I do remember that.

Up until then I had thought Ken's parents were just dull people, but after that I started to see that something else was going on underneath their dull exteriors. I know I shouldn't be saying much about other people's boring personalities considering my own, but in an odd sort of way I'm actually very well qualified in this area. Sometimes we unpopular wallflower types are just brimming with intuition and powers of observation. We stand over to the side and see things other people miss.

I noticed it again later—the unmistakable contrast in my mother-in-law's behavior when her husband was with her and when he wasn't. And it wasn't hard to figure out why. My father-in-law's technique of handling women and children could be summed up in one word: repression. Or oppression. Or suppression. Take your pick, or better yet, add them all together and stir them up into one potent brew. The perfect recipe for every head of house. Keep those subordinates in their place!

Have I said that Christine was my mother-in-law's first name? And her husband's was one of those odd family names that boys sometimes get stuck with for a first name: Schuyler. I shook their hands the first time we met, two hours before our wedding rehearsal was scheduled to begin. I say *scheduled* because it was delayed by another hour. My mother, suddenly seized with the certainty that two rolls of film wouldn't be enough for the evening, sent my father out to get two more rolls. "Everybody knows that at least three out of every five pictures aren't any good," she said, as if she had actually run tests and tallied the results. And as Dad was backing out of the driveway, she flung open the door and called out, "And don't have a wreck, for heaven's sake!"

Which is exactly what he proceeded to have, believe it or not. When he called on the phone from the drugstore, Mother thought he was teasing at first. "That isn't funny, Brandon," she said. "Now get on back here with that film." It wasn't anything major, just a smashed taillight on the car he rear-ended in the parking lot, but he had to wait around for a policeman to come and write up a report and listen to both sides of the story, and so forth. "Well, isn't this par for the course?" Mother said to us when she hung up the telephone. To Ken's parents she said, "I had a feeling something like this would happen. I never should have let him go." No one pointed out that she had actually *made* him go.

We laughed about it later—well, Juliet and I did, and my brother, Greg. I don't remember Mother ever seeing the humor in it. Daddy got to the church late for the rehearsal and threw everything off schedule. You can't have a wedding rehearsal and leave out the part where the father walks the bride down the aisle and speaks his lines about giving her away. The delay wasn't really a major deal, but when it's your oldest child's wedding, a mother just naturally wants things to run like clockwork. Mother was peeved about the whole thing and showed it.

When Daddy finally arrived, Greg called out, "Hey, Dad! Where ya been? You look like a wreck!" I think Juliet and I were the only ones who laughed. Everybody in Ken's family was sitting together on one of the front pews, and I remember how they all looked quickly at Mr. Landis for his reaction. He didn't smile. Maybe he was wondering if the hotel was going to charge extra for having to hold the dinner, or maybe he thought Greg's comment showed disrespect for authority or disregard for the value of time, or who knows what?

Anyway, the hotel restaurant was gracious about it. Daddy made a public apology to all of us when he arrived, very sweet and sincere, and the rest of the evening went smoothly in spite of the fact that Mother's smile was very strained the whole evening. I'm sure the restaurant staff must have wondered about the high percentage of solemn people in this wedding party.

Of course, the very next morning, my wedding day, Daddy got the news about the medical tests, and the biopsy followed a couple of days after that, and then Mother didn't have much reason to smile about anything for a long time. My father's decline and death completely set her back. His little mishap in the drugstore parking lot must have seemed mighty piddling to her compared to what happened in the days and months that followed.

It was a coincidence, I suppose, that a book of William Meredith's poems titled *The Cheer* was published the same year Daddy died. In the book—Ken had given it to me for Christmas that year—was a poem called "Give and Take," which I read for the first time on the very day of Daddy's funeral, which was the day after Christmas. The poem's subtitle was "Christmas, after a death in the family," and when I read the poem that day after what we'd all been through that Christmas in Georgia, I felt like William Meredith had crawled inside my skin.

There's no way to describe going through the Christmas season when your father is dying and then watching his casket descend into a hole in the ground, but Meredith comes as close as anything I've ever heard. He compares his loss to having to rewrap a nice Christmas present and give it back. That may sound like a weak analogy just summarizing it, but let me tell you, the way he puts it is powerful. You'd have to read the whole poem to see what I mean.

He talks about Christmasy things like stockings and tinsel and the smell of spruce but uses them to point out the swift passage of time that brings the end of everything we hold dear. The green Christmas wreath is replaced by another. "How dark the hemlock wreath," he writes. How dark everything when you've lost the kind of father I had.

Looking back on it, I know I was selfish with my grief. I didn't share it with my mother as I should have. I fled back home to our basement apartment in Columbia, to my classes and my job at the gift shop, and I left her to wander through those first several months all alone in the dark. Juliet returned to Paris in January, where she was studying ballet for a year in a cultural exchange program, and Greg went back to Piper College to continue his freshman year. I could have stayed out of grad school second semester and helped my mother, but I didn't. I'll always regret that.

But back to my in-laws. As I said, I shook their hands the first time I met them before our wedding. Though born and raised in the South, I'm not the openly affectionate type like Juliet is. She treats everybody like a member of the family—hugs and kisses on the cheek and such. And for a guy, Greg is pretty much into touching, too. He'll slap a back here, grab an elbow there, or lay a hand on a shoulder. I'll admit it—I've never liked hugging other people any more than Ken has. But it's just a personality trait, not a character flaw as Juliet would have you believe.

I couldn't bring myself to call my in-laws Mom and Dad the way lots of people do, but I don't know that they ever really wanted me to. I already had a Mom and Dad, although I didn't know at the time of the wedding that my father wasn't going to live the year out. I didn't want to call anybody else by those names, ever. You shouldn't be expected to do that in my opinion. There ought to be other titles of address for in-laws, something completely different and neutral. There are enough words in the English language that you shouldn't have to double up that way. Or you could make up brand-new words. Somebody ought to do that—make up names for in-laws.

So we were visiting my in-laws for the first time in Newton when I first called my mother-in-law "Mrs. Landis." It was in early September after we had been married in January. The Landises had moved from Orangeburg that summer to Newton, where Piper College was. After Ken had gone through four years at Piper, Mr. Landis said it didn't make good sense to pay room and board for his children when they could just as easily live at home and save all that money. I think he was hoping to get a job at Piper in some capacity, but that never worked out.

We had driven to Newton from Columbia to stay overnight before heading to Georgia to see my parents. By this time Daddy was failing fast.

When I called her "Mrs. Landis," she shook her head, I recall, and cast a quick glance at her husband, who was sitting at the kitchen table reading the sports page of the newspaper. "You can call me Christine," she said, half whispering, and when he looked up at her over the top of the paper, she said, "Don't you think that would be all right, Schuyler?" She had grown up in Minnesota, so I guess she wasn't as horrified as my mother was about the idea of young people calling older people by their first names.

Mr. Landis frowned, I remember, and didn't say anything for a few minutes but went back to reading the paper. A little while later he folded up the paper, noisily drained his coffee cup, and said, "I guess it will be all right if she calls you Christine." He didn't look at any of us when he said this. I couldn't help wondering what he would do if I were to throw myself prostrate on the rug in front of him and say, "Oh, thank you, thank you, my lord, for your most gracious permission." I only thought about it, though. I was always imagining sassy comebacks that I was too polite to deliver. With Mr.

Landis, fear was part of it, too. I could well imagine him giving me a swift kick for my impertinence.

"What is it with your father?" I had asked Ken during that short visit. "Why does he act so mad all the time?"

And, of course, Ken's answer was "I don't know." He was saying that even back then. I think that answer is encoded into the brain of every male on the face of God's green earth. When I tried to pump him, he made a face. "He's always been that way," he said. "We just learned not to mess with him."

Schuyler Landis had been a champion swimmer in his youth, and in his mid-forties his physique still bore the evidence. Big muscular chest and arms, and a quickness on his feet. He usually looked at you with his eyelids partly closed, like a lizard sunning itself on a rock. You half expected to see him flick his tongue out. He'd stare at you without a trace of expression on his face. Except for the rise and fall of his massive chest, he hardly seemed to breathe. I've never known a man to breathe so slowly and quietly. His lungs had to be enormously efficient. I could picture him swimming underwater for long stretches of time without having to come up for air, then appearing suddenly and silently like a monster from the deep.

When he rose from his chair, however, it was always quick. Everybody would flinch from the surprise of it, and I think this pleased him. He liked to keep people guessing. For a man of his height, his feet were small, and I always wondered if that hadn't kept him from setting records in swimming events. It would seem that a swimmer would benefit from having big, broad, flipperlike feet. I never asked him, though. With his small feet he walked lightly as if accustomed to sneaking up behind people.

Though I fell into the use of Christine for my mother-in-law quite easily, never did I call my father-in-law Schuyler. Nor did he invite me to. It was always Mr. Landis if I called him anything at all. Usually I avoided him. I wasn't surprised to learn that he had named all five of their children, thus putting on display for the whole world his utter lack of creativity.

Ken's name was the most original; they all went downhill after that. Even Ken's was pathetic in a way, though, for his full name was Ken Charles Landis. Not Kenneth, but just plain Ken. Mr. Landis despised the nickname Kenny and forbade anyone at home to call him that. When I found this out, I started calling him Kenny sometimes, though never in the presence of Mr. Landis, of course.

After Ken came his brother James William, then another brother named John Robert, and a few years later two sisters a year apart, Sue Ann and Mary Jane. So there you have Ken's siblings—James, John, Sue, and Mary. No nicknames allowed for any of them either, of course. They sound like the names in an old first-grade primer: "*James, John, Sue, and Mary go to visit Grandfather and Grandmother.*" If they'd had a cat and dog, no doubt Mr.

Landis would have named them Tabs and Fido. They didn't have a dog or cat, of course. It shouldn't surprise anybody that the Landis kids weren't allowed to have pets. Or go to summer camp. Or have friends over to spend the night. Or do a hundred other normal, healthy things that make a happy childhood.

All five children had left home as soon as they could, which was following graduation from college. As the oldest, Ken was the first to go to Piper College, followed at regular intervals by the other four, all of whom worked at various jobs around campus to help pay their tuition. Mr. Landis believed in education, but not free education. It was his firm belief that everything came at a cost, and the higher the better—unless it was something *he* was paying for. He required all five children to pay for half of their college expenses except for his youngest daughter, Mary, who was a senior in high school when Mr. Landis left home one day with two large suitcases, the family car, and a violinist who was only a year older than his other daughter, Sue.

Mr. Landis earned his living repairing instruments and teaching clarinet lessons for several music stores in Newton and Camden, and this young violinist also taught lessons at one of them. That's how they met. I suppose he thought that as a musician himself, he had found more of a soul mate for himself than Christine, who had nothing going for her except that she had borne him five children and kept his house as neat and sanitized as a clinic for some twenty-nine years.

What goes on in the mind of a man to do something like that? For twenty-nine years he's a dictator at home, controlling every single detail from the way his bacon is fried to how many minutes are allotted for showers, and then one day he gives up his kingdom for a long-haired fiddler the age of his daughters.

Maybe a better question would be what was going through the young violinist's mind to do such a thing? Surely she didn't really know him. After it happened, I used to lie in bed at night and wonder how long it would take the poor girl to realize what a horrible mistake she had made. *Does she know yet?* I'd ask myself. *Is she lying in bed beside him right now wondering how she could have done something so abysmally stupid? Has she felt the first wave of repulsion roll over her when he reaches out to touch her? Does he let her call him Schuyler, or does he insist on Master?*

Christine weathered the abandonment quite well, actually, and though no one came right out and said it, I think we all knew that as soon as the shock wore off, she was probably going to feel like a liberated woman. She had certainly earned it. The courts were good to her—gave her a fair share of their assets, which turned out to be a lot more than she knew they had, and provided support for Mary, who was still under eighteen. I'm sure this part of the whole thing—the money distribution—must have sorely grieved Mr. Landis. He had tried to shield and conceal several of his investments and holdings, but Christine's lawyer was good and flushed them all out.

Ken and his brothers feared that their father would try to come back and take over again after the violinist tired of him, which we all knew was bound to happen sooner or later. It turned out to be sooner. Less than a year was all it took, but Mr. Landis merely found another woman and moved with her out to Nevada. We weren't sure whether it was the casinos he wanted to be near or the easy access to divorce.

The last we heard, he was still out there in Nevada. Who knows if wife number three stuck with him. If she was smart, she didn't. Of course, if she was smart, she wouldn't have married him in the first place. What's wrong with a woman who can't see through a man like that the minute she lays eyes on him?

I don't have much sympathy for such wives, I'm afraid, but my heart goes out to the children. The wives should have done their homework better before jumping into marriage, but Schuyler Landis's five children didn't have a choice. If I had met Ken's father earlier than I did, I might have had second thoughts about marrying his son. Sons of such fathers have to pay heavily. They never ever get off scot-free.

So Christine is left high and dry at the age of fifty—only in this case "high and dry" ends up being a good thing in comparison to what she knew before. She's set free from the asylum, her shackles are removed, the strait-jacket is ripped off. She moves out of their latest house, which held only furniture and appliances that Schuyler Landis had chosen, all arranged exactly as he had mandated.

The only moments of freedom she had ever felt in any house were in the big dormitory-type room upstairs when they lived in Orangeburg, where all of her children had taken their turn hearing her read nursery rhymes before bedtime. It's a wonder Mr. Landis didn't find a way to put an end to that, but I'm guessing he was too lazy to climb the stairs and probably didn't even know they were having a good time up there. They no doubt learned to have their fun very, very quietly.

I wonder if Christine ever read them the rhyme that goes "Clap hands, clap hands! / Till Father comes home; / Then quick to bed, / For playing is done." Or this one: "Old Father is dead, that poor old man, / You'll never see him more. / He used to wear a long sad face / When he came in the door." Or "Mother must stand at the tub, tub, tub, / The dirty clothes to rub, rub, rub, / She boils them till they're clean, clean, clean, / So Father can dress like a king, king, king." As I said before, whoever put those rhymes together wasn't operating under the illusion that life was all fun and games.

After the divorce Christine moved to Charleston and bought a small renovated beach house an older couple was selling because their days of trekking to Charleston for the summer were over. Ken tried to talk her out of it, warning her about hurricane season and flooding and all, but she wanted to hear the ocean, she said. She had lived cooped up in a house a hundred miles inland for twenty-nine years with a man who betrayed her, she said, and she was ready to take off her shoes and walk on the beach and get the hem of her dress wet if she wanted to. And who could deny her that little bit of pleasure? Besides, we could all come visit her, she said, and have a cheap vacation at the beach anytime we wanted to.

But we didn't. Ken mentioned it several times, but I was good at finding excuses. It wasn't my idea of a family vacation to go stay at Christine's house. While my heart should have been overflowing with sympathy for her, it wasn't. Everything about her irritated me, especially the fact that she had let herself be walked all over for almost thirty years by a man like Schuyler.

Back to the week she visited us seven years ago. It was in the fall, October I think, and Jennifer had left home to go to college several weeks earlier. The old family standby, of course—Piper College.

I guess I haven't mentioned yet how Ken ended up at Piper College. Schuyler Landis had met a man when he worked as a typesetter's apprentice for a newspaper in Baltimore during his high-school days—the man was the owner of the newspaper, actually—who happened to be one of the sons of Randolph Shelby Piper, the founder of Piper College. As a high-school kid looking to make it big, Mr. Landis had been highly impressed with this young newspaper owner who drove a convertible and wore flashy clothes. He assumed that such a wealthy, intelligent, self-confident man must have come from good stock, and he thought if he sent his sons to the college that this man's father had founded, they would surely make something of themselves.

Mr. Landis had always wanted to live in the South anyway. He thought Maryland was a wishy-washy place to be from—neither North nor South— and I guess I forgot to mention that his middle name was Lee, as in Robert E. His mother was a native Virginian, and even though he grew up in Maryland, Mr. Landis had always fancied himself a Southern gentleman, although if there's anything I'm sure he never was, it was gentle.

Anyway, when he finished a degree at a music college in Baltimore, he packed up and moved himself to Orangeburg, South Carolina, where he met and married Christine, then found odd jobs playing the piano and clarinet in bars and restaurants by night and learning the instrument repair business by day. Eventually they moved fifty miles away to Newton, which was his goal all along since that's where Piper College was located.

He probably thought he had a pretty good chance of being hired at Piper, being a fair enough musician, and they did hire him on a limited basis to help out with instrument repair but not to teach. The music department was pretty small in those days. Anyway, he attended all the concerts on campus and of course sent all his children there.

And my family was big on Piper College, too, my father having attended there on the GI Bill after World War II. His father knew one of the board members somehow. So it was always taken for granted that Jennifer would go to Piper. Even though they didn't offer a law degree, they did have a good prelaw program by the time she enrolled, so she did that and then went to the University of South Carolina afterward for law school.

So anyway, Jennifer was away at college during Christine's week-long visit. Travis was eleven and in sixth grade that fall. Ken had given up his job at the middle school in Derby a couple of years earlier, having been wooed to the college position he now holds. It's a small college, privately funded, originally a Presbyterian school but now dissociated from any religious affiliation. Harwood College it's called, and it's located on a large, beautiful tract of land the Presbyterians were smart enough to purchase when land was cheap and Greenville hadn't yet started attracting every type of industry you can imagine. German, Japanese, French—you name it, we've got it in the Upstate.

The Southeast is full of these small, private liberal arts colleges, and some of them are quite fine. Others limp along. Many should close up shop and send their students somewhere more promising, though they never will, of course. Within a fifty-mile radius of our house in Berea, there must be more than a dozen colleges. This is the absolute truth.

There's Harwood, where Ken teaches, and Clarke-Forsythe, where I go for my poetry class. Also a Methodist university, a couple of community colleges, a women's school, a business college, and several others. And they all have their own emphasis: vocational, Catholic, minority, fine arts, and so forth.

Well, I keep getting off the subject, almost as if I don't really *want* to talk about my mother-in-law. But I'm going to. I have to. Every day I keep praying, "Open my eyes," and every day I see her face float up in front of me. I don't see any way of taking that other than as a sign from God.

I know there are exceptions to what I'm about to say, but I think the relationship between a woman and her mother-in-law is just naturally fraught with problems. From the minute you start dating a guy, I think his mother deep down wishes you'd drop off the face of the earth. You're just a kid at the time, of course, so you're not aware of any of this animosity at first, and most middle-aged women can cover it up so well that you might even think your boyfriend's mother really, really likes you. But don't let them fool you. Potential mothers-in-law see you as the spoiler they've been dreading ever since their son was first placed in their arms in the delivery room.

Like I said, this isn't always the case. There's another substitute teacher I run into from time to time, when we're called to the same school on the same day, whose name is Kathy Kramer. I heard her say once in the teachers' lounge that she had gone to Atlanta and spent a whole day shopping with her mother-in-law the weekend before, and she went on to say she felt closer to her mother-in-law than to her own mother. And she had all the appearances of telling the truth. So it does happen.

Back in college my roommate, Laurie, met the mother of a guy she was dating pretty seriously her senior year. We were still rooming together at the time, and when she came back to the room that night, she told me she was going to have to break up with Jeremy. When I asked why, she said it was because of his mother. "Didn't she like you?" I said, and she laughed.

"Like me?" she said. "She adored me. She gushed about how perfect I was for Jeremy. She fawned over me all night and praised me up one side and down the other." And when I asked her why that was such a problem, she said something I think made good sense. "Any time a guy's mom is that nice to you, it's a danger sign," she said. "It shows she's getting desperate. You gotta wonder what's wrong with her son that makes her so eager to get rid of him." Now, doesn't that seem logical? Laurie had a head on her shoulders.

I was glad Jeremy's mom had come along when she did because I never thought Jeremy was right for Laurie. I even started calling him Germy right to Laurie's face. I tried to point out some obvious character weaknesses, but she was blinded by his biceps. He played football and acted like that qualified him for all sorts of special favors. I told her he was a cretin, and she said no, she didn't think he'd ever been over to the Mediterranean area. He's probably sprawled out on a couch somewhere right now clutching the remote control and hollering, "Woman! Bring me a cold beer!"

That mother-son bond is a funny thing. You want it to be strong when you're on the mother end, but not when you're the wife of the son. I've always wanted Travis's bond with me to be unbreakable, but I've always wanted Ken's bond with Christine to snap right in two.

And I have to be honest. I have to look ahead and realize that someday some woman might be thinking resentful thoughts about me the way I've thought about Christine. Of course, I see no imminent danger from prospective daughters-in-law as I write this, since the girls aren't exactly waiting in line for Travis. I wonder if he's even spoken one word to a girl at Piper.

Anyway, Christine and I tiptoed around each other that week she visited us. I was convinced from the moment she arrived that she was trying to compete with me, but she did it in such small, subtle ways that you could never really catch her at it. Ken thought I acted petty the whole week, but he didn't see and hear the things I did. He was gone most of the day, and she knew how to act innocent when he was around.

All week long she asked questions, rarely looking at me. Her eyes darted everywhere. "Do you always fold Travis's shirts instead of hanging them?" "Do you prefer these small biscuits to the bigger ones?" "Is that painting on the wall upside down?" "Did you use whole milk in this custard?" "Have you ever tried using regular starch instead of the spray kind?" "Would you like me to dust all your picture frames?" "Do you think Travis is getting enough sleep?" "Do you think you'll ever color your hair?"

On and on and on it went all week. And what she was really saying, of course—speaking of the art of translating, I'm pretty good at it myself—was "Anybody knows you should hang shirts instead of fold them." "These little biscuits are barely big enough to taste." "Abstract art is ridiculous," and so forth. But all her questions sounded so soft and courteous on the surface that if you listened to only the tone and not the actual words, you'd think she was just as sweet and guileless as a dove. Even if you looked her in the eye, you'd think the same thing. I guess living with a man like Schuyler Landis for all those years had taught her a thing or two about how to disguise her true feelings. Or I don't know, maybe it was all my imagination. You start to lose your objectivity pretty fast when you're around your mother-in-law.

While I cleared away the dishes, she sat at the table with Ken after supper every night and plied him with questions, too, but only about the things she knew would interest him. She asked about his students, his private lessons, his conducting, his upcoming concerts, his writing, his brass quintet, his traveling, his views on investments, his favorite band works, his golf games, and so on. She would sit there every night and hang on every word he said, one elbow propped on the table, her bright eyes fastened on him the whole time he was talking.

I'm sure Ken talked more those seven days than he had in the previous seven years. He talked as if the floodgates had been opened, as if he'd been deprived of human contact and had finally found someone to listen, as if he'd been a mute all his life and suddenly discovered his voice.

And it wasn't just Ken she tried to woo away from me. It was Travis, too. She used my sewing machine that week and made a bathrobe for Travis out of plush royal blue velour, after making a gentle speech implying that any boy or man who doesn't have a bathrobe isn't being properly taken care of. Travis loved it, of course, and for a long time after her visit he would take his school clothes off and put that royal blue bathrobe on every day. Then he'd sit in the living room wearing it as he practiced his piano and trumpet. Before long I started washing it frequently in hot water, and it soon faded and then grew too small for him.

From Silver Aslant

14

Sometime around the first of April I started singing in the choir at the Church of the Open Door. Here's how that happened. In late March, Margaret Tuttle invited me to her house "for a bite of dessert" after one of our evening poetry classes at Clarke-Forsythe. We had gone out together after class a few other times, but always to a coffee shop or restaurant. But she had made a pie, she said that night, and wondered if I'd come over to her house and have a piece before I went home.

I accepted, although I told her I wouldn't stay long. I knew she got up early to go to her job at Emma Weldy Elementary School. I also knew I would be getting up early because I was substituting for the next two days at Berea Middle School for an English teacher who was out of town for a funeral. English classes have always been my favorites for substituting.

We had gotten into a discussion in class that night at Clarke-Forsythe about "suitable subject matter for poetry." Somebody had asked Professor Huckabee his opinion about a poem that dealt with the awakening of adolescent sexuality in pretty raw terms. The poem was in the textbook we were using, and Professor Huckabee had skipped over it as we discussed the chapter for the night: "Telling the Truth in Poetry."

The young man who asked the question had distinguished himself by this point in the semester as a libertine and a sloppy thinker, which often seem to go together. Other people in the class gave each other looks of "Oh no" whenever he started talking. He referred to himself as A. R., though Professor Huckabee always read his name as Albert Romaine Waddell when calling roll.

A. R. made outrageous statements he couldn't back up and more than once had been corrected by Professor Huckabee but in such a mild, polite way that A. R. never seemed to catch on that he had made a fool of himself.

It was clear that he thought he was smart enough to take Professor Hucka-bee's place. Earlier in the semester he had declared Allen Ginsberg to be his favorite poet and "Howl" the greatest poem in the English language, so that tells you a lot about him right there.

So A. R. shocks everyone on this particular night by reading several really embarrassing lines of this poem out loud in his deep bass voice and then saying, "I think that's great poetry because it's *honest*. Too many of the poems we've been reading in class are stuffy, like the poets are too hung up or timid or maybe just too *out of it* to use the real, everyday language of the people. They're a bunch of wimps." A. R. was wearing a sweatshirt that night with the words *SHAKE IT LOOSE* printed across the back, along with a picture of a buxom girl, apparently dancing, whose clothes were in the process of flying off. He had looked around at the other students, waved a hand, and said, "Okay, okay. I know. Just call me the class reactionary."

I'm not sure how many people caught his misuse of the word *reactionary*, but Margaret glanced at me and raised an eyebrow. I've heard other people make this same mistake, so A. R. isn't the only one who thinks *reactionary* is a synonym for rebel or independent thinker or someone who bucks tradi-tion. They don't know that it's actually the opposite. A reactionary is against progressivism or liberalism; he wants things to stay as they are.

I've heard people do the same thing with other words—like *temerity*, for example. It sounds like it might be something akin to timidity, but it's as far from that as you can get. And *enervate*—that's another one. I once heard a secretary at one of the schools where I sub say she had raked leaves for four hours straight the day before and loved every minute of it because "cold weather always enervates me." She obviously thought the word was a syno-nym for *energize*. If she'd been enervated, though, she certainly wouldn't have been outside raking leaves for four hours.

Anyway, we had quite a little discussion after that, with a few people taking A. R.'s side, but most of us agreeing with Margaret, who finally summed up what the rest of us were trying to say. She sometimes stood in class when asking a question or venturing an opinion, and she did so on this night. She turned slightly so that she could be heard from her seat at the end of the front row. She looked only at Professor Huckabee as she spoke, how-ever, and he looked right back at her. By this point in the semester I think Professor Huckabee adored Margaret. He knew she was the leader of a po-etry club and often asked her after class how the group was coming along.

Margaret spoke clearly, and the words fell from her lips, as always, in shapely clusters. I love to hear her talk. It always seems so effortless. "To be sure, a poet or any other writer *can* say whatever he chooses," she said. "He may choose to use offensive language to discuss offensive topics. An artist likewise has the freedom with paint and brush to depict in graphic detail on canvas those aspects of man which are bestial. I suppose there are those who would claim that such bold realism qualifies such works as great, yet the question we may reasonably pose is this: Though the artist in any genre *can* deal with any subject as vile, seditious, scatological, profane, or gory as he wishes, does this mean that he *should*? Does artistic freedom compel us to bring into the open every aspect of human behavior and thought, both high and low? Does an artist not have a moral obligation to his fellow man to lift rather than degrade?"

She paused. "I suppose we could debate what constitutes uplifting and degrading for weeks and not reach a consensus, even in a group as small and relatively homogeneous as this one, but I believe we would all agree on one point, and that is that the artist must not forget the power of the 'withheld image,' to borrow a term from John Frederick Nims. A great deal may be suggested rather than directly stated, and this is what good poetry does so well. This is what Professor Huckabee has been teaching us these past weeks."

She paused again to nod and smile in his direction, then continued. "Even tonight he showed us how deftly Edwin Arlington Robinson led us to understand that the miller and his wife both took their lives in his poem 'The Mill.' As readers, we discovered it for ourselves, however, rather than having the scene portrayed in grisly detail."

She appeared to be finished, but before she sat down she added one other thought. "And Robert Frost's poem 'The Silken Tent,' which we read last week—does that not relate to this very subject? Does Frost not suggest clearly that freedom and bondage may be compatible, that in allowing ourselves to be placed under certain restrictions we may find ways of liberating our powers of expression?" She shook her head and glanced at A. R. briefly. "Speaking one's mind plainly without restraint may severely undercut artistic effect." She sat down, and though I didn't look around, I'm sure there was more than one dropped jaw in that room.

Professor Huckabee appeared profoundly grateful to Margaret for her speech and even jotted something down in his notes as she spoke. Then, though the point was already beautifully made, he picked up her theme when she sat down. "One of the most poignant love scenes I've ever read," he said, his eyes fixed on his desk, "is found in the fifth canto of Dante's *Inferno*. Instead of describing the amorous scene between the lovers, who had been reading together, Dante writes, 'That was the end of our reading for the day.' "

Then he colored slightly, cleared his throat, and looked down at his notes to resume his planned lecture. I had noticed on the first night of class that Professor Huckabee wore a thin gold wedding band, so I assumed he had a wife waiting for him at home. I have often wondered what Mrs. Huckabee is like. I've wondered if he discusses his classes with her or reads poems to her at bedtime.

A. R. didn't push the matter any more that night, and we went on to discuss the whole business of artistic freedom for several more minutes before turning to a fascinating little six-line poem by Howard Nemerov titled "Because You Asked about the Line between Prose and Poetry." Now this is important, so don't start skimming here. The metaphor in the poem is watching birds feed in a freezing rain that suddenly turns into snow. The poet is talking about how subtly it changes from "silver aslant"—which is rain, of course—into floating white snowflakes. The line between rain and snow is blurry for just the briefest of moments, the poet says, and then suddenly you see the change of motion, from falling to flying, and you know it's snow.

I could write fifty more chapters about this whole subject of lines between things. I've been looking for the lines in my marriage, you see. Or I guess it's the *big* line, singular, I'm looking for. At what point did things arrange themselves so that Ken was open to infidelity? When was he *first* vulnerable, and how did it come about that his ties to home were weaker than the pull of temptation? Was there a specific point in time, something that happened, or was it more a period of time during which things slowly evolved? But even then, what first occurred to initiate that period?

Don't ever let anybody tell you that sorrow destroys your ability to reason. Even when you're hurting, you can *think*, and maybe you can think all the more clearly because unimportant things tend to fall away when something really big throws itself at you. Your analytical powers start working double-time as you sort through stuff in the past. At least that's the way it was for me. Maybe my analyses weren't all that accurate, but I couldn't help considering them.

Anyway, when I got to Margaret's house after class that night, it was about nine o'clock. Thomas was eating peanuts and watching a program on television when we walked in, and he stood up to greet me. He'd already had his pie, he said, and recommended it highly. "Rosie sure has a magic touch in the kitchen," he said and smiled at Margaret proudly. "Here, let me take your books and pocketbook for you," he said, and Margaret let him. He took them into one of the bedrooms, and Margaret led me into the kitchen.

We resumed talking about the line between prose and poetry as Margaret heated water for tea and cut each of us a slice of pie. Then we turned to talking about lines in general—when a child steps over the line into adulthood, when a person becomes old, when a work of art is finished, when God's kingdom on earth will be done, and so on.

"Have you ever crossed a line in your relationship with Thomas?" I asked at length. We were both eating our pie—chocolate praline—by now and sipping our tea. I knew where this question would lead, and I was stepping into it willingly.

Margaret talked briefly about her marriage. "It has not followed a conventional timetable," she said. "I do not intend to sound trite, but my love for Thomas is new every day." She went on to tell me about the line she had crossed from living with Thomas as a brother to loving him as her husband. "I was blind for many years," she said, almost sadly I thought. But she smiled afterward and said, "But my sight has improved immensely."

We sat quietly for a few moments, during which we heard Thomas laugh at something on television. Margaret lifted her eyes to mine and seemed to hold her breath as if gathering her courage. "You know it is not my habit to pry," she said, "but do you mind telling me about your marriage?"

She knew by now, I'm certain, that my marriage was on rocky ground. I had never told her outright, but women can sense these things about other women. It had been six weeks since I had first come to her house for dinner that Sunday in February, and we had seen each other regularly at our bi-weekly poetry classes and at church. I had recently begun attending Sunday evenings as well as Sunday mornings.

"My husband left home a little while ago," I told her now. She didn't reply, and I kept talking, giving her a summary of the events beginning with my driveway revelation the day Ken accidentally called me on my cell phone. I didn't tell her it had been my idea for him to move out of the house.

"I am sorry," Margaret said when I finished. She reached across the table and laid her palm against the back of my hand, hesitantly, almost shyly, as if she wasn't sure how to do it. "Do you love your husband?" she asked.

I can't explain why I turned my hand over at once and clasped hers as if I were drowning and she was offering to help me into the boat, but that's what I did. As I've said before, I'm not much for touching, and I don't really think it comes easily for Margaret either. But there we sat that night holding onto each other's hand as if we'd done it all our lives.

We talked for an hour at her kitchen table, and she never let go of my hand the whole time. I'm a proud person. It's not easy for me to let anybody else know about my problems. I had kept everything under wraps for all this time except with my mother, who's like a bloodhound and can sniff out trouble from only the tiniest scraps of evidence.

And as I've said, my circle of friends is pretty small. When you throw all your time and energy into your children, you wake up one day and realize you don't have a whole lot of friends to fall back on. I knew a lot of people by name, of course, but I didn't really *know* them. I had mingled with a lot of other parents over the years, but everything we talked about was sur-face—the soccer team's new uniforms, homeroom parties, the band's candy-bar sales, renovations to the school gym, and such things. Sometimes I had even sunk so low as to talk about a troublesome teacher.

The only friendship I came close to cultivating was with Polly Seacrest, my former neighbor over in Derby, and that was only because we were thrown together and she was easy to talk to. So my continual worry over

Travis's lack of friends was partly because of the condition of friendlessness itself as it affected him, but also because of what it reminded me about myself. Like any parent that's ever lived, I wanted him to have what I didn't. I wanted Travis to be things I wasn't.

Not that I was a social outcast. Not at all. I was friendly enough in school, as I've said, and consistently polite, but what it all added up to, as I've also said, was boring. I didn't have the kind of quick humor that makes a kid popular. I never did exciting things the way other kids at school did— or even as my own brother and sister did. Greg got into a fight during football practice in eighth grade one day and came home with a black eye and swollen nose. "The other guy looks worse," he told Juliet and me proudly. And Juliet probably held the record in school for being sent out of class the most times for talking.

But I was the big sister who always did what she was supposed to do— made good grades, did her chores at home, showed responsibility, said "yes, ma'am" and "yes, sir" to grown-ups, all that boring stuff. I loved it when Greg or Juliet got into trouble, not because I had a mean streak but because it opened up such an interesting side of life. It was like turning over an ordinary old gray rock and finding the underside teeming with biological wonders. Greg and Juliet were acting out a part of me that was smothered. I just didn't have the courage to do anything but behave myself.

But here's a funny thing. With kids at school now, when I'm subbing, I can be all the things I've never been with my peers. I'm confident, outgoing, articulate, even witty sometimes. I act like I have it all together. Nothing escapes me in the classroom, but nothing gets me all bent out of shape either. A lot of times the kids will remember me from other days I've subbed, and they'll even look glad to see me when they come into the classroom. But then I step inside the teachers' lounge during a free period or after school, and I clam up. I can't think of anything to say, and I assume the other teachers aren't much interested in someone who's always just passing through.

But it's different with kids. When I used to go to Jennifer's and Travis's classrooms in elementary school to help with parties or serve as a teacher's aide, I felt right at home. I was always friendly and easygoing with them, interested in them but not pushy. The boys on Travis's baseball or soccer teams would barely give Travis the time of day, but they'd tease around with me. Life is strange. You can feel like several different people living in one body.

So back to Margaret and me sitting at her kitchen table. I pour my heart out to her, and I can't begin to say how good it is to feel the love and concern of someone you really respect and trust. It feels as though I've been carrying a load of cement blocks on my back but have been allowed to set them down for a rest. She asks me if I'd like to talk with the pastor of the church, Theodore Hawthorne, or his wife Edna. She says she'd be glad to mention it to them, but when I shake my head and tell her I'm not ready for anything like that, she nods and says she understands.

I tell her I need to go, and she asks if we can pray and read a passage of Scripture first. I say yes, that's something I am ready for.

She doesn't pick a finger-pointing passage, like one of those addressed to women about having a meek and submissive spirit, but she chooses one from the book of Zechariah, of all places. I've read parts of the major prophets by now, but I haven't read anything yet from these little books of the minor prophets clustered together at the very end of the Old Testament. As she starts to read, I'm thinking this is an odd passage for her to pick, and she admits as much. After she finishes reading the entire twelfth chapter, she stops and gives her head a little shake.

"I know these verses deal primarily with the return of Christ and the establishment of his kingdom on earth," she says, "but I believe they may also be applied to our present lives." She reads the first part of the seventh verse again: " 'The Lord also shall save the tents of Judah.' " She looks at me with a rueful smile. "Forgive me. I have no skill in counseling. These verses must seem highly irrelevant to your circumstances. I cannot begin to explain why they came to my mind."

"Except that God put them there," I say.

"Of course," she says, nodding. "God put them there." She looks down at her open Bible once again and very deliberately reads aloud the tenth verse, where God says he will pour out "the spirit of grace and of supplications" and that the delivered remnant shall look upon him "whom they have pierced."

We talk a little about this verse, and she tells me that although Satan has besieged me and wants my troubles to destroy me, she believes God will bathe me with his grace and save our home—this is exactly what she says, *save our home*—if I will keep my eyes turned to him. " 'He that is feeble among them at that day shall be as David,' " she reads again from the eighth verse, and then adds, "David was only a shepherd, but he was mighty in God's strength." She shakes her head again and says, "I fear that my words sound empty in spite of the fact that my heart is full. There are those who are trained to comfort, encourage, and exhort, but I—"

I interrupt her. "Your words are just right," I say.

Before I leave, she prays with me. She calls me by name in her prayer, and her words are like water in the desert. And she's still hanging onto my hand this whole time. She may not be a trained counselor, but God has anointed her this night to minister to me.

As we walk through the living room to the front door a minute or two later, we pass by the piano. On the wall above it hangs a cross-stitched poem I had noticed before. I stop to read it again. I could have guessed it was by Archibald Rutledge even if the poet's name hadn't appeared at the end.

"Good old Rutledge," I say to her. "I have his *Deep River* collection at home." I say the last line aloud: " 'Some wildflower in my heart.' "

"The cross-stitch was a gift from my friend Birdie Freeman," Margaret says. "She was the one who taught me to play the piano." She lays a finger on one of the keys and sounds a single note. "She taught me many other things as well."

I imagine Margaret playing to Thomas in the evenings from the book that's open on the piano. She sees me looking at the book—a collection of Mozart—and asks if I enjoy music. I tell her I love it but have always wished I knew more about it, that I've learned a little bit just from being married to Ken, that what little bit I know gives me great pleasure. She asks if I would ever consider singing in the choir at church, and I laugh.

"I've never sung in a choir," I say. "I've never had singing lessons of any kind. My sister was in the school choir a couple of years, but I was always on the tennis team."

"Our choir director is always looking for new voices," she says. "Judging from your speaking voice, I am willing to guess that your singing voice is equally lovely." I don't think anybody in my whole life has ever told me I have a nice speaking voice, and I tell her so. "Well, I suppose people have seen no need to state the obvious," she says, "although those are often the very things that need to be stated."

So this is how I end up joining the choir, which meets before church on Sunday nights at the Church of the Open Door. I arrive early and enjoy it intensely. I sing alto, which is much more interesting I think than soprano. I sit between Fern Tucker and Shirley Grimes, both of whom attend Margaret's poetry club. Fern's voice is a little on the strident side, but Shirley's is pleasant and true to pitch. I lean slightly toward Shirley as we rehearse each week.

The director, Willard Scoggins, is a man I've known for years, although I never knew he was a choir director until I first visited the church back in February. I knew he was a librarian, of course, but not a choir director. This just shows how limited our view of a person is. Before then I had seen him regularly at the Derby Public Library, where he works, and once when I helped with a used-book sale—the time I came across the little book of Elizabeth Barrett Browning's sonnets. I even had a memorable conversation with him, though I'm sure he doesn't remember it.

He's a jolly-looking man. That's the best way to describe Willard Scoggins. I've never asked him, but I can imagine that he's had numerous invitations to dress up in a red suit and white beard at Christmas. He's a little overweight, though not nearly so much as he used to be, and he has a round, rosy, jovial face.

He was the assistant librarian back when I first saw him some ten or twelve years ago but is the head librarian now that Mabel Weatherby has retired, thank goodness. That woman was a dragon. I asked her once, very politely of course, if she had plans to expand the poetry collection at the library. She looked me up one side and down the other, then said, "I believe we have *quite* an adequate poetry collection. No one has *ever* complained of any scarcity of volumes in the eight hundreds."

Oh, to be bolder! "I'm not complaining!" I wanted to say. "All I did was ask a simple question." But I didn't say anything, of course. Later I would think of several splendid retorts, but at the time my entire vocabulary flew right out the top of my head. I left the circulation desk, seething that the poetry lovers of Derby were at the mercy of such a dry stick of a librarian, and walked back to the poetry shelves.

A few minutes later who should appear at the end of the aisle where I was standing but the congenial Miss Weatherby herself. I was browsing in a volume of imagist poetry I had already read several times and was comparing William Carlos Williams' longer first version of "The Locust Tree in Flower" with his revised published version that was only thirteen words long. I didn't even see her at first.

I jumped when she spoke. "Was there something in particular you were looking for?" she asked, much louder than you'd expect from a librarian. "Maybe I could steer you to some excellent anthologies you've overlooked." I almost laughed. As if I didn't know every volume of her paltry poetry collection like the back of my hand.

I found my voice then, maybe because I felt fortified by the tall bookshelves instead of being exposed in the open area by the circulation desk, where everybody could see and hear me. "Well, to start with," I said, "I've been wanting to find the complete poems of Blaise Cendrars, but I guess I'll have to order them over in Greenville." She frowned a little and took in her breath. "You know, the ones translated and edited by Ron Padgett," I added.

"And I'd really like to read some of Laura Riding's poetry, too," I continued. "I know a collection of it was published sometime in the last six or seven years, but I suppose it's considered too obscure for our library, even though I think it would really be interesting to read the poems of someone who publicly denounced the writing of poetry after she herself had written poetry for all those years, don't you? I've been wondering what kind of poetry someone like that would have written."

Miss Weatherby took a few steps forward. I saw that she had in her hand a slip of paper and a stubby pencil, which she was holding out toward me. As she came closer, I couldn't resist adding, "And Mina Loy and Joseph Ceravolo—I don't find any of their works on the shelves either. Oh, and Melvin Tolson and John Wheelwright and Leopold Sedar Senghor—I'm particularly interested in finding Senghor's 'Elegy of Midnight.'"

"Please write down the titles for me," she said stiffly, "and I'll locate them for you." Which she did eventually. And even if her efforts were stingy and grudging, I was grateful. She retired soon after that, and Willard Scoggins took over as head librarian.

I met him at the spring book sale a few months later as I was unpacking a box of donated books in the basement of the library. He was passing through, greeting all the volunteers. I remember not wanting to talk to anyone that day because a blood vessel had burst in one of my eyes. A mature adult shouldn't be bothered by something like that, I had told myself that morning, but evidently I wasn't a mature adult.

I kept my eyes turned downward and hoped no one would address me. Other people might show up at work with a problem like mine and say something like "Hey, everybody, look at my *eye*! Can you believe this?" then laugh it off and go about their business. But I retreated to the table at the far end and tried not to look at anybody.

Willard didn't know about my eye, however, and he came right up to the table where I was sorting books and greeted me cordially. "Oh, here's a gem," he said, picking up a book from the nonfiction stack. " 'The Miracle of Terry Cloth.' " He laughed heartily. "Now, why do you suppose a person would ever want to let go of a treasure like this?"

One of the other volunteers, a silly woman with one of those little-girl double names like Dee-Dee or Zuzu or Gigi, piped up and said, "Maybe the person just felt like throwing in the towel." Everyone laughed, and I'm sure she was proud of herself.

I reached into my box and pulled out another handful of books, and I must have made some kind of sound when I caught sight of the book on top because Willard Scoggins, who had put the terry cloth book down and was moving on to another table, stopped and came back. "What have you got there?" he said. I set the other books down and opened the small black volume of sonnets.

"This is unbelievable," I said. "It's a collection of Elizabeth Barrett Browning—but *look* at it." And then I asked the same question he had. "Why would anyone get rid of something like this?" I closed the little book and ran my hand over the cover where *E. B. Browning* was stamped in gold on the front. On the spine were the words *The Poetical Works of Mrs. Browning*. I must have looked almost desperate as I clasped it to me and turned my eyes to his, forgetting for the moment about the broken blood vessel I didn't want anyone to see. I actually heard my voice quiver as I asked, "May I buy this one? I don't care how much it is. I want it."

Willard Scoggins' face bloomed with joy as we stared at each other. Then he laughed, raising his eyes to the ceiling and lifting his hands as if catching rain at the end of a drought. "Ah, someone who understands the value of a book!" he said. "Someone who knows that a man is never poor who has books." Then he took a step closer and whispered, "The book is yours for a dollar. Put it in your purse right now. Don't waste a single moment. Pay the dollar later."

Before he turned to leave, he leaned forward again and said, "You've seen the French film *Babette's Feast*, haven't you?" I shook my head no, and he said, "Oh, you have to. It's all about the exquisite power of art. We have it in our video collection." Then before I could even thank him, he was gone, disappearing up the basement stairs instead of waiting for the elevator.

"Well, what was that little *tête-à-tête* all about?" Dee-Dee, or whatever her name was, called from two or three tables down.

I just shrugged and turned to put my new book in my purse. And here's what was going through my mind. Never in a million years would I have expected somebody like Willard Scoggins to understand the "exquisite power of art." I knew, of course, that as a librarian he must love books, but I had known so many librarians who loved them only as merchandise to be cataloged, shelved, inventoried, and horded. One librarian I remember distinctly from my childhood in Burma, Georgia, always made me feel as though she begrudged me every book I ever checked out, as if she were positive she'd never see the book again and deeply regretted having to entrust it to the care of someone as irresponsible as a child.

But anyway, Willard Scoggins looked so ordinary, so unworldly, so blithely Unaware that his swift and generous response shocked me. There could be no mistaking the fact that he truly loved books. He clearly wasn't the man you'd expect him to be, judging from his brown polyester pants, short-sleeved white shirt, and short green necktie. Later I wrote him a letter to thank him for the book of sonnets and included five suggestions for volumes of poems to add to the library's collection. He wrote back and thanked *me* for my letter, and when I went back to the library a month or two later, all five books I had suggested were on the shelf.

And now here I am singing alto in Willard Scoggins' church choir. I know he doesn't remember me from the book sale incident, but someday I might tell him how well I remember him. I keep the little black book of Mrs. Browning's sonnets on a table in my living room, along with a small volume of Keats, Hawthorne's *Mosses from an Old Manse*, and an old copy of Eliot's *Silas Marner*.

They make a nice little collection, the kind you see set out just for looks. On the same table are a pewter candlestick, a bird's nest filled with miniature silk roses and ivy, and a scrimshaw letter opener. Nobody would ever guess from the artful little arrangement that I've read every word of those four books and still pick them up often just to feel them in my hands. May my grandchildren or my nieces and nephews who read this someday know the thrill of holding a book they love.

But the thing about Willard Scoggins is this. First, he looks like what I used to think every Christian looked like—not exactly the picture of contemporary fashion or sophisticated tastes, if you know what I mean. Not that I *still* think that. I'm learning that my cookie-cutter image of Christianity has been about as far off as assuming everybody in Texas wears a ten-gallon hat. But here's my point. Even if Willard is a little overweight and needs a wardrobe update, I like the man. I liked him at the library the first time I met him, long before I knew he went to church and called himself a "born-again believer."

I liked him because he looked past my exterior, my unsightly eye, right into my heart. And when a person does that, who cares if he's wearing brown knit pants that are a little too short? I'm not saying a person should *try* to look dumpy, but there's so much more to a person than what you see on the outside. You just never can tell for sure what people are really like. Looking at Willard's broad, open face, I never would have guessed he had an artist's soul.

And years ago, looking at Ken's handsome face and steady brown eyes on our wedding day and hearing him say "I do" when the minister asked if he promised to love and cherish me for the rest of his life, I never would have guessed that he would break his word and betray me. If there's one thing you learn going through life, it's that people surprise you at every turn. Sometimes the surprises are pleasant and sometimes they're not.

One Far Fierce Hour

15

Before I climbed into my car the night I ate pie at Margaret's house, she placed her hand on my shoulder and told me that she'd pray for me. I believed her. It never occurred to me to doubt whether she meant it. Everything about her, from the touch of her hand to the depth of her gaze to her long patience in hearing me out at the kitchen table, testified to her sincere concern. I may not have had an abundance of close friends in my lifetime, but I knew I had one now.

I forgot to record what my answer was to the question Margaret had asked me earlier in the kitchen: "Do you love your husband?" It wasn't an easy question to answer. Not that I didn't know the answer, but to say that I loved a man who obviously didn't love me anymore wounded my pride. I nodded my head, though, and whispered, "Yes, I think so."

If someone had asked me that question a year ago, I'm not sure what I would have answered. Probably yes, since it would have been the expected answer for a woman who had been married to the same husband for over a quarter of a century. A yes would have been the easiest answer, to prevent follow-up questions. If I had been required, however, to answer truthfully, straight from my heart—if there were some kind of clairvoyant gong, say, that would sound at any falsehood—I might have stalled and stammered and ended up saying, "Give me a little time to think about it."

So where does love go when it sinks to the bottom like that? And how does it so suddenly resurrect itself when your husband appears to be done with you? Thinking about all this makes love seem unstable and fickle, like a sprite playing hide-and-seek. If you love someone, it ought to be steady and constant. Love is supposed to last through thick and thin, for better or worse, all that. You're not supposed to need more time to think about whether you love someone.

Still, if the truth were known, I couldn't have declared promptly and confidently a year ago that I loved Ken. A year ago was a horrible time, though. I wasn't in my right mind a year ago when I was facing the loss of Travis.

Margaret walked with me out to the driveway. She closed the door of my car after I got in, and I rolled down the window to thank her again for the evening. She smiled and nodded, then said, "Keep reading your Bible, Elizabeth." And after I started the car, she said, "I believe the Old Testament Prophets would make good reading." I must have looked surprised because she added, "I know it must seem like a curious suggestion, but the Prophets have a great deal more to offer than the foretelling of doom." She laid a hand on my open window and leaned closer. "There are beautiful stories of grace to be found in the Prophets."

"Which ones?" I asked. I had skimmed through parts of Isaiah, Jeremiah, and Ezekiel, but they seemed an odd recommendation for someone whose husband had been unfaithful. The Book of Psalms would have seemed a better choice or one of Paul's encouraging epistles.

"Read some of the minor prophets," she said. "Read them straight through." She smiled. "Start with Hosea."

Have I mentioned yet how beautiful Margaret is? And when she smiles from somewhere very deep and private within her, she's so lovely you can hardly stand to look at her, yet you can't tear your eyes away, either. When I was a teenager, I would have scoffed at the idea of any woman Margaret's age being called beautiful, but I know a lot of things now that I didn't know back then. When I was a teenager, thirty seemed old, and I thought you might as well curl up and die after you turned forty.

I put the car in reverse and started backing up. "Okay, I'll give old Hosea a whirl," I said.

She waved and called, "We have a prayer service at church tomorrow night, you know. We could sit together."

I waved back noncommittally. I was going cautiously with the church business. Although I was attending the Sunday services more or less regularly now, I still didn't know what to make of the people. There were so many of them and so many different types. Sitting right in the middle of them all made me nervous, so I preferred to sit at the end of a row and slip out quickly.

It was odd, really. I wanted to participate, but not too much. I wanted to go to the services, but I didn't want to be cornered and barraged with greetings and questions. I wanted to sing in the choir, but I didn't want to engage in long, friendly chats after choir practice. I was polite as always, and I talked to Margaret and Thomas and to Barb Chewning every now and then, but to others I mostly just smiled and said things like "I'm fine, thank you."

And Hardy Biddle—of course I talked to him whenever the opportunity arose. I loved Hardy. He was the whole reason I had come to church the first time. I think about it now and am filled with wonder. If it hadn't been for a simple invitation from a teenage boy, I probably wouldn't be a Christian today. The first time I talked to him after my conversion I said to him, "Well, Hardy, you've got another star in your crown," referring to the song he had sung with the other three boys that Sunday in February. And he had studied me closely first to see if I meant what he hoped I did, then raised his hands like the folks on Channel 16 do and said, "Hey, I love it! I been havin' bad dreams about a starless crown! Welcome to the glory gang, Mrs. Landis!"

Aside from these few people, though, I didn't mingle much. I had attended one Wednesday night prayer meeting and had sat in amazement as church members rose to their feet and shared their requests publicly, some of them about very personal matters. I wondered what everybody would do if I stood and said, "Please pray for me. My husband is having an extramarital affair with a woman who has long hair and drives a blue Mazda." It would have taken a team of wild horses, though, to drag me to my feet to say anything at all during request time on Wednesday night. Some things were too private.

So anyway, I drive home from Margaret's that night, and I pull into the driveway and unlock the door and go inside. I stand completely still right inside the door for a full minute listening for worrisome sounds, which is something I never used to do. Then I lock the door behind me and walk through every room of the house and finally arrive at the master bedroom and go into my pink bathroom. I start running a tubful of hot water and then walk back through the house once more.

I turn on the light in Ken's study and stand in the doorway not even knowing what I'm looking for. He used to sit right here at the desk for hours every night after supper. While other men were watching the news on CNN or a game on ESPN, he would usually be back here writing music. Or sometimes he would have a band score spread open on the desk, and he would be conducting with his baton or marking something with a red pencil. He never even saw me walk by. The door would always be wide open, but it might as well have been locked and bolted. When he was in his study, Ken might as well have been in Outer Mongolia.

After my bath, I do start reading Hosea, very slowly. This is different stuff—heavy and symbolic, yet compact and powerful. It's a rich meal for late night, but I make it through three chapters. It appears that the prophet Hosea had some problems in his marriage, too, if I can take any of this literally. As I turn off my light a little later, I keep hearing the passage from Zechariah that Margaret read to me at the kitchen table. I know I'm mixing it up, the way you do when you're barely hanging onto consciousness, but the words that keep coming to me as I fall asleep are these: *"And I will save your tent and pour out my spirit of grace upon you."*

The next afternoon I've finished my day of subbing at the middle school. I haven't been out here to Berea Middle School for a long time. It has been a reasonably good day in the life of a substitute teacher. I had four classes of seventh graders, and the teacher's lesson plan said to "review prepositional phrases for fifteen minutes and discuss literature (G. K. Chesterton—pp. 302–310) for the remaining time." That was it.

I suppose some substitutes would have panicked at such sketchy instructions, but I knew my way around teachers' manuals well enough by now to feel sure I wouldn't have any trouble filling up a class period. In fact, I knew I could wing an English class if I got into a jam, but there was no need to do that. I used the teacher's free first-hour period to read the material for the literature portion of class. I wasn't too worried about the prepositional phrases part.

It was an older literature book they were using, and over the years I've generally found these to be the best. The story was an excerpt from Chesterton's *The Innocence of Father Brown*, which seemed a tad advanced for today's seventh graders. I wondered if they were supposed to have already read it, and if so, how many of them actually would have. And—here was the best part—there was a poem by Chesterton on the last page of the assignment. Oddly, in all my years of obsessing over poetry, I couldn't remember having read much of Chesterton's.

I could detail the way the lesson unfolded in each of the four classes, which, as anybody who teaches middle school knows, will be different every time the bell rings and a new class files in. Actually, "files in" is a joke. More like tumbles in or storms in or whirls in or piles in. Anyway, that's probably why the teacher left such sparse instructions for the substitute. She knew there was no way to map it all out for twelve- and thirteen-year-olds. You'd be wasting your time. Better just have a general idea of the war plan and save your energy for the battleground.

I managed to keep everybody marginally engaged in the lesson by starting off with a little contest in which I read a newspaper article as fast as I could, and the one who could write down the most prepositional phrases from the article got to pick something out of the prize sack I carry around with me sometimes when I sub. I know the prize sack sounds juvenile, but it works, believe me. I even use it with high schoolers on occasion, and never once has anybody turned down a package of M&M's or a Fruit Roll-up for winning some kind of competition.

In the contest the phrases had to be verbatim—no extra words or close approximations. One kid threw a little fit and pounded his fist on the desk when I told him I wouldn't count "in twenty years" because the article had said "in almost twenty years." "It's the same thing!" he shouted. Everybody looked at me to see how I would handle the fist pounder. You could feel something very delicate being weighed in the balance.

I stared at the boy for a full eight or ten seconds, which seems like forever in a classroom where everybody is holding his breath waiting to see if a teacher is up to the challenge, then I said slowly and quietly and very, very politely, "If I tell you I'll give you twenty dollars but then give you only fifteen, you might say it was unfair. And if your father grounded you for twenty days but let you off after fifteen, you might say he showed mercy. In either case, you wouldn't say 'twenty' and 'almost twenty' were the same thing. Five dollars less in your pocket or five bonus days of freedom do make a difference."

The trick is, you don't pause after you make your point, but you just pick right up and go on as if you've spent enough time on the delay already and don't mean to waste a second more. The boy who had spouted off still looked angry but slightly confused also. He probably didn't even understand a word of what I said, but he must have sensed that the rest of the class was on my side because he slouched down in his seat and didn't say anything else.

The story excerpt about Father Brown, the priest-detective, went okay in all four classes. They had read a Sherlock Holmes story the week before, and we compared the two sleuths, as suggested in the teacher's manual. I'll have to admit that I hurried through the story somewhat to get to the poem.

When I called their attention to the poem on page 310, I distinctly heard groans in each class and saw eyes start to glaze over. By seventh grade a kid has often formed the opinion that a poetry lesson is as far removed from real life as an Egyptian mummy and even deader. I don't blame this on the kids, but on the teachers. Of course, the teachers were probably victims themselves of an unimaginative teacher somewhere in their own past who either browbeat or sedated them with poetry.

But somehow I managed to salvage the end of each of the four class periods. Or, to give proper credit, the poem salvaged it. It was a charming little poem in ballad form. That is, it was written in quatrains rhymed *abcb* with an alternating four- and three-beat meter. Probably very few of the seventh graders at Berea Middle School could tell you today what ballad form is, even though I did take great pains to explain it that day, but I'd wager that every one of them could tell you the title of the poem we discussed that day: "The Donkey."

Oh, we had a lively twelve minutes with that poem! G. K. Chesterton wasn't any slouch of a poet, let me tell you. "The Donkey" made us all sit up and smile for the first three stanzas, but then a lot of the students quit smiling and looked puzzled after we read the last stanza. Me, I felt like doing something wildly out of character, such as galloping around the room swinging a lasso. I love that last stanza. A few students caught it, of course, and that's what made it so much fun.

The donkey is talking in the poem, you see, and he's describing how things were when he was born and what he looked like and sounded like, and it's all very witty. It even provoked a few sound effects from the students, which I overlooked. You can't make a big deal out of every little infraction when you're working with middle-school kids.

So you're going along enjoying this little monologue by the talking donkey when all of a sudden he turns on you in the last four lines and lets you know *which* donkey he is. Not just any old common barnyard donkey. When he tells you in the last line that he remembers his special hour, when there were palms laid at his feet, it dawns on you. This was the donkey that carried Jesus into Jerusalem on Palm Sunday!

Imagine—a poem with religious overtones in a public school literature book. Like I said, it was an older textbook. And I was the lucky teacher who got to be there that day, which was another example of being rewarded for saying yes to somebody's request. Or maybe it was all planned out by God "before the beginning of time," which is something Theodore Hawthorne at church likes to say. Maybe God planned exactly which days the regular teacher would be absent, then planned it so I'd be the one to get the principal's call. And even while I'm writing the words *maybe*, I'm scolding myself. Maybe? What am I talking about?

The donkey has a great line in the last stanza when he describes that crowning day of his life as "One far fierce hour and sweet." Who could say it better? I wish I could thank Mr. Chesterton personally for a splendid twelve minutes at the end of four different class periods in seventh-grade English at Berea Middle School. Who knows, maybe he'll be in heaven and I can someday.

And since it's April, the timing is perfect. Palm Sunday is coming up in only four days, and Easter Sunday is a week after that. So I ask the students if they know what each of those days celebrates in Christianity. In the last class of the day, a boy in the back row tells me he's a Jew and doesn't celebrate Easter, and I can't think of anything appropriate to say at the moment. "I'm sorry" comes to mind, but I know I shouldn't say that if I want to keep subbing in the public schools around here.

Somebody else in the back pipes up and says Easter is when the Easter bunny was born, and everybody laughs. Somebody offers that Palm Sunday is a special holiday in Florida. More laughter. Somebody else asks why Easter always comes on a different date. So I briefly explain the deal about the vernal equinox and the full moon, then ask again if anybody knows the meaning of Palm Sunday and Easter.

A girl who sits in front of the Jewish boy says, "Isn't Easter something about Jesus dying?" And before I can even nod, another boy, a redhead named Philip Biddle, raises his hand and says clearly, "Palm Sunday was the day Jesus rode into Jerusalem on a donkey and all the people cheered and called him king, and then a few days later they nailed him to a cross and he died, and three days later he came out of the tomb alive just like he'd said he would, and that's what Easter's about. It's the Day of Resurrection."

And then, as if right on cue, the bell rings. "Remember to read the next story for tomorrow," I say as they scramble to get their books together. On the way out the door, a big overgrown boy sticks a foot out and trips a kid half his size, and the little guy swings his backpack at him. "Ooh, he's so vicious!" says the big guy. "I almost felt a breeze."

From the back of the classroom I hear a girl squeal, "I lost my earring! Help me find it!"

Watching the seventh graders leave the classroom in various stages of disarray, I wonder again whose idea it was to have kids this age move from room to room for their classes. I see three pencils and a book on the floor, along with two jackets slung over the backs of chairs. "Take your stuff with you!" I call. "Does anybody know whose jackets those are?" A pale boy with a flaming crop of pimples turns back to claim one of them. Somebody teases him for wearing a jacket when it's so hot.

"Hey, thanks for speaking up," I say as Philip Biddle walks past me at the door. He looks to be in a hurry, but he stops long enough to smile at me and tell me the poem was cool. He has a slightly worried look, though, as if his mind is somewhere else.

The two of us know each other from church. Philip is Hardy Biddle's little brother. Hardy introduced us one Sunday out in the parking lot after church. "This here's my baby bro, Philip, aka Pip, aka Flip, aka Fill-er-up," he had said. And without missing a beat, Philip had said to me, "Oh, and you must be the teacher my brother Hardy the Har-Har told us about, except you're not nearly as fat and mean looking as he described you."

Hardy had encircled Philip's neck with one large hand. "That's about a C minus, Flip," he said, then explained to me in a confiding tone, "I'm trying to teach Pip the Squeak the finer points of humor, see, but he's a slow learner. Everything he says is so *formulaic*." He shook his head and clapped Philip on the back. "It's a hard job I've taken on, but somebody's gotta do it. Don't get discouraged, Flip, I'll keep working with you. You'll catch on sooner or later."

Another kid calls to Philip from the hallway now. "You playing today, Phil?"

"Yeah, I think so," he says, then adds, "I've gotta call my mom, though. I forgot my cleats." I watch him weave his way down the crowded hallway toward the school office.

When I get to the office to check out a few minutes later, Philip is using a telephone at the front counter. This is the one the kids are supposed to pay a quarter to use. Philip has the receiver to his ear but isn't saying anything. He's nibbling on his lip and frowning. There's the usual after-school tumult going on in the office, with kids and teachers going in and out and the phones ringing and the secretaries paging people over the intercom. I see a teacher escorting a boy into the principal's office, and the door closes firmly.

"Hurry up, I gotta use the phone," somebody calls to Philip. A small line of three or four has formed behind him.

He hangs up and covers his face with both hands, then runs them up through his hair. "She's not home," he groans to nobody in particular.

I walk over to him. "Can I help?" I say.

He looks up at me forlornly. "Nobody's home," he says again.

"What do you need?" I say.

"My cleats. I forgot 'em at home, and we've got a game in thirty minutes." He remembers something and brightens. "Maybe I can call my dad." Then he remembers something else. "Nah, that won't work. He's over in Spartanburg today."

"Can I help?" I ask again.

He looks hopeful. "I need my cleats from home. The coach won't let us play without 'em."

"I could give you a ride home," I say. "Can you get in the house?"

He nods excitedly. "I know where the key is."

"Let's go," I say, and we head for my car in the teachers' parking lot.

I start to worry even before we get into the car. I've met Philip's parents at church and have talked briefly with his mother a couple of times in the last month when she's been out on walks with Barb Chewning, but I wonder what they'd say about my giving Philip an unauthorized ride home. I worry about this all the way to their house on Brookside, which is only two streets away from my house on Windsor. From the little bit I know about her, Catherine Biddle isn't a woman I'd care to get on the wrong side of.

I ask myself what I would have thought about a substitute teacher giving Travis a ride home when he was in seventh grade. This makes me see all the more clearly that this isn't a good idea. I should have at least told someone in the office what I was going to do. What if I have a wreck and Philip gets injured? I'm not acting like a responsible adult, and I know it. I can see myself getting ushered into the principal's office when I get back. I can imagine the door shutting firmly.

Once we get to his house, Philip is out of my car and back in it within three minutes. "They were in the garage," he says, panting slightly. "I always keep 'em by the back door." He holds the cleats in his lap, both hands firmly clasped on top of them as if restraining a wiggly puppy. As I drive back to the school, he talks about first one thing and then another. The game, which starts in only twenty minutes now, is a makeup game against North Greenville Middle School. Philip hopes he gets to play center halfback, his favorite position, but last game the coach put him in as left wing because he has a good left foot. Not many of the seventh graders get to play the whole game, he says, but he's hoping he will today. One of the starting eighth-grade mid-fielders is out with a sprained ankle. Philip's brother Hardy plays striker for Berea High, he tells me, and he's scored seven goals already this season.

His dad never played soccer in school, he says. "They didn't even hardly know what it was down in Mississippi," he says. "He was real good in base-ball and football and basketball, though. One time he scored thirty-eight points."

"That must have been in basketball, huh?" I say, and he grins. His dad still plays racquetball and jogs, he tells me.

I ask about his aunt Della Boyd, and he says she mailed him a book about hummingbirds last week. She left her hummingbird feeder in Philip's care when she moved, he says, and she wants him to report to her as soon as the first one arrives. The book says they'll probably come to South Carolina sometime this month, so he's got the feeder filled with a mixture of water and sugar. "She's got herself a feeder, too," he says, "and we're going to see who gets the most birds." He sighs a little. "She lives in Yazoo City, Missis-sippi, now," he says, and I tell him that I got to know her a little bit before she left Berea.

Just two Wednesday nights ago, in fact—the night I attended—Della Boyd got up in prayer meeting a day or two before she was to leave for Mis-sissippi and told everybody that she finally understood the whole business of sin, confession, salvation, and eternal life, and she credited Hardy with finally making it clear to her. This is another thing they do on Wednesday nights at this church besides telling each other all about their troubles. They share praises—that's what they call it.

"Does anyone have a praise to share?" the pastor will say, and people start popping up to tell about all kinds of good things that have happened to them. These are never the result of chance or modern science or wise plan-ning or any kind of natural cause-effect relationship; they're always straight from God's hand.

This strikes me as a perfectly reasonable way for a Christian to live life, but I'm still working on the other side of it. Do the bad things come from God's hand, too? I keep hearing people at church give prayer requests and then say things like "God has taught me so much through this," which must mean they think this was all something God brought to their lives.

"Aunt Della bought me this before she left," Philip says, pushing up his sleeve to show me his watch.

"Wow, she gives nice gifts," I say. "I liked your aunt Della a lot."

He nods and rubs the face of his watch with his shirt cuff. "She's nice," he says. "I wish she was still here." He turns away to look out his window. I wish I could stop the car and give him a hug, but I'm pretty sure his parents wouldn't like that. I grip the steering wheel tighter and concentrate very hard on driving carefully. This is a sweet kid riding in the car with me, and I want to deliver him safely to the soccer field for his game.

We made it back to the school, and I decided to stay for the soccer game that afternoon. I didn't have anything better to do when I got home, and I suddenly wanted very much to watch a soccer game. I like soccer. For a team sport it's probably my favorite to watch, although baseball is a close second. Football is way down at the bottom of the list, and basketball and hockey are in the middle somewhere.

Soccer is such a smart, graceful sport when played right. Of course, I was fairly certain a game played by seventh- and eighth-graders wasn't going to be the prettiest sight in the world, but some hint of the sport's vast potential for beauty was bound to be there somewhere. If I was lucky, I might even get to see somebody make a goal, the kind where the ball is worked through the gaps in the defense and then kicked with enough power to bury itself in the back of the net and make it billow. There's nothing in the world of sports to compare with the sight of a soccer ball finding its mark. This will sound silly to anybody but a soccer lover, but there's a special kind of passion about the way the net receives the ball so silently yet so fully.

So I found a spot on the bleachers in among all the parents. These were the same kinds of bleachers I used to sit on when Travis played in the county league in seventh grade. His middle school didn't have a soccer team back then, but I signed him up every year from third grade on to play on a county team, and I took him to every game.

Twisters, Hurricanes, Raiders, Lightning, Mustangs—those were some of the teams Travis was on. I can close my eyes and imagine it's six, eight, ten years earlier and Travis is getting ready to play. He could have been great on the front line, but none of the coaches ever tried him there. They usually put him in as a fullback, and that was all right with him. He liked stopping goals more than trying to make them.

I don't see either one of Philip's parents. Most of the parents here are moms. Afternoon games don't make it easy for dads to come. I know from experience, though, that mothers can be every bit as cutthroat as fathers, so I'm in no way expecting a quiet low-key crowd in the bleachers. Some of the things I've heard come out of the mouths of moms at soccer games would curl your hair.

The game starts, and I see that Philip is playing left wing. Six boys stand along the sidelines with the coach, and you can see in every tense little muscle of their bodies that they're aching to get into the game. The woman sitting next to me looks glum. From the way she's squinting toward the sideline, anybody can tell her kid is one of those standing by the coach.

Philip's team is wearing bright yellow jerseys and black shorts, and the other team is decked out in royal blue. "Go, yellow, work the ball!" one of the few men in the crowd calls. His voice is reedy and resonant, and several people glance back at him. "You can do it, guys!" a woman with a high, sharp voice yells.

The Berea boys look smaller than the boys on the other team, and somebody behind me says, "How old are those other boys anyway?" I remember one game Travis played in where a parent on the opposing team demanded proof that our goalie wasn't older than he was supposed to be. Luckily the coach had photocopies of all the birth certificates to show the referee, but the game got off to a late start, and there were bad feelings between the two teams and all the parents because of it.

Philip's team might be smaller, but they appear to be better. The ball stays on their half of the field during most of the first fifteen minutes. Just as Philip receives a pass from a midfielder and sprints down the sideline toward the goal, I hear a woman yell, "Go, Philip! Take it all the way!" I look back and see her walking toward the field from the parking lot shading her eyes. It's Philip's mother, Catherine. She looks like a million dollars as usual. Catherine Biddle is one of those put-together types.

She stands apart from the bleachers, watching Philip take the ball in. I watch her watching him, and I know exactly how she's feeling. I see the way she leans forward, as if to help him out, and I know if I could see her eyes they would have that hungry, desperately hopeful look every mother has when she watches her child compete. I can feel the pounding of her heart and that tight feeling that something heavy is pressing on your chest. I know what's going through her mind, too. *Come on, Philip, baby, make a goal. You can do it, sweetheart, I know you can. Do it for your mother.*

How well I remember those days when nothing seemed more important than getting that ball into the net—or keeping it out if you were the mother of a fullback or goalie. Mothers of goalies have my deepest sympathy and admiration. I would be a nervous wreck today if Travis had been a goalie.

Mothers waiting and watching on the sidelines—if you could harness all that emotional energy and turn it into electricity, the light from Earth would illuminate outer space all the way to Pluto. And not just mothers of athletes. Think of all those mothers in history who have watched their boys go off to war or off to sea or off to climb mountains or off to build bridges or mine gold or explore continents. I heard once what Charles Lindbergh's mother said when her son started his epic flight across the Atlantic: "For the first time in my life, I realize that Columbus also had a mother." I've never forgotten that.

It's a warm April day on the soccer field. I close my eyes and almost forget that Travis is away at college now. It's easy to pretend that he's out on the field in front of me. I remember how I used to close my eyes exactly like this when things got too nerve-racking at a game, when the ball was perilously close to going in and the fullbacks were stumbling all over themselves trying to clear it. And games that ended with a shoot-out were the worst. I closed my eyes for every shot when that happened. You can always keep track of the score by the reaction of the other parents.

Philip crosses the ball beautifully, but the striker shanks it, and it goes twirling off away from the goal. A blue guy gets to it and sends it back down the field, but the yellow center halfback traps it and passes it again to Philip. He dribbles around a blue guy and sprints back toward their goal.

Catherine takes a step forward and yells, "Okay, now, do it again! Take it in! That's right, keep going!" Both hands are raised now to make a visor over her eyes. I know if someone were to come up behind her right this instant and say, "Who are you?" she would probably answer without even thinking, "I'm Philip's mother."

The Blood Flowing Back

16

On the way home from Philip's soccer game, I decided I wanted a barbecue sandwich from a place in Filbert called C. C.'s. It's the same barbecue place where Travis worked during his last year of high school. This is the kind of impulsive thing I had been doing more and more lately. Another night, for instance, while I was sitting at home in the den after the evening news went off, a sudden hankering to see *Bringing Up Baby* struck me, and I got up and drove to Nick's Flicks over in Derby, rented the video, and came home and watched it. I'm sure I was the only person in the world who ever cried while watching that movie. I kept remembering how much Ken had laughed when we first saw it together in college.

Another night I had a powerful urge to hear my brother's voice. I hadn't spoken with Greg in over two years, ever since he moved out to Wyoming, a shock from which my mother still hasn't recovered. Imagine this. A man teaches P.E. and coaches high school football in Georgia for twenty years, then decides one day to quit and move his family to a ranch in Wyoming. Knowing Greg, the only thing that surprised me was that he had stayed in Georgia so long doing the same thing. So I called him on the telephone one night and asked him to step outdoors and describe everything he could see from the front porch of his ranch house. And he did.

Another impulse. At the end of March sometime I had remembered a picture I drew back in eighth-grade art class in Burma, Georgia, of a Victorian house, and I had promptly decided to buy some art supplies and do some dabbling. At my age! All because of a picture I remembered painting thirty-five years ago. Who knows why these things pop into your mind, but it did.

I've always loved looking at art, but something had happened in junior high to make me feel for a little while as if I could actually do more than just look at it. The teacher, Mr. Bingham, wasn't the kind of man you'd expect to be teaching art. He looked more like a wrestler—muscular and frighteningly masculine. Nobody goofed off in art class, let me tell you. Mr. Bingham's voice was incredibly deep. If you were putting men in groups according to the parts they sang, there would be tenors, baritones, basses, and Mr. Bingham.

But I had loved him in spite of the fact that I was scared to death of him. I had painted the picture of the house with vivid colors of tempera paint—bright blues, oranges, yellows, greens—and the paper had rippled and buckled as its heavy load of paint dried. My father had pronounced it a masterpiece when I brought it home, but my mother had asked me whatever possessed me to make it so *gaudy*. Daddy took issue with her and declared the colors to be perfect. "It has such verve and vivacity," he had said, holding the picture out at arm's length. "It couldn't be any other way and be right." Daddy knew a thing or two about art in any medium. "It sings an aria," he had said. I've always remembered his exact words.

So anyway, this picture came to my mind, and I remembered how much I had enjoyed painting it. I had sat next to a girl in art class that year named Penny Peach, whose favorite subject to draw was food. The curious thing was, she was really skinny, which makes me wonder, looking back on it, if she had some kind of eating disorder, some obsession with food that allowed her only to look at it and dream about it, but not eat it. I wonder if Mr. Bingham ever suspected anything like that. But maybe drawing food was just a predisposition stemming from the fact that she had an edible last name. Penny never talked to anybody but just sat in class drawing these round, sumptuous fruits or golden loaves of bread or roasted turkeys with the legs sticking up and little foil caps on them. Whenever Mr. Bingham walked by, she would hunch over her picture and cover it up so he couldn't see it in progress.

But anyway, it was my own picture of the two-story gingerbread house that led to my impulsive action that day, but before that it was some zebras. It all started with zebras. Let me explain. You see, I had subbed at Derby High School that day—consumer math and economics—and on the way out that afternoon I had walked past the art room. Glancing in, I saw a huge mural of a zoo in progress, and a kid was just finishing up the zebras.

The remarkable thing about those zebras wasn't so much their lifelike size and careful proportion, although those were pretty amazing for a teen-aged artist. The main thing, though, was their color. Instead of white and black, the boy had painted the zebras turquoise and black. I stopped right in the doorway and stared. I couldn't help it. I wasn't staring because the color was all wrong; I was staring because it was exactly right. It was totally unpredictable yet totally right. That's the way good art always is, whether it's a painting or a poem or a piece of music or whatever. It surprises you, yet it seems inevitable. You can't imagine it any other way.

Standing in the doorway, I remembered then and there what my father had said all those years ago, and when the zebra artist turned around and saw me, I smiled and, before I realized what I was doing, said, "It couldn't be any other way and be right." The boy looked a little stunned, the same way I felt, but he did manage a mumbled thank-you before I turned and walked quickly down the hall. With every step I could hear my father's voice as he praised my Victorian house picture and clamped it onto the front of the refrigerator with two big daisy magnets.

As I pulled out of the parking lot a few minutes later, I wondered what had happened to that picture. Maybe my mother had thrown it away. She didn't like a lot of clutter, and she never had taken to that picture. "Let go and it'll grow on you, trust me," Daddy had told her, but it never had. She had moved it from the front to the side of the refrigerator within a few days. It troubled her that I would paint a house such *unnatural* colors, and I think she was worried that it revealed some deep psychological turmoil within the only one of her three children she thought was truly stable.

As I drove along slowly after leaving the high school, I remembered clearly the feeling of sitting in art class all those years ago and watching the house take shape as a pencil sketch first, and then I remembered the moment of excitement and power when I dipped my brush into the brightest blue I could find and laid it against the paper. So instead of turning in the direction of home, I drove straight to an art supply store in Greenville that afternoon and bought some paper and tempera paints and a couple of brushes.

I had no idea what I might try to draw, but the zebras had reminded me of something I had almost forgotten—that life still had a few nice surprises. Maybe the art supplies would just sit in the bag I brought them home in, but maybe someday I would have whatever it took to crawl out of my hole and try another painting. It had been a long, long time since I had drawn that picture in eighth grade, but something like that ought to be one of those things you can't lose the knack for, like riding a bicycle.

I've always loved the innovative use of color. Sometimes I catch people staring at the colors and textures of clothes I put together, such as when I wear my lime green Ellen Tracy silk jacket with a maroon denim skirt. I have never spent as much money on an article of clothing as I did on that lime jacket. I bought it a year ago, when I thought I was going crazy, as an act of defiance—against Ken or myself or Travis or life in general, I'm not sure which. I think I intended to shock Ken with the bill first and then take it back later for a refund. I didn't, though. I put the jacket on one day and fell in love with it. It's too bad expensive things have to fit so well and feel so good when you wear them. It only encourages you to buy more. Ken never said a thing about the receipt. I put it on his desk in his office, and the bill got paid without a word. I don't know if he ever even noticed I had a new jacket in a knock-your-eyes-out color. He never let on if he did.

I like muted colors, too—tans and grays and browns and creams and faithful old black and white. And pastels. And trusty, standard crayon colors. And jazzy tropical colors. And hybrid paint-store colors with goofy names like "harvest mist" or "calypso swing" or "pigeon breast" or "clay canyon." The point is to mix them all together, to touch the tip of your brush into different colors when you're putting an outfit together or decorating a room or painting a picture or doing needlework. Forget the whole concept of matching. Any color matches any other one if you do it right.

Which reminds me of the way Emily Dickinson approached rhyme. Did you ever notice how Emily Dickinson seemed to think any vowel sound rhymed with any other one? She used word pairs like *time* and *ran* as rhymes and *me* and *say*. Read her poems, and you'll see what I mean. *Ring* and *sun*, *wait* and *not*, *balls* and *fuse*—I could go on and on. They say she wore mostly white dresses, but with such an adventurous approach to rhyme, I'm not sure I believe that. Well, maybe she did wear white dresses, but I'll bet she wore bright red underwear. The kind of poetry she wrote, you just know she had to have had a daring streak. I can't imagine Emily Dickinson disapproving of wearing lime green and maroon together or some of my other color combinations like royal blue and orange or yellow and pink or red and dark brown.

That's one of the fundamentals of art in my opinion. You take things that normally don't go together and you create a context where they do. If I ever became a painter, that's what I'd do. I'd paint a green cat sitting in a purple tree, and somehow make it seem like they couldn't possibly be any other color.

So I start out talking about a barbecue sandwich, and now here I am painting purple trees. That's the way it goes. Everything's connected to everything else. So back to my sudden craving for a barbecue sandwich after Philip's soccer game. He made the goal, by the way, the one his mother was cheering for: "Take it in! That's right, keep going!" He drove it in with his left foot, right past the goalie.

As I drove to the barbecue place in Filbert, one of those talk shows was on the radio. I never used to listen to the radio, but ever since Ken left, I was doing that more and more. I guess I didn't like the silence in the car. Anyway, the person phoning into this talk show was asking the one who had all the answers—a medical doctor and family therapist all in one—why she thought her ninety-year-old mother was suddenly refusing to eat.

"She'll knock the spoon right out of my hand when I try to feed her!" the woman said.

"Does she say anything?" the therapist asked. They called her Dr. Vivian.

"Oh, you can't understand a word she's saying anymore," the woman said. "She just babbles like a baby or screams like she's throwing a tantrum. She's as healthy as a horse, though. She had a doctor's appointment a few weeks ago, and he said she's healthier than a lot of *fifty*-year-olds he's seen. She'll probably outlive all of us. But now here all of a sudden she stops eating! My sister thinks she might be acting out a death wish, but I'm wondering if she's got some kind of blockage that makes it hurt when she swallows."

They went on talking this way, Dr. Vivian asking questions and the exasperated daughter answering. Then Dr. Vivian says something curious. It's about zebras, which is funny since it was only a little while ago that I saw the turquoise-and-black zebras on the mural in the high-school art room.

"Let's make sure we're not looking for zebras" is what she says.

"Looking for zebras?" the caller asks.

"It's something an old doctor friend of mine used to say when I was in a private practice in Abilene," Dr. Vivian says. "Every time we'd be discussing unusual cases, this doctor would always say, 'Let's make sure we're not looking for zebras.' It meant make sure we're not stretching for some kind of rare condition when it might be something really simple. You always want to eliminate the obvious things first."

And do you know what? She starts asking the woman about her method of feeding her mother and finds out she's only recently started feeding her because a few days earlier her mother had tipped over a glass of orange juice and spilled oatmeal all down the front of her housecoat during breakfast. "That just did it," the woman says. "I knew she couldn't feed herself anymore, so I started doing it for her."

Well, it didn't take a ten-minute call to a syndicated radio talk-show doctor to figure that one out, I thought. That woman's mother was mad over the loss of her independence. That's why she was knocking the spoon away and screaming. Dr. Vivian enlightened the woman and then made some suggestions about how they could make it easier for her mother to keep feeding herself without spilling things.

"Think about it from her point of view," Dr. Vivian told the woman. "That's pretty good advice for any problem, by the way," she said. "If we can learn to look at things from the other person's angle, chances are we can solve most of our problems pretty easily." Something wiggled around in my memory. Who else had said something like that? Not that it was a new concept, of course. Maybe it had been Theodore Hawthorne at the Church of the Open Door. That would be something he might have said the week I attended the Wednesday night prayer service. Before prayer requests and praises he gave a short devotional on family life. He made it all sound so easy.

As Dr. Vivian was moving on to the next caller, I latched onto the memory. It hadn't been Theodore Hawthorne who said that, but Margaret Tuttle, and it had been weeks ago now, back in February when we were talking on the telephone one night. I had asked her about husbands and wives and happiness, and she had said something about learning to see through each other's eyes.

There was plenty I wanted to see through my *own* eyes, though. Ever since I can remember, I've wanted to have long-distance X-ray vision. I used to wish this all the time—that I could see anything I wanted to see at the exact moment I wanted to see it. As a kid on Christmas morning, for instance, I'd suddenly wish I could see Roy Rogers and Dale Evans opening their presents. Or during school I'd be suddenly struck with the desire to see what Captain Kangaroo was doing right that very minute. I'd wonder what kind of house he lived in when he wasn't on television and if he helped his kids with their homework. I used to wish I could see Jacqueline Kennedy at bedtime. Did she wear a nightgown, I wondered, or pajamas?

My mother used to get put out with me about this, I remember. Once over Christmas break in fifth grade I kept wondering what my teacher was doing. Mrs. Eden was a favorite teacher of mine, and I must have said twenty times a day, "I wonder where Mrs. Eden is right now" or "I wonder what she's doing" or "I wonder if she got any new clothes for Christmas." I thought nobody dressed as fine as Mrs. Eden, who was partial to the color blue. My mother finally got fed up and said, "Oh, stop it, Elizabeth! Mrs. Eden is probably lying drunk in a gutter somewhere!"

But right now I wished I could see inside the house of that old woman whose daughter had called Dr. Vivian for advice. It was close to suppertime now, so her daughter was probably getting her tray ready. I wished I could see that ninety-year-old woman lifting her own spoon to her mouth, concentrating to get it there safely and then chewing slowly before she tackled another bite. There would be something very satisfying about seeing an old woman eat her supper bite by bite, progressing at whatever rate of speed she wanted to go. And there shouldn't be anybody there prodding her to eat more of this or to try some of that or go faster or take bigger bites. There was no dignity in being prodded. She should be allowed to eat what and how and when she wanted to. Her ninety years surely had earned her that privilege.

And Ken. How many times in the past several weeks had I been seized with the desire to be able to see him and observe him *right then* without his knowing it. As I pulled into the drive-through window at C. C.'s Barbecue over in Filbert, I felt it again. I wished I could see what he was doing right then, right that very minute. I wondered if he was eating his supper or maybe sitting in his office at his computer or lying on a sofa watching the news or reading the paper or grading essays. Maybe he was playing his trumpet or writing out music or studying a band score. I wondered if he was with *her*.

I ordered my barbecue sandwich and then pulled around to the pickup window. The girl handed it to me in a sack and smiled. She had a choppy, lopsided haircut and one of those smiles where too much of a person's gums show. "That'll be $3.56," she said. She had a nice voice, though, and as she handed me the sack, I caught the sparkle of a diamond ring on her left hand. Isn't that the way it goes? A woman doesn't have to be much to look at for some man to go after her and court her and buy her a diamond ring and get her to the altar.

The Filbert *Nutshell* and the Berea *Bugler* are full of these stories when they print up all the weddings for the week and show the pictures of all the brides. Some of them say things like "The bride attended Berea High School and is currently employed at Kentucky Fried Chicken" or "The bride is a graduate of Southeast Cosmetology School and is employed at Earlene's Cut 'n Curl in Seneca." Which is okay—perfectly, wonderfully okay. My point is that for every kind of woman, there's a man pursuing her. Anybody can get married. The trick is to stay that way, and the real trick is to stay that way happily.

So I head home with my barbecue sandwich, and another urge hits me hard as I pull into the driveway fifteen minutes later. I go inside, pick up the telephone, and dial the number for Travis's dorm room. I suddenly want to see Travis, but since I can't see him, I want to hear his voice. It's partly due to seeing Philip Biddle's soccer game earlier today and seeing Philip's mother with that hungry look of hope on her face. It took me back to the days when Travis was Philip's age. How could those days have disappeared so fast? Sometimes I stand at my kitchen sink and watch the water swirl down the drain and think, "That's how long you get to have your children before they're swept away from you."

Ken suggested once that I try to keep my phone calls to Travis to a minimum. This was seven months ago or so, back in September, after Ken had loaded all of Travis's things into the car and taken our only son over a hundred miles away from home to live in a dormitory among hundreds of other boys who were far too young to be on their own and far too immature and unfocused to dedicate themselves to a course of study. I had stayed home that day. I would have no part in something so wrong. I can hardly remember anything about that day except how cold I felt even though it was still August. I do remember another thing. I saw the Piper College course catalog lying on Travis's desk as I walked past his room, and I remember picking it up, then ripping the pages out and throwing them into the trash can.

Travis had chosen his major by flipping through that college catalog one day. I watched the whole deliberation, which took all of about two minutes. This was a year ago after his application to Piper College had been sent in and he had received his letter of acceptance. They were asking him to declare a major.

"This sounds like a good major," he had said, running his finger down a page of the catalog. "I think I'll major in physical therapy." And that was that. I was in a daze as I watched him. Physical therapy? I could name a dozen things he was better suited for—music, literature, biology, for example. The fact that it was altogether the wrong major for him troubled me mildly, but not nearly so much as the fact that he was acting so independent. And *acting* is exactly what it was. If there was anything Travis wasn't, it was independent.

His choice of physical therapy was no doubt based on an experience he'd had in ninth grade. He had hurt his knee in a soccer game after another player had mistaken it for the ball. It swelled up like a balloon, and he had had to be on crutches for a couple of days, then go to physical therapy for several weeks. The physical therapist happened to be a very, very nice guy—tall and skinny and very funny. After the first visit, Travis couldn't wait for those appointments. After each one I'd hear him in his bedroom imitating Champ's voice, which was a sprightly tenor full of Deep South inflections. That was the therapist's name—Champ Trotter.

I knew the number of mothers who had sent their sons off to college was enormous, and I knew I couldn't be the only one who saw this step as grossly premature. I knew all about boys' maturity rates lagging behind girls', but I also knew that out of all the immature high-school senior boys applying for college, Travis had to be at the low end of them all. I mean, the kid had never even had a *date*. He still had a stuffed bear in his bedroom.

Ken and I had exchanged words more than once about the whole idea of college for Travis. My argument had been practical. A year of work after high school would give him time to catch up, to be ready to take on the responsibilities of college, to decide what he wanted to study. Why, some boys worked two or three years before going to college, I pointed out, and those were the boys who afterward were ready to settle down and concentrate on their schoolwork and not waste their parents' hard-earned money floundering around academically and changing their majors five or six times.

Ken hadn't even half listened to me. His mind was made up. "He needs to learn to stand on his own two feet," he had said to me. Although it was probably just a coincidence that he was staring straight at *my* feet when he said this, he spoke in a tone of voice that clearly implied that I was somehow to blame for Travis's immaturity. This had been a repeated theme throughout the entire eighteen years of Travis's life, of course. Ken was always telling me I did too much for Travis, either saying it outright or giving me these looks or sighing and walking out of the room.

Standing there facing Ken a year ago, I remember thinking at the time how easy it was to understand women who were driven to madness by their husbands, who one day laid their hands on a gun and committed a violent act. I remember feeling my insides twist into knots when I realized there was absolutely nothing I could say that would change Ken's mind. It's as good as done, I thought. Travis will be carted off to college in the fall as sure as water is wet. And he was.

Men are always so certain that their opinions are the only ones that matter. And to make it worse, Travis sided with Ken this time. Of all the times! All his life he had been mine, had stuck right beside me, had been my ally, had been easy to talk into agreeing with me, had confided in me as much as boys confide in anybody, had depended on me, had appeared to enjoy my company, sometimes unnaturally so, like the times he'd call out "Hi, Mom!" in a crowded hallway when I happened to be substituting at his school or the times he'd actually come and sit with me in the cafeteria. And what was worse, I saw that nobody even teased him about eating lunch with his mother. I'm not even sure anybody noticed. It was as if everybody expected Travis Landis to do an uncool thing like that.

But anyway, when it counted most, Travis turned around and took Ken's side. He actually wanted to go away to college, he said. I had stared at him with my mouth hanging open. Here he was, the same kid I'd had to bribe to go to camp for the first time in his life the summer before eighth grade, who never would have been on a soccer team if I hadn't signed him up and physically escorted him to the field, who was too shy to ask questions in class, who got sick at overnight parties, who was so nervous the first day of his first job that he lost his breakfast, who delayed learning to drive because he loved his bicycle, who tried to talk us into letting him stay home when his senior class went to Washington, D.C., whose date on prom night was the television—this kid was saying, "I want to go away to college."

And when I asked him why, he had shrugged his shoulders and said, "I don't know, I just do." All through his life I had had to push him to do new things, and now all of a sudden he decides he wants to do this huge new thing all by himself a hundred miles from home. Ken took it as a long-overdue sign that Travis was beginning to grow up, but I took it far too personally. I know that. I felt the way you'd feel if you had sacrificed your life savings to give somebody something really precious and expensive and then that person later said to you, "Oh, that? I never did really like it, so I gave it away."

In sending Travis to Piper College, I felt that I was losing the only thing that was truly mine, and I took it hard. I couldn't see how I would even want to get up in the morning after he left home. I doubted that I could ever be happy again. I started letting things go around the house, and some days I would find myself still wearing my nightgown in the middle of the afternoon. I'd forget all about going to the grocery store and suddenly discover we were completely out of something important, like milk or bread or toothpaste.

All that was last spring, and that was when Ken had started looking at houses. We moved that summer as Travis got ready to leave home. Normally

I like nice things for the house—good furniture, accessories, artwork—but I couldn't summon the energy to care about any of it. All I knew was that my son was leaving home and things would never again be the same.

So you can imagine what it was like in those first months after he left. I acted like people do when someone they love dies. I literally made myself sick. I quit cleaning the house and cooking meals. What was the point? A little dust never hurt anybody, and I couldn't stand the thought of food. How could you cook for just two people anyway? I would notice all of a sudden that the laundry hamper was stuffed full and clothes were hanging out the top.

And as I listen now to the first ring of the telephone in Travis's dorm room many miles away, I stare up at the ceiling of my kitchen. Suddenly a sharp picture comes to my mind with amazing clarity. It's from a poem I read a good ten years ago, a poem by Michael Blumenthal titled simply "A Marriage." It was in the anthology by Helen Vendler called *Poems, Poets, Poetry*, and I can see the book now—a red-and-white soft-cover. I still have it on a shelf somewhere. It's the sight of my ceiling, of course, that gives rise to the memory of the poem, for the central analogy in "A Marriage" concerns a ceiling.

I remember thinking ten years ago what a simple yet perfectly *right* parallel Michael Blumenthal had hit upon when he created his metaphor of two people helping each other hold up a ceiling so the house won't fall down. I made no connection between the poem and my own marriage at the time, but I liked the metaphor nevertheless and thought it appropriate for the idea of marriage in general.

The phone in Travis's room was still ringing, and I was still seeing those two people in the poem taking turns holding up the ceiling, each one relieving the other so he could take his arms down for a while and feel "the blood flowing back." I'm not sure how many times I let the phone ring as I stood there staring at the ceiling, but I know it was a lot. Any other day I would have hung up after five or six rings, but the poem had taken me out of the present long enough for someone on the other end to finally get curious or awake or annoyed enough to answer, "Hello!"

It was hard to read the tone. Not angry really, but somewhat challenging, as if saying this better be a call worth answering. It wasn't exactly what you'd call cordial. You wouldn't train the receptionist of your business to answer the phone this way. But it wasn't Travis, I could tell that. I wondered for just a moment how Travis sounded when his roommate's mother called and he answered the phone. More polite than this, I hoped.

"Is Travis there?" I asked.

"Hey, is this Stacy?" the voice asked, sounding a little friendlier.

Now, here was an interesting question. Why would somebody named Stacy be calling Travis? Surely it wasn't a girl. I tried to think if I had ever known any boys named Stacy. "No, this is his mother," I said.

The voice changed, got slightly higher in pitch. "Oh, well, he's . . . uh, he's around here somewhere if you . . . want me to check." It was the tense tone kids use when they're caught in a situation where they have to be polite but want to hurry up about it. It was the tone that said, "I've got far more important things to do." He was silently begging me to say, "No, no, don't bother. I'll try again some other time."

So I'm sure he had to have been disappointed when I said instead, "Yes, thanks, I'd like to talk with him, please, if you can round him up. I'd really appreciate it."

I heard a sigh and then, "Well, I'm not sure . . ." No doubt he was chastising himself for his hasty overture of courtesy.

"If you can just check around, that would be great," I said. "I'll wait." What was a dollar or two of waiting time? I thought. I was finding that money didn't mean nearly as much to me as it used to.

"Okay, hold on," the voice said after another sigh, and I heard a clunk, then something that must have been the opening of a door, then a muffled bellow, "Hey, Landis! You out here anywhere? Anybody seen Landis?" I heard a slam, which must have been the door closing because everything got very quiet. For all I knew, Travis's roommate might have just decided to leave the dorm and go hang out somewhere fun, far away from telephones where parents were always trying to track you down.

My eyes traveled from the ceiling down toward the kitchen door leading into the carport. Don't ask me why, but another picture came to my mind— not from a poem this time but from real life. I could see Ken walking into the house through that door back in August, returning from his trip to Piper College to deliver Travis. I was standing at the sink filling a juice glass with water, which I then began to sip slowly.

He closed the door behind him but didn't say anything. I could tell he was just standing there watching me from across the kitchen. I didn't want to look at him, but I finally turned and glanced in his direction more out of curiosity than anything. What I felt at that moment was so close to hatred that I don't know what to call it. He had taken Travis away and had come back without him. I didn't see how I could ever let him near me again.

He was standing just inside the door holding two things. One was a bouquet of flowers—a wild mixture of colors. I knew it was just a lucky guess on his part. There was no way he could have known I would prefer something like that far more than your standard dozen red roses. He wasn't the type to bring me flowers, so it was a subject we never discussed. I had never told him I thought a bouquet of roses, all alike, all predictably perfect, wasn't my idea of beautiful.

The other thing he was holding was a book. He started walking toward me then, holding the book out as a peace offering. He was smart enough to try his strongest defense first. I wanted to slap it out of his hands, but my curiosity got the best of me, and I made the mistake of looking down at the cover. It was a paperback copy of *Nine Gates*, Jane Hirshfield's essays on poetry. This was another lucky guess on his part. He had probably popped into a bookstore on his way home and said to a salesclerk, "Quick, I need something under ten dollars about poetry."

He would have no way of knowing I didn't already have this book, but I didn't. I knew about it, though, had seen an advertisement for it recently, and I knew that I wanted to read anything Jane Hirshfield had to say about poetry. It was a horrible struggle I went through at that moment, wanting to refuse the book, to stomp my foot and say, "No! You can't pacify me this easily!" I wanted to grab it from him and throw it back at him as hard as I could. But I knew if I grabbed it from him, I'd never be able to let go of it, certainly not to throw. You don't throw books, especially books about poetry.

All was still quiet on the other end of the phone. I realized I could stand here waiting for Travis for hours. I could imagine a charge for twenty dollars showing up on my next phone bill.

I couldn't remember putting Ken's flowers in water, but the next day they were in a vase on the kitchen table. Ken must have done it because the vase was perfectly centered on the table. I stopped once and took a good long look at them. They were really spectacular, a splash of color against the dark paneling in the kitchen. There must have been a dozen different kinds of flowers and a tall, wispy kind of greenery artfully arranged among them. I remember reaching out my hand and almost touching a bright fuchsia flower, but I drew back at the last minute.

Over the phone I heard the muted thump of footsteps running down a faraway corridor, and suddenly Travis was there. "Hey, Mom, what's up?" He was panting, but I knew it was from the running, not from eagerness to talk to me. For a moment I couldn't get the sight of Ken out of my mind, holding that bouquet of flowers in one hand and the book in the other. Maybe I would try painting those flowers with my new art supplies. I'd make it a closeup view, not one of those cool, arm's-length still-life pictures. This painting would be impressionistic, with thick dabs of brilliant color all over the paper. It would be a riot of emotion. In spite of the bright colors, though, it would be an angry picture.

On the other end Travis spoke again. "Mom, you there?"

In Shadowy Silent Distance

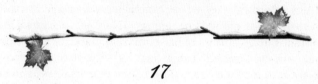

17

Let me tell you how I lived my life with the knowledge that my husband loved another woman. This is grossly simplified and probably not at all the way others live through such an experience, but this is how it was for me. I think the pain hit me hardest in the morning when I first woke up and at night when I was by myself. During the daytime hours I could usually throw myself into something else and stand apart from the ugly, gaping wound of my marriage, but by nighttime I was back with it again, bleeding and limping. It was no way to live, compartmentalizing my day like that, but that's how I tried to do it.

No. Reading that paragraph over, I realize I'm not coming anywhere close to getting it right. This is because it was never the same from day to day. The daytime hours were full of land mines, too. I'd see or hear something that reminded me of Ken and what we used to have, and I'd feel like my heart had been hacked in pieces and scattered abroad like bad seed. Then maybe at night I might open my Bible and read something like the passage I stumbled across one night in the fourth chapter of Acts, and the darkness would lift a little.

Here's what I read that night. Peter and John had been persecuted for preaching the gospel, then grilled by the Sanhedrin, then ordered not to preach anymore, then finally released. They immediately went to the other Christians and reported all that had happened to them, and during this talk somebody pointed out that they were only being treated as Jesus Christ had been treated. But that's not what hit me. It was the fact that they acknowledged *God* to be the one who decided beforehand that Jesus was to be abused by everybody—Herod, Pilate, Gentiles, Jews, the whole world. "For to do whatsoever *thy hand and thy counsel* determined before to be done." That's exactly what it says.

I admit it—I was still wrestling off and on with the question of why my life had suddenly grown so much more difficult when I supposedly had God on my side now. It kept coming back like an especially pernicious weed, cropping up again whenever I mowed it down. I knew I wasn't the only person who had ever wondered about this, and I felt it was a fair question so I didn't feel guilty about it. I was a new Christian and wasn't wise yet to Satan's crafty use of doubt.

But here's what happened. Every time I opened my Bible with this question troubling me—*every single time*—I would find something like that passage in Acts 4. So there was only one conclusion to draw, and I kept drawing it over and over: God did allow bad things to come into people's lives.

Of course, I had to follow the line of thought to its conclusion. The mistreatment of Jesus ultimately had a good end. Therefore, bad things *could* turn out good, or at least they could have some kind of positive outcome not evident at first glance. It took a lot of faith, I decided, to be a Christian every minute of every day, to reject the temptation to curse God and despair when life took a turn for the worse. I wanted to *see* the reason for my present trial, to understand why God had allowed it, to be offered some kind of hope that life wasn't as bad as it felt. But God withheld such enlightenment from me.

My decision, then, centered on whether I was going to trust in a God who didn't let me in on the big master plan but permitted me to suffer in ignorance. And I decided that this question led to another bigger one. Was God really powerful enough to trust? I truly believed he was stronger than the forces of Satan, that he could turn the tide of evil with a single command as easily as he created light in Genesis 1. But was I willing to trust him to bring something bad into my life in order to bring about his own good purposes? Would he really follow through, or might he get distracted with the rest of the world's problems and forget he had left me stranded high and dry?

I kept thinking it through. I'd go over and over it. Jesus' suffering had brought about good for *other* people. So sometimes, I reasoned, bad things that happened to a Christian might turn out to benefit others rather than himself. This required not only trust but also selflessness to be able to say, "All right, God, you can let this happen to me if it will do something good for someone else." Could it be, I wondered, that my losing Ken's love would in some way help somebody else? I'll be honest—it was hard to be interested in helping anybody else. Oh, I had heard all about the J-O-Y principle by now—Jesus first, others next, and yourself last—and though I agreed with it in theory, practice was another matter.

But I kept coming back to this: If I believed in God's omnipotence and his love for me, I had to believe he knew what he was allowing to happen to me. I tried to keep clinging to this even on the days when the dam burst and my feelings swept over me, which was most days.

Maybe all of this sounds very cerebral. Maybe people who are suffering aren't supposed to think so much. This is the way my mind worked, though. It had to make sense up to a point. Of course, plenty of times my feelings clouded my thinking, but it helped having a friend like Margaret, who would tow me out of the ditch and direct me back to the road. Many times she was the one who suggested certain passages of Scripture for me to read.

What would I have done without Margaret? It surprised me to think of how many people's *names* I knew when I really didn't know *them* at all. I tried to do some thinking about why I had opened up to so few people in my lifetime. I never assumed people would be interested in me. Other people's abilities always seemed worthier than mine. Everyone else was a lot more fun than I was.

This may sound strange, but even with my good grades in school, I never stopped thinking they were somehow a stroke of luck, that I really wasn't as smart as people thought I was. It wouldn't have surprised me a bit if the principal in high school had called me in one day and told me I wouldn't be delivering the salutatorian's speech at graduation after all, that they had discovered all my grades had somehow gotten mixed up with somebody else's and I was really number 438 in our class of 500 instead of number 2.

And later in college, if the dean had announced at the end of my senior year that due to a huge programming error, the computers had been recording all C's as A's during the entire past four years, I would have said to myself, "Well, I suspected all along I was just a C student." This is something I picked up from my mother, I suppose.

But all that aside, Margaret became my friend. Not that we saw each other or even talked by phone every day. Sometimes three or four days went by without any communication, but she was always there, faithfully waiting for me whenever I needed to talk. Often she would call me at just the right time, as if God had told her, "Pick up the phone and call Elizabeth. She needs you." And I got the idea that Margaret herself didn't have an abundance of close friends, so in many ways we were alike.

It was Margaret, by the way, who suggested I write all this down. "It will help you gain perspective," she told me. She spoke from experience, she said, for she had written an account of a watershed of her own. In fact, hers grew to be the length of a full-fledged novel, though it was a true story, of course, and as she put it, "Wonder of wonders, my husband's niece, through some fortunate connections she had with a publishing house, managed to get my story in print."

It was no wonder to me, though, for I have read the book she wrote. And though I just *might* know a little more about poetry than Margaret does, you'd never guess it to hear us talk or to compare our writing. My words don't sing as Margaret's do, and I have no hopes of getting my story published. It halts along on clubfeet compared to hers. But she was right to advise me to commit my thoughts to paper, broken and clouded as they are. Writing things down forces you to step away from them and look at all the angles.

But back to the phone call I made to Travis at his dorm. We talked briefly in general terms—"How are you doing?" "Oh, fine," and that sort of thing—and then I asked him casually, "So who's Stacy?"

He didn't answer right away but made sounds as if chewing on something crunchy. I heard what sounded like the snap of a pop-can tab and then several quick, slurpy inhalations, as if preventing an overflow. At length he asked, "Who said anything about Stacy?"

"Whoever it was who answered the phone," I said.

"Oh, *him*—that was Gus. Don't pay any attention to Gus. He's not even *awake* half the time."

I dropped it, but I felt a great distance between us, more than just the miles that separated his dorm from our house. And this distance wasn't closing. It was getting wider and wider. I should have felt hopeful, of course. If Stacy was a girl Travis was interested in, this should be the cause of great rejoicing. So why didn't I feel happy?

Travis's spring break was coming up over Easter, and we talked a little about that. His father had already called him, I learned, and had given him permission to go to Myrtle Beach with "some guys." This took me completely by surprise. I didn't even know Ken and Travis had telephone conversations. I had assumed all along that Travis would be coming home. I had been wondering, in fact, how I should explain his father's absence from home that week. I couldn't decide if I should go ahead and tell him the truth or wait until he came home in the summer.

"Didn't Dad tell you about the beach?" Travis asked. "Didn't you hear us talking on the phone that night?" It was clear that Ken hadn't said a word to him about our living arrangements.

I said no. "Who are these other guys?" I asked.

"Just guys from the dorm. One of them's in my biology class. Dad remembers his parents from the Groovy Age." That was what Travis always called our high school and college days. He thought *groovy* was the funniest word he'd ever heard in his life. "Tell me you're kidding, Mom," he used to say to me, holding his sides in mock hilarity. "Tell me you didn't really use that word in normal conversations." And I'd fire back, "As if anybody your age would know what a normal conversation was."

I hadn't realized until now how much I was counting on Travis coming home for Easter. Ever since February I had been planning our first talk during spring break. I was going to take him out to eat over at Juno's in Greenville. It was one of his favorite places, although most of the customers were over sixty. Or maybe it was *because* most of the customers were over sixty that he liked it so much. The place is a hole in the wall with mismatched tables and chairs, dusty light fixtures, missing ceiling tiles, and a hand-printed sign over the door that says, *YAWL COME BACK*. And people do, believe me. It's a regular mecca for senior citizens.

Travis used to sit there with very bright eyes, taking it all in as he ate his heaping plateful of catfish, country ham, fried chicken, macaroni and cheese, okra, collard greens, crowder peas, and so forth. It's that kind of food. He liked to overhear what the people were saying at the other tables and would often repeat entire conversations at home, complete with all the local dialect: "I told Violet, I said, 'Ain't no way Skeet's gonna have them thangs planted 'fore Labor Day, so your hopes is doomed to be dashed, honey.'" Travis had a gift for mimicry.

So while other kids his age were hanging out at a pizza place or the sandwich shop over next to the Diamond Movie House, my son was eating down-home cooking at an old-folks' restaurant. There had been a time when I had resisted going to Juno's because it seemed so unnatural for Travis to like it so much, but I had slowly given in over the years. The staff all knew us by name now.

I had so much to tell him that just wouldn't work over the phone. He had no idea yet that my whole view of life had been turned around since my first visit to the Church of the Open Door two months ago, just as he had no idea that Ken had left home. I kept meaning to write him, but every time I'd start to, I'd put it off. Same with Jennifer. I hadn't told her yet either. Not because I was ashamed of my salvation, not at all. It was just too hard to summarize two big things like those in a few sentences. How do you go about saying to your children, "Your father loves another woman, and I'm a born-again Christian now"?

I know Travis heard the disappointment in my voice, but I hung up before I could start crying. I could probably have made him feel guilty. I knew how to do that, and he was the kind of kid it usually worked on. I could probably have gotten him to feel so bad he would change his plans to go to the beach and come home after all. But I don't know, maybe I *couldn't* do that anymore. Maybe my power over him was completely gone. I knew I wasn't ready yet to find out. As I hung up, my thoughts were running in every direction. I knew Travis was growing up, and though it was something I wanted, it was also something I didn't want. Any mother can understand that.

My barbecue sandwich was cold now, and I wasn't hungry anymore, but I nibbled around the edges of it anyway as I sat at the kitchen table staring at the phone and thinking. To know that Travis was actually making plans with friends for the first time in his whole life should have been something to celebrate, but the idea of him partying on the beach for a week wasn't. My heart told me nothing good would come out of that. But who could blame him for accepting such an invitation? Aside from a general "Be a good boy" kind of teaching, I had given him no solid reason to object to such a use of spring break. Being the kind of kid he was, he'd never been in on any kind of wild partying, but what was to keep him from it now that he was on his own?

I went to bed early that night but didn't sleep much. I had an awful picture in my head of Travis with a can of beer in one hand and a marijuana joint in the other. No, I was stuck in the Groovy Age. Marijuana was probably passé. It was other stuff now. Crack, coke, other names I didn't even know. I kept thinking of how I had failed to equip my children for life. All my hours of doing all the right things as a concerned mother seemed so useless now, like a little bit of powder on a tired old face.

Speaking of which, a few days after talking with Travis—the day before Easter actually—I looked into the mirror and saw clearly that I had let myself go. Part of me suggested that it was easy to see why Ken would stray to more pleasant fields, and another part snapped back quickly, "Don't let him off the hook with such a trite old excuse." I thought of the thin, homely face of my former neighbor, Polly Seacrest, and I could hear her husband Morris saying to her, "Hey, beautiful, come here and give me some sugar." Plenty of men with decidedly nongorgeous wives are faithful husbands.

I had been passably pretty in years past, but I couldn't fool anybody now into thinking I had lived anything less than my almost-fifty years. To young people, of course, this seems ancient. For example, I was subbing recently in a writing class—one of the new offerings at Filbert High School. Expository and Creative Composition was the actual title of the course, and it was supposed to be an English elective for advanced placement juniors and seniors. They were assigned to write all kinds of things—business letters, arguments, comparisons, and descriptions on the expository side and stories, poems, and plays on the creative side.

One student had written a story that he volunteered to read aloud the day I was there. He was obviously very proud of it and eager for praise. It started out with a scene in which the protagonist, a burger flipper, had to wait on an elderly customer whose hands trembled, whose voice quivered, whose legs were barely able to support him even with the aid of a cane, and whose hair, in the student's own words, was "like a thin white cobweb." The old man, of course, couldn't decipher the menu board, and the protagonist had to recite practically every item and its price very slowly at top volume before the customer feebly croaked out his order of a small hot dog and a cup of water. Naturally, the scene elicited laughter from the rest of the class.

The story proceeded to another customer, the construction-worker boor who groused about everything from the size of the cups to the length of the wait for his special-order burger. The entire story was simply a series of episodes featuring stereotypically difficult customers, no doubt inspired by the writer's after-school job at Burger King. I couldn't be too hard on the student, though, since the following bit of advice was printed in gigantic letters over the chalkboard in this teacher's classroom: *WRITE ABOUT WHAT YOU KNOW!* The kid was simply writing from the little bit of experience that he had.

During the class discussion that followed, someone mentioned the first customer and told the writer she thought he had done a really awesome job of describing the old man. Out of curiosity, I asked the students just how old they imagined the old man to be, and the writer himself thought a moment, then answered, "At least fifty." And he wasn't trying to be funny! Kids can be so stupid. "You'll be there before you can turn around twice," I wanted to tell them. But things like that don't mean anything to kids. They have to find out for themselves. And they do eventually. I'd like to have a conversation with this young writer thirty years from now. Or maybe twenty years. If he's smart, he might have caught on by then.

That same day I was looking through this same teacher's ungraded papers, and I saw a paper another student had written that caught my attention. It was an argument with the thesis "People should not be allowed to drive past the age of sixty." I wanted to find out who this kid was so I could follow him and run him off the road into a concrete culvert. Or I'd put him in a roomful of senior citizens and let him read his paper aloud to them, then watch him try to get out alive.

So the day before Easter I decide I need to spruce myself up, as my mother likes to say. It had been a hard day, with my mind returning over and over to the picture of Travis riding to Myrtle Beach with a carload of college guys all bent on debauchery. I look in the mirror that afternoon and say out loud, "Haircut—you need a haircut." This gave me a project, something to take up my mind. Even the best haircut, though, can't disguise the buildup of years on a person's face. I knew I wasn't any match for the youngster I imagined Ken had fallen for.

These days I found myself thinking a lot about getting old. Remember, I was still living every day with the knowledge that a woman with cancer had died in the same bedroom where I slept at night, had bathed in my pink bathtub, had walked down my hallway, had laid her hand on the same light switch, had swept my front steps, had planted a garden in my backyard. And I was still passing the casket store almost every day or so, too. What's more, the proprietor of the store had recently decided to prop all the lids of the caskets *open*, probably to display all the options for linings. It was creepy, though. You half expected to see someone rise up and wave.

Old age is sneaky. First you're young, and then all of a sudden without warning you're old, or else getting there really fast. The picture I see is that of a young girl preening in front of her mirror while old age in the shape of a grizzled old man watches her from a dark corner. He's rubbing his hands together and murmuring to himself, "I'll have her, that I will, and soon, too," and she's totally oblivious to him. There's a poem called "Piazza Piece" by John Crowe Ransom about this. Everybody should read it.

I think often, too, of Thomas Hardy's poem "The Convergence of the Twain" and how the *Titanic* was cruising along so confidently, all sleek and young and luxurious, totally unaware of the iceberg that grew "in shadowy silent distance." That distance closes quickly, mile by mile, until the fatal collision, and the contest between ship and iceberg is a short one. So is the contest between a woman and time. Time's foot is heavy in its "heedless stroll over brow and breast and hand"—that's from another poem, one called "At Cape Bojeador" by Dorothy Richardson.

So it's Saturday, the day before Easter Sunday, and I do something else impulsive. First I try calling Theresa Dillman across the street. Just last week I saw her in her front yard cutting Macon's hair as he sat in a kitchen chair under a dogwood tree with a dish towel draped around his neck. It made perfect sense after I thought about it. Outdoors like that, they wouldn't have to sweep up all the loose hair from the floor. I'm hoping maybe she'll give me a haircut even though I don't know if she'd do it. Maybe she was just experimenting on Macon. Maybe she had never cut anybody's hair before that. I don't get any answer at her house, however, so I imagine she's off somewhere with Macon. Maybe she's with him in his apartment above the mattress store, helping him pack up to move in with her.

It's three in the afternoon, but I feel myself getting more determined about the haircut instead of giving up. I look up the number for Dottie's Be-Beautiful Style Shoppe out on Highway 11. Dottie Puckett goes to the Church of the Open Door and has run a beauty shop in her home for as long as I can remember. I never knew her before I started going to church, but I've passed her house hundreds of times and have seen the beauty shop sign by her mailbox. I'm sure people joke about the color of her house, but I admire it. It reminds me of my picture in eighth-grade art class. Who says a house can't be aqua blue?

So the color of her house has nothing to do with why I've never gone there for a haircut, or why I've always driven all the way to Greenville for my haircuts. The real reason has to do with the name of the shop. Would you trust your hair to anyone who would name her place the Be-Beautiful Style Shoppe? There's no chance in the world anyone like that could be Aware. That's what I'd always thought before I met Dottie Puckett or heard anybody talk about what kind of hair stylist she was. I assumed all she knew how to do was give tight perms and blue rinses.

Dottie answers the phone herself, and I apologize for calling at the last minute like this and tell her I'm sure she doesn't have time to work me in this afternoon for a haircut and that it's okay if she doesn't because it's not really all that important and . . . and then she interrupts me and tells me she did have a cancellation phoned in earlier today and if I can come at four-thirty, she'll be glad to put me down.

So that's how it came about that I was seated in Dottie Puckett's black vinyl swivel chair on the Saturday afternoon before Easter when I ran up against Eldeen Rafferty, the likes of whom you've probably never in your entire life observed at close range, maybe not even from a distance. Afterward, I felt as if I had been standing too close to a cannon when it was fired.

Though I have a fertile imagination, I could never have dreamed up such a person as Eldeen. You know those articles in *Reader's Digest* called "My Most Unforgettable Character"? Take them all, every single one of them, and stack them up against Eldeen Rafferty, and the whole lot will be so insubstantial by comparison that you could blow them away like a little bit of dust off a tabletop.

This wasn't my first encounter with her, of course, since I'd seen her at church regularly and also at the March meeting of Margaret's poetry club several weeks ago. That night, however, I had come late and left early, so I didn't get the full impact. She was sitting on the other side of the room also, so the cannonball whizzed over my head instead of passing right through me as it did here in Dottie's beauty shop, where she was up close and personal, as they say—at one point less than twelve inches away from me as she aimed her finger at me and spoke in her great, megaphone-like voice.

Eldeen wasn't there for an appointment herself, but she had come with her daughter, Jewel Scoggins, who plays the piano at church and is married to the choir director and librarian, Willard Scoggins. The most conspicuous thing about Jewel is that she's pregnant, which is a word my mother would frown at if she heard it coming out of my mouth. She always taught Juliet and me to say "expecting" since, in her opinion, "that *other* word is something only trashy people say."

So anyway, Jewel Scoggins is going to have a baby, which is especially noteworthy since she's in her late forties, somewhere around my own age. I try to imagine being pregnant right now, and I can't decide why I suddenly feel as if something has got me by the throat. Is it because I'd like to be or because I know it's impossible? I try to imagine calling Ken up and saying, "Hey there, Ken, boy, have I got some news for you. Are you sitting down?" I wouldn't be the first woman to use that trick to try to get her man back, but in my case Ken would know it was only a trick. It takes two to make a baby, and if I had lost several fingers in a meat slicer, I could still count the number of times on one hand that Ken and I had been that physically close in over a year.

"April is the cruellest month," according to T. S. Eliot in *The Wasteland*. He's got a good point, too. April presents you with beauty everywhere you look, but it doesn't erase all the heavy December memories crowding your mind. It seems mean for April to dazzle you with lovely sights when everything else about your life is anything but lovely. And you know all that April loveliness is really only a dream anyway, that it will all vanish as it has countless other times. And in the end you'll be left again with what comes after—sweaty summer, sad autumn, and cold, ugly winter.

Last April, a year ago, as the azaleas were in full bloom and birds were building their nests, I tumbled down a long steep hill and landed at the bottom a total wreck. With the knowledge that I would be losing Travis in a few short months, I retreated from life. I had been retreating from Ken for years but was still somewhere on the same continent with him. After last April came and went, however, we were on opposite sides of the world. It's an amazing fact that a husband and wife can sleep in the same bed night after night, yet he can be at the North Pole and she can be at the South. Both places are mighty cold, you know.

And of course, when *this* April rolled around, I wasn't even sleeping in the same bed with Ken anymore, not even in the same house. So I get to walk through my yard and watch the whole world turn green and put forth buds and leaves, and I get to smell the lilac bush Dorothy Sherman planted in our backyard many years ago when it was her garden and gaze in silent awe at the iris bed that has come to life. I have no idea what all the varieties are called, but that iris bed is a spectacle. It's not a group of ladies sitting prim and proper at an afternoon tea party. It's a square-dancing troupe with red petticoats and glittery shoes.

There are purple irises so dark they're only a whisper from black and others that are pure white or champagne pink or canary yellow. And that's only scratching the surface. There's one with a royal purple center and white outer petals, another that's deep maroon and gold, and others the colors of fruit—peach, plum, blueberry, and pineapple. I get to stand and look at all of this and then go inside to an empty house. Oh yes, T. S. Eliot knew a thing or two about April.

So anyway, Dottie is just finishing up with Jewel Scoggins when I arrive for my appointment, and Eldeen is stationed on the sofa, which is upholstered in the most unbecoming fabric you could imagine, the color and texture of a burlap potato sack, a color my mother would admire, however, because it would hide the dirt. In fact, she'd probably approve of the texture, too, since it would last four or five lifetimes. Practicality is one of my mother's strong points.

I sat down on the other end of the sofa, grateful to be wearing slacks so the fabric wouldn't leave scratch marks on my legs. Eldeen was wearing a bright pink tent of a dress and large black sandals with white socks. She fixed her eyes on me as Dottie introduced us from across the room. And smiled. The smile has to be in a separate sentence, you see, because of the fact that it was such a peculiar smile. Her whole face was stretched into something that resembled one of those rubbery, wrinkled Halloween masks.

It was one of the most painful things to look at, yet fascinating, too. I could imagine young children shrieking with terror when she smiled at them.

You could almost have thought she was making a face at you, but it was a smile, clearly. She nodded at me the whole time Dottie was talking and made noises deep in her throat, like the purring of a very large cat. When Dottie was done, Eldeen scooted over on the sofa so she could take my hand in both of hers. "I been wantin' to get a chance to welcome you to our church fellowship ever since I first laid eyes on you," she said to me. I yielded my hand without delay since, number one, she had taken me completely by surprise, and number two, it was clear that she meant to have it whether I submitted or she had to take it by force.

"The first time you was at church," she went on, "I said to Jewel, I said, 'I sure want to greet that visiting lady who's settin' over there on the other side,' didn't I say that, Jewel? But the crowd pressed in after the amen, and I couldn't begin to get through the thick of it, with folks a-stumblin' all over theirself to get out into the aisles, so I just been bidin' my time waitin' for my opportunity, and here it's come a-rap-tap-tappin' at my door, like that old blackbird in that poem I read in Joe Leonard's English book by that same feller who wrote all them scary stories about people being sealed up and buried in wine cellars and one-eyed black cats and masquerade balls where Old Mr. Death comes all dressed up in party garb and what have you. Joe Leonard's my grandson, and he takes some of the most *interesting* subjects in school. I like to read his books when he's not studying them."

She paused and clasped my hand tighter. "But anyway, like I was saying about my opportunity finally a-comin', usually it does work thataway, you know, if a body can only hold out, but I get so antsy a-waitin' for them poky old opportunities to come along I can hardly stand it! Sometimes I have to prod 'em along!" She lifted her eyes to the ceiling and closed them for a brief interval. "Thank you, dear Jesus," she said right out loud, "for seeing fit to bring Elizabeth right here and plump her practically in my lap so's we could have us a proper meeting."

She opened her eyes again. "I hated to *beller* 'cross the sanctuary," she said, "besides which, you couldn't of heard me in all that hubbub, but I sure have had the urge to, I'll tell you what! After Brother Hawthorne pronounces the benediction, you just scooch outa church faster'n I can get my old legs to start ambulatin'! I said to Margaret one day, I said, 'Margaret, tell that new little lady friend of yours to stay put in her pew after the service so's I can get through the throng to talk to her,' but she must not of remembered."

I was beginning to realize that the term "brief chat" was probably a foreign concept to Eldeen. "And then last month," she went on, "when the Women Well-Versed met over at Geneva Fowler's house, I was so hopin' to have my chance, but no sirree, it wasn't meant to be. I no more'n turned around and you had up and gone—pffft!—just *gone* like a monkey up a tree.

How glad I am, oh, how happy and glad I am that I decided to come along today to visit with Dottie while she gave Jewel a shampoo and set. This is just the Lord's way of tellin' me, 'Eldeen, you better get up and get out amongst folks as long as you got breath in your body!' "

By now she was just getting warmed up, let me tell you, and in the minutes that followed I actually began feeling a little dizzy even though I was sitting down. It wasn't until later that I asked myself this question: Is Eldeen immensely, incomparably Unaware, or could she be deceptively Aware, operating on a whole different plateau of Awareness than I ever dreamed of?

I was already suspecting by now that my categories were far too broad and simple. Maybe there were people who were Aware yet unaware that they were Aware. Now there was an interesting possibility. And what about the Unawares? Could there be people who were Unaware yet *aware* that they were Unaware? There had to be other huge dimensions of Awareness and Unawareness to accommodate somebody like Eldeen. She scrambled things up considerably. I'm remembering now what she said to me right before Jewel managed to get her off the sofa and guide her out the door.

"You got you a husband and children?" she asked me from the door.

I told her I did.

"And are they born-again believers?" she asked.

I told her no.

"Then I'll pray for 'em!" she all but shouted. "I'll bring 'em before the holy throne of God and beg him to bring them to the mercy seat."

I thanked her.

"What's their names?" she demanded.

I told her.

"I'm gonna start today," she said. "Right this very day I'm addin' Ken and Travis and Jennifer to my prayer book, and I'm not gonna let go of prayin' till they come to Jesus, all three of them." She started rummaging in her purse and pulled out a crumpled piece of paper and a pencil. "Here, Jewel, write 'em down, will you? Ken and Travis and Jennifer." She looked back at me and said, "I got arthritis and can't hardly read my own writing." Then for some reason, she narrowed her eyes at me and asked, "Is your husband livin' with you?"

I could have lied, but I didn't. I was sure Margaret hadn't told her, but somehow it didn't matter to me if she had. People were beginning to find out, I was sure of that. Someone in the teachers' lounge at one of the schools just this past week had given me a look that had pity written all over it. Small towns like Derby and Filbert and Berea don't keep secrets well. I was surprised it had taken this long.

"No, he isn't," I said.

She shook off Jewel's hand and waddled over to the black swivel chair where I was now seated. She pointed her finger right at me and bent forward. "I'm gonna pray that you and him will get your marriage patched up. No, not just patched up, but *healed* like new! The Lord Jesus can do it, too! And I know he *will*, for it's not glorifyin' to his precious name that a sacred and holy union should be busted up by Satan and all his evil emissaries!"

She leaned in even closer. "And then after God sends your husband back to you, I'm gonna pray that he'll be drawn to the fold by your good works and shinin' light at home. That's the way it happens, you know, Elizabeth. They say a wife might be the only Bible her ungodly husband will read, and by the bright beam of her testimony at home she can woo him and win him to the Savior's arms."

Well, I was worn out by the time she left, let me tell you, but I heard her voice for days and days afterward. "No, not just patched up, but *healed* like new!" she had said.

PART THREE:

Go and catch a falling star,

Get with child a mandrake root,

Tell me where all past years are,

Or who cleft the devil's foot.

....

JOHN DONNE

With Low Sounds by the Shore

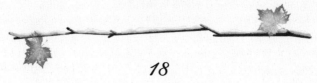

18

It used to make me mad that with four brothers and sisters Ken was the one who got stuck with doing everything for his mother. The plain truth is that two grown men and two grown women made conscious decisions to throw off all responsibility for their own mother, leaving their big brother holding the bag.

I suppose James, John, Sue, and Mary couldn't help being warped in one way or another from the ordeal of living under their father's very large and very heavy thumb, and as they wiggled out from under it, one by one they took off for cities far removed from South Carolina—Seattle, St. Louis, Albuquerque, and Bakersfield, California. No more small-town life for any of them, no more of the Southeast, and for sure no more family visits. If I had to bet on it, I'd say the four of them have seen the inside of a good many psychotherapists' offices. No, I'd better retract that bet, because if they're anything like Ken, they'd never in a million years admit they had any problems. Denial flows like a strong current through the Landis bloodline.

As far as I know, none of them to this day keep in touch or ever see each other at holidays. They scattered like buckshot fired from their daddy's rifle, like the wreckage of a plane that ends up all over kingdom come, like fallout after a nuclear explosion. James and John both married, but I guess Sue and Mary hadn't been much impressed with marriage in general after observing their mother's short end of the matrimonial stick, and they both opted for the single life. One of them is a realtor and the other one is a piano teacher, both graduates of Piper College, of course.

The only thing I know about James is that he and his wife own a Mexican restaurant in Albuquerque and have no children, whereas John is a mechanic for Boeing in Seattle and has three daughters. Which means that Travis is the only male grandchild to carry on the Landis family name. Lucky Travis, who gets to drag Schuyler Landis's revered surname around for the rest of his life.

So the chicken who roosted closest to home got to look after the mother hen once his brothers and sisters had all flown the coop one by one. Mary did call her mother every now and then, and Sue sent her a fruitcake and a tin of assorted chocolates every Christmas, but James and John didn't even do that much. Silence was the name of their game, and they were very good at it. I bet their wives know a thing or two about silence, too.

It's all a matter of transfer, I suppose. Christine was a dutiful mother, and I don't doubt for a second that she loved all five of her children deeply, but maybe she couldn't show it to all five at once. Maybe the younger four transferred their negative feelings for their father to their mother. Sometimes the innocent are guilty by association, you know. Maybe they thought Christine should have stood up to their father more on their behalf, and because she didn't, they saw her as a partner in his tyranny. I don't know any of this as a fact. I'm just guessing.

Anyway, I'm not in any position to be judging the way other people handle family conflicts, being the closed-up type myself. The only reason I ever blew up at Ken on occasion was that I knew he wouldn't answer back. There's great freedom in knowing you won't be called on to defend anything you say. If Ken had been like his father, I never would have had the nerve to unleash my words on him. And of course, when I finally saw that my words made absolutely no difference anyway, I fell back into what came most naturally—that is, I retreated into my own world. This withdrawal has comprised the longest and most recent stage of my married life.

How Ken escaped being emotionally ruined by his father is a great mystery to me. The oldest child generally bears the brunt of a father's oppression, from what I've heard, but somehow Ken weathered his childhood. He learned early the run-for-cover and keep-it-all-inside technique. When I hold up my gentle and good father next to Schuyler Landis, I know my childhood was one long sunny spring picnic in the country compared to Ken's.

So two people who bottled things up inside, except for brief private uncorkings by one of them, got married and were naïve enough to think they'd live happily ever after. When Ken and I started dating regularly in college, Laurie used to shake her head and tell me it was all wrong, that I needed to marry somebody loud, adventurous, and intellectually mediocre, a "let-it-all-hang-out" kind of guy so our kids would have some kind of balance. "Poor kids," she'd say. "Two brains whose tongues the cat got for parents is going to be a real drag." Laurie didn't have a clue what the term *misplaced modifier* meant. She'd sum up these little speeches with a singsongy "BORing!" and head out the door to go rock climbing with some guy who wore a bandanna and ponytail or rode a unicycle to classes or spoke Swahili or what have you.

I tried, I really did, to fill up our home when we were first married. I wore myself out thinking up things to talk about, but a lot of times it just felt artificial. It didn't work. I could talk the livelong day, and it wouldn't make any difference. But I've already gone into all this. Ken wasn't going to turn into Mr. Ready Communicator when he'd been the Silent One all his life.

Before I was married, I had always thought I'd lie in bed at night with the lights off and carry on long intimate conversations with my husband. This was a dream of mine from the time I was old enough to think about getting married. I thought I'd tell my husband everything—reveal my deepest secrets, admit my disappointments, share my hopes for the future. It wasn't a question I thought to ask Ken before we married: "Will you talk with me into the night?"

I guess I thought all husbands and wives naturally did this. I had grown up hearing my parents do it. Their bedroom was next to mine, and I can still remember hearing the murmur of their voices long after their light was off. They talked a lot during the day, too, though. I guess I should have known people were basically the same at night as they were during the day. Ken didn't talk much during the day, so why did I expect him to at night? The things we expect before marriage are funny. And sad, too.

Once when I was twelve or thirteen, I came into the kitchen behind my parents. It was on a Saturday during the summer, I remember, and we had eaten a big breakfast of bacon and eggs before loading the car for a three-day trip to Savannah. A lot of families wouldn't have bothered with such a breakfast before leaving for vacation, but that's the way we always did it. Mother always packed sandwiches for lunch, too, so we wouldn't have to waste time and money stopping to eat.

Anyway, on this particular day my parents were standing at the sink with their backs to me. Mother was scrubbing the skillet with an S.O.S. pad, and Daddy was standing behind her and a little to the side with one arm resting lightly on her shoulder. He had on plaid Bermuda shorts and sandals with socks. He was leaning down as she talked, but I could hear what she said quite clearly. She was crying as she said it. "I *knew* I would start my period today. I just *knew* it! It's so *irritating*! And now I'm going to feel like a big fat beached whale the whole time we're there!"

Daddy nibbled at her neck and said something I couldn't hear because I was backing out of the kitchen by now. I hurried back to my bedroom and closed my door softly. What a great marvel it was to me to discover that my mother would actually say words like those to my father. I felt as if I had learned something very grown-up, and I'm sure an expectation was planted that day. When I was a married woman, I would talk about private things like that with my husband. That's what married couples did, I thought. It made me wonder, too, what kinds of things my parents talked about at night in bed. If my mother would say something like that in broad daylight in the kitchen, there was no telling what they spoke of in the dark.

Things didn't turn out that way for me, of course. At first I thought maybe it would just take some time for Ken to warm up to these kinds of shared confidences about very personal things, but it never happened. He acted embarrassed about the silliest things. He wouldn't even go down certain aisles in the grocery store, and once when an anchorman on the six o'clock news announced, "A new study on PMS after this word from our sponsors," Ken blushed bright red and fell all over himself trying to find the remote to change the channel. If somebody walked up to him today and said the word *menopause*, he would turn around and run.

When Jennifer was born, he felt light-headed in the delivery room and had to leave. Conveniently, he didn't even have to put in an appearance the next time around because Travis came two weeks early while Ken was out of town at a summer band directors' workshop out West. He supposedly tried to get a flight home but couldn't make it in time. I always suspected he hadn't tried very hard. By the time he got home, the worst parts were over, except for breast-feeding, which always embarrassed him. Yes, this was a married man who acted this way. I'm not inventing one word of it.

These are the things I think about—Ken's siblings, Christine, my parents, Ken's hang-ups—after I come home from Dottie's Be-Beautiful Style Shoppe with my new short haircut. Here's how it all starts, and yes, I know I'm going backwards here, but it's my story and I get to do that. There's a wonderful sense of liberty in knowing I don't have to follow anybody's rules about telling things in order. If I were testifying in a court of law about a criminal act I had witnessed, I'd drive them all crazy—judge, lawyers, jury, everybody. They'd have to make charts to figure out the sequence of events.

But I'm not in a court of law. I'm sitting on my own sofa in the den with the newspaper—two of them actually. Our subscription to the Greenville *News* ran out back in March, and I threw away the renewal notice. The weekly copies of the Filbert *Nutshell* continue to arrive every Wednesday, however, and the Derby *Daily* every Friday. No one around here seems to think it the least bit odd that the Derby *Daily* isn't published daily. I think maybe that was the plan in the beginning, but somewhere along the line they dropped the plan and kept the name.

Anyway, the Filbert *Nutshell* and Derby *Daily* are far more interesting papers than the Greenville *News*, which has gotten so cosmopolitan that it's not much fun to read anymore. The front page of the *Nutshell* always features a column called "Out of Commission," which lists residents who have recently had surgery or been hospitalized. "Dorothea Yonkers is showing improvement following back surgery on April 5," you might read, or "Tommy Sharp had his appendix removed on the 7th and was able to go back to school on Monday." I don't know many of these people, since I don't live in Filbert, but I love reading about them.

And the pictures on the front page! They're priceless. The Derby *Daily* has the best ones. I run across a lot of names in the Derby paper of people I used to know when we lived there. The picture I'm looking at now, for example, shows an eighth-grader at Derby Middle School named Chris Corkle receiving a trophy for winning the county geography bee on the question "La Pérouse Strait is between the island of Sakhalin and what country?" The answer was Japan, and he had even specified the northernmost Japanese island of Hokkaido in his answer and informed everybody to boot that Sakhalin was part of Russia. I remember Chris Corkle from the times I've subbed at Derby Middle.

Right next to the geography-bee picture is the column called "Sheriff's Report," in which all the arrests and accidents for the past week are listed. So you see Chris Corkle smiling with his shiny trophy, and then you shift your eyes over two inches and see a picture of Ralph Armstrong's 1977 Ford pickup smashed into a mailbox on the corner of Graybill and Filo. Ralph Armstrong used to help Morris Seacrest from time to time on remodeling jobs.

Down near the bottom of the front page is another picture of the oldest member of the Derby Methodist Assembly, ninety-eight-year-old Rosetta Fay Verdin, holding the youngest member, two-month-old Alexis Maria Presley, at the church's seventy-fifth anniversary, and the caption goes on to say, "Rosetta shed tears of joy when little Alexis was placed in her arms. 'You never get over the thrill of holding new life,' Rosetta said as onlookers also wiped their eyes." You would never find anything like this in a big-city newspaper.

And remarkably, you'll see poems in these two papers from time to time. I found out from Margaret that they are to be laid to the credit of a contributing editor named Joan Dunlop, who happens to be Margaret's niece by marriage, the same one who helped her get her book published. I've met Joan twice—once at the poetry meeting I attended back in March and again at church, when she visited one Sunday with her husband, Virgil, who teaches at Berea Middle School. I had seen him at Berea Middle but never met him until our introduction at church. The world is a small place, especially in this part of the Southeast. The same people are always looping back around in a different role it seems.

"Oh yes," Virgil Dunlop said when Margaret introduced us. "You subbed for my friend Bruce's science classes one day, and the kids all wanted you back the next day. They asked Bruce why he couldn't stay sick longer." I knew he was stretching it, but I smiled anyway. Virgil and Joan attended another church over in Filbert, one closer to where they live, they told me, but occasionally they liked to visit Margaret and Thomas's church and "after Margaret twists our arms really hard, we usually give in and accept her invitation for dinner," Virgil said.

Anyway, Joan Dunlop is employed by both the *Daily* and the *Nutshell* to cover regional arts, I learned from Margaret, and she often slips in a poem or two as fillers. Not cheap stuff either. Once it was Louise Glück's "Wild Iris," for instance, and another time Tess Gallagher's "Black Silk." The poems, of course, are one of the main reasons I keep subscribing to both papers. The other parts are entertaining, but the poems are nourishing.

Inside the Derby *Daily* is a favorite column of mine called "Twenty-Five Years Ago This Week," where you'll read fascinating tidbits from the *Daily* archives of a quarter-century ago, such as "Becky Belle Winslow was installed as a Rainbow Girl in a ceremony at the Derby Civic Club" or "Jimmy Hornaday turned ten on April 10 and brought treats to school for his classmates" or "Mr. and Mrs. Cleo Fetters are visiting the latter's mother for a week before moving to Oklahoma." I had just smiled over the announcement that "Carla Olson is the only tenth grader with a perfect score in grammar on the spring achievement test" when my eye caught the next item. "Christine Landis from Newton visited her new granddaughter, Jennifer Gail Landis, last week. Jennifer's proud parents are Ken and Elizabeth Landis."

So once again it comes back to Christine. The circle goes round and round, and when it stops, Christine is always there. I think about that visit of hers twenty-five years ago. Though I'd like to forget them all, each one of her visits has stamped itself into my mind, which is the way it usually goes. The things you most want to forget are the things you can't.

Jennifer was six months old by the time Christine came to see her for the first time, and I was ready for her to leave the minute she stepped inside the nursery and said very sweetly, "Oh, are you using disposable diapers instead of cloth ones?" Thankfully she didn't stay but two days since Schuyler had said she couldn't leave before Thursday and had to be home for the weekend.

Ken adored his mother, have I said that? Unlike his brothers and sisters, he never once mixed up his feelings for her with those for his father. I'll never know the unabridged story of Life with Schuyler Landis, of course, but I think Ken and Christine held each other up through each battle. There were no open counterattacks, but they were in silent cahoots through the whole thing. During those years, they hunkered in the same foxhole, and after Schuyler left, they saw each other as veterans of the same war, having been wounded in a thousand ways but in the end alive and honorably discharged. Old army buddies.

Christine could get Ken to talk all right. Often I learned things about him from overhearing his side of their phone conversations. That's how I found out he was wanting to switch from teaching in the high school to the middle school, for example, and I heard him tell her about the job offer from Harwood College before he even told me. I first heard about the piece he had been commissioned to write for the South Carolina All-State Band when he told her about it over the phone. I heard him tell her they had offered him three thousand dollars for it, but he couldn't help wondering what they'd pay somebody like Alfred Reed for an original grade-six band composition. "Not that I think I'm in Alfred Reed's league," he had told her, "but three thousand is chicken feed when you consider all the work."

But strangely, it really wasn't the talking that bothered me most. It was the times when she visited and I saw them together, just sitting quietly and contentedly in each other's presence like an old married couple, as if they didn't need to talk to be communicating. Somehow their happy silence was far louder than their actual conversations. I hated every minute I had to spend in her presence and always imagined myself far, far away.

It was a curious poem to cling to, but whenever I was around Christine, I used to recite "The Lake Isle of Innisfree." I once considered William Butler Yeats the finest poet who had ever lived, and for a long time I thought "Sailing to Byzantium" was the one and only perfect poem in the English language. I've broadened my view considerably since then, even though I still think he's a mighty fine poet. Anyway, he somehow took me worlds away from Christine.

So I would flee to the Lake Isle of Innisfree, and in reciting the lines over and over, I could block out Christine's presence. By the time I got to the "lake water lapping with low sounds by the shore," the words were more than words. All those different vowel sounds, the liquid consonants and hushed sibilants, the lulling rhythm *became* the lake itself, and on it I was floating away to a peaceful island far beyond the messy business of mothers-in-law. It's a mysterious thing to me even now how that particular poem always had such a soothing effect on me in spite of its clear implication at the end that Innisfree is ultimately unattainable. It's all a dream. It's a hunger that will never be fed. It worked for me, though. That poem was an ointment to my soul.

If there were an Innisfree where life was reduced to its simplest components of shelter and food in lovely and carefree aloneness, I would have paid any amount to get there during Christine's visits. As it was, I could only recite the poem and try to hang on until she left. I was grateful to Schuyler at such times that he would yank back on her leash after two or three days and demand that she come home. When he finally abandoned her, however, she would often come for a week or ten days. "The Lake Isle of Innisfree" got a real workout during those visits.

I can't help wondering now if we ever could have become friends if I had tried even a little bit. I wonder if we could have sat and talked for hours as she and Ken did, if we could have helped each other through rough times, could have exchanged understanding looks across the room.

After her emancipation from Schuyler, Ken would sometimes visit his mother on the way to or from a judging or conducting event. Not that

Charleston was on the way to anyplace, but that's how he always put it: "I'll go by Mother's on my way back from Sumter," he'd say.

Christine's last phone call comes back to me often. "Tell Ken to give me a call, will you, Elizabeth dear?" I hear those words in my sleep sometimes, and for sure I hear them during my waking hours. It was five years ago during an ice storm in January. Ken was driving home from a band clinic in Charlotte, where he had been a guest conductor at a two-day event involving eight private high schools in North Carolina. Christine called at ten o'clock that night before he made it home.

It was a Saturday night, like this one I realize now, only four or five hours later. There was a new moon that night, so the sky was pitch-black. Under the streetlight near our house, though, the world shone like glass. I imagined I could feel things all around me contracting and splintering with the ice. Travis and I were home watching a movie we had gotten at the library— *Swiss Family Robinson*—and hoping the power didn't go off. I had the flashlight and candles laid out just in case. In the movie the girl had just shown up on the Robinsons' island pretending to be a boy when the telephone rang. I thought it might be Ken, saying he had decided to stop at a motel along the way instead of trying to make it home.

I answered and heard Christine's voice instead of Ken's. I thought at first that we had a bad connection, but I soon realized she was just talking softly. She sighed when she heard my voice on the other end, and she kept sighing faintly after every sentence or two. Christine wasn't above appealing for sympathy in this way. I had heard her put on what I called her bedridden voice more than once. She started off making small talk the way she usually did whenever she got stuck talking to me on the phone. I didn't have a whole lot of patience with her right now, however, and I told her as soon as I could that Ken wasn't home.

She caught her breath a little at that, and after a pause she asked where he was. "Well, didn't you say you were having freezing rain around there?" she said. I told her we were. "He doesn't need to be on the roads on a night like this," she said anxiously. "The weather map shows sleet and ice all over the state, you know." She sighed.

"Yes, I know," I said. "I'm actually expecting a call from him any minute, telling me he's stopping somewhere overnight." I paused and added, "When the phone rang, I thought it might be him, in fact."

She didn't pick up on my hint to free up the line. "I've felt so tired for the past couple of days," she said.

I could have made myself sound concerned, but I didn't. "I know how that feels," I said.

She sighed. "I haven't even been out of the house most of the week except to get the newspaper."

"Well, it's been too cold for anybody to get out," I said. What did she expect—to go beachcombing when it was twenty degrees?

"I ran out of milk yesterday and couldn't even make myself go to the grocery store." I knew she hardly ever drank milk anyway so took this as another plea for sympathy.

"It's supposed to warm up a little tomorrow," I said.

She sighed again. "I probably need to go to the doctor, but I don't feel like it."

Travis laughed out loud at something on the movie, and almost at the same moment I thought I heard the crack of a branch in the backyard, followed by a thud. We didn't have nearly as many trees at our old house in Derby as we do now, but there were a couple of tall pines near the back fence. I braced myself for the lights to flicker, but they didn't.

"I'd better go check on something," I told Christine. "I think one of our trees might be going." The year before, a tree in the Seacrests' yard next door had toppled right over onto their storage shed and smashed the brand-new ten-speed bicycle Morris had bought Polly for her birthday—a present which she didn't act a bit appreciative of. She was pregnant at the time and in no mood or condition, she said, to be wheeling around the neighborhood "like a pumpkin on a perch."

"Well, I was sure hoping to talk to Ken tonight," Christine said.

"Sorry," I said. "I doubt if he'll even make it home tonight." I knew I was repeating myself.

She sighed. "It sure is quiet around here." This was her way of saying she was lonely. I was sure it was one way she got Ken to invite her to come for visits. She hadn't been to our house for well over a year now, which suited me fine, but we had gone to see her for one day the summer before, and of course, Ken had stopped by to see her any number of times. She was never satisfied, though. No amount of time was ever enough. I'm sure Christine would have liked to spend every weekend with us. Once she had even said, "It's getting so hard to keep up with everything that needs to be done around the house," which I was sure was just her way of saying, "If I lived in the same town as you, I'd have some help."

"I need to go," I said to her again. "I think I just heard another limb fall in the backyard."

She sighed again, this time vocalizing a little so that it came out as a soft moan. "Well, tell Ken to give me a call, will you, Elizabeth dear?"

I didn't commit myself. She had just talked to him three days ago. "Well, I don't even know if I'll talk to him tonight," I said.

"Just have him call, please," she said again. "I need to talk to him. I'm not feeling well."

When I finally hung up, I felt myself relax, the tightness in my throat loosening and my breathing coming easier. I stuck a bag of popcorn in the microwave and poured two glasses of Coke for Travis and me, but by the time I got back to the movie I had lost interest in it and didn't hear half of what Travis said in his attempts to catch me up on the plot. When Mrs. Robinson decided to stay on the island with her husband in their tree-house home, when she could have gone back to the comforts of England, something in me admired her for just the briefest moment before something else made me think she was a moron and this whole movie was as far from any semblance of reality as you could get.

It was over an hour later when Ken got home. He had crept along at twenty miles an hour for most of the way, he said, and had passed dozens of cars that had slid off the road. I mean to be honest in everything I'm writing down, so I won't lie and say I forgot to tell him to call his mother. I did forget about it when he first walked in, but when I remembered a little while later, I just didn't tell him. I knew she'd be calling him again or he'd call her in the next day or two, so it didn't matter anyway.

But she didn't call again, ever. And Ken didn't call her either for four or five days, and when he did, he didn't get an answer. He figured she was out somewhere.

She was out all right. It was all pretty gruesome. She lived at the end of a row of beach houses, and the people next door were in Florida for a couple of months, so it was like something you'd read in one of those cheap paperback mysteries. And just like in one of those books, it was the mailman who first suspected something. A funny smell, he said. He'd gone up to the door to leave something that wouldn't fit in the mailbox. Christine was always ordering things through discount catalogs and sending in coupons for free thirty-day trials of beauty aids or kitchen knives or what have you. The front door was open about twelve inches or so, which was odd for January.

According to the coroner's report, it was a heart attack. He estimated the time of death sometime between midnight and noon the previous Sunday, which meant that she had died only hours after telling me she hadn't been feeling well. She had collapsed by the front door, apparently as she was preparing to toss some bread crumbs into the yard for the birds. That's exactly the kind of thing she'd get it in her mind to do at midnight in the dead of winter. A plastic bag containing two pieces of crumbled toast lay on the floor beside her. The telephone was on a table nearby. If Ken had called her as soon as he had gotten home that Saturday night, he would have gotten to talk to his mother one last time. Maybe he would have made her call 9–1–1. Maybe she wouldn't have died of a heart attack within a few hours.

After it was all discovered, Ken asked me point-blank if I had talked to Christine during his absence. I told him the truth. "Did she complain about feeling bad?" he asked.

I hesitated and said, "No more than usual," which sounded a lot more heartless than I intended. I never told him she had specifically asked for him to call her.

To say that Ken was preoccupied over the next few weeks would be putting it mildly. After he received the news about Christine on Friday, he drove down right away to make all the arrangements, and we had a small private burial in Charleston, which none of her other four children could fit into their schedules, naturally. After that Ken spent several days at her house going through things. I offered to stay and help, but he shook his head.

He hardly spoke to me after he got home, nor I to him. It wasn't that he was mad at me—he was just absorbed in his loss. Her death knocked him off his feet emotionally. He didn't talk about it, and I didn't either. I don't think he blamed me for her death—I really don't think that entered his mind—but I blamed myself, privately, of course. We both retreated to our separate spaces while he grieved and I nursed my guilt.

And he felt guilty, too. He had meant to call her before leaving for the conducting trip to Charlotte, but he'd gotten busy and decided to wait and call her from there, which he hadn't. The two days were packed from early morning until ten at night, and by the time the clinic was over, the weather had turned bad and he was concerned about making it home, and then he had things to tend to at the college after being away for a few days, and so forth and so on.

I felt deep down that Christine's death was one of those big dividing lines in a marriage. If we could reach out to each other and hold on tight through it, we'd be all right. Sometimes a big loss will drive two people away from each other, but sometimes it will build a bridge between them. But you start building a bridge in the middle of the water—did you know that? The two people have to start together, and they have to work as a team. For sure they have to talk as they make their way to shore together.

When we lived at our old house in Derby, we used to buy a real Christmas tree every year, but at some point my mother convinced me that an artificial tree was much more practical and a lot less trouble. The "lot less trouble" appealed to me in particular, so after Christmas one year I bought one on sale that looked like it had snow on the branches, and we still use it. We've probably had it at least fifteen years now, and here's something funny I discovered when we moved from Derby over here to Berea last year.

In the course of packing things up, we had to roll up the area rug in the living room. I don't think Ken and I had spoken more than a dozen sentences to each other during the entire week prior to moving, but one day when Travis was away at work, he asked me to help him move the couch and coffee table off the rug so we could roll it up. I'll never forget the surprise of seeing a number of fir needles on the hardwood floor under the rug after we had rolled it up. They weren't fake ones from our fake snow-laden Christmas tree either. Those were long, thin, and flat, all uniformly cut, with a texture like sateen ribbon.

These, on the other hand, were shorter, stiffer, and a little fatter, with a tiny nub where they had been attached to a tree. I even imagined a faint smell of long-ago evergreen, though they were mostly brown and dry now. They were obviously real fir needles from a real tree. I stood there holding several of them in my palm and trying to figure it out. When Ken asked, "What's that you've got?" I said, "Oh, nothing" and stuffed them inside the pocket of my jeans.

We hadn't had a tree like this in over a decade and a half, but that's the only place they could have come from since I had never been one for decorating with fresh greenery indoors. I remembered how bad some of our trees used to be about shedding their needles. So these must have fallen off one of those trees and gotten brushed against the edge of the rug by the vacuum cleaner or people's feet or whatever, then gradually worked their way farther under until safely hidden from sight. And now suddenly we roll back the rug and bring them to light many years later.

So I guess this answers the question "How often do you take up your rugs and give the hardwood floors a thorough cleaning?" I'm pretty particular about a clean house, but when it comes to hardwood floors, I'm an around-the-edges housekeeper. Unless the rugs are small and washable, they pretty much stay in place. I mean, how's the hardwood floor underneath going to get dirty if there's a rug on top of it? That's my reasoning, and I think it's altogether logical.

But here's the point. I'm thinking now about how those needles under the big rug in the living room are a perfect picture of the way Ken and I have always handled our problems. Brush them off, look the other way, step over them, shove them aside, hide them, and pretty soon you'll forget about them. They're still there, but they're under the rug, and if the rug is big enough, you can sweep an infinite number of little problems under it.

I'm still sitting on the sofa with the two newspapers in my lap, weighed down with heavy thoughts, when I hear a car door slam in the driveway. My first thought is Ken, but I can't imagine him coming over on a Saturday night when the chances are so good I'd be home. Somebody rattles the kitchen doorknob and knocks lightly, and my heart is suddenly in my throat. That was always what Travis would do when he'd forget his key. He'd rattle the doorknob with one hand and tap with the other.

I turn on the kitchen light and see him bending down peering through the small panes of the kitchen door. I see my son's face and suddenly feel things leaping around inside me. I open the door, and he throws a duffel bag in ahead of him, then takes his sneakers off at the door as he always does. I stand there staring at him. My son has come home for Easter.

"What happened to the beach?" I say.

"I don't know," he says. Of course, what else did I expect? But then, remarkably, he goes on. "I decided it was a waste." Then he grins at me. "Hey, your hair shrank."

I throw myself at him, surprising both of us, and he puts his arms around me clumsily. Like his father, hugging doesn't come easily for him. He's trying, though, he really is, sweet kid. "You sounded so—oh, I don't know, like worried or sad or something when we talked on the phone," he says. My ear is pressed to his chest, and I can hear his heart beating as he speaks. I want him to keep talking. I want to feel his arms around me for a long, long time.

The Birth of the Simple Light

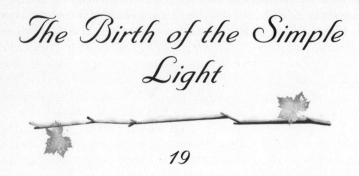

19

Travis and I sit across the table from each other. I have fixed him a toasted cheese sandwich and poured him a glass of milk. He's hungry as always, and I'm hungry, too, but in a different way. I think of a poem by Gwendolyn Brooks that talks about the "gobbling mother-eye." It's a sad poem, really, about the regrets of a woman who has carried children in her womb but never let them see the light of day. Gwendolyn Brooks wrenches your heart in two in that poem.

I've had my own time of suffering because of unborn children, but I'm not sad right now. Travis has come home for spring break. He's grown over the past eight months since he's been at college, even since Christmas. A little bit of it is actual height and maybe five pounds in weight, but more of it is depth. I see that he's not a boy anymore. It's odd to feel something verging on shyness with your own son.

I've got something to say to anybody who's grumbling about the slow pace of this story. And to anybody who wants to lay it aside because it's disjointed. Here's what I have to say: Don't. A story goes forth in its own way. It takes its own sweet time to do whatever it's going to do, which sometimes, granted, might not be all that much. But you can't impose outside standards on it. You can't take it through a neat little checklist to make it presentable, then shoo it out the door all trim and shiny faced to make a good impression on the world.

It's a lot like your child. The more you try to get him ready to step out into life, the more deficiencies you see to correct. Of course, I know Anne Bradstreet beat me to that comparison over three centuries ago in her poem "The Author to Her Book," in which she called her book of poems her "ill-form'd offspring," whose face she attempted to wash, only to see more smudges.

But the point is, you can't force your story to be a compact, tidy, shapely thing when it's a long messy network of tangled wires. I'm doing the best I can with it, but something like this takes time. In writing it all out thus far, I'm afraid everything seems too neatly segmented. You have to deal with things separately when you write it all down, but in reality it's one big jumble. The days are divided into different parts, yes. There's the time I'm home, the time I'm away teaching, the time I'm at church, the time I'm at poetry class or with Margaret, and so forth. But the hurting part doesn't happen just when I'm at home, and when I go to church I don't block out everything else and meditate only on spiritual thoughts. It's all mixed together.

Every minute of every day is dragged down and held back by the heavy anchor of my broken marriage. Even as I consider the metaphor of the anchor, though, I ask myself, "But isn't an anchor good?" Can it be that my ship is being stalled here for a purpose, that someday the anchor will be hauled up and I can skim across the sea under a blue sky? I find that I am not completely my mother's daughter, for I feel something I can call by no other name than hope. The Bible is a book of hope, you know. You can't read it as much as I've been reading it these past months and remain an obdurate pessimist. Mine is a cautious hope, however.

Though my marriage is uppermost in my mind, I can and do think about other things, of course. I can even smile when I see the sky go pink and blue at twilight or hear the bird in our backyard whose hoarse call sounds exactly like *uh-oh!* or read a poem by Dylan Thomas, whose words are put together in the most highly original way of any English poet. I can read his elaborate syllabic poem "Fern Hill," for example, with its greens and golds, its stars and barns, its owls and orchards, its pebbles and stables and rivers and foxes, and hear music. I can feel how it "must have been after the birth of the simple light" in Eden and can contemplate both the mercy and judgment of time. That poem is the most curious mixture of joy and sorrow I can think of, but mostly I feel joy when I read it, joy that anybody could write something so beautiful.

I can even laugh out loud when Macon Mahoney shows up at my kitchen door wearing one of Theresa's aprons and asks if I have any sesame seed he can borrow "for a culinary masterpiece" he is designing, or when a kid in a government class asks if I remember what it was like when Prohibition was repealed, or when Bernie Paulson at church prays aloud for God to forgive "all our sins and falling shorts."

But behind every thought, every smile, every laugh is the ever-present knowledge that Ken is gone. It's not something I forget, not for a single moment. When I open my eyes in the morning, it's there, and when I close them at night, it's still there. And if I get up in that long hollow part of night, sometimes that's the worst time of all.

I can hear my readers stirring around restlessly and saying, "Okay, let's get on with it." I can hear Jennifer saying, "Blah, blah, blah," the way she does when somebody on talk radio can't get off a boring subject like tax hikes or illegal immigration. I can see Travis's glazed look when he retreats from my speeches to the more interesting world of his imagination. Young people like a story that moves, but let me tell you young people something. Sometimes you just have to slog through something long and hard. Everything in life isn't quick and entertaining. And it's during the slow times that you sometimes learn the most.

But I'll try to get on with it, though I'm not making any promises. As my mind wanders hither and yon, I nevertheless have a distant goal in sight. I'm going somewhere, trust me, but the trip might be more than just a short day's ride. "As if I hadn't already figured that out," you're saying.

"You don't have to walk across the back forty just to get to the barn," my father used to say when my mother got bogged down in the details of a story she was telling him. But if you're surveying the whole farm so you can draw up a map, or if you're having it appraised for resale, or trying to find something you lost while driving your tractor, the back forty might yield some mighty important evidence. So I'm not going to take shortcuts. If you want to read that kind of story, I can give you some titles, and you can enjoy a nice little afternoon's light diversion, but don't try to fit this one onto a collapsible framework like that.

Which brings me back to the child analogy. You can't force a story to do what you want it to do any more than you can force your child to present himself a certain way to the world, to have a certain personality and demonstrate certain attitudes. I can state this without equivocation because, as I've said earlier, I've had lots of experience in trying to do exactly this with my son.

On the few days when Travis didn't ride his bike to school for some reason, I would pick him up at Derby High School. I'd get there early so I could watch the end of the school day from my parked car, and I'd try to piece together clues about how other kids managed to seem so socially adept. I'd study their strategies as they came out of the building in twos or threes or sometimes whole groups the size of a soccer team.

They always seemed to know the right steps, as if they were following a fiddler's calls at a barn dance. Sometimes they kept walking as they talked, reaching over to swat at each other playfully or one of them turning around to walk backwards, staying just slightly in front of the others and, of course, continuing to talk the whole time with large gestures. There were shrieks of laughter that sometimes signaled them all to stop and lean in closer to hear what somebody had to say. It looked so easy the way they'd hang a wrist over somebody's shoulder and put their heads together.

They might stand in a circle for a while, the girls tossing their heads to make their hair do whatever it was they wanted it to do, the guys with their hands in their pockets, their shoulders hunched forward. And the whole time they were talking, their eyes were constantly turning to scan the nearby parking lot to see who was driving by, checking out what kind of car they were driving, who was peeling rubber, whose music was making the pavement vibrate, and all that.

My observations never lasted long enough, though, because Travis would always show up too soon. He'd walk out of the building by himself usually, always pausing to look up at the sky first and then locating my parked car before striding straight past all the other students, making a beeline for me. Travis walked alone through life and seemed perfectly content to do so.

If he came out with someone else, it was usually an accident of just happening to fall into step with a total stranger. They'd take one quick look at each other and drift apart as soon as possible. Once when I saw him actually say something to another boy as they came out together, I felt a brief spark of hope.

"Who was that?" I asked him when he got in the car.

"Who?"

"That boy you were talking to," I said.

"I don't know."

"Well, what were you talking about?"

"Nothing," he said. "He thought I was somebody in his physics class, but I told him I wasn't taking physics." Then, without any conscious effort at changing the subject, he'd say something like "Look at those two squirrels" or "It smells like rain" or "Hey, that gingko dropped all its leaves last night." Gingkos do that, you know. They'll hang onto their yellow fan-shaped leaves until the temperature gets to a certain point one fall night, then the next morning all the leaves will be on the ground.

That was Travis—the only high-school senior in the world who would rather hang out with birds, squirrels, clouds, rocks, or trees than with another living person his own age. He loved biology—made an A in it without half trying. Most of the stuff he already knew from years of reading and observing and from watching the Discovery Channel.

Well, so much for that. A kid will be who he is, Mr. Congeniality or Mr. Recluse or something in between. And a story will be what it is. But one thing in Travis's favor—and I'm realizing this more with every passing day— is he's a lot nicer than I've given him credit for most of his life. I've been so busy wishing he were more like my idea of "normal" that I've forgotten at times to appreciate the things about him that are really very, very good. "Don't wish your life away"—that was something my mother used to say when we were growing up and wanted something to be different from the way it was. I keep forgetting her advice, though.

So by this time in April it's been eight weeks since the day in February when I found out Ken loved another woman. And here's how it is on the day before Easter. I'm still plodding along. I'm getting through each day somehow. I'm still praying every day for my eyes to be opened. I'm still wanting God to illumine my steps. I'm still reading my Bible and trying to make it part of the way I think and act, trying to make it a core subject and not just an extracurricular.

But I still sit around in a daze a good part of the time, too. Finding out your husband doesn't love you anymore isn't something that comes with a "how to" guide. Maybe somebody needs to write one. I can see it on the bookstore shelf now along with all those others with yellow and black covers: *How to Lose Your Husband for Dummies*. Nobody could write something like that, though. The rules have got be so different with every case.

For example, Juliet called me recently, after Mother told her about Ken, and told me all about a friend of hers who had hired a private eye to follow her "skunk of a husband" around and collect hard, cold evidence of his philandering ways so she could "take him to the cleaners" when court time rolled around. The detective found out all about the other woman—or *women* in the case of Juliet's friend's husband—and drew up a long documented list of the man's goings and comings at all hours of the day and night. He collected phone numbers and gift receipts and copies of motel registers and all kinds of things.

Juliet was astounded when I told her I didn't know who the other woman was. "Don't you *care*?" she practically screamed, and I told her yes, I did. I cared very much, but the *fact* of Ken's unfaithfulness was all I could handle at the moment. I couldn't begin to face the details yet. I think I may have hung up before Juliet was finished. She was right in the middle of a sentence when I gently replaced the receiver and walked outdoors to sit in the swing in the backyard. Oh yes, you're thinking, I see how polite you are, hanging up on your own sister.

So anyway, I'm muddling along on the eve of Easter when suddenly the door opens and Travis is home. He comes in hauling all his stuff, including dirty laundry, and he hugs me and tells me he changed his mind about going to the beach because I sounded sad on the telephone, and then he wanders off down the hallway while I fix him a sandwich. I wipe my eyes with a paper napkin and blow my nose as he leaves the kitchen, and I wonder how many other freshman boys would hear something in their mother's voice over the phone to make them give up a trip to the beach.

Within seconds I hear sounds from his bedroom of Doc Severinsen playing Schumann's "Traumerei." Travis took all his favorite CDs to college with him, but he left this one at home, along with two or three dozen more. Travis travels light through life. He took his small boom box but decided to leave his stereo system at home, which suited me fine. You don't take expensive things away to college if you're smart.

Anyway, Travis turns up the volume now, and down the hallway floats a lyrical line from Doc Severinsen's trumpet that makes you forget that Doc began his career playing in a swing band. This doesn't swing; it hangs suspended, catching the light just so, like something exquisitely fine and breakable just out of reach.

Add "Traumerei" to that list of the world's most beautiful melodies I wrote down earlier. I thought of another one, too. It's a mazurka by Debussy, or maybe that's the only title it has: "Mazurka." It was a piano piece Travis worked on in high school. Whenever he played it, I would stop whatever I was doing and sit down. If I closed my eyes, I would see a field of white lilies against a backdrop of dense cool forest. I found out later when I heard the piece on a CD that it was supposed to be played much faster than Travis played it, but I preferred his tempo. One thing Travis could always do was wring feeling out of the piano. His repertoire wasn't very wide, but it was deep.

But back to "Traumerei." Add it also to the endless list of sensory impressions that make me think of Ken. He played this piece in his senior trumpet recital at Piper College. "A child's dream state" is what Ken said it was supposed to suggest. I close my eyes now and see dozens of silk scarves in all colors slowly swirling through space. I'm thankful it's a short piece, and after it's over I start breathing again and put Travis's sandwich in the frying pan. I know what comes next on the CD, and it's harmless—the flashy "Carnival of Venice."

A few minutes later Travis sits down at the kitchen table, and I sit down across from him and watch him eat. I'm hungry myself, but this is food enough right now. He has never liked to talk much during meals, but maybe he's trying hard to do what he thinks will please me because he starts telling me about his freshman lit-comp class and a paper he wrote the week before about Graham Greene's story *The Destructors*. I'm afraid to say anything much, afraid he'll stop talking. When his glass of milk is half empty, I get up to refill it.

"Where's Dad?" he says casually. I don't read anything into this. Travis knows all about Ken's frequent absences from home.

"Away," I say. I bring his glass back to the table and sit down.

"I was wanting to talk to you guys about something," he says. "Will he be home tomorrow?"

"Probably," I say. I mean to call his office and leave a message that his son is home and wants to see him. That will get him here. Meanwhile, I know I can press Travis to go ahead and tell me whatever it is, but I decide not to. Things are different between us now in some indefinable way, and I'm not as sure of myself as I used to be. I wouldn't want to hear my son say, "No, I'll just wait and tell you when Dad is here." I can imagine his saying this now, although as recently as last September I was always the one who heard things first. Sometimes Ken never did hear them if I chose not to tell him.

"I was wanting to talk to you about something, too," I say, and he looks at me and cocks one eyebrow the way he used to do to be funny. He listens as I start telling him about the change in my heart, my new understanding of God's plan for mankind, the faith and grace at work in my life. Then, realizing how vague and timid I'm sounding, I talk very pointedly about Christ and his atoning work on the cross. His eyebrow goes down. When Travis listens hardest, he doesn't look at you, so I know he's listening hard right now. He's frowning just a little, staring at the last quarter of his sandwich in his hand.

When I finish, I quit talking, which is something I haven't always done after I've covered a subject. That used to be one of Jennifer's main complaints: "Okay, okay, enough already! You've said it a hundred times! Don't treat me like I'm retarded!"

It's a trick parents have. To make themselves perfectly understood, they often feel compelled to find a dozen ways to repeat their point. They'll say it once, then think of a better wording and add that, then think of an illustration and tack that on, then remember some related transgression of bygone days and work that in, then make grim prognostications about consequences of not following their advice, then go back to the main tune and saw on it again in a different key. Parents are masters at the musical concept of Theme and Variation.

Travis and I sit across from each other silently for a full minute after I've finished speaking. Without looking at me, he eats the rest of his sandwich in two bites and drains his glass of milk. When he finally speaks, it's not at all what I expected, although I'm not sure I could say what I expected. "Stacy's a Christian," he says. He looks at me now, and his look tells me not to push him for more, so I don't. His hands are laid flat against the table on either side of his empty plate, and he's tapping the table with one index finger. After a few seconds he adds, "She's this girl I know at school."

"The one you denied knowing anything about?" I want to ask, but I don't. I can't think of anything appropriate to say. All sorts of thoughts crowd in on each other. I've wanted Travis to have friends for so long, and now here I am not at all sure I like what I'm hearing. Of course, a girl can be just a friend and nothing more. I tell myself to be glad that Travis has met a girl named Stacy. Maybe she's in one of his classes and is engaged to somebody else.

But even if she's more than just a friend, it hits me how remarkable it is that she's a Christian. Out of all the girls at Piper, Travis is attracted to one who's a Christian. I had never even thought to pray for this.

"She didn't like the beach idea, either," Travis said.

I nodded. He was probably looking for a more dramatic reaction, and he stared hard at me, waiting for something else. I nodded again. We sat in silence for another long moment.

"You want a shake?" he asked all of a sudden. "My treat. I'll drive." I knew he was thinking of a place over in Derby called Darlene's Kreamy Kones that makes real shakes and malts that are so thick you have to use a spoon for the first half.

"Sure," I said, then, "Will you go with me to church tomorrow morning?"

He shrugged and frowned. "Church? Oh, I don't know, Mom. I don't—"

"Tomorrow is Easter Sunday," I said. I picked up his plate and glass and carried them over to the sink. "I sing in the choir, but you could sit in the back and we could get out early."

"All I got with me is stuff like this," he said, looking down at his shorts and sandals.

"We'll think of something," I said. "Anyway, they don't have a guard at the door to turn people away if they're not dressed right." I looked back at him from the sink. "It would mean a lot to me."

He shrugged again, curled up one side of his mouth, and shook his head the way he always used to, then rolled his eyes and said, "Oh well, the moat's low and the drawbridge is down," which is an expression he picked up from something he read years ago. I have no idea how it was used in the book where he read it, but he always used it to mean, "Okay, okay, I'll do it." I was hoping it still meant the same thing.

When we got in his car a couple of minutes later, I noticed the sun visor was broken on the driver's side and hung down at a crazy angle that looked as though it could seriously interfere with his view of the road. He didn't seem to pay any attention to it, and when I asked about it, he said simply, "Oh, that—it broke." Travis had always been the kind of kid who would make do. He used to do things like tie the ends of broken shoelaces together multiple times, or write with just the pen refill after the pen itself broke, or tighten the spit valve on his trumpet with a rubber band, or make tomato soup out of ketchup. This was the kind of thing that drove Ken crazy, and he had given Travis any number of lectures on the subject.

In fact, Ken and I had quarreled about it more than once. Ken saw Travis's makeshift repairs as careless and lazy, whereas I saw them as resourceful and considerate of others, resulting from his being so naturally accident prone. "He's learned to get by without bothering anybody about all his little mishaps," I'd point out. Once when I wasn't home, he had bandaged a large cut on his leg with a clean dustrag and masking tape, and another time he had stapled his shirt cuff together when he discovered the button missing. I thought he deserved credit for all this, but Ken said it revealed a slipshod way of approaching life. "Take the time to do it *right*," he was always telling Travis. This was just another big difference between them.

We got all the way to the end of our street where it meets DeLaney before Travis remembered he'd left his wallet back at the house. It could have been worse, I reminded myself. We could have been all the way over in Derby before he realized it. I hadn't even bothered to bring my purse, so I couldn't offer to pay. Not that he waited for me to. No, he slapped the dashboard once, hard, then said one word—"Money!"—and shoved his car into reverse.

And that's the way we rode the whole way back home—two and a half blocks—in reverse. Most people would pull into somebody's driveway to turn around and then head back home frontward, but this was typical of Travis. I could have said something, of course, and a year ago I wouldn't have hesitated to do so. But this was now, and for some reason it seemed altogether appropriate, even inevitable that we should be riding backwards down the street. It struck me that this was like the ending of a good poem. Nothing you could have ever foretold, but once it was there, it felt like a prophecy coming to pass. It had to be this way.

I thought of the time when I was a kid and something happened to the transmission of our Oldsmobile while we were on vacation. I don't remember all the details, but I do remember Daddy driving the car—one of those sixties models with enormous tail fins—several miles through moderately heavy traffic going backwards. For some reason, reverse gear was the only one that would work, and Daddy was saving a towing fee by getting the car to the repair shop on his own. Try to picture it. A big family car going *with* the flow of traffic on a two-lane road in the middle of the afternoon, but turned around backwards, along with the people inside it, of course. Naturally Daddy had to drive slowly, with his head twisted around to see where he was going. Mother, Greg, and I were humiliated, but Daddy and Juliet thought it was great fun. They talked about it afterward as the highlight of the whole vacation.

I didn't think I had ever told Travis this story, but here we were all these years later riding down our own street going the wrong way—or rather, going the right way, but backwards. I realized that Travis was reminding me more and more of my father as the years went by. I knew they would have been big buddies if Daddy had lived.

But all that's irrelevant. Travis and I were riding down Windsor Drive backwards, and it was only starting to get dark. It was April, so the daylight was lasting until eight or so. The streetlights were already on, however, so I could see the houses clearly. We weren't talking. Travis was turned around, concentrating on staying between the curbs.

Thankfully, no other cars were on the street at the time, either parked or in motion. I was glad for that, considering the fact that Travis wasn't the best driver even under optimal conditions. He had passed his driving test the third time by the skin of his teeth. Strangely, though, I was very calm at this particular moment. Feeling the way I did, that this whole experience was somehow foreordained, I suppose I felt that we were removed from any possibility of calamity.

I had seen all these houses many times, of course, and realized now that I actually knew more about my Windsor Drive neighbors than I had thought. I knew that the Nestbergs at the end of the street, whose name was on their mailbox, always left their porch light on all night every night and most days, too, and that the Yokims next door to them had a deaf son. I knew that a woman lived alone in the house with green siding and shutters and that she had several cats. The Pratts across the street from the cat woman were an oddly matched couple, he being close to six-feet-five and she barely topping five feet.

These are the kinds of things I'd learned about my neighbors farther down the street, and I rehearsed them as we passed each house, getting closer to our own. The Underwoods had awnings over their windows and a birdbath right smack in the middle of the front yard. Furthermore, it was a well-used birdbath, not one of those that sits empty or full of dead leaves and stagnant water. I had seen Mrs. Underwood hosing it out regularly and filling it with clean water, and the birds rewarded her by flocking to it.

I know, I know. I'm doing that "back forty" thing again, but I want you to get a clear sense of this backward trip down our street on the night before Easter. On we went, past the Ingles' house with the new roof and the one next to it that was almost completely obscured from view by two gigantic magnolia trees in the front yard.

Because we were going a little slower than usual and because I wasn't driving and was free to look around, I had the sensation of seeing things with exceptional clarity. I even saw a few things I had never noticed before. The two-story house with the big planter of pansies by the front porch, for instance, had a tree fort in an oak in the backyard, barely visible from the street, and a lamp in the Burnsheins' side window had an amber shade. I saw irises beside a carport, all of them a lemony yellow, and wind chimes hanging at the corner of another house.

This is a skimpy summary of what I saw, but it's enough. Here's the point. By the time we got back to our own driveway, I felt that I really knew my street, that I could walk down it blindfolded and know exactly where I was each step of the way. And all of this had come about without my trying to make it happen. It had come simply by observing it backwards.

I had always been interested in doing things backwards. Daddy used to make home movies as we were growing up, and after we'd watch them, I'd beg him to let us watch them backwards. For several years I was passionate about palindromes, those sentences that read the same way frontwards and backwards. I thought "A man, a plan, a canal—Panama" was the cleverest of all, and the famous one on a sign at a beet root cannery came in a close second: "Red root put up to order." I wrote a poem once in college about an old man who grew young, and then later I started experimenting with writing poems backwards, starting with the last line and working toward the first.

So anyway, here's what came to me as Travis pulled into our driveway, or rather backed in, barely missing the azalea bush next to the mailbox. The thought that presented itself to me was this. Maybe seeing our street backwards was God's stamp of approval on my backwards search through my marriage. More than once I had thought of the verse that said, "Forgetting those things which are behind" and wondered if God was trying to tell me not to keep looking into the past but to try to look ahead. Now I felt sure that looking backwards wasn't bad, that sometimes it was the only way to move forward.

Does God do this? Does he cause your son to forget his money so you have to go back home? Does he block from your son's mind the natural course of action—that of turning the car around—in order that you can ride down the street backwards, in order that you might see things you had missed before and consequently realize that examining the past might yield valuable insight into the present?

Does God remind you, as he reminded me when Travis and I returned home later with our milk shakes, that you had never finished reading the book of Hosea? I had left off some weeks earlier in the middle of the book, after the seventh chapter, where God talks about the falsehood, treachery, transgressions, wickedness, pride, deceit, rebellion, mischief, and *adultery* of Israel. Frankly, I had begun to wonder why Margaret would recommend such a book to me, though I never asked her.

But first, I left a message at Ken's office about Travis being home, and then Travis and I watched back-to-back reruns of *Happy Days*, *The Dick Van Dyke Show*, and *The Mary Tyler Moore Show* on Nick at Nite. I didn't care about the programs themselves, of course, but I wanted to be in the same room with Travis. He lay on the floor, and I sat on the couch watching him. At eleven I told him we'd need to leave for church around ten-thirty the next morning, and I went to take a bath and get ready for bed.

When I went into my bedroom, I saw my Bible on the nightstand, and that's when the thought came to me as clearly as if it had been spoken aloud: "You never finished reading Hosea." So before I even ran my bath water, I sat right down on the bed and opened my Bible to Hosea. Not to the chapter where I stopped, though, but to the last chapter of the book. I usually didn't skip ahead to the ends of books the way my mother did, but for some reason tonight I did. Maybe I was still in a reverse frame of mind.

And do you know what? Here's what I read in the last chapter of Hosea. I read words like *gracious*, *mercy*, *heal*, and *love*. God was apparently done with his anger. He talked about sheltering Israel under his shadow, making them grow as the lily, the vine, the green fir tree, giving them the strength and fragrance of the cedar. I read that last chapter five times before I went in to take my bath.

I bathed slowly and quietly. And here is the prayer I prayed: "Restore to me my marriage." But even as I prayed it, I knew it wasn't right. It wasn't my marriage. It was ours. And so I revised it. "Restore to us our marriage," I prayed, though I realized I was praying for a joint venture without the consent of the other person.

I wanted to see the whole twenty-eight years of my marriage, but I knew I couldn't. My memory is imperfect. I prayed, however, that God would show me the scenes I most needed to contemplate. "Take my hand, God," I prayed, "and lead me. Open my eyes to what you want me to see."

Free of Our Bridges

20

I've done more reading and thinking about the translation of poetry. Margaret and I also had a talk about it after one of our poetry classes with Dr. Huckabee, during which we had read and discussed selected passages from Robert Fitzgerald's translation of the *Odyssey* and three or four of Richard Wilbur's fine translations of French poetry.

Margaret said several things that night about translation that impressed me all over again as to her intelligence. "It seems to me that translation is a dangerous business" was one thing she said. She talked about the risk of missing the heart of the poem, of being so consumed with the mechanical aspects of word exchange, of parsing the sentences and pinning down denotations, verb tenses, and the like that the main similarity between the original poem and the translation might end up being the number of lines.

She smiled, then added, "I suppose a translator will always face the risk of offending those who love the original in its own language."

"I guess William Tyndale found that out the hard way," I said, and we laughed, though probably we shouldn't have. Being burned at the stake is no laughing matter.

We went on talking for a while, and then Margaret said, "Actually, I believe any attempt to reduce life and the universe into lines of poetry might be considered an act of translation." This was the second thing she said that struck me. She was absolutely right, of course, and many a good poet has raved in frustration at his inability to capture essences with mere words, even in his own language. I think of Robinson Jeffers' lament in the opening line of "Love the Wild Swan": "I hate my verses, every line, every word."

I know exactly how Robinson Jeffers feels. Every attempt at poetry writing I have ever made has fallen so far short of the mark that I've wondered why I even bother to try, yet I know for a certainty that the very next time I feel that slow boil inside me of words clustering themselves together and calling out to be set to the music of poetry, I'll try again. But at least I don't thrust these poetic attempts—I have notebooks full of them!—into other people's faces and demand a response.

And I guess it applies not only to poetry but to any kind of writing. Every time a writer tries to put some experience, memory, feeling, or observation into words, even in his own native tongue, he's translating in a sense. He's changing the intangibles of life into printed matter.

So as I write, I translate the images of my marriage into written words in the hopes of finding meaning. Many scenes have rolled across my memory in the days since I rode backwards with Travis down Windsor Drive. That night after I went to bed, in fact, I went through reels of film. Nothing was in order, but I took special care to observe each picture, to let it unfold at its own pace.

I saw myself in Christine's kitchen that first time Ken and I visited after we were married. Schuyler had left the house for a while, and Ken was upstairs, so the two of us were alone. I was sitting at the table looking through a *Smithsonian* magazine, and she was at the stove stirring something. When I glanced up, she was staring at me. She smiled and looked away quickly, but a few minutes later I caught her staring again.

She looked back at what she was stirring and said, "I never dreamed Ken would marry such a pretty girl." She spoke so softly I thought I might have misunderstood her, but she looked back at me after she said it and nodded her head. "I know he loves you for more than your looks, but I'm very happy he found such a pretty wife."

I didn't know what to say, so I didn't say anything. I remember looking back down at the magazine and reading the same picture caption over and over. It was in an article about some island in Indonesia, and the picture showed what looked like a mist rising over a small lake at sunset, but the caption read: "Mosquitoes rise en masse at twilight ready to begin their quest for flesh." I thought of how nice something could look on the surface when the real meaning was deadly.

After a few more minutes, she quit stirring, set the lid on the pan, and came to sit with me at the table. "I was surprised when Ken showed me your engagement ring last summer," she said. I stopped reading the picture caption and looked up. "He was so excited when he brought it home that day," she went on. Then she reached over as if to take my left hand. I closed the magazine and pushed my chair away from the table a little so that I wasn't quite so close to her. I didn't go so far as to pull my hand away and place it in my lap, but neither did I extend it to her.

"I was worried when he showed it to me," she said. "I didn't think you would like it, and I asked him why he didn't get a diamond. When he told me you didn't want a diamond, I couldn't believe it." I must have looked offended because she hurried on. "I mean, it's a very lovely ring, but you don't see many ruby engagement rings, and I was sure hoping he hadn't gotten mixed up about you not wanting a diamond. Sometimes men don't listen very well."

And do you know how I translated her words? I took them to mean that she thought there was something wrong with me for wanting a ruby engagement ring, and within five minutes I had gotten up from the table and left the kitchen. I heard her saying, "Elizabeth, I hope you don't . . ." as I walked out, but I never knew how she finished the sentence.

I wonder now how different things might have been between us if I had smiled at her and said, "Thank you" when she told me I was pretty, if I had let her take my hand, if I had told her I wanted a ruby because it was Ken's birthstone, that a diamond solitaire looked cold and hard to me, whereas a ruby looked like something warm and alive.

That memory had no sooner left my mind than another took its place. It was much later now. Jennifer was around ten, and Travis was a toddler. We were at the Columbia Zoo, standing in front of a railing that surrounded the seal pool. We must have asked someone to take the picture for us because all four of us are in it.

It never struck me before how much that snapshot says about our family. Jennifer is holding Ken's hand and leaning against him. I'm standing next to her on the other side, which means she's leaning away from me. I'm holding Travis, who looks sleepy and has his head on my shoulder. But the way I'm holding him! It's not an easy, natural kind of holding, but almost a clutching. It looks as if I'm afraid he's going to try to get away, though the only thing he appears interested in doing is staying right where he is with his head on my shoulder. Maybe my real worry wasn't so much that he was going to get away as it was that someone was going to try to take him from me.

I see a Christmas memory, too. I'm opening a present, a huge one, something Ken got gift-wrapped at a department store. I lift out a coat. It's a very soft camel wool. Ken is watching me out of the corner of his eye as he helps Jennifer insert batteries into a Game Boy. I hold up the coat and examine it a while. It's a nice coat and probably very expensive, but it isn't exactly what I would have chosen. I would have gotten something darker—navy or charcoal—with a higher collar.

It amazes me now that I couldn't summon up some Christmas spirit and do a little acting for Ken's sake. A person should be able to do that on Christmas Day. I could have praised the coat and been very honest about it. It had a lot of classy touches—beautiful buttons, a matching neck scarf, a rich brown satin lining, generous length. But I didn't. I don't think I said much at all, and Ken never asked me point-blank if I liked it. I think he already had his answer to that.

I did wear the coat a few times that winter but not much. I kept going back to my old one, and the next winter it hung in the closet most of the time. When I finally did get it out to wear it one day, I discovered three evenly spaced moth holes on the lapel. Connected with a line, they would have formed a perfect equilateral triangle.

None of these pictures does me justice. I complain to God late into the night that I haven't been a *bad* wife. I ask for happy pictures, but these are the ones that keep rewinding and playing. I'm not the one who has committed adultery, I remind God, as if he may have forgotten that. I've kept our house well. All those years of cleaning, cooking, laundering, helping with homework, chauffeuring, sticking to a budget—Ken couldn't have asked for more!

I got up around one in the morning, which would now have been Easter morning, and I walked quietly down the hall past Travis's bedroom and into the kitchen. I poured myself a glass of milk and walked into the den. I opened the blinds and stood there in the dark looking out into the backyard. I took small slow sips. The milk was so cold it hurt my throat. The moon must have been bright that night because I could see the shapes of trees, the birdbath, the rocks along the old paths.

Sometime toward the end of March, Ken had come over one Saturday while I was playing a tennis match. I got home before he left, and I remembered now that I had stood right here at this same window and watched him in the backyard with the leaf blower. He didn't know I was home, and I didn't tap on the window or call to him. I watched him as he finished clearing all the dead winter leaves and debris off the paths and out from under the bushes. He blew it all into one huge pile over toward the side of the house.

When he finished, he set the blower down and went to the middle of the yard. He stood there for what seemed like a long time, looking all around as if trying to visualize something. He even paced off some distances, then went back to the middle and studied some more. At one point it looked like he was talking to himself.

Drinking my milk now in the earliest hour of Easter Day, for some reason I began to think of all the gardens in my mother's nursery rhymes when I was a child. I even whispered the lines aloud.

"The maid was in the garden / hanging out the clothes."

"Mary, Mary, quite contrary, / how does your garden grow?"

"In a garden deep in Spain, / sat a little maid named Jane."

"Oh, whither sat young Jack by night? / Upon a garden wall so white."

"G was a garden all greeny and fine, / H was a hunter ready to dine."

"I had me a hen, the prettiest ever seen, / She went to the garden to plant me a bean."

"Willy Boy, Willy Boy, / where are you going? / Out to my garden, / To see what is growing."

I stopped, although I knew I could think of more if I tried. I thought of all the gardens around the world in the history of mankind and all the work that had kept them pretty. That was one thing about gardens. They didn't keep themselves. Look what had happened to our backyard after Dorothy Sherman took sick and died. Part of a verse I had read many weeks ago came back to me now: "*Mine own vineyard have I not kept.*"

I finished my milk, but still I stood looking out into the dark. I thought again about Ken clearing out the backyard, then standing in the middle and turning in different directions as he looked it over. It didn't take a fortune-teller to see that he had plans in mind. As I wondered whether the backyard would ever be a garden again, I also wondered if I would ever see it. Maybe Ken was drawing up plans with *her*, consulting her about her favorite flowers, making plans to add a fountain, a gazebo, a small greenhouse.

There in the middle of the night it came to me again how useless it was for me to say, "I mean to have my husband back" if his heart was set on someone else. But then, I reminded myself again, God could change people's hearts. He had changed mine.

It was close to two o'clock before I got to sleep. Before leaving the den, my thoughts turned to the day ahead. Easter Day. The day of Christ's resurrection. I thought about the early hours before dawn on that long-ago day in the garden of tombs. I thought of Mary Magdalene and the other women who rose early to take spices to anoint the body of Jesus. I imagined their quiet passage through the streets, their immense sorrow over the death of their Lord, their hushed conversation as they neared the garden, and one of them must have asked, "How are we going to move the stone to get into the sepulcher?"

As I walked through the hallway later to return to my bed, I stopped for a moment beside Travis's door. Another thought struck me. God brought my son home to be with me on Easter Day! This was the kind of God I had. I recalled a sermon Pastor Hawthorne had preached recently from the book of Jeremiah, taking as his text the third verse of chapter thirty-three: "Call unto me, and I will answer thee, and show thee great and mighty things, which thou knowest not." I remembered thinking what a wonderful verse that was to be tucked into the middle of a book of doom and gloom.

I moved away from Travis's door and returned to bed. I fell asleep with a picture in my mind. Travis was walking along a mountain trail away from me. I was standing behind watching him go. He turned and smiled and waved, then disappeared. I didn't run after him or call to him but turned back and walked toward home. In my picture, the home I walked toward was made of logs, set up against a tall mountain. I distinctly remember that there was smoke curling out of the chimney, and as I drifted into sleep, I remembered hearing somewhere that when a child draws pictures of houses with smoke coming out of the chimney, it's a sign that he has a happy home.

Another thing Margaret said about translating poetry that night was this: "So much of a poem deals with echo and shadow. A translator's fidelity to the original, therefore, must go beyond mere text and form into those murky regions of intention, tone, innuendo, connotative nuance, ambivalence of mood—all the secrets that a good poem whispers to the patient, aware reader."

Ah, there was one of my favorite words—*Aware*. I've hardly even thought about it lately, however. Some things dawn on you slowly, but this one just came to me one day recently, like a voice from heaven. *How silly it is to label people that way, how arrogant to think that your two little categories can account for all the variables of humankind.* It's something that has just fallen away like a piece of clothing you've worn out and don't have use for anymore. Or maybe you just take it off because the seasons have changed.

Something that struck me about what she said concerning translation was that I saw in an instant how applicable it all was to my attempts to translate the tragedy of my marriage into meaning. It *was* a risky business. And maybe I was trying so hard to analyze all the parts and find some kind of structure that I was missing the heart of the matter. I had been praying for my eyes to be opened, yes, but I didn't want to see anything bad about myself. I only wanted confirmation that Ken was at fault. It had all been about *his* transgression, *his* shortcomings, *his* mistreatment of *me*.

I suddenly knew, though, that I had to be willing to look within, long and hard. I had to see our marriage as a two-person package, and I was one of the two in the package. What had I done, or not done, to make our marriage what it was? *Forget Ken's betrayal for a while*, I told myself, *and open your eyes to everything that came before it.*

There's so much between the lines of a good poem. And there's so much beneath the surface of a marriage. I don't know how other women cope with the disintegration of their marriages, but I know that I have to find the meaning of it in the large sense. I have to translate all those intangibles into printed matter, which is what I'm trying to do by setting it all down in this record.

"Well, this is one long, redundant, circuitous piece of translation," you're complaining, and I'll grant you that. But, remember, marriage isn't a little three-line Japanese haiku. It's an epic poem handed down through many generations. If you give yourself to translating poetry, you will end up with a broader knowledge of language, so if I give myself to translating my marriage, maybe I'll end up with a deeper understanding of love.

And I must go beyond the surface to the murky regions, as Margaret said. I must explore shadows and listen for echoes. I must be willing to pull things from inside and bring them out into the sunlight, separate and examine all the threads so tightly plaited. "Fidelity to the original"—that's an important concept in the translation both of poetry and of problems. It was ironic, I thought, that the word *fidelity* was one I had to keep thinking about to get all this straight. It was a word Ken obviously hadn't been much concerned with.

Okay, enough already. That's something else Jennifer used to say when I'd get started dissecting a situation. "Okay, okay, enough already, Mom. Leave something to our imagination. You don't have to draw us a diagram on the chalkboard." So enough already. I see these connections between our discussion of translation and my marriage, and I tell them all to Margaret, who listens without interrupting me and then says, "That was beautiful." Which it wasn't, it most definitely wasn't, but I wasn't going to argue.

"Translation it is that openeth the window to let in the light, that breaketh the shell that we may eat the kernel." This is from the Preface to the King James Bible, and I think of it as I open the kitchen window on Easter morning. It's before eight o'clock, but in spite of my short night, I'm wide awake. It's a bright crisp morning. I stand at the window and count thirty-eight full-blown irises with many more ready to open. I remember a question Margaret asked me the night we discussed translation. She had walked me to my car and stood by as I unlocked the door and got in.

"After you have completed your translation, are you prepared for grace?" she asked before I closed the door.

I looked up at her. "Prepared for grace?" I said. "I've already received it, remember?"

"I do not mean the receiving of it, but the giving of it," she said. I knew already this was where she was headed.

"You can't extend grace to someone who's not interested," I said, but I knew this wasn't true. I hadn't been in the least bit interested in salvation through the atoning work of Christ that day back in February when I went over to Margaret's house for Sunday dinner, yet before I left, I had received from God's hand abundant grace. His willingness to extend it preceded my desire to take it.

Margaret could have pointed out my error, but she didn't. I'm sure she must have known that I was already reconsidering my words.

As I stand by my kitchen window on Easter morning, however, something inside me keeps insisting that a husband who has strayed needs to learn a lesson, and where's the lesson if his wife simply says, "That's okay, hon, I forgive you"? I'm ashamed to acknowledge it, but I can easily understand the expression *sweet revenge*.

As you can tell, my anger was still plenty hot on Easter Day. Prepared for grace? I don't think so. Not by a long shot, as my mother likes to say.

I remember what Polly Seacrest said one time when we were having one of our neighborhood chats over in Derby. Angie and Mack Nesbitt lived across the street from Polly and Morris, and as we were sitting on Polly's front steps that day, we saw the Nesbitts pull into their driveway in separate cars, one right after the other. The Seacrest kids were racing in a circle all around Polly's house, with Estella terrorizing Edwin and Eaton as usual, pretending to be a monster who was going to catch them and "snuff out their breaths," as she put it.

Mack Nesbitt flung his car door open and went inside, but Angie walked across the street in her candy-pink stretch pants and calmly informed us that she and Mack were splitting up, that they'd been to see a divorce lawyer that very day. Neither Polly nor I had known quite what to say, but finally Polly said bluntly, "What happened?" And Angie told us Mack had been consorting with his secretary at work for over a year. What a tired old horse of a story that was, I thought. Surely Mack could have come up with something more creative.

And then Polly said perfectly seriously, "I would kill Morris if he did that." Angie and I looked at her, and she nodded. "I mean it. I swear I would literally kill him somehow. Maybe strangle him while he was sleeping or put poison in his coffee, or maybe just shoot him point-blank with his hunting rifle or stab him in the back with a butcher knife. I don't know how I'd do it, but I'd kill him for sure." Just then Edwin and Eaton whizzed by again with Estella in hot pursuit roaring, "I'm gonna stomp on you and claw the living breaths out of your throat!"

"There you go, that's another idea," Polly had said, nodding. If Angie hadn't been standing right there looking so stunned, the echo of her news still lingering in the air, Polly's words probably would have been funny. "Yep, any husband of mine would suffer big time if he did something like that," Polly said. "Then I'd take his sorry carcass over to that secretary's house and dump it on her front lawn and knock on her front door and say, 'There you go, sweetheart, there's your lover boy. He's all yours.'" She nodded emphatically. "That's exactly what I'd do." I didn't doubt Polly a bit, that she'd do something like that, and I don't think Angie doubted her, either. Of course, I couldn't begin to imagine Morris Seacrest looking at another woman, so Polly's threats weren't going anywhere.

Anyway, all this zips through my mind on Easter morning, And I chide myself briefly. I want Easter Day to be special. My son is home, and in less than three hours I'll be standing with the choir to sing "Christ Arose." This should be the happiest day for Christians, a day of ultimate grace, not a day filled with thoughts of unfaithfulness and revenge. I decide to read my Bible and clear my mind before I get Travis up.

Even as I return to my bedroom, though, my thoughts go back to Angie Nesbitt. I never would have dreamed back then, hearing her talk, that someday I'd be in the same boat. Of course, it isn't Ken's secretary in my case, because he really doesn't have one. There is a secretary for the whole music department at his college. Emmie Lou Baddorf is her name, but she's sixty-two years old and built like a fifty-gallon hot-water tank. Here it is April, and I still don't know who Ken's been consorting with. I'm getting ready to learn, though. For a while I've felt myself inching closer to the point of finding out.

I got my Bible from my bedroom and took it to the den. I didn't open it, though. I sat on the sofa holding it in my lap, running my hand over the cover. Many people had given much that this book could be translated.

And here I was back to translation. I wanted a translation of my troubled marriage, as free from self as I could make it. *Stand aside,* I heard a voice say. *Don't impose your will on the picture as it takes shape. Don't force an interpretation. Be willing to go where you don't want to go.*

The truth is always there somewhere. Sometimes it's buried under many layers of other stuff, and sometimes it's far away, across a great gulf. Rainer Maria Rilke wrote a little poem to his Polish translator, I've heard, to release him from the old curse that brands a translator a traitor. He gave the translator his trust, assuring him that the absolute truth of the work would still breathe out of the lines regardless of the Polish words he chose to use. "Free of our bridges," he wrote, the "unsayable" does exist and will emerge.

I had done an awful lot of thinking about my own trouble since February, of course, but I had protected myself. Anything that got too close or self-incriminating I'd lock back up. I had made myself think I was being really open, looking truth in the eye and facing everything squarely, but I wasn't really. I'd take a little peek maybe, then shut my eyes again. All that business about my mother-in-law, for instance. I had felt something akin to self-righteousness when I forced myself to think of my relationship with Christine and put it into words, even admitting my part in her death. But I never got to the heart of that whole thing.

Say it now, I told myself sitting on the sofa, and I did. I let go and said it right out loud. "I hated Christine because I was jealous," I said. "I was convinced she had more of my husband's heart than I did, and because Christine had Ken, I was all the more determined to have Travis. He would be all mine. I wouldn't share him."

Every one of these words felt like it weighed a ton. The truth is often heavy. I had never admitted any of these things, much less spoken them aloud, and releasing them somehow made it a little easier to breathe. The air in the den seemed light and clear.

Up to this point I knew my thoughts had been here, there, and everywhere, random and without directionfulness. That's a word one of Travis's teachers used one time in a note home. "Travis daydreams alot in class," she wrote, "and lacks directionfulness." I had been tempted to write back a snippy note: "The term *a lot* is two separate words, and there's no such word as *directionfulness*." But I hadn't. I had asked Travis what he was doing in class that made his teacher think he was daydreaming, and he said, "Nothing." This was his other standard answer besides "I don't know."

In truth, his answer was probably very accurate, though. *Nothing* was most likely exactly what he was doing in class. If I hadn't tutored him at the kitchen table and supervised his homework and study, his grades would have been abominable.

For the record, let me say that Ken didn't agree with this. More than once he stated the opinion that the reason Travis was unfocused in school was because he knew I'd reteach everything at home. I could see now that he was probably right. And backing up a few sentences, maybe his grades wouldn't have been so bad if I hadn't helped him. Maybe after the initial shock of flying solo, he would have spread his wings and gained new heights. Maybe I kept him earthbound with all my tutoring.

But anyway, back to my translation project. I wanted to be free of my bridges, free of my lifelong obsession with finding just the right words to say something. I knew I was perfectly capable of verbalizing something to death. I often got so consumed with *how* I was saying something that I had to bend *what* I was saying a little bit in order to get it to fit a pattern.

To be honest, this was the problem with a lot of the poetry I had tried to write. The words themselves were lush and beautiful, sometimes extravagant and cleverly turned, but taken together, they rarely added up to what I was really trying to say. I was too intent on how my words could function as emblems within a dazzling form, so I ended up skating around the edges of truth. I was still such a beginner in so many ways, still looking down at my shiny new skates and sticking close to the well-frozen perimeter instead of venturing onto the broad, dangerous, thinner stretch of ice in the middle of the lake.

But I wasn't going to do this anymore. I was going to look for plain, honest ways of saying what I knew to be so. Sitting in my den on Easter morning was a moment of decision for me. I knew it wasn't going to be easy, though. There on the sofa I prayed right out loud, "Keep showing me scenes from my marriage. Help me to look at them squarely and admit the truth."

Maybe somebody reading this is already saying, "Hey, you can't pray something like that. You can't make some vague, general request like that of God."

But here's what I have to say about that. Why not? I can't see why God would balk at such a prayer. If he could make the walls of Jericho fall, if he could open up the Red Sea, and if he could make manna fall from heaven and the sun go backwards and Lazarus walk out of the tomb alive, would somebody please tell me why he can't bring to my mind pictures that will enlighten my understanding? If I read my Bible right, that's one thing God wants us to have—understanding.

Travis got up while I was still in the den. I heard him running water in the bathroom. Here was another change. He used to wait for me to wake him up on weekends. After his shower, he found an old short-sleeved blue

Oxford cloth dress shirt in the back of his closet that still fit him and, amazingly, a pair of navy corduroy pants he could wear with them. Not exactly right for the season, but it didn't matter to either of us. The pants were ones I had bought him after Christmas a year ago, but he'd never liked them because the legs were too baggy or the pleats in front too full or some such tailoring defect.

Travis is an odd bird when it comes to clothes. He's not really picky about name brands and that sort of thing, but he latches onto favorite items and wears them with unabashed frequency while politely ignoring other nicer, more expensive things I bring home.

He put on a red necktie he'd worn a few times in high school, and if you didn't look down at his old brown Docksiders, he actually cut quite a presentable figure for church. The night before, on Saturday, I had left a message on Ken's answering machine in his office, telling him Travis was home for a surprise visit. I figured he'd check his messages during the next few days. So ten minutes before time for us to walk out the door for the Easter service, I hear a car in the driveway. This is typical of Ken's timing.

Travis is drinking a glass of milk and eating a doughnut from the box we had brought home from the Donut Castle on the way back from getting milk shakes the night before. He's sitting at the kitchen table reading the Sunday comics as he eats, giving no hint whatsoever of the talk he's going to initiate later that day. I wish I had known so I could have prepared myself, but that all comes later.

Before we know it, Ken's there, unlocking the door with his key and walking into the kitchen. I step out of the bedroom, where I'm getting dressed, and I hear him say, "Hey there, so you didn't go to Myrtle Beach after all, huh?" I hear a muffled slapping sound as if Ken and Travis are embracing and one of them is thumping the other on the back, though I can't imagine this. I can't remember that last time they hugged each other.

Somehow we end up going to church together, the three of us. It has been decided before I get out to the kitchen in my yellow linen suit. I have no idea how it all came about. Ken probably asked Travis why he was dressed like that, and Travis probably told him and maybe suggested he come along so he wouldn't have to suffer alone. And Ken probably gave in because he couldn't think of a good excuse, having no golf game set up for the day.

Anyway, we're somehow suddenly all three in Ken's car driving toward Derby, with me sitting in the front and Travis in the back like it always used to be. Ken gives no sign of having noticed my new haircut, which doesn't surprise me. The next thing I know I'm sitting in the choir looking out at the congregation, and Travis and Ken are sitting side by side four rows from the back on the center aisle. Most of the other men are wearing suits, of course, but Ken is wearing an open-necked polo shirt—pale cream with light blue stripes. The clock says that it's a minute before eleven. Everybody in the sanctuary is still talking, though, and people are still milling about. Pastor Hawthorne and Willard Scoggins are conferring in low tones on the platform.

I watch as Eldeen Rafferty comes into the sanctuary through the double doors at the back, stopping first to say something to the usher, an elderly man about half her size. She towers over him and leans in to say something directly into his ear, then squeezes his arm and moves on. The usher looks shaken after she has left. She stops again near the back and waves her bulletin at someone sitting in the middle of the same pew as Ken and Travis.

Then she looks intently at Ken and Travis and bends forward to ask something. I can see her mouth fall open, then stretch into her peculiar smile, which always looks like the expression you'd expect on the face of someone who just slammed the car door on his finger. She reaches forward, taking Ken's hand in one of hers and Travis's in the other, and then shakes them both at the same time.

I can imagine what she's saying, though I can't hear her, of course. "Why, I been prayin' you'd come and pay us a visit here at the Open Door, but I never dreamed we'd be so blessed as to have the *both* of you turn up on the *same day*—and Easter Sunday to boot! If that doesn't just fill me with pure wonder and delight to meet my friend Elizabeth's kinfolk! You're just as welcome as you can be, and then some!" And so forth and so on.

Pastor Hawthorne gets up to start the service before she's done, and I can imagine Ken and Travis feeling dazed as she finally lumbers away to find her seat closer to the front. And here's the thought that sweeps over me as I look at Ken and Travis sitting in my church on Easter Sunday. *I want this to happen again.*

I want my husband and son to come to church with me regularly. And I don't stop there. I want Ken and Travis to accept God's gift of salvation—and Jennifer, too. I want us to be a family united for eternity.

That Sunday in the choir I say these words to myself: "I want my husband back." No, not just back living in the house with me, but I want him in a way I've never really had him. "I want my husband," I say again, dropping the "back." I don't just want to be married. I want a new relationship with the man I love. This is what I wish on Resurrection Day.

And even as I wonder whether this can ever be, considering what has come to pass between us, I say it again. "I want my husband." I imagine the words hanging in the air like the dense, richly sweet fragrance of the lilacs blooming in our backyard right now, the ones planted and tended years ago by a woman I never knew, the ones grown tall and sparse from neglect, all but choked out by the encroaching redtips nearby but whose few blossoms reach high for sunlight and bend forward from their own weight.

In a Room With Paintings

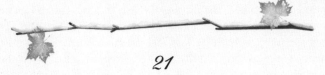

21

"The other woman" has a sinister sound. I have seen her with my own eyes now. She doesn't *look* all that sinister—early- to mid-forties, medium height, a little pillowy around the hips, long hair that has obviously been touched up with color since it's a youthful honey blond, almost exactly the color mine used to be, in fact, before it started fading. I guess Ken suspended his rule about no long hair past thirty-five when he met her.

I find out that she's a teacher at Harwood College, where Ken teaches. According to my source, she joined the faculty just last fall after returning to the States from the heart of Africa, where she lived with some tribe that had no written language until she came along. I'd like to have seen her hair during those days. I doubt if she wore it down over her shoulders, as she does now. It was probably yanked up into a tight little sweaty wad on top of her head during that year in the jungle.

She's a linguistics scholar, and the tribal language project was her doctoral dissertation. Doctor Snipe is what the kid called her. It pleases me just ever so slightly that her last name isn't what I'd call a pretty name. Have you ever noticed that only a few of the words that start with *sn* are pretty words? Most of them have negative connotations. Sneak, sneer, snide, snitch, snivel, snort, snoop, and so on. I hope her first name matches her last. Let me back up and tell how I found out about her. This is fresh information, learned only a few nights ago.

It's curious, but now that I know who she is, have set my eyes on her and observed her from the balcony of a dark auditorium, something settles down inside me. I quit imagining a glamorous young model and readjust the picture to the more ordinary-looking Dr. Snipe. I should have sought her out earlier, I guess. But then it doesn't really matter all that much what the other woman looks like. The fact remains that she has *something* that attracted your man. Actually, I guess it might be a little more threatening if you know it's not just her looks. Still, it helps me in some strange way to have seen her.

It's early May now. A few days ago on my way home from subbing for a Spanish teacher at Derby High, I had an idea. It originated from the Spanish classes I had just taught. This teacher, who had snapped her neck pretty badly in a rear-end collision over the weekend, was big on the idea of immersing language students in the culture of Spain and the Latin American countries instead of just teaching them words in a list. The wet method versus the dry, she called it.

In her lesson plan for the day she had written "Play selections of twentieth-century music and show pictures of contemporary art." She didn't elaborate on these plans by listing common characteristics of twentieth-century Spanish and Latino artists or ideological influences or parallel trends in literature or socioeconomic concurrences or historical context or any of that, but fortunately, I discovered when I went to her classroom that morning that she had already collected all the samples and had them stacked neatly on an audiovisual cart beside her desk.

Now here was a happy development. I can't count the number of times teachers have written something like that in their lesson plans without giving the substitute a clue as to where any of the materials actually are. Either this woman had a premonition that she wasn't going to be at school on Monday, or else she was extremely well organized.

Señorita Verde was what the students called her since *verde* meant green and her real name was Janelle Greene. They didn't look any too excited to see me sitting at her desk when they walked in, let me tell you, which let me know she was probably either a very good teacher or a very lax one. If she was good, they were very likely dreading a lousy lesson from a substitute who probably thought *que* rhymed with *due* and who didn't know a *perro* from a *gato*, and if she was lax, they were probably afraid that a substitute would expect too much out of them. Luckily I had taken three years of Spanish back in high school and had worked through two more years with Travis not too long ago, so at least I wouldn't embarrass myself with the pronunciations.

Señorita Verde, I learned from a freshman girl in the first-hour class who evidently adored her, was engaged to be married to one of the math teachers at the same school, Vince Rivers. Señorita Verde had jet-black hair and "these real thick eyelashes, like a night-club singer," the girl told me, while Mr. Rivers was "a blond California hunk." Ninth graders these days talk as if they've seen the world. "So next year we'll have to call her Señora Rios," the girl said importantly, rolling the *r*'s. This girl made it very clear that I was a mighty poor fill-in for the lovely young Señorita Verde.

Well, on to the point of all this. One of the musical selections I played for the Spanish students reminded me of something, which in turn led to my

seeing the "other woman," Dr. Snipe. It was a piece called "Huapango" by
Jose Pablo Moncayo, and I recognized it right off. Ken's band had played it
at Harwood four or five years back when he put together a program of music
from around the world.

"Huapango" was the first piece they played that night, and it lit a fire
under that whole concert, believe me. It was a Mexican fiesta in full swing.
Jose Pablo Moncayo had figured out a way to adapt the scientific concept of
spontaneous combustion to music. He knew how to turn notes on a page
into a roaring blaze. I had never seen the printed music for the piece, but
each page should have been stamped with a bold red warning: *FLAMMA-
BLE.*

I had no trouble filling up each class period. There's another advantage
of substitute teaching. You can play around with the lesson plans. For example, though Señorita Verde hadn't said to do this, I took the liberty of
having the students try composing short poems inspired by "Huapango." In
English, though, not in Spanish. I told them to describe a scene they imagined taking place, and I stressed the importance of images. Here is a poem
one student wrote. I copied it down and saved it. The kid who wrote it had
a buzz haircut and wore glasses an inch thick. When he read his poem aloud,
other kids smirked.

> Lanterns sway from the branches.
> The flames of the campfire leap in the night
> Like the slapping waves of the lake beyond.
> The storm clouds roll by,
> The black sky turns starry, and
> Overhead the silver crescent moon smiles
> As the children of Zamora dance in the sand.

Not bad for a sophomore boy. Not bad for anybody. It suddenly dawns
on me as the first-hour class leaves and I'm still hearing "Huapango" in my
head that this is the time of year when Ken's band gives their final concert.
In the past it was always sometime during the first or second weekend of
May.

And I also remember that during the week leading up to the concert they
always used to have two or three evening rehearsals in the auditorium where
they would be playing. When Travis was in middle school and high school,
he and I used to go to some of these rehearsals and sit in the balcony. This
is the first week of May, so maybe the concert is this very week. This important thought leads to another: *Maybe this timely realization means that you're
supposed to go to one of the rehearsals.* An answer comes right on its heels. *No,
Ken might see me.* The reply is just as quick. *Not if you sit in the balcony and not
if the auditorium is dark like it used to be during rehearsals, and even if it's not, and
he does see you, so what?* I'm not even sure why I want to go to one of Ken's

rehearsals, but I know suddenly and certainly that I do.

By this time, as I've continued thinking backwards through my marriage, I've seen more pictures and have been busy trying to translate them. I prayed that God would show me scenes, and I mean to tell you he's answered my prayers abundantly day and night. Some of them have been hard to look at, but I've forced myself to do so, and I've talked a lot of things over with Margaret, and I've admitted some things.

To illustrate, here's something I made myself say out loud just last week: "I've lived my entire life as a cautious person, always afraid to step into new territory because I might fail." This is very true. I know, for instance, that this is one reason I never pursued art further. I loved it but was scared I wouldn't ever be good enough to do anything worthwhile. So all my life I've looked at art from the sidelines.

In museums you see those red velvet ropes draped between little brass poles positioned in front of paintings to keep people from getting too close. When I was a teenager, my father took me to an art gallery in Atlanta, and I've never forgotten watching a woman in a glittery gold shawl step right around one of those ropes and put her nose six inches from a painting called *Berries on a Table*. It was a painting of a basket on an old wooden tabletop. The basket was tipped over, and raspberries, blueberries, and cranberries spilled out onto the table. The woman had to crane her neck to look up at it, of course, so the view couldn't have been very clear, but still I couldn't help admiring her. To step around a barricade that way!

I've always stayed behind the ropes, and when I look at Travis's life, I can't help seeing with my improving vision that I've transferred this mindset to him. So much of what I've done has suggested to him, "Stick with the familiar and safe."

I think about all the new and dangerous things I was too afraid to deal with. That's why I had always guarded my private space from Ken, why I didn't want to move to a nicer house, why I never worked to keep up my friendship with Polly Seacrest after we moved, why I preferred to read poetry instead of pushing myself to write more of it, why I subbed instead of committing myself to a regular teaching position, why I clung to Travis even when I knew it was time to let go, and on and on it goes.

Even though my willingness to help out with book drives, bake sales, YMCA luncheons, school committees, and all of that might seem like a contradiction, it's not, believe me. I think I've deceived myself about this over the years. You see, I'm not afraid to volunteer for something that requires carrying out somebody else's orders. Give me a job and I'll do it really well. I'll organize my little section meticulously, answer questions politely, and clean up after myself. That doesn't take any courage to speak of. Even singing in the choir at church is not scary, because I'm in a group doing what the person in charge says to do. That's easy.

But personal relationships—now that's where the real risk in life is. Find-ing out you're not as important to someone else as that person is to you—that's terrifying. Or finding out that something that comes from deep inside the very center of yourself has no merit in the eyes of others—I can't imag-ine being brave enough to place yourself in a position to find that out.

So anyway, back to my point. I decide I want to step out of my cautious world for a few moments and sneak into one of Ken's band rehearsals. I'm not exactly sure why—maybe to observe my husband doing something he loves, maybe to make myself take a risk now that I've recognized and admit-ted this weakness of mine, or maybe simply to hear live music.

Travis's visit over Easter reminded me that I hadn't heard much music lately. He and Ken always used to keep the house filled with music—no, flooded and overflowing with music is more like it. I used to call out things like "I wish you two would get together on what you're listening to!" Neither one of them ever heard me, though. From Travis's bedroom the sounds of a swing band might be cranking out "Tuxedo Junction" or "Little Brown Jug," while I might hear the strains of Edward Elgar's "Enigma Variations" coming from the living room. There's a contrast for you!

Then Travis might change and put on Wynton Marsalis playing some-thing soulful, maybe "Sometimes I Feel Like a Motherless Child," while Ken switched to one of Dvorak's Slavonic dances, and then Travis might move on to John Williams' *Star Wars* music, while Ken put on some Mozart. Ken liked opera, too. Once I distinctly remember hearing Kathleen Battle singing the part of Sophia from *Der Rosenkavalier* in one room at the very same time Natalie Cole was belting out "Orange-Colored Sky" in Travis's room.

Consider the fact that both Travis and Ken like to play their music loud, and you can sympathize with me. Thankfully, since Ken was often writing his own music, he didn't play his tapes or records or CDs as much as Travis did his. I always saw this music thing as a metaphor for their whole relation-ship, since the two of them were never on the same wavelength.

Anyway, I find myself wanting to hear music again, and I don't waste any time making plans. During my lunch break later that day I call Harwood College from the teachers' lounge and ask the dates and times of the band rehearsals. The woman I talk to first connects me to the music building, and Emmie Lou Baddorf comes on the line. She doesn't recognize my voice and assumes I'm the mother of a town student. "I know these kids have a lot to try to keep track of, poor things," she says to mark time as she shuffles around trying to find the calendar.

"The poor things will have a lot more to keep up with after they graduate and find out what real life is like," I want to say. Finally Emmie Lou locates what she's looking for and tells me there's a rehearsal the next night, Tues-day, and another one Thursday night, and the concert is Friday night. I con-gratulate myself for guessing right.

I decide on the Tuesday night rehearsal because Thursday night is my last poetry class with Dr. Huckabee, and I don't want to miss that.

So the next night, thirty minutes after the rehearsal is scheduled to start, I pull into the parking lot in front of the Felix Zane Auditorium at Harwood College. I'm wanting to make sure that everyone is in place on stage so the chances of my being seen are less. I go in the side door by the green room and hear the sounds of music immediately. Then it stops abruptly, and I hear Ken's voice saying something I can't understand, and the music starts again. My heart is racing as I realize how adventurous I'm being. I find my way to the balcony stairs and climb them. I don't run into anybody else, which is what I had hoped for.

I open the balcony door and slip through. The door closes silently, controlled by some kind of air pressure device. Even if it had creaked and scraped, though, it would have been covered up by all the other sound whirling around. The band is playing something bombastic that I don't recognize, and everybody's eyes are glued to the music, which is part of the reason why Ken stops them again.

"You've got to listen to each other!" he says with a tone of exasperation. "Things are sticking out all over the place! Trumpets, there are other instruments in the band besides you, and I'm pretty sure the composer wanted them to be heard." Some of the players smile and look chastened, while others look as if they're not even listening to him. One clarinet player runs a rag through her instrument as if this little break is just for her convenience, and two of the percussionists are whispering in the back.

The stage is lighted, of course, but the auditorium itself isn't, and the balcony is even darker. After Ken gets them started again, I move away from the door and sit down in the second row. I sit in that one spot for over an hour, watching those fifty students get a workout from Ken. I haven't seen him conduct in a long time, and I love the way he does it with such purpose yet with easy grace.

He doesn't let anything go. Ken doesn't put up with silliness, and they all seem to know it. "You're late!" he bellows at one point when the French horns enter timidly. He cuts everybody off, and the clarinet player picks up her rag again. "You can't wait for somebody else to start it!" Ken points his baton at the four horn players. "I've seen you play basketball, Palmer," he says to one of them. "You don't stand around and wait when somebody passes you the ball and the clock's running out." Palmer laughs and says, "But that's easier." He holds up his horn. "This thing doesn't bounce." There's a weighty pause as if everyone is shocked by Palmer's ill-timed flippancy.

"I'm very tempted to see if it does," Ken says at last, and everybody breathes again and laughs. Then Ken taps his baton on his stand to start again. "Dunk it this time," he says to the horns right before he gives the downbeat. It's funny how you can tell they're smiling even with their mouths all jammed up against their instruments.

Another time the whole band muffs a cutoff and crashes. Ken drops his arms and throws his head back. After a moment of silence while still looking at the ceiling, he says very quietly but intensely, "There's an old game children play called follow-the-leader." Nobody is laughing or talking now. The clarinetist with the rag doesn't move a muscle. Ken looks around at every band member. "I'm the leader," he says. "You have to follow me. You need me. You can't do this without me." He lifts his baton again. "We'll start at letter F and go to the end." This time they all follow him as if he's the Pied Piper, and it's perfect.

"I had every confidence that you could do it" is all he says afterward, but you can tell he's very pleased. They move right on to the next piece, which he announces as "Circus Polka," and start going through it.

He gives them two short breaks during the rehearsal, but mostly he works them measure by measure through five or six different pieces. I look at my watch sometime around eight-fifty and decide I'd better go so I won't get caught still hanging around when the rehearsal ends. I stand up to leave and then see something that makes me sit down again.

A woman is walking slowly down the side aisle of the main floor below me. Even in the dim light, I can tell she's watching Ken. When she gets to the second row, she stops and stands for a few seconds. Several of the players notice her, and then when Ken stops to fix a tricky rhythm that's giving the flutes trouble, he glances over and sees her. She gives a little wave, but he doesn't acknowledge it. I feel my throat go dry.

She's got a sweater tied by its sleeves around her shoulders, and she's wearing pants. She sits down at the end of the second row and turns her body toward Ken, leaning forward in her seat and propping one elbow on the seat in front of her. I don't miss the irony of this whole thing, believe me. Here I am, his wife of almost thirty years, hiding in the balcony, afraid of being seen, while this woman parades right down front and *waves* at him. We both choose the second row to sit in, and we're both here to watch Ken, but everything else is completely different.

I know I need to leave, but I can't take my eyes off her. She's nothing like what I had imagined her to be. I am suddenly overwhelmed with a desire to know her. I feel myself getting ready to do something impulsive. Ken starts the band up again, and I slip out of the balcony. I go downstairs to the green room, but it's empty. I walk outside and go around to the front doors. They're all locked, but one of the doors on the other side is open. This must be the door she came in through.

I see the hallway leading back to the dressing rooms, and I follow it. Meanwhile the music plays on with stops and starts. At one point I hear Ken yell at the top of his lungs, "Softer! This section is a lullaby! You don't want to wake up the baby!" I know at the end of this hallway is a big control desk where the stage manager usually sits, and I'm happy to see a young man stationed there now. He appears to be reading a big book spread out in front of him. Maybe he's a student worker and gets to study on the job, though I can't see how anybody could study at a band rehearsal.

From where I'm standing now, I can see the players sitting in the back of the band, but they don't see me. I get the attention of the stage guy and motion to him. He comes over, and I say, "There's somebody sitting out in the second row of the auditorium. I need to know her name." The logical solution for him to suggest would be for me to go out there and ask her, but he doesn't.

He ambles onto the stage behind the percussionists and stands for a few seconds pretending to look up at the lights. Then he walks to the other side of the stage and does the same. The rehearsal goes right on as if they're all used to stagehands moving around.

He comes back to where I'm standing, and we step back into the hallway. "That's Dr. Snipe," he tells me. "She's a teacher here."

"Oh" is all I can think of to say.

"She's new this year," he says, and he goes on to tell about her year in Africa with the linguistics project. "I don't have her for any classes," he says, "but my roommate does." He pauses. "Do you need to get a message to her or something?" He looks at me curiously as if he's starting to wonder who I am and what I'm doing slinking around the building. Maybe he's wondering if he should call campus security.

"No, no," I say. "I just needed to know her name is all. It's nothing, really," and I turn to leave, then call back softly, "Thanks a lot for your help." I hurry out to the parking lot, eager to get away before the rehearsal ends. I'm also looking for something I'm quite sure I'll find, and I do. It sits a little lopsided under a huge oak tree where the roots have started to push up against the asphalt. It's a blue Mazda. I can't resist stopping and looking in it as I pass by.

It's dark by now, but the parking lot is well lighted. I don't really know what I expect to see when I look into the car, but I find that it's remarkably neat, with nothing lying on the seats or floors. This doesn't surprise me. Ken would never be attracted to anyone messy. The only thing I see that's the least bit unusual is a large rabbit's foot dangling from the rearview mirror. It's so big that I wonder if it's fake. Or maybe it came from some rare jumbo breed of African hare, maybe considered a delicacy by the natives she worked among. Maybe they roasted it over a ceremonial fire as they sang the chant of the new moon or something. Maybe they covered their shields with its skin to ward off evil spirits. Maybe they gave her this fellow's foot as a good-luck token before she left.

My hands are shaking as I pull out of the parking lot. I wish I could say that I prayed aloud or recited verses of Scripture, but I didn't. Not right then. *I have seen the enemy* are the words that keep going through my head. I wish I had thought to ask if she was married, but the stage guy was getting suspicious enough without that.

It's funny that the other woman has turned out to be a fellow teacher of Ken's. That was never something I worried about. From time to time I used to worry about his college students, all those pretty twenty-year-olds who sat in his classes or in his band and looked up at him with their big adoring eyes. Polly used to tell me things like "I bet those girls at Harwood think he's It! You better make sure they know he's married, girl." I wonder if Ken's students know he's carrying on with Dr. Snipe. They would have to suspect something if she'd show up at a rehearsal and sit right down front.

I see another picture as I drive home. It is probably triggered by the memory of Dr. Snipe sitting in the second row, leaning forward toward Ken as he conducted, looking as if she were trying very hard to restrain herself from rushing up to the stage and throwing herself at him.

This picture is only a small one but incredibly detailed. I see myself sitting in our bedroom in our old house in Derby. This house is nothing elegant, trust me, but it has a certain dignity, like an old car that has been well maintained. Margaret has a car like this—a 1967 black Ford that Thomas keeps "polished and purring," as he likes to say. This is totally irrelevant to my point, though.

Back to the picture. I'm in our bedroom propped up in bed against my pillows reading a book of poems by Jane Kenyon. It must be some seven or eight years ago. The book, *Constance*, is a new one I have just purchased. I am turning the page to begin reading a poem titled "Otherwise," and by the time I finish it, I'm breathing hard. Here's why: I had eaten a peach with my cereal that very morning, I had spent the next three hours after breakfast working on a poem about my father, I had set silver candlesticks on the table that evening when I served German pot roast for dinner, and I was now lying in bed "in a room with paintings."

And you're saying, "So what?" Well, here's the point. Jane Kenyon's poem "Otherwise" mentions all these things—the peach, the satisfying work, the candlesticks, the paintings on the wall. What she's saying is this: "Today I enjoyed all these things, but I know these days won't last." She's looking back and ahead at the same time, and joy and sorrow are pulling hard in opposite directions.

As I drive back home after seeing Ken conduct his band, I'm seeing myself clearly as I sit in bed late at night holding that book of poetry and staring around our bedroom at the artwork I've picked up here and there. I wouldn't know Jane Kenyon if I passed her on the street, but I know this poem was written for me. I know exactly what it's trying to tell me, too. It's speaking quietly but emphatically. "Be thankful for what you have right now." It's as if I'm standing over in a corner watching myself. I see myself turn my eyes toward the bedroom door, which is closed.

I know what's on the other side of that door. Jennifer's bedroom is directly across the hall. It's the summer before she goes away to college, and I'm certain her light is still on. She has no lights-out time anymore.

Travis's room is next to hers. His light has been out for a couple of hours already. He has never fought going to bed the way Jennifer always has. He loves his evening routine—a long bath, a snack, a chapter from a book I read to him, and another twenty or thirty minutes of reading on his own, usually with a record playing at the same time. He has some of Ken's old LPs that he plays over and over, odd things for an eleven-year-old—the Norman Luboff Choir singing sea chanties, cowboy songs, Early American folk songs, music of the British Isles.

This house is small, remember, much smaller than the one we live in now. Down the hall from Travis's bedroom is the living room. We have no den, so this room gets a lot of use. At one end of the living room, beside a door leading into the kitchen, Ken sits at his desk. I know he's writing a band arrangement called "For Heroes and Monarchs," and I know it's almost finished. He hopes to have it published and, in fact, succeeds at this the very next year. One advantage of revisiting the past, you see, is that you already know the future.

I know I could open our bedroom door, walk down the hallway, go into the living room, and put my arms around Ken's neck. I know beyond a doubt that he would put his pencil down and turn to me. I know that without saying a word I could lead him back to our bedroom. I know I could close the door and say to him, "This moment is precious, and we won't always have it. Let's love each other as if we understand the value of every day. Let's gather wood together and lay a fire to drive away the cold that has crept into our home." And even though it's summer, I feel quite sure that Ken would catch my metaphor and would labor with me to chop wood and carry logs inside by the armful to build a fire.

I see myself set the book of poems on the bedside table, then push back the covers and place one foot on the floor. I see myself hesitate, then pull my foot back up. I hear Ken in the hallway. It's late and he's coming to bed. I've missed my opportunity. I realize immediately that this isn't at all true. I can meet him at the door, pull him into the bedroom, and make my speech. He's actually making it easier for me by coming to me. I hear him coming closer, and I see myself on the edge of the bed in a moment of indecision before I quickly turn out the lamp and cover myself up.

He opens the door and stands there a few seconds in the dark. "I saw the light under the door," he says. "I thought you were still up."

I could have done it then. It wasn't too late. I could have turned the light back on, held out my arms, and said it then. Or even fifteen minutes later when he came out of the bathroom and got into bed. I could have moved over to him and whispered it in the dark.

But I didn't. By that time I had asked myself why I had to be the one to say those things. Why couldn't *he* feel the cold and do something about it? He got into bed and reached over to touch my nightgown. He still hung onto that funny little ritual of his—clutching a handful of my nightgown and holding onto it until he went to sleep. It was sort of sweet, really, but tonight it irritated me.

I have nighttime and X-ray vision in this picture I'm seeing. From my corner vantage in the bedroom, I see myself roll over, turning away from Ken, and yank my swatch of nightgown out of his hand. I sigh and squeeze my eyes shut, and he lies still. There is no sound in the darkness.

While the Sun Walked High

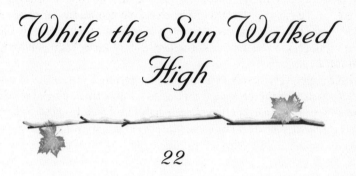

22

When Ken and I were in college, I went to watch him play soccer one night. We had met each other at the end of the previous school year and had dated a few times, and now it was the end of September, and we were juniors. We hadn't seen each other over the summer, but I had thought about him every day. He must have still been interested in me, too, because as soon as we got back to school that fall, he asked me out, and we started dating again. So one Saturday in late September, a cool evening, I walked over to the athletic field where the Piper soccer team was playing St. Francis, a Catholic college.

Ken wasn't a starter but was subbed in with about fifteen minutes left in the first half. He was a midfielder, and if he had spent as much time practicing his soccer skills as he did his trumpet, he could have been really good. As it was, he was well above average—good speed and good instincts. I didn't know much about soccer at the time, but I liked to watch it and could see the intelligence and patience it must take to play it well. For some reason Ken had decided to wear a knit cap that night. He's always been funny that way, wearing caps and gloves and wool scarves. Just another way he insulates himself.

He saw me in the bleachers and caught my eye but didn't wave. He's not the waving kind. He did nod, though. I was sitting in the third or fourth row close to the middle of the field. The cheerleaders were lined up to my left and the extra players to my right. After Ken went in to play, he must have found that his cap was too hot, and before a throw-in he yanked it off and tossed it over past the sideline. It landed right in front of the bleachers not far from where I was sitting, and I looked at it for a few moments before deciding to get it and keep it for him. It was a rust-colored cap—I remember that clearly—the kind you pull down snugly over your head.

Just as I stood up to go get the cap, one of the cheerleaders, a perky petite blonde named Kelley, left the lineup, ran over to Ken's cap, and picked it up. She shook it off, then pulled it down over her long, straight blond hair and ran back to get in formation with the other cheerleaders, who all laughed at her. I sat back down, amazed at her audacity. Not only amazed but also angry. I was sure Ken had meant for me to get his cap, not a silly cheerleader. And I was also sure he didn't want someone else wearing his cap. He'd have to wash it now.

She even had the nerve when the whistle blew for halftime to call to Ken as he was coming off the field. "Hey, Ken! Like my cap?" I wanted to charge down there and choke her. I didn't remember ever feeling such fury before. Of course, I kept my seat and fumed in silence, and after the game she gave Ken his cap back with a flirtatious little thank-you. She knew she was cute, and she flaunted it. I wished her all manner of ill, then tried to act as if it didn't bother me when Ken came over to talk to me afterward.

I guess I would have given Ken up to the cheerleader back there on the soccer field if he had acted the least bit attracted to her. He didn't, though. He took his cap from her and turned it over in his hands, looking at it as if it had been contaminated. I remember feeling gratified, even though I did wonder if he would have done the same thing if he had seen *me* wearing it. I had never known a guy with such old-womanish standards of cleanliness, and it struck me as very quaint and endearing in the early days of our courtship. More recently it has struck me as weird and irritating.

I was reminded of this little incident as I drove home from the band rehearsal. It had been my first real experience with jealousy in a dating relationship, which might seem a bit overdue, but I had never really had a dating relationship before this. I had learned along the way, you see, that guys aren't much drawn to girls who consistently outshine them in grades and sports.

I guess the bright boys had always seen me as a rival for academic awards and scholarships, and from what I could tell, most of the athletic boys went either for the cute and spacy types who thought of school as one big social event or for the girls who didn't have very good reputations. You'd think the boys on the tennis team at Burma High would have liked to date someone who could go out on the court with them and play a couple of decent sets, but they all seemed to resent me, especially after the coach put me in as a sub for the boys' number-four player who was sick on the day of a school match against the former state champions, J. M. Brighton High. And especially after I beat the Brighton number-four player that day in two easy sets, 6–2, 6–1. The guy complained, of course, that it wasn't fair, that he couldn't play his best against a girl and all that.

But to get back to my point, I felt the same seething rage toward Dr. Snipe as I had toward Kelley the cheerleader, except this time it was about a hundred times hotter. This was ripe, mature rage. It wasn't just a knit cap she had snatched from me, but my husband. For just a few seconds, my anger at Ken was overshadowed by my anger at this woman. She had taken something that was mine. This kind of response was something new. Oh, I could be plenty aggressive on the tennis court when I was pounding on a ball, but that was impersonal. When it came to people, it was totally different.

As I said, I probably would have surrendered Ken to Kelley without a fight all those years ago when I was insecure, cautious, and young. But driving home now with a picture of Dr. Snipe in my head, I feel myself grabbing the steering wheel tightly and gritting my teeth. My breath is coming fast. Something as hard as steel is replacing my backbone, and I sit tall. I feel my insides filling up with resolve.

I'm very aware that this is something especially big that I'm thinking right now. I lean forward, staring at the road, and here's what is going through my mind: *I'm not giving my husband up meekly. I've been married for twenty-eight years, and I want to make it to thirty, then thirty-five, then forty. I want a 24-karat gold necklace on our fiftieth anniversary.*

I've made Ken's life an easy one in many ways. In twenty-eight years I've cooked a lot of meals, washed a lot a clothes, scrubbed a lot of floors. When brass players empty their spit valves, they sometimes miss the newspaper on the floor, and with two of them in the house, my mop rarely had time to dry out.

Over the years Ken has been free to teach, conduct, compose, travel. I've stayed home and sewn buttons on his shirts, folded his underwear, taken his pants to the dry cleaners when he's dripped valve oil on them. I've even washed the cars and done yard work on occasion. Several times I've climbed up on top of the roof to clean out the gutters when he was out of town. I haven't been a lazy wife. I've contributed.

Maybe there are lots of things I haven't done that I should have, but I'm not thinking of them right now. I'm thinking of all the ways I've helped him, and this isn't the time for being modest and humble. If Ken Landis had paid someone to do all the housekeeping chores I've done, he would have shelled out a small fortune.

I won't be put out to pasture. My throat tightens as I think of Donald Hall's poem "Names of Horses." This poem always affects me this way even though I'm not a horse lover. I never got into those books about horses—*Black Beauty, National Velvet, My Friend Flicka*, all those—but I have to sit down and catch my breath every time I read "Names of Horses." It's such a brutally truthful poem. Donald Hall tells the story of a horse's life with such heart-aching plainness, listing in monotone quatrains all the work the horse does through all the seasons of the year—hauling, pulling, mowing, haying.

On Sundays he got off easy, having only to pull the buggy two miles to church.

Read it. You'll feel your throat tighten, too, when you come to the end. Read what happens when the horse gets old and starts to stumble, how he gets his own special place in the meadow—in a grave with goldenrod growing on top. Even if you don't care a whit about horses, you'll feel something almost like a moan coming out of your mouth when you read that last line, where Donald Hall names the horses of his childhood. And it's because you'll put your own name in there somewhere. We live our lives, and then we die. One day the horse was serving a useful purpose "while the sun walked high in the morning," and the next he was mingling with tree roots. We all have that in common—horse or man.

I'm not ready for the pasture, though. The sun is still too high in the sky. I don't mean to see our marriage shot behind the ear, then rolled into a sandy grave. The days are still long and useful, and I want them back. Not just the days themselves, but Ken. Something like a sudden hot wind hits me now as I remember again that it takes two for reconciliation. There are three people in this mess, and I'm outnumbered two to one. "You can't force him back." I hear a taunting voice reminding me of this. I drive on, fluctuating between determination and dismay.

By the time I arrive home, I've come to my senses again and remembered that I'm not outnumbered two to one at all. I have God on my side. It would be a despairing situation but for this one wonderful fact. And don't judge me harshly for temporarily forgetting this. My guess is that all Christians, even the veterans, have to keep reminding themselves that the battles aren't theirs alone, that they don't have to figure it out all by themselves. Maybe someday I'll reach the point where I can say right from the start, "Okay, God, I'm trusting in you to help me."

As I pull into my driveway, I remember the passage in the second chapter of Hosea that speaks of the restoration of Israel. "And she shall sing there, as in the days of her youth." I know the verses well, for I've read them many times now. God promises to give his people a song of joy *there*, in a wilderness and in a valley of trouble. That's where Israel will sing! The valley of trouble turns into a "door of hope." That's what the verse says.

Once inside, I waste no time praying. You don't have to get on your knees to pray earnestly, but I do this time. I kneel beside our bed, and I pray a very simple prayer. "Please turn Ken's heart back to me." That's all. I say it over and over, and somewhere in the middle of it all, I realize I'm crying. Partly because I'm happy that I've finally latched onto the hope that has been waiting unclaimed for me since February and partly because I know I still have many painful miles to travel. As I get up from my knees, I recall another verse from that same chapter of Hosea. "And it shall come to pass in that day, I will hear, saith the Lord." I go to bed that night with one thing settled. I have prayed, and God has heard.

A week or so later something happens that might seem irrelevant, but it's not. It belongs here. I see very clearly why God has brought this into my life, for it opens my eyes to something. Margaret tells me to write my thoughts as they come, and this is what I'm doing. "As you write, your ideas will begin to coalesce into a meaningful pattern," she told me. "As your thoughts come, don't fret over chronology or relative importance or style or structure. It is important to put into words the things that are in your heart. Unity and design will come." So I stop and start and digress and retrace and shift verb tenses, but in the end I'm trusting that the story will hang together, that all the separate stitches laid here and there will combine to make the garment whole.

So here's what happens in the middle of May. I get a telephone call from a woman I've played against in the YMCA tennis tournament two seasons in a row, and she invites me to join her tennis team. She sounds nervous on the telephone, her voice a little too fast and high pitched, and she talks on and on explaining how the team thing works, about having to get a rating so you can be verified to play in the USTA events, which include city and district matches, then state playoffs, then sectionals, then nationals.

Some teams play during the week and some only on weekends, she says, her team being a weekday team, specifically Mondays. Some of the teams are sponsored by country clubs or sports complexes, but theirs is independent, so you don't have to join an expensive club and pay monthly dues to belong and all that. Two of their singles players recently left the team for health reasons, one because of a bad knee and the other because of foot surgery, and last year they lost their "number-one singles gal" because she "got bumped up to 4.0 at sectionals," all of which combines to mean that their team is hurting for singles players.

This is only the bare minimum of what she says, believe me, but I'll let it go at this. Finally she stops and asks, "Would you be willing to meet me for lunch one day in the next week or so and talk about joining our team?"

I feel like an inner tube that's been overinflated. You know how too much information dispensed at one time can do that. But I don't want to give the wrong impression about this woman. From what I remember about her from our two matches, she's a nice person. She shook my hand after both matches, looked me in the eye, and congratulated me for winning, then even hung around a little while and asked about my family, my work, and all that.

Some of the women I've played haven't been nearly so gracious. Some can't wait to get in their cars and leave after grumbling briefly about why they played so poorly that day—allergies, new tennis shoes, wind, blisters, elbow trouble, wrong racket, and so forth. And some just rush off without saying much of anything, giving you the impression that they lead very busy, productive lives and only barely managed to fit this trivial little match into their schedules.

This woman didn't do that, though. She was pleasant, with a round face and clear, steady eyes. I didn't get the idea that she was being friendly just out of politeness either. It had taken a while for me to figure out who it was she reminded me of, but the second time we played, it had come to me suddenly, with the sense of something locking securely. Miss Kitty on *Gunsmoke*. That's who she was. I could see her sitting in the saloon with Marshal Dillon and Chester, a woman with a big heart, always there to listen and sympathize.

But getting back to the phone call. After she tells me all about the tennis team, called the Holiday Winners because they usually have their practices at the Holiday Inn courts in Greenville, she asks me to lunch, and without even stopping to think about it, I accept.

To summarize, we meet for lunch at a deli over in Greenville, and she repeats some of what she told me over the phone, plus some new stuff. Their team is a 3.5 team, and they've gone to the state championships two years in a row and even made it to sectionals in Mobile, Alabama, last year, where, she tells me again, their ace singles player "got bumped." This means the woman is no longer eligible to play on their team but has to find a 4.0 team to join. The Holiday Winners play other 3.5 teams all over the area, one over in Anderson, one in Simpsonville, one in Fountain Inn, and several others in Greenville.

She explains the fees for joining the U.S. Tennis Association, the process for getting verified, the team expenses, uniforms, practices, and all that, and then right before taking a big bite of her shaved ham on rye, she says, "So would you like to join our team?"

I nod and say, "Yes, I think so." It's as simple as that. But here's the whole reason I've written all this. She says something now that completely takes me back.

Her name, by the way, is Bonnie Maggio. She starts laughing while she's trying to chew her bite of sandwich and finally manages to swallow it and say, "I can't believe it was this easy." She goes on to tell me how reluctant she was to call me in the first place.

"Why?" I ask her.

And without even hesitating she says, "Oh, you know, because you're so intimidating." She says three other women on her team had played me in the YMCA league over the past years, but when my name was mentioned as a replacement for one of their singles players, none of them wanted to be the one to call me.

"Why?" I ask again. I'm still trying to take in the word *intimidating* she just used to describe me. It doesn't make sense. Polite, boring people are never intimidating.

Bonnie looks me right in the eye over the table and says, "Oh, I guess we were all afraid of you."

I know the same word keeps coming out of my mouth, but I can't help it. "Why?" I ask again.

"Oh, you know," she says, looking now as if she wishes she had never started down this path. She picks up a potato chip and examines it closely before taking a bite.

"No, I don't know," I say, leaning toward her a little. "Why would you be afraid of me? Just because I won a few tennis matches? I lost some, too, you know."

She smiles. "Not many, I bet."

"Enough," I say. I want to finish my sandwich, but I've got to get to the bottom of this. "Why did you call me intimidating just now? I'm about the least intimidating person I can think of. And what's there to be afraid of?"

She shook her head and took a quick drink of her tea. "Okay, okay." She cast her eyes toward the ceiling and said, "When will I ever learn to keep my big mouth shut?" Looking back at me, she said, "It's more than your tennis game, though that's plenty scary to anybody on the other side of the net. It's just . . . the way you're so . . . well, you know, standoffish, sort of. Not in a bad way, really—oh, I'm getting myself in deep, aren't I?"

She stopped and raised both hands. "Okay, let me try again." I could tell she was trying to choose her words with great care. "You just seem to hold yourself a little bit away from people, you know? Closed off, sort of. Not like you think you're better than other people or anything. I'm not saying that. But it's like you're just not really . . . available and, well, not *interested* in opening up. Like you've always got other things on your mind. Like you're standing back evaluating everything. I'm not saying you're stuck-up, really I'm not, not at all, but you just give the impression that you're a little distant and . . ." She shrugged and trailed off, looking at me helplessly.

"Standoffish," I said.

She shrugged again. "I don't know. Yeah, I guess, sort of." She smiled, her blue eyes very bright and her whole face crinkling up. "But here's what I'm trying to say," she said. "Here's the important part. I can see now how all those impressions were totally wrong." She was really trying hard, and I felt myself wanting to help her out. "And isn't that the way it is so much of the time?" she went on. "We judge each other on such a little bit of evidence."

I nodded. "Very, very true." I felt like my head had been turned upside down and shaken. What a revelation to hear somebody tell you when you're just shy of having lived a half a century that you're a totally different kind of person than you've always imagined yourself to be! I had always, always, thought I was the most courteous, nonthreatening, agreeable person in the world. Not very exciting to be sure, but certainly interested in other people and ready to meet them halfway if they showed any inclination to friendliness. Sincere, kind, shy—these are all words I used to think applied to me. Not intimidating, standoffish, and distant.

Questions came tumbling at me. It was as though a curtain had been raised and the whole stage was flooded with lights. If I really was *perceived* as standoffish, could this be why I had never had many friends? Why I rarely dated before Ken? Why I spent Friday nights in the library in college? Why Polly Seacrest was the only neighbor I'd ever been close to? Why the other teachers never engaged me in conversations at the schools where I subbed?

And what if it wasn't just a perception? What if I really was standoffish, distant, aloof? Could this be why Margaret and I felt at ease together, each of us seeing so much of herself in the other? Could this be why Ken rarely confided in me? And why I rarely confided in him? Why I retreated to my poetry and grew silent a few years into my marriage? Why I gave my husband up to his music and his mother?

I looked up to find Bonnie Maggio studying me uncertainly. She was drinking her tea through a straw, frowning ever so slightly at me. "I'm sorry, Elizabeth," she said. "I sure didn't mean to offend you. I'm always saying lots more than anybody wants to hear." She set her cup down. "It's like I slip and say one thing, then another, and then there's no turning back the tide." She sighed. "But, really, I didn't think I was saying anything you didn't already know."

"I'm not offended," I said. "It's just so unbelievable. I wish somebody had told me all this a long time ago."

"Yeah, it's funny, isn't it?" Bonnie said. "I remember a girl in school calling me Fang because one of my teeth was coming in on top of the others, and it had never even bothered me before that. But from then on, I would cover my mouth when I laughed so that no one would see my teeth. That went on for years."

She shook her head. "But I don't even know why I mentioned that." She smiled at me, and I could see that at some point in her life, she must have gone to an orthodontist to correct her crooked teeth. "I guess what I'm trying to say is that sometimes it's hard to see all the little things about yourself that other people see," she said. "But I sure don't want you to think I go around telling people how to improve their personalities. My own needs too much work for that." She put another potato chip in her mouth and chewed a few moments. "I'm sorry, Elizabeth. I'm always saying stuff I shouldn't."

"You don't need to apologize," I said. "Really, you don't. You were honest, and that's good. I'm not offended, really." I smiled at her. "Shocked and astounded maybe, but not offended."

"So you haven't changed your mind about being on the team?" she asked.

I shook my head. "No. When do we start?"

So God uses Bonnie Maggio to open my eyes wider. I'm beginning to see myself as I really am. Not only have I tiptoed through life cautiously for fear of not succeeding, but now I learn that I've also put on such an air of cool self-sufficiency that I've come across as being in need of no one or nothing. This is a moment of illumination for me. I can look back and see past events in light of this new truth.

I remember sitting in the choir on Easter Sunday morning and looking out at the congregation during the offertory, which was a trumpet solo by one of the Chewning boys, and thinking how strange it was that I could name most of the people by now, after having attended only two months, yet Margaret and Thomas, and maybe Hardy Biddle, were the only ones I felt that I really knew. And it wasn't because the people weren't friendly. I was always being greeted and spoken to and welcomed and urged to come to the fellowships after church or to Sunday school parties, but big social gatherings were one of the few things I found it easy to say no to.

We sat in the choir loft during the entire service that Easter Sunday because we sang several numbers interspersed throughout everything else—Scripture reading, teen choir, PeeWee choir, a brief but eloquent sermon on "The Empty Tomb," a dramatic monologue by Fern Tucker, the trumpet offertory, Hardy's quartet, and the observance of Communion. I remember wincing during Theodore Hawthorne's sermon when he said, "And this same Jesus, who lovingly gave up his life on Calvary and then victoriously took it up again on the third day, now lives with God the Father, overseeing the affairs of man."

The affairs of man—I glanced at Ken sitting near the back. Was God overseeing Ken's affair? I had to hang on to the belief that, in some big way I couldn't begin to understand now, he was doing exactly that.

The people of the Church of the Open Door were a mixed lot. I had learned that by now. There were the classy types—the Gills, the Harrelsons, a new family named Peterson—and the ordinary, cornbread-and-pinto-beans people like Bernie Paulson, Fern Tucker, and the Farnsworths. And though I spoke to all of them, our fellowship usually ended after a few polite words.

How I loved to watch them all from my post in the front row of the choir. This was the only drawback I had found to singing in the choir—I was sometimes distracted from the service by the sights before me. And when you're a newcomer, there's so much to wonder about! Not just the nosy, minor things like whether Grady Ferguson wore a hairpiece or just had hair that grew in a little lopsided, but bigger things, too. Like why didn't Marjorie Eckles' husband ever come with her? I kept meaning to ask Margaret about that.

And were Curtis and Barb Chewning really as happy and contented as they seemed? How about Blake and Catherine Biddle—they were such a nice-looking couple they almost seemed out of place here with everybody else. Not that they were perfect. Catherine had a blunt way of speaking at times, and Blake looked as though he always had a lot on his mind, but they had two of the nicest sons in the world and a beautiful daughter, too, so they must be doing something right.

From the choir I could see everybody, and my mind was always busy. What was it like to be in Dottie Puckett's shoes, I often wondered, having buried your only daughter less than a year ago? Did she ever get angry at God? You sure couldn't tell it from the look on her face if she did.

And Edna Hawthorne—did she have any problems at all besides being a little overweight? Her life seemed so perfect. And pretty, soft-spoken Jewel Scoggins—was she worried about having a baby at her age? Had she ever said an unkind word in her whole life? Did her mother ever get on her nerves with all her talking? I couldn't imagine living in the same house with a woman like that. I'll admit it—every time I saw Eldeen Rafferty coming toward me at church, I went the opposite way.

But now that I think about it, I've never once gone to any of these people at church and initiated a conversation. Isn't that confirmation of what Bonnie Maggio told me about myself? It's like she said—I've kept my distance. I've displayed good manners on all occasions, have replied when spoken to, have volunteered to bring a flower arrangement for the sanctuary, have taken a couple of turns helping in the nursery, have put money into the offering plate, have sung in the choir, and have even prayed for many of these people by name after hearing about their needs, but I've done exactly what Bonnie said. I've stood off to the side. I haven't shown a personal interest in them and have turned aside any attempt on their part to get too close to me.

I know how a blind person must feel if he were to suddenly look up and see trees, birds, sky. It's an astonishing thing to have your eyes opened to what everyone else has known all along. It's almost three o'clock in the afternoon as I'm driving back to Berea after saying good-bye to Bonnie outside the deli. I have a sudden urge, a need actually, to talk to Margaret, and not just by telephone. I turn off Highway 11 toward Filbert. I know my way to her house by now. I'm hoping she's home from work.

I finally turn onto Cadbury Street in Filbert and feel a surge of relief as I see Margaret's black Ford in her driveway. I pull in behind it and get out of my car. Her front door is open, and I hear music. I take this as a sign that I was meant to come. *Thank you for being here* are the words that go through my mind as I approach her door.

What Scent of Old Wood

23

I stood awhile outside Margaret's front door that day listening to her play the piano. She was playing hymns, stopping after each one to turn a few pages and start a new one. I could name them all. A few of them I remembered from my spotty church attendance as a child, but most of them I had learned only in the past three months. It surprised me all over again every Sunday that they sang such a wide variety of hymns at the Church of the Open Door, but I suppose it only reflected all the different types of people that attended. To be honest, some of the songs struck me as comical and some as theologically anemic. Whoever had written some of the words had one big idea in mind: They have to rhyme.

One Sunday we sang four songs during the morning service: "His Banner Over Me Is Love," "Love Lifted Me," "The King of Love My Shepherd Is," and "Jesus, Lover of My Soul." Talk about different types! You couldn't find four better songs to prove my point. I guess Willard Scoggins tries to pick something for everybody. Some of the children giggled as they did hand motions to "His Banner Over Me Is Love," but everybody was thoughtful and meditative during "Jesus, Lover of My Soul."

When I come across fine poetry in the hymnbook, I read it over many times. That's another distraction besides looking at the congregation from the choir loft. I sometimes stop singing and just read the words. "The Sands of Time"—that's one of my favorites in the hymnbook. I also like "I Sing the Mighty Power of God" and "O for a Thousand Tongues" and "There Is a Fountain." And "Jesus Paid It All"—simple words but powerful. And "Be Thou My Vision" and "Spirit of God, Descend upon My Heart." Also "Guide Me, O Thou Great Jehovah" and "A Mighty Fortress"—these are all lovely poems. It has been a happy discovery, let me tell you, to find some real poetry in the hymnal. I don't know exactly why, but I wasn't expecting it.

After I've taken in the words, I'm ready to add the music, but by then we're usually done with that song and on to something else. So here's what I want to suggest to Willard Scoggins someday. First, announce the hymn and then have everyone turn to the page and read the words silently. Next, have someone stand up and read the words aloud. And don't rush any of this. A church service shouldn't zip along like the six o'clock news.

Then have the organ and piano play through it while everyone reads the words again silently. Finally, have everyone sing it together. The way it is now, it usually hits me too hard and fast to do its full work. It's like one of those quick, violent thunderstorms that's over almost before it gets started, before the ground has time to soften and accept it. What I like is a good slow, soaking rain.

So anyway, I must have listened to Margaret play six or seven different hymns. I know the last one was "When I Survey the Wondrous Cross," played very thoughtfully so that I heard not only the chords but also the words very clearly in my mind. When she played "And pour contempt on all my pride," something made me raise my hand and knock on the screen door. She stopped immediately and came to the door.

Margaret has a beautiful smile, and it was especially beautiful as she swung open the door and invited me in. Margaret isn't the kind to pretend, so when she said, "What a delight this is, Elizabeth," I felt she meant it. She was still dressed for work, wearing a white dress and soft-soled shoes. Her hair was combed back behind her ears, and if she hadn't been dressed like a nurse, she might have looked almost glamorous. Her face has a kind of movie star beauty that doesn't seem to belong in Filbert, South Carolina. She has no idea how pretty she is, which makes her even prettier.

I stepped inside, and she invited me to sit down, which I did. She couldn't have been expecting my next words, but she didn't let on. "I've just found out I'm not who I've always thought I was," I said.

Her eyes are a deeper blue than Bonnie Maggio's, with a touch of violet. As she looked at me, they twinkled even though she wasn't really smiling anymore. I think she was trying to figure out where I was headed with my startling news. If she had been a different kind of person, somebody like, say, my old roommate, Laurie, or my sister, Juliet, she might have come back with something witty like "So who are you—the maharani of Bhutan?" She didn't say anything, though. She waited for me. Margaret is one of those people who know the virtue of quiet patience.

We were both sitting on the couch, as we had been on the day of my salvation. "Do you think I'm standoffish?" I asked her. She lifted her chin slightly, and the smile crept back. "Be honest with me," I said. As if she wouldn't be. But then before she could answer, I explained. "See, I've always had the idea I was really polite, and since polite people are usually boring, I never made a lot of friends, but then somebody up and tells me just today that she's always thought I was intimidating. Standoffish was another word she used." We stared at each other a moment. "So, do you think she's right?" I said. "Am I standoffish?"

Margaret has a good sense of humor, though not everybody knows this. She crossed her arms and frowned a little. "You are no more standoffish than I am," she said. We looked at each other another long moment, and I'm not sure which one of us started laughing first. Our laughter was an admission of what we knew we were and what we acknowledged each other to be.

So, okay, I'm standoffish. I think you always know in your heart when you hear the truth about yourself. When Bonnie Maggio spoke, though I resisted her words at first, something told me she was right. I felt the same sense of wonder yet deep-down acceptance you'd feel upon witnessing a prophecy come to pass. Part of me was saying, "It can't be" while the other part was saying, "It is." It was as if a storm had come up during a picnic. I didn't want it to be true, but I knew it was, and denying it didn't change the fact that the rain was coming down in sheets.

But it wasn't enough to know it in my heart, so I went to Margaret for verification. But really, I tell myself now, there's no need to overdramatize this. It's not as if you've come to discover you're an extortionist or a sadist. There are worse things than being standoffish. And when you think about it, it doesn't have to be a permanent condition.

Margaret and I talk for about an hour. She asks me how my translation project is going, and I tell her some of what I'm learning as I progress backwards through my marriage. I tell her that Ken and I never learned to talk beyond the mere exchange of information concerning the daily business of life and that I'm not certain whether this is a cause or a symptom of our weak and sickly marriage, but for sure it's a fact. We lived in the same house for many years but never gave each other keys for our secret rooms.

I don't try to blame Ken, nor do I heap all the blame on myself. It's funny how I've suddenly dropped the need to allocate the blame for what has happened. I've shed it like an old skin. You reach a point where it doesn't really matter who contributed most to the failure. I don't doubt for a minute that there are cases in which a husband or wife is truly and purely innocent of all guilt in the breakdown of a marriage, that it's totally the fault of the other person. But in my case I have come to see that I had a part in it. Twenty percent? Forty? Sixty? What does it matter now? Whatever my part, it completed the hundred percent.

So I simply tell Margaret the plain facts, how both Ken and I over the years found private places all our own where we never invited each other. How neither of us ever went knocking at each other's gate to gain entrance, how the overlap between our two circles gradually became less and less, and how the only remarkable thing about Ken's affair with another woman is that it took so long to happen. I've never before put all of this into words that I spoke aloud to another person. I hear a loud hum inside my head when I stop talking.

Here's something I'm beginning to learn about sharing personal things with a close friend. You don't always need or want a lot of comment in return. Certainly no great visible outpouring of sympathy. Sometimes all you want is the kindness of her silent presence. And other times, although this doesn't really make sense logically, a friend can minister to you best by talking about herself.

This is what Margaret does now when she says, "I understand precisely what you have said. I am only now learning to talk to my husband." She isn't shifting the subject at all. She's not wanting to turn the focus on her own problems. Margaret isn't the windy type who likes to hear the sound of her voice as she holds forth. She's talking about me as she speaks of herself. I sense that I'm hearing something she hasn't told any other woman, and I listen with great reverence.

"At Thomas's suggestion, we began taking evening walks last summer," she says. "It was a peculiarly emotional time of my life, for I had lost a dear friend a few months earlier. At the same time, however, I was at last giving place in my heart to a deep love for my husband—a love which I had suppressed since the day we were married."

She pauses, then continues slowly. "We began walking together each evening at sundown," she says, "and our love grew. I found that I could not walk beside him under God's great merciful sky and keep silent. It was as if the open air and our matching steps released my tongue, and I began to talk to Thomas for the first time in our marriage. I did not pour out my heart all at once, but I began to empty it drop by drop." She stops and gazes toward the piano for a brief moment, then adds, "And I found him to be a large and ready receptacle."

Had Margaret's hair suddenly caught on fire, I couldn't have been more surprised at her words. I had assumed that her relationship with Thomas was one of long and happy intimacy, the miracle of oneness achieved by only a blessed few and impossible to explain in human terms, the kind of devotion I had seen in my parents and in Polly and Morris Seacrest, the kind of marriage I predicted for Theresa Dillman and Macon Mahoney. I suspected it might exist in some of the married couples at church—the Hawthornes maybe and Willard and Jewel Scoggins and the Chewnings—but you can't tell just by Sunday behavior.

Not only did Margaret's confession surprise me, but it also encouraged me, as she must have known it would. I knew Margaret was in her fifties, and Thomas had to be close to twenty years older than she was. If two people their age could learn to talk, why couldn't anyone? Why couldn't Ken and I? Houses could be raised from rubble. Gates with rusty hinges could be opened. Gardens could be planted in old fields.

When I was a girl, I had once watched my father patiently work on a window that had been painted shut. He went all around it first with a razor blade, then took a small paint scraper and went around again, tapping delicately with a hammer and carefully chipping away the dried paint. Then he wrapped the head of the hammer in a rag and once again went all the way around the window frame inch by inch, gently knocking loose any remaining paint. Then he put down his tools, set his feet apart, took hold of the bottom sash, and pulled. When it finally gave way, it made a loud, splintery-sounding pop, and more flecks of paint went flying. I sucked up all the dried paint with the vacuum cleaner, and even though I was a child at the time, I realized I had observed a lesson in restrained, methodical persistence.

Margaret doesn't advise directly. That's not her way. She's a parable giver. I go away from her house that day with more hope. Just as surely as they can disintegrate, relationships can also rejuvenate. People can change. Windows can be opened. God has once again shown his goodness. Through the Bible he gives me hope from heaven, and then he gives me a friend to illustrate how it works on earth. Margaret invites me to stay for supper, but I don't. I want to get home.

Before I leave, she says to me, "Remember the poem Professor Huckabee read at the end of our last class." This isn't a question; it's a statement. Maybe I'm wrong, but I think Margaret is a unique Christian in the way she mixes everything into her religion. Or maybe I should say she mixes her religion into everything. She can be talking about a passage of Scripture and suddenly weave in a reference to a novel she's reading, or she can be talking about a poem we studied in our poetry class and flow right into a point Harvey Gill made in her Sunday school class.

I like this about her. One of my misconceptions about Christians has always been that they had no appreciation for aesthetics, that any interest or aptitude they had in music, art, drama, or literature had to be compromised and diluted by their rigid doctrinal creed. Born-again Christians and genuine artists were two completely different groups of people in my way of thinking. I had heard of exceptions, of course, but even people like C. S. Lewis didn't altogether disprove my theory. After all, he drank, smoked, and married a divorced woman. Wouldn't these facts elicit a collective "tsk-tsk" from the ranks of fundamentalists? Sure, he grew up in England and moved in academic circles, so it's only natural that he would come at Christianity from a whole different mindset, but still—well, I can't remember where this was going now.

And anyway, I need to get back to what I was saying about Margaret. She has just prayed with me in her living room, and then she looks up and says, "Remember the poem Professor Huckabee read." I do remember it, of course, and I instantly know exactly what she's driving at. It's a poem by William Stafford titled "You Reading This, Be Ready."

Before he dismissed us that last Thursday night of class, Professor Huckabee cleared his throat, dismounted his stool, and stood before us. He was wearing patent leather lace-up dress shoes. I remember that clearly because I was staring at them the whole time he was reading Stafford's poem in his well-measured schoolteacher's voice.

When he finished, there was a hush. Even A. R. Waddell, the know-it-all, didn't have anything to say. "Thank you for your faithful attendance and kind attention during these past weeks" was the only other thing Professor Huckabee said before he turned and collected his things and left the room. It didn't seem abrupt or discourteous at all for him to leave ahead of us. I watched him go and felt a pang of sadness that such a richly scenic journey was over.

No one called out to him or tried to stop him for one last question. He wasn't the kind of teacher you chased down in the hallway to chat with. In fact, I'm sure some people thought of Professor Huckabee as standoffish. Maybe that's one reason Margaret and I liked him so much, besides the fact that he's a master of his subject. I know one thing. If I were to ever teach a poetry class, the very last thing I would do at the end of the final class would be to read William Stafford's poem "You Reading This, Be Ready."

By reminding me of the poem, what Margaret is saying in her indirect way is this: "Remember to meet each minute of every day with great alertness. Be ready to see and hear and feel something new every time you turn around, with every breath you take." Which is just another way of saying, "Appreciate every moment you're alive and use it to become more alive in some way." Which may be just another way of saying, "This is the day which the Lord hath made; we will rejoice and be glad in it." Some will accuse me of stretching the point here since I don't know anything at all about William Stafford's religious beliefs. It's clear, though, that his poem isn't just talking about how to read poetry, but how to read life.

And isn't this the real meaning of Aware? I'm not talking about my earlier snobbery of labeling people. The principle of Awareness comes straight from the Bible. It means living with the knowledge that our days are as a vapor but are full of opportunities and challenges and setbacks and advances and wonderful gifts. They're all part of life, and as we spend our days, so we become. William Stafford's poem is packed with questions, but when he asks, "What scent of old wood hovers?" he's not really asking so much as he is telling. The things of today become part of us forever. The past is the present, and the present is the future, or as Flannery O'Connor put it, "Everything that rises must converge."

And speaking of setbacks, something happens on the way home from Margaret's that day. I drive into Derby and stop by the library. It has come to me recently that I've never watched a video Willard Scoggins once recommended to me, *Babette's Feast*, and I decide I'll get it right now on my way home.

I want to check out *The Collected Poems of Marianne Moore* also. I can go only so long between immersions in this book. I need to buy my own copy, but I've checked out the one at the Derby library so many times now that I feel it's my own. I imagine it as a child of mine in boarding school whom I bring home periodically for short, happy holidays. There's a smudge of chocolate on page 67 that dripped from my spoon one day as I was reading and several puckered water spots on page 123 from my bath one night.

Beside the poem "Carriage from Sweden" on page 99, some other reader has written in a round, childish script, "I like this one," and every time I see it, I can't help wondering what exactly the person liked about it. I wonder if he noticed all the intricacies of form in this poem—the syllabic pattern, for instance, and the subtly concealed internal rhyme in the first line of each of the twelve stanzas. You could read that poem a hundred times and not notice those things, and you could read it every day for a year and not get to the bottom of everything it's saying.

So I stop at the library, find both the video and the book, then leave. Here's when the setback happens. My car won't start. It grinds away sluggishly but won't catch. Now that I think about it, it has been taking a little longer to start lately. Well, okay, Mr. William Stafford, I think. Here I sit with all my senses alert, experiencing this moment to the hilt. Now what? How am I going to use this moment to become more alive? I sit there a minute going over the options. I'm a smart woman. I can figure this out. I'm guessing it's the battery.

If I had known this was going to happen, I could have left a note for Ken on the kitchen table three days ago when he came over to mow the lawn: *My car is getting hard to start*. He would have seen it, checked the battery, and taken care of it for me before leaving to go back to his apartment at the Home Away from Home. But I didn't know, of course, and now I'm stuck in the parking lot of the Derby Public Library.

I realize it could be worse. It could have happened on my way to teach one morning, and then the principal would have had to scramble around and find a substitute for the substitute. It could have happened last week when I ended up parked right next to Marvella Gowdy's maroon Pontiac at church. She tried to engage me in a conversation after church, which could have gone on indefinitely, since she was cut from the same cloth as Eldeen Rafferty. The two of them are good friends, in fact. If I had gotten into my car and found the battery dead, who knows how much more of her talk I would have had to endure? She probably would have rounded up Eldeen and brought her out so they could both keep me company while somebody checked the battery. She might have dragged me home with her for Sunday dinner.

Or, even worse, it could have happened when I left Ken's band rehearsal that night, and I could have still been sitting in the parking lot when Ken and Dr. Snipe walked out hand in hand, though I couldn't imagine him holding hands in public. I *could* imagine the look on his face when he saw me, though. "Why, Elizabeth, what are you doing here?" I wonder if he would have introduced me to Dr. Snipe.

Stop it, I tell myself. You're getting carried away. None of these things happened. You're here right now at five o'clock at the library. Then a very simple fact dawns on me. I have a cell phone, the same one Ken called me on that day in my driveway back in February. I could call Margaret or Pastor Hawthorne or Theresa Dillman or a service station. Or I could go inside and see if Willard Scoggins is still here. I didn't see him in his office when I was at the check-out desk, but maybe he was somewhere else in the building. I know he would be happy to help me.

Or—and this comes to me last for some reason—I could call Ken. I know his office number, and I have his cell phone number written down in my purse. His number at the motel is written on a slip of paper on the refrigerator back at home, but that's not going to do me any good now.

I remember the day Ken wrote it down for me. I had come home from a tennis match one Saturday in late March to find him cutting down a small tree in the backyard that was dying. By the time I was out of the shower, he was packed up and gone, but I saw the piece of paper on the refrigerator with his phone number and apartment address on it, along with the words *In case you need to reach me.* Very efficient and businesslike. I had almost snatched it off and torn it to shreds, but I hadn't. I had the sense to know I might actually need it someday.

I look toward the street now and see cars lined up at the stoplight. This is a bad time of day. People are getting off work and thinking about supper. I'd hate to bother Margaret and Thomas. There's a gas station only a few blocks away over on Fredericks Road, but they would probably charge a lot for a service call.

I watch a mother and her two small children come out of the library and head for the Jeep Cherokee parked next to me. They're talking animatedly, and I hear the mom say, "We'll get Daddy to grill us some hot dogs for supper. How about that?" They get in their car and close the doors, and the engine comes to life immediately. As they back out, I see one of the children waving a big picture book around excitedly in the backseat. The mom is laughing and saying something over her shoulder.

She has no idea what it could be like, I think. She's just taking for granted that her husband is coming home after work to grill hot dogs. I ought to jump out and flag her down and say something like "Be alert!

Appreciate what you have right now! Sit down and read to your children as soon as you get home! Savor every bite of your hot dog! Talk to your husband! Take in deep breaths of fresh air and be glad!"

I watch her pull out of the parking lot and disappear into the stream of traffic on the street. I start to wonder about her life—where she lives, what her name is, where her husband works—but then I remember my problem at hand. I've got to do something other than watch all the library patrons come and go.

What if I do call Ken? Will I seem helpless? Or maybe like I'm wanting attention? Like I staged it all somehow? What if he drove over, turned the key in the ignition, and it fired right up? I realize that while I'm worried about inconveniencing everybody else, I'm only worried about what Ken will think of me if I call him. Stop it, I tell myself again. Act like an adult and dial his number.

I try starting my car again just to make sure, and it sounds even weaker, so I slowly punch in Ken's office number on my cell phone. As I punch the last number, it comes to me again that God surely has a plan for me right now, sitting here stranded with a dead battery, that if he's the God of the whole universe then he has to be concerned with even the accidents in our lives. I also realize that if I really believe in God's involvement in my life, I'll stop using the word *accident* so freely.

Ken's office phone rings six times, and I hang up when the voice mail takes over. I find his cell phone number and try that. Maybe he's just left his office and is in his car, but I find myself thinking like my mother. *If I have only two of the three numbers where he can be reached, no doubt he'll be at the third one, the one that's back home on the refrigerator.* I'm so full of gloom that I'm temporarily unable to think of what to say when he answers before the second ring.

"Hello?" he says again when I don't respond the first time. "Who is it?" I can hear music playing in the background. This is no surprise. Ken would never drive anywhere without music. It used to be the radio or a cassette, but the car he has now has a CD player. Whenever we used to be in the car together, I would have to raise my voice if I wanted him to hear me.

For a long time after we were married, it made me mad that he was so rudely cutting off any opportunity for conversation by playing his music in the car, but gradually I got used to it. In the days when we took family vacations, Jennifer often complained about the volume of the music, saying it interfered with her reading or sleeping, but Travis never did. He stared out the window and listened hard, his eyes wide and bright. This is one of the few ways Travis is like Ken—he can get lost listening to a piece of music.

Sometimes riding with Ken I would start talking out loud, carrying on my own dialogue with myself, but not loud enough for him to hear over the music, unless it suddenly got soft or ended abruptly, at which time he might hear me say something like "Oh, really, so you've found that butter works a lot better than margarine in that recipe?" He might turn to me then and say, "What?" And I would wave a hand and say, "Oh, never mind." Not once did I ever try to explain to him how it made me feel for him to build a wall between us with his music. You would assume somebody would already know something like that.

"*Royal Fireworks*," I say to Ken now over the phone. That's the music I hear playing in the background. It's easy to recognize. It sounds just like something written for a king of England and played on a barge floating down a river, with fireworks lighting up the sky in celebration of something military. Sometimes I form a picture when I hear a piece of music, and from then on I never forget the piece. Even if it's something obscure I heard thirty years ago, if I made a picture in my mind to go with it, I would recognize the music immediately. I could name it on a game show and win thousands of dollars.

I remember hearing *Music for the Royal Fireworks* years ago when Ken played his trumpet in the orchestra in graduate school, and then many years later he conducted a transcription of it with his band shortly after he took the job at Harwood. Every time I hear it, I see a picture of a bunch of bassoons on a barge with fireworks exploding all around. The bassoons are because Ken told me that Handel's original instrumentation was heavy on the bassoons.

I like the band version of *Royal Fireworks*. Sometimes transcriptions fall flat with bands, and other times they take off and fly. Sometimes they fly too high, though, and then they melt and crash. Some arrangers don't understand the concept of balance and moderation and appropriateness. They know when to push but not when to pull back.

When Travis was in middle school, his band director had them play a transcription of Debussy's "Girl with the Flaxen Hair" at one of their concerts. It was embarrassing. Not just the fact that the clarinets squeaked in every other measure, but the whole poorly conceived arrangement never should have been. You'd think somebody would have halted it at some point along the way—either the arranger or the editor or the publisher or the band director. Someone should have said, "This just shouldn't be." I wonder if any group of players has ever risen up in mutiny against their conductor and said, "We won't play this. It's a parody and a desecration."

Some pieces ought to be left in their original form and medium. I could imagine Debussy tearing his hair out by the roots as he listened to the Derby Middle School Band slash his art to ribbons. It was hard for Ken to go to Travis's concerts. He never could enjoy them as a parent. He was too busy watching the conductor and analyzing the arrangements. After this particular concert, I remember he talked with the conductor up front for a long time. Other parents were lined up behind him waiting to shake the conductor's hand, but Ken never noticed. Afterward he was so preoccupied I had to remind him to say something positive to Travis about the concert.

I never asked Ken what he'd said to the conductor, a man named Billy Thornton, who was a friend of his. I hoped Ken had been tactful, but I doubted that he had. When it comes to music, Ken has definite opinions that he voices freely. Being a friend, though, maybe Billy took it okay. He knew how intense Ken was and how he had a special interest in the band program of Derby Middle since that's where he used to teach before Harwood.

Well, anyway, all this zips through my mind as I hear Handel's *Royal Fireworks* over the phone. It gets softer all of a sudden, so Ken must have turned it down.

"I'm sorry?" he says. This is always what he says when he doesn't hear something the first time. Not "Pardon?" or "Please?" or even "What did you say?" but "I'm sorry?"

I'm tempted to say, "You sure are," but instead I say, "*Royal Fireworks*. That's what's playing."

He pauses. I'm not sure he recognizes my voice. Maybe he thinks it's Dr. Snipe, the way he did that other time. He's being cautious, though. "Yes, it is," he says but nothing else. Maybe he's trying to figure out which woman he knows that would be most likely to recognize *Royal Fireworks* over the phone.

I help him out. "It's Elizabeth. I've got a dead battery, I think. I'm at the library over in Derby, but I can call somebody else if you can't come. I know it's kind of a bad time." I'm trying to sound natural, but my throat feels dry, and I think I may be talking too fast.

There's a pause, during which I'm sure he's trying to think of how to say he can't come. I'm already busy thinking of what to do next and planning how to sound casual and offhanded when he gives me his excuse.

When he says, "I'll be there in ten minutes," all I can think of to say is "Okay."

Range After Range of Mountains

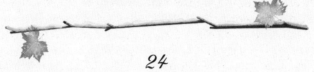

24

Pulling into our driveway a half hour later, we sit for a while in silence. Ken has decided to bring me home and take care of my car tomorrow, which is a lighter day for him. Tonight there's a recital he has to attend, and it starts at seven o'clock, so he's a little pressed for time.

One of his senior trumpet students is giving the recital, and Ken anticipates a shaky performance. The boy has been sick off and on for several weeks, he says, and the recital has been postponed twice already. Tonight it will take place even if the kid has to be carried out on a stretcher, Ken says. I can tell without his actually putting it into words that Ken thinks a good part of the boy's sickness involves his dread of getting up onstage in front of a lot of people. Ken doesn't have much sympathy for people who have stage fright.

"He never should have majored in music," he says now. "That's like a professional athlete who can't handle competition." I've heard him say things like this before about musicians and stage fright. "That's like a fire fighter who can't stand heat" or "That's like a pilot who's afraid of heights."

I can't help thinking of Travis. The first time he played his trumpet in a recital in seventh grade he cracked an average of one out of three notes, and others he just didn't play at all. His piece was "Red River Valley," but the only way you would have known this was that it was printed in the program. I was mortified for him, and I don't think Ken ever got over the incident. I had a theory about it but never had an opportunity to test it because Travis never again played a solo in public.

He continued to take private lessons with the band director at Derby High, Charles Beatty, who kept telling me every time we talked that Travis had "fine potential." In fact, three years after his one and only recital, Travis was second-chair trumpet in Mr. Beatty's band at Derby High. "He's got all this music inside him," Mr. Beatty told me once, "but he seems to have trouble getting it out when he's in public." Mr. Beatty tapped his head. "It's all up here." Travis could play a section of band music flawlessly in his private lesson, Mr. Beatty said, but if he asked him to do it as a solo in band rehearsal, he froze up. "We'll keep working on the mental part of it," he told me.

As I said, I had a theory about his miserable public performance in seventh grade. I think Travis panicked because he knew his father was in the audience. If Ken hadn't gone to the recital that night, I think Travis would have breezed through "Red River Valley," and then, having succeeded at his first solo performance, he would have been ready for more.

Ken had decided early on, like the moment Travis was born, that his son would play the trumpet and he would teach him at home. He never asked Travis if any of this was okay with him. Ken had an old cornet he'd been saving for Travis to start on, and I guess he had his heart set on the two of them going on tour and playing duets someday. So the summer Travis turned ten the lessons started.

The word *fiasco* isn't strong enough to describe how they went. Ken was all keyed up about it, determined from the first day that Travis was going to be a virtuoso, that the bio paragraph on his first concert program would start out "Taught by his father, Ken, from an early age, Travis Landis has been described by Wynton Marsalis as a 'rising star in trumpet performance whose extraordinary musicianship outshines anything you'll hear in your lifetime.' "

By the end of the first lesson, Travis was in tears. You must understand that this was a kid to whom things came fairly easily and who already had exhibited a deep interest in music. He had been playing the piano for two years and had done exceptionally well. He took lessons through a music store over in Greenville, and his teacher, Miss Elliott, praised him highly. She was a young woman in her twenties, thin as a broom handle and bursting with energy. As I watched him practice at home, I marveled over his devotion and the sense of awe with which he turned the pages of his book and placed his fingers on the keys. The look on his face when he sat down at the piano after school every day wasn't that of a little boy. He looked like a wise old man approaching an object of great beauty.

So I watched all this at home. The songs he played were simple, of course, but he put his heart and soul into them. "The Little Red Cart," "Barnyard Talk," "The Balloon Man," "Spooky Night"—I'm sure whoever wrote those songs never dreamed they could be played with such depth of feeling by an eight-year-old. Ken wasn't home much when Travis practiced, but I know now what he was thinking whenever he did hear him play. He was thinking very practically of what a good foundation this was providing for the trumpet lessons that were coming. Piano for Ken was just a means to an end.

Another thing about Travis was that he was sensitive to criticism but rarely let on. He was good at pretending not to care too much, but underneath it all he wanted desperately to succeed. This is why his piano lessons filled him with such quiet rapture. He was so naturally gifted, and Miss Elliott praised him so generously that he approached every lesson with anticipation. None of the timidity with which he faced his peers in a social setting, not an ounce of the fear I saw when I took him to his first swimming lesson or soccer practice, no holding back at all. At his piano lessons he was a different child. Or maybe that was the child he really was, and all those other withdrawn, introverted Travises were the impostors.

Miss Elliott stuck dozens and dozens of gold stars by his name on a chart she kept on the wall of her studio, and she hugged him after every lesson. He didn't pull away either but sometimes even leaned into her. When she told us after three years that she was getting married and moving to Texas, I felt like crying. I knew it would never be the same with another teacher, and it wasn't. Mrs. Starkey taught piano just to earn a living, and she moved the children in and out of her studio like she was the foreman of an assembly line. She made Travis nervous, and he never loosened up and really played for her.

I remember seeing him look off toward some faraway point and vanish in spirit when Mrs. Starkey broke in with something like "No, no, no. Now remember to use that *fifth* finger for the D—no cheating!" I tried to tell her once that Travis seemed to be regressing in his piano skills and that he responded best to a lot of encouragement and praise, to which she frostily replied that she did not "sling praise around indiscriminately" and that "teaching means correcting bad habits, not just patting the little darlings on the back."

But I'm getting things out of order. Mrs. Starkey came later, a year or so after the trumpet lessons started. On the day of the first trumpet lesson, Travis was still ripe for teaching. It was a Saturday morning in the middle of summer. Jennifer had graduated from high school a month or so earlier, Ken had received word recently that a publisher wanted to buy a collection of folk dances he had arranged for intermediate band, and I had won the annual YMCA women's tennis tournament. So it was a happy summer for us all.

Travis liked being out of school. I had made up a little routine for each week, and he liked that, too. One day he'd write a story, another day I'd give him a tennis lesson, another day he'd draw a picture, another day he'd do a science experiment, and so forth. I had him help me, too, with chores like washing the windows, dusting the baseboards, and things like that. He kept busy—he also played the piano, rode his bike, read, worked on puzzles, listened to his story tapes and old LPs, and watched reruns of old TV programs like *Bonanza* and *Gunsmoke*. *Kojak* and *The Rockford Files* came later, when he was in middle school, and then he got hooked on *Columbo* in high school. Some people are born before their time, but Travis was born after his.

So anyway, he was having himself a good summer that year he turned ten. One thing I never remember Travis saying as a kid was "I'm bored—there's nothing to do." Jennifer said it—oh, she said it enough for both of them! But I don't think it ever entered Travis's mind to be bored. He found something to do all summer long, every minute of the day and usually all by himself. We did the summer baseball thing and even some summer soccer, but mainly he kept to himself.

I think he was looking forward to starting trumpet lessons and learning a new instrument. And since this one had only three valves to push down, I'm sure he must have expected it to be easier than the piano with its eighty-eight keys.

I knew the lessons were coming, of course. We all did. Ken had told Travis for several years that they'd have their first lesson when he turned ten. Maybe I could have done something to help, but it never occurred to me to give Ken a few pointers about teaching Travis—his own son! I had nothing to offer about the instrument itself, of course, but looking back on it, I could have shared some tips about teaching styles that possibly could have prevented the disaster. If Ken would have listened to me, that is. That's something I'll never know. He approached that first lesson as if he were at Normandy directing the D-day invasion and the whole future of mankind depended on his orders being carried out.

Nothing showed me more clearly than that botched trumpet lesson how little Ken understood Travis. I was away at the grocery store when it started, and by the time I got home it was past repair. Ken was Mrs. Starkey multiplied by a thousand. When I stepped inside the kitchen door with a bag of groceries in each arm, I heard Ken say, "No, I said tighter! Your lips have to be tighter and harder and flatter to get a buzz! This is the most important part, Travis. If you can't get a decent buzz, you'll never get a decent sound. Now look at how I do it and then try again."

I set the groceries down and listened. Travis tried again, and Ken stopped him again with another lecture. "Tighter and harder"—that's what he kept saying. Travis's lips evidently weren't getting that way, but Ken's voice sure was. I walked over to the doorway between the kitchen and living room, where they were having the lesson, and as soon as I saw Travis's face, I knew Ken might as well pack up that cornet and take it to a pawn shop. You could see it in his eyes that Travis was trying for all he was worth to produce a buzz that would please his father.

And the funny thing is, Ken has taught hundreds of beginners to play the

trumpet. And he's a *good* teacher. He really is. He used to teach a lot of private lessons at home, and I used to admire his self-control. There were times,
honestly, when it seemed like the only true thing to say to a kid would have
been, "That sounds like a wounded animal that needs to be put out of its
misery," but he never would. He'd always come up with something like
"Okay, good. It's coming. Let's try it again, and don't be afraid to blow more
air in a nice steady stream. That'll make your tone even better." And off the
kid would go, blatting out yet another horrendous attempt.

But I guess the objectivity and calmness he had teaching other people's
kids flew right out the window when Travis was the student. Anybody reading this who's a father, take note. Teaching your own kid takes a special measure of self-control. Instead of stepping in closer, you'd do better to take a
few steps back. In fact, you'd probably do even better to let somebody else
teach your child. You're not the only capable teacher in the world!

Of course, no one else will have his best interest at heart the way you do,
but neither will anyone else have quite so much at stake if he doesn't succeed the way you hope he does. A parent is sometimes so intent on getting
to the destination that the trip itself is wretched for everybody—and you
might end up overturned in the ditch.

People have always praised Ken as a trumpet teacher. He has always
known exactly how hard to push a kid, and he's not the kind of teacher who
spends too much time talking or showing off his own skills instead of letting
his students play. But something had gone completely haywire that day. I
was absolutely astounded to hear him interrupt Travis again right away and
launch into yet another speech about the importance of the proper embou-
chure, after which he said, "Now listen to me play and watch my mouth."
Then he lifted his trumpet and played the call to colors with a vengeance,
followed by a couple of furious octaves of the chromatic scale.

He must have seen Travis's eyes fixed on me in the doorway because he
turned around abruptly. "Oh, hi. I didn't hear you come in," he said.

"I'm sure you didn't," I said. "You were much too busy."

His voice took on a defensive edge. "We're having a lesson here."

"Is that what it's called?" I said.

We stared at each other. I saw Travis's pinched face behind him, his eyes
begging me not to make his dad mad. Travis hated confrontations.

I tried for a light tone. "Well, why don't you guys call it quits for today
and take it up again tomorrow? I could use Travis's help unloading the groceries."

Ken sighed. "And maybe after that he could put on an apron and help
you bake brownies," he said. He twisted the mouthpiece off his trumpet and
put it away in the case. He closed the lid and snapped it shut, then yanked
the cornet away from Travis and put it away. He didn't say another word,
and I knew he wouldn't. His mouth was set in a thin, rigid line.

This was how our arguments went. We rarely had them, but when we did the words were few and spiteful. Neither of us ever apologized later, and we never ever brought up the subject for further discussion. We turned to other things and left the words hanging in the air like the strong heavy odor of something cooking. They usually dissipated after a few days, absorbed into the walls and ceilings like the smell of cabbage or burned bacon.

So anyway, we're sitting in the driveway now after a pretty quiet ride from the Derby library, accompanied by a Vaughan Williams CD, and Ken politely turns off the engine of his car so he doesn't seem to be rushing me to get out. He has only an hour and a half before the recital, so he's no doubt eager to be on his way, though he tries not to show it. He appears to be studying the carport, frowning as he does so. It's uncharacteristic that we would have such an untidy carport, because both Ken and I like things to be neat, but I guess you just learn to overlook some things. Every time I pull into the driveway and walk through the carport to the kitchen door, it bothers me, but once I get inside, I always forget about it.

We still can't use the carport for its intended purpose because of all the other stuff lined up around the edges—the lawn mower, a fold-up Ping-Pong table, some old window screens, a bin of firewood left over from winter, two storage cabinets with boxes of tools stacked on top, things like that. It's not all helter-skelter and trashy looking, but you can't help noticing that it's definitely not used for a car.

I look toward the Yarnells' house and see that Eunice has once again changed the color of the ribbons on her door wreath, the rabbits, and the lantern post. Now they're all yellow. I can't imagine a person spending her time like that. But then I look down at the book of poetry in my lap and realize she probably can't imagine people spending their time the way I do.

I think of that poem of Marianne Moore's that I like so much: "The Steeple-Jack." A lot of people would read that poem and think Miss Moore was a crazy woman for spending all that time just to describe this person doing this ordinary job in a little New England seacoast town. She goes into such *detail*! Everything from how much a lobster weighs to a cataloging of all the flowers that grow along the shore to the markings on the back of a newt.

The steeplejack's name is C. J. Poole, she says, and he's "gilding the solid-pointed star" on top of the steeple. She even tells us what the star stands for in the very last line, which opens up a whole new dimension to the poem. I'm already making plans to read this poem first tonight, line by line very slowly, both silently and aloud. While Ken is listening to his student stumble through his senior trumpet recital, I'll be reading Marianne Moore. I might get around to watching the video, and I might not.

How we spend our time tells us what we are, I suppose. Before I can stop myself and for no good reason, I say to Ken, "The details of life are so important." I'm thinking of irretrievable moments in the past, both sad and happy, that have led to this moment right now of sitting in the car together in the driveway right before I get out and we go our separate ways.

I'm thinking along totally different lines than he is, obviously, for he nods and answers, "But we could get rid of a lot of that junk in the carport. Some of those details aren't very important."

The way Marianne Moore arranges a stanza is like a sculpture. Look at how she lays out her poems on the page sometime. She liked to have fun with design, but she was also interested in saying something that mattered and saying it in a fresh, memorable way. Somebody once called her "the greatest living observer." She wrote poems about subjects nobody else ever considered as poetic material, everything from steamrollers to anteaters.

Objective observation—that's what her poems look like at first glance. But they always lead deeper to some simple yet rich insight. You could say it this way: Read a poem by Marianne Moore, and you don't just see the flower. You see the roots also, close up, with clumps of dirt clinging to them and all the little threadlike tendrils branching off the taproot. "Imaginary gardens with real toads in them"—I think of that line from Moore's poem "Poetry." That's what a poet should present to the world, she says.

I stubbornly stick to my own wavelength and say the line aloud to Ken. "Imaginary gardens with real toads in them." It's awful to be saying something and have no idea why you're saying it. Maybe I'm thinking that if I can't really talk to him, I'll just do a little flummoxing to fill up air space. I don't recommend this, but this is what I did. I should have stopped and prayed about what to say, but I didn't.

"Or real gardens with imaginary toads," Ken says back to me. I realize all of a sudden that he sounds really tired. I wonder if he sounded that way when he first got me from the library, or if it's just happened since pulling into the driveway.

I know I should stop talking, but I keep on. We're both staring into the carport now. I try to inject some pep into my voice, by way of contrast I suppose. "If you study the details of life, the images, the luminous particulars, you'll find the truth," I say. That's a phrase I picked up from Jane Kenyon—"luminous particulars." I like the way it rolls off my tongue. I look over at Ken. "I've been trying to study the details lately."

Still staring straight ahead, Ken says, "Right now I feel like I'm getting buried by details, and there's nothing at all luminous about them."

I have no idea at what point we both realized we were deliberately pretending to dodge each other, which made no sense whatsoever considering the seriousness of what we were going through. It was a grossly inappropriate time to be teasing, but I guess that's what it amounted to. I can't tell you how odd this is. Ken and I haven't teased for a long, long time. I try to remember the last time we laughed together, and I come up blank.

"I'm looking right now at the pictures and trying to see them for what they are," I persist. "But I'm trying not to hunt for symbols."

"I *am* hunting for cymbals," Ken says. "Our newest pair disappeared after the last concert." I'm tempted to ask him how the "Circus Polka" went at the concert just to see the look of surprise on his face and hear him ask, "Hey, how did you know we played that?"

I hear Macon's van start up in Theresa's driveway across the street, and I glance behind me. I see Theresa run out of the house and get in the van. Then Macon activates the sound effects he's rigged up, and from the speaker mounted on top of his van we suddenly hear what sounds exactly like a train whizzing past a railway crossing—clanking bells, clacking wheels, blasting whistle.

Ken turns around quickly. "What the—?" He watches Macon back out and head down the street. "I'm sure there are laws about stuff like that," Ken says. "Turn something like that on in heavy traffic, and you'd cause a pileup." I remember that Ken has never met Macon. I briefly consider trying to describe him but decide not to. Theresa and Macon's wedding is next weekend. I wonder if the other people on Windsor Drive have any idea what they're in for with Macon Mahoney soon to be a resident in our neighborhood.

I take hold of the door handle. "Well, thanks for coming to get me," I say. "I guess you need to get on your way." I sound like a teenager being dropped off after an awkward first date.

I remember this next part really clearly now. Ken didn't make any move to start the car. He had turned back around and was studying the carport again. "I called that guy again a couple of months ago about turning it into a garage," he said. "He gave me a price, and I said I'd get back with him." He sighed again. "I never did, though."

I wasn't interested in garages right now. I opened the door. "I can pay for the battery," I said. "I don't expect you to. I'm still subbing, you know. I've got money for car repairs. In fact, I can give you money now." I unzipped my purse.

"No!" He said it so suddenly and sternly that I flinched. He turned his head and looked out the driver's window, across the front yard. "I don't know how much it'll be," he said, more softly now. "I'll just charge it. I'll call you tomorrow sometime. Are you going to need to go anywhere before then?" He still wasn't looking at me.

"I have a couple of things lined up for tomorrow afternoon, but I can get by if it takes longer." I had planned to look for a wedding gift for Theresa and Macon sometime tomorrow, and I was supposed to play tennis with Barb Chewning at four, but she had offered to drive.

I got out of the car and leaned down to look back in at Ken. He was still turned away, gazing out at the yard. His shoulders were slumped forward. How is it, I wondered, that you can be so mad at someone for something he's done and yet feel sorry for him at the same time? Some kind of parallel was stirring in my mind. Oh yes, it was that thing Harvey Gill had said in Sunday school about God hating the sin but loving the sinner.

I tried hard for an instant to remind myself that Ken had made a premeditated decision to break his marriage vows. He broke the seventh commandment and committed adultery. For three months now he had caused me to envision horrible scenes that no wife should have to imagine. No one held a gun to his head and forced him to do any of this. He did it of his own free will. So feeling sorry for him didn't make a bit of sense.

"You okay?" I said.

"No." He said it so low I barely heard it.

I didn't know how to follow that up. Maybe you're thinking the logical thing would have been to ask why, to give him the opportunity to explain that no. Or maybe logic had nothing to do with it. Maybe it would have been the *Christian* thing to do. Whatever, I was neither logical nor Christian at the moment. I said good-bye and slammed the door. Still he sat there. I walked slowly around the front of the car and started toward the carport, then for some reason turned back. Something pricked at me. He was looking at me now. That was typical. He would look at me from a distance through the glass, but face-to-face I got only quick sideways glances, if anything.

I walked back toward his car, to his side, and stood at his window. He shifted his eyes away from me, of course. Too close for comfort, as the old saying goes. He started the motor, though, and rolled the window down halfway. "Guess I need to go," he said. "I've got to change clothes . . . and all."

Margaret gave me a book to read recently, the story of a missionary to China named James Fraser. She said it had done her heart much good to read about the fervor this young man had in sharing the gospel with the Chinese mountain people, of the arduous living conditions that to him were not a sacrifice but only part of the great joy of doing what God had called him to do. I was reading the book at night in bed now after my Bible reading. Just the night before, I had read in James Fraser's own words the description of negotiating a steep mountain path in a heavy mist.

Then the mist cleared suddenly, and a magnificent view presented itself to him. As far as the eye could see, there was "range upon range of dark mountains, swathed in cloud," he wrote.

As soon as I read that, I lifted my eyes to one of the pictures on the bedroom wall beside the dresser. It was a watercolor painting I had bought more than ten years ago at a student art show at Harwood. One of Ken's band members, a flutist, was an art major, and when he told me about the girl's art show, I went.

"Unusual" was all Ken had said about the show, but after I saw it, I immediately thought of dozens of other adjectives to add. Full, free, intelligent, vibrant, innocent, crafty, haunting, witty, and harmonious were just a few.

Not all of these applied to every piece, of course. It was a staggeringly brilliant and diverse art show for someone barely past her second decade of living. I couldn't believe the pieces had been executed by the plain-looking little person who sat fourth chair in Ken's flute section, who rarely smiled and who wore barrettes in her hair. Her name sounded nothing like that of a famous artist: Peggy Fletcher.

She had prices on her work, modest ones, and I bought a watercolor she had titled *The Fog Lifts*, in which she had depicted range upon range of mountains stretching into the distance with wisps of white clouds scattered here and there and a narrow strip of pale blue sky beyond. It's only about sixteen inches square, but you feel like it goes on and on. The frame is irrelevant.

I looked at that painting on my bedroom wall, and as I heard the echo of James Fraser's words "range upon range of dark mountains," I heard also the opening of a three-line poem I had read just a few days earlier by Gary Snyder, who had climbed the Sierra Matterhorn: "Range after range of mountains." How similar were the thoughts of missionary and poet as they viewed the world from great heights. In their own way, both were declaring their wonder over the created world, over being part of that world, over having a special work to do, and over loving that work. And really, isn't that enough to fill anyone with wonder?

So all of this floods my mind right now as I stand beside Ken's car. I could so easily be filled with despair, but instead I know very certainly right this minute that I, too—spurned wife of Ken Landis—am part of God's created world and that I have a special work to do. Something opens up inside me. When you lift your eyes to the mountains, you start to see all kinds of things.

"Are you okay?" I say to Ken again. "Do you need anything?"

He gives a half smile, half grimace and cuts his eyes up at me. "Maybe something to eat," he says, but he immediately shakes his head. "No, just kidding. I'm going to grab something before the recital." He steps on the brake and shifts into reverse. He doesn't go, though.

"All I have is stuff for sandwiches," I say. "You want a sandwich?"

He shakes his head again. "I don't really have time."

"It's the least I could do to thank you for rescuing me."

He's still shaking his head. He takes his foot off the brake a little, and the car inches backward.

"I could make you a grilled cheese with bacon," I say.

The car stops. I see him look at his watch. "Well, I guess it *would* save me having to stop," he says.

"The bacon's the precooked kind, really lean," I say. "It wouldn't take long. I'll use the griddle instead of the oven." It used to be a debate between Jennifer and Travis as to which sandwich was better—grilled cheese or toasted cheese. "You could be eating in ten minutes," I add.

"Well, I . . ."

"I've got some chips and Coke," I say. I'm not sure why, but it seems very important all of a sudden for him to eat a sandwich here and for me to make it for him.

He shifts the car into park and turns off the engine. "Okay," he says, getting out, "you talked me into it."

He doesn't seem to know what to do when we go inside, so he steps back out into the carport while I get his sandwich going. I hear him moving things around out there.

It's been a long time since I've served Ken a meal, I realize. Even before he left in February, I wasn't doing much of that. It had pretty much stopped the summer before he took Travis away to college. Travis had worked from two o'clock till ten that summer, so he wasn't home for supper. Combined with my despair over losing him, his absence at supper had taken away all desire to put meals on the table.

I can hardly remember what happened during those months after Travis left. I do remember saying to Ken one day, "I hate to cook" and walking out of the kitchen at suppertime. I went to bed at six o'clock that day, and Ken got in his car and left. I woke up many hours later when he got into bed, but I pretended to be asleep.

The griddle is hot now, and Ken's sandwich is put together and ready to grill. I watch my hands lift the spatula, then slide it under the sandwich. I hear the hiss when I lay the sandwich on the griddle. How can it be, I ask myself, that you hate to cook yet receive such pleasure hearing the sizzle of buttered bread on a hot griddle? How can it be that you actually want to be doing this right now for the man who has broken your heart? And how can it be that you are standing here daring to imagine that he will someday be home for good? I have no answers for these questions.

I'm turning Ken's sandwich over a minute later when I hear the words of the missionary once more: "Range upon range of dark mountains, swathed in cloud."

You climb a lot of mountains in a marriage. Range after range. Sometimes you lose sight of where you are. Maybe a fog rolls in, or the sun goes down and darkness settles in. You have to keep your eyes on your feet because the terrain is so rugged. The days are long, but you live for the one when the mist will clear and you'll see the whole panoramic view spread before you. In the nighttime, though, you can sometimes catch the glimmer of a star through the clouds above.

The Colored Night Around

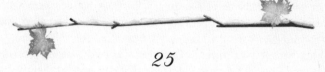

25

Ken says one thing that surprises me before he rushes off that night to attend the trumpet recital. I putter around in the kitchen while he wolfs his sandwich. I wipe down the griddle and put away the cheese and butter. I twist the bread wrapper tight and put it in the freezer. I put some things in the dishwasher, and when I do, I see a saucepan I used over a week ago to heat up some soup. I can go a long time these days before running the dishwasher.

"Aren't you eating anything?" Ken says between bites. But this isn't what he says that surprises me. I'll get to that.

"I'm not hungry yet," I say. "I'll eat later." I might and I might not. Sometimes I don't eat supper, and I don't even realize until bedtime that I'm hungry. By then it's too late and too much trouble to fix something, so I usually don't bother. I might drink a glass of milk and eat something sweet, but I don't tell him this. Ken has always been big on substantial meals at regular times.

I think of something I've been wondering a lot lately, and before I can chicken out, without even stopping to choose my words, I say, "How long has it been going on between you and her?" I wouldn't dream of looking at Ken as I ask this question. I'm still over by the sink, wiping the counter now, making a real production out of it by pulling the canisters out and wiping behind them, then wiping down the canisters themselves. I guess it tells a lot about a person as a cook when your countertops get dusty.

He doesn't answer right away, and I'm beginning to think he's going to ignore the question, which is something he's been known to do. He finally clears his throat, however, and says simply, "Since right before Christmas." I hear the chink of ice cubes as he shakes his glass.

"There's more Coke," I say, wondering how such a thing can come out of my mouth at the same moment I'm calculating the time frame of my husband's affair. So it had been going on almost two whole months before I finally caught on in February, and now it's five months old. I try for a moment to remember if anything happened around Christmas that should have warned me, but nothing comes to mind.

In fact, I can't remember much at all about Christmas except a desperate all-day-and-into-the-night shopping marathon at the mall, trying to throw together some semblance of a normal Christmas before Travis got home from college the next day. I spent way too much, I also remember that, and even duplicated a sweatshirt I had given Travis for his last birthday.

I think hard, trying to recall Christmas Day. We opened presents that morning, and I baked a turkey and a pumpkin pie, among other things—the first meal I had cooked in months. The three of us ate together at the dining room table in the middle of the afternoon. Jennifer didn't make it home for Christmas but came for a few days around New Year's.

What else? Oh, yes, Travis and I had gone to the tennis courts and hit for an hour or so late that afternoon. It was chilly but not so bad after we got moving. Ken stayed home and worked in his study—or that's what he said. Anyway, he was there when we left and there when we came back. Around nine o'clock that night Travis and Ken were back in the kitchen eating turkey sandwiches and leftover pie.

I remember Travis making a big deal over the food that day, telling me how good it was, saying the stuff he ate in the college cafeteria was a travesty. He had always liked the word *travesty*. He used to use it all the time in high school. Everything was a travesty—school projects, the neighbors' new yellow shutters, a teacher's hairstyle, fast food, local politicians, his failing score on his first attempt at the driving test, and so forth. I think the reason he liked the word so much was that it had his name in it. He would have thought it was a fine thing if his middle or last name had started with a *t* so the whole word would have fit. Travis T. Never mind that the word had undeniably negative associations—all the more fun in Travis's opinion.

Well, anyway, he went on and on about how good Christmas dinner was. Ken didn't say much, but he ate as if it were his last meal—or his first one in a long time, which to be honest wasn't far from the truth. I hadn't done much in the kitchen for a good while, as I said earlier.

Which brings me to what he says that surprises me. It wasn't the part about how long his affair had been going on. That didn't really surprise me. I had prepared myself for anything up to ten years on that one.

I guess what he says should make me mad, but mostly it just surprises me. He finishes his sandwich, takes the last gulp of his Coke, and wipes his mouth with the paper napkin I put beside his plate. I walk over and pick up his plate and glass. He balls up his napkin and drops it onto the empty plate, then pushes his chair back. I remember these small actions as if I'm seeing them in slow motion on a screen. He's looking at me cautiously, as if afraid I'm going to ask another question he'd rather not answer. Maybe he's wishing he had time right now to discuss the matter of divorce, since I seem to be in a calm, receptive state of mind.

"Thanks, Elizabeth," Ken says. "That was good." I go back to the sink and start rinsing off his dishes. He goes to the door and stands there with his hand on the doorknob. I look across the kitchen at him. The thank-you is surprise enough, but this isn't the big thing, which is coming. I can't remember the last time Ken thanked me for anything, but to be fair, I haven't done much in the way of thanking him, either. I guess you get out of the habit of that when you live with somebody for so long. I realize that this admission further undercuts all my earlier claims of politeness.

So he's turning the doorknob now and opening the door to leave. We're still looking at each other across the kitchen. It's been maybe five seconds since he's said, "Thanks, Elizabeth," but it seems longer. Then he says it, right before he steps out of the house and closes the door behind him. He presses his lips together and shuts his eyes as if recalling something painful, or maybe blissful. "I miss your cooking," he says. The next thing I know, his car is backing out of the driveway. I'm holding the glass from which he drank just moments earlier, and I'm staring at the door through which he just left.

Remember way back at the very beginning of this convoluted narrative when I said my story might make you angry? Well, I'll be getting to the big reason I said that, but here's one reason right here for starters. Husbands are supposed to appreciate their wives for their inner beauty, right? For the delicate touches they add to a home, for the warmth of their companionship and the glow of love that radiates from their eyes, for their capacity to turn the business of life into an art.

So when a man has been deprived of his wife's singular charms for three whole months, albeit having comforted himself with another woman's allurements, if he were going to *say* something to his wife to communicate even a twinge of regret or the smallest sense of loss, he would do well to focus on some aspect of her interior worth, her character, her *self*. Right? To say to her, "I miss your cooking" is thoughtless and self-centered. All you're really saying is "I miss having my appetite satisfied." You're speaking from your stomach, not your heart.

So by all rights—and even if you're a young person reading this, you can understand my point—I should have been furious at Ken. Surprised, too, yes, but mostly furious at his gross animal-like maleness. So this should make me mad at Ken, right?

But do you know what I felt as I stood there in my kitchen staring at the kitchen door and hearing Ken's words ricochet around inside my head? I felt glad. Not a vengeful sort of glad that he was suffering to some degree by feeling dispossessed of one of the good things of life—good cooking—but glad that he missed *my* cooking. What it must mean, I thought, or at least what it might mean, was that Dr. Snipe either didn't cook for him or what she did cook wasn't very good.

By all rights, I should be feeling insulted, but instead, I am feeling complimented. I was completely aware that it was all wrong, yet I couldn't help it.

Anybody reading these pages has my full permission to be angry about this. I agree, it's an offense to women everywhere. But let me warn you—this is only the beginning, so you might want to reserve your anger for later. Don't use it all up now.

And here's part of what was behind my feeling glad. I knew that Ken was reaching back in his memories to earlier years because, as I've already said, I had done very little cooking for almost a year, ever since the summer before Travis left home. To know that Ken was remembering those earlier years told me he was thinking about some of the good things we had together. And even if it was mostly mealtimes he was remembering, it still made me glad because mealtimes are about more than just food. He couldn't be remembering only the food. Surely the picture had to include the rest of us sitting at the table. Surely once in a while my face rose before him and something I said came to his mind.

But right away I scold myself for stretching what he said. I need to stop doing this. One minute I'm determined not to hunt for symbols and hidden meanings, and the next minute I'm swathing four simple words with layers of suggestion.

Wasn't it Ezra Pound who said, "The natural object is always the adequate symbol"? It's hypocritical to detest poems that are too heavily abstract, I tell myself, yet to generalize everything you see and hear in life, to force a symbol by transforming a specific phrase like "your cooking" into "you." So let Ken's words mean just themselves and nothing more. "I miss your cooking." That's all he said. Okay, that's enough. For someone who hasn't ever really talked to his wife, it's at least something.

It's not terribly specific, and it's totally unromantic, but I latch onto it as if it's a cloudburst and I'm a withering crop. I know, I know—it's pathetic. I should be throwing things and screaming, but instead I'm tenderly holding those four sorry words in my hands, stroking them over and over like an especially adorable kitten.

As I stand at the sink, I think of all the ways a husband can talk to his wife. Ken's father talked to Christine almost exclusively in the imperative mode. He gave orders brusquely and succinctly, and she carried them out.

Morris Seacrest teased Polly half the time and praised her the other half. I never heard even the least bit of irritation in his voice when he talked to her, although I wouldn't have blamed him at times. She pretty much did what she wanted to, and he cheerfully went along with her. Maybe he was a little too worshipful, I don't know. Maybe it would get on your nerves after a while, but I used to think Polly was one lucky wife. Of course, she thought the same thing about me. Once she watched Ken walk from his car to the front door of our house and said to me, "I always used to dream of marrying the silent, sexy type. Hope you know what you got, girl." I knew what I had all right—Mr. Zipped Lip. Mr. Brick Wall. Mr. Mole in a Hole.

My sister and her husband have an interesting way of communicating. It sometimes wears you out to be around them, but it's entertaining at the same time. Both Juliet and Tony are very smart and very opinionated, so their conversations often sound like arguments, though they aren't really. Usually after everything is said and done, they strike some sort of compromise, except for the time Tony was offered the job in New Hampshire and Juliet said she'd rather have molten lead poured up her nostrils than move to the North. They still live in Virginia, and Tony seems perfectly satisfied, especially since the company that offered him the job in New Hampshire folded after a year.

But the freedom with which they speak to each other! Once I heard him say to Juliet, "You are the most stubborn woman on the face of the earth!" and she shot back with "And you wouldn't be where you are today without this stubborn woman!" He responded with "And *you* wouldn't be where you are today without *me!*" and she shouted, "So what's your point?" He bellowed, "So we *need* each other, just like I've been trying to tell you!" Which wasn't at all what he had been trying to tell her, but Tony knew when he was in a corner. Ten minutes later they walked out onto the back porch, where the rest of us were sitting, and they were holding hands!

And then there were my parents. The way Daddy talked to Mother was something I've often wondered if I just imagined. Maybe I idealized it after he died so as to keep his memory unspotted. I don't think so, though. Daddy was a gentleman through and through in his dealings with Mother. He let her name the dance, but he always led, never once stepping on her toe. He let her bluster and grumble according to her melancholic bent, but the final word was always from him—strong, positive, and kind. I never once heard him lecture or rebuke her for a gloomy prediction, but he would always follow up what she said, gently tempering her words with words of his own.

After Daddy died, I remember seeing Mother look around after she had spoken, straining forward just a little as if listening for his counterremarks. I think she still listens for him. She'll make a grim statement, then pause ever so slightly, holding her breath, waiting for him to set things straight.

I remember when Mr. Bingham, my eighth-grade art teacher, explained the concept of complementary colors on the color wheel, I immediately thought of my parents. I was only fourteen at the time, but I grasped the meaning of complementary colors before the words were all the way out of

Mr. Bingham's mouth. Daddy is yellow and Mother is purple, I thought. Daddy is red, and Mother is green. Daddy is orange, and Mother is blue.

I had been watching my parents very closely for a couple of years by that time, aware that they had a life of their own completely apart from Greg, Juliet, and me. Some children don't ever realize this, but I suspected it from an early age and knew it for sure by the time I was a teenager. All those after-dark talks were probably what gave me my first inkling. Once I even got a glass from the kitchen and held it up to the wall between my bedroom and theirs. I should be ashamed to admit this.

Well, I'll tell the whole truth. I didn't get only one glass, but two. I got one made of glass and one made of plastic and told myself I was doing a scientific experiment, although I was smart enough to know which one would be the best conductor of sound.

They were talking about Greg, who would have been seven or eight at the time. Mother had gone to see his teacher that day and was worried that Greg was still having trouble reading. "I wish he'd get a teacher with some *experience* one of these years," she told Daddy, who reminded her that this was only Greg's third teacher in his whole school career and that his kindergarten teacher had been a thirty-year veteran. "But most of those years were in other grades," Mother had said.

I could hear most of what she said through the plastic glass, but the glass one was better, of course. I listened for less than a minute before I was overcome with shame at what I was doing. Next thing you know, you'll be hiding under their bed, I told myself. As I tiptoed back to the kitchen to return the glasses, I couldn't help wondering if anyone had ever done that—hidden under their parents' bed to see what they did after the lights were out. The thought was tantalizing, but, oh, how awful if you got caught!

Many years later when I read a book of James Dickey's poems in college, I came across "The Celebration," in which the speaker sees his parents at a carnival, but they don't see him. He follows them for a while, marveling over the fact that they're not asleep at home as he had thought they were, but that they're here in the middle of all this noise and light and sawdust, his mother leaning on his father's arm and laughing at something he says.

He can hardly believe it when his father, whom he considers old and incompetent, wins a teddy bear for his mother at one of the games, and after they board the Ferris wheel, he watches them rise and fall as the great wheel turns "the colored night around." For the first time in his life he sees his origin for the miracle it is. This is where I came from, he thinks as he watches them swaying from their perch fifty feet in the air.

The first time I read that poem, I felt a shaft of truth pierce right through my heart. It was so sharply, shiningly beautiful that it hurt. You can feel that same swift pain with music and art, but it always strikes me more suddenly and with more blinding intensity when it comes through poetry. Poetry gives you elements of music—rhythm, pitch, harmony, dynamics—and it paints pictures besides.

So anyway, my parents knew how to talk. I can close my eyes now and see Daddy pulling Mother close to him and murmuring into her ear. I can see her look up at him and ask him something, and I can see him bend to her and talk earnestly. Having a father like mine, I guess I expected too much from Ken.

I guess I should at least be grateful that Ken didn't take after his father and tyrannize everybody, and I don't know that I'd want him to be as silly and adoring as Morris Seacrest either. Polly told me once that she sometimes just went into the bathroom and locked the door on Sundays when Morris was home all day following her around and asking her questions and hugging on her. And I can't imagine getting into shouting matches with Ken the way Juliet and Tony do. They're *talking*, yes, but, oh, the outlay of energy, the shattering of serenity!

There are times in everyone's life, or there should be, when you see things the way they really are, not the way you suppose them to be or want them to be. So I'll start and stop with this. Ken misses my cooking. Period. Don't push it further, I tell myself. "I miss your cooking"—those were his exact words. I used to be a pretty good cook, I'll go ahead and say it. Mostly I stuck with the standard things—chicken, ham, roast beef, round steak, pork chops—but there's lots of room in there for variety and experimentation.

So I'm standing alone in my kitchen, and Ken's gone now, driving his car down Highway 11 away from Berea and back toward Spartanburg. He'll pass the intersection at Utica Corners, maybe glance to his right and see the casket store and notice the satiny pink lining of the one propped open closest to the front window. Perhaps he'll shudder at the sight of something so private being exposed like the inside of someone's mouth or a gaping stomach wound. Or maybe the pink will make him think of something pretty, like the early tinges of dawn or rose petals. I know he has to *think* metaphorically, being a musician, but he never talks that way, of course.

Maybe as he drives on, he will think of charcoal clouds against a pearly sunset sky and listen to a CD of Pachelbel or Scarlatti. Maybe he'll roll down the windows to feel the mild evening breezes. These are images I can see whirling around in my head like the swinging seats of a Ferris wheel. Think about these, I say to myself. Don't look for symbols. Don't try to interpret or make connections or forecast. Just be content to see, hear, feel, smell, and taste.

Eventually, though, there has to be more. Anyone knows that. With all due respect to Ezra Pound, natural objects are splendid in their place, but the human heart longs for things to be put together into a whole design. And wouldn't Mr. Pound agree? Images are good, but if they don't link up with a bigger idea somehow, they just squat on the page and take up space. Besides, Ezra Pound went further than mere images himself when he wrote about the young river-merchant's wife watching for her husband's return. He arranged those images into a mural about love and longing.

In fifteen minutes Ken will be at his apartment, and he'll change his clothes, then go to his student's recital. Then what? "I miss your cooking." I hear it again. I'm done in the kitchen now. I look around and think of how little use this room has had since we moved here. It's a bigger kitchen than we had in Derby, a lot more counter space and cupboards, a more open feeling, the kind of kitchen I used to think I'd love. On the pass-through window between the kitchen and den, I see the book of poetry and the video I got at the library. I pick up the video.

Babette's Feast. The combination of the unique name and the evocative word *feast*, with all its pleasurable connotations, makes a nice title. I read the summary on the back. It interests me that the feast is a literal one. Of course, no doubt there's another stratum of meaning aside from the actual food, but the description lets me know there's plenty of real food in this feast. This is what I'll do tonight. I'll watch *Babette's Feast*. It's from a story by Isak Dinesen, the woman who wrote *Out of Africa*. I wonder if Margaret has ever read this story. I must ask her.

I'm not going to tell the whole plot of *Babette's Feast*. For one thing, everybody needs to see this video for himself, and for another, I hate to read summaries of stories. As if a story is nothing more than a sequence of events. It's like someone showing you a skeleton and saying, "This is John Burgess." You totally miss the essence of John Burgess.

An hour and a half later I have watched the video once, and an hour and a half after that I've watched it a second time. When I say I've watched it, I mean it in the fullest sense. I don't often truly watch television, but I do listen to it and glance up occasionally to catch a quick illustration. But this is different. It's a French movie with English subtitles, so following the plot requires that you watch the screen at all times.

It's a story full of symbols, but I'm not sure what they mean. I can usually reduce a work of art to its theme in short order, but this one is ambiguous. There's a conservative religious sect in the story, which interests me. As you would expect, this one is portrayed without sympathy, as is the case in most bestsellers and blockbusters. In most stories, plays, and films, a religious group is nothing more than a refuge for lunatics and perverts. The one in this video is on that order. It's a small group whose members are small minded. Nothing new here.

There's a French servant named Babette who prepares a Feast for the congregation. We must capitalize this Feast. Every detail is rich and colorful. The Feast is the focal point of the whole story, and its preparation and execution are magnificently depicted. The sensory appeal was as astounding the second time I watched it as it was the first.

Even for those not interested in the message behind art, the painstaking and elaborate lengths to which Babette goes in serving this sumptuous banquet are reason enough to watch this movie. Forget, if you want to, trying to figure out what the author of the story is saying. Just kick back and revel in the incredible Feast cooked in a cramped kitchen and laid out on a rustic table by a servant in a remote Danish seacoast town.

But for those who do happen to care about what a story or poem or picture or film is communicating about life, you'll need to watch this one more than once. It's all about art. Willard Scoggins, who recommended it to me, praised it, yet I could just as well imagine him condemning it. The message could be something a Christian could either embrace or shun—that's how equivocal this movie is, at least the way I see it. It could be saying that art can enhance spirituality, or it could be saying that art can replace spirituality, and I don't need to tell you that those are two very different themes.

I want to watch the film a third time, maybe with Margaret, and pick up more clues as to the author's intent. Art can deepen and then reflect one's love for God, or art can become one's god—which one is it? I want to study the two sisters further, listen again to the general's speech at the dinner table, and review every excellent detail as Babette prepares her incomparable Feast.

I can't help seeing Babette as a Christ figure, although I have no idea whether Isak Dinesen meant her to be. Babette gives all that she has, and in so doing makes the poor townsfolk rich in spirit. But maybe I'm straining after symbols again. For sure, though, her Feast is a work of grace. The congregation gets something wonderful for nothing. They haven't done anything to earn it. They simply open their arms and receive it, or their mouths in this case. Through her art Babette causes the blind to see.

This whole thing about art has been on my mind these past few months. Since my salvation, I've heard a lot at the Church of the Open Door about idols and false gods. "Anything that comes between you and your personal relationship with Christ is an idol," Pastor Hawthorne has said on more than one occasion. He has gone on to list several possible idols: another person, a new home, a car, a job, a hobby, and so on. And I've done some serious thinking. Is my love of art—of poems and paintings, music and drama—an idol? Does it keep me from loving God more?

I remember the extreme religious fervor of the Moffett family, who used to live next door to us in Georgia. If somebody offered them their choice of an original Matisse or a Thomas Kinkade print, they'd point to the print and say, "That one. That's *real* art." And as for music, I can think of only one adjective to describe the music that typically wafted across the driveway from their house: *twangy*.

They would no doubt call Marianne Moore's poetry the foolish babbling of a heathen, and they would never watch *Babette's Feast*, because they were convinced that all movies were from the Devil, along with a lot of other things that seemed like fun to me. I remember Mrs. Moffett stopping my mother one day when she was taking Juliet to a ballet lesson and telling her that Jesus didn't approve of "flaunting your body around on a stage in tight clothes."

I haven't seen anything this fanatical at the Church of the Open Door, but I sometimes wonder what Pastor Hawthorne would think if he knew I once spent an entire paycheck on an oil painting of wild jasmine vines. A couple of years ago I subbed for a U.S. History teacher for two whole weeks, and when I got paid for it, I cashed the check, then drove straight to a gallery in Greenville that was featuring a regional artist and laid down every penny plus twenty dollars extra for the painting, which I had seen the week before.

I remember feeling like crying when I walked into the gallery and saw the painting still there, and when I carried it to my car a few minutes later, I was afraid the earth couldn't contain me, that I would float right up into the sky and never be seen again. I hung the painting in our living room, and for months afterward I would go stand in front of it and completely lose track of time. That happened before I became a Christian, but the thing is, I can imagine doing it all over again today if I saw another piece of art I loved as much. Would Pastor Hawthorne say this was idolatry?

I look at some of the other people at church and see their devotion and zeal acted out very actively and publicly, whereas my own commitment seems so timid and private in comparison. If I didn't spend so much time reading and writing and observing, could I be a better Christian? Sometimes after reading poems or essays about poems, I wonder if I should have spent the time reading my Bible instead. The thought has come to me often: Do I love God more than I love art? Would I give up poetry for God?

But other thoughts crowd in after the second time through *Babette's Feast*. Has God asked me to give up poetry for his sake? Can't the love of art open our eyes to the glory and majesty of the Creator? Can't it cause us to be more discerning of truth and beauty? Can't it provide a broader point of contact with unbelievers? Can't it therefore supplement our love of God? Before the film is rewound, I hear the answers to these five questions: no, yes, yes, yes, yes.

It's going on ten o'clock when I finish the movie for the second time. Seeing all that food twice in close succession reminds me that I haven't eaten since my lunch with Bonnie Maggio. I know I shouldn't eat a heavy meal this late at night, but I'm hungry. The strangest craving comes over me all of a sudden for tuna salad. Maybe the idea was planted by the setting of the film.

Somebody ought to do a survey of what people eat after they watch certain movies. There must be a correlation. Watch a Western movie about stampedes and cattle roundups, and you want a steak. Watch *Charlotte's Web* or *Babe*, and you want a ham sandwich. Watch a movie set in a fishing village, and you want tuna salad.

The way I make my tuna salad is not complicated. I put an egg on to boil. I get a can of tuna out of the pantry, then drain it and put it in a mixing bowl. I spoon in just enough mayonnaise to hold it together, then add a little sweet pickle relish and mix it all together. I pour myself a glass of Coke, which I shouldn't do at ten o'clock at night, and get out the bag of chips I served with Ken's sandwich several hours earlier. While I wait for the egg to finish, I sit down at the kitchen table and read three of Marianne Moore's poems: "No Swan So Fine," "Four Quartz Crystal Clocks," and "The Mind Is an Enchanting Thing." This is one smart woman writing these poems. I wish I had known her, maybe lived next door to her or served on a committee with her.

I'm dicing the egg a few minutes later, thinking about Moore's concept of "conscientious inconsistency," when Ken surprises me for the second time that day. He shows up at the kitchen door. I hear him tap, and I almost slice my thumb off. I've been intending to get wooden blinds to cover the panes on the top half of the kitchen door, but I haven't gotten around to it. When I look over and see Ken's face against the panes, I'm glad there are no blinds. I wouldn't want to stand at the kitchen counter and wonder who was there at this time of night.

I remember how I liked to look at things through my bedroom window as a child, like my mother's jonquils in the backyard. You could see the whole world so clearly, and you could focus on what every detail looked like. You weren't distracted by all the outdoor sounds. Ken says something now through the glass, but I don't catch it. I know he has a key, and I motion for him to come on in.

" . . . need to get something," he's saying as he swings the door open.

I nod and resume my dicing. He walks past me into the hallway. He's wearing his navy suit with the wide pinstripe. The tie is one I gave him, silver gray with small navy polka dots, which he thought was too flashy when he first saw it. He wore it, though, and got compliments on it and kept wearing it. Ken is a neat dresser, tasteful and conservative, very professional and put-together.

I mix the egg into the tuna, then start spreading it onto a slice of bread. I hear Ken back in his office opening drawers, then coming back down the hall.

"You just now eating?" he says.

I nod again. "Time got away from me," I say.

He has a file folder in his hand. "I meant to get this the other day," he said. "I need it . . . for something coming up." He's standing about three feet away from me watching me put my sandwich together.

I cut the sandwich in half, then take it over to the table and sit down. He moves slowly toward the door, glancing at my plate. "There's more tuna if you want it," I say.

He sets the folder down on the table and says, "Well, okay." He gives a short laugh. "I guess the other sandwich wore off." Then, as if afraid I'd feel bad, he adds, "It was good, though." I suddenly have the feeling that if I were to open the folder he just laid down, I'd find something really insignificant, some trifle he doesn't really need all that badly. Or maybe nothing at all. Maybe it's completely empty. With sudden dread I wonder if he has come back tonight to talk about divorce.

"The bread is on the counter," I say in case he's thinking I'm going to make his sandwich for him. "And how was the recital?" I ask as he takes off his suit coat and hangs it on the back of a chair.

"Not as bad as I expected," he said. "But not good either."

I suddenly think of something I hadn't thought to ask before. "Will Travis have to give some sort of recital his senior year?"

Which reminds me of unfinished business from an earlier chapter. I don't apologize for this. It's the way I tell my story. One thing reminds me of something earlier, a dropped stitch in the narrative, and I have to loop back and tighten it before I go on.

When Travis came home for Easter back in April, we had a talk that Sunday afternoon, the three of us. After church we went to Juno's for dinner, and then we came home, and Travis told us he wanted to talk to us about something. As far back as I can remember, Travis had never once initiated a discussion with us about anything.

It was a funny feeling that day, sitting down at the kitchen table, this same table I'm sitting at now with my tuna sandwich. Travis waited till we were both seated, and then he sat down. We all took our normal seats, as if it were a regular suppertime. The atmosphere was totally different, though. It was completely turned around. I don't know how Ken felt, but I felt nervous, as if this were a job interview.

Travis lightened things up at first with a little impromptu monologue. Or maybe it wasn't impromptu. Maybe he had written it out and memorized it ahead of time. He delivered it Columbo style, the puzzled expression just verging on stupidity, the bumbling apologies, the slow roundabout approach to his subject. "I hate to bother you, sir, ma'am," he started out, nodding at each of us, "but the fact is, well, I've been doing some thinking about a few things, see, and well, it just doesn't add up. So if you don't mind, I mean I hate to inconvenience you like this, but I need to have just a little word with you about some questions I have, and I'm hoping you can help me out here."

He had it down pat. With a good makeup artist, Travis could pass for a young Peter Falk any day.

I remember looking at him during this introductory part and thinking, "This kid should be an actor." Which was very, very curious, considering what it was he wanted to talk to us about.

The Trumpet of a Prophecy

26

Our Sunday dinner at Juno's was a little awkward, as you'd expect. I didn't think Travis would notice, though. Juno's was a small place with a low ceiling, and that day it was even more crowded than usual, with all the elderly customers descending at once to celebrate Easter Sunday. You should have seen the finery! Seersucker suits and bow ties, patent shoes and silk pocket handkerchiefs, floral prints, earbobs, matching pumps and pocketbooks, even a few extravagantly trimmed spring hats—these old folks were decked out.

Travis's eyes were bright and alert as we went through the buffet line. We heard one woman behind us say to somebody, "My grandson's so sweet, I could eat him with a spoon," and another woman, whose hat was shaped like the hood of a hair dryer, said, "I tried for years to grow raspberries but couldn't ever get pea turkey." A man already seated near the line shouted, "Turn your hearing aid down, Bonner! Folks'll think there's an air raid!" I couldn't help sympathizing with Bonner. If he turned it down, he wouldn't be able to hear anything above the din. A woman in front of us must have been describing a funeral because I heard her say, "Oh, and he *did* make such a handsome corpse!"

Thankfully, the noise made it easier not to talk much once we got seated, so we didn't bother trying. Neither Ken nor Travis had ever been much inclined to talk when there was food in front of them anyway. Even with Ken and Travis both going back for seconds, we were all three finishing up our peach cobbler with vanilla soft-serve ice cream exactly forty minutes after having sat down. And we were back home by two o'clock or so, which was when Travis summoned us for the talk around the kitchen table.

After a little while he dropped his Columbo persona and just turned into Travis again. He looked at the pepper grinder in the middle of the table as he talked. Travis was always bad about not making eye contact, and I saw college hadn't changed that. He was planning to switch his major—that's what he wanted to talk to us about. I had known all along that physical therapy was the wrong major for him, so I wasn't surprised.

Physical therapy was okay, he went on to say, but it was a little boring, and he'd found something he liked better. Ken asked him what it was. He had a satisfied look on his face as if he'd known all along that this day would come. Last summer when Travis had chosen his major, Ken hadn't been too worried. Just let him do it, he'd said. Travis was picking something out of a hat for now, but he'd change after the first year. It didn't matter anyway, Ken said, since you don't do much toward your major during your freshman year.

In the seconds before Travis answered, I tried to anticipate what his new major was going to be. I found myself hoping it wouldn't be related to music. *Please don't let it be music,* I prayed. I knew Travis would never measure up to Ken's expectations if he majored in music, especially if it had anything to do with trumpet. Surely he knew that. He couldn't have forgotten all the stress we'd been through over the years when he wasn't playing something the way Ken thought it should be played. Surely he wouldn't choose something his father had absolutely no objectivity about.

Besides, a music major would mean a solo recital, wouldn't it? And he didn't do recitals—surely he remembered that. He had changed a lot since last fall, but I couldn't imagine him putting himself through that. I could picture Ken getting up and walking out in the middle of Travis's senior recital or else standing up and shouting, "You're rushing those sixteenths, and that whole passage should be tongued not slurred!"

Or musical composition—surely that wasn't what he was thinking about, was he? He had played around with it some his last year of high school, had written a piano piece called "Cauldron Brew," a couple of brass ensembles, and even a transcription of some Bartok dances for band. I'd hear him calling out questions to Ken from his bedroom. "Hey, Dad, what key is an English horn written in?" or "How low can a tuba go?" I even remember Ken looking over something Travis had written one time and saying, "This isn't half bad." But still, I couldn't see Travis picking a major his dad was so close to.

"Drama," Travis said.

Ken and I stared at him. I thought he might be teasing. It used to be one of his tactics growing up, to prepare us for bad news by telling us something really farfetched that was even worse. When he was just a little kid, for example, he dropped a carton of eggs on the kitchen floor one time, then came outside where I was spray-painting a patio table and told me the refrigerator had fallen over and everything inside had spilled out onto the floor. When he lost my library card, he told me he had given my Visa card to a man at an intersection holding a sign that said *WILL WORK FOR FOOD.*

And once when I asked him how he did on a chemistry test, instead of coming right to the point and telling me he had made a D, he started out by saying with a perfectly straight face that he had been expelled from school that day. I would always fix him with a level gaze and ask him what had *really* happened, and he would keep modifying the story until he finally got around to the truth.

But the usual signs of his teasing were missing this time—the way he narrowed his eyes to slits and scrunched in one corner of his mouth. He was looking at us now, going back and forth between Ken and me.

"With a minor in creative writing," he said, then added, "I tried out for a play a couple of months ago and got a part."

He couldn't be serious, but it didn't make any sense that he'd be making something like this up. "What play?" I said. I was trying not to show on my face or in my voice how impossible I thought it was. Ken was sitting there with his brow furrowed and his mouth slightly open.

"It's just a one-act," Travis said. "*Hello Out There*. That's what it's called." "By Saroyan?" I asked.

His eyes lit up. "Yeah, you know it?" he said.

I nodded. I had read the play years ago but never seen it. I remembered only two main characters, with several minor characters appearing at the very end in a jailhouse showdown. He must be one of these, I concluded, if he really was in the play at all. I still suspected him of tricking us.

I recalled the drama majors at Piper College in my day—they had a reputation for being intelligent, haughty, and clannish. Or weird, to sum it up in one word. They would always look over your head as if someone far more interesting was coming along behind you. They hung out in a back corner at Father Barlow's and engaged in role-playing games while they drank flavored teas and ate pears and wafers. Not seeming in the least bit concerned about what others thought of them, they exuded a private sense of having figured out the meaning of life, which they guarded as their collective secret.

One of them, a boy named Jedediah Dunwoody, sat next to me in American Romanticism and always wore a black turtleneck to class, even on the warmest days. Once he looked at me solemnly during class and whispered, "Your face is like a burnished medallion." I didn't ask him to elaborate.

I couldn't see Travis as a drama major. I couldn't imagine him drinking hot tea, eating pears, and telling girls their faces were like medallions. Ken immediately took Travis's announcement for the truth, which it in fact turned out to be, and began to attack it from the purely practical standpoint.

"And what would you ever do with a degree in *drama*?" he asked Travis. It was easy to tell from his tone of voice that Ken thought a major in drama was equivalent to one in sandcastle building.

"Oh, I don't know," Travis said. "Maybe a little Broadway, a little off-Broadway, a couple of movies a year, eventually get into directing, producing, that sort of thing." He had his hands clasped behind his head and was speaking to the ceiling. It jolted me, looking at him sitting like that, to see how much he resembled his father. I had never been able to understand how people could think the two of them favored, but I saw it clearly now. Ken's mother had been the worst about it, always saying things to Travis like "My, my, I look at you and think it's thirty years ago."

"This is no time to joke around," Ken said now.

"I'm not joking," Travis said, and I knew in that instant that he wasn't.

"When I chose a major," Ken said, "I was thinking about what I wanted to do for the rest of my life. You don't want a degree you can never use."

Ken is a very, very smart man, but he has never caught on during the past almost nineteen years that the surest way to get Travis to tune him out is to lapse into his lecturing mode. With Jennifer, he always talked in a very reasonable, controlled, respectful tone, and she listened. She even sought his advice. But something happened when Travis was born. By the time he was walking and talking, Ken's manner with him was sternly instructive. Maybe it's the way he thought a father should deal with a son, so as to toughen and sharpen him. It was no doubt the way his own father had dealt with him.

It had the opposite effect, though. Travis seemed to wilt whenever Ken started in. He refused to reply and often cried when he was younger, which annoyed Ken to no end. In a way, though, Travis did toughen up in that he grew obstinate and held on even tighter to whatever behavior or attitude was being targeted, although adopting more subtle, evasive ways after that to throw his father off track. More and more he learned to retreat into his own world. Ken would start lecturing, and Travis's eyes would glaze over. I don't think a father ever understood his son less than Ken did Travis.

"It's a waste of good money," Ken went on to say, "to get a degree in something you can't make a living from." He was starting to gesture more now, which always happened right before he started talking louder and faster. "I could tell you story after story of people who graduate from college without ever settling on anything useful. And they flounder around trying to find a job in some dead-end field before they eventually have to go back to school to get the training they should have gotten the first time through, so they can support a family."

That's one thing about being a teacher. You always have a ready source of illustrations in your students to prove almost any point you're trying to make. Ken cited one of these now. "I have a student in two of my classes right now who's almost thirty, taking conducting and music ed courses after drifting around for eight years trying to do something with a degree in piano performance." He had slid into louder and faster by now. "This guy thought he'd be giving solo concerts at Carnegie Hall as soon as he graduated, but he found out that good piano players are a dime a dozen. He tried selling pianos on commission for a while but could barely make enough to pay his rent."

"Exactly!" I wanted to cry. This was ironclad proof for something I've believed for years, that boys right out of high school are too young to know what they want to do for the rest of their lives. In my opinion the solution was simple. Let them wait three or four years until they can decide, then start college when they're twenty-one or so. By then they'd have a little money in their pockets and a little sense in their heads. Ken's solution, though, was to find something practical you could do to make money, anything for which you had even a modicum of aptitude, then set your mind to it and get a degree in it, find a job, be satisfied, and live happily ever after.

"And creative writing is the same thing," he said to Travis, leaning in closer as if he knew he was losing his audience. "What does a person do with *that*? Sit down at a desk the day after graduation and start writing the next great American novel? And what does he do to support himself while he does that for several years? Get a paper route? And let's say he actually does finish a book. After the first twenty publishers tell him they don't want it, then what?"

Ken shook his head gloomily. "It's all very idealistic, Travis, but real life doesn't work that way. If you change your major to something like drama or creative writing, you're digging a hole you'll never crawl out of." He laid both hands on top of the table as if that were the end of the matter.

As usual, Ken had taken things to the extreme. Travis was clenching his jaw, still staring up at the ceiling. I wished I could read his mind. I doubted that he was listening anymore. Maybe he was reviewing his lines for the play he'd tried out for. "What made you try out for the play?" I asked.

He shrugged. I was expecting "I don't know," but after a pause, he said, "I saw a purple light blinking in my head, and I heard a high-pitched whirring sound when I looked at the announcement on the bulletin board."

Ken made a sound of impatience. "You're acting silly now. And even if you did see lights, it was probably a warning not to do it!" He paused for a breath and then lowered his voice. I could tell he was making a conscious effort to act calm. He leaned back and adopted a tone of reason. "Actors spend their lives pretending to be somebody else, Travis," he said, as if it grieved him to impart such sad news. "What kind of a life is that? Why don't you find something where you can be yourself?" He shook his head slowly and spoke even more softly. "Do you know how many unemployed actors there are in the world? They had a part in a high-school play and thought they'd be the next Jimmy Stewart or Harrison Ford."

"I know myself a lot better than you do." Travis spoke slowly and clearly. He was looking right at his father now. The kitchen was deathly still as the two of them stared at each other.

I reached over and laid my hand on Travis's arm. "I can see you doing a wonderful job on-stage," I said. "I've never thought of it before, but it makes perfect sense." And it was true. He had always had a flair for capturing voices and mannerisms. I wasn't amazed that he had won a role in a play but that he had gotten up in front of people and auditioned for it.

"I think it's something to be thankful for," I said, turning to Ken. "Travis has a talent for this—I feel certain of that. Look at what it's already done for him." Surely Ken could see the obvious. This wasn't the same Travis who had left for college back in August.

Ken pushed his chair back and stood up. "Of course, I might have known you'd take up for him. He could come home saying he wanted to major in bungee jumping, and you'd think it was the greatest thing you'd ever heard of."

It came to me in a flash that Ken's response to all this was more disappointment than anger. It had never dawned on me before, but I was absolutely sure at that moment that he must have always harbored the dream that Travis would eventually enter the field of music. Which was funny considering how little real encouragement he had given Travis along the way. No doubt Ken would have found some argument for any other major, even something as practical as accounting or computer science. The intensity of his objections didn't have all that much to do with drama or creative writing. I was sure of that. It wasn't so much a matter of what Travis had chosen, as what he hadn't.

Ken walked toward the door. Before he could lay hold of the doorknob, however, Travis said something else that stopped him cold. "Where are you living now, Dad?"

I suddenly felt sick. Ken shot a look of reproof at me, but I shook my head and spoke quietly. "I haven't said a word."

"You should have told me," Travis said. He sounded much older than a college freshman, and I wondered if Ken felt as ashamed and rebuked as I did.

It was true. We should have told him—and Jennifer, too. Ken and I had had over two months to come to some kind of understanding about what was going on, but we still hadn't talked it out together. So I guess part of the reason we hadn't told our children anything yet was that we didn't know exactly what there was to tell. We could have fallen back on other excuses, too: "We didn't want to worry you," "We've been preoccupied," or "It was too painful to talk about."

The main reason, though, was that both Ken and I were master avoiders of anything unpleasant. The danger in hiding the truth, of course, is always that the news will fall harder the longer you wait. So now our son had to come home and discover it for himself.

Looking at him now, I hated what we had done to him. I saw him gallantly trying to act like a grown-up, speaking with terse authority and looking us in the eye. Yet I also saw something else that broke my heart. I saw fear. He might be three inches taller than his father now, with a deeper voice and a bigger shoe size, and he might be finally gaining confidence and independence at college, but he was also scared. He was a little kid who had lost his parents in a crowd.

"How did you know?" I asked him.

He sighed, then lifted one foot and pulled up his pant leg. "Socks," he said. He had gone to Ken's bureau to borrow a pair of socks to wear to church that morning, he told us, and found the drawers mostly empty. He had then looked in his father's closet, which was in the office bedroom, and found the same. And the desk looked too neat—he could tell Ken hadn't used it in a while. Then the phone calls all added up, too. Ken had been calling him at odd times, by himself, and I had seemed distracted and sad whenever I called.

Ken came back to the table and sat down again. He took off his glasses and rubbed his eyes wearily.

"So what's going on?" Travis asked. "Are you gonna tell me now?" He looked from Ken to me. "Does Jen know?"

I shook my head. "No, I haven't told her anything either. But I was planning to tell you sometime this week. I was going to wait for the right time. When you showed up last night, I was so . . . surprised I couldn't think straight. But I made up my mind to tell you while you were home, and I was going to. I promise I was."

We all sat there silently for several moments. "So tell me," Travis finally said. He looked right at me, his dark eyes wary. Was it only minutes earlier that I was deploring his lack of eye contact?

"I think your father should do this," I said. "I don't have a whole lot of information."

Without his glasses, Ken looked vulnerable, his deep-set eyes beseeching and childlike. He gave me a long look, then turned to Travis. "I met a woman several months ago," he said. He pressed his lips together and looked away. "Your mother and I . . . were having some problems after you left for school, and . . . then I met this other person, and then your mother found out, and . . . well, I'm staying at a motel now."

Travis shook his head very slowly. "You can't do that," he said. "You can't be with anybody else but Mom." When Travis used to cry, he did it silently but with his whole heart. He would bury his face in a pillow and shake with sobs, but he wouldn't make a sound. He didn't have a pillow now, and he wasn't shaking with sobs, but his eyes were bright with tears. He held his head very high to keep them contained. "You and Mom have to . . ." He trailed off. His voice was tight and thin. He kept his eyes on Ken, never once looking over at me. "You can't do this," he said again, almost kindly, as if he were asking a favor.

It's a horrible thing to see the grief of your child and to know you can't make it go away. I wanted to put my arms around him and hold him close, but I didn't dare. I wasn't even sure how he would take it if I did. For all I knew, he might push me away.

But this was something he had to face alone. I knew that to try to comfort him would somehow have wounded him further. I imagined the heartache at this table as a moldy, rotting piece of fruit dragged out of the garbage and cut into generous wedges. We each had our own large slice and were commanded to eat.

What happened during the next thirty minutes was something that should have taken place many weeks earlier, between only Ken and me instead of as a three-way conversation. Travis asked the question one of us should have asked long before. "So what happens now?" Later, I looked back on it and marveled at the role Travis took. I also felt deeply sorry that he had to do it. I know nothing he had taken at college thus far had prepared him for this, so he must have had the strength somewhere inside him the whole time. I guess we don't give our kids enough credit most of the time.

But I'm ashamed to think of the weight we placed that day upon our son. And how he took the burden without flinching. Except for the shine in his eyes, his face was set in stone. I talked first. I said I didn't know what happened next because I barely knew what had happened already. I summarized what little I knew—that Ken had been seeing another woman, that he had moved to a motel in February, and that we hadn't yet discussed a divorce. I talked to the tabletop. I couldn't look at Travis.

Ken took over, also addressing the tabletop, pointing out that the reason I didn't know much was because I didn't want to sit down and talk about it, to which I hotly responded, "As if you really do yourself." Ken claimed that he was ready any time, and I said no, he was content to avoid it as long as I was, that he couldn't initiate a heart-to-heart talk if his life depended on it, that he might sit down and make a charade of it the way he tried to do back in February, but all it would amount to was skirting around the edges of the real problem.

He had *wanted* to talk that night, he said, but I had been in another world. No, I said, the only thing he had really wanted that night was another piece of pizza.

No child should have to hear his parents having a conversation like this. Travis listened without comment, then turned to Ken. "Why did you do it?" he said. His voice was full of wonder and great sorrow, which must have caught Ken off guard. If he had been challenging and angry, Ken would have known better how to respond. After all, he was the one who gave any lectures that were to be given around here, who pointed out errors and asked probing questions. I fully expected him to tell Travis that a son had no business asking his father why he did anything.

But he didn't. He appeared to be thinking over an answer, and I dreaded hearing it. I dreaded Travis hearing it. Finally he said, "I fell into it without meaning to. Your mother and I weren't . . . talking, and I was lonely . . . I guess. It was winter, and . . . I don't know."

Of course, it always comes back to that. *I don't know.*

"Winter isn't bad," Travis said, which seemed an odd reply. Ken and I both looked up at him. "And it's not bad to be lonely," he continued. "It gives you lots of time to think."

Ken leaned forward. "You'll find out someday that you can run out of energy to think about things when you've already thought about them over and over. There's nothing more to think. The landscape's all the same. Everything's cold and dark." This was an amazing speech for Ken, who always spoke literally, rarely bothering with metaphors.

"Winter isn't permanent," Travis said. "Everybody has to go through winter, but it doesn't last forever."

" 'If Winter comes, can Spring be far behind?' " I heard myself say it, yet could hardly believe I had. What a silly, sentimental thing to say at a time like this. We all seemed to be saying such strange things—Ken waxing symbolic, Travis hung up on winter, and me quoting Shelley's famous line from "Ode to the West Wind."

"Exactly," said Travis. "Things can get better. You can work things out. People make mistakes all the time but then fix them."

"Ah, 'the trumpet of a prophecy,' " I said. It was another line from Shelley's "Ode." Thankfully, Travis didn't seem to catch what I meant. Oh, the foolish innocence of youth. They toot these little platitudes and think they've blown a mighty trumpet. There was no way Travis could know how far short the word *mistake* fell from what had gone on between Ken and me. He had no idea what kind of impossible miracle-working power it would take to "fix" such a mistake.

Travis persevered earnestly. "It doesn't have to be the end. You can work it out."

"You have to *want* to work it out, Travis," I said.

"But don't you?" he asked. He was suddenly full of fire. "What about what you were telling me last night? If you're different now, how come you don't want to fix things up with Dad? Didn't you tell me God had forgiven you and taken you into his family? Okay, so how come you can't do that? And what about all those things that preacher at church said this morning? He kept talking about all this power Christians have. The resurrection power—wasn't that what he called it? So do you believe all that stuff? Then how come you can't work it out with Dad?"

"I mean you have to *both* want it," I said. "And your father doesn't want it. One person can't fix a problem like this."

Travis turned to Ken for his response. I felt as if I were slowly suffocating.

In that moment I knew what Ken was going to say, and I wondered briefly how other wives through the years had had the strength to bear these words from the men they had given themselves to. I thought of the vast volume of pain generated by all the words in conversations like this one. I guess I was bracing myself by imagining what a small part of the whole my own portion would represent. I pictured an ocean of seething black liquid and an eye-dropper poised above it ready to release another milliliter.

I heard Ken take a deep breath. I wanted to run out of the room, but I knew it was time, finally, to hear it. I guess I thought I could take it now that Travis was sitting here with us.

"I never said I didn't want it," Ken said.

It was hard to absorb the words at first. I let them replay in my mind. I sat there taking them apart and putting them back together. I reviewed what had been said before, to make sure I had the context right.

He never said he didn't want what? The problem to be fixed? I kept backing up and going over and over it, and that's the only thing I could come up with.

"See, Mom," Travis said. He was tapping lightly on my arm, trying to get me to look at him. "See, Dad says he wants to work on it."

So on Easter Sunday I find out that Ken might not want a divorce. I feel myself wanting to laugh, to make a farce out of this, to say, "Oh, okay then, come on back home, and we'll just pretend that nothing has happened. We'll start over with clean white paper and a sharpened pencil and write a brand-new fairy tale that has a handsome prince and a beautiful princess in it who live in a splendid castle and love each other devotedly."

But as Ken said earlier, this was no time to joke around. In spite of what I had just heard Ken say, my heart felt like a great slab of stone. It's not that simple, I wanted to explain to Travis. Forgiveness and restoration are very, very big words. You don't just decide you're ready to receive them. And you don't just decide you're ready to give them either, even when you might know you should.

It's odd how you can want something yet at the same time resist it. Lots of times you want the end product, but you hold out against doing what it takes to get there.

In matters of forgiveness, there's a whole jungle to hack through before you get to the treasure. And sometimes the treasure isn't even there. The *X* on the map was just a hoax. You follow all the directions and you dig a hole all the way to China, but there's nothing there. Or maybe your compass was broken or you misread the directions.

Or maybe you even get mixed up on purpose because deep down you really don't want the treasure. So you put on a big show of trying, but you know all along that you're digging nine hundred miles from where the treasure really is.

PART FOUR:

And though the last lights off the black west went

Oh, morning, at the brown brink eastward, springs

GERARD MANLEY HOPKINS

Across the Glittering Sea

27

So much happens at a kitchen table. I think about how many kitchen table scenes my story has already had. I'm back to mid-May now. Several weeks after Travis told us in one breath he was changing his major and then in the next urged us to work out our marital difficulties, I'm eating a tuna sandwich at that same table and watching Ken make one for himself. He tells me yes, Travis will certainly have to give a senior recital of some kind when he graduates. It's a requirement for all the arts.

I remember Jedediah Dunwoody's senior drama project at Piper College. He stood up in our American Romanticism class and invited all of us to attend the "mythological chimera" he had written and directed, followed by an "illusory soiree" in the lobby. Ken had to practice for his upcoming trumpet recital, so I went to the chimera and soiree by myself.

Even if he hadn't told us, I would have known Jedediah had written the play himself, which he titled *The Color of Ether*. The characters spoke in a cryptic, affected way, imitative of Jedediah's own speech, and the dialogue was full of attempts at metaphoric subtlety, which resulted only in nonsense. The characters were genderless gods named after letters of the Greek alphabet—Alpha, Mu, Gamma, Theta, Omega, and so forth—and they all wore billowy pastel pantaloons and armored breastplates.

I remember nothing of the plot, which was absurd, but I do remember that Delta said to Kappa at one point, "Your soul is a platter of sweet cream," and Kappa answered, "Yea, sweeter than much fine cream." I quoted these lines to Laurie, who thought they were hilarious and copied them down for future use with one of her boyfriends. I wonder if Jedediah ever looks back on his twenty-one-year-old self now and is embarrassed, or if he's still going around saying things like "Your eyes are twin citadels" or "My spirit is a deeply riven canyon."

There was no actual food at the soiree following the play because college policies prohibited serving food in the auditorium. Long tables were set up in the lobby, however, and the pantalooned gods floated around with silver pitchers pretending to pour nectar into tiny communion cups. They also carried silver trays and served invisible macaroons in little frilled cupcake papers, which kept blowing off the trays onto the floor. So everybody left with a plastic communion cup and a cupcake paper, both empty.

I try to imagine what kind of senior project Travis will choose. Maybe he could stage a *Columbo* episode. Maybe he could do all the sound effects while his cast pantomimes the action of a basketball game. Maybe he could write a play set in a restaurant where old people eat.

Three weeks have passed since Travis went back to college after his spring break. Ken has continued to come home off and on, maybe a little more than before, but every time we've seen each other, Ken's words "*I never said I didn't want it*" have hovered between us. We haven't talked about it further, of course. We're both still eyeing each other from opposite corners, trying to read past, present, and future from the scrappiest of evidence.

I don't know if Ken said what he did because after four months his affair with Dr. Snipe was losing its appeal or if he was just trying to mollify Travis at the moment. Either way, I figure he was just looking out for himself. If he wants me back simply because he's tired of her, I'm not much inclined to rejoice.

For some reason it makes me think of the new dishcloth I bought one time. It was thick and nubby, like a washcloth, and I used it for weeks until I realized I really didn't like it. I liked my old ones better, which were limp and thin and easy to slide around inside glasses and bowls. So one day I put the new one away and got out one of my old ones again. Maybe Ken just wants his old dishrag back. Maybe the new, fancy one is too hard to get used to. I am not flattered to realize that I have things in common with an old dishrag.

I talked with Margaret a few days after Travis left in April. Our poetry classes were still in session then, and we had been going to the Second Cup Coffee Shoppe most Thursdays after class. We usually talked about the poems Professor Huckabee had discussed in class or others Margaret was planning to present to her poetry club. But that night I turned to a more personal subject.

I remembered something she had asked me weeks ago: "*Are you prepared for grace?*" I told her now that the idea of grace had been on my mind a lot lately, and I asked her the question I had been asking myself for several days. "What if someone does something so horrible to you that you can never trust him again," I said, "but then one day he decides he wants you to forgive him? Does being a Christian mean you have to?"

She gave me a long steady look. "Has your husband asked for your forgiveness?"

I shook my head. "Not in so many words. I have no idea what's going on, really. I'm just trying to think of all the possibilities. But if he did, would I be obligated to take him back? I don't see how I ever could after what he's done. Every time he went somewhere, I'd be sure he was sneaking around again."

Margaret looked thoughtfully into the palms of her hands before she answered. "I, too, have known suffering, though not the suffering of a husband's infidelity, and I, too, have struggled with the matter of forgiveness for wrongs against me. This is one of life's great tests, and I do not have the answer key." She paused as if the words were being dredged up from a deep place.

She lifted her teacup as if to drink but then set it back down. "Is a Christian obligated to forgive? It is no easy question you are asking, Elizabeth. We might get to the answer, I suppose, by asking other questions. Is a Christian to be like Christ? Did Christ forgive those who abused him? Does God forgive us daily for our failures? The parallel is perhaps imperfect, but if God's forgiveness rested in our trustworthiness, would we not stand outside the reach of his grace? When I seek his forgiveness for a sinful action or word, to what degree can he trust me not to commit the same transgression again?"

I didn't like what this implied, yet I couldn't find a loophole. "So you're saying forgiveness is a matter of the will?" I asked. "Just do it because it's right? Seventy times seven times if necessary?"

"So you have read Christ's answer to Peter?" Margaret said.

I nodded. "Oh yes, I've read every verse about forgiveness listed in the concordance. The only thing the Bible doesn't tell me is how to *want* to do it. And if it doesn't come from the heart, it isn't the real thing, is it? I mean, I can put on all the outward signs of forgiving, like actually saying, 'I forgive you' and then doing all kinds of nice things for the person and never bringing up the past and all that, but if I still bear a grudge against him inside, then it's all a sham, right? And how can anybody really forgive and forget? Can you *will* yourself to forget? If we could forget, the forgiving part would be easy, wouldn't it?" I knew I was talking too fast and jumbling my thoughts together, so I stopped to take a breath. "I'm praying for God to open my eyes," I said, "but I still feel like the blindfold is on a lot of the time."

Margaret smiled sadly. She stirred her tea a bit and then set her spoon down. "This is slippery ground," she said to me at length. "I feel incapable of guiding you. A shepherd must have the wisdom and patience of long experience. He must be strong yet gentle. I am still picking a path through so many of life's hard places that I fear I will lead you astray. Will you not consider going to our pastor and his wife for surer counsel?"

I told her I wouldn't, not yet. I just wanted her opinion. But the matter of forgiveness is so much more than mere opinion, she replied, and I told her I knew that, but I wanted to start there for now, so would she please just answer? I was probably a little unfair in adding, "Friends do this, you know—share opinions."

We talked a long time that evening, and we shared more than opinions. She asked me many questions, and I lost track of time and space in answering them. I took detours and ended up many times on the "scenic route," as my father used to call it when Mother began embellishing her side of a conversation with too many details. "Can we get off the scenic route and back on the main road?" he would ask her.

Margaret never made any attempt to redirect me, though. She simply listened. A few times she made observations. Though she kept her voice neutral, I bristled at one remark in particular, or rather a question. Margaret often comments in the interrogative mode.

"Do you think it at all possible that over the years your love for your son eclipsed your love for Ken?" she asked.

"No more than his love for his mother eclipsed his love for me," I replied quickly.

I came back to the thought later that night. *Be honest,* I told myself. If both were contributing factors, which one had contributed more to the breakdown of our marriage—my excessive devotion to Travis, if it could be called excessive, or Ken's excessive devotion to his mother? And going back further, had I lavished my love on Travis because of all the attention Ken gave his mother, or had he drawn closer to his mother because I was so consumed with Travis? Here was a chicken-and-egg dilemma.

Think, I told myself. *How was it between Ken and Christine before Travis was born?* I can barely remember the years before Travis. Even the first seven years of Jennifer's life—my own daughter!—are something of a blur now except for a few scattered memories I can't even put in order. My most vivid recollection of her babyhood is the day I realized she was Ken's child more than mine.

I always felt that my role as mother was narrowly limited with Jennifer, that she thought of me only as a nursemaid, teacher, and chauffeur. I remember at times being overcome with love and hugging her suddenly to me, only to feel her pull away impatiently. Oh, she loved me, I don't doubt that, but I could have been a hired hand instead of her mother for all the affection she showed me. She wasn't that kind of little girl.

I had always resented the fact that Ken gave his mother attention and emotional energy that rightfully belonged to his family. I had even said out loud to him once, "You give her more of yourself than you give your own children."

He hadn't answered, but I wondered now, looking back, if he had ever wanted to say to me, "And you give more of yourself to your children than to me, so it all evens out."

I couldn't imagine him ever saying words like this, of course, and I wasn't even sure his mind could assemble thoughts like these. Ken was a composer of the first degree. He could put together all the intricate parts to make up a densely textured piece of music. He could study a score and then pull out every little nuance of the music from a group of sixty players. He could take apart a student's arrangement and critique it measure by measure, citing specific reasons for its success or failure as a musical whole. He could do all of these things expertly, but when it came to analyzing and hashing out relationship problems, he couldn't find his way out of the thicket. He couldn't even make it to the end of a straight path.

I kept coming back to the question, though. How was it between Ken and Christine before Travis was born? Schuyler had run off with the violin teacher by then, so Christine was living by herself. Suddenly something very, very simple came back to me as I thought this through. It was Schuyler's leaving home that had made Ken so solicitous of his mother. That was when she started clinging to him as her eldest son, and that's when he started calling and visiting her so much.

It was hard to believe I could have forgotten this very obvious cause-and-effect sequence. I know, I know—for being so smart, I sure am dumb. I'm certain I must have caught the connection at the time, but I guess the passing years have a way of dimming things like that.

Before Schuyler left, I can't remember thinking that Christine had any special hold over Ken. After the abandonment, which turned out to be her liberation, I briefly felt sorry for her—I do remember that much. I think I saw her sudden attachment to Ken as fairly normal, considering how ill prepared she was for living alone. I'm sure I expected things to ease up once she got used to being on her own. I didn't dream that the end of her marriage would have such an unraveling effect on ours.

Another question Margaret asked that night before we parted was "Could it be that over the course of your marriage, you have held back from opening your heart to Ken the way you have opened it to me tonight?"

"He wouldn't hear a word of it even if I did," I said. "He'd be too busy with his music."

She continued as if I hadn't spoken, gazing into her empty cup as she spoke again of how difficult it had been for her to talk openly with Thomas. "I know I have told you this before, but it seems relevant again," she said. "I am by nature introspective and a keeper of secrets. I have brooded over my past and have dragged it through life like an iron ball." She sighed. "I regret this, for it stunted my marriage." She lifted her eyes to mine and smiled. "In the last year it has begun to grow, however, in large part because I have learned the joy of sharing my heart with the man who loves me. You know that I do not offer advice unsought, Elizabeth, but I speak to you now out of a deep knowledge of my many failures as a wife."

All I could think of to say in reply was "It takes two to talk," to which she readily agreed.

"Yet one person has to speak the first word," she said.

Margaret's words have played through my mind over and over since that night at the Second Cup. She hasn't pried in the weeks since then but has patiently waited for me. She has been content to talk about anything I've brought up—a new poem I ran across, a class I subbed for, a piece of music I heard, a passage of Scripture, a sermon Pastor Hawthorne preached, a linocut of Macon Mahoney's I plan to buy, and so forth. Margaret is an ideal friend. I'm discovering this more as time passes.

I watch Ken now as he spreads tuna salad on his sandwich very methodically. He lays the other piece of bread on top, lining it up precisely, then presses it lightly and slices the sandwich in half. I'd be willing to bet there's not a millimeter's difference between the surface area of those two halves.

Looking at him standing at the kitchen counter, I think of what I said to him at the table that day when Travis was home: "You couldn't initiate a heart-to-heart talk if your life depended on it." I ask myself now when had I last initiated a heart-to-heart talk with him. The old pot-and-kettle saying comes to mind, but I push it away. I'm not the one who's committed adultery, I tell myself, which, though it's absolutely true, somehow seems worn out and beside the point.

Something else comes to my mind right now. Last Friday, a week ago, I arrived home after teaching to find three small rosebushes planted beside the driveway in a strip of dirt newly tilled and mulched. They aren't the formal, perfect, elegant roses that unfold themselves in slow motion. These bushes are small and low to the ground, with roses that open up eagerly around a yellow center and start dropping their petals almost immediately. There's something endearing about a flower so ready to give itself.

"I like the rosebushes," I say to Ken as he brings his sandwich to the table and sits down.

He nods. "They're carpet roses."

I'm almost done with my sandwich as he takes his first bite. I try to remember the symbolism of white roses. On Mother's Day when I was growing up, Daddy would always order Mother a corsage and take us all out for dinner. At some point during these dinners Mother would always mention the rules about the colors of roses in corsages. Red roses meant your own mother was still living—I think that was it. Pink meant something else, and I'm pretty sure white meant your own mother wasn't living anymore. I couldn't imagine Ken choosing the color of the roses based on their symbolism, though, and I was sure he hadn't thought of Mother's Day, which was last

Sunday, when he planted the bushes two days earlier.

"Most roses bloom later, but this is an early variety," he says. "They were on sale at Lackey's."

Ah, I should have known. The red ones were probably a couple dollars more. That's okay, though. White roses suit me better than red ones. White ones don't put on airs. They make a suggestion instead of an announcement. They're friendlier, more like a puppy than a cat.

"What did the guy play at his recital tonight?" I ask Ken.

He makes a face. "Easy stuff—'Prelude et Ballade,' 'Petite Piece Concertante,' a couple of others. He made a stab at Hummel's 'Concerto in E-flat.'" He shakes his head as if to say it was a very weak stab with a very blunt instrument.

I know the Hummel piece. Travis worked on it last summer during his final series of lessons with Mr. Beatty before leaving for college. We wanted him to play it in the recital Mr. Beatty scheduled for all his private students last August, but Travis declined, politely but firmly. "Me and recitals, we don't go together, remember," he had said. Ken had slammed the kitchen door and gone out into the carport after that discussion and had spent over an hour shoving boxes around and violently hammering something.

"Did you already know Travis was playing in the band?" I ask now. This is something else Travis told us a few weeks ago over Easter. At the beginning of second semester, he auditioned for the Piper College Band and is now sitting seventh chair, playing the third trumpet part. He told us this off-handedly, as if he were telling us he had bought a new spiral notebook. I was shocked. I wondered what other surprises he was going to spring on us.

"No," Ken says. I can tell he doesn't know whether to be glad or frustrated. He had tried to get Travis to join the band back in September, but Travis was convinced he wasn't good enough to play in a college band and claimed he'd be too busy with classes to keep up with his music. There had been more hot words over this—from Ken, not Travis. Travis had just tuned him out and let his eyes travel back and forth across the ceiling as if following the flight of a lazy horsefly. He did take his trumpet with him to college, but I imagined it sitting in a corner gathering dust and cobwebs.

But this was the funny part. When Ken asked him at Easter what piece he played for his audition to get into band, Travis said, "Part of the Hummel." I know Ken was tempted to say, "You mean the same piece you refused to play in a recital last summer?" He didn't, though. He asked him if he practiced it before the audition, and Travis said, "Sure. I brushed it up and played it for Mr. Beatty. He gave me some tips."

"Mr. Beatty?" Ken said. "How did you do that?"

"Easy. Like this." Travis acted out putting a trumpet to his lips and buzzed the first several notes of the Hummel.

"I mean, when?" said Ken. "What did he do, drive all the way to Piper and give you a private lesson at the dorm?"

"Nah," Travis said. "I went over to his house at Christmas."

Well, this was news. He had known at Christmas that he wanted to join the band, and he had laid plans to accomplish it. Surprise upon surprise. I wondered if there had been clues at Christmas that I could have picked up on if I hadn't been so distracted.

"I played it for him the day before the audition, too," Travis added. "On the phone." This makes me laugh, imagining Travis dialing Mr. Beatty long distance from his dorm room, then setting the receiver down and picking up his trumpet to play over the phone. I guess that explains one of the mystery phone charges that showed up on his school bill.

"Didn't you sit eighth chair in your college band?" I ask Ken now.

"Only a little while," he says quickly. "I was first chair my senior year."

I remember, of course, but I'm bringing it up to make a point. I don't want him to expect more out of Travis than he did out of himself as a freshman.

We sit quietly for a few minutes, and Ken finishes his sandwich. I think of the old dishrag again and get up quickly. I set my plate in the sink harder than I need to and let the knife clatter on top of it.

Ken clears his throat. "I meant for the rosebushes to be a gift," he says. "For Mother's Day."

I turn on the water forcefully. I know I should probably thank him, but I can't get the words out. I'd rather have the rosebushes than a dozen cut roses any day, but to receive a gift so indirectly annoys me. Was I supposed to *know* they were meant as a gift?

"Travis sent a card," I say. I'm letting Ken see how other people do it, how they communicate in some way when they're giving a gift. "He wrote a poem for me. And Jennifer called Sunday night. She sent me a couple of books and a pair of gloves."

"Gloves?"

"Gardening gloves. She thinks I might like to plant some things in the yard." Jennifer likes our new house. She's seen it only once, in January, but she immediately envisioned the backyard as "a garden to die for," as she put it, dead and brown and neglected though it was back then.

Ken gets up and brings his plate to the sink. He drains the rest of his Coke and sets his glass in the sink, too. I watch the water swirl around inside the glass and fill it up. He's standing less than a foot away from me, and I'm suddenly, irrationally afraid he's going to reach out and touch me. I stoop down and open the door of the dishwasher. He quickly moves back, then leans over and picks up dishes from the sink, where the running water has almost rinsed them clean, and starts arranging them neatly in the dishwasher.

I see our reflections in the window over the sink. I look closed up and angry. The set of my mouth is hard. Ken's head is bent in concentration as he gets those glasses and plates in just the right slots.

Out of the blue an idea comes to me, but I resist it. *Do it,* I tell myself, but nothing happens. I hear Margaret saying, *"Someone has to speak the first word."* And I think, *Then let it be the chief offender.* I recall something else Margaret said to me that night: "Grace is the ultimate gift. It is the precious ointment poured out of a free heart—free from the bondage of self-love. We have received it gladly from the hand of God, and so should we give it." How easy it is to make a pretty speech like this, I think.

It's irritating in a way that something that makes no sense logically is so foundational to Christianity. I see it running like a mighty river throughout the entirety of Scripture, underpinning the Law and the Prophets, blooming radiantly in the Gospels, and resonating in the Revelation of John on the Isle of Patmos.

"Grace greater than all my sin" is what the song says. I sang the words in choir just two weeks ago. I look at Ken's reflection in the kitchen window and think, *Grace greater than all your sin.*

I turn the water off, squeeze my eyes shut, and force myself to speak words I don't want to say. "Would you take a walk with me?"

Riding down the freeway, I often feel a sudden panic when I see a truck approaching an overpass. In my head I know the road engineers have carefully planned it so that the overpass is high enough for a truck to drive under, but there's always that moment of doubt when I see the test coming. What if there was a mistake made on this one, and it's just a couple of inches too low for a really big truck like this one? Or what if this truck was manufactured wrong and sits up just a little higher than every other truck on the road? What's going to happen when it hits the overpass? Will the truck fly apart? Will the overpass collapse? And what about all of us riding along in the cars nearby?

I feel that same tightness right now as I hold my breath and wait for Ken's answer. Part of me wants him to say no. Then I can tell myself that I made an effort and was rebuffed. It would be a relief in a way. *Say no,* I'm thinking. *Say you have to hurry back to take care of something you forgot. Say you have a band composition to finish or an exam to type.*

But he doesn't. "Well, okay" is what he says instead. He sounds a little puzzled as if I know something he doesn't. As if he's waiting for me to explain a riddle. "Listen, buddy," I want to say, "I have no idea why we're going for a walk, but let's do it fast and get it over with."

Ken takes his tie off and changes from his good shoes into an old pair of his work sneakers in the carport. We step outside together a couple of minutes later and smell rain. I feel a few light drops on my head. I don't know when this started, but I see it as an excuse to back out. "Oh, it's raining," I say, hesitating at the end of the carport.

"It's barely sprinkling," he says, holding out a palm. "I don't mind getting a little wet if you don't." I wouldn't expect this from Ken, being as particular as he is.

"Your good clothes will get wet," I say.

"They're going to the laundry anyway," he says.

I shrug and we walk out onto the driveway. I lift my face to the sky, and I like the way it feels, like a fine mist from a spritz bottle.

"Which way?" Ken says at the end of the driveway.

I choose right. We can walk the three blocks down to DeLaney and then decide whether to go farther or turn back. I look down our street as far as I can see and wonder what we will have talked about by the time we get to the second streetlight. Maybe we will have walked silently the whole time.

As we set off, I remember when Travis drove down our street backward not so very long ago. I'm not sure my backward look through our marriage has been very successful. I've seen plenty of pictures from the past, some good and some bad, but I'm not sure I've had any grand revelations. Or maybe I just haven't let myself admit what I've seen.

It comes to me again that my habit of looking back may have been a handicap in a lot of ways. I've always had trouble with the concept of starting each day fresh. "Forgetting those things which are behind"—I remember those words from Philippians again. I glance over at Ken and say to myself, "Oh no, you don't get off that easy, buster. We don't just *forget* about it."

We've passed two houses now and haven't said a word.

"Everything's so linked together, isn't it?" I finally say.

Ken nods. "Oh yes, it is," he says. "It definitely is."

"All those islands 'across the glittering sea,' " I say.

He nods again, though I'm sure he has no clue what I'm talking about. He surprises me, though, by saying, "Yep, they're all connected."

Which is exactly what the poem is talking about—Muriel Rukeyser's poem "Islands." It's in one of the books Jennifer sent me for Mother's Day, a new paperback by Herbert Kohl called *A Grain of Poetry*. The point is, you look at islands from the shore or from a plane or boat and you think of them as being separate, but they're not. They're all connected by the ocean floor, just like the land that links mountains together. That's what islands are— they're mountains that happen to be standing in water, that's all. You've got to learn to look at things from all directions, including underneath.

I think of Ken and me. For many years it has seemed like we've been separate islands, but I imagine myself going underwater now, and I see that we've got a lot of land connecting us. It's called the past. And the present. And maybe the future.

A Thousand Days of Words

28

I have something to put in writing. Every time I've thought of putting it down on paper, I couldn't. I tried to write a poem about it once and couldn't get past the first line: "Too soon she left me." We all have private places where no one else enters, and this is another one of mine. This is one of the places I've never invited Ken. In the beginning I didn't really intend for it to be a secret. I could have shared it with Ken, with my mother, with Juliet. But for some reason, I never did, and then the time for sharing was gone, and I knew it wouldn't come again.

I didn't mean to set it down in this record, but now I see it belongs here. This will say a great deal about me and about our marriage. It's another picture, but a strange and solitary one. I'm by myself in the middle of the day. Jennifer, who will be four soon, is asleep. She rarely takes naps anymore, but this day she does. Ken isn't home, but I can't remember why. It's the last Saturday afternoon in the month of November, and it has been raining all day. I'm ironing a shirt, I remember that clearly. It's a blue oxford dress shirt with a button-down collar, and I've just finished one sleeve.

It happened fast. I remember a horrible heavy pain. When I looked out the bathroom window ten minutes later, it was raining harder. Everything outside looked sad and bedraggled, and I heard Jennifer crying in her bedroom. That was always how she woke up from a nap.

It will seem odd to anyone reading this that I've written twenty-seven chapters, have gone woolgathering hither and yon, but never mentioned a word about this before now. But everybody has rooms they keep locked, and this has been mine. I've always guarded it possessively. No one else could possibly care as much about it as I do, so I kept everybody out.

As Ken and I walk down our street now with the mist swirling about us, I think of all the ways we're connected. The faces of our children rise before me—Jennifer and Travis. And there's another one I see, though I never actually saw her. She's a sunny, bright-eyed child, the way I imagine her. Her hair is blond, and she has a dimple in one cheek. She's shorter than Jennifer, with delicate bones and very fair skin. I've always called her Annie, though she never had a name, of course.

There, I've committed it to paper. I can see my readers already shaking their heads, ready to judge me. This is why I never speak of it. The pain cannot be explained, but it is enormous and never diminishes. This will confirm to anyone reading this that I'm an emotional woman, one who enjoys wallowing in grief, who magnifies every sentiment into melodrama. It is completely unreasonable that I should think of Annie as my daughter, should have dreams about her, should have invented a whole childhood for her and given her a face and physique, a personality, talents, fears. Many years ago I even gave her a birthday, which is coming up in June, a few weeks before Travis's.

I regret already putting this down in writing, trying to reduce something as complex as my feelings about my unborn daughter into letters of the alphabet. I can't begin to comprehend how something so small expelled from my body can stay so long in my heart. Others will accuse me of a woman's particular weakness, that of seizing a moment of sorrow and enlarging it into a great maudlin trophy to be proudly borne throughout a lifetime.

Ken knows nothing of Annie, even though she's his daughter, too. He never knew she lived inside me for eight weeks. She was midway between Jennifer and Travis, which makes her almost twenty-two. When he came home the next day, I was in bed, and he just thought I had a touch of something. I remember him taking over with Jennifer. I can still hear them laughing in the kitchen while I lay in the bedroom. I stayed in bed two days, went to the doctor the third day, and grieved in silence every day after that.

I wonder what Ken would say about it if I suddenly divulged this information to him. Probably nothing. He'd probably take his breath in suddenly, then blush in the dark and stare down at the pavement until a decent space of time had passed, then look up at the sky and say something like "Well, I think I see a break in the clouds up there. Tomorrow ought to be clear and sunny."

A dog barks from a backyard along the way. Headlights come toward us, and I recognize Macon Mahoney's van as it comes closer. He and Theresa wave. I wave back, and Macon activates the sound system. It's a cello rendition of "Beautiful Dreamer" with the strident caws of crows in the background.

"How old is that guy? Thirteen?" Ken says. "He must have too much time on his hands. Who is he anyway?"

"That's Macon, the man Theresa Dillman's marrying next weekend," I say. "He'll be moving in across the street."

"Oh, great. I can't wait to hear the rest of his repertoire," Ken says.

"Maybe you won't have to," I say. I don't know exactly what I mean by this, and evidently Ken is afraid to ask, because he doesn't reply.

The streets are wet, and our sneakers make squishy sounds as we walk. It strikes me that even the finest mist can soak things down if it keeps up long enough.

We walk a little farther, and a silly idea suddenly pops into my head. It comes from something Margaret told me about her walks with Thomas. Every time they walk, she said, she makes herself reveal something private to Thomas—some hope or fear, maybe a regret from the past or a happy memory. It can be anything, as long as it's something she's never shared before. It's a requirement she sets for herself.

So without stopping to talk myself out of it, I say, "Tell me something I don't already know."

"What?"

"Something about you . . . something I don't know," I say. "Just anything."

"My feet are getting wet," he says, pointing to the sneakers he's wearing. "These things have holes in the bottom."

"No, something bigger," I say, shaking my head. "Something from your heart."

He's quiet for so long that I begin to think he's not going to answer. But then he sighs and says, "I've been a fool." Very matter-of-factly, just like that. "I've been a fool."

"I said it had to be something I didn't already know," I say.

I can tell he doesn't know how to respond. He doesn't know whether he ought to laugh or just keep quiet. He plays it safe and goes for something in between, one of those indiscriminate sounds deep in the throat that could be anything from chuckling to choking on a bone.

We walk on, the mist turning into a drizzle. "We could have brought an umbrella," he says.

"Yes, we could've," I say. For some reason, though, I'm glad we didn't. I like this new feeling of being out in the elements without protection. An umbrella would just be something to fiddle with, to be a distraction, to hide under.

Ken starts to say something, then stops, then clears his throat. "You must hate me," he says finally.

"I hate what you've done," I say, feeling a sudden swell of virtue for answering this way. Isn't this what Christ says to sinners? He loves the sinner but hates the sin, right? I'm quickly filled with shame as I realize how unlike Christ I really am, how I've wanted Ken to suffer as I've suffered, how hypocritical I've been, alternating between reading my Bible and thinking up ways to get even.

We come to DeLaney and without discussion turn left onto the sidewalk. Cars go too fast for conversation along here, so we walk in silence except for the sibilant whistle of tires on the wet asphalt. I close my eyes briefly and lift my face, thinking how pleasant this cool wet air would feel in different circumstances—during a long, hot tennis match in July, for example. I open my eyes and remind myself that it's only May, that Ken has slept with another woman, and that I live alone. I hear the same words from the Song of Solomon that I often hear at night. *"But mine own vineyard have I not kept."*

I don't know why, but something about the glow of the headlights through the drizzle suddenly makes me think of a lonely soldier coming home after a long war and wondering if his sweetheart is still waiting for him. Or worried that his sweetheart will be able to tell somehow that he's been unfaithful to her. For some reason the number half a million comes to my mind, and I wonder if over the course of history this many soldiers have been untrue to their wives and girlfriends while away at war.

I am stunned for just a moment at the hairpin turns my mind is capable of making, certain that I've lost my ability to make sense of anything, that this is what it must feel like to go crazy. I picture my mind as a wide level plain with a heavy fog rolling in and every thought a lost soul stumbling around trying to latch onto something solid. I wonder if a person who loses his mind ever suspects that's what's happening, or does he just think he's a little mixed up about details?

Stop it, I tell myself. *Think of what's happening right now. Quit getting sidetracked. Ken is trying to say something important.* I realize all of a sudden that what he's saying, though it's not much yet, is a result of something as simple as my asking him to speak to me from inside his heart. Would he have said anything if I hadn't asked? I wonder. Would he have said important things a long time ago if I had only asked earlier? This gives me something to think about. Then I ask, But should a wife have to bear the burden of initiating important discussions? Should she have to beg for revelations? Shouldn't they be her due?

I muse over this for several seconds as cars zip past us. And then one comes barely crawling along, five or six cars lined up behind it bumper to bumper, the silhouettes of the two heads inside small and just clearing the dashboard. From the size of the heads, they could be young children out for a lark, but from the speed of the car, there's no doubt that they're old people fearful of the dark and the slick roads. I wonder where they're going and why they're out so late—and then feel an instant flash of annoyance. *Get back to the main point,* I tell myself.

We come to Brookside and turn left. We aren't walking fast, just ambling along. I wonder how many other couples in the whole state of South Carolina are taking a late-night walk right now. Twenty? Thirty? I have no idea what a good guess would be. How many of those other couples, I wonder, are struggling to put thoughts into words, to interpret the future from those few words? I can well imagine that we're the only such couple. I see all the others walking along easily, bantering or talking about their kids or vacation plans or new gutters.

"She's leaving, Elizabeth," Ken says. This falls onto the damp night air with no prompting from me.

"Leaving? Who?" I want to make him put it all in words. I'm not going to let him get by with hinting.

"Her. The person I . . . you know, the one who . . . the woman . . ." He trails off, apparently unable to put a tag on Dr. Snipe. I give him no help, angry that he's too cowardly to come out and say it, yet grateful, too, that I don't have to hear the words. I'm not even sure how I want him to fill in the blanks. "The person I've been having an affair with"? "The one who's been spending nights with me"? "The woman I left you for"? None of these are things I want to hear him say.

Ken sighs again. "She was just *there*, Elizabeth," he says. "I didn't even notice her for a long time."

We're approaching the Biddles' house now, as well as the Chewnings' right across the street from it. The Chewnings' living room light is on, and I see someone sitting by a lamp, apparently reading. I see Barb standing in front of another window that looks like it could be in the kitchen, her head down as if washing something at the sink. I imagine running up to the window and tapping on it. That's something Barb herself might do. We could talk through the window about our tennis match for tomorrow, and I could tell her my car has a dead battery and I'm glad she's planning on driving. I don't, of course. Lights are on all over the Biddles' house, too. Evidently nobody's in a hurry to go to bed on a Friday night.

Ken is waiting, as if hoping I'll say something. When I don't, he continues. "Things were so . . . cold at home back then, and we weren't ever . . . together. And then one day she comes to my office—she's a linguistics professor—and asks if I have a stapler she can use. Hers is jammed, she says. And she stops by again the next day, and she brings me a doughnut another day. Says she bought two and doesn't want the other one. And stuff like that. She was friendly, and lonely, too. She didn't know many people here. And I was . . . like I said, I was a fool. You were always . . . so far away, and I just let one thing lead to another."

This was a lot of words for him to say at one time, and he stops as if winded from the exertion.

"*I* was always away?" I say. "You weren't exactly around a lot yourself. I'm not the one who goes out of town all the time, remember, or hides away in the back room writing music. You're not pinning all this on me."

He shakes his head. "No, I'm not. Not at all." He turns and looks away from me toward the houses we're passing, then adds, "It's funny how you can be in a place but not really live there at all, you know?" He runs one hand over his face. "I've had a lot of time to think things through lately, and . . . well, it's so easy to mess up. Not to be careful with what you've got."

I realize something at that moment, something that's sure to be old news to everyone else. *So much time is spent separated from those you love.* I think about the last year of our marriage, before Ken moved out in February. In the mornings he would leave before seven-thirty on the days he had his eight o'clock conducting class and sometime around eight-thirty on the other days. If I was subbing, I'd usually leave before he did. He would arrive home anytime between six and nine o'clock at night, usually closer to nine than six as the year wore on. I know now, of course, how he was spending those extra hours before he got home, but at the time I didn't really think about it. I guess I thought he must be working late—the same thing a million other two-timed wives think.

By ten o'clock I'd be in bed reading, and by eleven I would turn out the light. I could see the ridge of light at the bottom of our bedroom door, shining across the hall from Ken's study, but if I rolled over and turned to the wall, the room was dark. I grew used to his nighttime sounds, the creaking of his office chair, the clearing of his throat, the opening of his closet, the clinking of a spoon in a bowl out in the kitchen, the running of his shower in the hall bathroom, and so forth. Sometimes I didn't even wake up when he came to bed. I used to think of our bed as a great expanse of sea and our bodies as two little boats drifting farther apart.

I do a quick total in my head. Sometimes as few as two hours a day, sometimes as many as five—that's how many waking hours Ken and I were together on the average day, *together* meaning simply in the same house with each other. Maybe a few more on Saturdays, maybe not. On Sundays he played golf and was usually gone by the time I woke up. I say it again to myself. *So much time is spent separated from those you love.*

I had run across a prose poem by Karl Shapiro just a week or so before our nighttime walk, and it comes to mind now as we near the cul-de-sac on Brookside. Prose poems usually irritate me with their blocky paragraphs instead of lines, but this one was different. It had the conciseness and color and sudden punch of a real poem.

The poem consists of four vignettes about people being separated from those they love. "The Two-Year-Old Has Had a Motherless Week" is the title and first sentence. The whole poem is about the way absences shake up our relationships, how the landscape always shifts between the leaving and coming back, and how the new terrain has to be stepped across carefully or sometimes evacuated altogether.

"A thousand days of words have passed." That's what Karl Shapiro writes in the last vignette. The speaker has come back to his brother's house after a long absence and found all the furniture worn out and in different places, and he realizes it's not just the things that are repositioned but his whole relationship with his brother. Although the poem says that a thousand days *of* words have gone by, what it really means is that a thousand days *without* any words have gone by for these two. The words that filled up all those days were spoken by and to other people, and now the narrator feels like a stranger to his own brother.

"It all comes back to words," I say aloud to Ken, who has no possible way of knowing what I mean. "Even two hours a day might be enough if there were *words*."

We don't actually walk into the cul-de-sac, but instead turn around and head back down the other side of the street. The drizzle has slowed now, almost stopped, in fact. Somebody has turned the dial to "mist" again. I feel that my hair has gone limp and heavy, like a wet fur hat.

"I'm so tired of words," he says wearily. "I can't tell you how tired I am of words."

"That's too bad," I say, totally without sympathy. "I don't see how you can be tired of something you use so little."

"Oh, those aren't the kind of words I'm talking about," Ken says quickly. "I *know* how important those words are—I know that now. I know there's no other way . . . to work things out. I know I haven't said enough in the past. I guess I always thought you didn't need me to talk. I guess I thought you were happy enough the way things were."

I never in a million years expected this walk to turn out like this. I never dreamed that asking Ken to tell me something I didn't already know would result in his saying all of this. I am astounded at everything that comes out of his mouth. I wonder what would have happened if we had gone on a walk in the middle of the day, though. Would he have said as much in broad daylight? I doubt it. I can't help thinking that the rain and the night have combined to make him feel safe. But nevertheless I am filled with awe to find that Ken Landis can talk, even if it is in the dark.

I wonder if all of this is too little too late. Or too much too late. I don't know if I could stand a chatty version of Ken. I can imagine telling him to shut up, which is something I would never let my children say. With every dam burst of words, I'd be thinking it was *her* influence, that she had somehow taught him that a woman needs plenty of talk, that words to a woman's happiness are like sunlight to photosynthesis. I wonder if a linguist would even think of a parallel like this, though.

She probably thinks only in terms of phonemes and diacritical markings and the way sound waves strike the tympanum of the human ear. I can imagine her explaining fricatives, nasals, and plosives with Ken by the hour, and for some reason this makes me laugh. I picture him struggling for air as she smothers him with her words. To go from a silent woman to one spewing great mouthfuls of words would be a shock to any man.

He looks at me. "What's so funny?"

"Oh, I was just thinking about something," I say.

"Okay, what?" he says. "It's your turn. I told you something. Now you tell me something."

"I wouldn't know where to start," I say.

"Try," he says. "Just think of something, anything."

"I was reading a novel recently," I say.

This is absolutely true. It was *Crooked Little Heart* by Anne Lamott. Margaret was ready to turn it back in to the library and thought I might like to see how a novelist had made the game of tennis such a big part of a work of fiction. Margaret thinks I should read more fiction than I do. She thinks an exclusive diet of poetry has turned my thoughts in upon themselves too much. She says novels are the literary equivalent of "getting out among people more."

Margaret wanted me to read this book, she said, so I could tell her if I thought the author really knew the game of tennis or had simply done a little research and was just bluffing her way through it the way she thought the writer of *Divine Secrets of the Ya-Ya Sisterhood* had done. So I read it, and it was clear to me that Anne Lamott had played more than a game or two of tennis to be able to write about it so convincingly. None of this relates to my point, though.

"That's it?" Ken asks. "You read a novel? That's the thing you're going to tell me?"

I hold up a hand. "I'm not finished." We walk past the Chewnings' house again, and I see that Barb is no longer at the window. I wonder if she's getting ready for bed. I can picture her in an old mismatched pair of her husband's pajamas. Barb is pretty in a natural, wholesome way, but she isn't into fashion.

"The husband in this book," I continue, "is a sensitive modern-day guy who's in touch with his feminine side, as they say, and he's always telling his wife things like she's his compass in life or the star by which he navigates his ship. Or he'll try to talk her through a spell of depression and help her analyze and fix it. Or he'll say he wishes they could be best friends again after a fight, but then the next day he might tell her she's undermined his sense of self-worth by something she said, and then he'll turn around and hug her and whisper that he understands exactly how she feels after some minor disappointment."

I stop, wondering if I can make my point or if it's even worth making.

"And?" Ken says.

"It's just all so unreal," I say. "I mean, I've been wondering through this whole book if the writer really *knows* any husbands like that. I don't think they exist. I don't think men are capable of verbalizing those kinds of things. I think people who write books like to fantasize. They like to make characters do things they wish people did in real life."

I know I'm making sweeping generalizations, but I press on. "I've tried to imagine you saying some of the things this husband says, and I just can't. I think men basically have a couple of things on their minds, and that's it. It never occurs to them to wonder what their wives might have on their minds, much less try to find out." I stop, realizing how useless this is. I might just as well be trying to talk to a Martian about the stock market.

I doubt if Ken has taken any of this in. He probably shut down as soon as I said the first word. I see him nodding, but I know all about nods, how they're often nothing more than cover-ups for lagging interest. My guess is that he's either thinking about where he'll buy the new battery for my car or wondering who he can get to complete their foursome for golf on Sunday.

I laugh dryly and say, "I think people who write novels mostly just write about dream worlds."

He looks at me, puzzled. "I've wished I could know what you were thinking lots of times."

"You could have tried asking," I say. We turn right again on DeLaney and head back toward home. A carload of teenagers flies by, all the windows down, loud rock music belching out like fumes. Though the clouds appear to be moving swiftly and a few faint stars twinkle overhead, I still hear thunder in the distance.

You never know what's coming, I think. You never know whether a storm is really passing or just circling back around for a new attack. Maybe storms never really pass. Maybe they just fall back for a while to gather their forces for another attack. When the weatherman talks about an approaching storm, maybe it's just the same old one that's been off visiting somewhere and is coming back for a reprise.

We don't talk until we get back on Windsor.

"It's hard to ask," Ken says. "I guess I think you'd tell me if it's anything you really wanted me to know." He shakes his head. "No, the real truth is, it's just easier not to ask. I get busy and just don't . . . pay attention. That's the sad, honest truth."

"I know," I say. And I do. How many times have I asked Ken what's on his mind? As he says, it's just easier not to ask. You get lazy in a marriage. It's discouraging that nothing gets better by itself. When you see how much work it all takes, it's easier just to let things lie where they drop.

"I've had time to think," Ken says again. "A lot of time. I'm so ready for school to be out. This is all so . . . stupid and twisted and . . . sorry." He stops in the middle of the street and holds out both hands. I walk ahead a few steps then turn around to face him. "Three months is a long time, Liz," he says. He hasn't called me Liz in ages. He looks down and addresses the pavement. "I'm so sick of that motel. I hate it. I haven't been able to write anything halfway decent the whole time I've been there. Everything comes out so flat and boring and . . . nothing holds together."

He lifts his eyes and looks straight at me, and I know right then exactly what he's asking. He's asking if he can come home so he can start writing music again. So he can quit paying rent and taking his clothes to the laundry and eating take-out food. He's asking it without really saying the words.

Macon's van creeps back down the street toward us. He pulls up beside us and rolls his window down.

"My betrothed hath kicked me out," he says mournfully. "On a Friday night she hath sent me home before midnight. 'O blackest midnight born!' How shall I pass the hours ere sunrise breaks, my regal Elizabeth?" One thing I've noticed about Theresa and Macon. His van is never in her driveway overnight. It's something unusual for a couple their age these days. He seems to expect no answer from me now, for he lets his van roll forward as he howls softly out the window. "Ah, e'en the stars mock my loneliness!" he moans and drives off, the chugging of his engine drowning out his faint caterwauls.

"Is he like that all the time?" Ken asks.

"Pretty much," I say. "He's part maniac and part genius. You should see his art." I think of the linocut Macon showed me recently of the beginning ballerina class, the one I plan to buy. Every little girl in that piece is an individual, and you can tell just by the way they're standing at the barre with their instructor which ones are going to make it and which ones aren't. And it's not what you'd think either. The little girl with the ribbon that's coming untied and one toe pointed just slightly inward will make it, but the one who's standing pertly with her hands extended in an obvious imitation of her teacher's won't. I don't know a thing about ballet, but I can tell that much. And the pumpkin sitting on the floor in the corner—that's an intriguing thing to be in a dance studio.

We begin walking again in silence. Macon's short speech seems to have derailed Ken's train of thought. Or maybe like me, he sees that we're only a block or so from home now. Maybe he feels the same sense of discouragement I do that we're almost back where we started and nothing has been resolved. True, we've talked more since we passed this way earlier than I ever thought possible, but I think now of how much more needs to be said. Our walk is almost over. In the cover of darkness we've spoken, but in not having looked at each other, it may be too easy to forget what was said.

Yet I realize that somehow this thought appeals to me. I think I might *want* to forget what was said. I'm not ready for Ken to come back home, to step past all that's happened and settle back in. I think again that would be too easy for him. Curiously, a phrase from the Pledge of Allegiance comes to my mind: "With liberty and justice for all." "You've had plenty of liberty," I imagine saying to Ken, "but don't think we're going to skip the justice part."

Three months is a long time, he had said. How little he knows, and how little he thinks I know. As if I don't have any concept of how long the last three months have been. As if I've been living it up while he's been pacing around his apartment unable to write. Oh, I know all about the last three long months, believe me.

I know about the six months before that, too. I know how long the months are when your son is loaded up in the car one day and driven a hundred miles out of your life. I know what it's like to walk by his room a dozen times a day and see it empty, to avoid looking at the kitchen table so you don't have to see the place where he used to sit, to watch the time get to three, four, five o'clock and not be able to stop listening for him to come home. This must be what it's like having a leg amputated but still feeling like it's there. Then every time you look down, you feel the loss all over again.

I know what it's like to hear the clock strike and know it's time to fix supper but to feel a dark force pushing you to lie down on the bed and close your eyes. I know what it's like to stand in front of a class of students and make yourself teach a lesson, but to be secretly studying every boy in the room and thinking the whole time, *Someday soon you're going to go away and leave a huge gaping hole where your mother's heart used to be.*

We walk up our driveway, and the motion light comes on. Ken stops beside his car, as if unsure of the next step. "Well, I guess . . . it's late," he says lamely. His hair is wet, plastered down from the drizzle, and he runs a hand over it. He looks toward the carport, then at me. "I guess I'll be back sometime tomorrow . . . with your car, you know."

"Aren't you going to get your shoes and things inside?" I say.

"Oh, right. I forgot." He walks ahead of me to the kitchen door and bends down to take off his old sneakers before stepping inside. "Yuck, I'm a wreck," he says, peeling off his wet socks. His suit pants are sadly droopy from the rain and his shirt rumpled.

I hate to think of him driving to Spartanburg like this. "Maybe there are some dry clothes in Travis's closet you could change into," I say.

"Good idea," he says and pads barefoot through the kitchen and down the hall toward Travis's room. I dump a load of clothes from the dryer onto the kitchen table and busy myself folding them until he comes back to the kitchen dressed in an old pair of jeans with one knee out and a red knit shirt Travis never liked. He's wearing a pair of tube socks with a hole in one toe and carrying his wet clothes on a hanger.

He glances at the clock on the microwave. "Well, it's late," he says again. "I'd better go I guess." I nod and pick up a dish towel to fold. "Elizabeth, I wish . . ." he starts, and I take the towel by the corners and snap it loudly. ". . . well, I'll talk to you tomorrow," he says. "It'll probably be before lunch sometime."

"That'll be good," I say.

Still he stalls. "Are those the gloves Jennifer sent you?" he asks, pointing to the pass-through window.

"Yes, and one of the books, too." I reach over and pick it up. *Planning the Southern Garden* it's called, one of those big books with a shiny cover, this one featuring a dazzling display of red and yellow tulips beside a decorative brick wall.

"Oh, I thought it was a book of poems she sent you," Ken says.

"She sent two," I say. "One was poetry, and one was this." I set the book back down. "She says she wants to help me with the backyard," I continue. "She wants to come home sometime in July when Travis is home. She sees a picture of our backyard in her head, she says." I shrug. "I never even knew Jennifer was interested in gardening, but evidently it's a new hobby she's picked up from somewhere. She told me she's had killer irises this spring. That's how she described them—killer irises."

Ken smiles and says, "Sometimes I worry about how she talks in the courtroom." Then he looks concerned. "Well, don't let her get too carried away," he says. "I've got some ideas for the backyard myself. Our irises all need to be dug up and divided."

I think of a really bad poem I read one time about a husband and wife laying out a garden plot together, planting tender seeds, watering them, pulling weeds, then finally gathering armfuls of ripe vegetables. It was a sappy, skippy little poem, of course, with a final stanza that pointed out the comparison between the couple's fruitful endeavors in the garden and the happy, rosy-cheeked children they had sown and reaped together.

A sudden image flashes into my mind of Ken and me side by side in the backyard, stooped over flower beds with seed packets and shiny trowels. I see us studying a plan Ken has drawn up, of walkways, a grape arbor, bee houses, a fountain with water bubbling out of a mermaid's mouth. I see the two of us sitting on a stone bench to rest, eating sandwiches and watching baby birds peer out of birdhouses while others splash and preen in the birdbath.

It isn't hard to imagine the kind of poem somebody could write about a man and woman planning a backyard sanctuary. Why, symbol upon symbol could be yanked out of such a scene—the grapes representing the cup of sorrow from which we all must drink, the bee houses the industry and sweetness of a good marriage, the birds the joy of hospitality, and so on. Oh, it could be the deluxe sappy poem of all time, the worst of the bad, an abuse of language never before seen.

"Are you okay?" Ken asks. "Is something funny?"

"Oh no," I say. "It's not funny at all. It's actually very sad what people will do with the English language."

Ken appears to think this over, then without speaking he slips into his dress loafers and opens the door to leave.

I pick up a bath towel to fold. I hold it against me as Ken steps out into the carport. I go to the door and watch him walk to his car in Travis's torn jeans, white socks, and dressy black tassel loafers. As I lock the door and turn out the carport light, I see visions of irises rising up out of the earth, each one dividing and spinning up into the sky. Irises of all colors—satiny white ones crowned with gold, frilly flamingo pink ones, rich indigo, coppery orange, buttery yellow, wedgewood blue.

Our irises, he had said. *Our* irises all need to be dug up and divided. Surely there's a symbol there, part of me says, while another part says, Enjoy the colors and let the symbol go.

Sweet Impossible Blossom

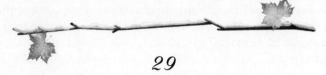

29

Hummingbirds ought to be the sweetest birds, wouldn't you think? I moved the feeder that had been left at our house when we bought it, and I hung it on a hook outside the kitchen window under the eaves where an old green plastic planter used to swing in the breeze. This planter is further evidence of something I've realized more and more about Ken and me, how over the years we've grown used to ignoring things we don't want to see or that are inconvenient to fix. That ugly green planter had been hanging outside the kitchen window ever since we moved into this house, almost a full year now. No doubt it had once held something green and alive, but when we moved in, it was a container of hard dirt.

Looking at it through the kitchen window, I had thought at various times of taking it down and throwing it away, of replanting something in it, or of replacing it with wind chimes, but I just never got around to any of it. Ken, too, had pointed to it more than once and said things like "We need to get rid of that thing." But between thinking about it and getting out there, something always happened.

So by the time you've looked at a green plastic planter hanging in the same place outside your kitchen window for almost a year, you just work it into the view as a permanent fixture, like a tree or bush or a fuse box you can't do anything about. But on the last Saturday of May, the afternoon I came back from Theresa and Macon's wedding, in fact, I pulled into the driveway, got out of my car—which by now had a new battery—and walked immediately around the house into the backyard. I reached up and unhooked the plastic planter, then took it directly to the garbage can and dumped it in.

Still dressed in my gold sandals and beige dress with the pearl buttons, I then carried a small stepladder from the carport to the opposite side of the house, where I climbed up to take down the empty hummingbird feeder. This was something else I had looked at a hundred times and thought about removing. I took it inside and washed it with a bottle washer and hot soapy water. Then I mixed one-fourth cup of sugar with a cup of water and boiled it. Philip Biddle had told me how to do it—one part sugar to four parts water. I had subbed in his Life Science class at Berea Middle School two days earlier when the lesson was about birds.

It was a shame, I thought, that five days before school was out for the summer the seventh graders were only on chapter seventeen out of twenty-four chapters in their science book, but I dutifully plowed through the chapter. Evidently the regular teacher, who had a history of back trouble during stressful times of the school year, was trying to speed through the rest of the textbook by covering a chapter or two per day. "Okay, get ready," I told the kids after the bell rang to start class. "Here's all you need to know about ornithology in one easy lesson."

The class Philip was in was full of questions, and somehow we got off on hummingbirds. Philip seemed to be the expert on this smallest bird, having received a whole book on hummingbirds from his aunt, he told us, and he shared a small store of his knowledge with us. He told us, among other things, that a hummingbird's heart beats more than a thousand times a minute during flight, that although the typical hummingbird needs only around ten calories of energy a day, this is like a full-grown man needing over two hundred thousand calories a day, that some species weigh only as much as a dime, that they have amazing memories and mean tempers.

"Mean tempers?" I said.

He nodded. "We have this feeder with three little places for drinking, but they won't ever share it. If one is already there, the new guy will try to drive him off so he can have it all by himself." He nodded again. "They're always fighting." Well, imagine that, I thought. Such tiny pretty birds, like little ornaments of iridescent glass, and they turn out to be fractious and bickering. Just another example of things being the opposite of what you expect.

I remembered the feeder hanging at the side of our house, and after class I asked Philip if he knew how to make nectar to go in it. He said you could buy packets or make your own out of sugar and water, then told me the proportions. Would it take long for them to find my feeder and start visiting regularly? I wanted to know, and he said he didn't think so. "I saw the first one at our feeder on Easter Sunday," he told me, his eyes bright, "so they've been back for a while. They fly south for the winter, you know."

I changed into a T-shirt and old pair of sweat pants while the sugar water was cooling, then added a drop of red food coloring afterward. As I stood at the kitchen counter stirring the water, my mind went back to Theresa and Macon's wedding just an hour or so earlier. Yet another example of things turning out different from what you expect, but not in a bad way. To be truthful, I hadn't known what to expect from a wedding in which Macon Mahoney was the bridegroom, but it was really a very beautiful ceremony, nothing weird or kooky, no humorous sound effects or silly speeches.

Though Theresa had a degree in vocal performance and taught Kindermusik full time, running classes in Berea, Filbert, Derby, and Greenville, Macon had insisted on planning the music for the wedding, she told me. His friend Richard, a fellow artist, played the cello, and Macon gave him a list of eight pieces he wanted him to play, including "Scarborough Fair," "All the Things You Are," and "When I Can Read My Title Clear," the last being his grandmother's favorite hymn. His grandmother, he had told me one day when I asked if he had one, had lived in the same three-room house near Black Creek, Tennessee, from the day she was born till the day she died. She was a midwife and preached every funeral in those parts but her own.

I had invited Theresa and Macon to visit the Church of the Open Door back in April, and Macon had tilted his head and studied me for a moment. "How very traditional to go to church on Sunday," he had said, nodding. "I might like that. I have a strong streak of tradition in me, you know." I raised my eyebrows. This was news to me. "Yes, I do," he said. "And so does Theresa. We like tradition a lot. We just might come to your church someday." He had looked down at Theresa and nodded again. "A walk to the kirk in your good company, my love," he said. "How quaint—and perhaps enlightening and refreshing to a jaded sojourner like me." They hadn't come yet, but I planned to ask again.

Anyway, Richard played eight songs on his cello, four before the ceremony, two during, and two afterward. Then he repeated all eight during the reception that followed. He was stationed on a wrought-iron bench beside a small circular bed of bright red zinnias. It was an outdoor wedding, of course. Another artist friend had furnished the backyard garden and had somehow secured several old kneeling benches from a country church to be used for rustic seating.

Theresa's tea-length dress was white with pale pink rosettes stitched onto the bodice, and Macon wore a charcoal gray tuxedo with tails and a special touch all his own—a red tartan plaid vest. You might think it would clash with the pink rosettes, but it didn't. That red tartan vest was one of those defining artistic details—unpredictable but totally right. The two of them made an incredibly good-looking couple. The minister read the ceremony from a black book, and at the appropriate time Theresa and Macon recited the vows they had composed themselves.

One of Macon's lines was "I do pledge my eternal reverence for the light of your soul and the wealth of your spirit." He spoke seriously, in a hushed voice, and had to pause often to catch his breath. This wasn't the Macon I had talked with in Theresa's front yard on Windsor Drive. I liked very much the fact that he was acting different now, nervous and solemn. I didn't want him to let even the flicker of an eyelash be flippant and lighthearted on an occasion like this.

When he kissed her at the end, he did it right. He lifted her veil with such tender awe that I had to look away. The kiss wasn't one of those embarrassingly long ones but was evidently full of meaning, for when they turned to face us afterward, Macon's eyes were full of tears. Macon's, not Theresa's. Imagine that.

A large oil portrait of Theresa in a long pale green dress, painted by Macon, was displayed on an easel on the deck where the reception table stood festooned with ivy and silver ribbon. An enormous spray of pink nymph gladioli adorned the center of the table. I imagined Theresa posing for the portrait, perhaps in Macon's apartment above the mattress store. A thought came to my mind. What would it be like to have a husband who could paint your portrait for a wedding gift? Such a tangible proof of his love, something you could hang on the wall and look at many times a day and think, *He did this with his own hands just for me.*

And then another thought slowly took form. Ken had composed a trumpet solo for my wedding gift. "Stella's Song" was a painting of sorts, a musical painting notated on paper and transferred to the senses in pure, perfectly pitched notes through the medium of a silver trumpet. Ken had written it out with his own hands just for me, then stood in front of many people and played it for me. I wondered now if I had sufficiently appreciated the beautiful, fragile cargo carried by those bars of music. I should have framed the original copy of the song and hung it above our bed as the work of art that it was. I should have hummed the tune many times a day, maybe written a love poem to fit the music.

Another thought rose up before me. Love poems—Ken had written some for me before we were married. He knew how much I liked poetry and told me he liked it, too. He even wrote me a few poems while we were dating and slipped them into one of my books or a pocket of my sweater, where I would find them later. It was almost beyond belief to think he ever did such a thing, but he did. It wasn't great poetry, of course, but it was from his heart. A few lines came to me now:

> I walked down a stone path tonight
> And looked up into a clear, dark star-ridden sky.
> A form was there of a ladle
> Overflowing and large,
> And a great hand
> Made to pour one huge drop.

What strange things the memory chooses to hold on to! I'm sure it all meant something back then, the ladle and the hand and the drop, but I can't remember anything now but the lines themselves.

I don't know how many minutes passed before I came to myself and realized I was still stirring the hummingbird nectar. Hummingbirds might
travel far and wide in their search for food, their wings beating almost four
hundred times a second, but my thoughts were capable of some pretty amazing flights, too. Hummingbirds had a great advantage, though, in being able
to drive off birds a hundred times bigger because of their speed and maneu-
verability. I wished I could drive away some of the heavy thoughts that kept
troubling me, the regrets and doubts and fears, all the painful memories of
the past three months, of the past twenty-eight years really.

I felt a constriction in my chest as I thought of Macon and Theresa beginning their long journey as husband and wife. I thought of them driving to
Charleston right now in Macon's van, outrageously decorated with enormous tin cans and multicolored streamers, and I thought of their wedding
night tonight and of the three-week honeymoon to follow, traveling up the
eastern seacoast to Maine. I remembered again the look on Macon's face as
he had reached out to lift Theresa's veil.

I tossed the spoon into the sink and leaned against the counter, trying to
clear my thoughts. Nothing like a wedding to make you go soft and sentimental.

I glanced over to the telephone. I knew all I had to do was call Ken and
ask him to come home, and he would be here before the day was over. Next
Thursday was the end of the month, and his rent would be paid through
then. Tomorrow was Harwood's graduation ceremony, and the school year
would be officially ended. Travis would be coming home soon, too, and we
could have a summer with all of us under one roof again. Jennifer would be
visiting sometime, probably in July, and I could go for a long walk with her
then and tell her about her father and me—the break and maybe the repair
of our marriage.

But something kept me back. I knew Ken's affair was over. A hundred
things told me that was a certainty. I knew he was sorry and wanted to come
home. I knew he loved me, though he never said it, and I knew I loved him,
though it was pretty crowded in my heart with all the anger and hurt pride
still smoldering there. What it came down to, I guess, was stubbornness and
wounded dignity, which is just another way of saying selfishness. His suffering had been nothing compared to mine, and some part of me wanted to
equalize things. It was just too easy for him to get to come home. To elude
"It," tag home, and be granted immunity. Home free.

I used a funnel to pour the cup of nectar into the feeder. It didn't even
fill it halfway, but that was okay. I was starting out slow. Who knew if the
hummingbirds would really come? No use in spreading a bounty when you
didn't even know if anyone was coming to the feast.

It had seemed illogical to me at first that Dorothy Sherman would have
put the feeder at the side of the house, and then it hit me. I remembered

where and how she had spent her last days—suffering in the bedroom where I now sleep. If the side window were open, she could have seen the feeder. I could imagine a large overstuffed chair pulled up beside the window, the blinds raised and draperies drawn back so she could observe the hummingbirds while she died. I wonder how much pleasure it gave her, though, if they were always fighting and driving each other off.

I had eaten a piece of Macon and Theresa's wedding cake very slowly while sitting on one of the low benches in their friend's backyard garden. People were all around, but I sat alone. A woman in a fuchsia caftan holding a plate and cup of punch had stopped in front of me, as if considering sitting by me, and said, "Wasn't that just the sweetest little wedding you've ever seen?" I looked up at her and couldn't think of a single word in response to such a vapid question. I think I smiled at her, but I can't even be sure of that. Anyway, she evidently decided she had no interest in sitting beside anybody who appeared to be a deaf-mute, and she moved on, much to my relief.

Macon had sought me out before I left. "There you are, Elizabeth," he said, coming toward me. "Somebody ought to take your picture and title it 'Serene Contemplation.'"

I shook my head. "No, no snapshots," I said. "I want a painting, something in the style of Monet."

"Yeah, okay, *Lady Eating Wedding Cake*," he said. He stepped back and made a frame out of his hands, studying me in mock seriousness.

"I like Theresa's portrait," I told him, nodding toward the deck. "I like it a lot."

"Thanks, and how did you like the wedding?" he asked.

For a moment I wondered if I was going to be able to get anything out. I opened my mouth, but no words came.

"Aw, you didn't like it, did you?" he said, but I could tell he knew better.

Theresa came up behind him. "There he is," she said to me. "I've been a married woman all of thirty minutes, and I'm already having trouble keeping up with my husband." The way she said the word *husband* touched me. I could tell she loved the newness of the sound coming out of her mouth.

"Elizabeth didn't like the wedding," Macon said, taking her hand. "She won't tell me why."

Theresa gave me a puzzled look.

"It's scary how well he can lie with a straight face," I said. Theresa smiled. "You two need to get away from here," I added standing up. "You don't have time to stand around and listen to how much I liked the wedding. Don't you have a honeymoon to go on? It's already two o'clock."

Macon looked at his watch. "We have reservations for dinner in Charleston at nine tonight," he said. "A restaurant on the water." He pulled Theresa closer to him. "We shall sup together at our marriage feast, wife," he said.

"Well, I should hope so!" she said, laughing. "Come on, they want us to open some gifts before we go."

As she pulled him by the hand down the garden path, he looked back at me and called, "'O sweeter than the marriage feast, 'Tis sweeter far to me . . .'" And then his words were lost. I heard a shriek of laughter somewhere behind me and a woman's voice: "Is there another punch bowl I missed somewhere? I was sure expecting something stronger than plain punch at *this* wedding! How *Baptist* of Theresa! I wouldn't expect that artist husband of hers to stand for it. Why, I thought artists as a lot were *perpetually* tipsy!"

Theresa and Macon went back up on the deck and began opening gifts. The first one was a beautiful black teapot with a glossy cracked glaze, made by one of Macon's artist friends. I left soon and drove home slowly. I kept hearing Theresa's words over and over in my mind: "My husband, my husband, my husband." And I kept hearing Macon's words: "'O sweeter than the marriage feast.'" I thought of all the days of living together that came after a marriage feast, how they could get sweeter but usually don't.

I took the hummingbird feeder around to the backyard and hung it on the hook by the kitchen window where the green plastic planter used to be. I looked up into the trees and spoke out loud. "Bless you, little friends. Come see me, and I'll fix more after this is gone."

As I turned to go back inside, I saw a white blossom unfurling on the small gardenia bush growing beside the crawl-space door. This was a surprise, since the bush looked totally incapable of living, much less producing flowers. It was bent over, practically lying on the ground actually, having been fallen on by a very hefty meter reader one day back in March.

I happened to be standing in the den that day when he had come tramping through the backyard, and for a moment I felt a prickle of fear until I saw him head toward the electric meter. I watched him stumble over the row of bricks around the crawl-space door, lose his footing, then fall right on top of the gardenia bush. He stood up, brushed himself off, took the meter reading, and walked toward the Yarnells' backyard next door.

I had never even come out to check on the bush. I had a lot more on my mind back in March besides a trampled gardenia bush. But now, here it is the end of May, and I see that it's still alive and well, even bearing flowers.

I walk over, kneel down, and lift the blossom to my face. Even though I've smelled gardenias before and know what to expect, the heavy richness of the fragrance astounds me. For some reason I think of magic carpets and genies wafting out of lanterns. I hear rippling water and strains of *Scheherazade*. I try to imagine the power and goodness and intelligence of a God who thought to give things certain smells and tastes.

I think of Li-Young Lee's happy poem "From Blossoms" and how the narrator of that poem is all but leaping in the air by the end as he holds a peach in his hands and thinks of the joyful expanses of life, wide-open spaces in which he can soar above the knowledge of death "from blossom to blossom . . . to sweet impossible blossom." I breathe in the scent of the gardenia once more and then rise to my feet. I think briefly of picking the blossom to take inside and put in water, but I know how quickly gardenias fade, how fast they go limp and their edges turn brown.

I have a sudden hankering for ice cream. I try to put it out of my mind. After all, I don't need any more sweets after the wedding cake I ate only an hour ago—a large piece with a sugary pink rose on top. The thought of ice cream keeps coming back, though. It must be its lifelong association with cake in my family. My mother always said a cake wasn't complete without ice cream.

I could be appalled by my eating habits if I stopped to think about it long enough. It's close to three o'clock and here I am fixating on ice cream. Even as I walk around the back of the house to go inside, I know I'll be in my car within a few minutes, heading to Darlene's Kreamy Kones over in Derby. I want real ice cream, none of the soft-serve stuff they sell at fast-food places.

I won't eat much supper tonight—I already know that. Maybe some popcorn and a Coke around nine or ten. I never used to eat like this when I was cooking for Travis and Ken. Back then I ate only at mealtimes—substantial, well-balanced meals with a meat and two or three vegetables. Now I eat odd things at all hours.

Sometimes I forget a meal, and then I might make up for it by stopping somewhere for a steak and eating it very slowly, along with a baked potato, a salad, a couple of rolls. Finishing a whole meal slowly seems like a great luxury, one I never knew I was missing when I was eating at the table with Ken and Travis, both of whom ate fast and were always done long before I was. I would look at my plate and lose interest in whatever was left.

I grab my purse now, lock the door, then get in my car. Maybe I'll stop by Lackey's Grass Is Greener Nursery on the way back from getting ice cream and look at some flowers for the front yard. The book Jennifer gave me suggests verbena and periwinkle. Maybe I'll buy them in little trays of six or eight plants and set them in the carport for Ken to see next time he comes over. I'm not sure I'd plant them right. Maybe he'll do it for me while I'm gone one day. I think about the garden where Macon and Theresa were married. I'd love to have a garden like that someday. A garden of my own.

When I back out of the driveway and head down Windsor toward De-Laney, I see Ken's car coming toward me. Too bad I haven't bought the plants yet. He could put them in while I'm away eating ice cream. We wave as we pass each other. He slows down, as if ready to stop if I do. But I keep going. All the way to DeLaney. I think about the look on his face.

It was the same one he wore last Sunday when I gazed out into the congregation from the choir and saw him again sitting on the aisle about five rows from the back. It's a hopeful, penitent, patient look, all wrapped up in one. Well, imagine this, I thought. Ken Landis comes to church uninvited on a Sunday morning. Had all the golf courses closed down for the day? I deliberately struck up a conversation with Nina Tillman after the service, and when I left, Ken was nowhere to be seen.

Driving to Derby, I think of Macon planting flowers in Theresa's front yard with her standing beside him. I know this is really the way it should be done. I think again of their three-week honeymoon to begin tonight and wonder if they have any idea of how important these early days are. All the days to follow will stack up on top of these, either straight or crooked.

It strikes me that I should have talked to them before they left and stressed the importance of speaking with utmost respect to each other. I should have warned them against too much joking around, too much familiarity and sarcasm, but also against too many long silences. I should have urged them to give each other privacy, yet not to let the circles of their lives drift apart, but rather to keep them closely intersecting.

I remember years ago reading an article in a magazine by a woman who married a pop singer, and she wrote about how on their wedding night he said to her something like "You look fatter with your clothes off." She said she knew at that moment that the marriage wouldn't last. I try to think of something, anything Ken said to me on our wedding night, but I come up blank. I know he didn't tell me I looked fatter than he expected, but I'm pretty sure also that he didn't tell me my gorgeous body far exceeded his wildest dreams. You'd remember something like that.

It wasn't exactly a storybook honeymoon. No cruise to the Bahamas, no tour of the British Isles. Instead, three days and two nights in Gatlinburg, Tennessee, in January—I do remember it was cold and we spent most of the time in our room on the back side of a Holiday Inn, which ran us $19.75 a night. On the second afternoon Ken got out of bed, I recall, and said, "Let's go for a walk," and I remember thinking he must be disappointed in what was going on in the motel room. But I wouldn't have made a joke like that out loud for the world.

I can imagine Polly Seacrest slugging Morris in the arm and saying, "Go for a walk? What's that supposed to mean? You tired of me already?" I can imagine Juliet pulling Tony back to bed and saying in a breathy, sultry voice, "Forget the walk, let's fly to the moon, you big handsome jerk." But not me. I politely agreed, and we went for a walk down to the shops along the street.

Maybe if I had started out saying what I thought on our honeymoon, our whole marriage might have taken a different course. Who knows? As it was, I said nothing but got dressed in the bathroom and came out to find him dressed and watching *The Price Is Right*. As we exited our room, a maid was approaching with a stack of towels. Ken turned his head and cleared his throat as we passed her, as if too embarrassed to look at her.

I remember catching sight of our reflections in a shop window a few minutes later and saying to Ken, "Hey, look, there's a couple of newlyweds." He glanced at the window and said sensibly, "No, not really. That's just their mirror image. The real newlyweds are right here." And he lifted my hand and squeezed it, then took me into the shop and bought me a navy sweatshirt with "Gatlinburg" imprinted on the front in big blocky letters.

I'm out on Highway 11 now, cruising along, when the thought comes to me that the little incident in Gatlinburg could very well sum up one of the main differences between Ken and me—my habit of looking at things obliquely, of examining causes and wrenching symbols out of everything, of inventing designs out of ordinary randomness, my love for colorful particulars exceeded only by my insistence on finding just the right words to describe them, then putting them all into an orderly pattern and extracting a principle.

I looked into the shop window and saw our reflections, whereas Ken looked down at our two hands and saw the real us. He works intimately with the symbols of musical notation, but the real thing for him is the music itself, not the symbols. I remember him holding up some pages of staff paper years ago on which he had just finished writing a new composition. I said something mindless like "Wow, look at all that music," and he answered immediately, "Oh, *this* isn't music, you know. Not really. It's only music when it gets off the page."

Which is similar, I guess, to the poet loving the poem more than the individual words. No, I realize this isn't holding together. I go back to Ken's putting notes together to compose a piece of music. It comes out as a grand design in the end, doesn't it, so in a way isn't he also busy extracting a principle out of particulars?

By the time I arrive at Darlene's Kreamy Kones, I'm disgusted with myself. Even in trying to delineate the differences between Ken and me, I realize I'm back to my old symbol-hunting obsession, trying to reduce things to "This means that," plowing through hedges and thickets in pursuit of parallels.

Mocha Almond Sundae is the flavor I decide on. Two scoops in a cup with a white plastic spoon. I'm the only one in the shop right now besides the two women behind the counter. I sit at a small table for two over in the corner and listen to the big band music being played over the speakers. It's the same recording we have at home. Glenn Miller's Orchestra playing "Kalamazoo," "Tuxedo Junction," "St. Louis Blues." I wonder what Ken is doing at home right now in my absence. Maybe he brought over some flowers to plant in the front yard. Maybe I shouldn't bother stopping for verbena and periwinkle on my way home.

I'm sitting there neatly sculpting my two scoops as I take small bites of

Mocha Almond Sundae when the door opens and a man walks in. He's very tall, probably six-five, with an athlete's build. He's holding a little girl, two or three years old, but she's not what catches your eye—not what you'd call cute at all, just rather plain with thin wisps of common brown hair that needs combing. But the man, well, he's drop-dead handsome, as my college friend Laurie used to say. I try not to stare, but I can't help it. He's wearing khaki shorts, a T-shirt, and loafers without socks. I find myself wishing I had changed into something nicer than my oldest pair of sweat pants before leaving home.

The man is walking up and down in front of the glass-front cases now, saying the flavors of the ice cream out loud, and the little girl is repeating them. I want him to finish so he can turn around again. He has thick black hair with the faintest threads of silver running through it, which is what makes me wonder all of a sudden if he's the little girl's grandfather. Surely not. He looks to be in his forties, but it's hard to tell exactly. Agewise, he could be a grandfather, of course, although he's hardly the picture that comes to mind when you say the word *grandpa*.

One of the women behind the counter says something to him and laughs, and then the other one chimes in and they both laugh, a little too loudly. Both of them have their eyes glued on him as if they're bird watchers and he's the rare ruby-billed saffron-crested night warbler. He makes his choice— one single cone of chocolate twirl and one of butter pecan—and the two women fall all over themselves getting them scooped up and wrapped with napkins, then taking his money and giving him change. It's funny to watch. As he turns to walk toward a table, one of them calls out, "And we got lots more if you're still hungry when you finish that!" It goes from funny to pathetic.

He sits facing me at a booth by the door. The little girl kneels on the seat across from him and starts attacking her cone sloppily. I see his eyes flick toward me, then return quickly to her. He smiles and says something to her, and she nods vigorously. He leans over to wipe at her cheek, but she turns away, lifting her elbow to ward him off. He glances over at me again, smiles, and shrugs. I smile back sympathetically.

This is when it hits me. A bolt out of the blue, as my mother used to say. Suppose, just suppose, I say to myself sitting here in Darlene's Kreamy Kones, suppose this man—this enormously attractive male—came over to my table right now and struck up a conversation. Suppose this man made small talk for a couple of minutes, then asked me my name, and then called me later tonight to talk some more. Suppose he found out I like tennis and came to watch me play one day, then dropped by my house to leave a gift another day—say, a half gallon of Mocha Almond Sundae, having taken note that day at the ice cream shop—and sent me flowers another day.

Let's say I'm lonely, not having had a lot of attention from a man in a good while, and I'm somewhat flattered by these signs of interest. Suppose he discovers that I like poetry and starts asking me questions, such as "What do you make of Berryman's 'Dream Songs'?" "Whose work do you like better, Anne Sexton's or Adrienne Rich's?" "What do the metaphysical poets and the imagists have in common?" And suppose that, finding a gleam in his eye when I answer briefly and timidly, I expand and begin to wax voluble, going beyond mere answers to discourses on rhythm, metaphor, form, tone. And all the while he listens raptly, interjecting other questions and admiring comments about the breadth of my knowledge.

Maybe he even convinces me to show him a few of my own poems, and though I bring them forth with great reluctance, assorted disclaimers, and numerous self-deprecating remarks, he reads them with a sense of awe and adoration, as if standing in the presence of a literary titan.

Okay, so here's where all this is leading. Here's the bolt out of the blue. How would I respond to such overtures from this man? Would something within me open up to receive more? Would I in turn show mutual interest in him? Could I be drawn away from my husband of twenty-eight years and be won by the affection of a devoted stranger?

And though I want to deny the possibility, to open my Bible to Exodus 20, point to the seventh commandment and say firmly, "I would never break this," I know the weakness of my heart, the old sins that beset me daily, the power of temptation. I imagine Satan lurking in the shadows, gleefully rubbing his hands together, and whispering, "Come on, say it! Say you'll never do it. Say you're too strong to fall. Say it so I can prove you wrong."

I see a parade of all my sinful thoughts and actions since the day of my salvation in February, all my omissions of good, all my words of pride and anger, my self-pity, my failure to trust in the Lord with all my heart, the continual leaning to my own understanding, my critical spirit, my doubt and fear. I see them all march by in a great noisy host, and I know how easily one more sin could slip into the throng. I believe God has sent this bolt out of the blue. I believe he wants me to acknowledge that I could be an adulteress.

I hear a squeal and look up to see the little girl's ice cream lying in a gooey lump on the tabletop, the cone in her hand empty. The man tries to scoop it up with his hand and restore it to the cone, but it's too soft and drippy now. The little girl is crying, and one of the women comes out from behind the counter with a spoon and a plastic cup and gets most of the ice cream up, then wipes the table with a big damp cloth while the other woman calls out to the man not to worry, that she's making up a new cone for Emily. Emily? I wonder if they already know *his* name, too.

I remember once a few years ago when I subbed in a geometry class over in Filbert, and during a free period I went to the teachers' lounge, got a Coke, and picked up a magazine to look through. The principal, who was new that year, came through and saw me sitting on the sofa. He came over and asked me how things were going, even sat down for a few minutes and asked if I thought I'd feel qualified to fill in for the art teacher, who was pregnant and having a hard time in the mornings.

I remember listening to his deep voice and wondering if he'd ever taken singing lessons and looking at his hands as they rested on his knees and thinking what powerful hands they must be. I found it hard to look at him directly because he had such clear blue eyes and such long dark eyelashes. Every time I went to that school to sub, I went to the teachers' lounge with the hope that he'd come through. When he did, he always made a point of greeting me cordially and asking if things were going okay, and I always felt tongue-tied and eager to please, like a freshman girl in the presence of the senior quarterback. He stayed only two years, then moved to Kentucky.

What if Richard Parton—that was the principal's name—had made it clear that he was interested in more than my services as a substitute teacher? Would I have resisted his advances? That was before my salvation, and though I was brought up to be morally upright, I had no real scriptural grounding. Could I not have easily fallen?

I was slowly lifting a spoonful of ice cream to my mouth when I was startled by a voice. The man was standing at the water fountain not more than three feet behind me. "Upsy-daisy," he said to the little girl. "There you go. Did you get enough?"

I glanced back and saw him wet a paper napkin and dab at her face with it. "Here, let's get all the sticky off," he said. Then he raised his voice a little, and I could tell he was addressing me. "I'd forgotten what a major project it was to eat ice cream with a three-year-old."

I smiled and nodded but said nothing. I finished my last bite of Mocha Almond Sundae, then got up to leave, depositing my cup and spoon in the trash bin by the door. As I got into my car, I could see the man standing up by the counter again, talking to the two women. The little girl was trying to pull herself up to look inside the cases at the ice cream.

For some reason the book of Hosea was on my mind as I drove slowly home. I thought of Hosea's wife, Gomer, a prostitute. I had always identified myself with Hosea in my earlier readings of the book, seeing myself as the righteous spouse betrayed by adultery. Perhaps I should take another look at the story, I thought, and see how it reads from Gomer's perspective.

I recalled a verse from the last chapter, one I had read several times for its lyricism. "They that dwell under his shadow shall return; they shall revive as the corn, and grow as the vine: the scent thereof shall be as the wine of Lebanon."

The Fall of Your Soft Song

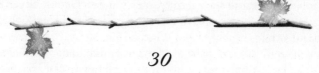

30

You'd think by the time you'd lived close to fifty years, you would know yourself inside and out. I realize now that this is a totally false assumption. It's possible, I'm convinced, to live an entire lifetime and die without seeing yourself for what you really are. The fact that I am altogether capable of being Gomer instead of Hosea, of doing to Ken exactly what he has done to me, has been slow in coming, but when it arrives, I feel as if I've been blown off my feet by the force.

"But I *didn't* do it," part of me protests.

"But you would have if the right man had come along and given you some attention," comes the answer. I think of the handsome man in the ice cream shop and the blue-eyed principal who moved to Kentucky, and I don't say anything back.

A week after Harwood's graduation, Ken leaves town for a two-week seminar up in Richmond. It's for college band directors, and some of the big names are there to give workshops and reading sessions. The idea is for the band directors to play in the band and sit under the baton of a master conductor. Harwood is paying for Ken to go. I misunderstand when he first tells me about it over the telephone. I think he's going to be one of the guest conductors, but he says no, he's taking his trumpet to play in the band and learn. "Learn?" I say. "What's there to learn when you've been conducting for umpteen years?"

I remember his reply. "Just because you've done something for umpteen years, Elizabeth, doesn't mean you've done it right."

Well, I already knew that, of course, but something about Ken turning into a student seems upside-down. He's excited about it, though, and has been practicing his trumpet for the seating auditions. He knows there will be a lot of competition in the trumpet section, as always. Trumpet players, even good ones, are hanging around every street corner, he always used to say. Your only hope is to be a *really* good one. I remember when he used to come home groaning after hearing all the band auditions for new students at Harwood. "Twelve kids show up and seven of them are trumpets!" he'd say. "I've already got way more trumpets than I need. I could stack them up like cordwood."

When parents of elementary kids ask Ken today what instrument their child should start on, he never recommends trumpet. Or flute either. School bands are overrun with trumpets and flutes, he tells them. They're the kudzu of band instruments.

Oboe, he tells them, or bassoon. Tuba or French horn are other suggestions. Of course, he didn't follow his own advice with his own son, but being a trumpet player himself, he just naturally assumed his superior talent would burst forth like the rising sun in Travis. He had his heart set on Travis going to the top, playing principal trumpet in New York or Chicago. He never dreamed his own son would break down during his first recital and make "Red River Valley" sound like one of those twentieth-century atonal pieces with shifting meters.

So Ken leaves town on the fourth day of June. And on the seventh of June, a Thursday, I see Alicia Snipe up close. At last I learn her first name—Alicia. It disappoints me a little that it's such a pretty name. I wish it were something clunky to match Snipe. I could have found out what it was weeks ago by making a simple phone call to Harwood, but something kept me back. I could think of "Dr. Snipe" back then only by gritting my teeth and clenching my fists and taking long slow breaths, but if I had had to deal with "Alicia Snipe," imagining Ken saying her name tenderly or even casually— "Hey, Alicia, hand me a pencil, will you?"—I don't know how I would have managed.

I recognize her immediately, but I can tell she doesn't have a clue who I am. I've seen her only twice before, once in her car outside a restaurant and once from the balcony of the auditorium at Harwood, both times from a distance and only from the side, not full face. Yet I know her at once. I wonder if women are better at this than men. I can often identify people from a great distance by their walk or the way they hold their head or flick their wrist.

So anyway, here's how the meeting of Alicia Snipe and Elizabeth Landis takes place. First, Bonnie Maggio asks me to practice with the tennis team I'll be joining in the fall. They already won the state playoffs in Charleston just the week before and are now getting ready for Sectionals, which are held in Mobile, Alabama, at the end of July. Only the team members from the spring season can compete, so I'm ineligible for this year. But they could sure use me to give their singles players some practice, Bonnie tells me. Their singles players are the weak link on the team, she says. One of them has a record for the most double faults in a single set, and another one has only one shot—the lob.

They practice on Mondays and Thursdays over in Greenville, she says, so I agree to help out. It's Thursday, June seventh, and I'm driving back from a two-hour practice, during which I have seen exactly what Bonnie means about the singles players being the weak link. It's just before noon when I decide to stop at Lackey's Grass Is Greener Nursery and buy a hydrangea bush for the front yard. I know I can do this much. I never got around to the verbena or periwinkle, but I know a nice hydrangea when I see one. I'll start out small with just one, and I'll plant it like I saw Macon do in Theresa's yard, and then I'll keep it well watered and watch it bloom. It will be my little yard project.

Actually, I'm surprised that Dorothy Sherman didn't plant hydrangeas in our yard years ago along with everything else. I wonder if she didn't like hydrangeas for some reason, but I can't imagine that. Hydrangeas are such mild-mannered, unpretentious flowers, beautiful but willing to stay in the background, hugging porches or the sides of houses, not at all like the peonies that flaunted themselves in our backyard a few weeks ago, opening their great white perfumed bosoms en masse in a display that seemed, as Jane Kenyon put it, "not quite decent."

Jane Kenyon, who wrote the poem "Otherwise" I talked about earlier, also wrote prose, which has been collected into a fine volume called *A Hundred White Daffodils*. She gave her short prose pieces lovely titles such as "Every Year the Light," "Childhood, When You Are in It," and "The Honey Wagon." In one chapter she talks about peonies, how they "loll about in gorgeousness" and "believe in excess."

Well, a little of that is all right, I guess, but I don't share Jane Kenyon's passion for peonies, which are always full of ants and always look a little ragged and blowzy, as if they've partied too long the night before. Hydrangeas are more to my liking. So I plan to buy one at Lackey's, and as I pull into the gravel parking lot I tell myself to be quick about it so I can get home.

After two hours of tennis, my shorts and shirt are sticking to me, my hair is limp, and any makeup I was wearing when the day started has long since been rubbed off with my tennis towel. So I'm not exactly a vision of loveliness as I walk along the aisles of plants and flowers. There was a time, I realize, when I never would have gone anywhere looking like this, not even to a plant nursery. I would have gone straight home and gotten cleaned up first, then gone back out.

I think about how particular I used to be, how organized and methodical, and I can hardly believe I'm living in the same body that other person used to inhabit. Up until a year ago, I actually used to write down in a special notebook which outfits I wore to the different schools I subbed in. I had each page divided into four columns with the headings "Date," "School," "Class," and "Outfit." So an entry might read, "October 12/Derby High/ Consumer Math/blue jumper, white blouse." I used to look at that notebook and feel proud. Now it seems like the most pitiful thing on earth.

After Travis left home, I didn't have the energy to keep up the entries. On the days when I decided to answer the phone in the early mornings, I was lucky to get myself dressed and to the right school. I was walking right on the edge of oblivion those days. It wouldn't have surprised me to look down one day in the middle of a class and see that I had on my bedroom slippers or had forgotten to put on my skirt.

Then six months after Travis left home, I went to church one day and met Margaret, accepted God's gift of salvation, and one night back in late February, discovered the Sermon on the Mount in the book of Matthew. When I came to the part about the lilies of the field, I read it over five times. It was a beautiful idea, expressed in beautiful words. I knew I would never again write down what I wore each day. I knew it didn't matter one crumb if I wore the same thing three times in a row to the same English class. Nobody was keeping track, and even if somebody were, I didn't care anymore. It was only one more way Christianity changed me, and this one came suddenly.

And I have evidence of the change. "Miss Jennings is sick today," I heard a seventh-grade girl say as she slammed her locker door shut a couple of weeks ago right outside the classroom where I was waiting to teach a history class. It was the second period of the day. "You mean we gotta have a *substitute*?" another voice said in the same tone she might have used for words like *ogre* or *cretin* or *psychopath* if she had known what they meant. "Yeah, it's that tall lady—the one with the yellow sweater," the first girl said. And the other one knew exactly who I was. "Oh yeah, her," she said.

I looked down at what I was wearing that day, and sure enough, there was the yellow sweater. I must have already worn it several times to this school. That's probably because it's always right in easy reach when I slide my closet door open and always has a little space on either side of it because I take it out and put it back so often. And, yes, I know it's just as wrong to be proud of not caring as it is to care too much, but I'll have to admit that it pleased me to hear this exchange. There's something refreshingly simple about being known as the tall lady in the yellow sweater.

All this aside, however, I'm still not eager to meet anybody I know here at the Grass Is Greener Nursery, so I locate the hydrangeas quickly and settle on a healthy-looking one with four perky violet-blue heads. I can imagine it multiplying and overflowing in our front yard, a great blue fount of heavy blossoms.

I pick up the container and take it to one of the counters inside, where I get in line to pay for it. It appears that half the population of Dickson County has turned out today to buy flowers and gardening equipment. I stand very still in line so as not to attract attention in my sweaty clothes.

A silver-haired man in front of me turns around and looks at the hydrangea I'm holding. He nods approvingly. "That was my mother's favorite flower," he says. "She had vases of them all over the house—pink, white, blue, purple, every hue cultivated under the sun." He speaks fluidly, with a coastal accent—Savannah, Charleston, somewhere down there. "Here, may I relieve you of your burden during the wait?" he adds, taking the pot from me and setting it in the top of his cart. I smile and thank him, although I didn't mind hiding behind it. He turns around to push forward his cart, which is full of pink and white begonias.

He turns back around a few seconds later and says, "Then they kept making their appearance all winter long, great bunches of them dried and faded, but still pretty in a . . . a rather matronly way. Crisp and colorless they were now, but still stately. She hung them in the attic to dry, my mother did, and when she died, we found dozens of them tied with colored ribbons and hanging from the rafters, patiently waiting their turn in a vase downstairs among the living folk."

Well, imagine this, I think. A poet standing right here in a plant nursery in the hinterland of South Carolina. "Your mother must have loved beautiful things," I say, and this is not a mindless comment. Any woman who kept hydrangeas in vases year round, who tied ribbons around them to hang in the attic, and who reared a son to talk like this was a lover of beauty. I can say that with assurance.

"Yes, she did." He looks at me for a long moment, then says, "A mother focuses the lens through which her children view life, you know. My mother did it for me, and my wife did it for our children." He turns around again, his head lowered as if deep in thought.

People are behind me in line now. The silver-haired man is the next customer to be served, but the woman in front of him holds up the line by crying out, "Oh, I forgot fertilizer—the very thing I drove all the way here to get!" and asks the cashier if she can get somebody to bring a bag to the check-out line, which necessitates an announcement over the intercom.

Mothers focus the lens through which their children view life. It's not a complicated analogy, not terribly original. I'm sure others have thought of it that way before. So why does it strike so hard?

"The fall of your soft song"—the line comes to me from something I read not long ago. When each new issue of *Atlantic Monthly* shows up in my mailbox, I look in the table of contents and turn first to the poems. By the time I have walked the length of the driveway back to the house, I've read the first one slowly. If it's longer and I haven't finished yet, then I stop walking and stand at the edge of the carport to read the rest of it before I go inside.

This one had a title both ordinary and intriguing. "You," it was called. "Me?" I said when I saw the title sitting so unadorned in the table of contents. I knew it wasn't *about* me, of course, but I felt very strongly that it might be *for* me. With a title like "You," you get the feeling that it's going to be a very personal poem, not a nature poem about rocks or pigeons or waterfalls, not a rhetorical poem about patriotism, not a witty piece of light verse with clever rhymes.

Peter Davison wrote it. He's the poetry editor of the *Atlantic Monthly* and has a collection of his own poems called *Breathing Room*. I don't know the man except as a name in a magazine, but I figure he's the one who picks the poems for each issue, and with the exception of a few slips, he does his job well. So he decides this particular month to include one of his own poems, which I think a man in his position has every right to do, and I read it with the wonder of someone stroking mink for the first time. I am amazed by the feel of it and have to keep going back over it.

In the poem a man is addressing his mother, but she's no longer living. She's the "you" of the poem. In curiously offset three-line stanzas, he lists briefly her many functions in his childhood, and then, with astonishment verging on rage, he ponders how she could have so completely disappeared from him—her arms, her kisses, her voice all beyond reach now. How could it all have vanished? he's saying—your smile, your fragrance, your words, "the fall of your soft song"?

And not only has *he* lost *her*, but part of his grief is for the fact that she has lost him. His whole developing self, so closely tied to her in so many ways, is something she isn't here to see and love and talk to. How can you not be here to *know* me? he's crying. It's the tone of a little boy but the sorrow of a man.

Which hits me now as I'm standing in line at a plant nursery. That's what poetry does. You read it once and feel the quake, and then as time goes on you feel the aftershocks. I see something now that I've never been smart enough to figure out before. A man has a mother first and then a wife. They are two different people with two different roles, and it's not a contest. A mother should let the man have his wife, and a wife should let him have his mother. He shouldn't have to choose one and turn his back on the other.

A mother focuses the lens for her children. She gets them ready for the long, strenuous trek through adulthood, for all kinds of weather and landscape—mountains, valleys, deserts. And if she has a son, she spends twenty years of her life preparing him for another woman. From the moment of his birth, she trains and molds him, clothes and feeds him, pours her heart and soul into promoting his success, only to turn him over at last to a wife, some twig of a girl who comes sauntering along after all the hard work is done and nonchalantly collects the prize.

Though neither of my children is married yet, I know it's got to be a different thing when a son gets married than when a daughter does. I imagine it as the difference between losing something and lending it. When a son marries, he's never truly yours again.

So why does a mother knock herself out for all those years when she knows what's ahead? Why was I so worried all that time that Travis was never interested in girls? Why didn't I remind myself that no girlfriends meant no wife in the end, which meant I'd get to keep him? But hadn't something told me all along that giving him up was unavoidable? And would I really want my son to live at home after he was a grown man? I tried to imagine Travis at the age of, say, forty, arriving home from work every day and walking down the hallway to his bedroom, coming to the table for meals, playing his CDs and watching reruns on Nickelodeon.

Well, it looked like I didn't have to worry about any of that, what with this person at college named Stacy calling him on the phone, encouraging him to try out for plays, and whatnot. Yes, she was the one who got him to try out for that play. He had finally told me that when he was home at Easter. It had nothing to do with a purple light and a high-pitched noise.

Part of me is still hoping Stacy is just a friend, an older-sister type who's taken a poor freshman boy under her wing, but it's hard to convince myself, especially considering the fact that he's coming home from Piper a full two weeks *after* he's out of school. "Stacy wants me to go to her house," he told me on the phone recently. "Her mom and dad said it's okay," he added quickly before I could think of anything to say. "Her dad's got a job he wants us to help him with. He's going to call you and explain it all."

The silver-haired man has paid for his begonias now, telling the cashier that the hydrangea belongs to the lady in line behind him. He lifts it out and puts it on the counter so she can scan the bar code on the plastic tag, then offers to carry it to my car, but I thank him and tell him I can get it. The cashier starts fumbling with the register tape, trying to install a new roll. "Just a minute!" she says irritably. "This stupid thing . . ."

The man gives me a gentlemanly nod and makes a motion as if tipping his hat, then picks up his tray of begonias and moves away. He steps slowly, bent to one side, and it strikes me that he's probably a lot older than I thought at first. The brightness of his eyes and his fluent speech covered it up when he was talking to me.

An impulse overtakes me, and I call to him. He's only a few steps away. "Oh, sir! Wait a minute." He slowly swings around to face me, a quizzical glint in his eyes, and I lean forward and say, "I will arise and go now, and go to . . ." I leave it unfinished on purpose. He frowns slightly and looks down at his begonias. For just the briefest second I think I've guessed wrong, and I'm embarrassed for him. For me, too.

I'm dimly aware that the cashier has just sighed and slammed something shut on her cash register. Then at the very same moment that I hear the beep of her scanner on my hydrangea, the old man looks directly at me, opens his mouth, and says very clearly, "Innisfree." He nods with slow satisfaction.

"Innisfree," he says again and turns to leave. It's funny, I think, how much I love the idea of men with artistic souls. My father. Professor Huckabee. Macon Mahoney. This man. I bet he knows nursery rhymes, too. A man like him must have heard them as a child.

I think of the mother who focused the lens for this man and wonder what her name was, what songs she hummed at home, what kinds of work she did with her hands, what she saw when she looked out her kitchen window. I wonder as I watch him leave whether his wife is still living, and if she is, if she fully appreciates what his mother did in his childhood and adolescence to prepare him to be the kind of old man he is now. I wonder if he's loved as he ought to be.

How rarely we think of what has gone on in a room before we enter it. We think everything starts with our arrival. I think of something my father tried to teach me growing up. He was the most courteous man ever born, and while my mother, the realist, concentrated on the rules of life, Daddy often tutored us in the graces. Mother's lectures often began with "Don't," while his began with "Do."

I remember him reminding Juliet and me that a lady always comes into a room quietly, that she waits to see if anything else is going on before she speaks. "Respect for the other world," he called it, the world outside your own immediate perception, that big domain that includes everybody else but yourself. "Remember, the play started a long time before you stepped onto stage," he would say.

So thinking about this, I suppose the next thought that comes to me is inevitable. Before the years of resentment piled up, did I ever stop to think of Christine's contribution to my happiness as the woman who shaped Ken's life? It dawns on me that Ken belongs in the list of men with artistic souls. Of course he does. Why did I leave him out earlier? He loves music and art and theatre. When we were first married, we went to plays and talked about them afterward. We sometimes went to art galleries on Sundays and, of course, to concerts by the dozens. And there were all those poems he used to write.

What part had Christine had in Ken's love of art? Schuyler was the musician, but I could well imagine her sitting with Ken as he practiced, applauding his successes, taking him to lessons. I could see her tapping out rhythms with a pencil, though meter must have come easily for Ken with all those nursery rhymes in his memory.

Had I ever considered what had gone on in the room before I entered it? Or did I view Christine as a rival from the beginning, somebody I had to shove out of the way as soon as possible? I'm almost ashamed to admit that this elementary principle has come to me so late: A woman owes a great deal to her mother-in-law. Some of the things her husband does might infuriate her over time, and some of those may have been passed straight down from his mother, but lots of the good things probably were, too.

At the same time I'm thinking all this, however, I'm fully aware that I deserve no credit for my sudden softness toward Christine. I haven't suddenly grown mature and reasonable. It's easy to have kind thoughts about your mother-in-law after she's dead.

"Were you going to pay cash, ma'am?" the cashier says to me, and from her tone and volume, I can tell she's repeating it. Someone behind me has a fussy child, and I hear her say, "Okay, okay, put a cork in it. We'll get lunch one of these days if this dumb line ever starts moving again!" I wonder what she would say if I turned around and asked her if she had ever thanked her mother-in-law? Thank *her*? she might throw back. She ought to thank *me* for taking the lazy bum off her hands.

"Cash, oh sure," I say to the cashier. I'm already digging for my billfold. I find my money, pay her, and pick up my hydrangea to leave.

I try to imagine Christine when Ken was a newborn. She must have known already that her marriage wasn't exactly the kind made in heaven, that Schuyler Landis was a hard man, and that the only change he was likely to undergo was for the worse. I try to imagine how a woman would be able to keep facing each new day with such knowledge bearing down on her, but then I know the answer in Christine's case. She had a son, and later two more, and then two daughters. With children, a woman can survive a marriage like hers.

Right after this is when it happens. I'm walking across the gravel parking lot when I see a blue Mazda turn in and park right next to my car. I turn around and walk behind a tall cart of potted petunias and pretend to be looking at them. But really I'm looking between two of the shelves and out into the parking lot. I see a woman get out of the blue Mazda and head toward the open side of the nursery where all the hanging plants are displayed. She doesn't even look my way, but I know at once that it's Dr. Snipe. I remember the way she walked down the aisle of the auditorium that night.

I can't help wondering why she's coming to a plant nursery if she's moving away. You don't buy new plants when you're leaving town. Maybe Ken was just telling me that. Maybe she's not moving after all. Maybe she'll still be at Harwood next year, stopping by his office all the time to bring him more doughnuts and borrow his stapler.

I quickly take my hydrangea to my car and put it on the floor in the back, and then without even stopping to consider why I'm doing this, I turn around and head straight for the hanging plants. For the next fifteen minutes I follow her around, stopping when she does and staying far enough away not to arouse suspicion. I don't get a good look at her face since I'm behind her, but I grow a little bolder as the minutes slip by, getting close enough to touch her at one point, so that when she asks a worker about the care of something she calls a "weeping fig," I hear him tell her it likes sun and needs plenty of water. He's going down the aisle of plants spraying them lightly with a hose.

She shakes her head. "Oh, I don't know if she'd remember to water it," she says. "She's kind of absentminded." She holds the plant aloft and tips her head from side to side to study it. Her long hair is swept back and bunched loosely on top of her head. It's thick hair, slightly curled, a uniform dark blond without the variations of shading you see in natural color. "I won't be here to remind her," she says. Her voice is lower than I expected. I can't explain the feeling of standing within reach of the woman you know your husband has touched intimately.

The worker, who has on a fluorescent green apron, shrugs and smiles. "Well, they're all going to need watering, ma'am," he says. "Unless you want to get her one of those silk plants we got inside."

"Oh no, I don't think I'd want that," she says. "I want something real." She speaks assertively, like a person who's used to lecturing in front of a class. She's wearing a white knit tunic top over khaki clam diggers, but the tunic can't hide the fact that she's big through the hips. I wonder if Ken likes the idea of big soft hips, if it seems more womanly to him than my narrow ones.

The worker moves away a little and continues spraying but calls over to her, "The weeping fig might be just the thing, really. With a plant like that, you can get used to watering it a little every morning, just make it part of your routine. You know, get a cup of coffee, read the paper, water the plant."

But the worker hasn't convinced her. She puts the plant down and walks over to the next aisle to look at the ferns. She's wearing white sandals, and her toenails are painted dark red. She tiptoes on the gravel. These details are fascinating to me for some reason. I know I'll think about them after I go to bed tonight. I'll imagine Ken watching her paint her toenails, and my heart will feel like ice.

I stand by the weeping fig she has put down and watch her make her way slowly down the adjacent aisle. Soon she's standing even with me on the other side of the ferns, and through the hanging baskets I finally get a good look at her face. I pretend to be examining a plant with amazing purple and fuchsia flowers that look like tiny Oriental lanterns. This whole situation suddenly seems like a hallucination. Surely such elaborate jewel-like blooms aren't really growing on a live plant. Surely I'm not standing here at a plant nursery staring at Dr. Snipe.

Her complexion is pale except for a spot of pink blush high on each cheek. As she squints up at a fern, I can see the pleats around her eyes, and when she purses her lips, ripples of wrinkles surround her mouth. It's one of those weathered faces, but motherly, maybe even close to grandmotherly. I can imagine her pulling a child into her lap, bending over to whisper something instructive.

There's no doubt that this woman has already walked down a considerable stretch of life. From the tilt of her chin, I wonder if she might take herself a little too seriously, enjoying the sound of her own voice, phrasing things in a teacherly way. As far as looks go, she's nobody you'd really feel threatened by, unless you knew for a fact, as I do, that your husband has been consorting with her. Then you'd look at her and think of all the ways you don't begin to measure up to somebody like her, who's been to Africa, devised a new written language, and earned a Ph.D.

Then you say to yourself sternly, "Stop it, Elizabeth. You're attractive. You're smart. You're thin. You're . . ." And then you interrupt yourself and answer back. "I'm boring. I'm selfish. I'm standoffish." One thing I've learned is that becoming a Christian doesn't sweep away all your self-doubts. I keep hearing Pastor Hawthorne say we're made in the image of God, but it almost seems like an insult to God.

So anyway, Alicia finally chooses a Boston fern and saunters with it to the check-out line. I cannot explain why I get in line behind her. I pluck a packet of pumpkin seeds out of a revolving wire rack near the check-out, so I'll have something to buy.

Imagine standing right next to the woman who's been carrying on with your husband behind your back. I see a bin of sharply pointed garden tools next to the seed rack, with a sign that says "Garden Dibbles—Ideal for Boring Holes for Seedlings and Bulbs." I close my eyes and picture the headlines in the Filbert *Nutshell* or Derby *Daily*: "Local Woman Attacked at Nursery with Garden Dibble."

My ears are ringing with all the talk around me, and suddenly I hear wind chimes—lots of them. Light chinks of glass, heavy gonglike tones, jingly bracelety sounds, hollow wooden tocks. People look around curiously. Alicia turns and meets my eyes briefly, then gazes past me. I turn and look, too. It's a tall skinny kid in plaid shorts. He's walking down an aisle under the wind chimes, batting at every one of them.

When it's Alicia's turn at the check-out, I move in closer. She writes a check, and that's when I see that her first name is Alicia. *Alicia D. Snipe* it says at the top. I can't read the address, which is in smaller print, but I watch her sign the check in a tall, compact, highly slanted cursive, dotting the *i*'s decisively.

And then, surprisingly, the cashier makes a chance remark that lets me know Alicia really is leaving town. This is a different cashier than the one I had earlier. This one is chatty and friendly, with big loopy earrings. She's chewing chartreuse gum, which seems like it would be against the rules for cashiers. "That's a gorgeous fern," she says to Alicia as she waits for her to get her driver's license out. "You gonna hang it by your front door?" The word *door* has two syllables the way this girl says it.

Alicia shakes her head. "It's not for me," she says. "It's for my landlord.

I'm moving back to Missouri next week."

"Aw, too bad," the girl says. "Missouri can't be nearly as nice as South Carolina." Can't is *cain't*, and nice is *nass*. Her chartreuse gum snaps fiercely.

Alicia smiles as she fits the cap onto her pen very deliberately. "Well, I appreciate a person's loyalty to his own part of the country, but, to be honest, I'm more than ready to move on."

Missouri? I think. You call that "moving on"? Who would want to live in a state that's hemmed in on all sides, right smack in the middle of the continent, with a name that looks like *misery*? The only thing I've heard of that's the least bit of an attraction there is that big arch. But of course I want her to move, so I'm sure not going to argue with her decision to go to Missouri.

She leaves with her fern. I watch her drive off in her blue Mazda and wonder what's going on inside her. Is she carrying around a heavy heart? Does she still love Ken? Did she ever? Or was he just a diversion, a passing fling who helped relieve the boredom of a slow year in South Carolina? Did she ever entertain the idea of marrying him someday? Did she know he still had a wife?

Thoughts zip around in my mind like electrons. Did she ever ask him questions about me? I wonder how things ended between them. Did she just suddenly grow tired of him and his silence, of all his fussy ways? Was she the one who put an end to it, or did he? I wonder if she has an ex-husband somewhere, maybe even children. I wonder if she's ever given up a son. I wonder if she ever reads poetry. If I said to her, "I will arise and go now, and go to . . ." I wonder if she would think a moment, then say firmly, "St. Louis."

A minute later I leave with my pumpkin seeds. Maybe I'll plant them when I get home. Put them in the backyard somewhere and have a whole pumpkin patch come fall. And then I'll cut one off the vine sometime in October and make a pie out of it. While I'm mashing up that pumpkin, I'll look back on this day in June and remember the time I stood behind Alicia Snipe and studied her up close.

Pumpkins symbolize potential and hope. Think about the pumpkin that turned into a carriage for Cinderella. One minute it was a plain old pumpkin, and the next it had sprouted wheels and was carrying her to the prince's ball.

I think about the linocut of Macon Mahoney's that I'm going to buy next week when I get my last paycheck for the school year. It's being held for me at a gallery over in Greenville. I can't wait to have it in my house to look at every single day. I love the pumpkin sitting over in the corner of the dance studio in that picture. It says so much about those little girls, especially the one who looks the least suited to be a ballerina. The look in that little girl's eyes says, "Don't give up on me. I'm the one who's going to the ball. You wait and see. My ride's waiting for me over there in the corner." She's the only one who has any idea why that pumpkin is there.

Just another example of things turning out upside down. Cinderella never expected to end up marrying the prince, but I did. It's a funny thing, but even with a generous supply of my mother's pessimism, I always expected growing up that I'd marry someone princely and that I'd be happy. I never once worried about ending up an old maid or being unhappily married.

And sure enough, my prince came along, and we got married. Then the "happily ever after" part started, and that's where things got turned around. After the marriage feast—that's where the hard part starts.

Driving home from Lackey's that day, I look back over the years since our wedding day, and I hear Ken's voice saying, "Just because you've done something for umpteen years, Elizabeth, doesn't mean you've done it right."

Every Farthing of the Cost

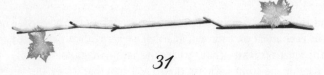

31

The grass is growing tall, and the first lightning bugs have arrived. I sit in the swing in my backyard at dusk and listen to the night sounds, letting the freedom of summer wash over me. I've decided to start coming outside every night to pray. There's something about being under the open sky, I've found, that makes it easier to put my thoughts into prayers. I have a lot to pray about these days. I feel an urgent decision bearing down on me.

Right now, though, I look up through the treetops to where the stars are beginning to wink and I breathe in the smell of June. *Time*—it's wonderful to have it. No more substituting for three months. I feel like someone has dropped a gift into my lap. It's wrapped in fancy paper with a silver bow, but it's not the kind of thing you tear into. You want to sit and ponder it for a while, admiring the shiny paper and considering all the possibilities inside.

Two different principals have asked me to consider teaching full time at their schools next year, but I can't think about that now. I remember Hardy Biddle's question to me months ago "You afraid of making a commitment, or what? How come you don't go after something permanent?" I'll think about that later. First I have to drink in the taste of summer and take care of other things.

I think about Ken's voice on the phone a few days ago. He called from Richmond to tell me his audition went well, that he made second chair and a jazz trumpeter and conductor from the University of Tennessee was sitting first. He was excited, and it wasn't hard to imagine he was a kid instead of a full-grown man. Mainly what I think about, though, is the question he asked right before he hung up. "Do you ever remember any of the good times, Liz?"

A long silence stretched between us, during which I considered pretending I hadn't heard him or didn't understand what he meant. But finally I said, "Well, yes. I do."

Another stretch of silence, then, "Me too."

He didn't ask me for details, but as soon as we hung up, I thought of the last good time we had together. I didn't know it was going to be the last, of course, and at the time I didn't think it was particularly outstanding, but it was good. It definitely was. Looking back on it, I could see it so plainly. I'm standing there with my hand still on the telephone, the connection broken between Ken and me, and suddenly I'm reliving the day we drove to the mountains almost two years ago. It didn't start out to be a good day, but it ended up very, very good.

It was the fall of Travis's senior year of high school, so we still lived in our old house in Derby. It was a Saturday, and Ken wanted Travis to help him with the leaves. We didn't have that many trees, but Ken's rule for October and November was to take care of the leaves in little increments every three or four days. Travis's preference was to wait until they had all fallen and then do them all in one swell foop, as he called it, but Ken always got his way, of course.

Travis was at the piano that Saturday morning playing a Brahms ballade when Ken came inside and said, "Let's get the front yard done now before lunch." It was a command, not a request. You would think that Ken, being a musician, would know better than to interrupt somebody like that right in the middle of performing a piece, but he had done it to Travis for years. It was as though he thought Travis's efforts at music didn't amount to much, that unless somebody was going to make it big in music, win scholarships and competitions and principal chair in the Philharmonic, then he might as well get up and rake leaves.

Here was something about Ken I didn't know when I married him: When something was on his mind that needed to be done, he relieved himself of it as soon as possible. He was a frontal-attack man when it came to work. And he had never been one to practice my father's suggestion of scoping out a room before you barged in talking. The Brahms piece was one of Travis's favorites to play, probably tied with Debussy's "Sunken Cathedral," and he was deep into it, so when Ken destroyed the mood with his sudden pronouncement, Travis sounded one loud horrendous chord and held the pedal down so it would reverberate.

I walked quickly from the kitchen into the living room. Ken was plugging an orange extension cord into an outlet by the front door so he could use the leaf blower in the front yard, and Travis was sitting motionless on the piano bench, his hands still splayed out on the keyboard, his jaw set like a rock.

I tried to think quick. I could see determination stamped on both of their faces. I knew Ken would win again, but I hated to see what it did to Travis.

I knew Travis well enough to know that from long practice he would let go of the piano keys and do what his father wanted, but I hated to see him jerked around like that. I wondered what kind of black thoughts would go through his mind as he silently raked leaves into little piles.

"Hey, wait a minute, can we go for a drive to the mountains first?" I said.

Ken looked at me as if I had suggested committing armed robbery. "First?" he said, shaking his head. "What do you mean, first? We've got to get the yard done. And I've got to do some writing this afternoon. I've got to start that big patriotic thing. They want it by the end of the year." As if that was anything new. I couldn't remember a Saturday afternoon he had spent doing anything else, and they—whoever they were—always wanted it by a deadline.

"We don't have to be gone all day," I said. "We could take the old high-way, drive into Saluda for lunch, stop for apples . . ." I knew he liked that route. It goes right past the Greenville Watershed, a beautiful reservoir tucked into a pristine setting. You drive along that road and feel as if you're sloughing off everything dirty and constricting, as if you're expanding into somebody different, somebody who could float if you unfastened your seat belt.

Travis released the pedal and looked over at his dad, who was still shaking his head but not so briskly as before. Ken stood by the front door, the thick coils of the extension cord looped neatly around his arm, which was bent at the elbow as if he were escorting a distinguished guest.

"The paper said this was the peak week for color," I said. "We could be back by two or so. That would still give you time to write." I paused, then added, "I heard the apples are good this year."

I used to make an apple strudel every fall when we got apples in North Carolina. I was hoping Ken would remember that and be tempted by the possibility.

Ken made a gesture toward the door. "But the leaves . . ."

" . . . would wait," I said. "Good grief, there aren't that many. Maybe Travis could even do them by himself after we get back." I looked at Travis, and he shrugged an okay.

Somehow the three of us had ended up in the car fifteen minutes later, driving toward the mountains, listening to the Boston Pops Orchestra play-ing John Williams' "Summon the Heroes" on the CD player in Ken's car. Considering the fact that Ken and I have always been so routine oriented, it still surprises me that we actually got into the car that day and went, that I came up with the idea spontaneously, and that Ken gave in. It was a postcard day—clear, crisp weather, a sky like blue ink, the hillsides flaming with au-tumn color. We didn't talk much, just watched the mellowing countryside drift by as we drove along. We opened the windows as we got farther up into the mountains.

We ate lunch at a place called The Poppyseed in Saluda, where a railroad track runs right alongside the main street. The Poppyseed used to be an old mercantile, with broad plank floors and lazy fans revolving overhead. Their specialty was something called "Molly's Burger," and we each had one. Whoever Molly was, she sure knew how to fix a burger. The waitress was a pale wisp of a girl with a blond braid down to her waist. She and Travis avoided each other's eyes, and when he gave his order to her, his voice cracked, which she pretended not to notice.

We walked through a shop next to The Poppyseed, where they sold everything from bubble gum to handmade pottery and local art. I bought a small framed weaving with a tag on it that said "Handloomed by Jimmie Nell Sinclair." It had every color imaginable in it with no perceivable pattern, the weaver's equivalent of a patchwork quilt I suppose. You had to know from looking at it that Jimmie Nell Sinclair was not a routine-oriented person. She had to be a fireball ready to follow a whim at the drop of a hat.

I think I bought the piece for inspiration, to remind myself that disorder could arrange itself into something uniquely beautiful if you let your imagination and some of your preconceptions go. It's funny that I would have to be reminded of something I had known for a long time to be true in poetry. I think I was beginning to see how segmented my life had been, how I had failed to transfer principles from one part to another.

It was a good day in every way. We stopped at a lake, and Travis and Ken skipped rocks. We took back roads and drove past harvested fields and farmhouses. Geese flew overhead, water sang in creeks, and all around us red and gold leaves floated down like confetti. We bought a bag of Arkansas Black apples at Heart Springs Orchard on our way back down, and that evening after Travis had finished the leaves and Ken had put in some writing time, I made an apple strudel, which we ate warm with vanilla ice cream. It's odd that I should remember the day as being so perfect when so few words were exchanged among the three of us, but it was. As I said, it was the last good time together that I remember.

I push myself a little in the swing now and look up to see the moon tipped on end like a lemon wedge in the darkening sky. Through the trees stretching out behind our house, I can see the lamp in Miriam Ramsey's window, and I tell myself I need to pay her a visit sometime soon. Since her nighttime scare months ago, she has come back twice—once shortly after that night with a pan of cherry-coconut crisp to thank me for helping out with her grandson's allergy attack and another time in April to give me a crocheted dishcloth and a jar of honey. She doesn't go to church, she told me, and for some reason I didn't ask why.

I need to go see her and take her something, but what do you give a seventy-year-old woman you barely know? I think of what my mother might like a neighbor to bring her. Maybe a tin of hard candy or some bubble bath.

Maybe a can of cashews or a houseplant. I make a note to do this as soon as possible. Maybe she would come to church if I offered to drive her. Maybe her reason for not going is as simple as not liking to drive, or not knowing how to.

I remember the shame I felt on a recent Sunday when Pastor Hawthorne preached a sermon titled "Neighborhood Missionaries." He went on at great length about the many ways we can demonstrate the love of Christ to those around us. I thought of all the people on my street, of how many opportunities I neglect as I pass their houses and keep right on going.

Eldeen Rafferty said "Amen" right out loud a half dozen times or so during Pastor Hawthorne's sermon, though I was sure she didn't need the message at all. She was no doubt the most zealous neighborhood missionary in the whole church. I could picture her taking her handmade pillowcases to every house on the street where she lived, dragging Joe Leonard over to mow their lawns, trim their hedges, wash their cars, inviting entire families over for cobbler or cookies and then drenching them in the mighty flood of her words.

I always felt as though I had a high fever whenever I had to be around Eldeen for very long, as though delirium could set in at any minute, but deep down I had to admire her. People came to church because of her persistence, and many of them came to Christ. More and more I was seeing that God uses all kinds. I saw people hugging her at church, seeking her out to talk to her, standing close to her, and soaking up her love. So I knew my reaction to her discredited me more than it did her.

She had given me a pair of her famous pillowcases shortly after our talk at Dottie's beauty shop, and every time I use them now, I see her big manly hands groping inside her purse and I hear her thick low voice saying, "Wait a minute, little lady, before you skedaddle away again. I got something with your name on it right here in my pocketbook." She pulled out a little rolled-up bundle secured with several rubber bands. "These here I stitched up special just for *you!*" she said, snapping off the rubber bands and pushing them onto her wrist. She held up the pillowcases and flapped them briskly so they unrolled. "See, they's little lambs a-skitterin' across the hillside so rambunctious they's about to fall all over theirself!"

She threw her head back and laughed with gusto, then immediately sobered. "I just love lambs and sheep, don't you, Elizabeth? Just think of all the ways God uses them to teach us lessons in the pages of the Holy Bible!" Her face creased into its usual anguished-looking smile, and she nodded vigorously. "He goes after little lost lambs like us and snuggles 'em in his bosom and brings 'em home to the fold." She gave a little shudder of pleasure and added, "It just makes me tingle all over to think of it!"

Without meaning to, I laughed out loud. I was sure she meant to say "tingle." I recovered quickly by laughing again and saying, "Oh yes, lambs are wonderful! And *these* are just . . . well, they're perfect." I took the pillow-cases from her and thanked her. Then before I could catch my breath, she gathered me in an embrace and said, "You're just as welcome as you can be, honey. Just as welcome as you can be! I hope they remind you of your gentle shepherd, the Lord Jesus, and give you peace all through the nighttime." And then she squeezed my hand and said, "And every day when I pray, I bring your family before the throne of God, too!"

I ought to learn from Eldeen, I tell myself now. School's out for the summer, so I have time. It will be good to get out and talk to my neighbors, to get my thoughts off myself. There's got to be something fundamentally wrong about living right by people and never talking to them. Eunice Yarnell next door has changed the color of her bows three times since I've last *spoken* to her. I'm not talking about an extended dialogue, but just a simple wave and "Hello, how are you?"

When I was growing up in Burma, Georgia, neighborhoods were a lot friendlier. Neighbors saw each other out in the yard and wandered over to talk. Even our old neighborhood in Derby was different from this one. Although Polly Seacrest was my main contact, I felt connected to the other neighbors through her. Polly talked freely to everybody up and down the street and then told me everything that was going on.

But our new street here in Berea is quiet and closed up, just like me. I'm ashamed to say that if I'm getting ready to go outside and I see Eunice or Wallace out in the yard next door, I usually wait until they've gone back inside before I go out. And it doesn't have anything to do with the Yarnells. It has to do with me.

The school year has tired me out. The last two days in the classroom reminded me of surrealistic art. Mixed up and meaningless. Nothing much happens of an academic nature during the final few days of school, and if I hadn't wanted the extra money for Macon Mahoney's linocut, I wouldn't have answered the phone those two mornings.

The first day it was girls P.E. at Derby Middle School, and the last day it was drivers' ed at Berea High. I played volleyball in P.E. with the seventh-grade girls, who begged me not to make them change into their gym clothes. I pretended to deliberate over it and finally told them I wouldn't if they would pledge exemplary behavior, which they did, and for the most part delivered on except for the usual silliness you expect from that age. I didn't tell them the regular teacher had already left word not to have them change and to leave plenty of time at the end of class for them to clean out their gym lockers.

The next day, the last day of school, I showed a film in drivers' ed—a repeat, judging from the kids' groans when it started. It was one of those gory ones that supposedly deter teenagers from driving too fast. I saw it five times that day. It didn't seem like a very upbeat way to end the school year.

On the way home I clutched the steering wheel with both hands and kept my eyes peeled for reckless teen drivers.

But now it's over, and I'm sitting in my backyard swing with summer before me. To be alone in the summer feels unnatural. Last year at this time Ken and Travis were both home, and here I am a year later all by myself. And here's the irony. If someone had asked me a year ago how I would like to have some time all by myself, say a week or two, I would have jumped at the chance. But today, right now, I've had my fill of it.

I'll admit it. I used to look at single women sometimes and envy their freedom to do whatever they wanted to do whenever it suited them. I've tasted that freedom now, had long days and nights of it—okay, maybe even enjoyed parts of it to some degree. But it's a heavy freedom. Living with people is better than living alone. I can't speak for everyone, but I can speak for me.

Everything costs something, even freedom, and "every farthing of the cost" has to be paid. It's odd that that particular line springs to mind, considering the fact that it's from a poem about illicit love. I'll never agree with Auden that "Lullaby" was the best title for that poem, but a poet has the right to choose a bad title.

Anyway, bad title notwithstanding, the poem does what good literature is supposed to do. It shows you different ways of looking at life and dealing with its blows. Auden's poem shows how desperate a person can get, how hungry for touch, how shortsighted on the one hand yet how keenly aware on the other of the inevitable cost. Stolen waters may be sweet for a moment, but payback time is coming, always coming. I wonder if Ken felt a sickness in the pit of his stomach when he thought of the price of what he was doing all those months. Or did he put the cost out of his mind like somebody on a spending spree?

I try to think back to a year ago to what it was like between Ken and me, but I can't come up with many details. All I hear is a great roaring silence. I remember passing him in the hallway sometime during that summer and moving as far over as I could so I wouldn't have to touch him.

By then I had already begun my descent into something so much like depression I don't know what else to call it. Women go through cycles, I know that, but I had never hit a low like this one. It was already settled that Travis was going away to college in the fall, and I felt like I was slowly being strangled.

I have no idea what I did with myself all day, but I went to bed early and spent the dark nights sleeping, alternating between near unconsciousness and troubled, fitful naps. I dreamed over and over of Travis walking across an ocean on what looked like stepping-stones but turned out to be alligators that rose up and swallowed him whole. I would wake up hardly able to get my breath, hearing horrible clacking sounds, like hundreds of spring-loaded traps snapping shut. I never told Ken about my dreams. I was way past telling him things, and he wouldn't have known what to say anyway. He might have even laughed.

We were getting ready to move a year ago, so I'm sure I must have wandered around the house sticking things in boxes, but I had no system to what I was doing. Ken did most of the packing. He packed the entire kitchen one day while I took down curtains. That was all I did the whole day. After it was over, I looked at all the boxes he had packed and stacked up against the wall, and I looked at the little pile of thin, faded curtains I had taken down, folded neatly, and set on the kitchen table, and I thought it was the saddest sight I had ever seen. I turned around and headed back to the bedroom to go to bed, and all I could think of was the word *curtains*.

I lay in bed and thought how you could take it apart and make it into separate words: *cat ruins, in a crust, car units, uni-carts, un-racist, narc suit*. My mind wouldn't stop. *Tina's cur, Ric's tuna, R. C. Austin*. When Ken came back to the bedroom and asked me impatiently if I wasn't going to wash the curtains before I packed them, I think I laughed. It had never entered my mind to wash the curtains. After he left, I kept on. *Can u stir? C. R. is a nut. Cart us in*.

I never really said good-bye to Polly Seacrest, the closest thing to a friend I had had for over six years. Polly and Morris had left for a month to rent a cottage with his brother's family up in Michigan. Morris just closed down his home repair business, and off they went. Before they left, Polly was busy trying to get everything ready for their trip, and when they got back, we had already moved. It was just as well, though. I couldn't have carried on a meaningful conversation with anyone last summer. I stayed away from people. The YMCA's spring tennis tournament was over in May, after which I zipped my racket up inside my tennis bag and stashed it in the closet. The thought of hitting a ball across the net seemed utterly pointless.

My mother would call me on the phone and say, "What's *wrong* with you?" and I would gather my wits enough to make some excuse or another—"I'm getting over a cold" or "It's just a touch of sinus" or "I'm tired, Mother, that's all." I reminded her that the school year was just recently over and a summer letdown was nothing unusual.

"I'm coming to see you," she'd say. "I'll do the cooking and help you with the packing." And I'd muster all my energy and say, "Oh no, no, please don't do that. I'm fine, really. I don't need any help. It's all under control." The thought of her coming to see me made me feel as if my throat was closing up. She kept telling me to go get checked for mono, and I told her I would, but I never did.

I knew the origin of my condition wasn't physical, and I wasn't about to go to anybody for help with the *other* kind of illness.

Lying in bed, I'd play word games to keep from thinking about other things. I'd try to make up my own palindrome without writing anything down but could never figure out the best way to start. Do you begin in the middle of a sentence and work out in both directions, or do you start at the two ends simultaneously? The closest I ever came was *Llama, level a mall*, which didn't even make sense, and *Ya, was Iris away?* which was another very sad effort.

But somehow the summer had passed. Then came the days after Travis left for college, but somehow those had passed, too, one at a time. Not happily nor profitably, but they had passed. Suddenly with a brilliant flash of shame, I remember driving to Greenville one day last fall in a melancholy trance and walking through stores in the mall, picking up things that caught the light a certain way or lay on a table with a kind of dignity, taking them one by one to a cashier and producing my charge card.

I wasn't totaling the costs, but somewhere in the recesses of my mind I knew the final bill would come, and for that reason the pleasure, even *as* I was indulging myself, was empty. That's my point, one I was reaching for a few paragraphs back. Something in the human soul, even one that's battered and stupefied, instinctively looks ahead and knows that *this* isn't the end. Sometimes with the hope of mercy, and sometimes with the dread of getting exactly what you deserve. Even those times when you're trying to convince yourself that you're having the time of your life, there's the nagging voice that says, "You'll pay for this."

Later I took my purchases out of the bags at home and set them around the house, hung them in my closet, put them in drawers, knowing full well that none of it could pump life into my hollow heart, knowing that my few hours of temporary pleasure would exact a large sum the next month. Everything costs something, and the cost, every farthing of it, will be paid. I despised my weakness. Other women could weather the storm of children leaving home and their marriages growing dull, but what was I doing? Dragging around in a stupor, then buying expensive things on a whim, that's what.

I'm not proud of how I handled it all, but it's done, and you can't put the milk back in the jug after it's spilled, which is my mother's version of the old adage. Before Daddy died, he was always quick to point out that you could clean it up fast, though, and go out and buy a brand-new gallon, and Mother would say, "Yes, but it might go bad the way that last gallon you brought home from Piggly Wiggly did!"

I make a note of something else to do this summer. I will drive to Georgia to visit my mother. I need to do that. I need to take a week and go places with her and help her in the kitchen and sit on the porch with her and talk face-to-face. She's worried now about what she calls my "extreme religion" and thinks I'm using it to run away from reality. I need to take my Bible and show her some things. I need to sit across the table from her and talk about

Ken. And I need to let her talk about Daddy, which was something I never did after he died. At the time I couldn't think of anything but my own loss. I gave her no outlet, which was selfish.

All over the backyard the lightning bugs are twinkling now. It's the perfect time of summer—the mosquitoes aren't bad yet. Another couple of weeks and I won't be sitting outdoors like this. I remind myself that I came out here to pray, but my thoughts want some time to swirl and mingle right now. I'm in no hurry. I mean to let them waft around in the night air like lazy smoke.

The lightning bugs remind me of the poem Travis sent me for Mother's Day a month ago. It was a childish poem, not a new one to me, but he had to have known it would be the perfect gift. And it was, of course. It was a poem he wrote in eighth grade titled "Bug Collection." I guess he's had it memorized all these years, or maybe he's kept a copy folded up inside his billfold. That's the kind of thing Travis would keep in his billfold. He asked his friend Stacy at college to copy it in calligraphy on nice paper, and he illustrated it himself with clever drawings of colorful bugs around the margins. Stacy is an art major, I've learned in recent weeks.

So that was it—that was his Mother's Day gift to me. He didn't spend much money on it, but he couldn't have pleased me more. He stuck it between two pieces of cardboard and mailed it to me in one of those padded mailers, and he even managed to get it to me on the Saturday before Mother's Day, along with a silly card that said, "Mom, you've given the world so much" on the front. Inside in huge letters it said, "ME!" I'm going to frame the bug poem and hang it in a prominent place on the wall.

It all took planning—the gift, the card, the mailing—and I'm not going to forget it anytime soon. I can't help wondering if Stacy was behind it all, but I prefer to think that it was completely the idea of my wise, thoughtful son, who has miraculously blossomed in an unlikely garden a hundred miles away from home, a garden I would have given anything to keep him out of a year ago.

Here's his poem. It's written in five-line stanzas with a pattern of 9, 9, 7, 7, 5 syllables per line. He made the whole thing up himself, content and form both. They had studied haiku in English class that year, and he was taken with the compactness of the word pictures. For days he even made up his own haiku and gave impromptu recitations at all hours. He might look out the kitchen window, point to the sky, and say something like "Sun, a fiery plate / Set on sky's blue tablecloth / Burns a hole in day." Part of it was deliberate artistic posturing, but the other was a genuine love of words.

Anyway, when his eighth-grade English teacher assigned a project, one of the options in lieu of the dreaded book report was a poem, which was listed as number fifteen out of fifteen choices. So Travis, still enamored of haiku, took the road less traveled and wrote a poem, devising his own syllabic stanza, then fitting it to a subject all boys seem to know well—entomology. Looking back on it now, I wonder why I worried so much about his lack of close friends when he could write poetry and dig down to the heart of a piano piece. What was I thinking?

He wrote the poem one Saturday in his bedroom with his door closed, and it didn't take all that long. The next time I walked by his room a couple of hours later, I heard him talking in two different voices, one high and Southern-belle syrupy, the other gruff and villainous. "Please, sir, don't, don't tie me to the tracks!" the first voice said, followed by a deep, perverse chuckle, then, "That train is a-thunderin' down these tracks in exactly two minutes, Eliza Snodgrass, and yor a goner 'less you say you'll be my bride." Where he got these goofy ideas, I'll never know.

Girlish screams, more wicked laughter, and the convincing sounds of screeching metal ensued, followed by what sounded like a mighty blast of steam as the train apparently stopped only inches away from Miss Snod-grass, who cried out, "Your wickedness has been thwarted, sir. Deliverance is at hand!" I would have bet money on the fact that he was holding a stuffed animal in each hand, using them to act out the little melodrama.

But this is all beside the point. Here's the poem, which Travis showed me two weeks later, after the teacher had written an A on the back of it with a perfunctory "Nice job!" scribbled beside it. "Understatement of the year," I said to Travis when I read the poem and saw her insipid comment.

BUG COLLECTION

Darting by with a whiz and a whine,
The vampire mosquito guzzles blood,
Bloats to the point of bursting;
When slapped, tiny gray body
Splotches your palm red.

Greedily eating fragrant roses,
Japanese beetle peers through petals,
Dressed in fine blue-green armor;
When stomped, iridescent shell
Crunches underfoot.

Buzzing fiercely out of paper nests,
Hornet makes ready tiny harpoon;
Zigzagging, then zooming down,
Black and yellow dive bomber,
When stirred up, strikes hard!

Lying in wait to capture its prey,
The mantis warlord sits patiently,
Posing as green twigs and leaves.
When a victim chances by,
Nabs it with vises.

Silently flashing on summer nights,
Firefly punches bright holes in the sky;
Hiding in bushes by day,
When sunlight fails, it wakes and
Blinks sporadic code.

Merrily chirping from dusk to dawn,
The black cricket hides in dark corners,
Plays an out-of-tune fiddle;
When startled, springs from tall grass
With a hopskipjump!

I loved it. It was a boy's poem, full of action and surprises. I never would have expected Travis to have the patience to write something so tightly constructed, to count out every syllable for thirty lines and think up metaphors for each insect, to use words like *iridescent* and *sporadic*, to know that *hopskipjump* wouldn't be right unless it was written as one word. And he hadn't asked for my help, had in fact rejected it outright, saying a *project* wasn't like regular homework where your parents could help. He had gone into his room and closed his door to do it.

Something knocks me over the head right now, and I feel slightly dizzy from the blow. I try hard to sort through it while part of me dismisses it as impossible and the other part says no, it could be true, so think about it. I remember an earlier attempt by Travis at writing a poem. It was in elementary school, somewhere around fourth or fifth grade, and he ended up crying at the kitchen table that afternoon.

I was there, helping as always. I remember how tightly he clutched the pencil, his hand shaking a little as he wrote each word, how he would brace himself after trying out a phrase, waiting for my response, how he tore a hole in the paper erasing the word *purple* to replace it with *lilac*, at my suggestion.

Here's what hits me over the head. Could it be that any part of Travis's performance anxiety was my fault? I had always blamed it all on Ken. Okay, now, don't get carried away here, I tell myself. *Think.* I close my eyes tight and try to remember all the way back to the debacle of his first trumpet recital. That was Ken's fault, wasn't it? I recall Ken's rigid posture as Travis stood up to play, the way he leaned forward and furrowed his brow as if the notes that came out of that trumpet the next minute were going to mean the difference between staying on the road or falling headlong over a cliff.

I remember Travis looking our direction right before he lifted the horn to his lips. But you know what I remember now that I never ever thought of in all the years before? He looked directly at *me*, not at Ken. He swallowed hard and licked his lips, then looked down at his music and slowly lifted his trumpet. I don't need to go into what happened next except to say that the notes that came out of his horn weren't the ones printed in the music.

But here's the question. What was on my face when he looked at me? Was it a demand for more than any child could give? Instead of "Have fun and do your best," did he read, "Be perfect"? What terrible burden had I placed on him? And what had I done and said afterward?

I remember Travis bending over his trumpet case after the recital, after the last student, a girl with pigtails, had played her piece, "Variations on Farmer in the Dell," flawlessly. I can still see him carefully laying his instrument inside, fitting the mouthpiece into the little hole, folding the flannel flap over the top just so, then snapping the case shut, and walking toward us with his head down. Why hadn't we walked toward him? I wondered now. I remember the thick silence in the car riding home.

But surely, surely I had encouraged him, hugged him, and told him not to feel bad, to forget it and keep trying. Surely I had assured him of our unconditional love. Surely I told him that lots of people get off to a slow start and then take off and fly later. Surely I told him about a couple of my own failures as a child—the time I entered a baking contest expecting to win and didn't even place in the top five, the time I tried out for cheerleader in junior high and got sick to my stomach, or the time I was in a tennis tournament in high school and lost 6–0, 6–0 to a girl who had been playing only a year and returned everything with little patty-cake shots.

Maybe I had even been part of Travis's difficulty making friends. Maybe I acted as if too much depended on it. Maybe I was even the reason why he turned into an indifferent student later in high school. Maybe he got so used to seeing my disappointment over report cards of A's and B's instead of only A's that he gave up and slipped down to B's and C's. I realize I'm breathing hard as these thoughts race through my mind. When I had prayed for God to open my eyes, I hadn't meant I wanted to see all this!

But maybe none of it is true. I need to sit down with Travis when he comes home from college and find out. He'll be home only for a couple of days, though. After he visits Stacy, he's decided to go back to Piper and take a four-week summer school course "to get rid of a requirement so I can get into my major courses next year." He told me this on the phone the other night, and I was stunned. Still am. I've never known Travis to have academic goals.

I've always been convinced that if I hadn't helped him, drilled him, looked over his homework, quizzed and tutored him, he never would have graduated from high school. The thought comes to me now, even as I try to push it away, that maybe he would have done better in school if he hadn't had so much help from me. I guess that's something I'll never know. I do remember holding Travis's high school diploma in my hand and thinking, *This is mine.* He had tossed it down on the kitchen table when he came home after his graduation ceremony, then shoved it out of his way a minute later when he sat down with a can of root beer and opened up the newspaper to find the comics.

And all of a sudden I remember very clearly one detail about Ken and me from a year ago, almost exactly a year ago in fact. It was the first week of June, and I remember the two of us going to Travis's graduation in separate cars and not even sitting together. I guess that says it all right there.

After summer school Travis plans to work at the summer camp Stacy's father runs in North Carolina, he told me over the phone. It's a Christian camp for disabled children called Running Brook, and Travis is going to work in the kitchen and help with programs and skits. After six weeks of that it will be time for school again. This is the way it's going to be now. When Travis left home last fall, he pretty much left for good. But, I remind myself, this is the way it's supposed to be. Your children grow up and leave home. It's been happening since the dawn of time. It has to be that way.

I sit very still for a long time. It's completely dark in my backyard now. I hear little rustling sounds and imagine it's the grass growing. Or maybe it's hummingbirds stirring around in the treetops. That's where they build their nests—in the lightest branches in the very tip-tops of trees. I saw the first hummingbird at my feeder today. He didn't stay long and drank with nervous, fitful sips, stopping often to look around. But he came, and I feel sure others will follow.

We've had rain lately, and things have taken off. Bustin' out all over, as the song goes. I might call Hardy or Philip Biddle and see if they'll come do our yard in the next few days. Ken mowed it before he left, but that was more than a week ago. He'll be coming back from Richmond in another week.

And what will I do then? What will he do? My thoughts have spun themselves out now, and I imagine them dispersing into the night, lifting like wisps of cloud. I am alone under the clear sky, ready to pray.

The Touch of Earthly Years

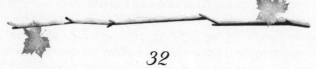

32

Several days have passed. I saw a book on Margaret's shelf earlier today when I sat in her living room. I saw many books actually, but the title of this one caught my eye in particular. It was a small unassuming paperback tucked in among larger books. I've found that it's often the people who don't call attention to themselves who have the most to offer, and I think the same might be said of books. *Things I Have Learned* was its title. Margaret let me bring it home with me, and I plan to read it soon.

The title put me in an assessing, ruminating, enumerating frame of mind. "I've learned some things, too," I told Margaret when she took the book off the shelf and handed it to me. It had been almost four months since the first day I sat here beside her on this same couch. When you consider a lifetime, four months isn't all that long. It wouldn't be long enough, for instance, to master a skill like carpentry or ballet or tennis.

On the other hand, you can learn a lot in four months. A person's whole view of life may change in four months. The things he considers important may completely reverse themselves. Past mistakes previously unrecognized may leap out at him like flashing road signs. A person may spend four months looking backward, during which time he may see many things he didn't notice the first time through, and then he may be ready to look forward.

It's a Saturday in the middle of June as I sit in Margaret's living room. Her job at the school cafeteria is done for the summer, and Thomas is away for the weekend visiting an ailing cousin in North Carolina. We have time at our disposal.

Margaret and I have begun taking walks together in the late afternoon, sometimes in my neighborhood and sometimes in hers. Today we're going to walk to a park in Filbert and watch a Little League game. We will be out of place, I suppose, two middle-aged women with no stake in the game—no sons, no grandsons, probably nobody we even know. But it's something we both want to do. Margaret had a son many years ago. He would be in his thirties now if he were still living. He could be one of the fathers of the Little Leaguers, maybe the coach.

When it comes to team sports, next to a good soccer game I'd rather watch baseball than anything, and preferably Little League. Professional baseball is way too smooth. It's beautiful and graceful, with everything moving in synchrony like a Mozart minuet, whereas Little League is like a twentieth-century piece Ken's band played one time called "Space Music," in which the different instruments made odd humorous sounds at random intervals. And for pure drama, there's nothing to match a fly ball lofted to the outfield in a Little League game. Time does funny things as that ball leaves the bat and sails up, up, past the infield.

Everybody has something different in mind for that ball. The parents of the batter want it to keep flying until it escapes the pull of gravity and is never seen again. The parents of the fielders, on the other hand, want it to develop a strong magnetic attraction to somebody's glove. It hovers over the outfield for what seems like several minutes, and you can almost hear the tension sizzling in the air as the outfielders stand rooted, staring upward, begging the ball not to fall in their direction. *Let it be some other guy who misses it, not me,* they're saying.

And then the ball starts its descent, picking up speed as it comes. You hear the other players shouting instructions to the fielder into whose territory the ball is clearly headed. "Back up!" "Go left!" "Get your glove up!" "Move under it!" You can look at the faces of all the people in the bleachers and pick out the parents of this boy. The mother might have hidden her eyes by now.

Meanwhile, the legs of the batter are pumping like pistons as he rounds first base and thunders toward second in a cloud of dust. You can find the parents of this boy, too, if you scan the faces.

I've been the mother of both of those boys, the outfielder and the batter—in the very same game, in fact. Travis was a good hitter when he set his mind to it, but mostly he just didn't seem to care all that much about it. Not nearly as much as I cared, for sure. In the field he was easily distracted—butterflies, airplanes, clouds, birds, small things in the grass. He knew how to catch a ball, found it quite easy, in fact, but often didn't see it coming in time. I knew he must be a source of frustration for his coach.

Ken and I were both there on the big day—the day our son pulled double-duty heroics. Travis caught a fly ball in left field in the third inning by holding his glove out and letting the ball plop right into the sweet spot. He hadn't even had to move his feet, so it didn't truly qualify as skill. But he did it nevertheless, and it counted as an out.

And then as a bonus he hit a home run in the seventh inning, which looked as easy as catching the fly ball had. He swung his bat and lofted the ball into center field. It fell about twenty feet behind the center fielder and rolled all the way to the fence before the boy chased it down.

We made a big deal out of that game, let me tell you. Ken hung around with the other dads after the game that day, talking and laughing, and I went overboard rewarding Travis with all sorts of things—I remember a pair of binoculars and a deluxe yo-yo in particular. We rode home in high spirits. Thinking back on it, I guess I should say Ken and I rode home in high spirits. Travis didn't really say much. I remember him sitting squashed over against the door in the backseat, staring out the window, his chin cupped in his hand. Later Ken complained at home. "He acts like he's in another world, like he couldn't care less about winning that game!"

Maybe he was too busy wondering why we acted as if we loved him more whenever he performed well than when he blew it. Actually, I doubt if he really had thoughts like those. Travis was a pretty simple kid, not a deep thinker. He must have felt something wasn't altogether satisfactory about that game and our extreme joy, though.

Anyway, Margaret and I are going to a Little League game at the Filbert public park a few blocks from Margaret's duplex. I tuck the book Margaret gave me into my purse, which I leave on her couch, and we head out the door.

"So you have learned some things?" she says as we head down Cadbury Street. We walk faster than Barb Chewning does when she is out for a stroll in our neighborhood. "If you care to share some of them, I am most willing to listen."

So as we walk, I tell my friend in no particular order some of the things I have learned over the past four months. The words tumble out like coins out of a jackpot. I have learned that I'm not as polite as I've always thought I was, I tell her, that sometimes I'm even perceived as stuck-up. I've told her this before, of course, but this is a good place to start. I've been afraid to offer too much of myself, I continue, but I've always thought it was other people holding back. I've learned that I have a lot of pride and that many of my smiles have been insincere.

On the other hand, I've learned recently that people are usually ready to open up to you if you take the first step. I've learned to say thank-you more and to look people in the eye. I've learned that there are lots of smart people in the world, smarter by far than I am. I've learned that my assigning of people into Aware and Unaware categories has been arbitrary, false, and snobbish, that a lot of Unaware people are miles ahead of me in the things that matter most.

I've learned that routine can be stifling, that sometimes you need to try something scary or totally out of character or do things in a completely different order than usual. I've learned that even if you don't reach the pinnacle of success in an endeavor, it can still be worthwhile to try. I got out my tempera paints a week ago and painted a picture of six colorful neckties jumbled together on the desktop in Ken's study. I actually went to his closet one night, took out six ties he had left behind, tossed them onto his desk, and then painted a picture of them. It wasn't a great picture, but I liked doing it and plan to do another one of something else. I might even take an art class.

I've learned also that a mother can totally lose her perspective and commit grievous wrongs while justifying her behavior as acts of love. Oh yes, for being so smart, I truly have been dumb in a lot of ways. I've put pressure on my children to be what I wanted them to be, and no doubt my high standards have often squelched any effort on their part. While Jennifer somehow managed to rescue herself, poor Travis had the temperament to make a perfect captive. But a light shines in the darkness! I've learned that children can turn into fine adults in spite of their mother's failures, that their stunted wings can grow strong and they can learn to fly on their own.

I've learned that beauty is everywhere, that it's a whole body rather than separate little dismembered pieces, that one kind of beauty is relevant to all others, and that art and living go together. It's been confirmed for me that the poetry I love so much can step off the page and go forth into real life, for it's more than beautiful language and interesting ideas. It has given me much comfort during the past four months.

I've settled the matter of Christianity and art. I know that one's view of God informs, shapes, and gives expression to his art and that art can be seen as both a gift to God and a gift from God, as Isaac on the altar and as the ram caught in the thicket. I've learned that God takes great pleasure in our happiness, that he isn't lurking about with a club in his omnipotent hand, ready to knock us out cold in the event that we seem to be having too much fun.

I go on and on listing the things I've learned, and Margaret inclines her ear and nods with understanding, often smiling and murmuring, "Yes." We pass water sprinklers and children playing tag. Dogs bark as we walk by their yards. One rushes at us, then stops and wags his tail when Margaret speaks to him quietly.

I've learned—and this is a big one, I tell Margaret—that though I've always considered myself a good girl in every way, my capacity for evil is limitless. I've learned that I am a sinner saved by the incomprehensible grace of a righteous God who loves me for all eternity, and in contemplating that fact, I feel both the warmth of harboring an intimate secret and, simultaneously, an unfolding of myself, a thrilling expansiveness and a bold desire to embrace the world. I've learned that my best efforts to do good are pathetic, but in spite of my weakness, my doubts, my wandering attention, my clouded vision, I am still precious in the sight of my Savior. I have learned of his infinite patience with me.

I've learned of the wonderful joy of friendship, I tell Margaret. Not that I've been the friend I should have been these past months, but I've seen in Margaret the example of how it's done. She raises her hand at this, as if to disagree, but I give her no chance to speak.

I hasten on. I have learned that a woman no longer in the sunshine of her youth can still bloom, can contribute, can make an enormous difference in the lives of others. I remind Margaret of last night, when this truth hit me with great force. She looks at me, her head to one side, as if puzzled and waiting for more.

So I lay it out for her, though I suspect she doesn't need the explanation. Last night, Friday, Margaret came to my house to walk. After our walk, I remind her, we ate together at my kitchen table. She brought over home-made vegetable soup, and I made sandwiches. During our supper the phone rang. Barb Chewning was on the other end telling me that Jewel Scoggins had just given birth to her baby an hour earlier. It was a healthy seven-pound girl, she said, and they had named her Rosemary Jean. After I hung up, Margaret and I sat in silence for a few moments, absorbing the news that Jewel was starting all over again on that long journey of motherhood, which turns out to be so short once it gets going. I think of the title of a band piece Ken conducted one time—"A Short Ride in a Fast Machine." That's motherhood.

A little while later we settled down to watch *Babette's Feast*, and at the end I asked Margaret how she interpreted the story, particularly Babette's final act.

"I see her as a dispenser of grace," she said at once. "Not that she is an altogether perfect figure of grace, for there is heavy emphasis on the work she does in order to offer and then create her artful banquet. On the other hand, God's gift of grace does involve work, does it not? Not man's works of righteousness, but Christ's atoning work on the cross. I see Babette's sacrifice as a beautiful enactment of grace, and the people's response, reluctant at first and then openly joyful, as a picture of man's inability to comprehend the depths of God's grace."

Margaret nods now. She remembers all of this, of course. Therefore, I repeat, I have realized that one woman can do a great and good work that may make an eternal difference. Teacherlike, I list the evidence for her. First, Margaret herself has been God's instrument in my salvation. There's no arguing that fact.

Second, Jewel has given birth to a daughter, a brand-new person whose soul will live somewhere forever. And like every mother, Jewel now has great power in her hands to shape that life into one with vast potential for the advancement of God's kingdom. Every birth is a miracle, but somehow this specific birth by a woman who is my own age makes me want to weep with gladness. I am struck with wonder at what a woman can still do after she's past her so-called prime.

Third, a woman like Babette, though she wasn't a real person, can give of herself in such a way that others see love and sacrifice and grace demonstrated right in front of their eyes. This reminds me that a woman has much meaningful work yet to do even after her children are gone. A woman can be used by God as an artist who draws large, vivid, specific illustrations of abstract truths from the Bible, enormous overwhelming truths like grace. I can be a woman like that, I tell Margaret. I can paint a portrait of Christ in radiant colors simply by choosing to give something for nothing, and doing it time and time again.

I'm getting to the end of my inventory now, the focal point of this whole thing, and I slow down a little. This next part is harder to say, but I know it needs to be spoken aloud. I've learned, I tell her, that in marriage it's a waste of time to review old pains and record the blame in two columns, then add it all up to see whose total is bigger. I've learned that I need to take off my rags of regret, wash myself, and put on clean clothes. I've learned that I need to let go of my status as victim. I've looked backward long enough. Now I need to look forward.

And I've learned that I love my husband. I don't just think I love him. I know I do. Back in February I was afraid I loved him only because of the competition from another woman.

"You know how anything out of reach is a little more desirable," I say, and she nods. "But then other days I'd go over all the ways he had failed me, and I'd be certain I didn't love him anymore, that I couldn't ever trust him again, and without trust you can't love somebody."

Then one night not long ago, I tell her, I woke up from a dream well past midnight and realized I had been having this same general dream for many weeks. In it I was being threatened by someone brandishing a knife in my face, or sometimes I was attacked from behind and knocked to the ground or dragged away bound and gagged by strong men. And as I struggled to get away, suddenly out of nowhere Ken was there, fending off the bad guys and lifting me to safety.

As I lay awake rehearsing my dream that night, I also realized I had slept on my side of the bed for several months now. Not in the middle as I used to do when Ken was away on trips, but completely on the right side. I rolled over and ran my hand along the mattress on his side of the bed. And I realized that I was saving it for him, that I was counting on him to come back.

When I tried to remind myself of how wrongly he had treated me, it was as if part of me said, "Oh, don't go into all of that again." And at that moment I knew beyond a doubt that I loved him. I don't tell Margaret this next part, but I even sealed it by saying out loud in the darkness, "I love you, Ken."

We walk in silence for a while. We're coming up to the park now and can hear the thunks of baseballs against aluminum bats, the boys' voices and shouts from the bleachers. "And your husband comes home from his trip tomorrow, does he?" Margaret says. "And you will tell him these things you have told me?"

"Yes, I will," I say. I have no idea how I'll be able to do it, having kept my heart closed for so long, but I know I will. I'll tell him tomorrow.

We stay for the entire game, and we're glad, because the best part happens at the very end, which is so often the case. It's the bottom of the last inning, with two outs and the team at bat down by one run, 6–5. Runners are on first and second, which isn't nearly as hopeful a fact in Little League as it might be in professional baseball. Ending an inning with stranded runners happens all the time in these games, except when nobody even gets on base that inning, which happens a lot, too.

A chubby boy they call Randy, who has struck out twice already, approaches the plate with the air of one destined to do it again. This same sense of gloom emanates from everybody on the team. The coach stands off to one side looking tormented, as if going through the rotation again, wondering how it could possibly have worked out to be Randy's turn to bat at such a critical time. All the boys on the bench are slumped over, elbows on knees, muttering and stirring up dust with their cleats. The boys on base stand rigidly with their arms folded, glaring at Randy as if he's playing a bad joke on them by walking up to the plate with a bat in his pudgy hands.

The first-base coach looks down at the dirt, pulls at the bill of his cap, and shakes his head. A couple of halfhearted "Go get 'em, Randy's" come from the bleachers, but even the parents, always the last group to give up hope, seem resigned to lose this game. I am startled all of a sudden when Margaret rises beside me, makes a megaphone out of her hands, and shouts, "You can do this, Randy! Fix your eyes on the ball and hit it hard!" Randy, who is in the process of shuffling his feet around in the red dirt by home plate, glances over at her, and other people turn around to look our way, too.

Here's what happens. After two balls and two strikes, at which Randy does not swing, the pitcher winds up to throw what he must surely hope will be the strike-out pitch. Just as he releases it, Margaret calls out clearly, "Swing your bat, Randy!" And marvel of all marvels, he does. Even more marvelous, he makes contact with the ball. He hits it a little on the early side, but that's okay. A stout fellow, he puts his whole torso into it, and it sails like a musket ball toward right field, shoulder high directly between the pitcher and first baseman, both of whom are so surprised by Randy's one shining moment that they can't react fast enough.

The right fielder is as shocked as everybody else. For some reason he had moved in and pulled over toward center field when Randy came to bat, so he's out of position to field the ball, which starts curving after it whizzes past the first baseman, then lands just inside the foul line and keeps rolling with the speed of a motorized racecar.

The runners on first and second, after a moment of disbelief, have already taken off, and Randy is lumbering down the baseline toward first. Everybody is Randy's friend now, cheering wildly and jumping up and down. The first-base coach joyously beckons him onward with great, flapping gestures, and the third-base coach is leaping around as if barefoot on hot asphalt, shouting for the other two runners to "Go, go, go!"

By the time the right fielder retrieves the ball and hurls it toward home, Randy is almost to third base, and the other two runners have already scored. So Randy wins the game for his team, and Margaret and I stay long enough to see him lifted, with no little effort, onto his teammates' shoulders and carried around in a celebratory procession. On our way out of the park, we pass a plump woman in a red gingham dress standing over by the fence. She's wiping tears out of her eyes. We don't have to guess who she is.

I think about the difference a few minutes can make. Randy is the team's whipping boy one minute, the hero the next. And the dividing line was that split second his bat came into contact with the baseball. So many changes can happen in an instant.

I can't help returning again and again to the afternoon in February when I sat in Margaret's living room and heard her clear presentation of the gospel, then bowed my head and accepted God's gift. It took only a fraction of time to be transformed into a child of God, but it made a difference for all eternity.

Now that I'm on the brink of my own act of grace, I'm suddenly seized with fear that something will happen to prevent it. Death, for one. Ever since my father died all those years ago, I've feared that most powerful of preventers. Ken is driving back from Richmond tomorrow afternoon following the closing concert of the conductors' seminar. Lots of bad things happen on highways.

There was a time in my childhood, even living as I did with a mother who looked for catastrophes to strike at any moment, when I never considered mortality. It just never dawned on me that death could come knocking at our door. I guess there comes a time in everyone's life when he wakes up to the fact that death is something real and close at hand.

"A Slumber Did My Spirit Seal." That's a poem by William Wordsworth that comes to my mind now. The speaker in that poem never expected the woman he loved to be taken from him. It's a short poem, broken into two quatrains, and the break between the two stanzas is a huge one. Before that white space he had no fear of death, for the one he loved seemed to him to be beyond "the touch of earthly years." After the chasm between the stanzas, he's a changed man who's been introduced to a terrible truth. The world has caught him by surprise and fallen apart on him.

Now I can only pray, very hard and without ceasing, that having decided what I must do, God will allow nothing to hinder me. I have no delusions about being beyond the touch of earthly years. I'm living with the keen awareness that something could happen at any moment to keep me from carrying out my plan. My prayer is brief but urgent: *Please, please, please.* God knows exactly what I mean.

It's almost six o'clock when Margaret and I leave the park. We walk back to her house, where I pick up my purse, say good-bye, and go to my car. She invites me to stay for beef stew, but I tell her I need to get home. I have things to do before Ken arrives tomorrow evening. She doesn't press me but stands in the driveway as I back out. When I pull away, she smiles and waves.

As I drive home, I pass Lackey's nursery and see a spectacular bed of deep pink lilies around the sign in front. *STARGAZER LILIES!* the marquee announces. *GORGEOUS BLOOMS! HEAVENLY FRAGRANCE!* Somebody had to think ahead in order for this display to happen. They had to plant bulbs at the right time and then wait for the spring rains to prod them to life.

"Even the dirt kept breathing a small breath." I remember the backwards poem I wrote in February when the cold winds whipped around my house at night. The idea comes to me now to go forward instead of backward, to start a poem with that line, to make it an impromptu poem, spoken aloud in the car as I drive from Filbert to Berea. Once spoken, it may be irretrievable, but that's okay. It will mean something right now, springing from my heart and falling on my ears only, and maybe it will be the seed for later poems. I speak slowly, not counting lines at first or fussing with meter.

> Even the dirt kept breathing a small breath,
> Under its frozen crust, through the winter rains
> And snows and brittle cold.
> And the sun was done with dark sleep and death,
> The sky bleached pale blue, clean of stains,
> Stretched out broad and tight.
> Something new stirred beneath the old
> Earth thick as muscle and black as night—
> A flutter, a faint beat.
> Within its walls the smallest seed can hold
> A banquet, can push its way to light
> And sing a sweet song.
> And from the ground with grace we eat
> And with gladness feast the day long.

It occurred to me after a few lines that I could rhyme the poem, and after that at stoplights I wrote down on the back of a grocery store receipt the last word of each line to get a pattern. Devising a poem aloud that way, I expected not to remember it, but I do. I remember every word. And in case I do forget someday, I have a receipt in my billfold on the back of which are scribbled the words *breath, rains, cold / death, stains, tight / old, night, beat / hold, light, song / eat, long.* I don't expect anybody else to care about this as much as I do, but the rhyme scheme pleased me: *abc abd cde cdf ef.* That makes two *a*'s, two *b*'s, three *c*'s, three *d*'s, two *c*'s, two *f*'s. Oh, the joys of symmetry!

I know the poem begs for revision, but I think of it already as a favorite old Christmas ornament—nothing extrinsically beautiful, maybe even a little tacky, but something you feature prominently on the tree every year because it has a special place in your heart.

I look up after repeating the last line aloud and find that I have pulled into the parking lot of the Winn-Dixie in Berea. Maybe it was suggested to me by the receipt on which I was writing, or maybe my poem has reminded me of the feast I must prepare.

I look at my watch. Twenty minutes past six. Tomorrow about this time, I will be saying grace.

Bringer of New Things

33

This chapter ends my written record, and I am eager to have it done. I want to meet my days with spontaneity, not with the wary, sizing-up eye of one who knows she will commit the day to paper. Margaret's advice to write it all down was good, but the season is over. A time to write and a time to refrain from writing. I must now get on with the business of life, which doesn't include hours each day of writing down my memories, reflections, feelings. I have other ways I need to spend those hours.

I have what amounts to a book in these many pages, and the accumulation of them has served a purpose. It was Margaret's niece by marriage, Joan Dunlop, who encouraged Margaret herself to write, and seeing the results, Margaret passed the advice along to me. "Writing until dawn" is what Joan calls the idea of writing your way through a trial, and I see her point. It has helped me get through the dark.

Like Joan and Margaret, I would recommend writing to a friend who's been knocked down and flattened by life, but the rule is, I'd tell her, you have to be honest, and you have to ask God to open your eyes as you write. It has surprised me these past months to learn how ignorant I've been about so many things in my life—Elizabeth Landis, the same one who used to think she was so terribly Aware. It's amazing how a person can fool herself. If you're not going to be honest, I'd tell this friend, don't bother writing about your troubles. You'll just end up wallowing. Honest writing elevates you just enough above the details to let you see further in all directions. Ironically, as you remove yourself from the truth to a certain degree, you are better able to pin it down.

It's late August as I write these final words. Winter passed, then spring, and now the summer is almost over and gone. I won't pretend that every day has been easy, that my journey of grace has been a smooth unwrinkled path, that I could draw a clear map for others to follow. My personal well of mercy doesn't always spring full and fresh every morning. Sometimes I pull up the bucket, and it's barely wet.

As I've said before, there will be those reading this who will end up angry at me, who will accuse me of turning back the calendar on the rights of women, who will object to my conclusions, to my methods, and especially to my tedious, rambling account of it all. But remember, as I've also said before, it's my story. It's not meant to be a recipe.

The story of my four months from mid-February to mid-June was that my husband was unfaithful, he moved out of our home, he regretted his infidelity, he asked to come back, I said yes, and he did. That's not the way it happens for everybody, I realize that. Reduced this way, it seems short and simple, but living through it was the hardest thing I've ever done. I feel as if I've toiled around the world on foot, stopping at only the bleakest places.

So to anybody reading this, take note. From my experience alone, I wouldn't presume to tell you how it should be with you. These pages simply tell how it was with me. Every graph of unfaithfulness is different. My husband's line peaked sharply and then plummeted.

A wife may be unfaithful, too, I've discovered, without ever looking at another man. Unfaithfulness may take many different forms. The line on my own graph rose to a plateau early in our marriage, where it remained high for many years. I didn't keep my garden, and it withered. And I don't need to tell anybody that *keep* can have two different meanings. If you don't take care of something, you can't hold on to it. I intend to have a garden again, a garden of my own, and I intend to take care of it so that I can keep it.

As I also said earlier, this story of mine goes against things I've always held dear—justice, logic, fairness, equality. Nevertheless, I know beyond question that its end is right and good. I said right and good, not easy.

So now I record the conclusion of the tale. I've waited over two months to write this final chapter, and with this I close.

You might remember that I had just composed a poem and had pulled into the parking lot of Winn-Dixie when I last stopped. So we'll return there. Before I got out of my car, I dug a list out of my purse. Oh yes, Elizabeth Landis was prepared for this little excursion to the grocery store. She had thought about it for many days, had wrestled with it late at night, had laid her plans.

Three nights before my trip to the grocery store, Ken had called again from Richmond. He had talked for some time about the seminar—the workshop sessions, the evening rehearsals, and of course the two guest conductors, one from Belgium and one from Norway. "Good grief," I told him, "couldn't they find anybody in the United States to do this?" These guys were "*really* good," he told me. "Like everybody on this side of the Atlantic is incompetent?" I said. He laughed. "Did they bring translators with them?" I asked, and he said no, they both spoke perfectly clear English. He said he had learned a lot and wished it wasn't summer so he could try some of it out on his own band before he forgot it.

His room was next door to a snorer, he said. Not your everyday average snorer but a blue-ribbon snorer and, coincidentally, a tubist. At first he thought the guy was practicing his tuba at night, something they had been asked not to do in the dormitory rooms. Over the couple of weeks Ken had been sleeping next door to the man, he had heard an astounding variety of snores besides the deep tuba tones—ones that sounded like someone revving a motorcycle, for instance, and others that sounded like a kazoo choir. But this is also irrelevant.

He went on to talk about the final concert they were giving on Saturday night. In fact, as I was walking across the parking lot toward the entrance of Winn-Dixie, I realized he was probably getting dressed for the concert right now.

It was going to be a good concert, he said. Shostakovich's *Symphony of Wind Instruments*, Grainger's *Lincolnshire Posy*, Schuman's *George Washington Bridge*, Gregson's *The Sword and the Crown*, and Holst's old chestnut, the *First Suite in E-flat*. No Sousa, no circus music, no Broadway tunes. Which reminds me of something. Too many marching band half-time shows have left the general public uninformed about band music. People who think only orchestras can play serious music should educate themselves by going to a good band concert sometime. There, Ken will be happy I stuck that in.

I walked up and down the aisles of Winn-Dixie, selecting things carefully and arranging them neatly in the cart. I was in no hurry that night. This had to be done just right.

Toward the end of his phone call three nights earlier, Ken had told me he would leave Richmond Sunday afternoon and drive home. There was a long pause, and then he had said, "I was wondering, Elizabeth, if . . ." Another pause, and then, "I was hoping maybe we could, I mean, *I* could come . . . well, I'd like to come home, Elizabeth. I wouldn't blame you if you said no, but I'm hoping you'll . . . Of course, I don't have any idea what's been going on in your mind. Maybe you don't ever want to live with me again, and I could understand that, I really could. I've been . . . well, I've said it before. I've been a total fool."

He stopped for a while, and I could hear him breathing hard into the telephone. I felt very powerful in that silent interlude. I knew I wanted him to come back home, but for some reason I couldn't let go and tell him so. Then he said, "I never loved her, Elizabeth. She . . . well, she *talked* all the time. I thought I'd go crazy."

He had mentioned this before, but I let him go on. He gave a little laugh. "Once she told me to repeat something I'd just said, and when I did, you know what she said? She said, 'Your glottal stops are a lot more forceful than the average person's, and did you know you just used a beautiful example of the phonetic intensive in that last sentence?'" I don't know if he expected me to laugh, but I didn't, even though I knew I'd probably think about it later and see the humor.

Then without a bit of warning he said something that made me flare up with anger. "I moved out of the motel before I left to come up here. I took all my stuff over to my office on campus." He paused a moment, then added, "I hated that motel." He had also told me this before.

I could have looked at it from his viewpoint and seen the logic. He was paying good money for the apartment at Home Away from Home, and if it was just going to sit there empty for two weeks while he was away at a seminar, he might as well move out and save the rent.

But I let my temper cloud my thinking. "So you were just *planning* on moving back home," I said. I could hear the tightness in my voice, the forcefulness of my own glottal stops. I kept going, not giving Ken a chance to reply. "You were going to start bringing your stuff back a little at a time, weren't you? Then you'd start hanging around the house more and more, and pretty soon we'd slip back into our old routine, and . . ." What I was thinking was, *And retreat into our own separate little worlds just like we used to*, but I wasn't sure I wanted to say it out loud.

"You're presuming a lot," he said quietly.

"*I'm* presuming?" I fired back. "What about you? Making plans to come back home without even talking to me about it—you're the one who's presuming!"

"Isn't that what I'm doing right now? Talking to you about it?" He sighed. "Or trying to. I've never been good at this. You know that, Elizabeth. I'm not much of a talker."

"Well, maybe it's time to learn," I said. "I'm getting awfully tired of trying to be a mind reader." Even as I said this, I knew how unfair it was. I knew I wasn't much of a talker either, hadn't been for years and years. If given the choice between discussing a touchy subject openly and ignoring it, I'd go for the easy way every time. Hadn't Ken just said he didn't have any idea what had been going on in my mind? That's because I hadn't been talking for a long, long time. At some point it had gotten to be too much trouble. As I've said before, Ken and I are too much alike in certain ways.

"Okay. So how do we start to learn?" Ken said. I noticed that he said *we*, not just *I*. "I'm not . . . well, like I said, I'm not good at this. I feel so . . . I don't know, so tongue-tied when I try to talk about things like this. It never comes out right, and finally I just give up." He sighed again. "How do you learn something like this when it's not the way you *are*?"

"Maybe a little bit at a time," I said. "Like doing dishes." He didn't say anything, but he must have thought, Whoa, what's she talking about now?

The fact is, a silly thought had just come to me, something I remembered with sudden clarity from the days when Jennifer and Travis were home and I used to fix big meals for supper every night. Supper would be over, and we'd get all the dishes over to the counter by the sink.

It might be one of those meals that makes for a big messy cleanup, maybe fried chicken or roast beef and gravy or pork chops with macaroni and cheese. You know, the kind of meal where you've dragged out practically every pot and pan you own, and you made way too much of everything, which means there are leftovers to scrape out of pans and put into little containers in the freezer, which you'll forget about until you run across them months later.

I remembered looking at the mess of dishes and pots and all the spills on the stove and the tablecloth and thinking to myself, How in the world am I ever going to get this cleaned up? And just *hating* the thought of starting. The smart thing to do would have been to organize the four of us into a clean-up crew. One person could have scraped plates and rinsed, another could have loaded the dishwasher, and so forth. It seemed so simple looking back on it now.

And I know exactly what you must be thinking. You're thinking, this woman was some kind of a near genius in school, and she couldn't figure this out? I guess I needed my old college friend Laurie there to look over the situation and say, "For crying out loud, get 'em in here to help you! Come on, *think*! Get a stopwatch and make a game out of it! Why should you spend all afternoon cooking it and all night cleaning it up? For being so smart, you sure are dumb!" Laurie had always said she was going to marry somebody rich so she could eat out every night. "Kitchen work wrecks a manicure," she'd say.

But anyway, in those long-ago days I used to see kitchen work as one of my main duties as wife and mother, and I didn't ask for help. After supper Ken would wander back to his desk, Jennifer would close herself up in her bedroom, and Travis would watch something on TV until I called him back to the kitchen for our nightly homework ritual.

So all by myself in the kitchen, I'd look at the heap of dishes, the leftovers, all the spots and spatters and gunk stuck in the bottoms of pans, and I'd take a deep breath and say to myself, "Okay, just start with something little." And it would usually be the silverware. I'd get it all in the sink, rinse it off, and stick it in the dishwasher. That always gave me the little push I needed. Then I'd do something else little, maybe the glasses, then something else and something else, and you know the rest. Before long, the job was done.

Oh yes, I know this is the stuff of little moralistic ditties. *"Tackle something small, and soon you'll do it all."* That could be the opening line. But really, this thing with the dishes happened night after night. I always detested facing all those dirty dishes, but it always got done a little at a time.

But I didn't go into it all with Ken on the phone that night. I just said, "Oh, never mind."

He followed up, though. "A little at a time sounds good to me." He was clearly open to discussing it.

It occurred to me right then that while some people are just naturally given to few words, others are probably trained to be that way. I wondered if Ken would have been more of a talker if he hadn't grown up in a house with Schuyler Landis. If you had to endure rebukes or lectures in response to everything you said, you'd probably quit saying much. If you were taught at home for twenty years or so not to ask questions, you'd probably not be inclined to initiate many discussions when you left home. When somebody got angry, you'd probably do what you'd done all your life: creep away and hunker down until the storm passed. How often we expect huge and immediate transformations in the people we marry.

I wheeled my shopping cart to the check-out line, which happened to be empty, and very carefully started placing each purchase on the moving belt. The cashier was much faster than I was and had to stop and wait for me several times. She was a piece of work actually, someone I could have enjoyed observing at length if I hadn't been so intent on my mission.

I had never seen her here before so figured she must be new. She was overweight and had an enormous crop of faded brown hair, very full and very, very frizzy. It had to be a bad permanent. No one's hair could look that way naturally. She also talked out loud as if nobody else was around. A regular running commentary in a funny stream-of-consciousness kind of street talk.

"And the lady heave out the big can of beans," she said, "and sit 'em up alongside the mushrooms, then git out the can of corn and the *little teeny, tiny* jar of pimientos and put 'em side by side just so. The lady ain't in no hurry, which suit me fine, 'cause I got all night. I just stand here a-tappin' my foot and a-hummin' a happy little tune 'cause everything's cool."

And she did actually start humming. When I looked up at her, I saw that in the middle of all that hair was a perky face with a pair of mischievous eyes. She was younger than I had thought at first glance. Her name tag said "Jennilynn."

I smiled at her. "I'm sorry I'm so slow, but it just won't do to throw everything together helter-skelter," I said to her. "This is for something special, and it has to be done just so."

"Lady must not hear good," Jennilynn said, looking off to the side as if addressing somebody else, " 'cause I done said I ain't in no hurry. She can take as long as she want 'cause I like ladies that use big words like helter-skelter. I like ladies that set things out dainty and proper. This lady got style. She do things just so. She probably one of them that puts a wreath on the hood of her car come Christmastime."

When she gave me my change at the end, she said, "And the lady give me five twenties, and I put 'em in the drawer here under this little springy clamp thing, and I give her back a ten and two ones and three pennies." By now a teenaged boy had wandered over to bag the groceries, but he appeared not to hear a word she said, not even when she said, "And then Big Bad Brian the Bagger finally come over and start doin' a little work for a change, and he know this lady awful particular, so he gonna be extra careful not to smash nothin'. Not to put them heavy cans on top of them eggs or nothin' like that." I guess Brian must have been used to Jennilynn by now, because he never gave any sign that he heard a word she was saying.

But there I go again. I had told myself I wouldn't digress anymore, not one single time, but see what happened? The lady forget her vow and go off rambling again. The sad thing is, I went back to that Winn-Dixie in Filbert five or six times after that and never saw Jennilynn again. The last time I went, I asked somebody about her and was told simply "Oh, *her*. She quit." I'm not surprised. They wouldn't appreciate somebody like Jennilynn at a grocery store.

Okay, to finish my story. I drove home and unloaded all the bags and put things away, then took a bath, set my clock for six o'clock, and went to bed. That ended the day before Ken got home.

The next day was Sunday. This is something I really like about this story of mine. It began on a Sunday and ended on one, and it's not anything I manipulated. It just happened that way.

On the phone with Ken that night, there had been a long, empty pause at the very end, and then I had finally said, "Well, you come over here to the house Sunday night around six o'clock, and we'll talk about it all."

"I'll probably get in around five," he said hopefully.

"Come over at six," I repeated, "and I'll be ready to give you an answer." I had so much to tell him that it scared me to think about it. How would I ever do it? Then my own words came back to me: *A little at a time*.

"We could go out to eat if you want to," he said. "That place over in Greenville maybe—the really nice one downtown near the Peace Center. Or any other place you want to go."

Oh, here was a man eager to please! "Well, we'll see," I said. "Come over at six, and we'll do something for supper."

There are different kinds of pity, you know. There's the kind you feel for the helpless—for sick babies, for old people, for victims of natural disasters. I remember the first time I saw that picture of the little Vietnamese girl running naked down a dirt road while her village burned behind her. I felt dizzy all of a sudden. I remember sitting down and putting my hand over my mouth. I was in college at the time, and I had never felt such sorrow for someone I didn't even know.

There's the milder kind of pity you feel for someone who suffers the embarrassment of public defeat, maybe in a sporting event. It might even be a person you dislike, maybe some tennis hotshot who obviously thinks too highly of himself and is favored to win but gets trounced instead. You get a little glimpse of what this match meant for this person, and even though you're glad he didn't win, you feel sorry for him. You know how it feels to want to win and not to.

There's the odd kind of pity you sometimes feel for truly bad people who are getting exactly what they deserve, and this kind doesn't even make sense. I remember reading an interview with a man on death row who was scheduled to die the next week for a murder he had committed twenty-three years earlier when he was nineteen. And I was mad at myself for what I felt when I looked at his picture in the magazine. Don't waste your pity on him, I told myself. But I couldn't stop. Something in his eyes broke my heart. They were such intelligent eyes. He could have been so many things, and yet he had to kill somebody and spend all those years in prison and then die in the electric chair.

Then there's the complex kind of pity you feel when somebody you love has failed, especially when the failure has in some way hurt you. If you don't watch it, the pity can go directly into anger and stay there. But the thing to keep remembering is that this failure could have been your own. It wasn't this time, but it could have been. And your own day of failure will come. The thing to pray for is grace, to give it now and maybe receive it later. For you will surely need it.

My mother disapproved of what I did that Sunday in June when Ken came home. Juliet also let it be known that I was making it far too easy for "the dirtball," as she let slip during a phone call. I hope to make them understand soon. The three of us are going to the beach together the second weekend in September. I have a lot to tell them.

Another thing I'm going to do next week is this. I'm driving over to Derby on Tuesday to visit Polly Seacrest. I called her up one day a few weeks ago, and the first thing she said was "Elizabeth, don't you *ever* move away without saying good-bye to me again! I still can't believe you did that!" She had to put the phone down twice as we talked, once to get their dog, Jester, out of the clothes dryer where Estella had hidden him from her brothers, and another time to turn off the smoke alarm Eaton had set off by trying to cook bacon in the toaster.

But back to my story. That Sunday I got up early and started dinner. I had already made a list of everything I needed to do. The menu had been drawn up several days earlier. Even when I told Ken to come home at six o'clock and we'd talk about getting something to eat, I knew exactly what we'd be eating and where.

It wasn't nearly as extravagant as Babette's feast, and I didn't spend my entire fortune on it, but if you asked Ken what the most memorable meal of his whole life was, I feel quite certain he would name that Sunday evening dinner in June.

I worked in the kitchen until ten that morning, then took time to go to church, after which I told Margaret and Willard Scoggins that I wouldn't be there for the evening service. Pastor Hawthorne preached from the ninth chapter of Isaiah that morning, and I remember well the beautiful verse he took as his text. "The people that walked in darkness have seen a great light; they that dwell in the land of the shadow of death, upon them hath the light shined." Later in that same chapter is the prophecy of Christ's birth, "For unto us a child is born."

I thought about the sermon as I worked through the afternoon. I pictured a great light called *Grace* penetrating the darkness of sin.

As I was setting the dining room table around four o'clock, I saw Macon and Theresa Mahoney pull into their driveway across the street. Their honeymoon trip was over. I stood at the window and watched them get out of the van and walk up to the house pointing to things in the yard. I had kept their flowers watered, and somebody in a red pickup truck, probably a friend of Macon's, had come by twice during the three weeks to mow their grass.

Theresa was wearing a pair of white Capri pants and a white shirt, and Macon had on black shorts and a black T-shirt. Dress-down wedding garb for the last leg of the honeymoon. I wondered if they had planned it this way. It wouldn't surprise me a bit. I thought about running outside to greet them, but I couldn't make myself move from the window. I remembered Macon saying to Theresa at the wedding, "We shall sup together at our marriage feast, wife."

At the front door I watched them stop while Theresa took out her keys and unlocked the door. I watched Macon sweep her up into his arms and carry her across the threshold. They disappeared inside, leaving the door wide open. Something inside me hurt. They had so much ahead of them. All those years that follow the marriage feast. They had no idea. They were starting from scratch.

And Ken and I were starting over. At least that's what I planned to propose to him that night over dinner. "Tho' much is taken, much abides." As I stood at the dining room window, these words came to me out of the blue. They were from Tennyson's poem "Ulysses." Ulysses knew a thing or two about starting over. He was an old king yet tired of sitting around. He was hungry for adventure. He wanted to sail the broad seas again. He looked up at the sun and thought of time. He saw the potential of each hour to be a "bringer of new things."

I remember one of my teachers in college denouncing Ulysses for wanting to leave his island kingdom in the hands of his son so he could venture forth again. She thought it was evidence of a weak sense of personal responsibility. I took up for Ulysses, though, and even wrote a paper defending him. My only criticism of the poem was that the last three lines were unnecessary. I wish Tennyson had ended it with "that which we are, we are."

Ulysses had a great outlook. You can't change the way things have been before now, but you can make them different from this day forward. It doesn't do any good to sit around moaning about what you've lost. You still have *something*, so use it. "Tho' much is taken, much abides." I like that even more now than when I first read it all those years ago. Back then I had no inkling what it really meant.

The hands of the clock kept moving around and around that afternoon. The hour was drawing closer. Six o'clock would be the "bringer of new things" for Ken and me. I prayed for him to keep his eyes on the road. I prayed for the words I would say when he walked into the house. I prayed for my rolls to rise and my pie to set.

I used my moss green Waterford tablecloth and arranged a centerpiece of white candles and small white roses, the ones Ken had planted for me in the front yard. I used Christine's china, which was white with a band of green scrollwork around the rim, edged with gold. I used my best sterling silverware and white cloth napkins. From the top shelf of our kitchen cupboard, I took down two crystal goblets. I washed them and put them on crystal coasters. My table was set for a gracious plenty.

I had gone through my cookbooks and recipe file to make up the menu. Like most men, Ken loves good food. I thought back over all the years I had cooked for him and tried to remember the things he had especially liked, which was harder to do than I thought it would be. He was always easy to cook for and seemed to like just about everything. I came up with a menu I knew he'd like, though, and I took pains to follow every step of each recipe, not taking any shortcuts.

I hadn't cooked a meal like this in a long time, so I was a little nervous that I might have lost my touch. It was a big undertaking, but I wanted it to be this way. A couple of ham sandwiches and a can of soup wouldn't have worked for this meal.

I stopped from time to time to wash up dishes so that by five-thirty the kitchen counter was clear and everything was ready. The rolls were laid out on a baking sheet ready to put into the oven. I had changed into a gray linen dress, put on silver jewelry, and combed my hair. I looked at myself in the mirror at five-forty-five and whispered, "Much abides."

Baked chicken with almonds. That was the meat. It was a recipe from my Williamsburg cookbook. You sprinkle it with cooking sherry just before serving. I cooked and served it in a covered white baking dish.

The salad was called Frozen Fruit Delight, and it had mandarin oranges in it, along with miniature marshmallows, lemon Jell-O, whipping cream, and a few other things. I put it into little molds, then froze it, served it on lettuce, and topped it with honey dressing. I remember how Jennifer used to tease me about making gelatin salads. "Jell-O is so *fifties*, Mom," she'd say, rolling her eyes, after which she would proceed to eat every bite of her fifties salad.

Three vegetables: corn puffs, which have a golden brown crust and a warm soft middle; a broccoli-cauliflower casserole with cheddar cheese sauce; and carrot soufflé, which is incredibly time-consuming to make but yields a beautiful delicate dish that's as light as air.

Crescent rolls for the bread. I kneaded the dough by hand for ten minutes, and after it rose I punched it down and rolled it into a large circle. Then I cut it into sixteen equal parts, rolled up each little triangle, curled them into crescents, and let them rise again. I set out a stick of real butter to soften. In case anybody reading this doesn't already know, you don't serve homemade crescent rolls with margarine.

Tea to drink. Strong and sweet. The kind of tea only southerners seem to know how to make.

And for dessert, I thought long and hard. Ken loves desserts. I had never made one he didn't like, so picking a favorite wasn't easy. I finally settled on cherry pie. I made my own crust, of course. You don't go to the trouble to make cherry pie and then use a store-bought crust. The cherries have to be the tart ones, and if you decrease the sugar a little from what the recipe says, it's even better. I add a little cornstarch to the flour to make sure it sets, and of course I do the lattice thing with the top crust. And you've got to have vanilla ice cream for the finishing touch.

So there you have it. That was the menu. Note, there was no appetizer. In my opinion, if a meal is cooked right, the last thing you want is an appetizer. A person has only so much of an appetite, and if you tease around with fluffy preliminaries, you're bound to take some of the pleasure off the other end. Whenever I go somewhere to eat and am offered an appetizer, I decline. "No, thank you," I say politely, but what I mean is, "Quit stalling and bring on the *real* food!"

I'm standing in the dining room straightening the napkins and silverware, which don't need straightening, when Ken pulls into the driveway. It's a couple of minutes before six. I walk quickly to the kitchen and put the rolls in the oven and set the timer, then return to the dining room window. I stand back a little so he can't see me.

He sits in the car a while, as if waiting until exactly six o'clock, as if he doesn't want to step out of line by even a second. I see him get out of the car, slowly. He's wearing a dark green shirt, open at the neck, and khaki pants. He closes the car door and stands for a moment looking out across the front yard, which Travis mowed when he breezed home last weekend. It was the weekend between visiting Stacy and starting summer school, and it had surprised me when he went out in the late afternoon that Saturday and started the mower. I hadn't told him to.

I thought at first it was all his idea, another sign of his budding maturity, but it turned out that Ken had asked him to. They had evidently been talking by phone on a pretty regular basis. I remember the puzzled look on my son's face that Saturday night when we talked over a spaghetti supper. He had been too hungry to shower before eating, and I remember the interesting combination of the fresh grass smell mingled with the spicy smell of spaghetti sauce.

Oh, I remember the moment well. I was stammering out an attempt at an apology for all the mistakes I made when he was a kid. I was well into it, trying to express how sorry I was, when he stopped me right in the middle of a sentence.

He had put his fork down and was shaking his head and waving both hands. "Mom, Mom, stop it," he said, leaning forward. "Are you having some kind of breakdown? Do I need to call 9-1-1?"

I started in again, telling him how clear it all was to me now, how I wish I hadn't held him back in so many ways, and he stopped me again. "Mom, this is a travesty. You're not making sense. You're making it sound like I shoulda been put in foster care or something. You were . . ." He stopped and shook his head again, looking at me incredulously. "Mom, you gotta believe me. It's *okay*. You were . . . you were a great mom. I was a happy kid." He looked confused. "I don't understand where all this is coming from. I never felt deprived."

Grace heaped upon grace! My mistakes, which were many, had bounced off my son like rubber balls, but the good things had somehow stuck like friendly burrs. Before he left to go back to college the next afternoon, Travis had hugged me of his own accord and right up next to my ear had said those simplest yet most precious words: "I love you, Mom." Then he had gotten into his car, rolled down the window, and said, "And Dad does, too. He told me so."

Ken is walking toward the house now. He looks tired and a little worried. Maybe he's trying to think of what he'll say when he opens the door and walks in. Maybe he's wondering what I'll say.

I close my eyes and see a broad green field. I smell the dinner I've prepared, and I hear my husband's footsteps in the carport. In a few minutes, before we eat our feast, we shall say grace.

Dramatic Fiction You Won't Be Able to Resist

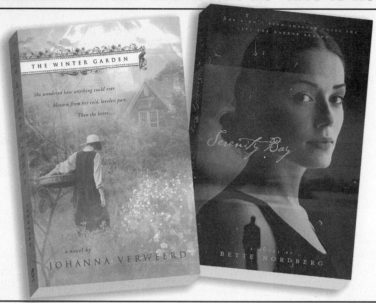

CAN LOVE AND HOPE BLOOM IN *THE WINTER GARDEN*?

To hide from painful memories, Ika Boerema loses herself in her work of designing gardens for other people. She has just begun planning a winter garden when the letter arrives—the letter that could change everything.

Written by her sister, Nelly, whom she hasn't seen in fifteen years, the letter alerts Ika to their mother's terminal illness. Will Ika return home for one last chance at rebuilding a shattered family, and can a heart that has never known love learn to love?

The Winter Garden by Johanna Verweerd

A SPINE-TINGLING ESCAPE FROM A LOVE GONE DANGEROUSLY WRONG

Encompassing all the elements that make for captivating fiction, including endearing characters, breathtaking suspense, and an unforgettable message, *Serenity Bay* has been called "riveting...a real page turner."

To the outside world, Dr. Russell Koehler was the ideal catch—charming, attentive, and attractive. And life in Serenity Bay offered the perfect setting for a young family. But eight years into marriage, Patricia knows her world is crumbling fast. With two children and no one to trust, Patricia faces the most frightening decision of her life.

Serenity Bay by Bette Nordberg